Noelle Stevenson • Shannon Watters • Carolyn Nowak • Brooke Allen

LUMBERJANES™

TO THE MAX EDITION

VOLUME TWO

BOOM! BOX™

Ross Richie...CEO & Founder
Matt Gagnon...Editor-in-Chief
Filip Sablik...................President of Publishing & Marketing
Stephen Christy...................President of Development
Lance Kreiter.................VP of Licensing & Merchandising
Phil Barbaro..VP of Finance
Bryce Carlson...Managing Editor
Mel Caylo...Marketing Manager
Scott Newman.......................Production Design Manager
Irene Bradish...Operations Manager
Christine Dinh.............Brand Communications Manager
Sierra Hahn...Senior Editor
Dafna Pleban...Editor
Shannon Watters..Editor
Eric Harburn..Editor
Whitney Leopard.......................................Associate Editor
Jasmine Amiri..Associate Editor

Chris Rosa...Associate Editor
Alex Galer...Assistant Editor
Cameron Chittock.................................Assistant Editor
Mary Gumport...Assistant Editor
Matthew Levine.......................................Assistant Editor
Kelsey Dieterich....................................Production Designer
Jillian Crab..Production Designer
Michelle Ankley.................Production Design Assistant
Grace Park...........................Production Design Assistant
Aaron Ferrara....................................Operations Coordinator
Elizabeth Loughridge.................Accounting Coordinator
José Meza...Sales Assistant
James Arriola...Mailroom Assistant
Holly Aitchison.................................Operations Assistant
Stephanie Hocutt....................................Marketing Assistant
Sam Kusek..........................Direct Market Representative

BOOM! BOX™

LUMBERJANES TO THE MAX EDITION Volume Two, September 2016. Published by BOOM! Box, a division of Boom Entertainment, Inc. Lumberjanes is ™ & © 2016 Shannon Watters, Grace Ellis, Noelle Stevenson & Brooke Allen. Originally published in single magazine form as LUMBERJANES No. 9-12, 14-17. ™ & © 2015 Shannon Watters, Grace Ellis, Noelle Stevenson & Brooke Allen. All rights reserved. BOOM!™ Box™ and the BOOM! Box logo are trademarks of Boom Entertainment, Inc., registered in various countries and categories. All characters, events, and institutions depicted herein are fictional. Any similarity between any of the names, characters, persons, events, and/or institutions in this publication to actual names, characters, and persons, whether living or dead, events, and/or institutions is unintended and purely coincidental. BOOM! Box does not read or accept unsolicited submissions of ideas, stories, or artwork.

A catalog record of this book is available from OCLC and from the BOOM! Studios website, www.boom-studios.com, on the Librarians Page.

BOOM! Studios, 5670 Wilshire Boulevard, Suite 450, Los Angeles, CA 90036-5679. Printed in China. First Printing. ISBN: 978-1-60886-889-6, eISBN: 978-1-61398-560-1

THIS LUMBERJANES FIELD MANUAL BELONGS TO:

NAME:_____

TROOP:_____

DATE INVESTED:_____

FIELD MANUAL TABLE OF CONTENTS

LUMBERJANES FIELD MANUAL

For the Advanced Program

Tenth Edition • April 1984

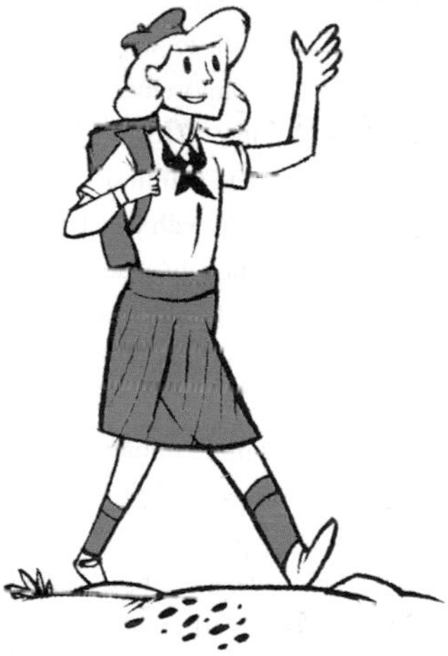

Prepared for the

Miss Qiunzella Thiskwin Penniquiqul Thistle Crumpet's

CAMP FOR [redacted] HARDCORE LADY-TYPES

"Friendship to the Max!"

A MESSAGE FROM THE LUMBERJANES HIGH COUNCIL

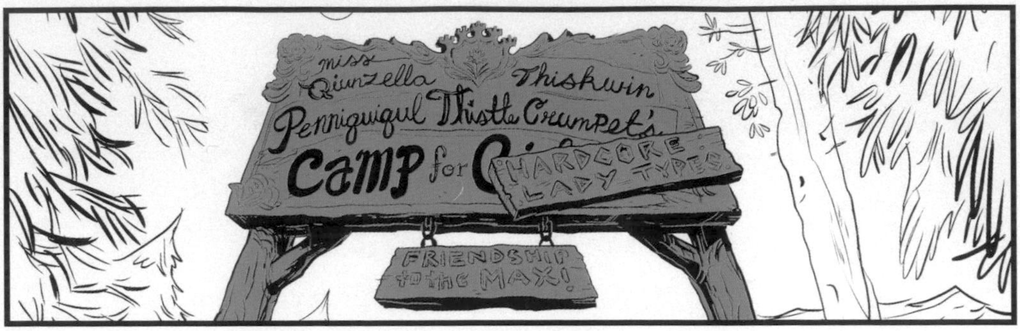
Miss Quinzella Thiskwin Penniquiqul Thistle Crumpet's
Camp for
HARDCORE LADY TYPES
FRIENDSHIP to the MAX!

It's not about the beginning of a journey or the end of the road, as much as it's about the path that you take from point A to point B. Sometimes it will be about the multiple paths you'll get to take in life and after.

We go through life making decisions, after all it's the choices in life that define us. Do I set my alarm early for tomorrow, do I wear flannel or cotton, which of these boots are better for this 20-mile hike? Some of these decisions are second hand nature that we don't even realize we're doing them, we are so confident in our abilities and experiences to trust our instincts when it comes to most of the decisions we make in life. Here at Lumberjane camp, we hope to prepare you for the choices that require more second-guessing.

Lumberjanes is not only camp but it is a lifestyle. It means something to every camper here, regardless of their background and without any consideration to their future. Being a Lumberjanes means something different to every individual at these camps, to every soul that passes through these wooden walls and to every creature that finds their ways to our campgrounds. Everyone and everything will have their own unique experience in these woods.

This camp is a choice, and the experiences you will have here are a choice, the friends that you make and bond with are a choice. But the best thing about these choices, about this camp, is that none of these decisions are wrong.

We want to celebrate everyone as an individual, everyone with their own unique lives and spirits. With their point of views that might be different or new but as a Lumberjane we are always willing to learn another perspective and embrace the unknown around us. This camp will not be the beginning or end for most, but we truly hope that it makes one great chapter in everyone's unique story.

THE LUMBERJANES PLEDGE

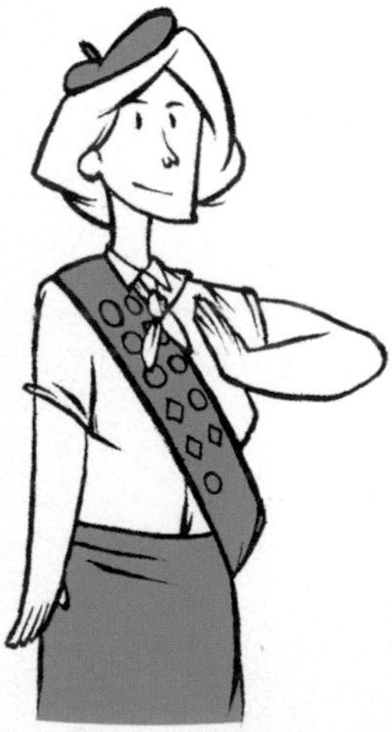

I solemnly swear to do my best
Every day, and in all that I do,
To be brave and strong,
To be truthful and compassionate,
To be interesting and interested,
To pay attention and question
The world around me,
To think of others first,
To always help and protect my friends,
[redacted]
And to make the world a better place
For Lumberjane scouts
And for everyone else.

THEN THERE'S A LINE ABOUT GOD, OR WHATEVER

LUMBERJANES™
TO THE MAX J EDITION

Created by **Shannon Watters, Grace Ellis, Noelle Stevenson & Brooke Allen**

Written by
Noelle Stevenson
& Shannon Watters

"If You Got It, Haunt It"
Illustrated by
Brittney Williams
Colors by **Maarta Laiho**
Letters by **Aubrey Aiese**

"Wrong Number"
Illustrated by
Aimee Fleck

"Ghost Girl"
Written and Illustrated by
Faith Erin Hicks
Colors by **Maarta Laiho**

"Bad Candy"
Illustrated by
Rebecca Tobin

"Lonely Road"
Illustrated by
Carolyn Nowak

"Tailypo"
Illustrated by
Felicia Choo

"Old Betty"
Illustrated by
T. Zysk

Illustrated by
Carolyn Nowak
(Chapters Ten through Twelve)
Brooke Allen
(Chapters Thirteen through Sixteen)

Colors by
Maarta Laiho

Letters by
Aubrey Aiese

Design by
Scott Newman
& Kelsey Dieterich

"Mixing it Up"
Written by
Shannon Watters
Illustrated by
Carey Pietsch

Character Designs by
Noelle Stevenson & Brooke Allen

Badge Designs by
Kate Leth & Scott Newman

Associate Editor
Whitney Leopard

Editor
Dafna Pleban

Special thanks to **Kelsey Pate** *for giving the Lumberjanes their name.*

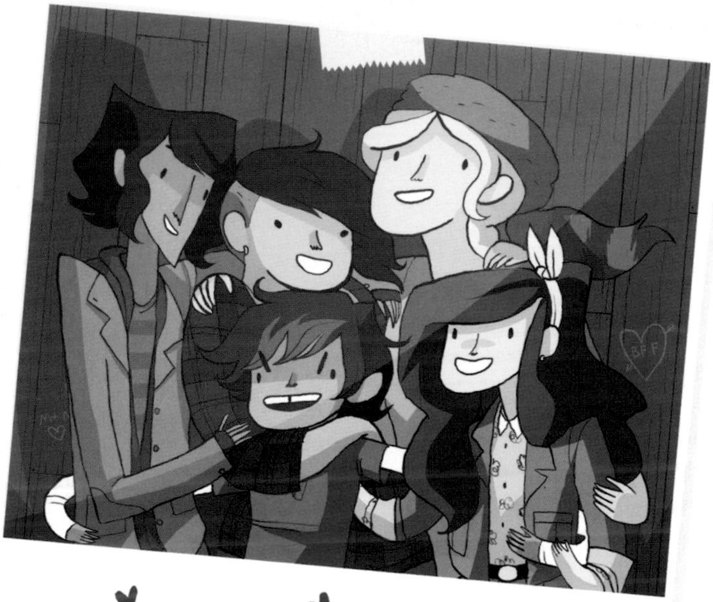
BFF

FRIENDSHIP TO THE MAX!

LUMBERJANES FIELD MANUAL
FOREWORD

What are we even doing, hanging out in the city, surrounded by concrete and traffic?

Huh?

Shouldn't we all be canoeing? Learning archery? Scratching mosquito bites? Shouldn't we be tucked into a sleeping bag in a canvas tent, hugged by deep dark forest, with a crowd of rowdy definitely-not-going-to-sleep friends, reading by flashlight?

Why are we posting on social media, when we could be telling ghost stories? Does that not just seem infinitely more fun?

I should be writing this sitting on a splintery dock, in a damp bathing suit, my feet dangling in the water of a crispy cold lake, my shoulders just a little sunburned.

I'm not. And the more I write, the more this seems just infinitely wrong.

Because come on guys, summer is where we all should be. Amiright? What's better than summer? SUMMER CAMP. Summer at camp is where it's AT. From the moment you arrive and your sneaker touches the soft floor of wood chips, from the moment you spot your bunk and you hear the first squeal of freedom, you know camp is sooooooo where it's at. (Even if you're homesick for the first three days and you have to leave the room with a counselor every time they sing "One Tin Soldier," it's still totally where it's at.)

Besides being a pretty kick butt comic peppered with golden nuggets of feminist manifesto and I'm assuming fully functional survival techniques, *Lumberjanes* connects readers to the paradise of summer camp; the joy of the thing we can't have all the time (because of seasons and this whole growing up thing). It connects us to that time of life that feels like forever when you're inside it and like a dream so many years later.

Lumberjanes is a gateway to our most adventurous, brave, big-hearted selves. Mal, Ripley, Molly, April, and Jo are the persons we can be, the brains, the champions, warriors, goof bally, spazzy investigators relentless, the best friends who stick together.

Noelle, Grace, Shannon, Brooke, and the many other incredibly talented contributors to *Lumberjanes*, know that the friends you make when you're a kid at camp are magic. They also know that when you embrace this magic there are no limits.

We should all be this kind of magic all the time. (During all four seasons. Although, yes, during winter and things like the "polar vortex," it's a challenge.)

We really should though.

In the meantime, I don't think it would hurt any of us if we all took the *Lumberjanes* oath, to be brave, to pay attention, to be interested and interesting (that's my favorite part), to protect your friends and make the world a better place. Let's just take the oath right now. Shall we?

Then it's cocoa and toasted marshmallows and well-earned badges for everyone.

Thank you *Lumberjanes* for giving us summer, for bringing magic and friendship and camp and good vibes all around.

I'm going to go search out a starry sky to lie under and read these comics.

MARIKO TAMAKI
Author of *Skim* and *This One Summer*

LUMBERJANES FIELD MANUAL
CHAPTER NINE

Lumberjanes "Out-of-Doors" Program Field

IF YOU GOT IT, HAUNT IT BADGE

"Because you weren't going to sleep anyway."

Things go bump in the night, it's basically the best time to go bump if one had to choose a timeframe. This is a lesson that every Lumberjane will learn as she continues on her path. Every Lumberjane should leave camp with the basic understanding of what is out there, how it could get you, and why it won't. She will encounter many problems through life and it will be this knowledge that will help her through. Scary stories are more than just a chance to give your neighbor goosebumps, they are also a chance for you to share your knowledge in a way that is not only fun, but entertaining. After all, aren't the best scary tales the ones that have a little truth to them? It should come as no surprise that both friendship and scary story telling are combined in the *If You Got It, Haunt It* badge.

Haunting is just a fact of life. Spirits are everywhere. Both living and long past, they often want to reach out to us in the only ways they know how. A Lumberjane will want to not only help these spirits, but with her friends, she'll be able to go above and beyond the call of a scout. And if she is unable to connect with the spirits as so many before her have, well then hopefully she'll at least be able to come up with a good story or two around the camp fire.

To obtain the *If You Got It, Haunt It* badge, a Lumberjane must have already received her *Up All Night* badge, and should have shown great promise in her creative thinking skills. A good picture might be worth a thousand words, but in the same amount of words, a good story is only the beginning. There are many things we can learn from the great storytellers before us. The women who put pen to paper and wove such intricate drama that their stories still stick with us to this very day. It is important for a Lumberjane to

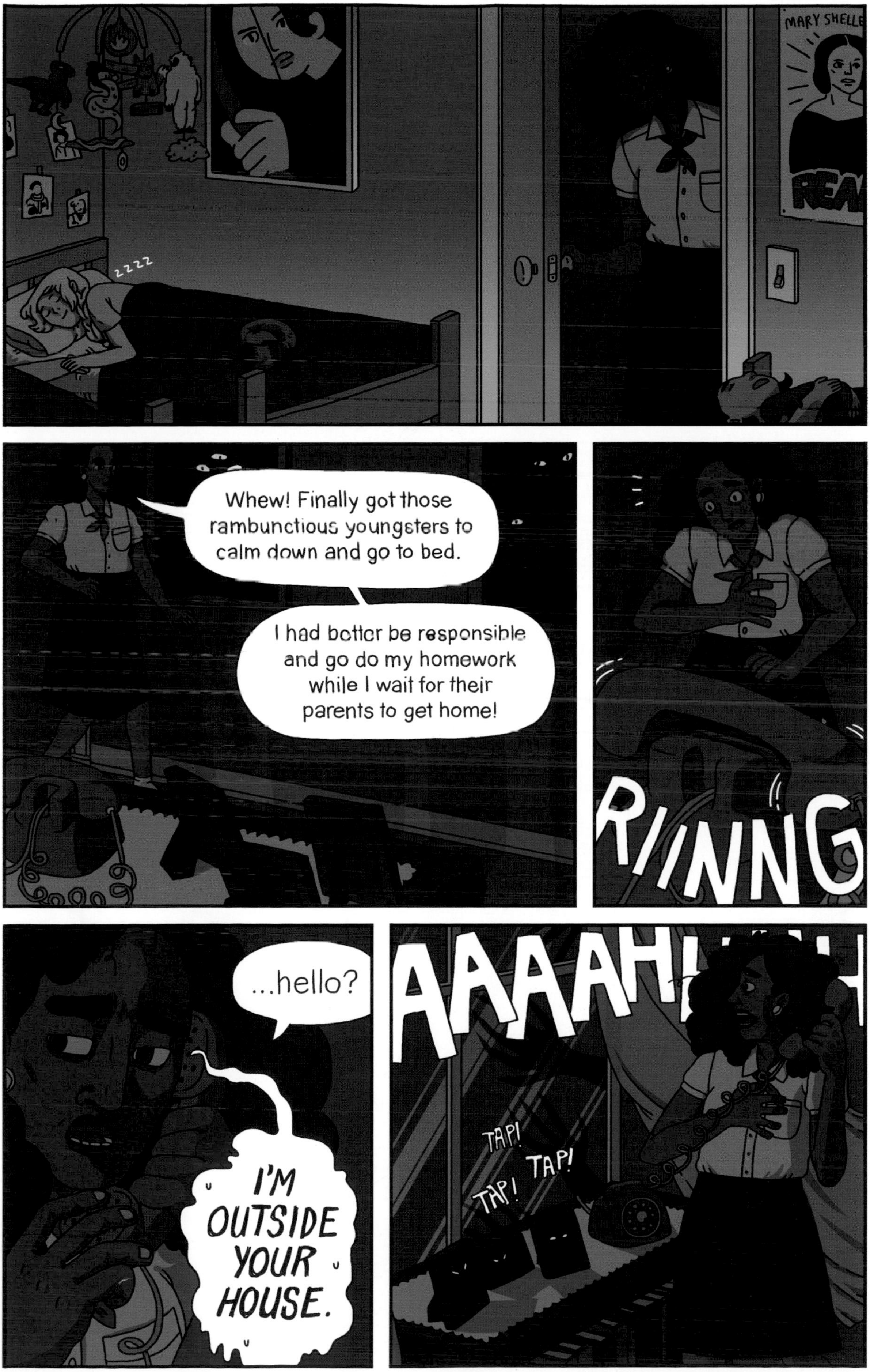
MARY SHELLE
ZZZZ
Whew! Finally got those rambunctious youngsters to calm down and go to bed.
I had better be responsible and go do my homework while I wait for their parents to get home!
RIINNG
...hello?
I'M OUTSIDE YOUR HOUSE.
AAAAH
TAP! TAP! TAP!

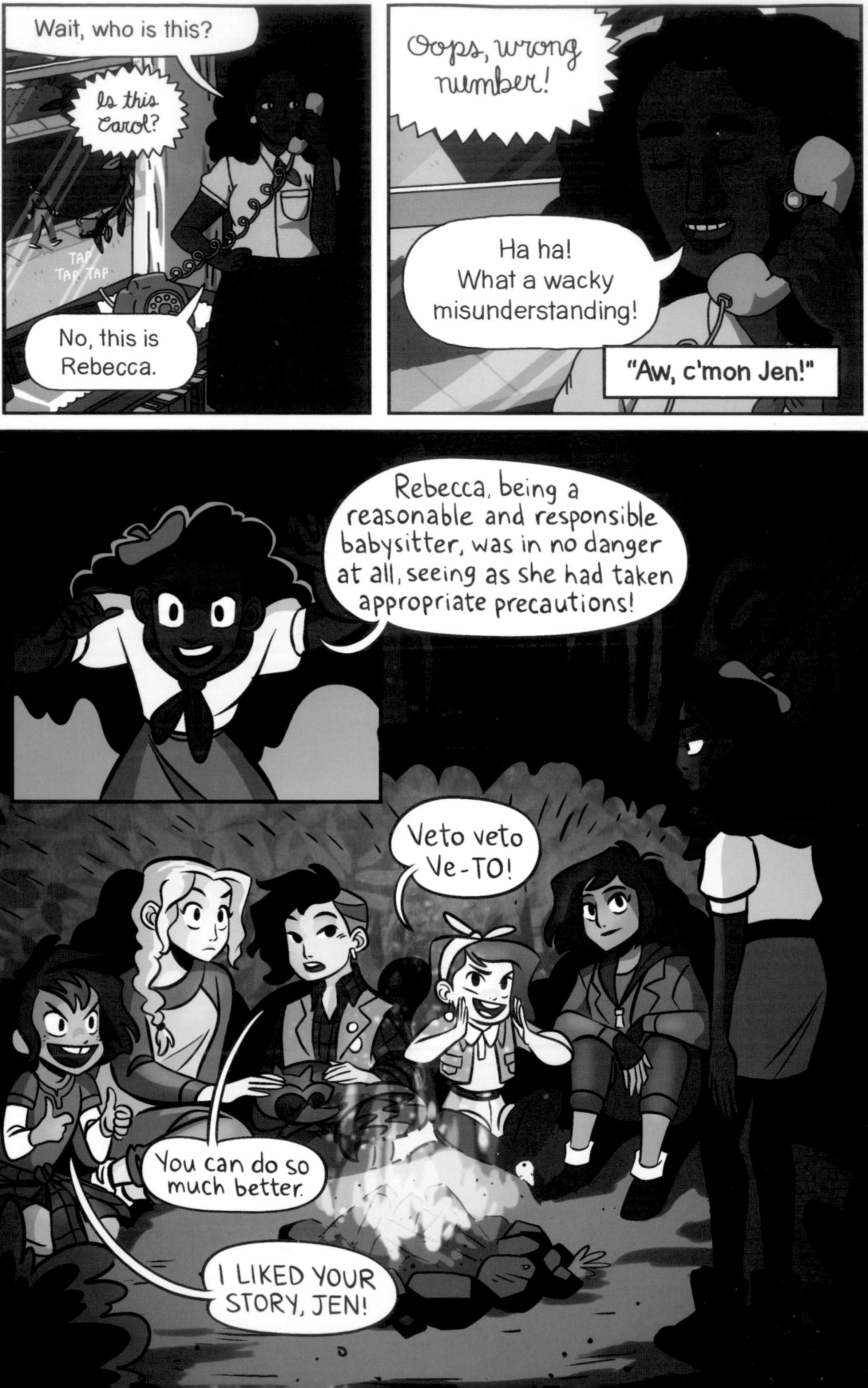
Wait, who is this?
Is this Carol?
TAP TAP TAP
No, this is Rebecca.
Oops, wrong number!
Ha ha! What a wacky misunderstanding!
"Aw, c'mon Jen!"
Rebecca, being a reasonable and responsible babysitter, was in no danger at all, seeing as she had taken appropriate precautions!
Veto veto Ve-TO!
You can do so much better.
I LIKED YOUR STORY, JEN!

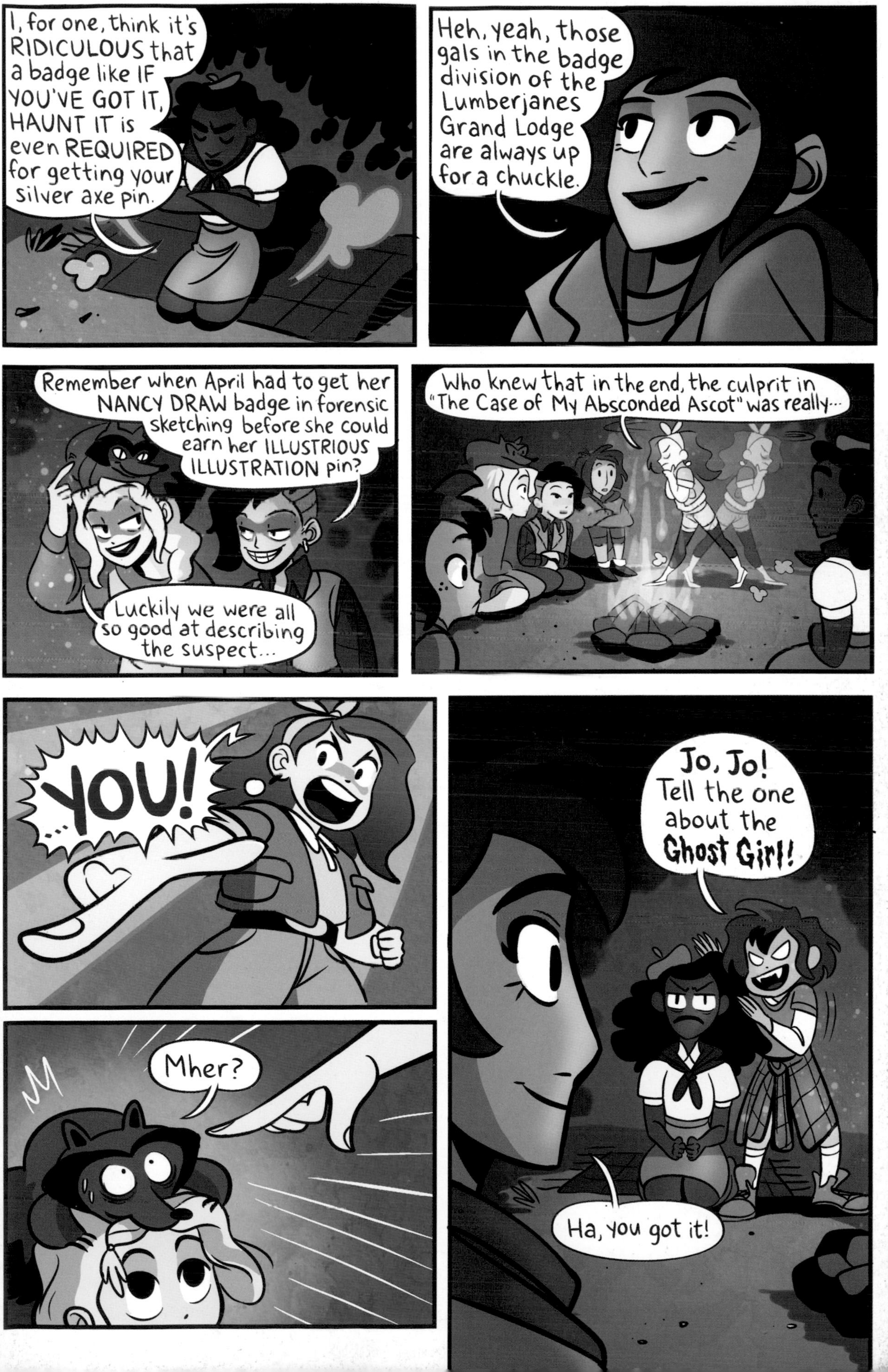
I, for one, think it's RIDICULOUS that a badge like IF YOU'VE GOT IT, HAUNT IT is even REQUIRED for getting your silver axe pin.
Heh, yeah, those gals in the badge division of the Lumberjanes Grand Lodge are always up for a chuckle.
Remember when April had to get her NANCY DRAW badge in forensic sketching before she could earn her ILLUSTRIOUS ILLUSTRATION pin?
Luckily we were all so good at describing the suspect...
Who knew that in the end, the culprit in "The Case of My Absconded Ascot" was really...
...YOU!
Mher?
Jo, Jo! Tell the one about the Ghost Girl!
Ha, you got it!

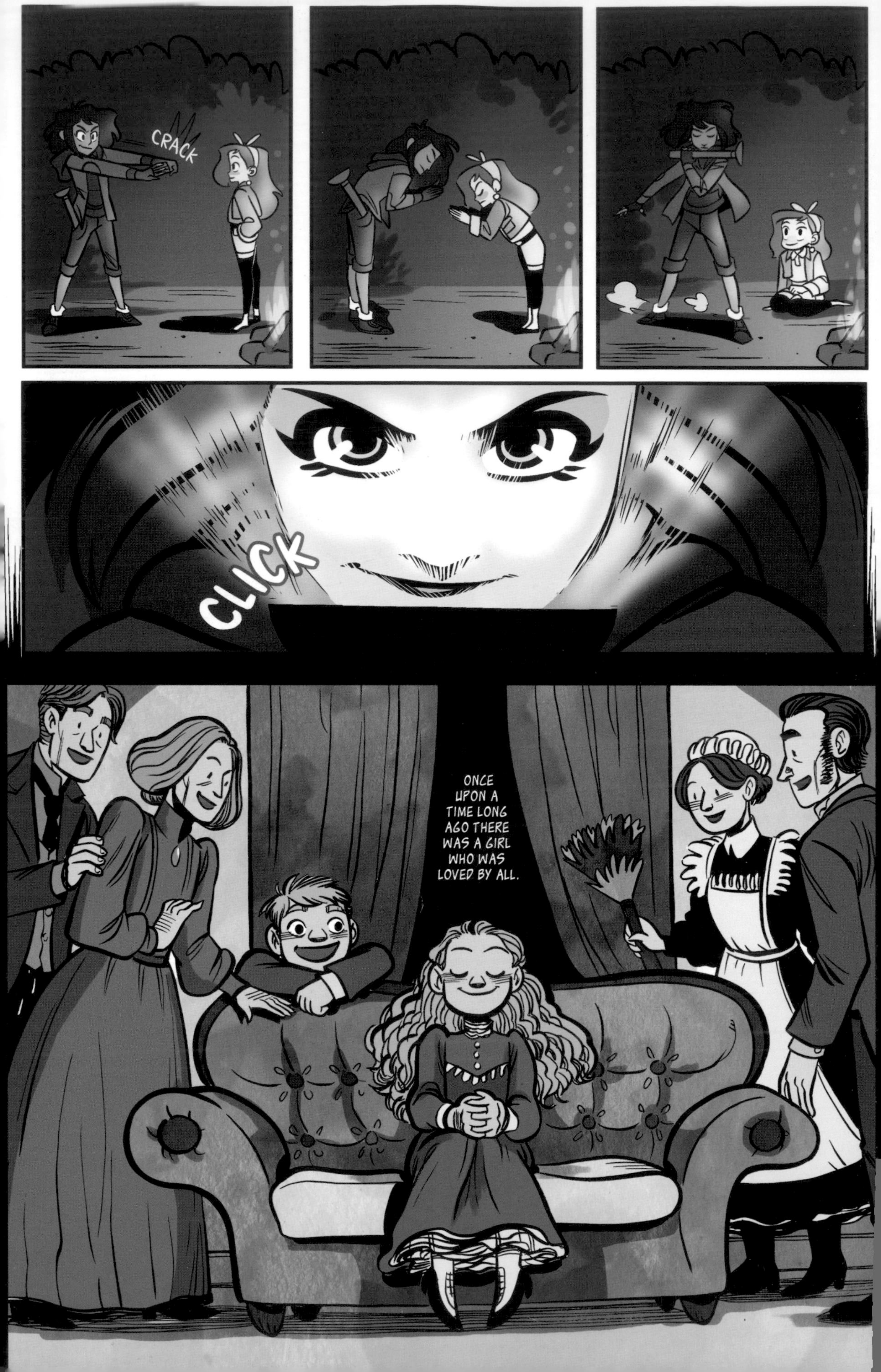
CRACK
CLICK
ONCE UPON A TIME LONG AGO THERE WAS A GIRL WHO WAS LOVED BY ALL.

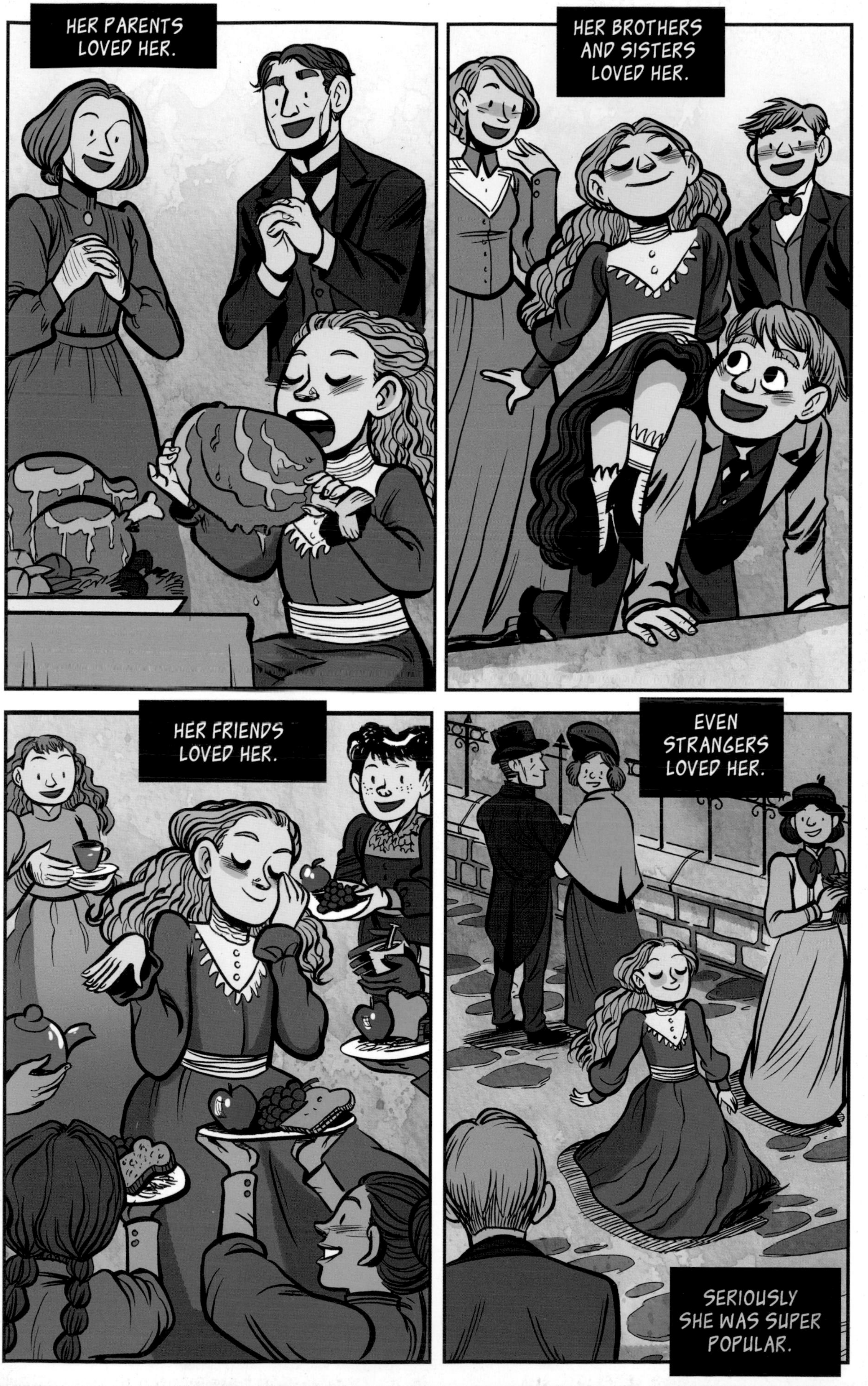
HER PARENTS LOVED HER.
HER BROTHERS AND SISTERS LOVED HER.
HER FRIENDS LOVED HER.
EVEN STRANGERS LOVED HER.
SERIOUSLY SHE WAS SUPER POPULAR.

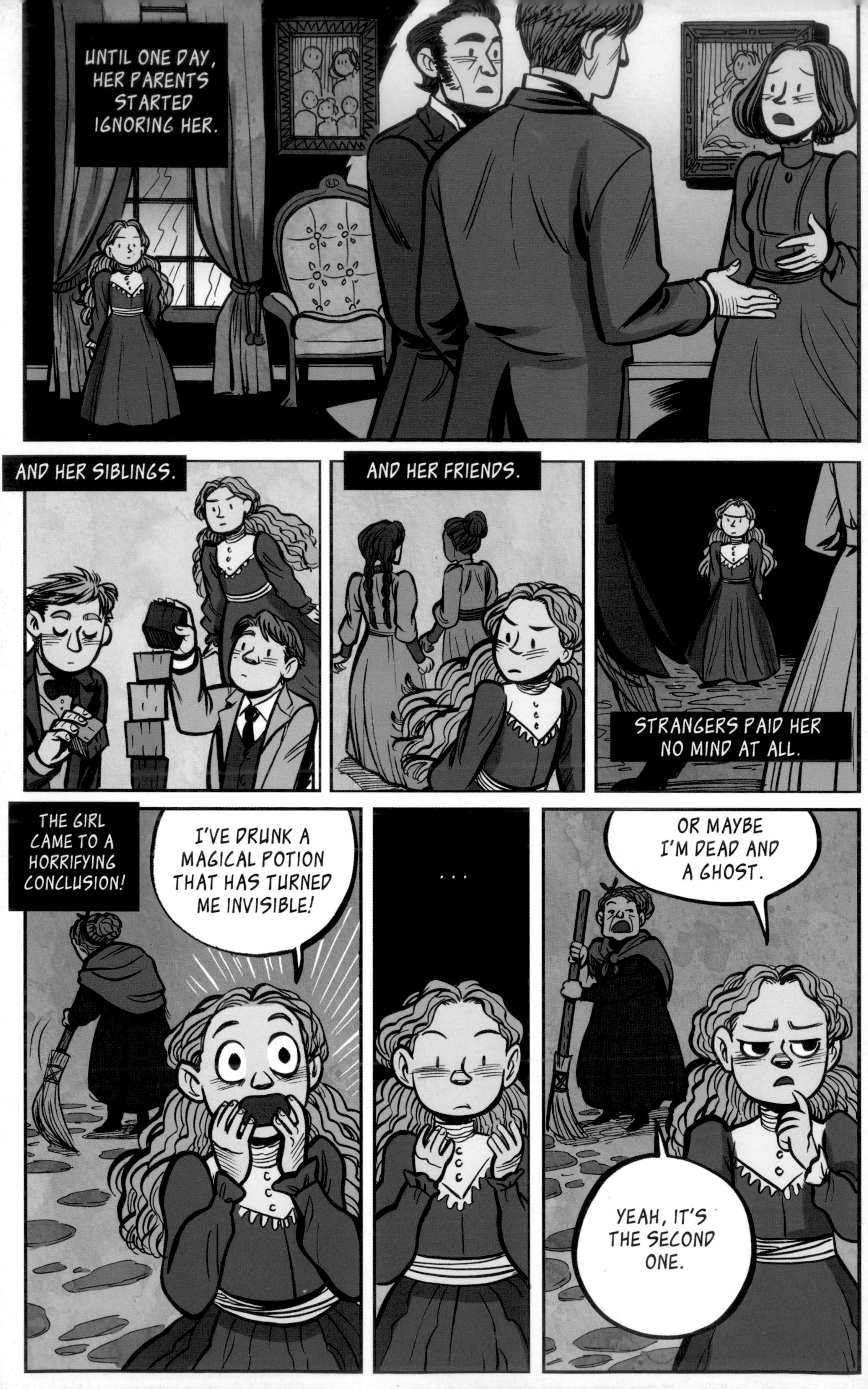
UNTIL ONE DAY, HER PARENTS STARTED IGNORING HER.
AND HER SIBLINGS.
AND HER FRIENDS.
STRANGERS PAID HER NO MIND AT ALL.
THE GIRL CAME TO A HORRIFYING CONCLUSION!
I'VE DRUNK A MAGICAL POTION THAT HAS TURNED ME INVISIBLE!
. . .
OR MAYBE I'M DEAD AND A GHOST.
YEAH, IT'S THE SECOND ONE.

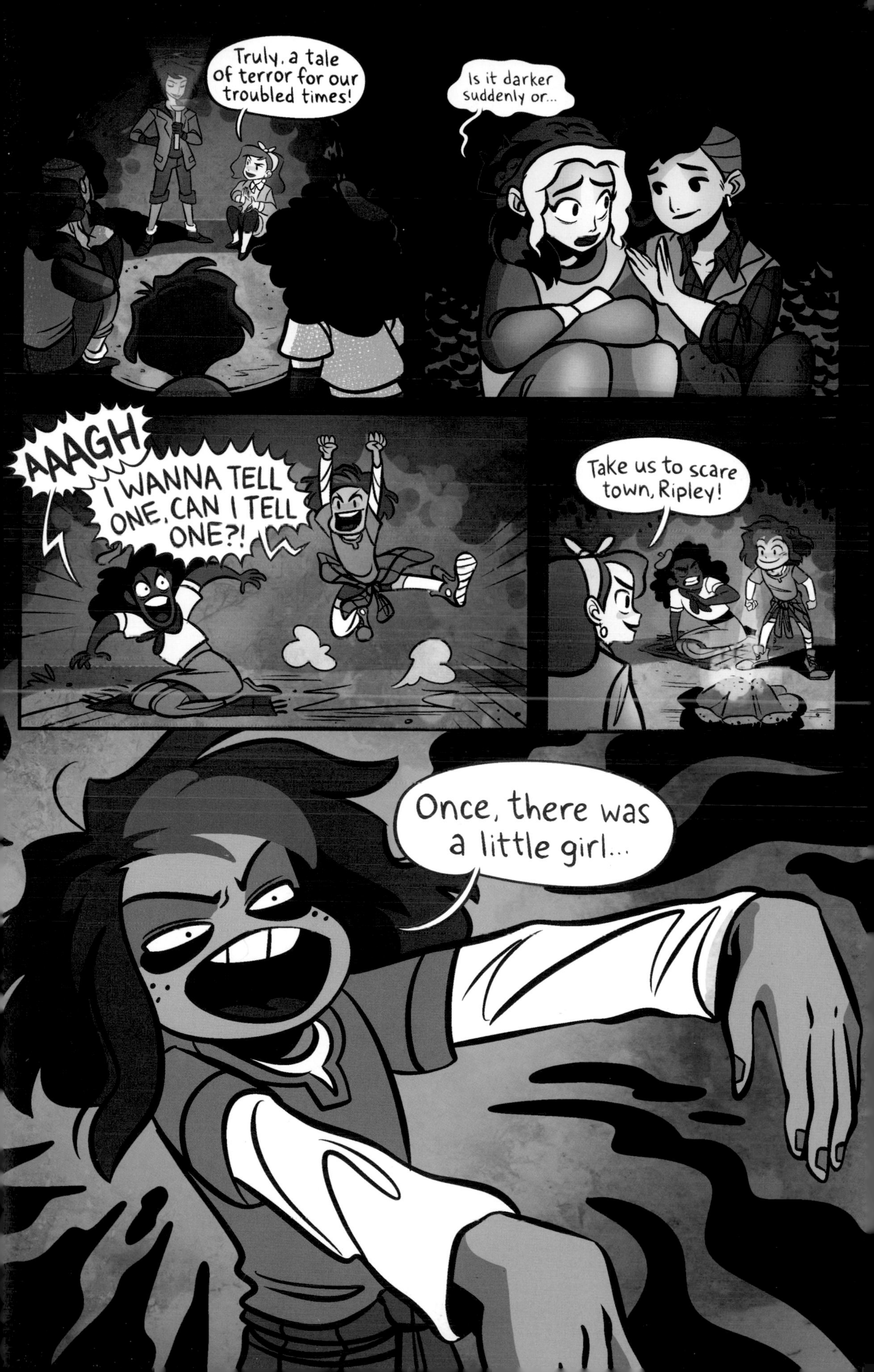
Truly, a tale of terror for our troubled times!
Is it darker suddenly or...
AAAGH
I WANNA TELL ONE, CAN I TELL ONE?!
Take us to scare town, Ripley!
Once, there was a little girl...

who had a whole bunch of brothers and sisters and great friends and an _awesome dog_ and maybe also a kitty and her life was super good. Every night she'd go to sleep in her own upstairs bedroom and a candy would be sitting on the windowsill just begging her to eat it because candy is delicious and _rules_.

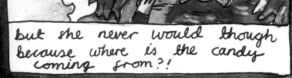

but she never would though because where is the candy coming from?!

one night she got home and there was the candy and it looked really good, it had a pretty wrapper and smelled like strawberries and chocolate so she ate it.

when she woke up she wasn't in bed anymore... she was in a giant room that looked like evil candy everywhere and she was all wrapped up and trapped in taffy. Staring at her was a lady who had a spider body and a mean smile.

you ate my candy and accepted my contract. now i'm going to eat you. to

there's no escape. you're never going to see any of your nice life again!

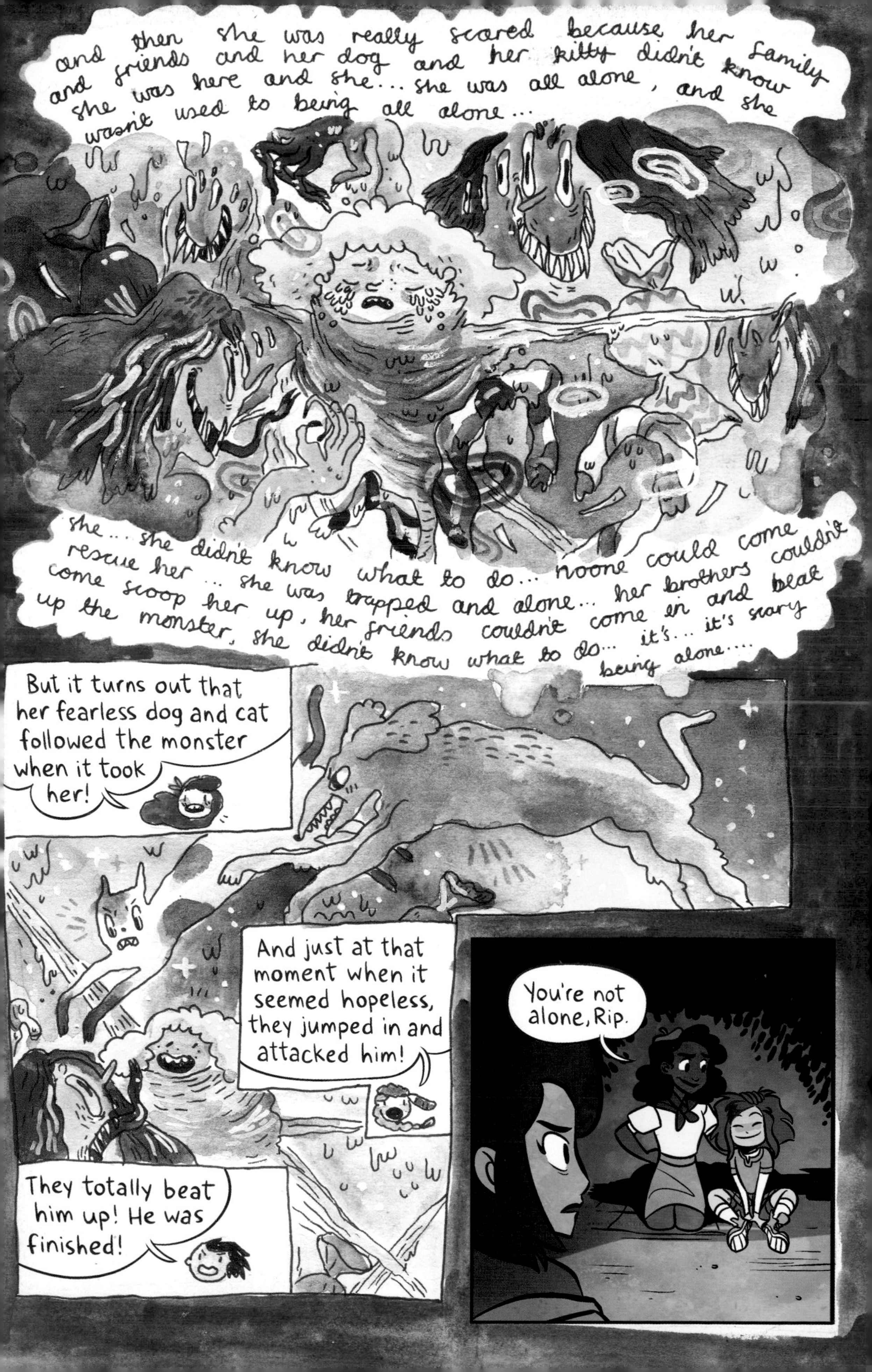

and then she was really scared because her family and friends and her dog and her kitty didn't know she was here and she... she was all alone, and she wasn't used to being all alone...
she... she didn't know what to do... noone could come rescue her... she was trapped and alone... her brothers couldn't come scoop her up, her friends couldn't come in and beat up the monster, she didn't know what to do... it's... it's scary being alone....
But it turns out that her fearless dog and cat followed the monster when it took her!
And just at that moment when it seemed hopeless, they jumped in and attacked him!
They totally beat him up! He was finished!
You're not alone, Rip.

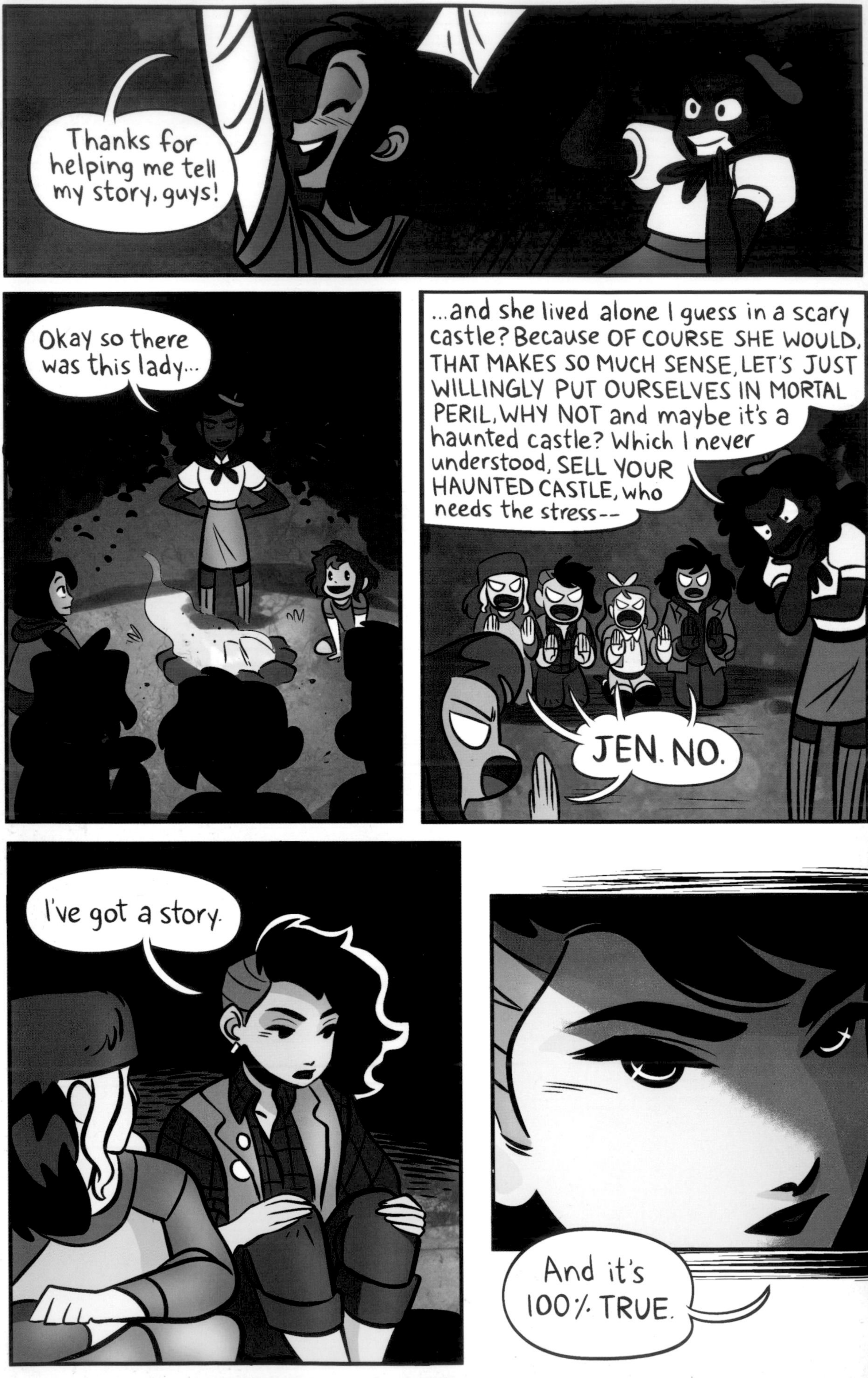
Thanks for helping me tell my story, guys!
Okay so there was this lady...
...and she lived alone I guess in a scary castle? Because OF COURSE SHE WOULD, THAT MAKES SO MUCH SENSE, LET'S JUST WILLINGLY PUT OURSELVES IN MORTAL PERIL, WHY NOT and maybe it's a haunted castle? Which I never understood, SELL YOUR HAUNTED CASTLE, who needs the stress--
JEN. NO.
I've got a story.
And it's 100% TRUE.

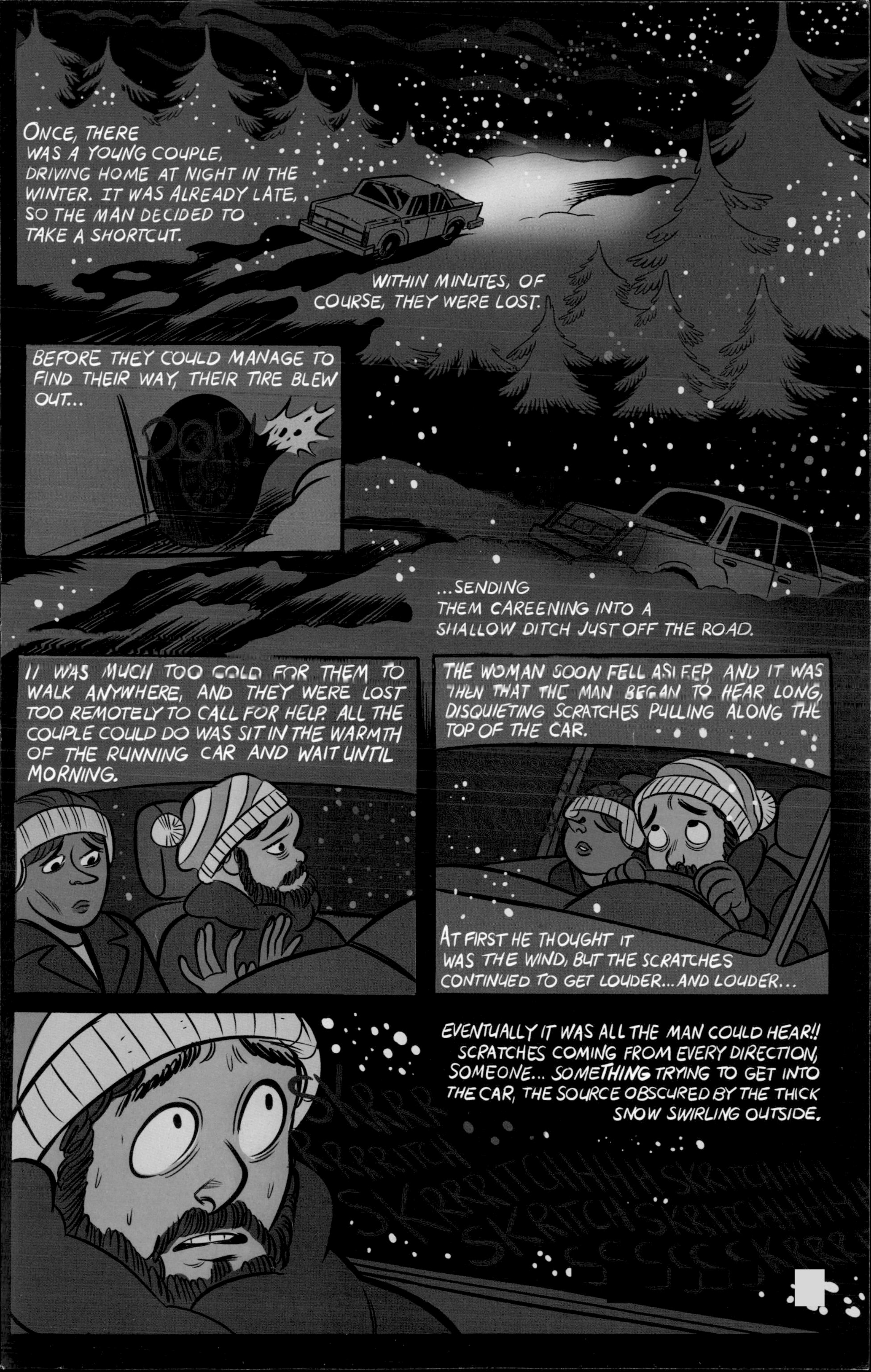
ONCE, THERE WAS A YOUNG COUPLE, DRIVING HOME AT NIGHT IN THE WINTER. IT WAS ALREADY LATE, SO THE MAN DECIDED TO TAKE A SHORTCUT.
WITHIN MINUTES, OF COURSE, THEY WERE LOST.
BEFORE THEY COULD MANAGE TO FIND THEIR WAY, THEIR TIRE BLEW OUT...
POP!
...SENDING THEM CAREENING INTO A SHALLOW DITCH JUST OFF THE ROAD.
IT WAS MUCH TOO COLD FOR THEM TO WALK ANYWHERE, AND THEY WERE LOST TOO REMOTELY TO CALL FOR HELP. ALL THE COUPLE COULD DO WAS SIT IN THE WARMTH OF THE RUNNING CAR AND WAIT UNTIL MORNING.
THE WOMAN SOON FELL ASLEEP, AND IT WAS THEN THAT THE MAN BEGAN TO HEAR LONG, DISQUIETING SCRATCHES PULLING ALONG THE TOP OF THE CAR.
AT FIRST HE THOUGHT IT WAS THE WIND, BUT THE SCRATCHES CONTINUED TO GET LOUDER...AND LOUDER...
EVENTUALLY IT WAS ALL THE MAN COULD HEAR!! SCRATCHES COMING FROM EVERY DIRECTION, SOMEONE... SOMETHING TRYING TO GET INTO THE CAR, THE SOURCE OBSCURED BY THE THICK SNOW SWIRLING OUTSIDE.

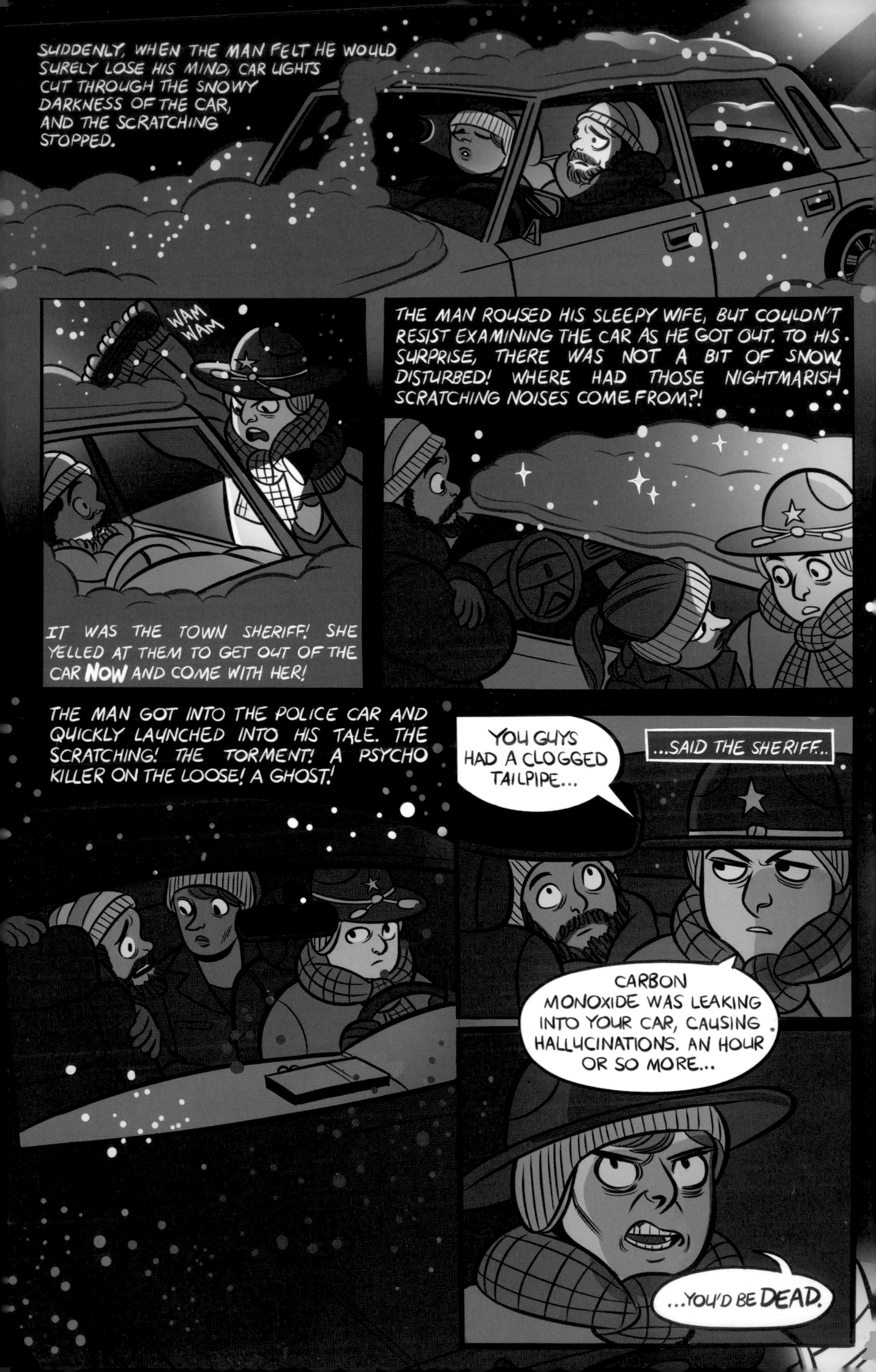
SUDDENLY, WHEN THE MAN FELT HE WOULD SURELY LOSE HIS MIND, CAR LIGHTS CUT THROUGH THE SNOWY DARKNESS OF THE CAR, AND THE SCRATCHING STOPPED.
WAM WAM
IT WAS THE TOWN SHERIFF! SHE YELLED AT THEM TO GET OUT OF THE CAR NOW AND COME WITH HER!
THE MAN ROUSED HIS SLEEPY WIFE, BUT COULDN'T RESIST EXAMINING THE CAR AS HE GOT OUT. TO HIS SURPRISE, THERE WAS NOT A BIT OF SNOW DISTURBED! WHERE HAD THOSE NIGHTMARISH SCRATCHING NOISES COME FROM?!
THE MAN GOT INTO THE POLICE CAR AND QUICKLY LAUNCHED INTO HIS TALE. THE SCRATCHING! THE TORMENT! A PSYCHO KILLER ON THE LOOSE! A GHOST!
YOU GUYS HAD A CLOGGED TAILPIPE...
...SAID THE SHERIFF...
CARBON MONOXIDE WAS LEAKING INTO YOUR CAR, CAUSING HALLUCINATIONS. AN HOUR OR SO MORE...
...YOU'D BE DEAD.

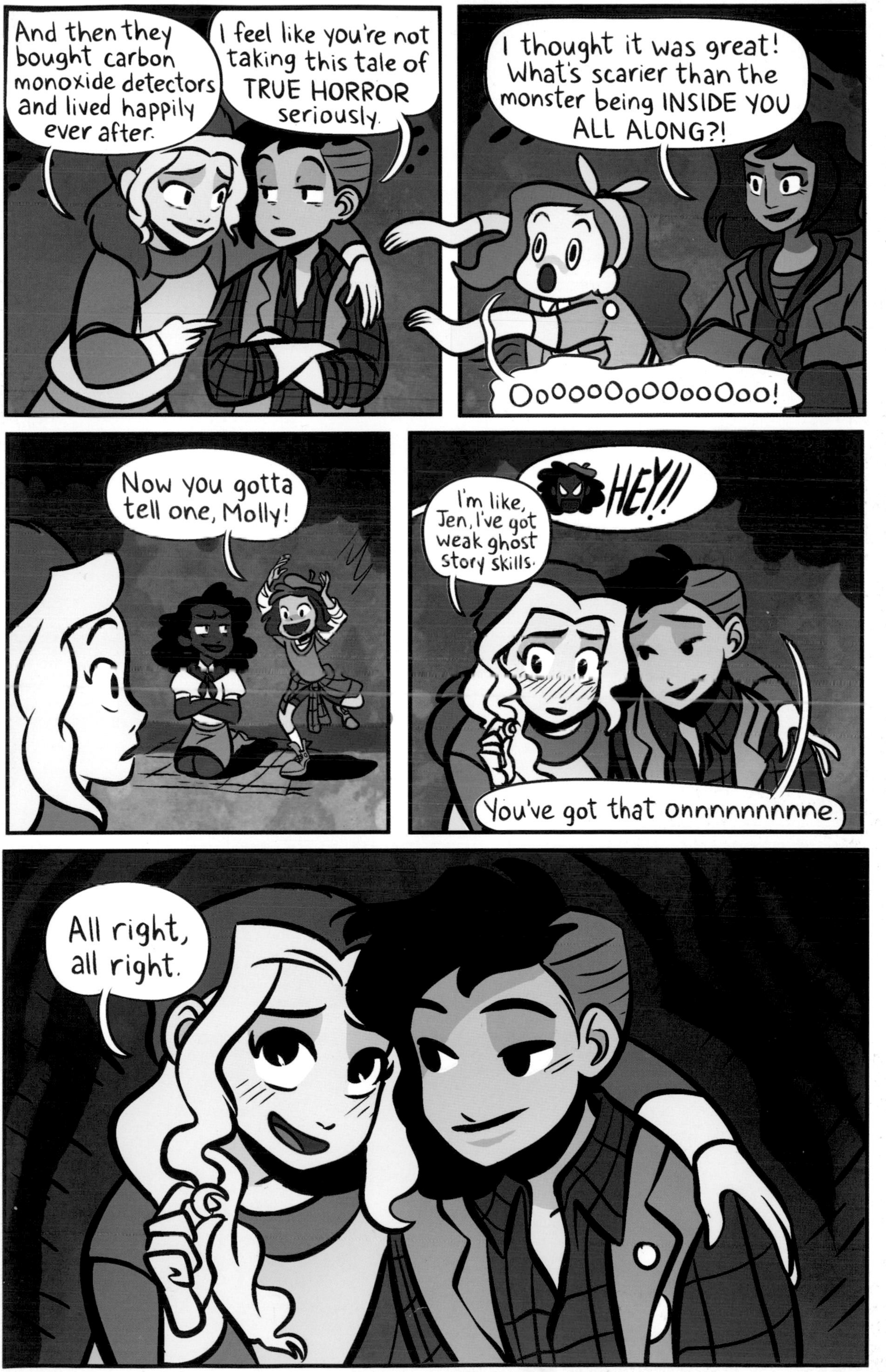

And then they bought carbon monoxide detectors and lived happily ever after.
I feel like you're not taking this tale of TRUE HORROR seriously.
I thought it was great! What's scarier than the monster being INSIDE YOU ALL ALONG?!
OoooooOoooooOoo!
Now you gotta tell one, Molly!
I'm like, Jen, I've got weak ghost story skills.
HEY!!
You've got that onnnnnnnnne.
All right, all right.

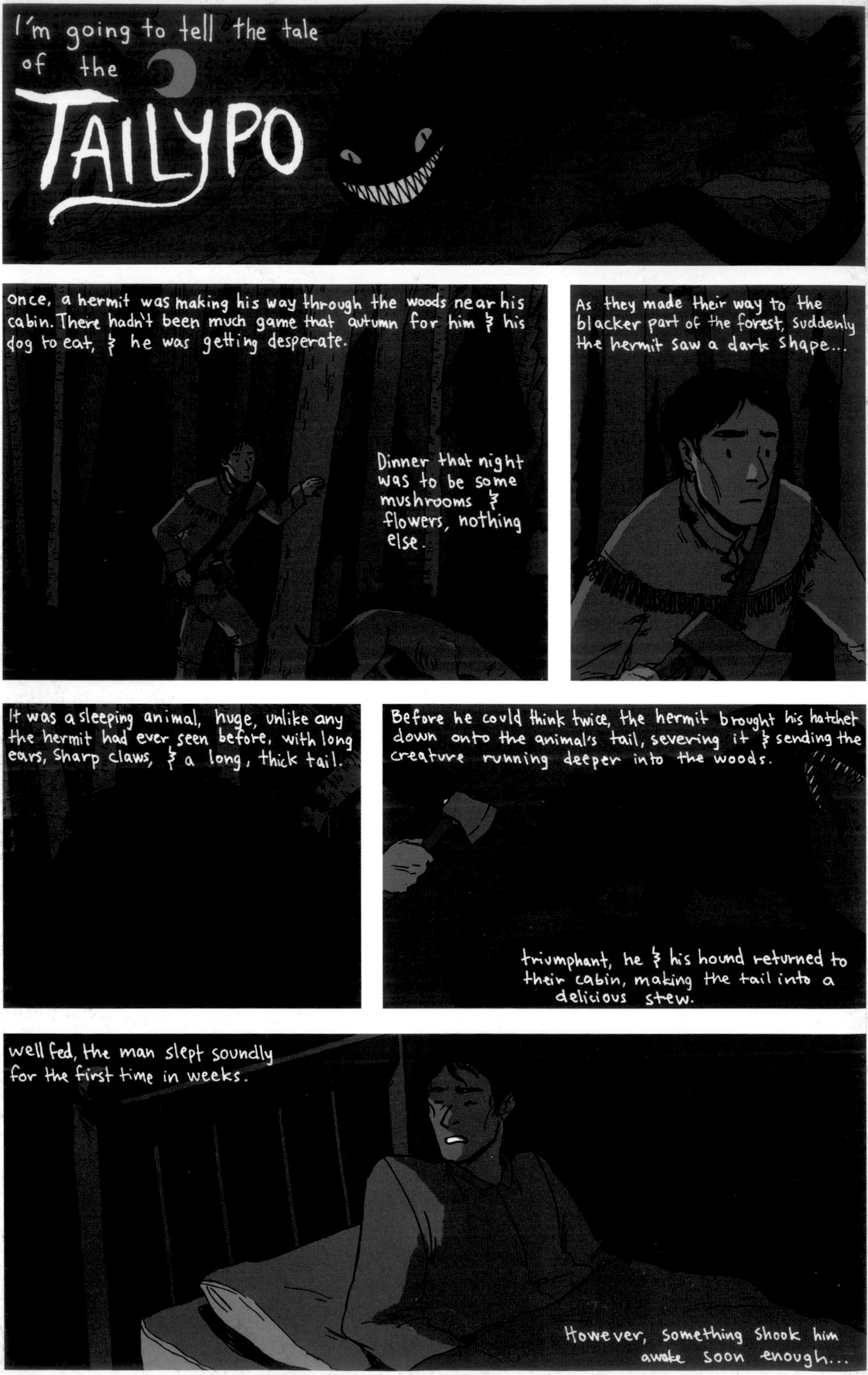
I'm going to tell the tale of the
TAILYPO
Once, a hermit was making his way through the woods near his cabin. There hadn't been much game that autumn for him & his dog to eat, & he was getting desperate.
Dinner that night was to be some mushrooms & flowers, nothing else.
As they made their way to the blacker part of the forest, suddenly the hermit saw a dark shape...
It was a sleeping animal, huge, unlike any the hermit had ever seen before, with long ears, sharp claws, & a long, thick tail.
Before he could think twice, the hermit brought his hatchet down onto the animal's tail, severing it & sending the creature running deeper into the woods.
triumphant, he & his hound returned to their cabin, making the tail into a delicious stew.
well fed, the man slept soundly for the first time in weeks.
However, something shook him awake soon enough...

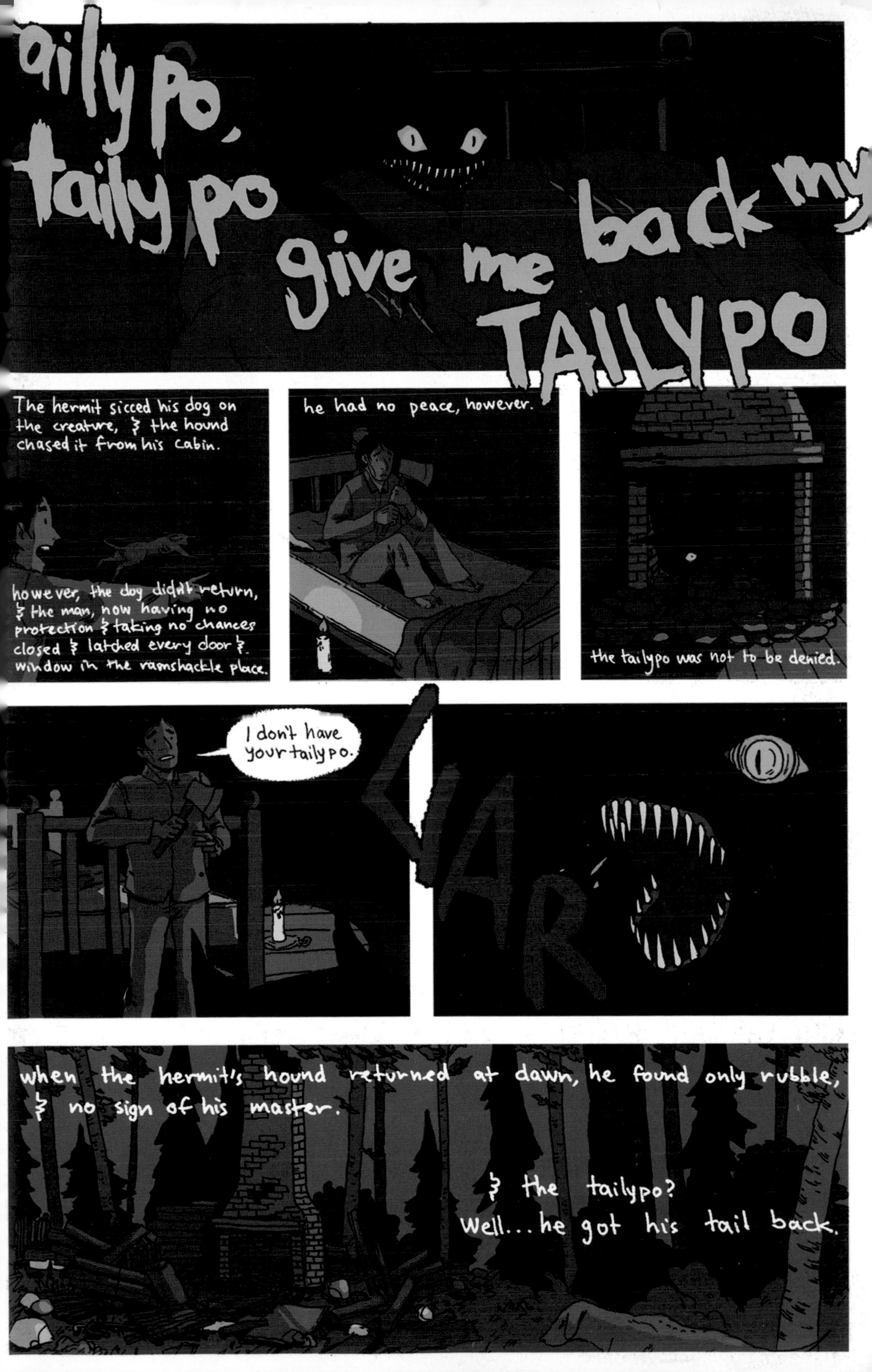

tailypo, tailypo
give me back my TAILYPO
The hermit sicced his dog on the creature, & the hound chased it from his cabin.
however, the dog didn't return, & the man, now having no protection & taking no chances closed & latched every door & window in the ramshackle place.
he had no peace, however.
the tailypo was not to be denied.
I don't have your tailypo.
YAR
when the hermit's hound returned at dawn, he found only rubble, & no sign of his master.
& the tailypo?
Well... he got his tail back.

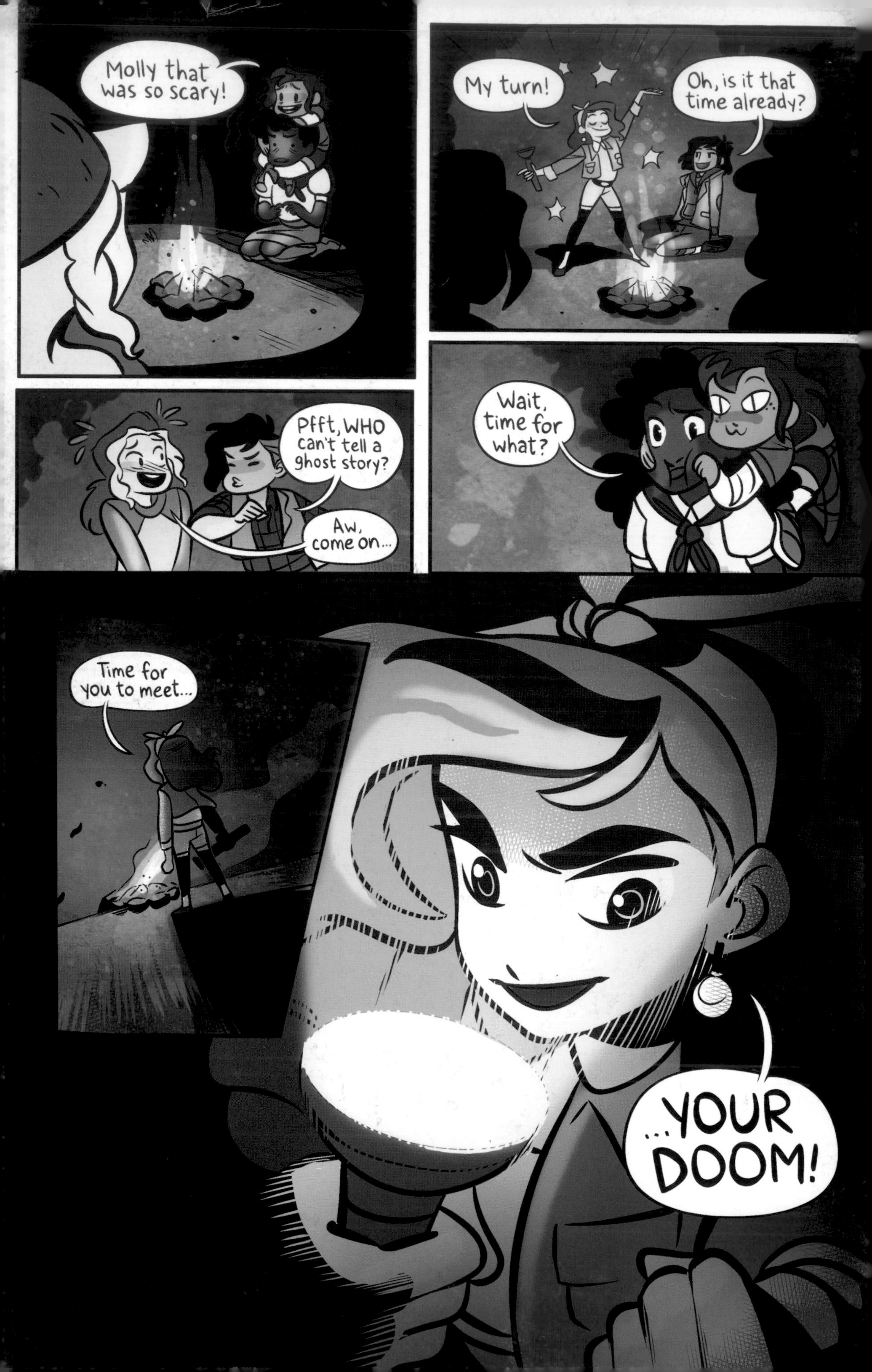
Molly that was so scary!
My turn!
Oh, is it that time already?
Pfft, WHO can't tell a ghost story?
Aw, come on...
Wait, time for what?
Time for you to meet...
...YOUR DOOM!

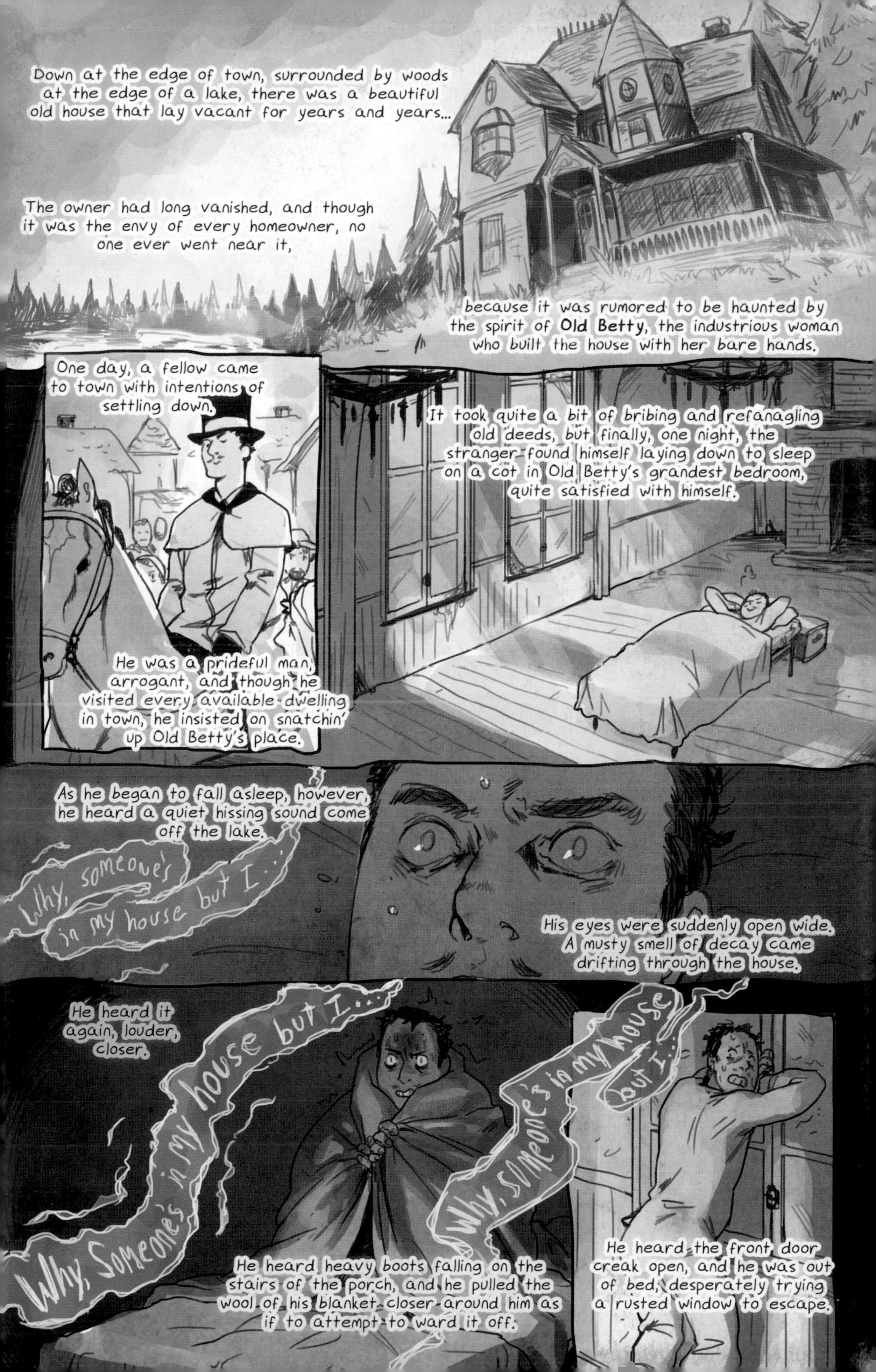
Down at the edge of town, surrounded by woods at the edge of a lake, there was a beautiful old house that lay vacant for years and years...
The owner had long vanished, and though it was the envy of every homeowner, no one ever went near it,
because it was rumored to be haunted by the spirit of **Old Betty**, the industrious woman who built the house with her bare hands.
One day, a fellow came to town with intentions of settling down.
He was a prideful man, arrogant, and though he visited every available dwelling in town, he insisted on snatchin' up Old Betty's place.
It took quite a bit of bribing and refanagling old deeds, but finally, one night, the stranger found himself laying down to sleep on a cot in Old Betty's grandest bedroom, quite satisfied with himself.
As he began to fall asleep, however, he heard a quiet hissing sound come off the lake.
Why, someone's in my house but I...
His eyes were suddenly open wide. A musty smell of decay came drifting through the house.
He heard it again, louder, closer.
Why, Someone's in my house but I...
He heard heavy boots falling on the stairs of the porch, and he pulled the wool of his blanket closer around him as if to attempt to ward it off.
Why, Someone's in my house but I...
He heard the front door creak open, and he was out of bed, desperately trying a rusted window to escape.

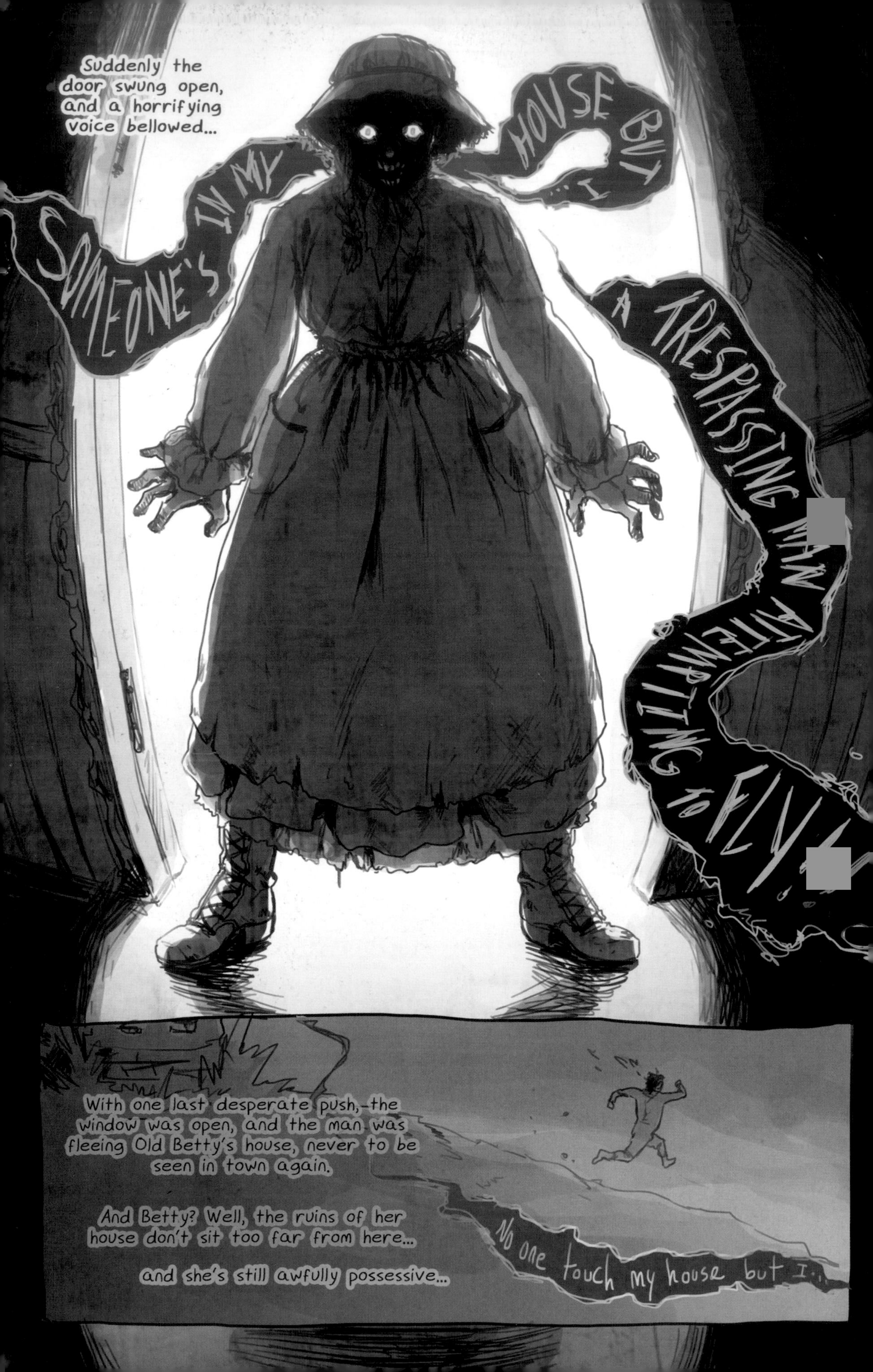
Suddenly the door swung open, and a horrifying voice bellowed...
SOMEONE'S IN MY HOUSE BUT I...
A TRESPASSING MAN ATTEMPTING TO FLY...
With one last desperate push, the window was open, and the man was fleeing Old Betty's house, never to be seen in town again.
And Betty? Well, the ruins of her house don't sit too far from here...
and she's still awfully possessive...
No one touch my house but I...

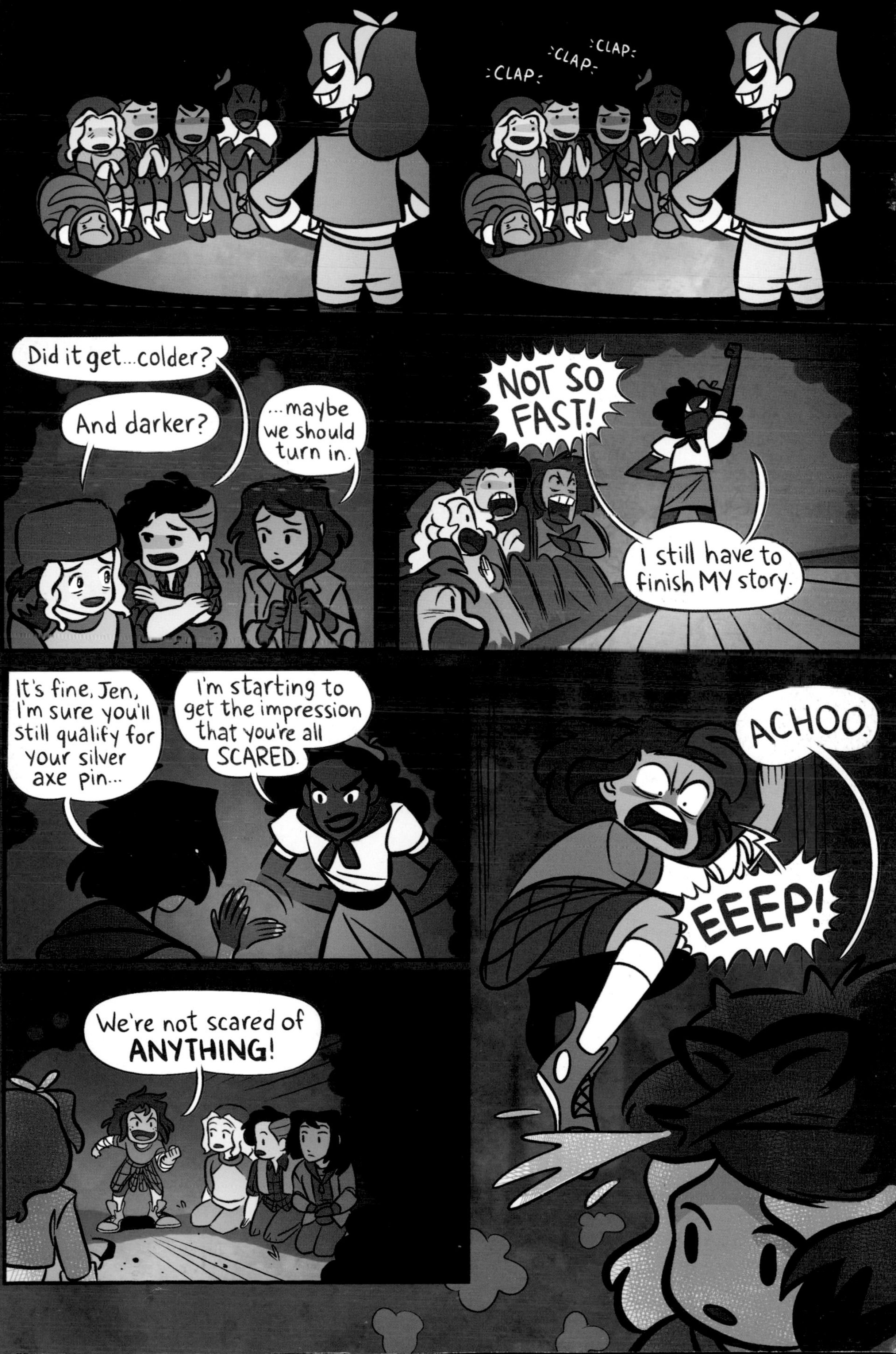
:CLAP:
:CLAP:
:CLAP:
Did it get...colder?
And darker?
...maybe we should turn in.
NOT SO FAST!
I still have to finish MY story.
It's fine, Jen, I'm sure you'll still qualify for your silver axe pin...
I'm starting to get the impression that you're all SCARED.
We're not scared of ANYTHING!
ACHOO.
EEEP!

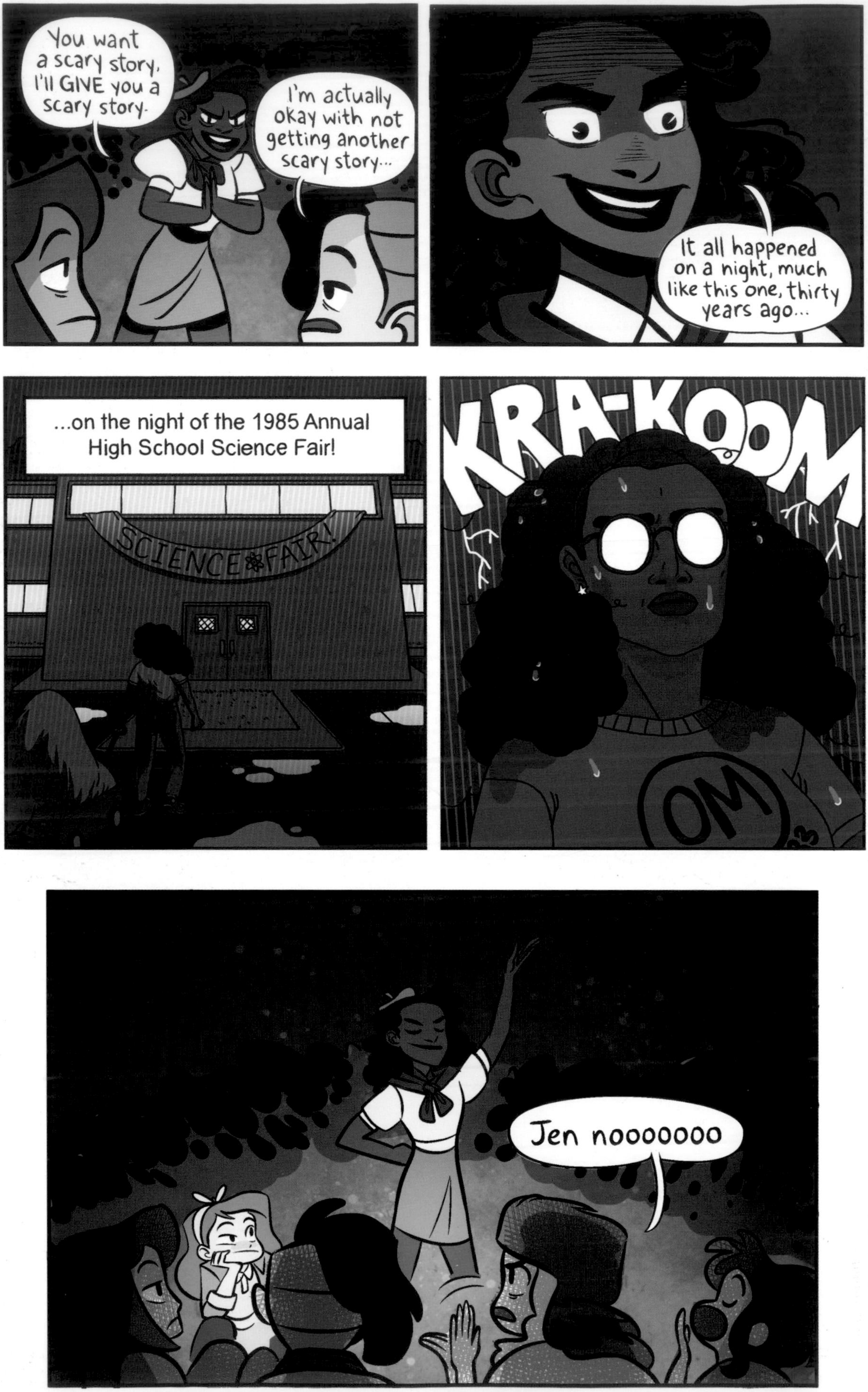
You want a scary story, I'll GIVE you a scary story.
I'm actually okay with not getting another scary story...
It all happened on a night, much like this one, thirty years ago...
...on the night of the 1985 Annual High School Science Fair!
SCIENCE FAIR!
KRA-KOOM
OM
Jen nooooooo

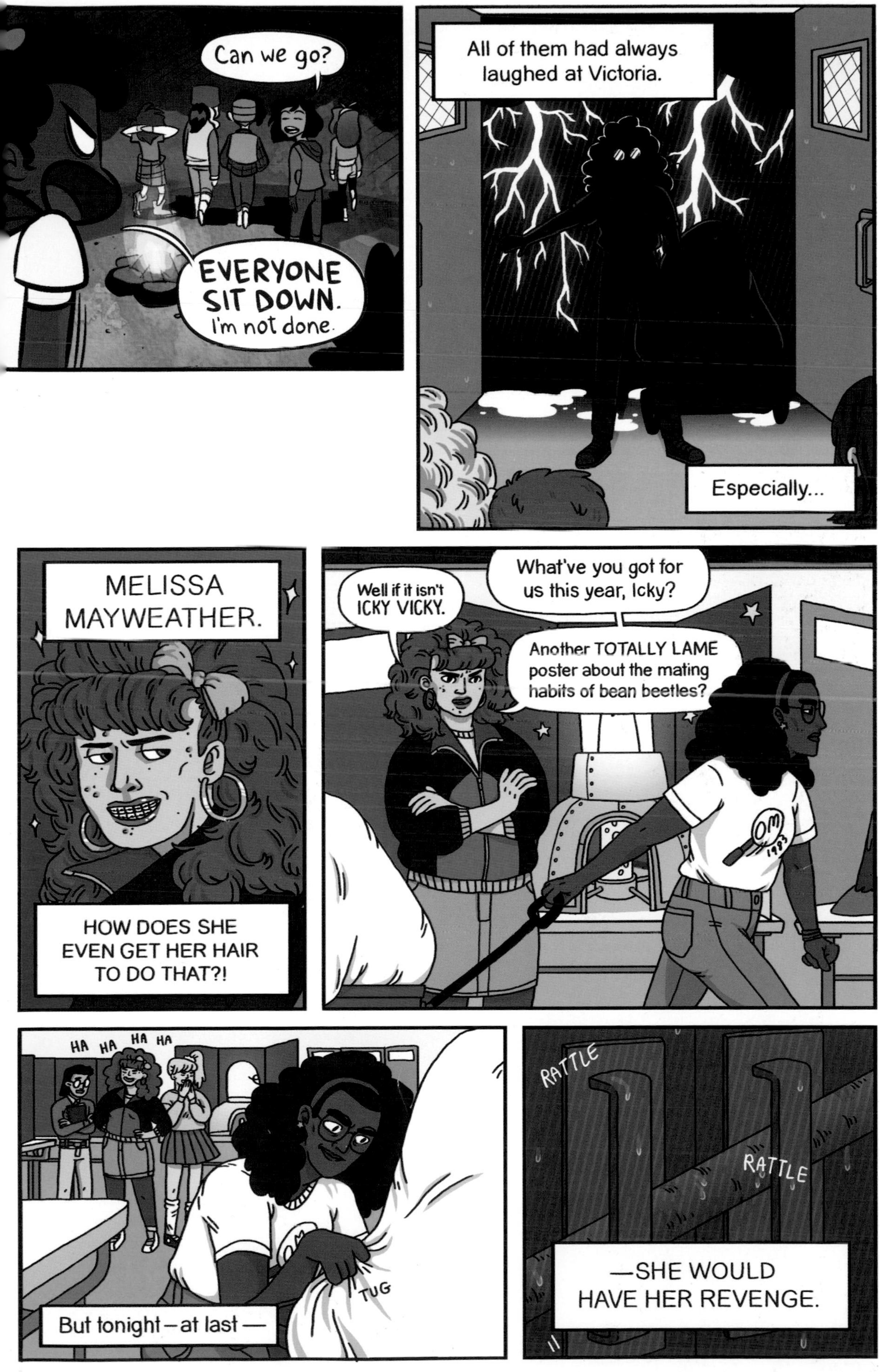

Can we go?
EVERYONE SIT DOWN. I'm not done.
All of them had always laughed at Victoria.
Especially...
MELISSA MAYWEATHER.
HOW DOES SHE EVEN GET HER HAIR TO DO THAT?!
Well if it isn't ICKY VICKY.
What've you got for us this year, Icky?
Another TOTALLY LAME poster about the mating habits of bean beetles?
OM 1983
HA HA HA HA
TUG
But tonight—at last—
RATTLE
RATTLE
—SHE WOULD HAVE HER REVENGE.

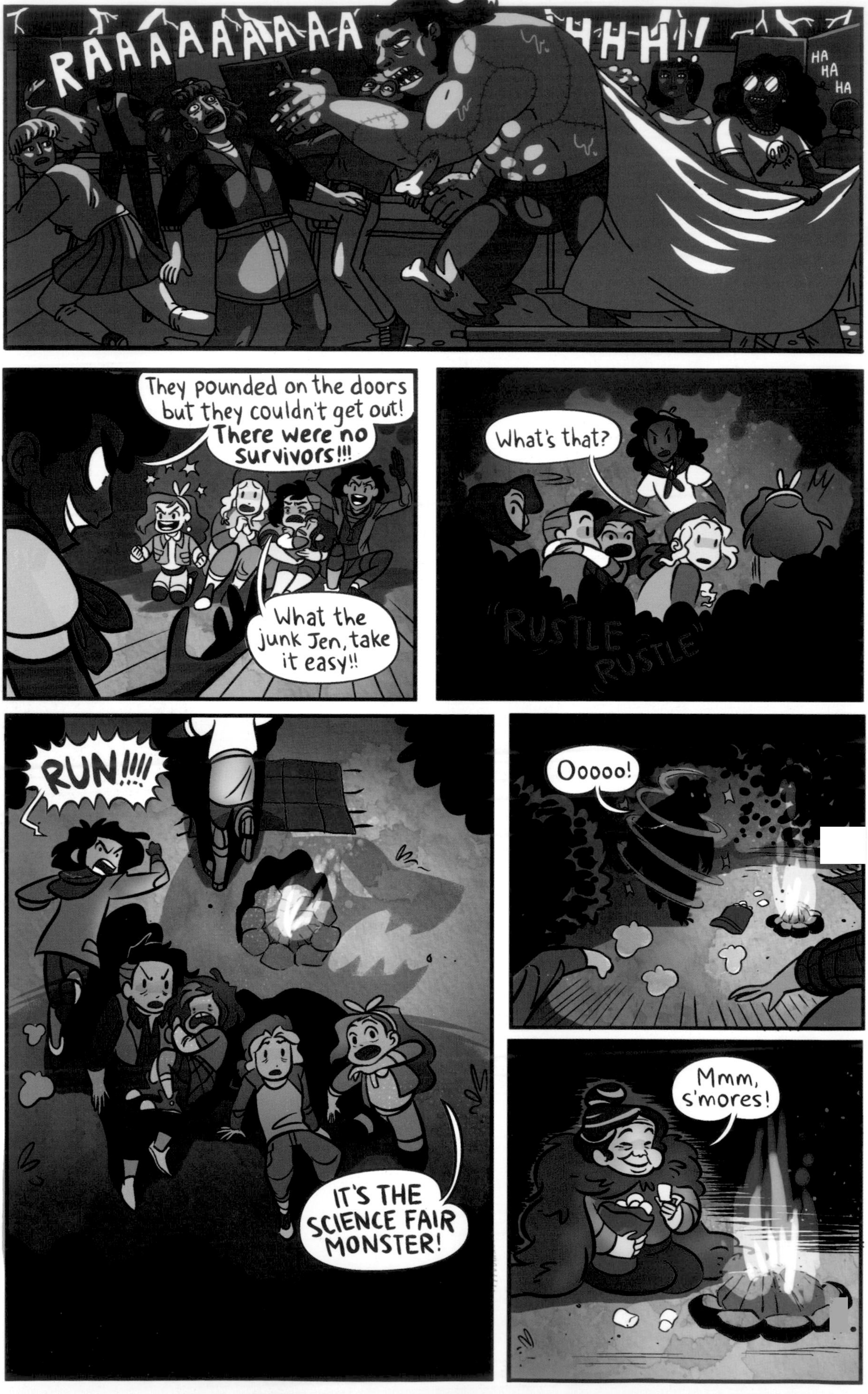
RAAAAAAAAA-AAHHH!
HA HA HA
They pounded on the doors but they couldn't get out! There were no survivors!!!
What the junk Jen, take it easy!!
What's that?
RUSTLE RUSTLE
RUN!!!!
IT'S THE SCIENCE FAIR MONSTER!
Ooooo!
Mmm, s'mores!

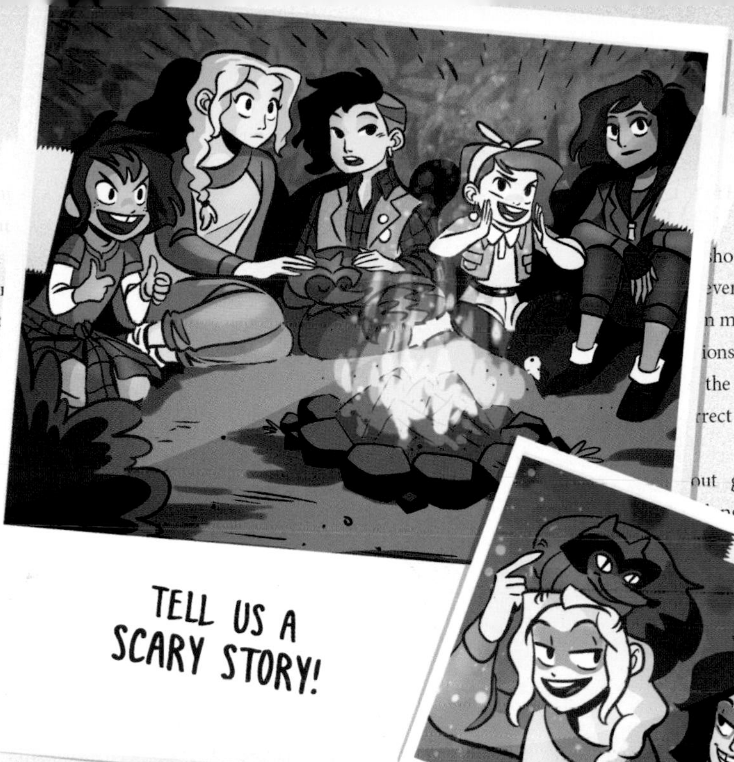
TELL US A
SCARY STORY!

will co...
Th...
It he...
appeara...
dress f...
Further...
Lumbe...
to have...
part in...
Thisk...
Hardc...
have ...
them...

...E UNIFORM

...hould be worn at camp
...vents when Lumberjanes
...n may also be worn at other
...ions. It should be worn as a
... the uniform dress with
...rrect shoes, and stocking or
...
...out grows her uniform or
...ng ...ster Lumberjane.
...a she has
... her
... her

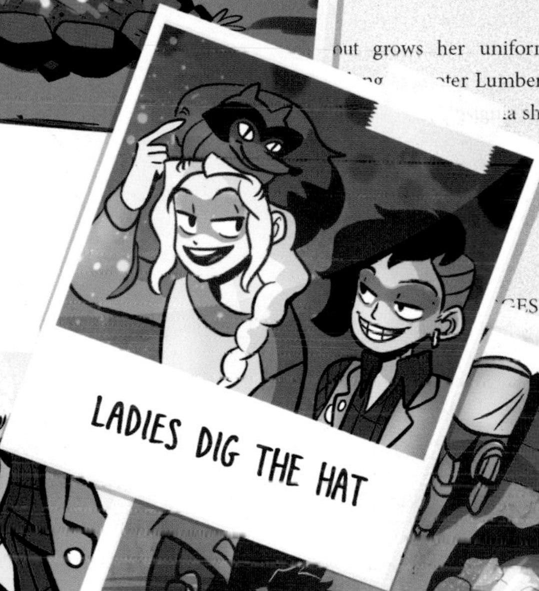
LADIES DIG THE HAT

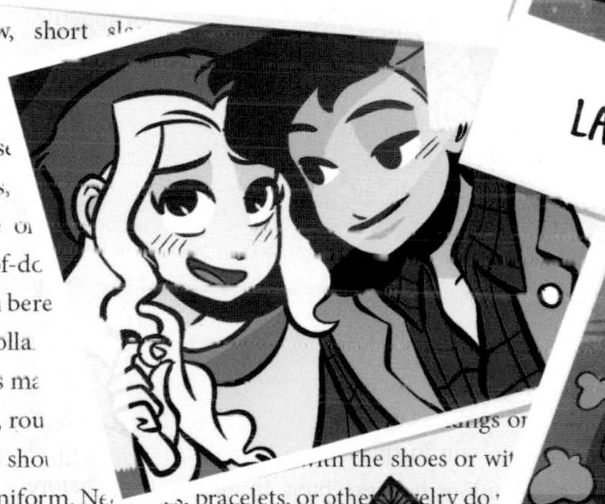

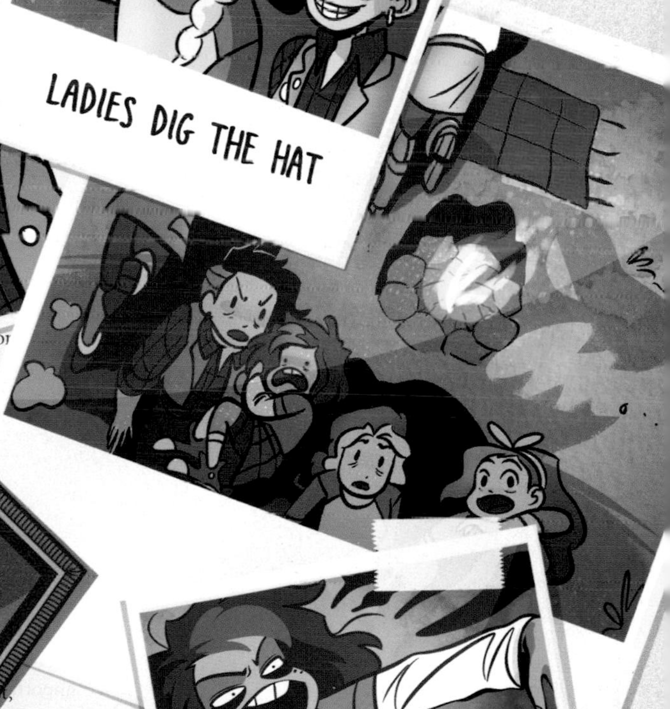

The ...
yellow, short sl...
emb...
the w...
choose...
slacks,...
made o...
out-of-do...
green bere...
the colla...
Shoes ma...
heels, rou... ...ings or
socks shou... ...ith the shoes or wi...
the uniform. Ne...es, bracelets, or other jewelry do ...
belong with a Lumberjane uniform.

...GES

HOW TO WEAR T...

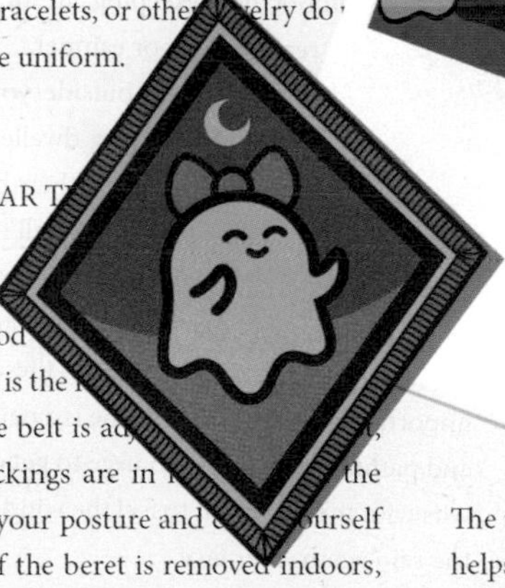

To look well in a unifor... uniform be kept in good ... pressed. See that the skirt is the ... height and build, that the belt is ad... that your shoes and stockings are in ... the uniform, that you watch your posture and ...ourself with dignity and grace. If the beret is removed indoors, be sure that your hair is neat and kept in place with an insonspicuous clip or ribbon. When you wear a Lumberjane uniform you are identified as a member of this organization and you should be doubly careful to conduct yourself in a way that will show everyone that courtesy and thoughtfullness are part of being a Lumberjane. People are likely to judge a whole nation by the selfishness of a few individuals, to criticize a whole family because of the misconduct of one member, and to feel unkindly toward and organization because of the

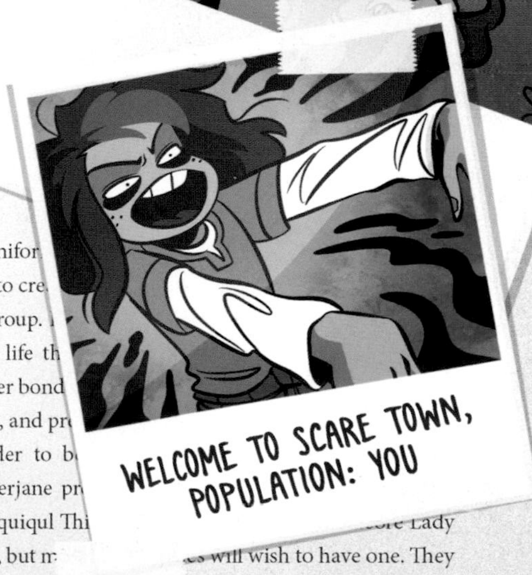
WELCOME TO SCARE TOWN,
POPULATION: YOU

The unifor...
helps to cre...
in a group. ...
active life th...
another bond...
future, and pr...
in order to b...
Lumberjane pr...
Penniquiqul Thi... ...ore Lady
Types, but m... ...es will wish to have one. They
can either bu... ...m, or make it themselves from
materials available at the trading post.

LUMBERJANES FIELD MANUAL

CHAPTER TEN

Lumberjanes "Cooking" Program Field

ABSENCE MAKES THE HEART GROW FONDANT BADGE

"Fondant gives the heart diabetes, it's the circle of life."

Everyone and everything needs food to survive. It is not something that is unique only to people or to creatures and it is something everyone must acknowledge. At Lumberjane camp, every scout will learn that while food is essential, that doesn't mean we can't have some fun with it first. Now while some ladies may have been taught that it is not polite to play with their food, the Lumberjane High Council disagrees. Everything is meant to be fun and exhilarating, we should constantly be learning and improving ourselves just as we should always be laughing. Life is meant to be fun and if that means we get to bake some cakes in the process then every Lumberjane should put on her best apron and go at it.

The *Absence Makes The Heart Grow Fondant* badge represents a skill that all Lumberjanes will be taught. As a Lumberjane it will be understood that every scout should be able to rely on just herself in any situation. That means

she should not only know how to handle a bear attack without harming herself or the animals around her, but she should also know how to create an elaborate cake that will entertain all her guests not only visually but as well as in flavor. The way around the kitchen will be no match for any Lumberjane as she masters her adaptability and her problem solving skills while at this camp.

To obtain the *Absence Makes The Heart Grow Fondant* badge a Lumberjane must be participating in a bake off. She will be given an already baked cake of her choice of flavor as well as the tools to mold her frosting to the design she prefers. Once the time starts the Lumberjane scout must completely decorate her cake in a creative style that will be judged by the leader of the class, and while all art is subjective, the instructions given before the bake off will be clearly given and understood by all participants. In the end, it will be the scout who

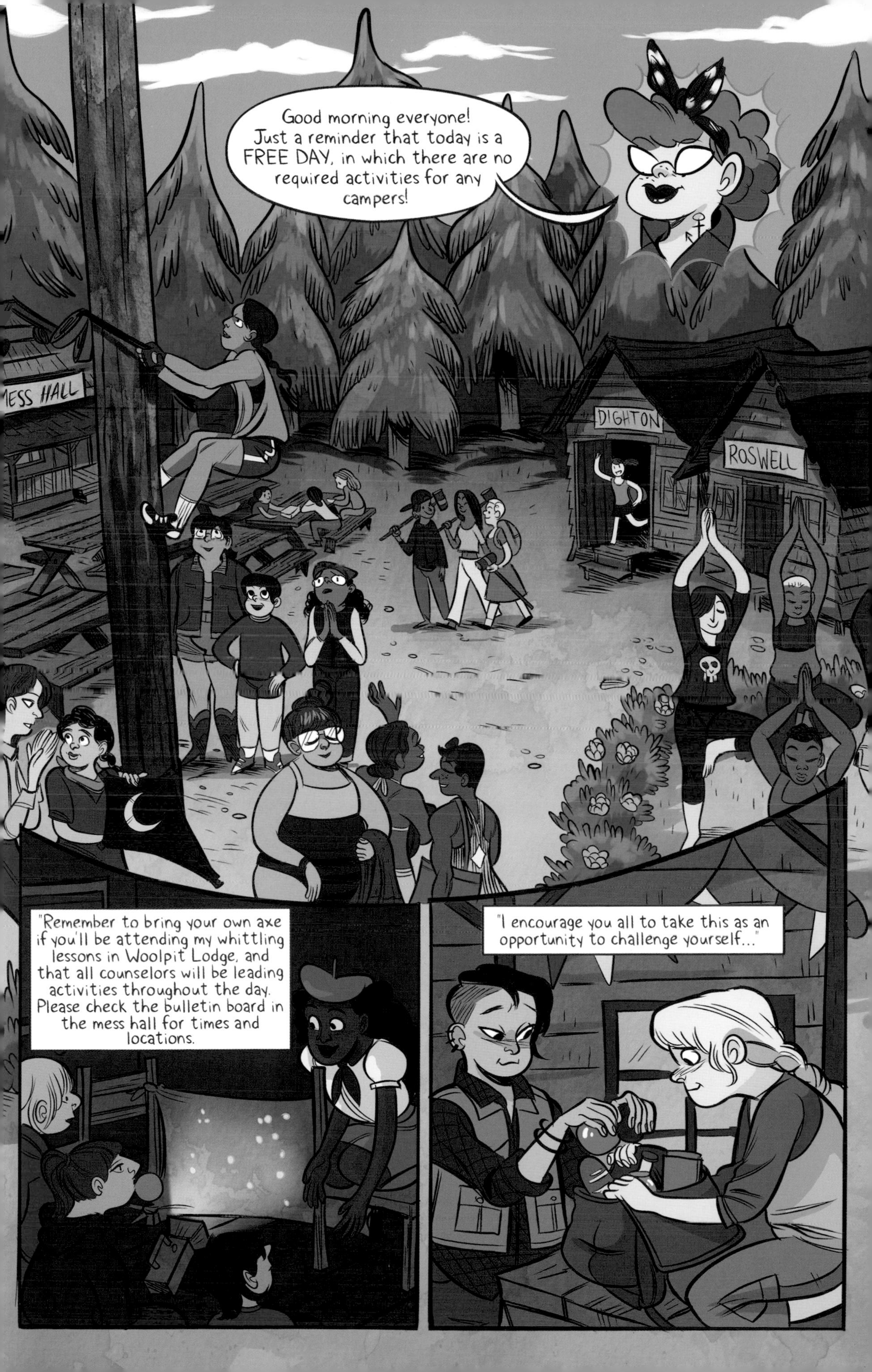
Good morning everyone! Just a reminder that today is a FREE DAY, in which there are no required activities for any campers!
MESS HALL
DIGHTON
ROSWELL
"Remember to bring your own axe if you'll be attending my whittling lessons in Woolpit Lodge, and that all counselors will be leading activities throughout the day. Please check the bulletin board in the mess hall for times and locations.
"I encourage you all to take this as an opportunity to challenge yourself..."

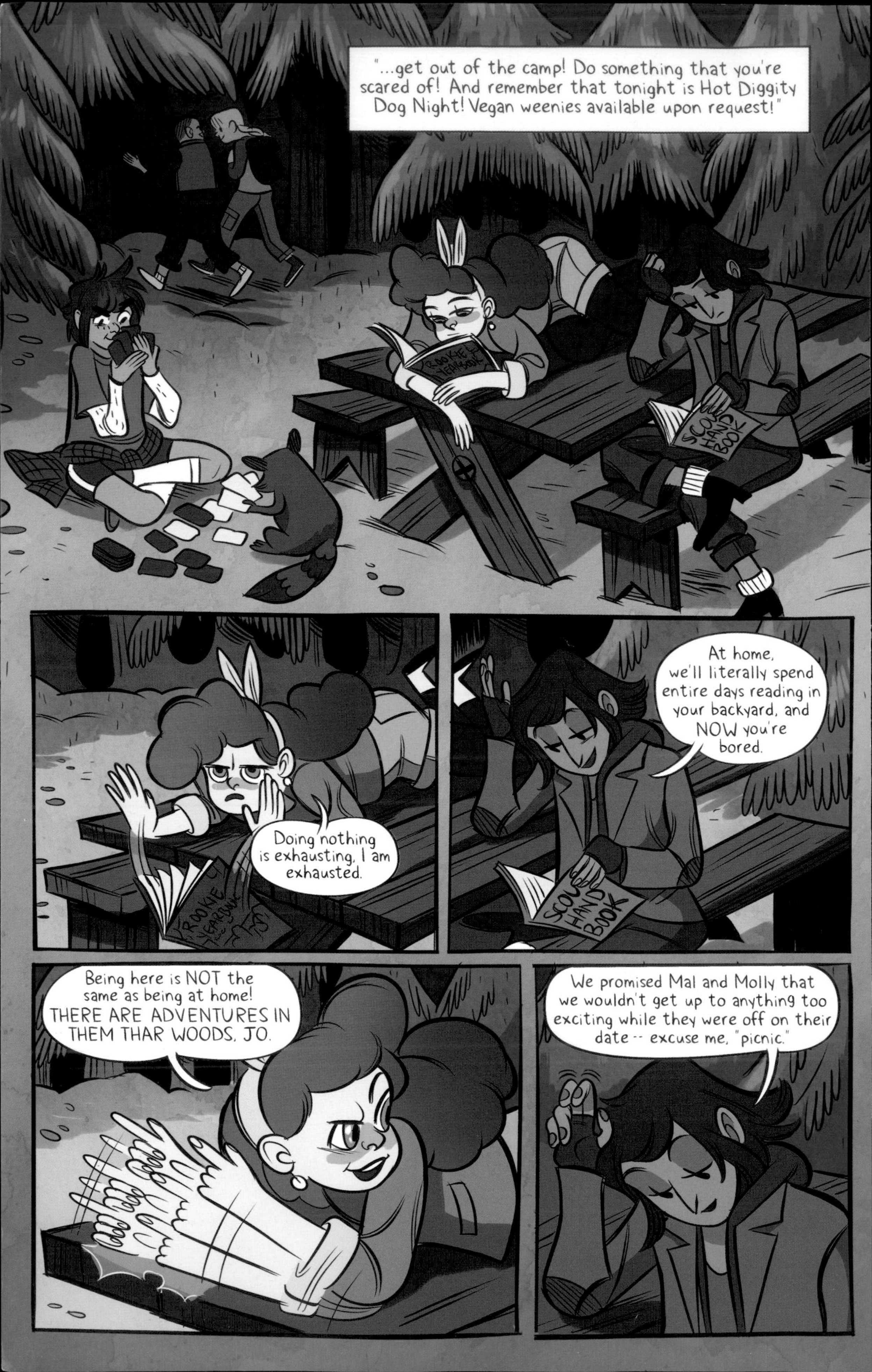
"...get out of the camp! Do something that you're scared of! And remember that tonight is Hot Diggity Dog Night! Vegan weenies available upon request!"
ROOKIE YEARBOOK
SCOUT HANDBOOK
Doing nothing is exhausting. I am exhausted.
At home, we'll literally spend entire days reading in your backyard, and NOW you're bored.
Being here is NOT the same as being at home! THERE ARE ADVENTURES IN THEM THAR WOODS, JO.
We promised Mal and Molly that we wouldn't get up to anything too exciting while they were off on their date -- excuse me, "picnic."

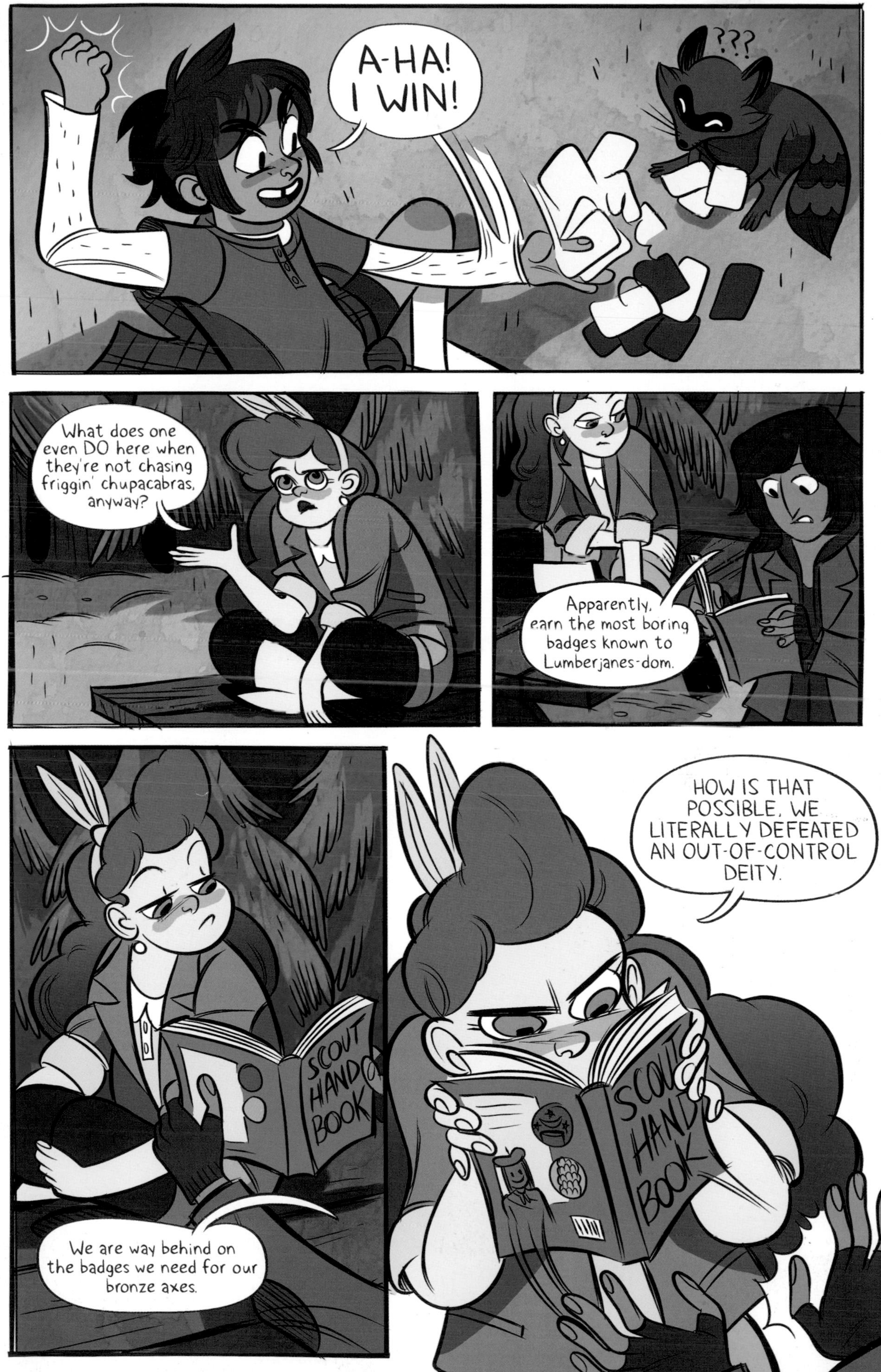
A-HA! I WIN!
???
What does one even DO here when they're not chasing friggin' chupacabras, anyway?
Apparently, earn the most boring badges known to Lumberjanes-dom.
We are way behind on the badges we need for our bronze axes.
HOW IS THAT POSSIBLE, WE LITERALLY DEFEATED AN OUT-OF-CONTROL DEITY.
SCOUT HAND BOOK
SCOUT HAND BOOK

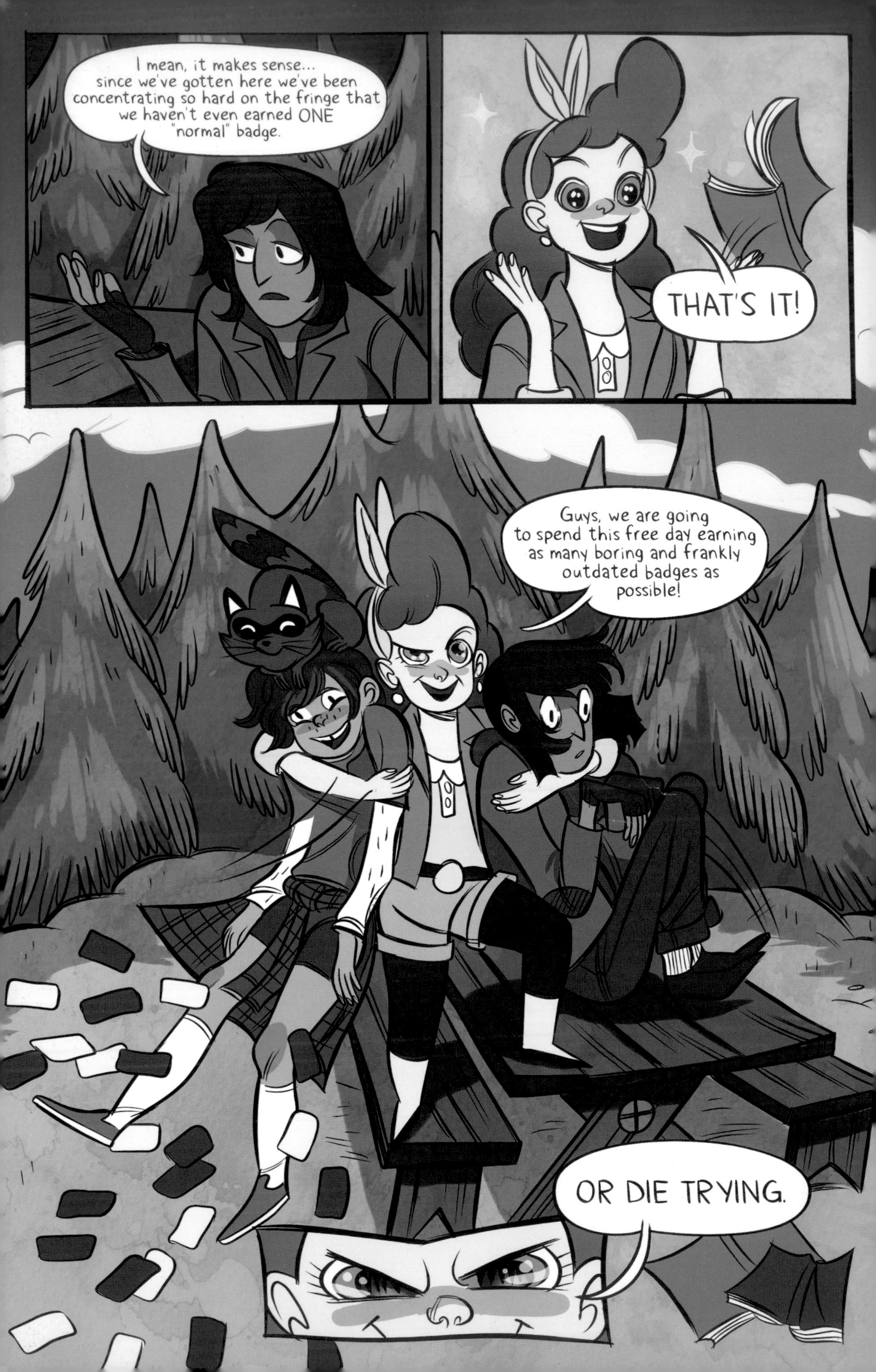
I mean, it makes sense... since we've gotten here we've been concentrating so hard on the fringe that we haven't even earned ONE "normal" badge.
THAT'S IT!
Guys, we are going to spend this free day earning as many boring and frankly outdated badges as possible!
OR DIE TRYING.

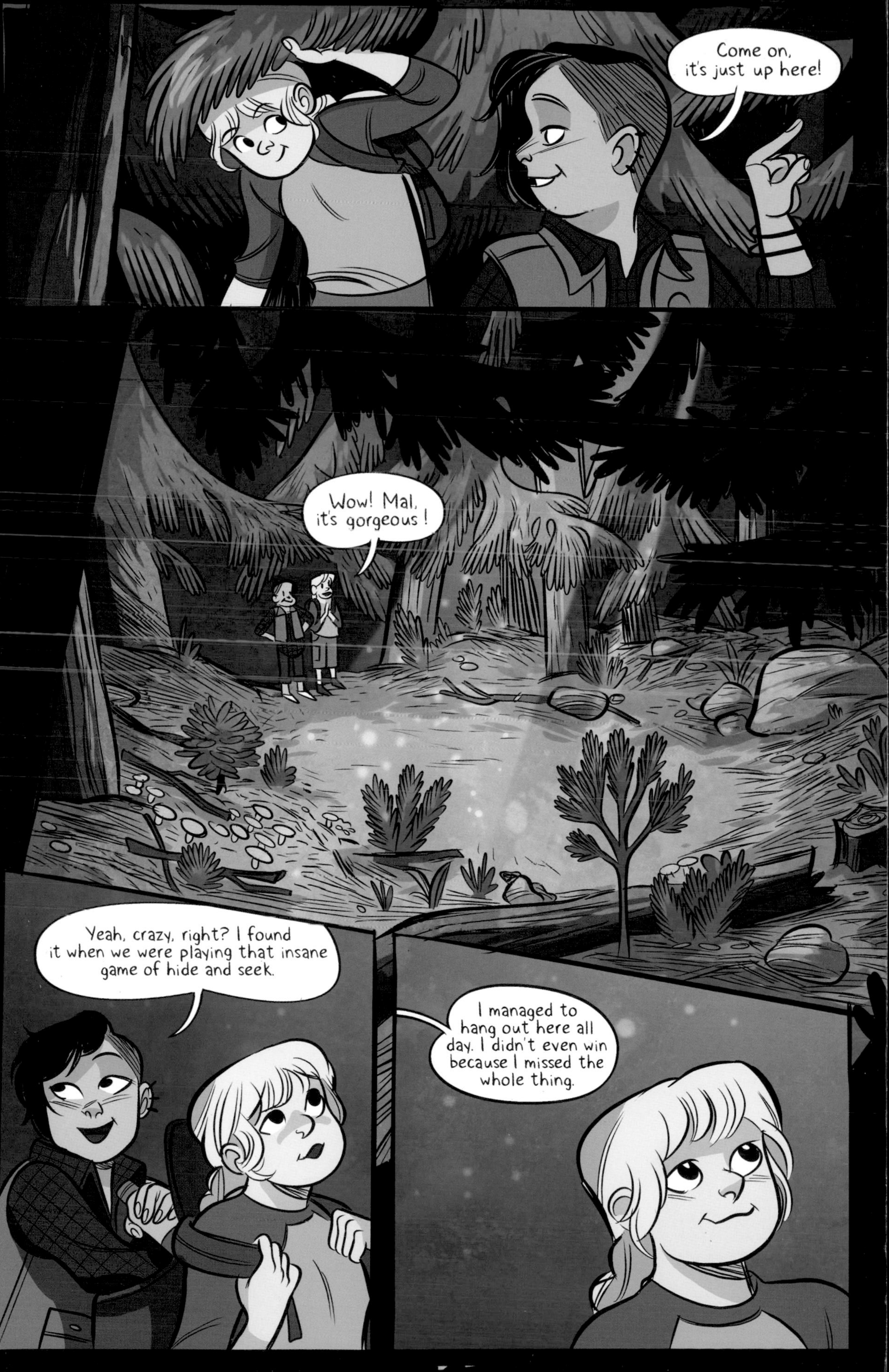
Come on, it's just up here!
Wow! Mal, it's gorgeous!
Yeah, crazy, right? I found it when we were playing that insane game of hide and seek.
I managed to hang out here all day. I didn't even win because I missed the whole thing.

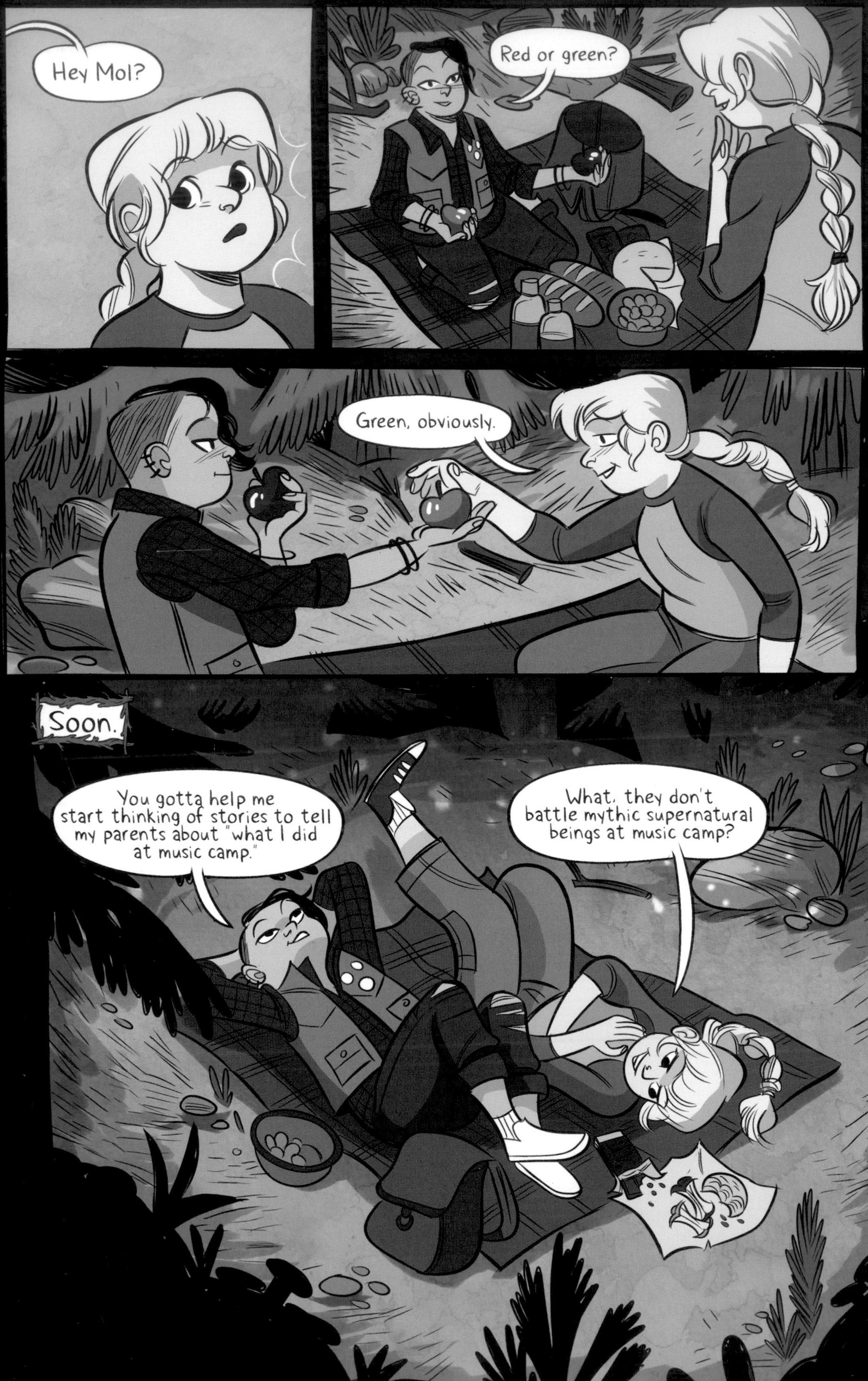
Hey Mol?
Red or green?
Green, obviously.
Soon.
You gotta help me start thinking of stories to tell my parents about "what I did at music camp."
What, they don't battle mythic supernatural beings at music camp?

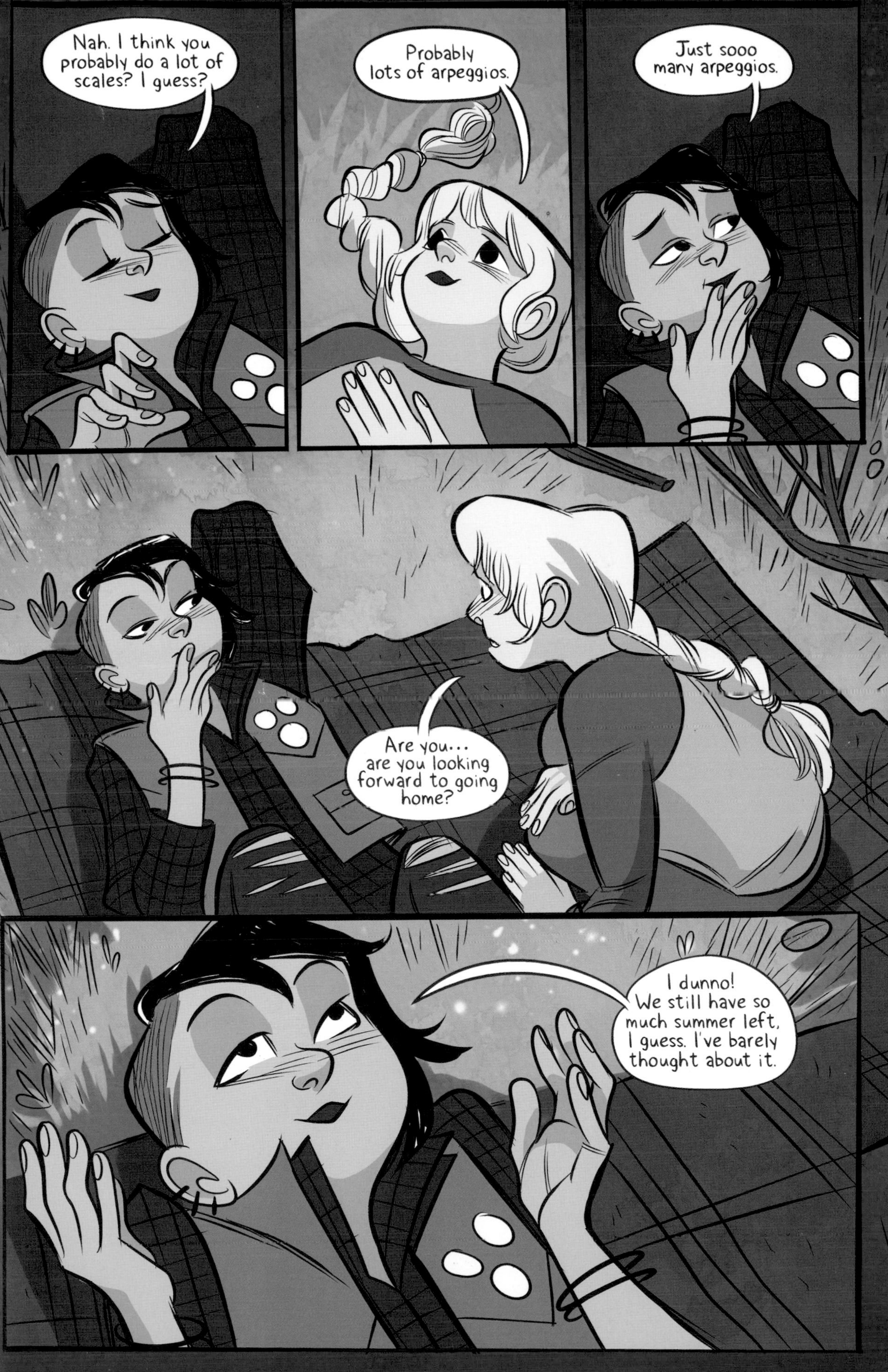
Nah. I think you probably do a lot of scales? I guess?
Probably lots of arpeggios.
Just sooo many arpeggios.
Are you... are you looking forward to going home?
I dunno! We still have so much summer left, I guess. I've barely thought about it.

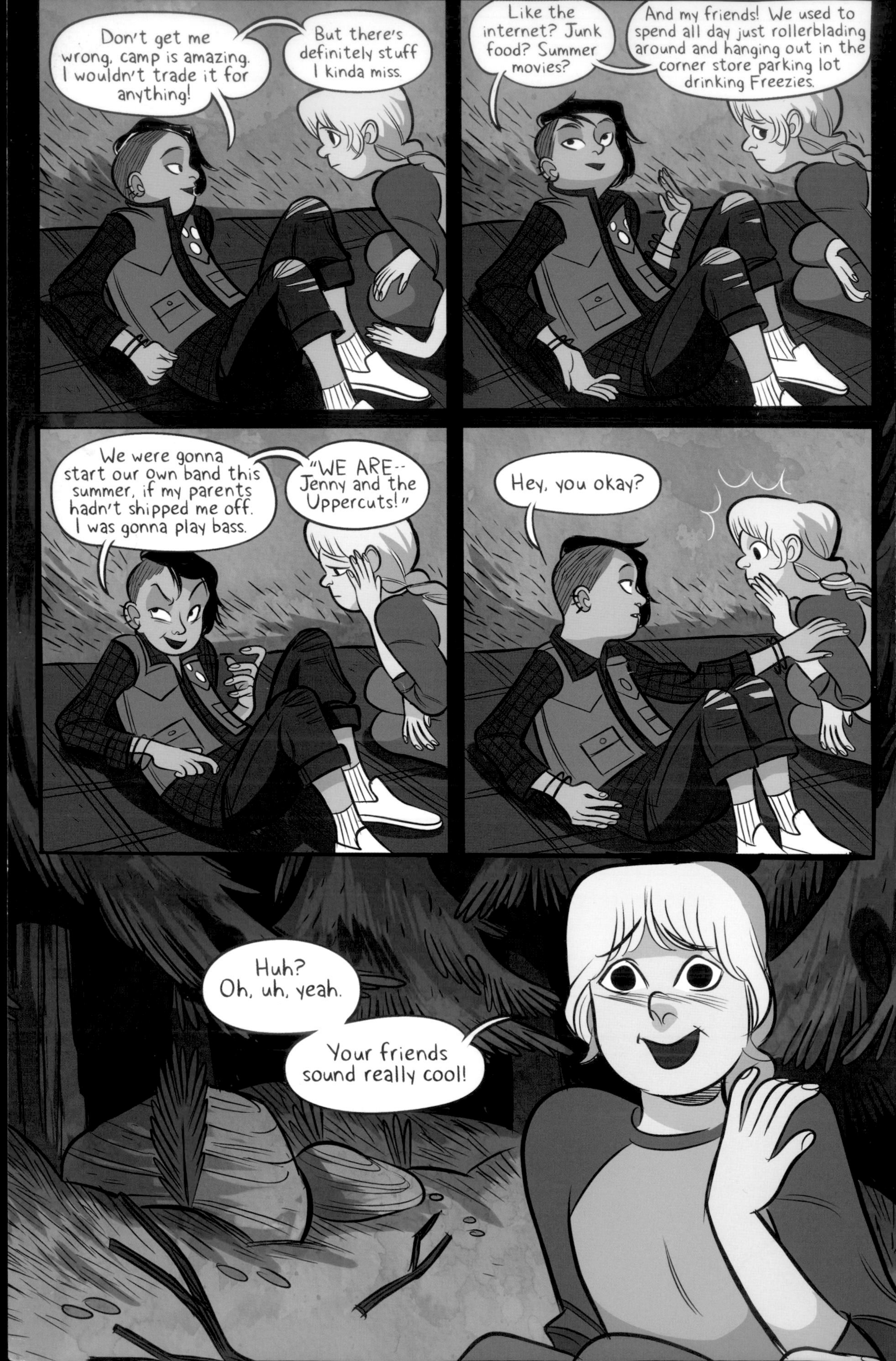
Don't get me wrong, camp is amazing. I wouldn't trade it for anything!
But there's definitely stuff I kinda miss.
Like the internet? Junk food? Summer movies?
And my friends! We used to spend all day just rollerblading around and hanging out in the corner store parking lot drinking Freezies.
We were gonna start our own band this summer, if my parents hadn't shipped me off. I was gonna play bass.
"WE ARE-- Jenny and the Uppercuts!"
Hey, you okay?
Huh? Oh, uh, yeah.
Your friends sound really cool!

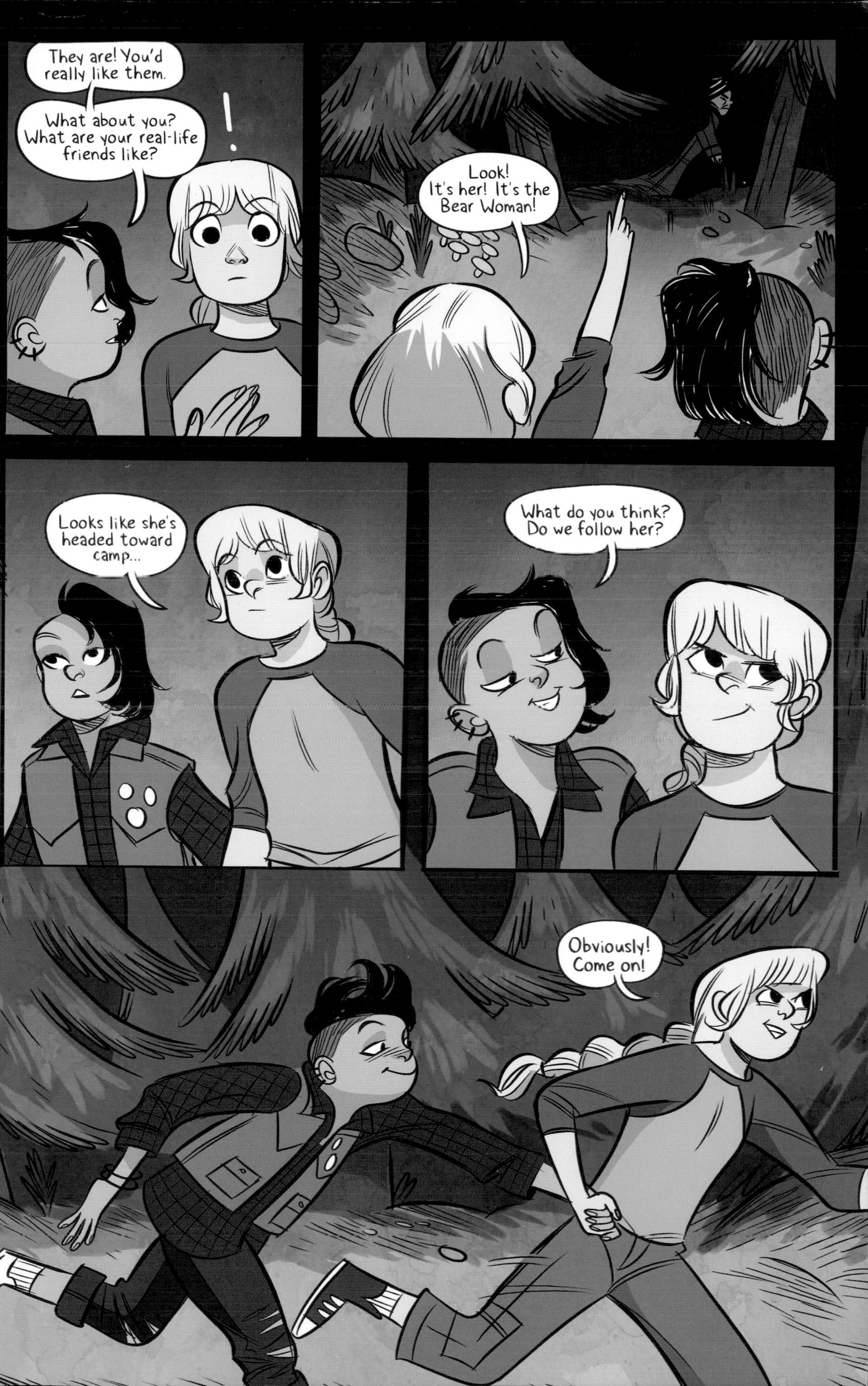
They are! You'd really like them.
What about you? What are your real-life friends like?
!
Look! It's her! It's the Bear Woman!
Looks like she's headed toward camp...
What do you think? Do we follow her?
Obviously! Come on!

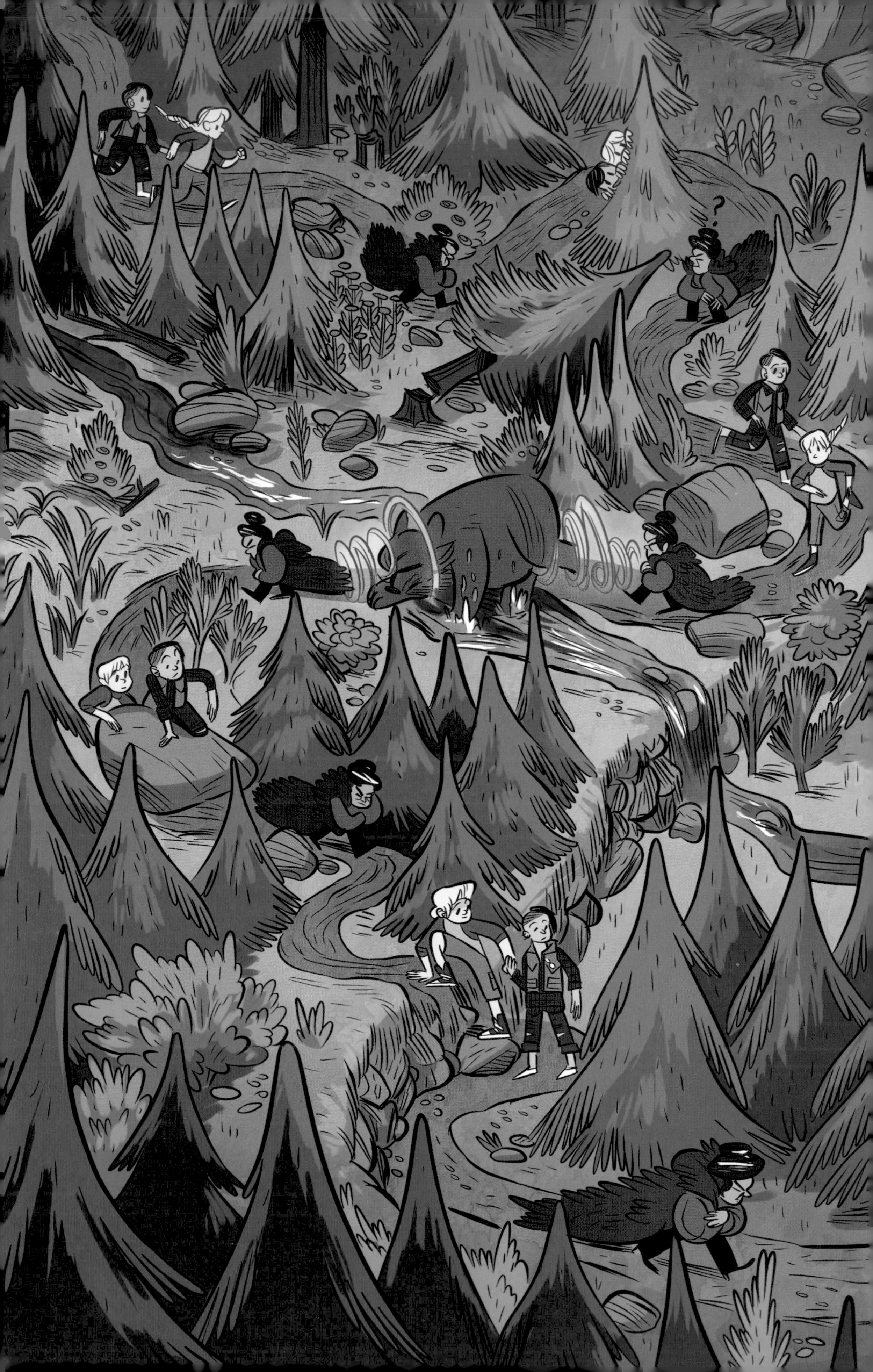

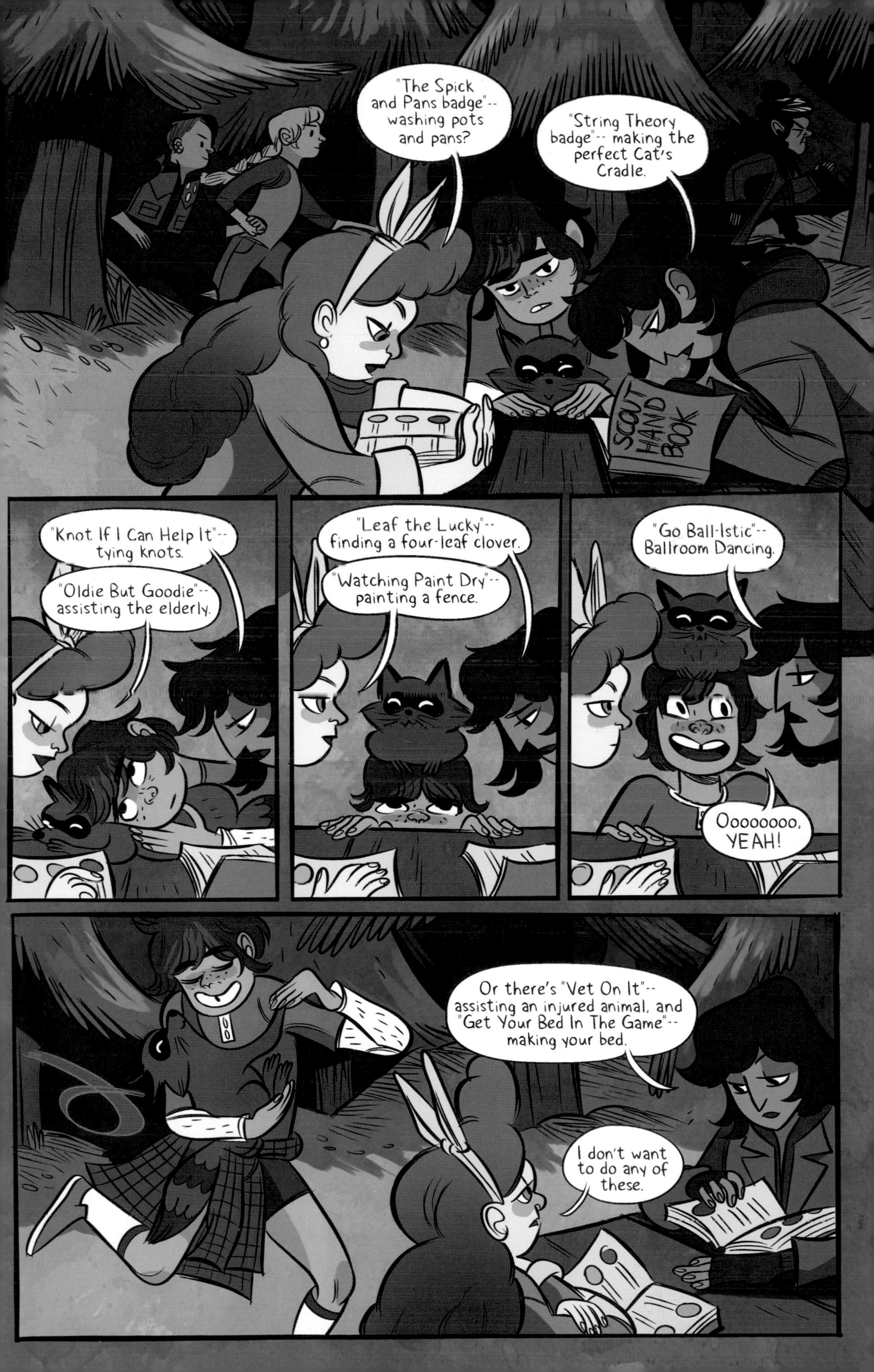
"The Spick and Pans badge"-- washing pots and pans?
"String Theory badge"-- making the perfect Cat's Cradle.
"Knot If I Can Help It"-- tying knots.
"Oldie But Goodie"-- assisting the elderly.
"Leaf the Lucky"-- finding a four-leaf clover.
"Watching Paint Dry"-- painting a fence.
"Go Ball-Istic"-- Ballroom Dancing.
Oooooooo, YEAH!
SCOUT HAND BOOK
Or there's "Vet On It"-- assisting an injured animal, and "Get Your Bed In The Game"-- making your bed.
I don't want to do any of these.

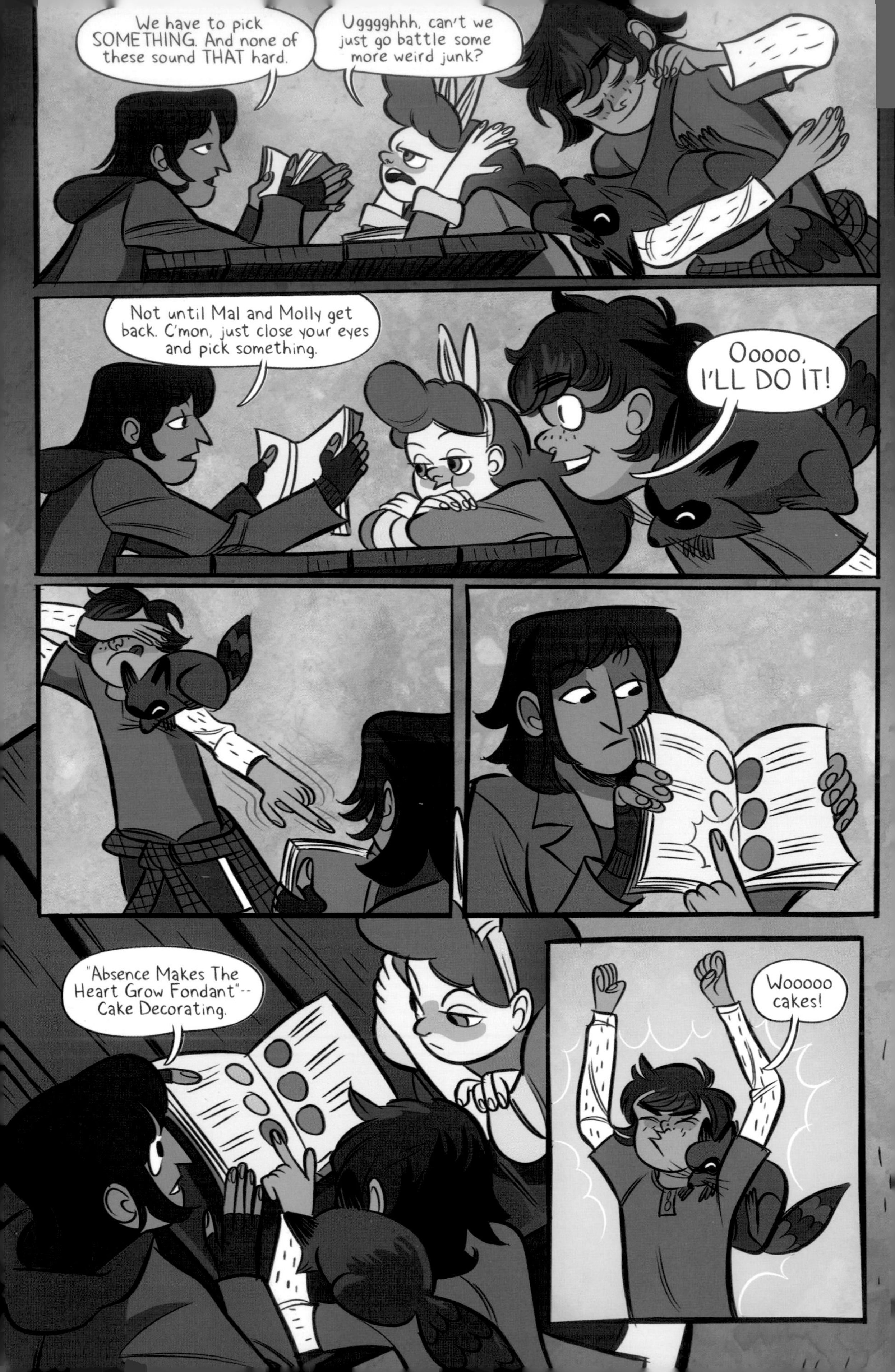
We have to pick SOMETHING. And none of these sound THAT hard.
Ugggghhh, can't we just go battle some more weird junk?
Not until Mal and Molly get back. C'mon, just close your eyes and pick something.
Ooooo, I'LL DO IT!
"Absence Makes The Heart Grow Fondant"-- Cake Decorating.
Wooooo cakes!

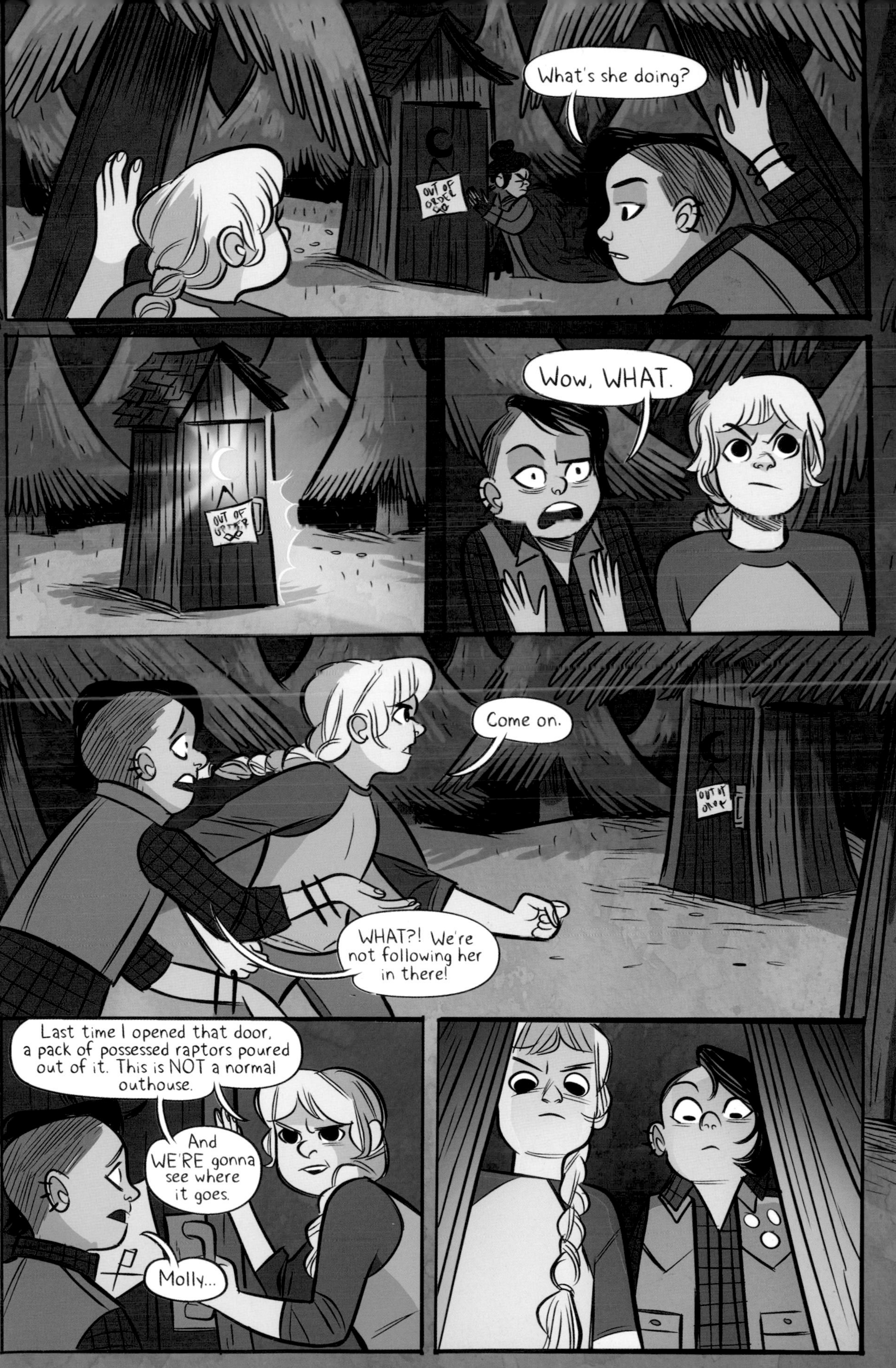
What's she doing?
OUT OF ORDER
Wow, WHAT.
OUT OF ORDER
Come on.
WHAT?! We're not following her in there!
Last time I opened that door, a pack of possessed raptors poured out of it. This is NOT a normal outhouse.
And WE'RE gonna see where it goes.
Molly...

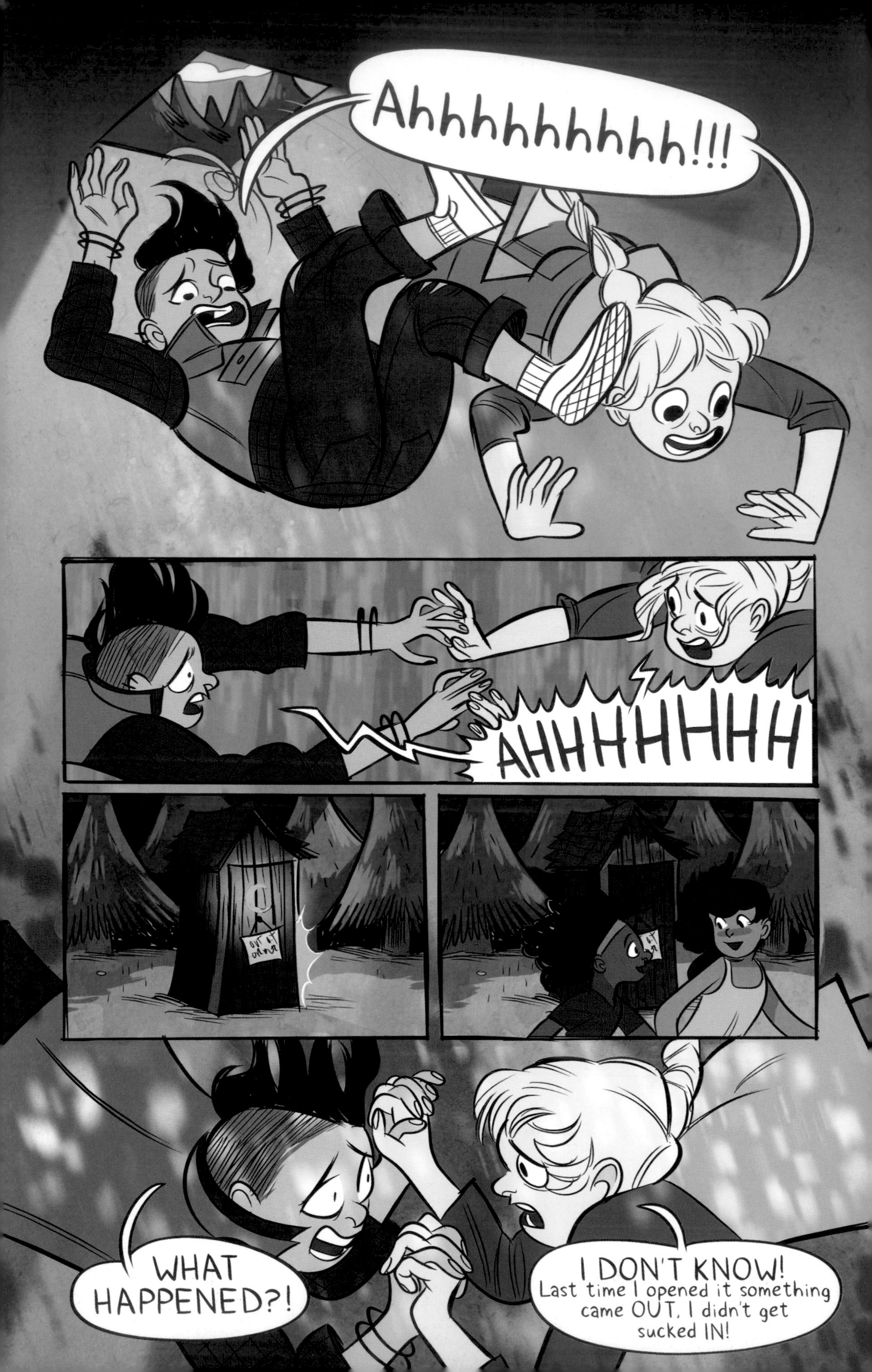

Ahhhhhhhhhh!!!
AHHHHHHH
WHAT HAPPENED?!
I DON'T KNOW! Last time I opened it something came OUT, I didn't get sucked IN!

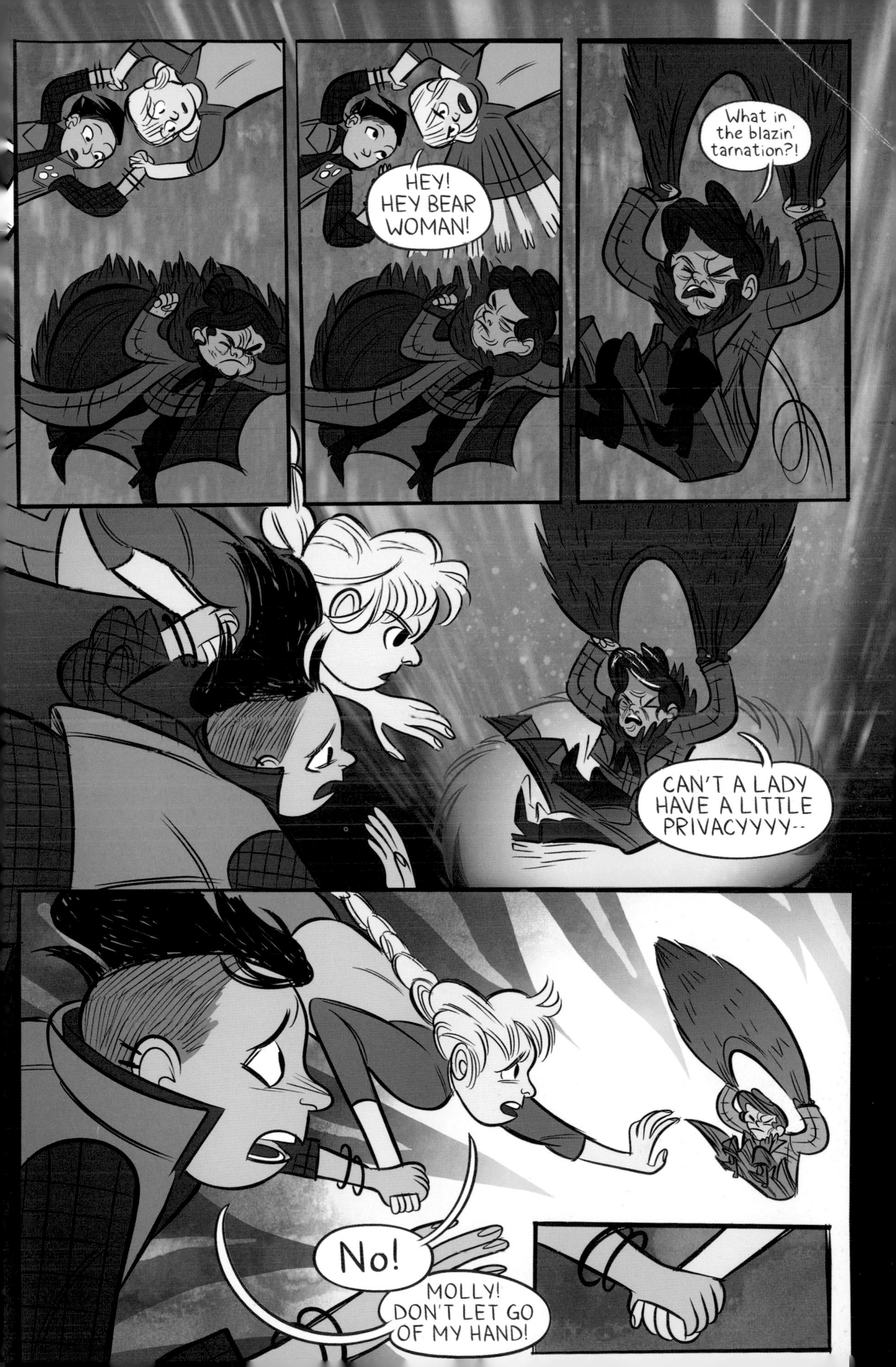
HEY!
HEY BEAR WOMAN!
What in the blazin' tarnation?!
CAN'T A LADY HAVE A LITTLE PRIVACYYYY--
No!
MOLLY! DON'T LET GO OF MY HAND!

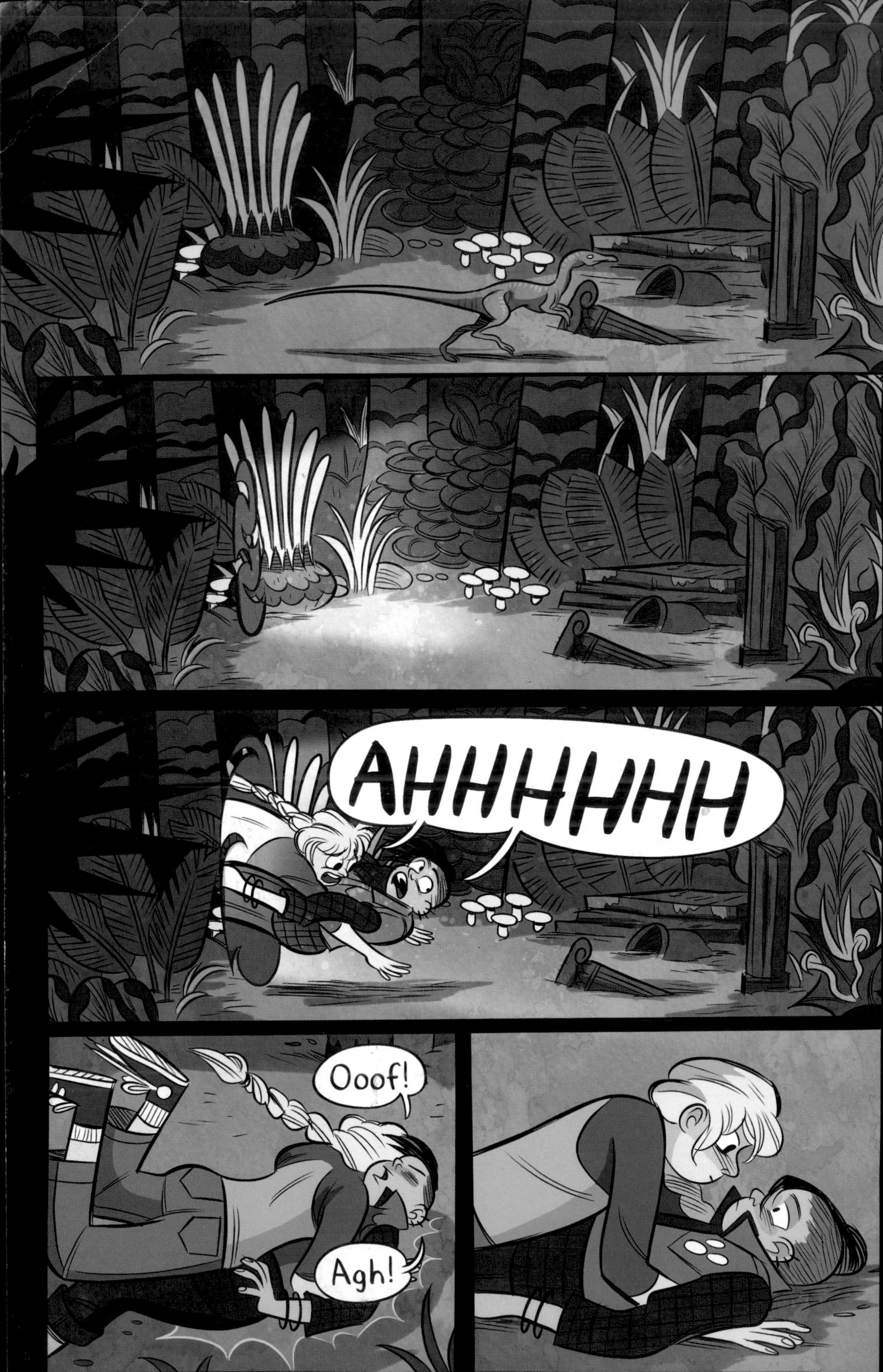
AHHHHHH
Ooof!
Agh!

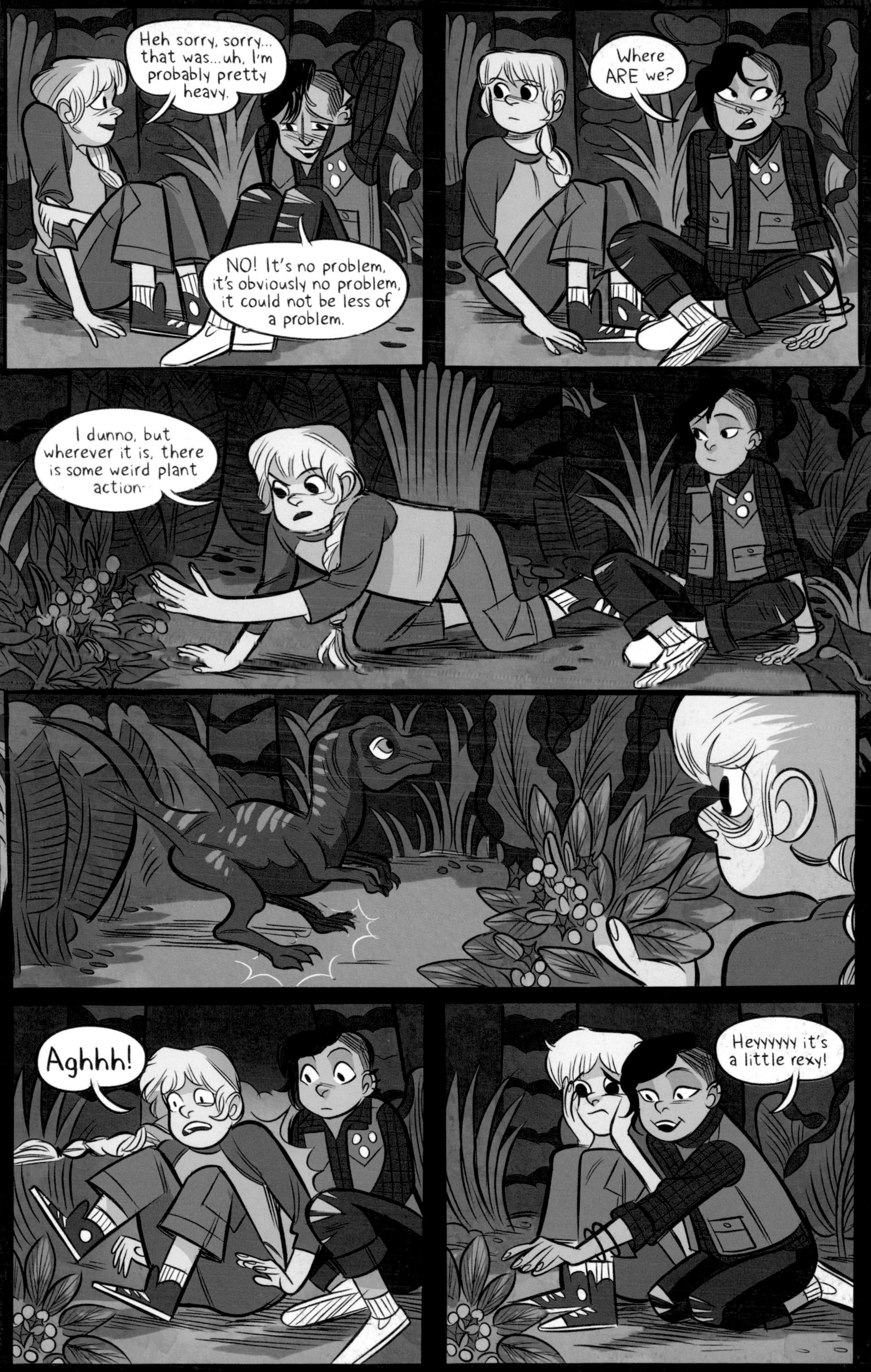
Heh sorry, sorry... that was...uh, I'm probably pretty heavy.
NO! It's no problem, it's obviously no problem, it could not be less of a problem.
Where ARE we?
I dunno, but wherever it is, there is some weird plant action-
Aghhh!
Heyyyyyy it's a little rexy!

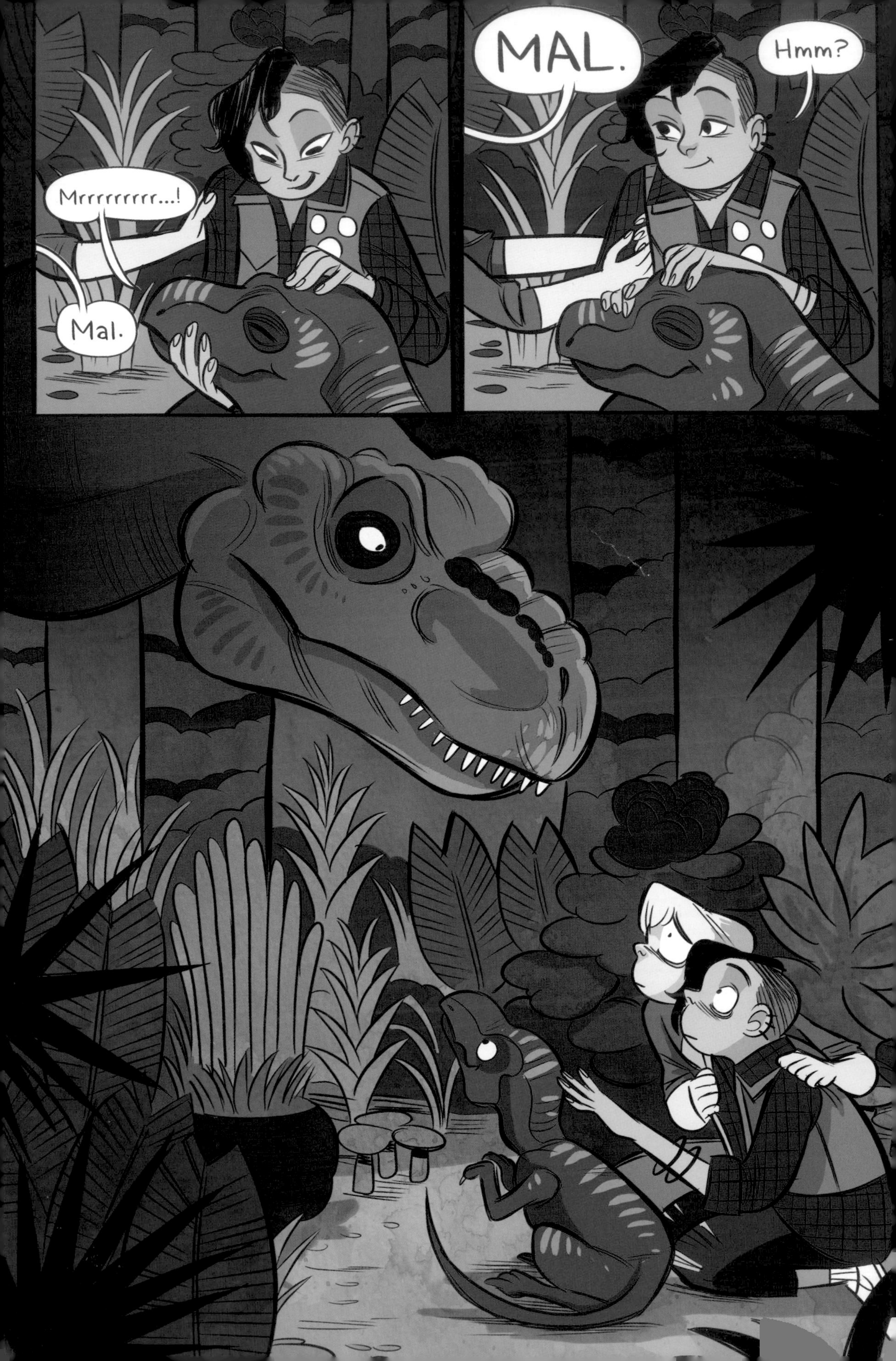
Mrrrrrrrrr...!
Mal.
MAL.
Hmm?

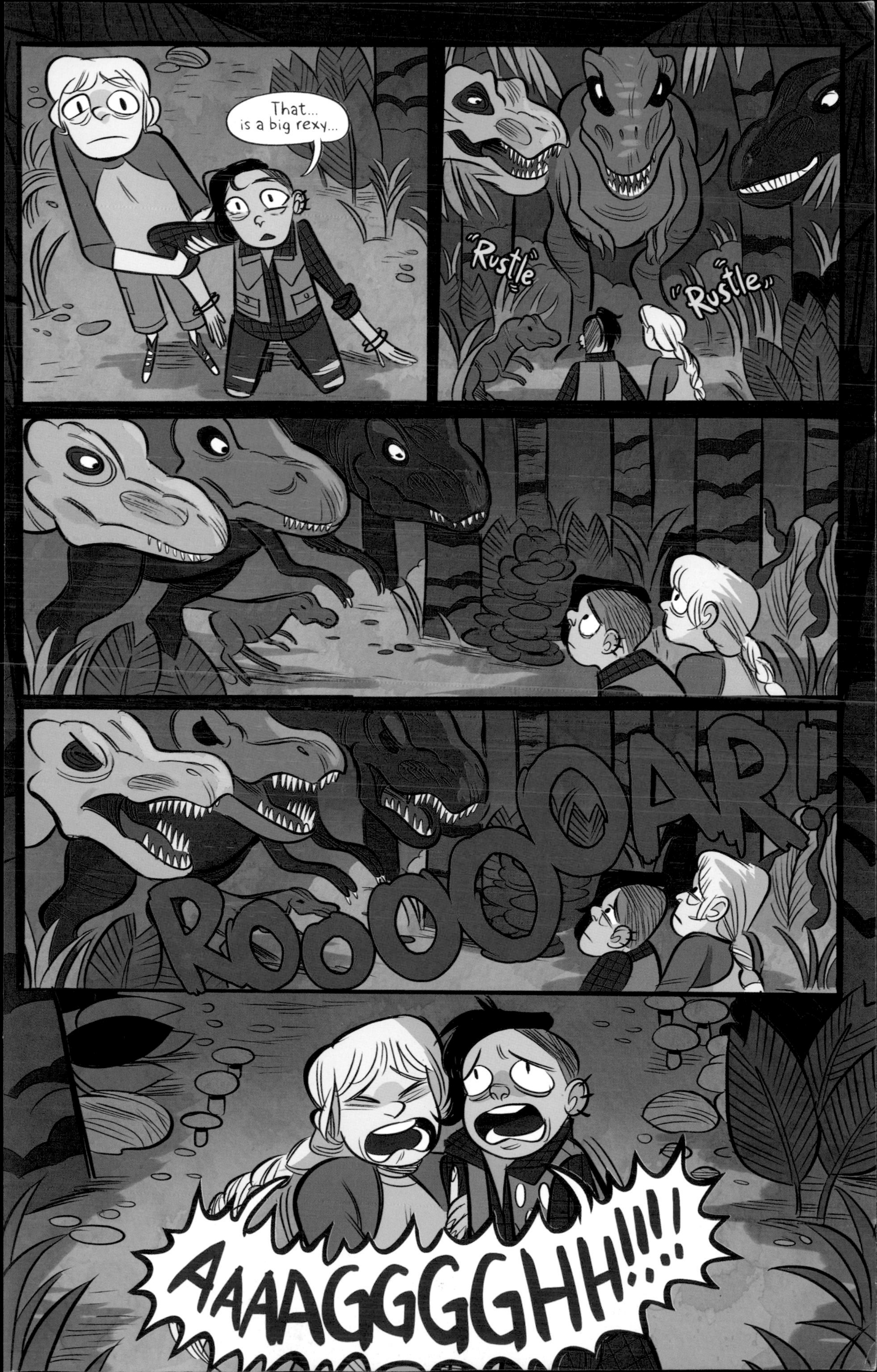
That... is a big rexy...
Rustle
Rustle
ROOOOOOAR!
AAAAGGGGHH!!!!

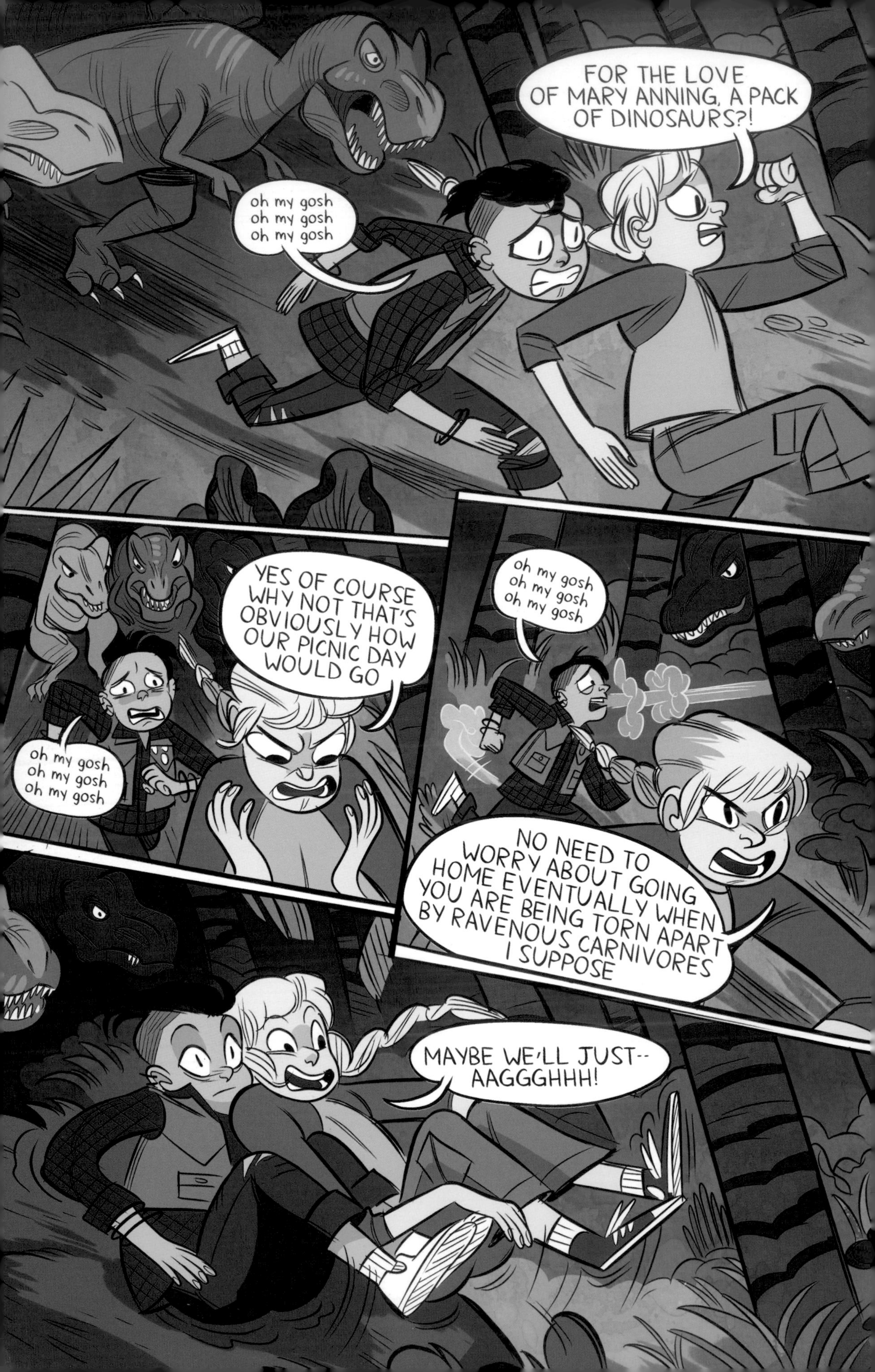
FOR THE LOVE OF MARY ANNING, A PACK OF DINOSAURS?!
oh my gosh oh my gosh oh my gosh
YES OF COURSE WHY NOT THAT'S OBVIOUSLY HOW OUR PICNIC DAY WOULD GO
oh my gosh oh my gosh oh my gosh
oh my gosh oh my gosh oh my gosh
NO NEED TO WORRY ABOUT GOING HOME EVENTUALLY WHEN YOU ARE BEING TORN APART BY RAVENOUS CARNIVORES I SUPPOSE
MAYBE WE'LL JUST-- AAGGGHHH!

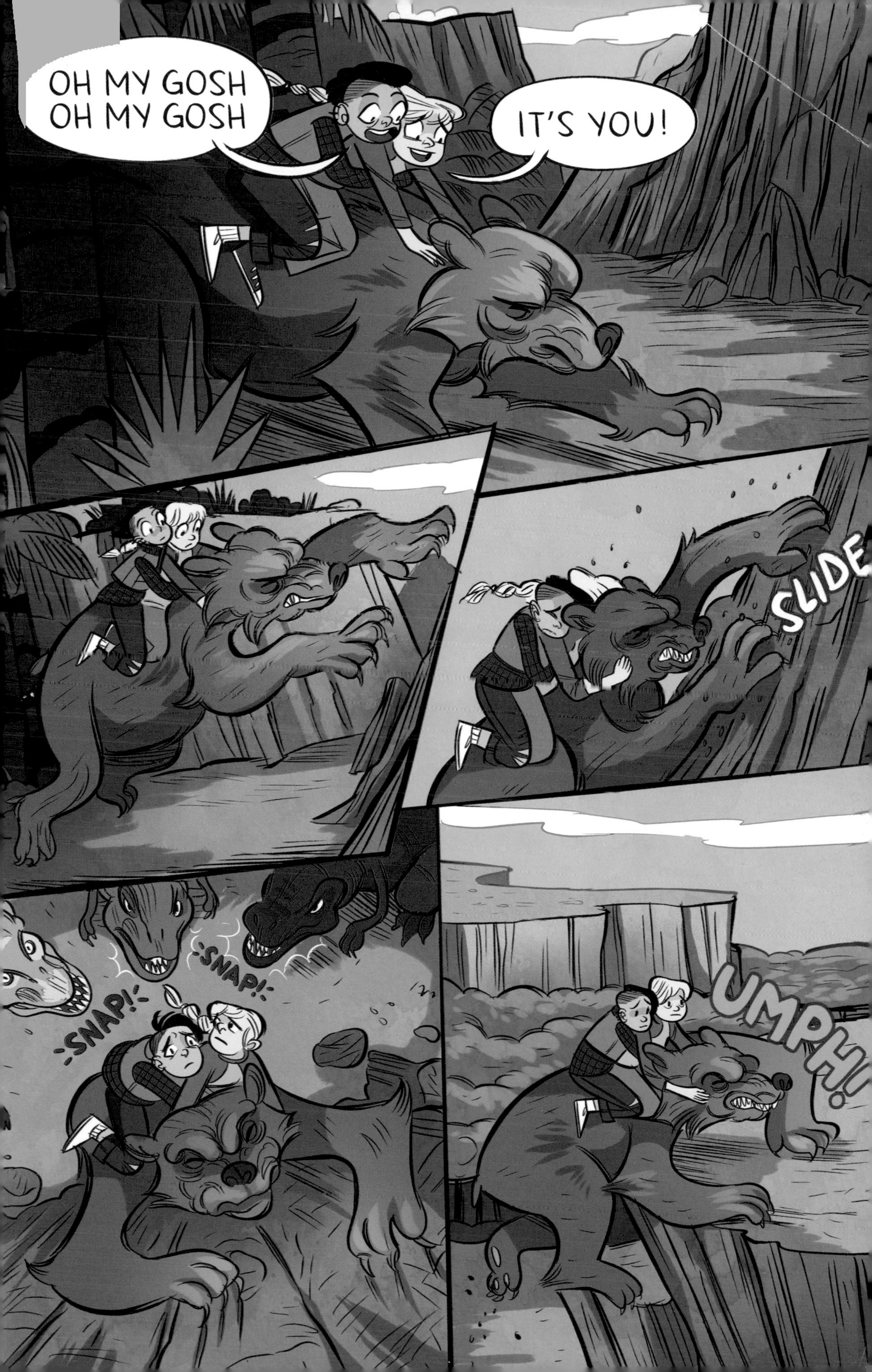
OH MY GOSH
OH MY GOSH
IT'S YOU!
SLIDE
SNAP!
SNAP!
UMPH!

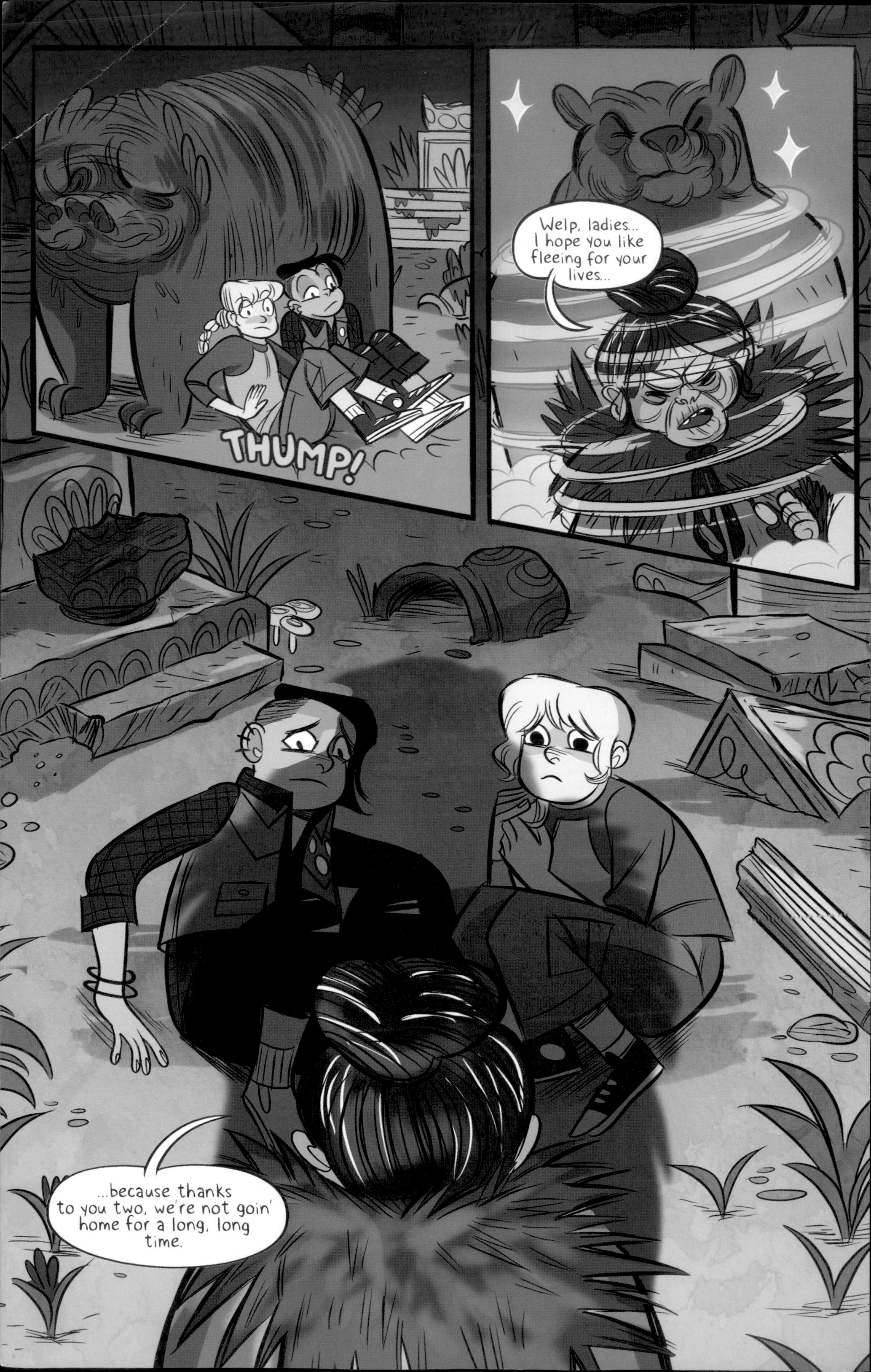
THUMP!
Welp, ladies... I hope you like fleeing for your lives...
...because thanks to you two, we're not goin' home for a long, long time.

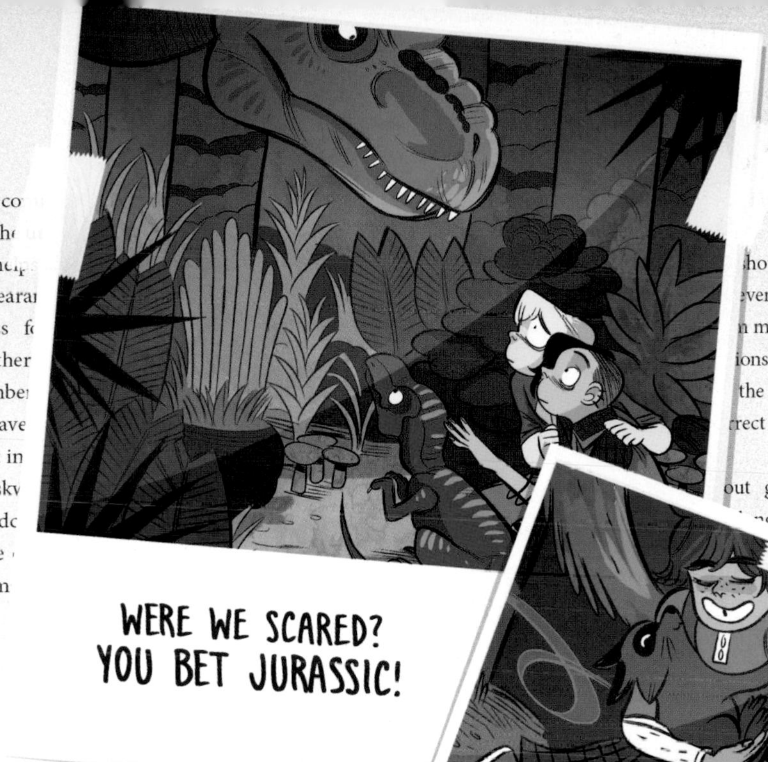
WERE WE SCARED?
YOU BET JURASSIC!

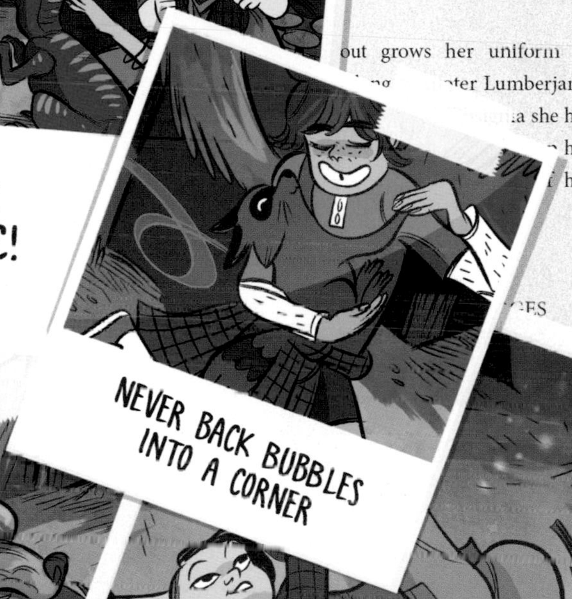
NEVER BACK BUBBLES
INTO A CORNER

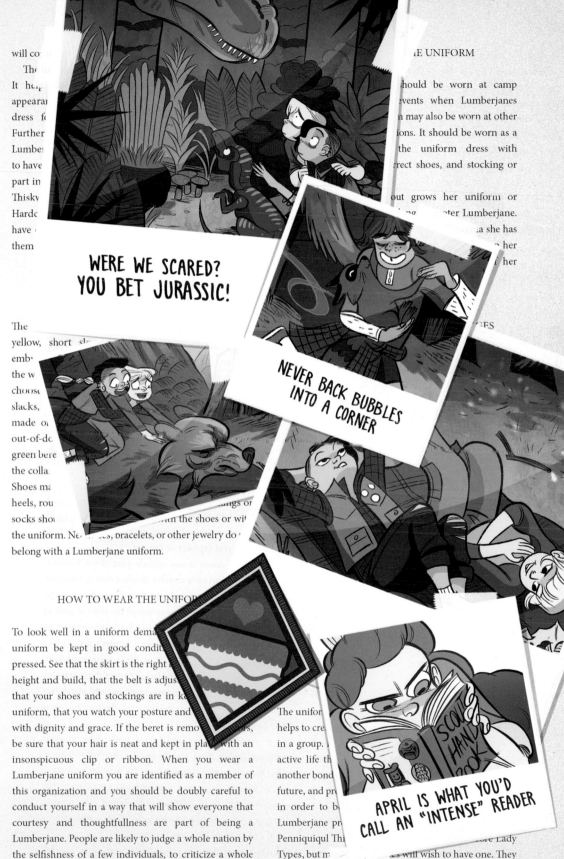

will co
The
It hel
appeara
dress f
Further
Lumbe
to have
part in
Thiskv
Hardc
have
them

HE UNIFORM

hould be worn at camp
events when Lumberjanes
n may also be worn at other
ions. It should be worn as a
the uniform dress with
rrect shoes, and stocking or

out grows her uniform or
ter Lumberjane.
a she has
her
her

CES

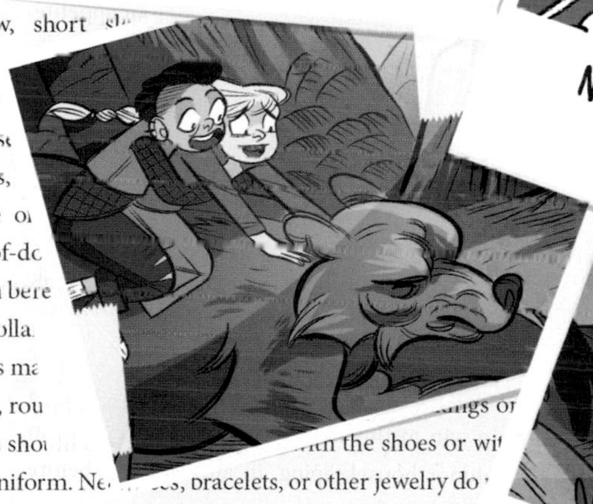

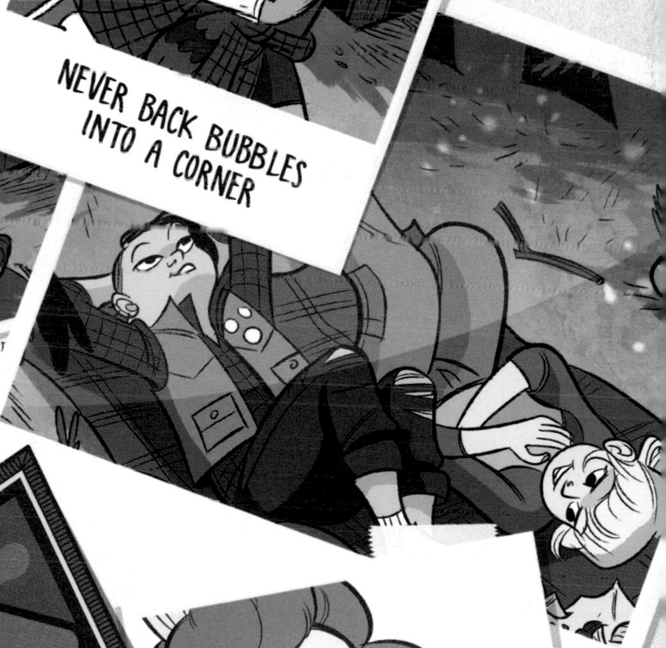

The
yellow, short sl
emb
the w
choos
slacks,
made o
out-of-do
green bere
the colla
Shoes ma
heels, rou … ings or
socks shou … with the shoes or wi
the uniform. Ne… ces, bracelets, or other jewelry do
belong with a Lumberjane uniform.

HOW TO WEAR THE UNIFOR

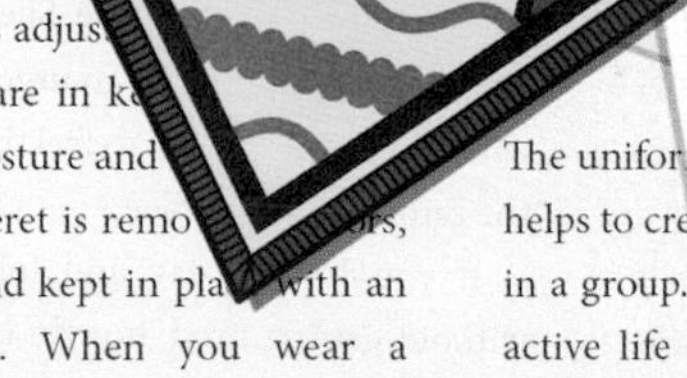

To look well in a uniform dema… uniform be kept in good conditi… pressed. See that the skirt is the right … height and build, that the belt is adjus… that your shoes and stockings are in k… uniform, that you watch your posture and … with dignity and grace. If the beret is remo… rs, be sure that your hair is neat and kept in pla… with an insonspicuous clip or ribbon. When you wear a Lumberjane uniform you are identified as a member of this organization and you should be doubly careful to conduct yourself in a way that will show everyone that courtesy and thoughtfullness are part of being a Lumberjane. People are likely to judge a whole nation by the selfishness of a few individuals, to criticize a whole family because of the misconduct of one member, and to feel unkindly toward and organization because of the

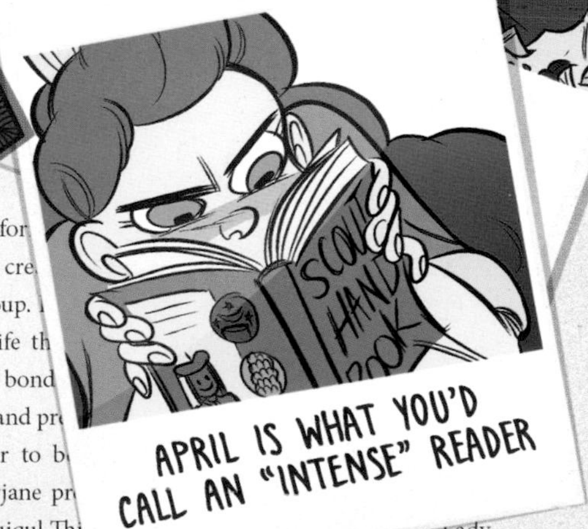
SCOUT HANDBOOK
APRIL IS WHAT YOU'D
CALL AN "INTENSE" READER

The unifor
helps to cre
in a group.
active life th
another bond
future, and pr
in order to b
Lumberjane pr
Penniquiqul Thi … ore Lady
Types, but m … will wish to have one. They
can either bu… the uniform, or make it themselves from
materials available at the trading post.

LUMBERJANES FIELD MANUAL

CHAPTER ELEVEN

Lumberjanes "Arts and Crafts" Program Field

GO BALL-ISTIC BADGE

"Dance like your life depends on it."

There are many things that a Lumberjane will learn while at camp, but one of the camp favorites over these many years has been ballroom dancing. Ballroom dancing is a stress reliever and will teach any Lumberjane scout to put the pressure of the world behind her. The feel and styles of ballroom dances brings the feeling of comfort and great social interaction. Not only that, but it has been shown to help Lumberjanes discover true passion and joy of their life. As a Lumberjanes, she will learn important ballroom dance elements, which include flexibility, superior mental ability, endurance, and strength.

The *Go Ball-istic* badge is not just another step for a Lumberjane on her personal journey in this camp but something much more. Just as many of the other Lumberjane classes will be able to teach and mold the scouts of this camp, it will be ballroom dancing that will show them that not is grace not a weakness, it is a powerful tool that can be used in almost any situation. The style of ballroom dances will make any Lumberjane more confident with a fresh sense of creativity, motivation and energy. The different forms of ballroom dancing not only give a great learning experience but will also show the importance of working in pairs and the ability to rely on a partner who is separate but at the same time an extension of the dancer.

To obtain the *Go Ball-istic* badge, a Lumberjanes must be able to perform one of the many dances available from start to finish with her partner. As partners, they will hold each other up and help each other if needed as they complete the dance to the best of their abilities. The lesson from this badge is something a Lumberjane will take with her for the rest of her life as she learns to understand the influence she will have on those around her. Confidence and strength is something that

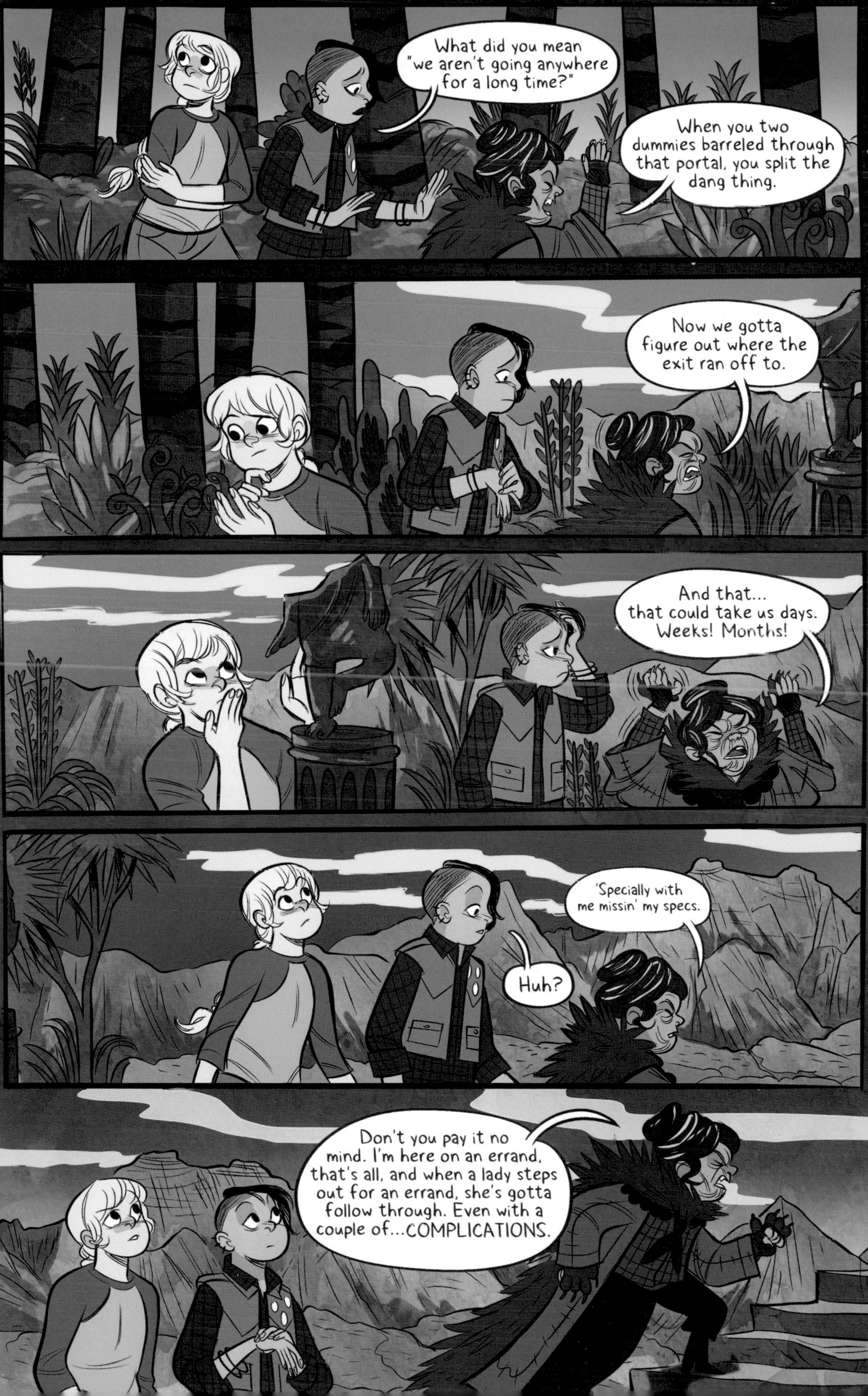
What did you mean "we aren't going anywhere for a long time?"
When you two dummies barreled through that portal, you split the dang thing.
Now we gotta figure out where the exit ran off to.
And that... that could take us days. Weeks! Months!
'Specially with me missin' my specs.
Huh?
Don't you pay it no mind. I'm here on an errand, that's all, and when a lady steps out for an errand, she's gotta follow through. Even with a couple of...COMPLICATIONS.

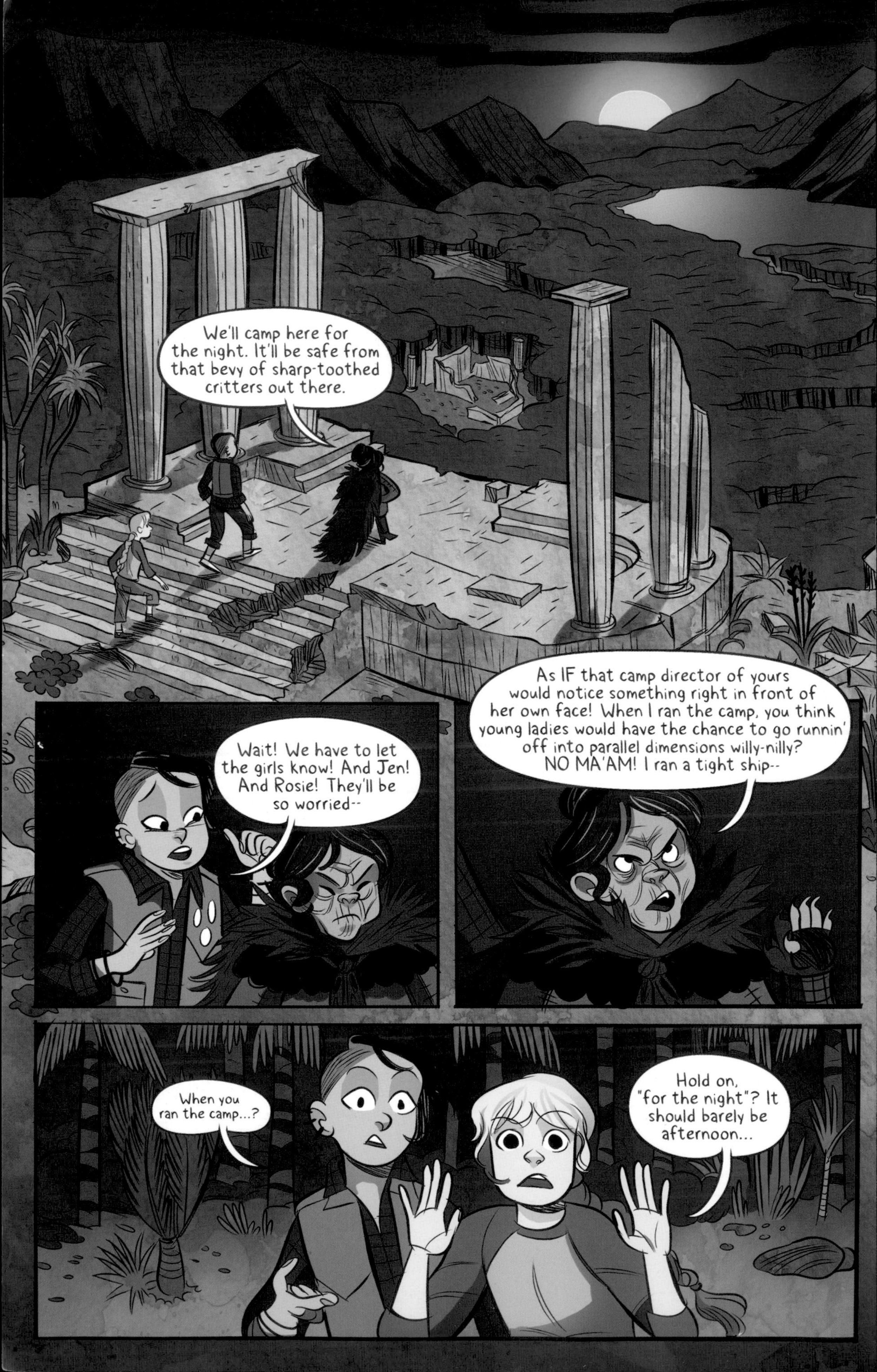
We'll camp here for the night. It'll be safe from that bevy of sharp-toothed critters out there.
Wait! We have to let the girls know! And Jen! And Rosie! They'll be so worried--
As IF that camp director of yours would notice something right in front of her own face! When I ran the camp, you think young ladies would have the chance to go runnin' off into parallel dimensions willy-nilly? NO MA'AM! I ran a tight ship--
When you ran the camp...?
Hold on, "for the night"? It should barely be afternoon...

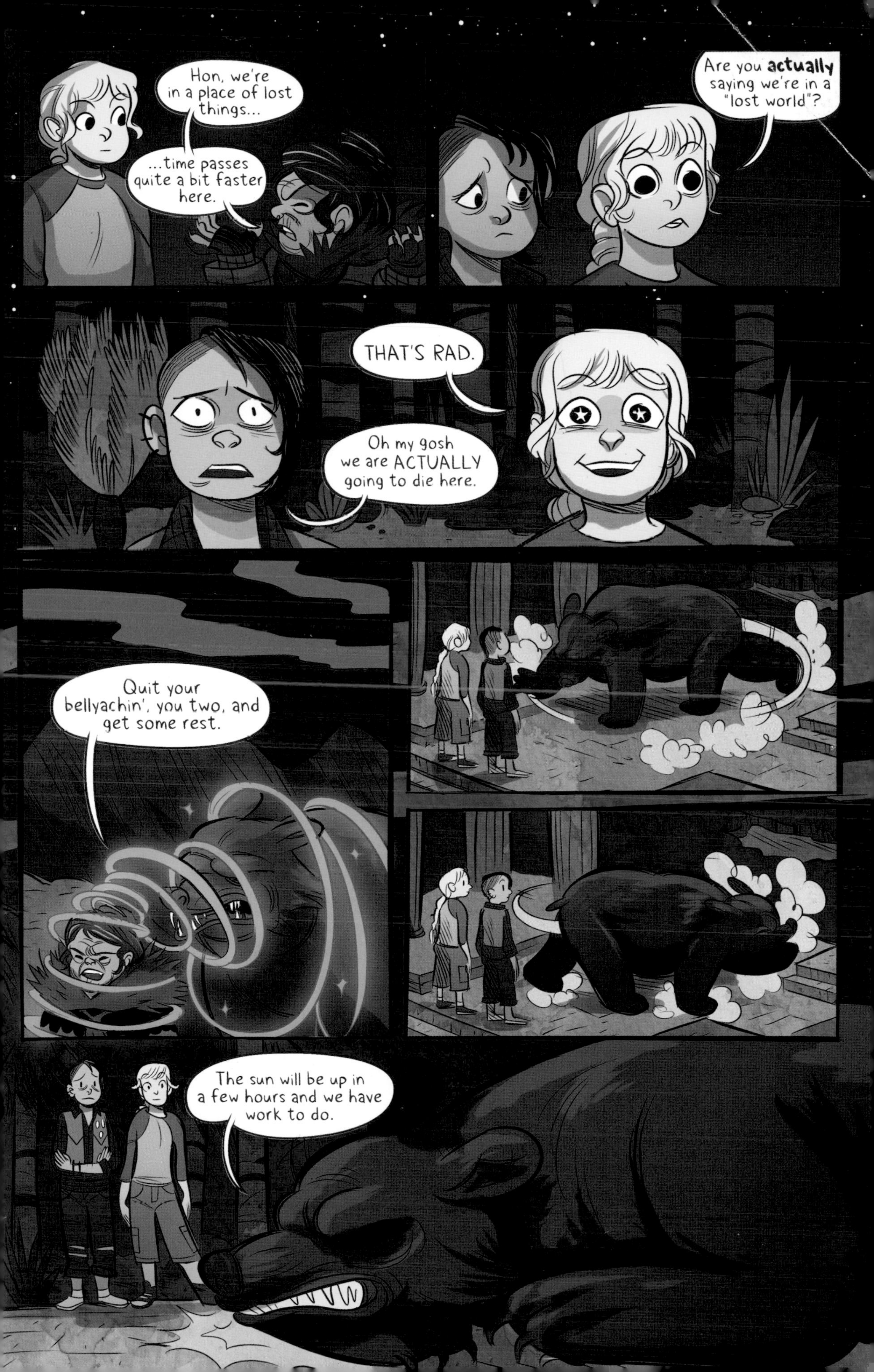
Hon, we're in a place of lost things...
...time passes quite a bit faster here.
Are you **actually** saying we're in a "lost world"?
Oh my gosh we are ACTUALLY going to die here.
THAT'S RAD.
Quit your bellyachin', you two, and get some rest.
The sun will be up in a few hours and we have work to do.

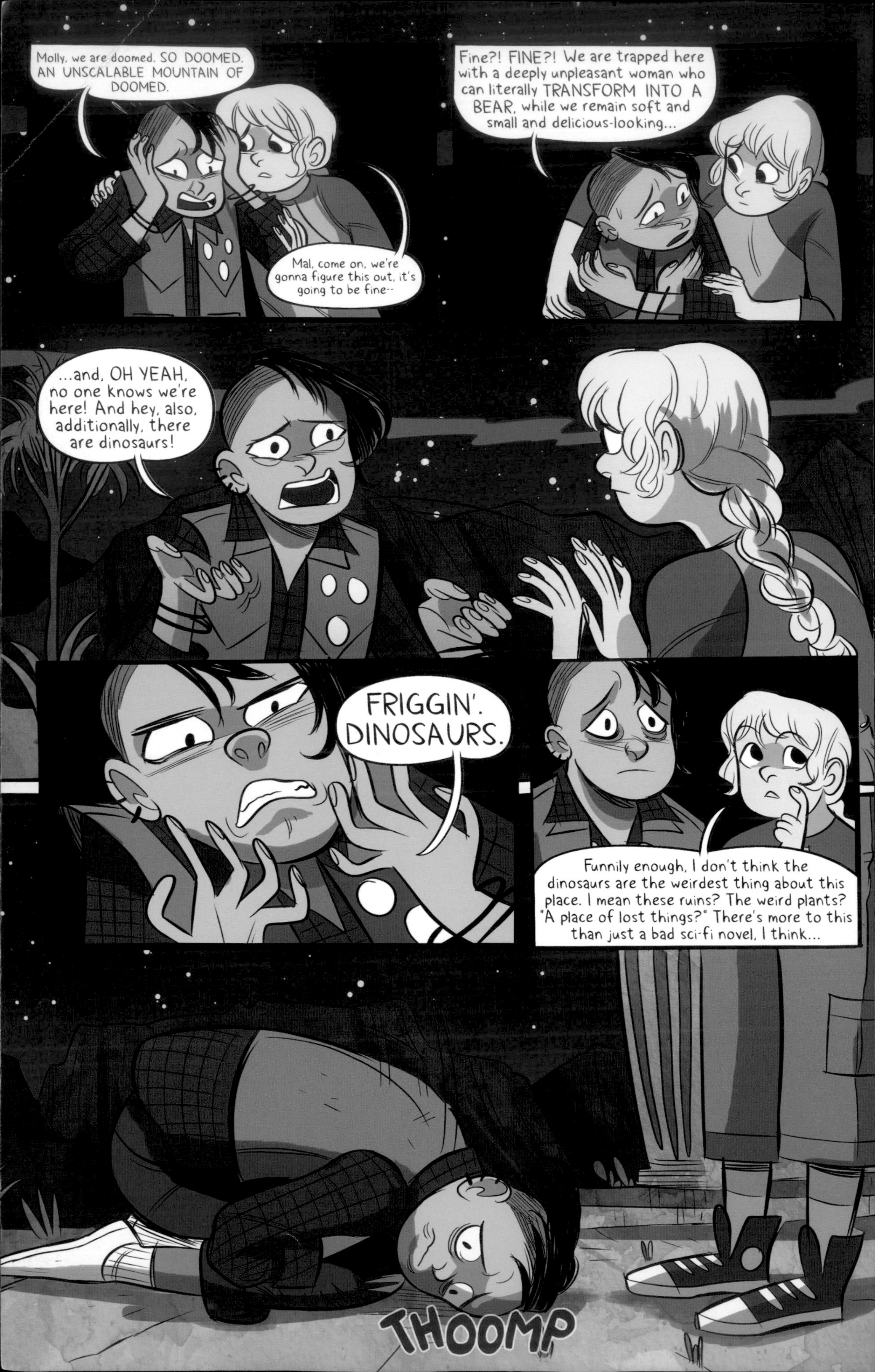
Molly, we are doomed. SO DOOMED. AN UNSCALABLE MOUNTAIN OF DOOMED.
Mal, come on, we're gonna figure this out, it's going to be fine--
Fine?! FINE?! We are trapped here with a deeply unpleasant woman who can literally TRANSFORM INTO A BEAR, while we remain soft and small and delicious-looking...
...and, OH YEAH, no one knows we're here! And hey, also, additionally, there are dinosaurs!
FRIGGIN'. DINOSAURS.
Funnily enough, I don't think the dinosaurs are the weirdest thing about this place. I mean these ruins? The weird plants? "A place of lost things?" There's more to this than just a bad sci-fi novel, I think...
THOOMP

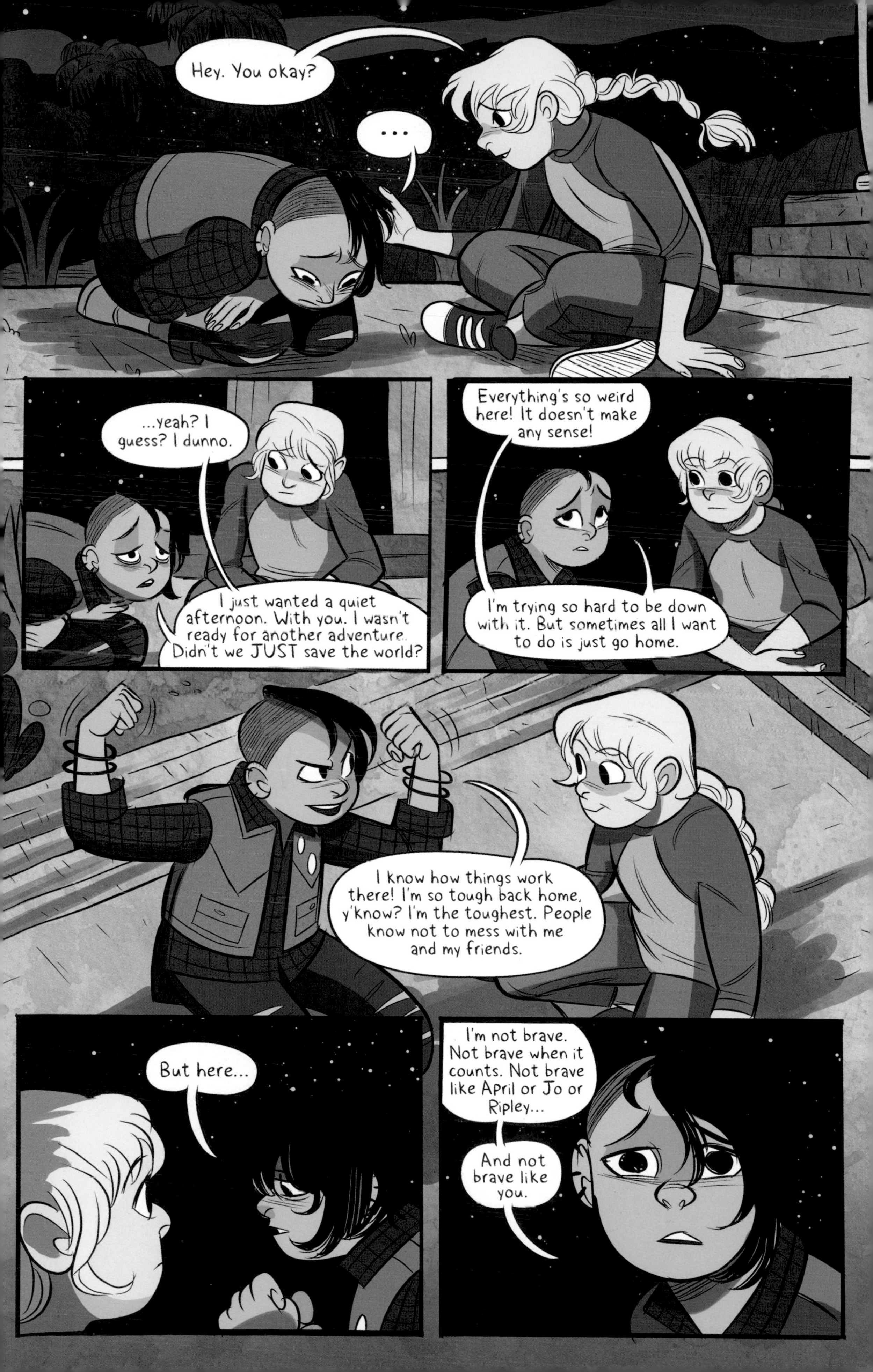
Hey. You okay?
...
...yeah? I guess? I dunno.
I just wanted a quiet afternoon. With you. I wasn't ready for another adventure. Didn't we JUST save the world?
Everything's so weird here! It doesn't make any sense!
I'm trying so hard to be down with it. But sometimes all I want to do is just go home.
I know how things work there! I'm so tough back home, y'know? I'm the toughest. People know not to mess with me and my friends.
But here...
I'm not brave. Not brave when it counts. Not brave like April or Jo or Ripley...
And not brave like you.

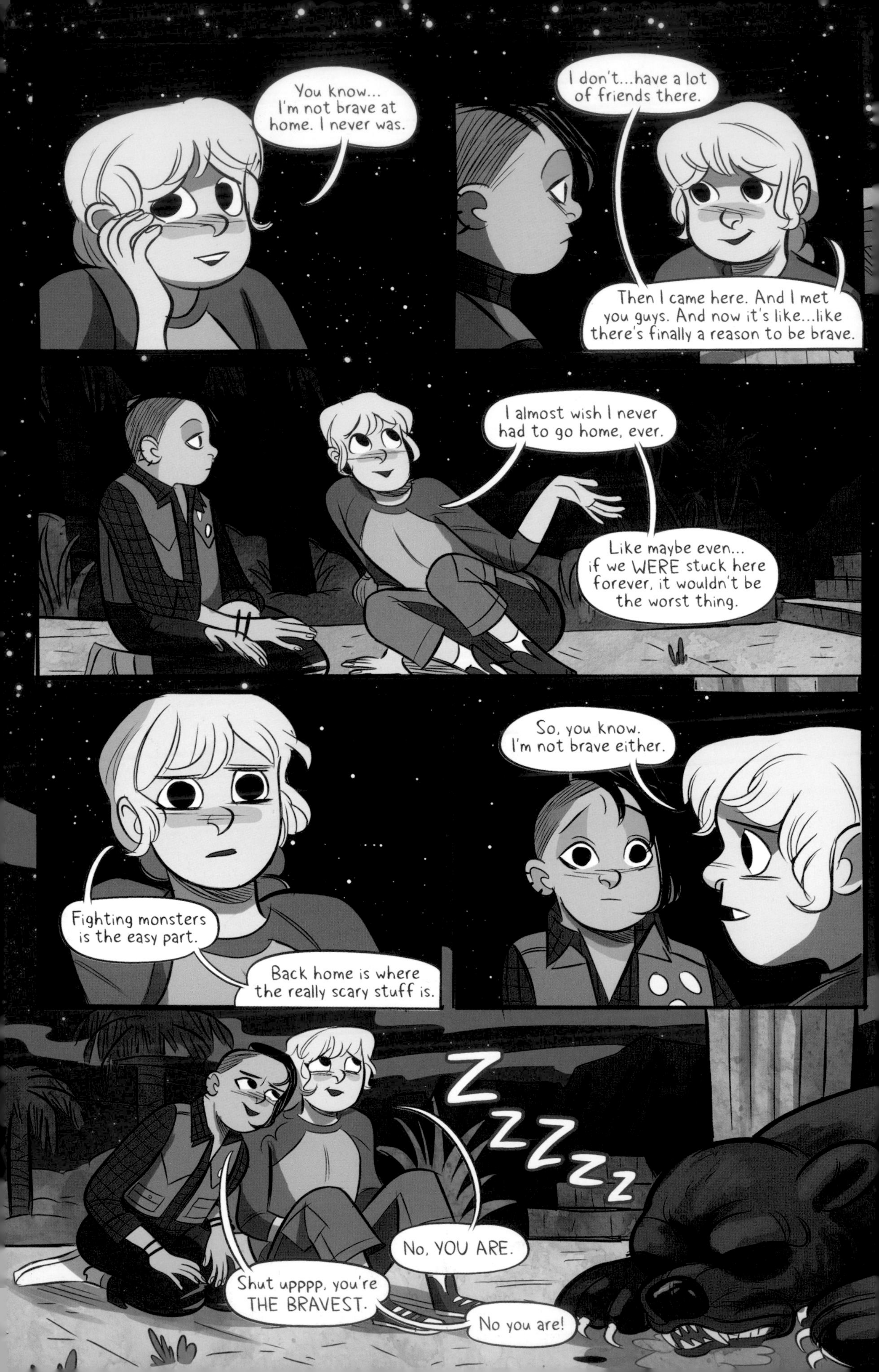
You know... I'm not brave at home. I never was.
I don't...have a lot of friends there.
Then I came here. And I met you guys. And now it's like...like there's finally a reason to be brave.
I almost wish I never had to go home, ever.
Like maybe even... if we WERE stuck here forever, it wouldn't be the worst thing.
Fighting monsters is the easy part.
Back home is where the really scary stuff is.
So, you know. I'm not brave either.
ZZZZZZ
Shut upppp, you're THE BRAVEST.
No, YOU ARE.
No you are!

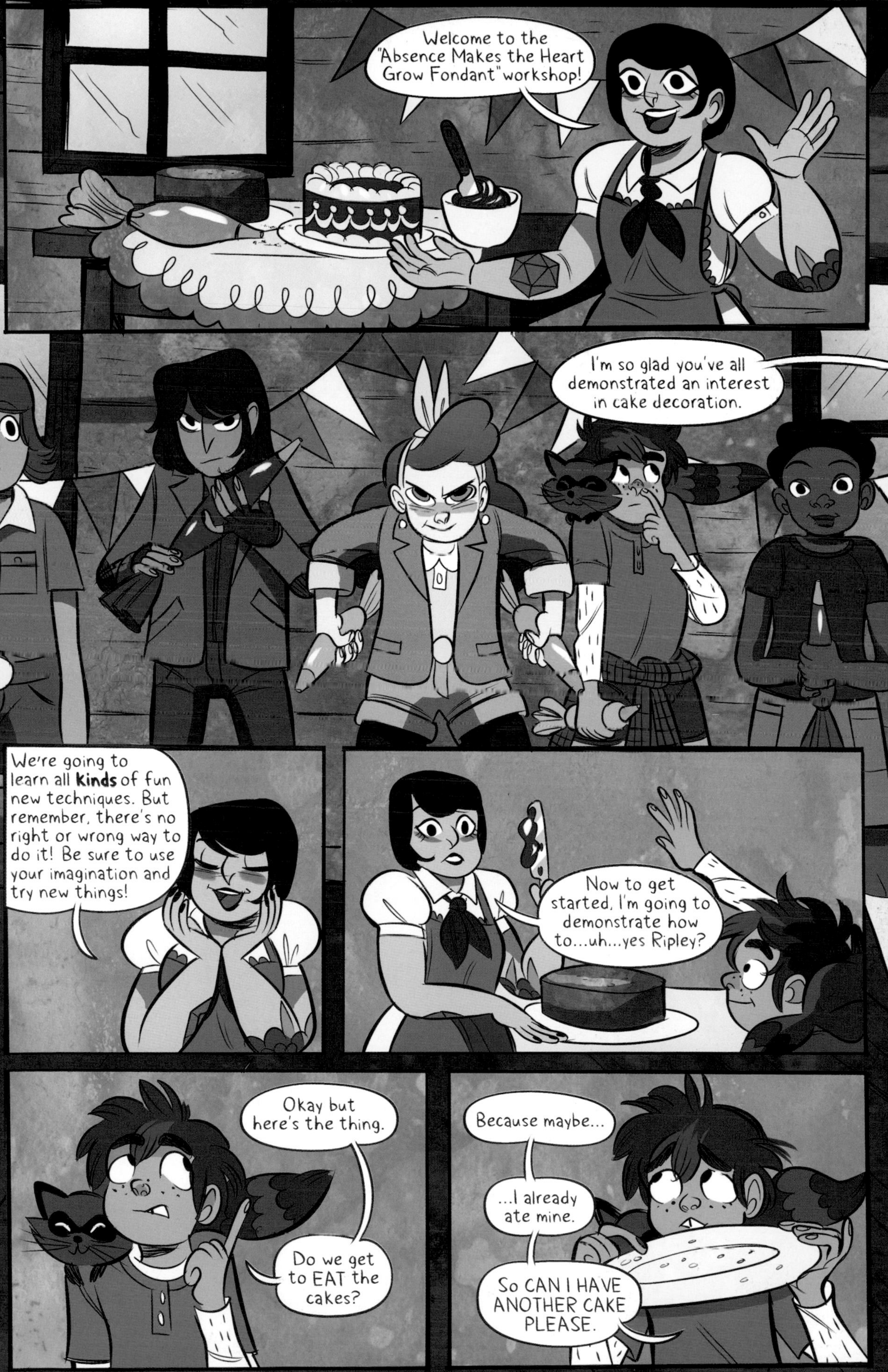
Welcome to the "Absence Makes the Heart Grow Fondant" workshop!
I'm so glad you've all demonstrated an interest in cake decoration.
We're going to learn all **kinds** of fun new techniques. But remember, there's no right or wrong way to do it! Be sure to use your imagination and try new things!
Now to get started, I'm going to demonstrate how to...uh...yes Ripley?
Okay but here's the thing.
Do we get to EAT the cakes?
Because maybe...
...I already ate mine.
So CAN I HAVE ANOTHER CAKE PLEASE.

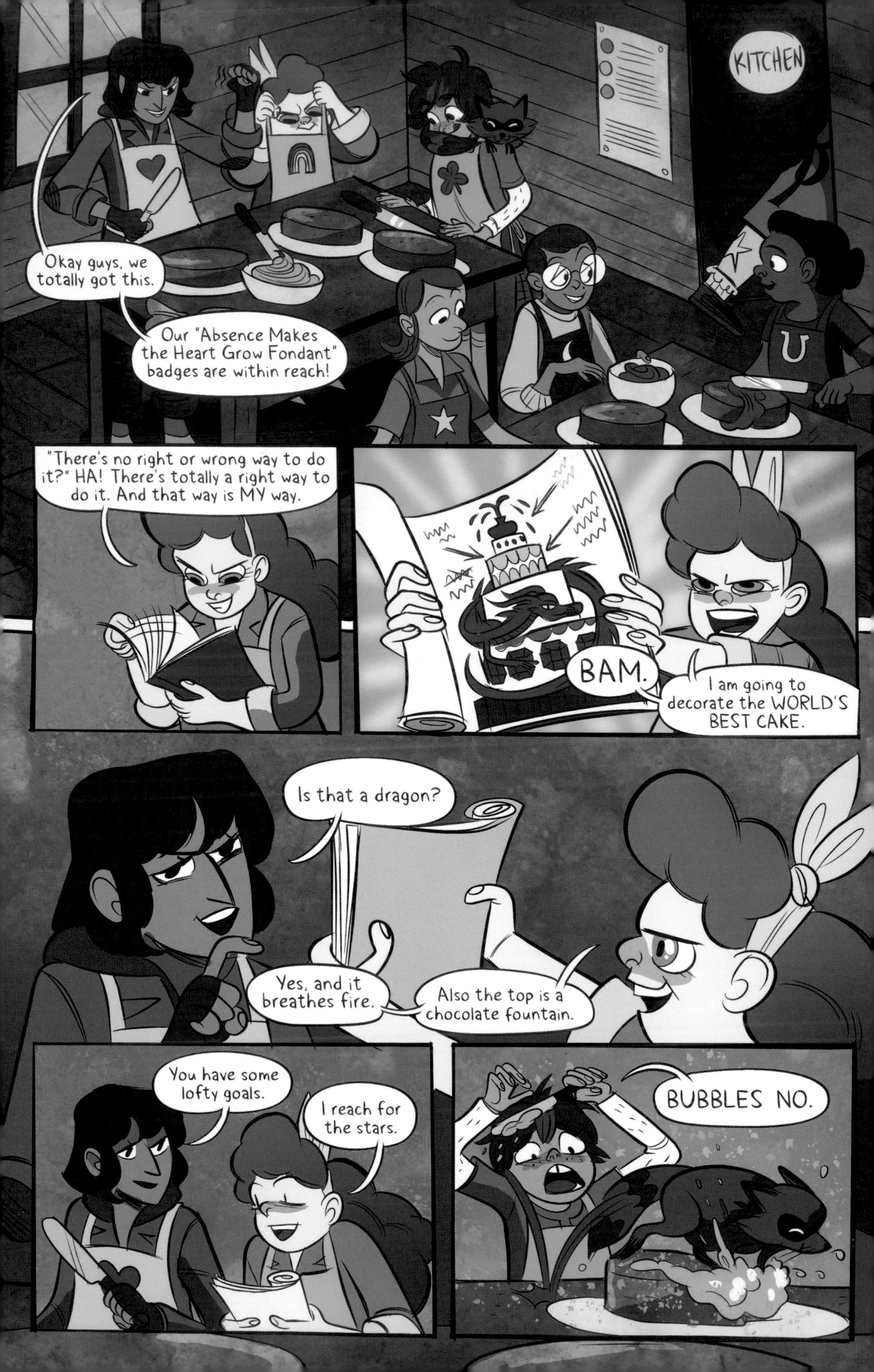
KITCHEN
Okay guys, we totally got this.
Our "Absence Makes the Heart Grow Fondant" badges are within reach!
"There's no right or wrong way to do it?" HA! There's totally a right way to do it. And that way is MY way.
BAM.
I am going to decorate the WORLD'S BEST CAKE.
Is that a dragon?
Yes, and it breathes fire.
Also the top is a chocolate fountain.
You have some lofty goals.
I reach for the stars.
BUBBLES NO.

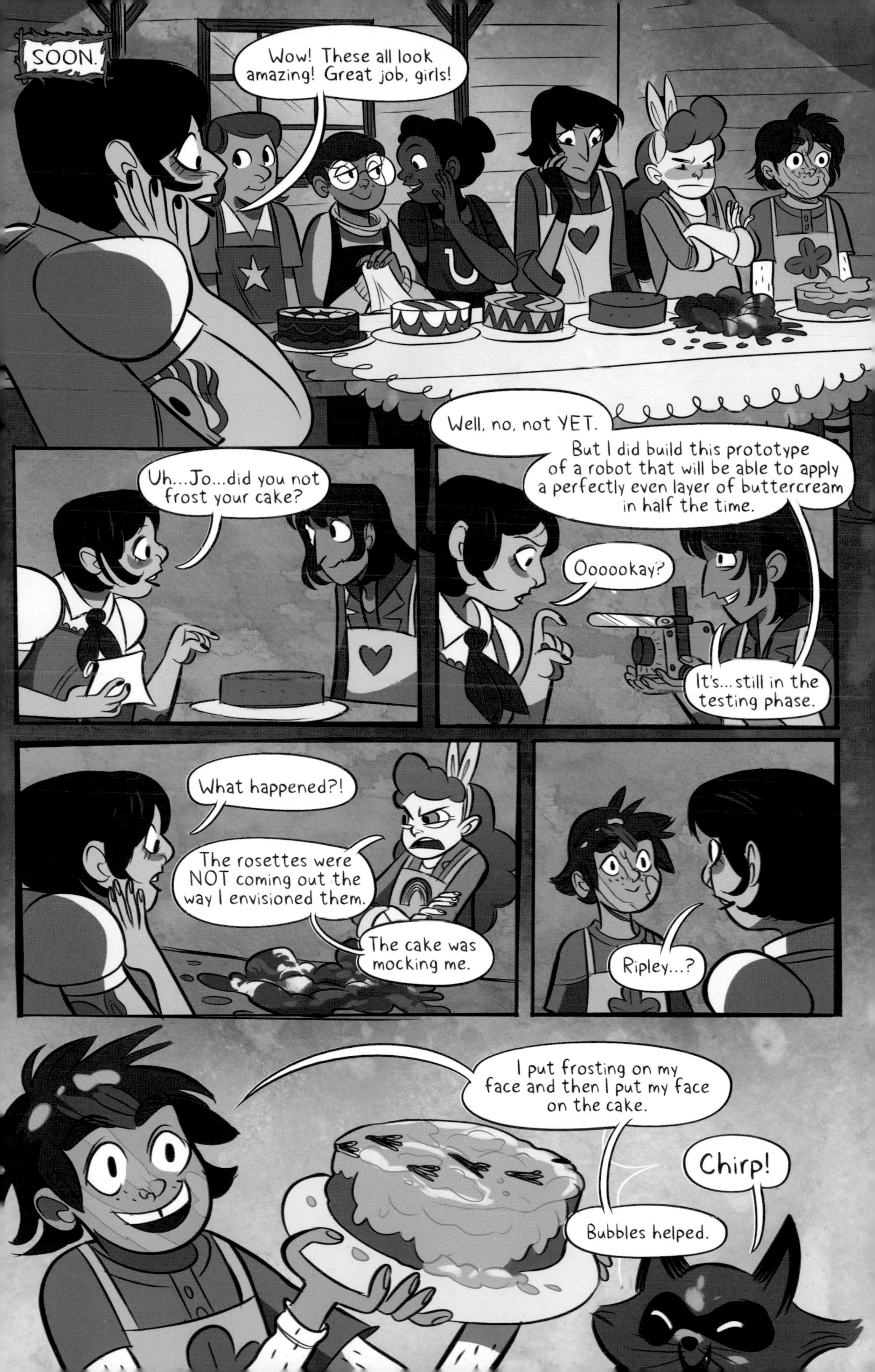
SOON.
Wow! These all look amazing! Great job, girls!
Uh...Jo...did you not frost your cake?
Well, no, not YET.
But I did build this prototype of a robot that will be able to apply a perfectly even layer of buttercream in half the time.
Oooookay?
It's... still in the testing phase.
What happened?!
The rosettes were NOT coming out the way I envisioned them.
The cake was mocking me.
Ripley...?
I put frosting on my face and then I put my face on the cake.
Bubbles helped.
Chirp!

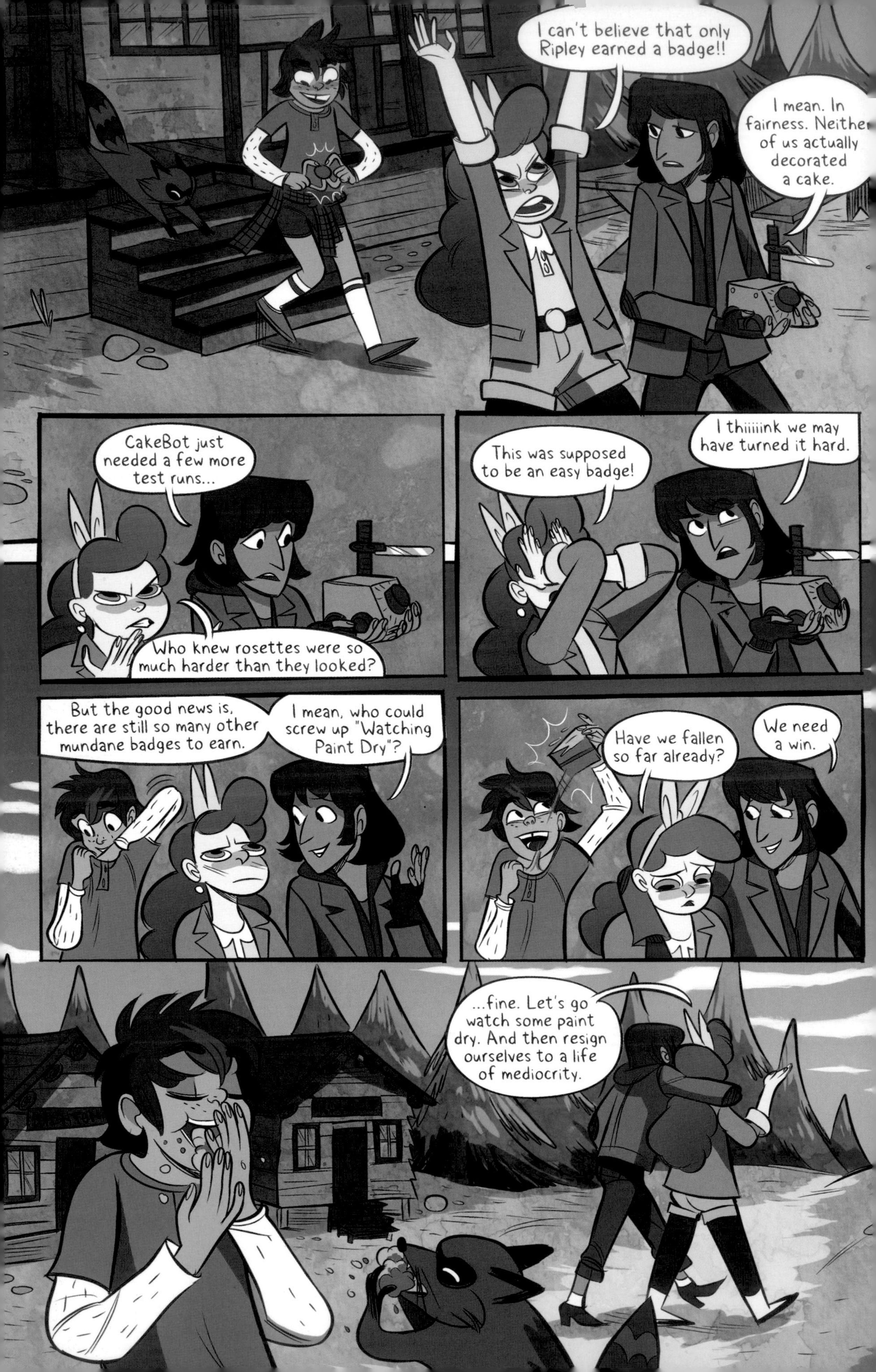
I can't believe that only Ripley earned a badge!!
I mean. In fairness. Neithe of us actually decorated a cake.
CakeBot just needed a few more test runs...
Who knew rosettes were so much harder than they looked?
This was supposed to be an easy badge!
I thiiiiink we may have turned it hard.
But the good news is, there are still so many other mundane badges to earn.
I mean, who could screw up "Watching Paint Dry"?
Have we fallen so far already?
We need a win.
...fine. Let's go watch some paint dry. And then resign ourselves to a life of mediocrity.

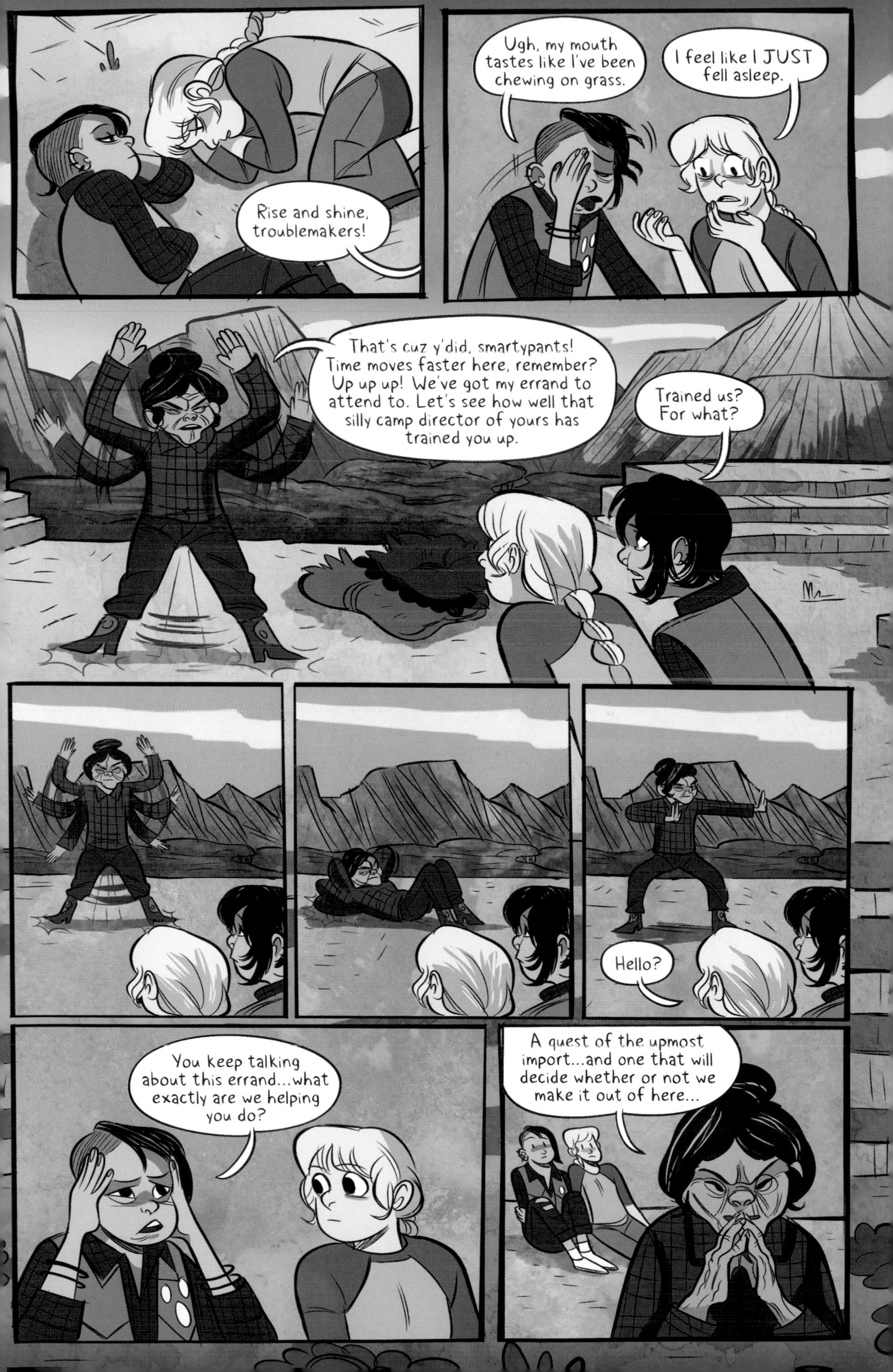
Rise and shine, troublemakers!
Ugh, my mouth tastes like I've been chewing on grass.
I feel like I JUST fell asleep.
That's cuz y'did, smartypants! Time moves faster here, remember? Up up up! We've got my errand to attend to. Let's see how well that silly camp director of yours has trained you up.
Trained us? For what?
Hello?
You keep talking about this errand...what exactly are we helping you do?
A quest of the upmost import...and one that will decide whether or not we make it out of here...

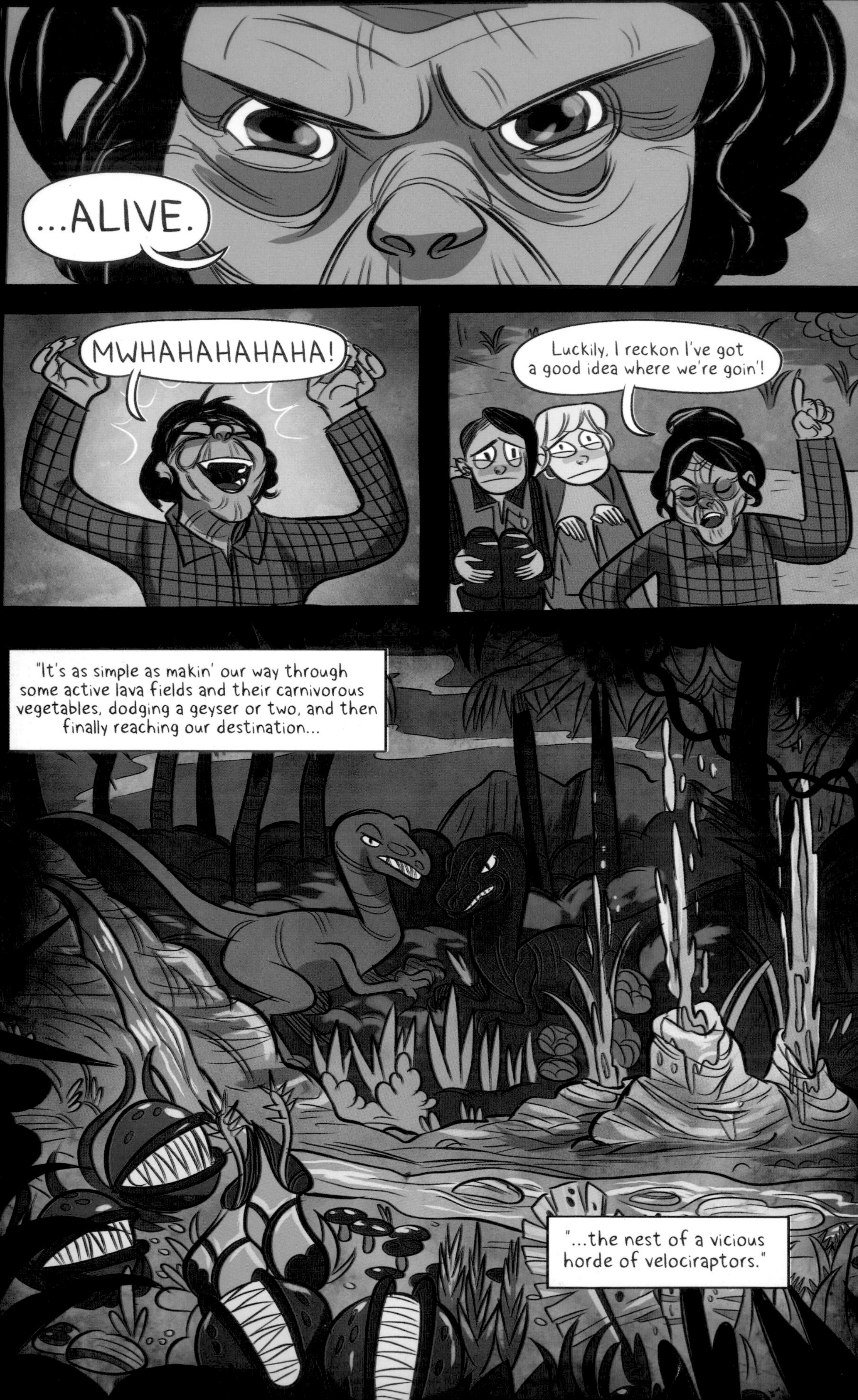
...ALIVE.
MWHAHAHAHAHA!
Luckily, I reckon I've got a good idea where we're goin'!
"It's as simple as makin' our way through some active lava fields and their carnivorous vegetables, dodging a geyser or two, and then finally reaching our destination...
"...the nest of a vicious horde of velociraptors."

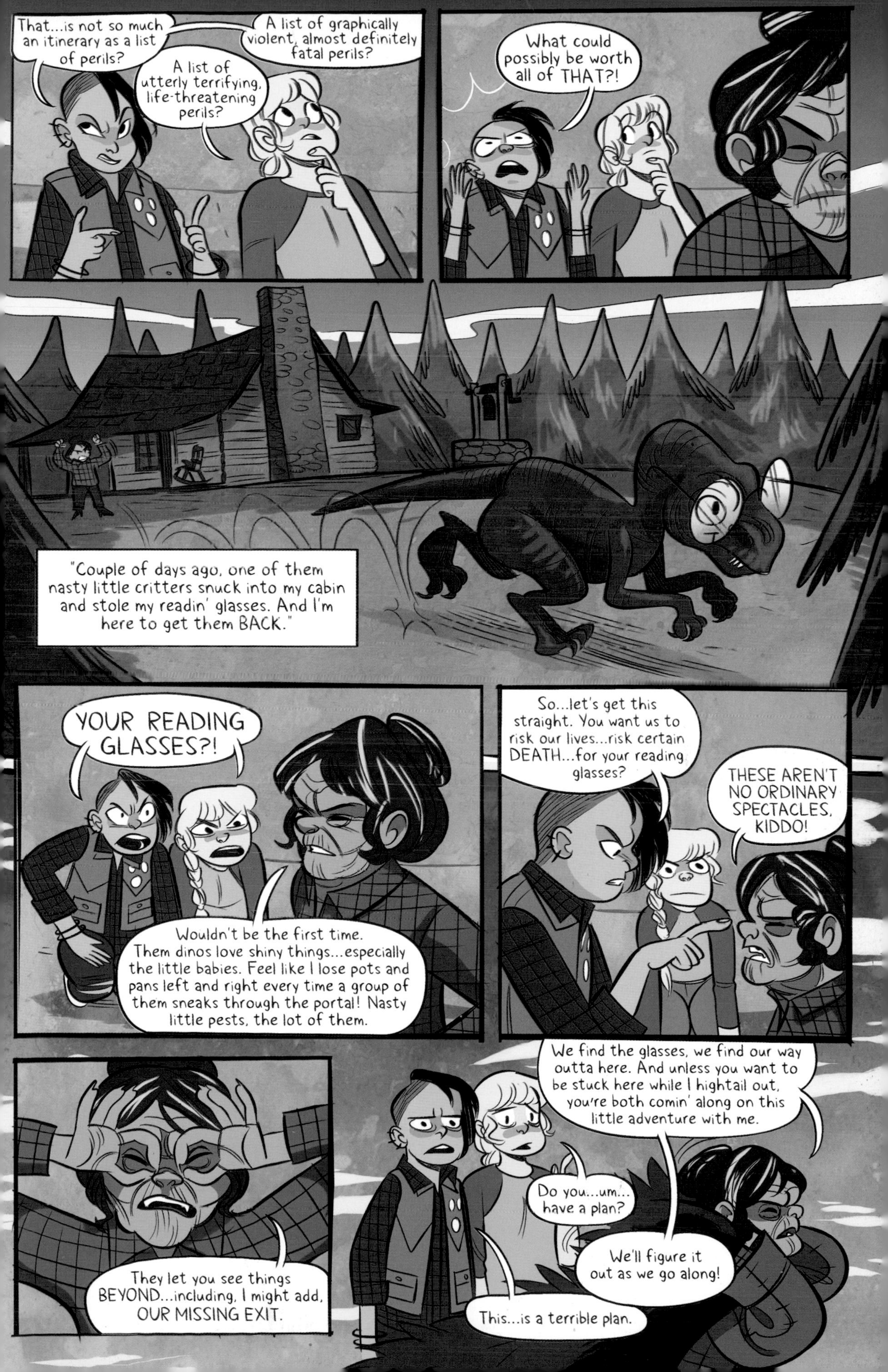
That...is not so much an itinerary as a list of perils?
A list of graphically violent, almost definitely fatal perils?
A list of utterly terrifying, life-threatening perils?
What could possibly be worth all of THAT?!
"Couple of days ago, one of them nasty little critters snuck into my cabin and stole my readin' glasses. And I'm here to get them BACK."
YOUR READING GLASSES?!
Wouldn't be the first time. Them dinos love shiny things...especially the little babies. Feel like I lose pots and pans left and right every time a group of them sneaks through the portal! Nasty little pests, the lot of them.
So...let's get this straight. You want us to risk our lives...risk certain DEATH...for your reading glasses?
THESE AREN'T NO ORDINARY SPECTACLES, KIDDO!
They let you see things BEYOND...including, I might add, OUR MISSING EXIT.
We find the glasses, we find our way outta here. And unless you want to be stuck here while I hightail out, you're both comin' along on this little adventure with me.
Do you...um... have a plan?
We'll figure it out as we go along!
This...is a terrible plan.

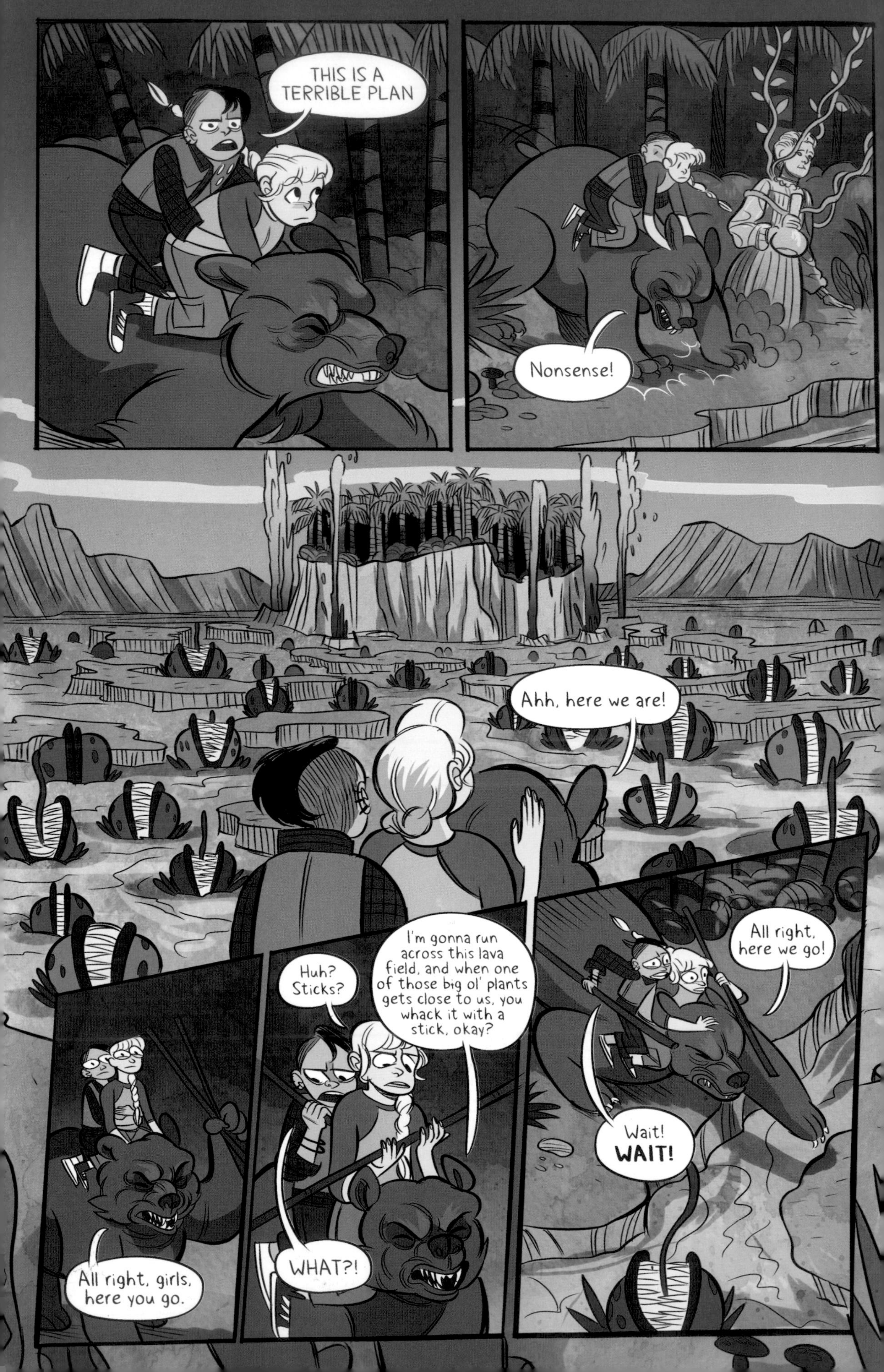
THIS IS A TERRIBLE PLAN
Nonsense!
Ahh, here we are!
All right, girls, here you go.
Huh? Sticks?
I'm gonna run across this lava field, and when one of those big ol' plants gets close to us, you whack it with a stick, okay?
WHAT?!
All right, here we go!
Wait! **WAIT!**

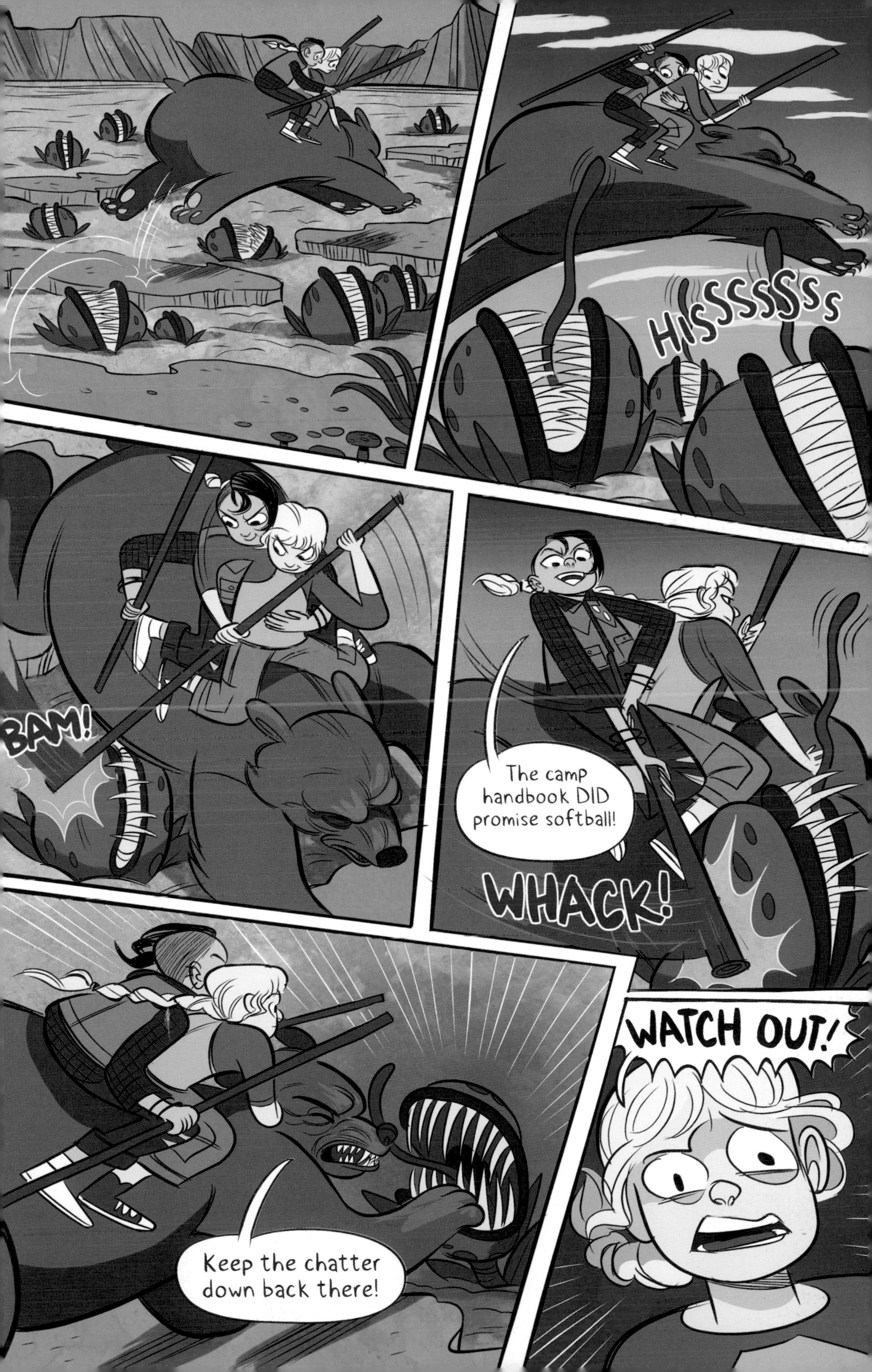
HISSSSSSSS
BAM!
The camp handbook DID promise softball!
WHACK!
Keep the chatter down back there!
WATCH OUT!

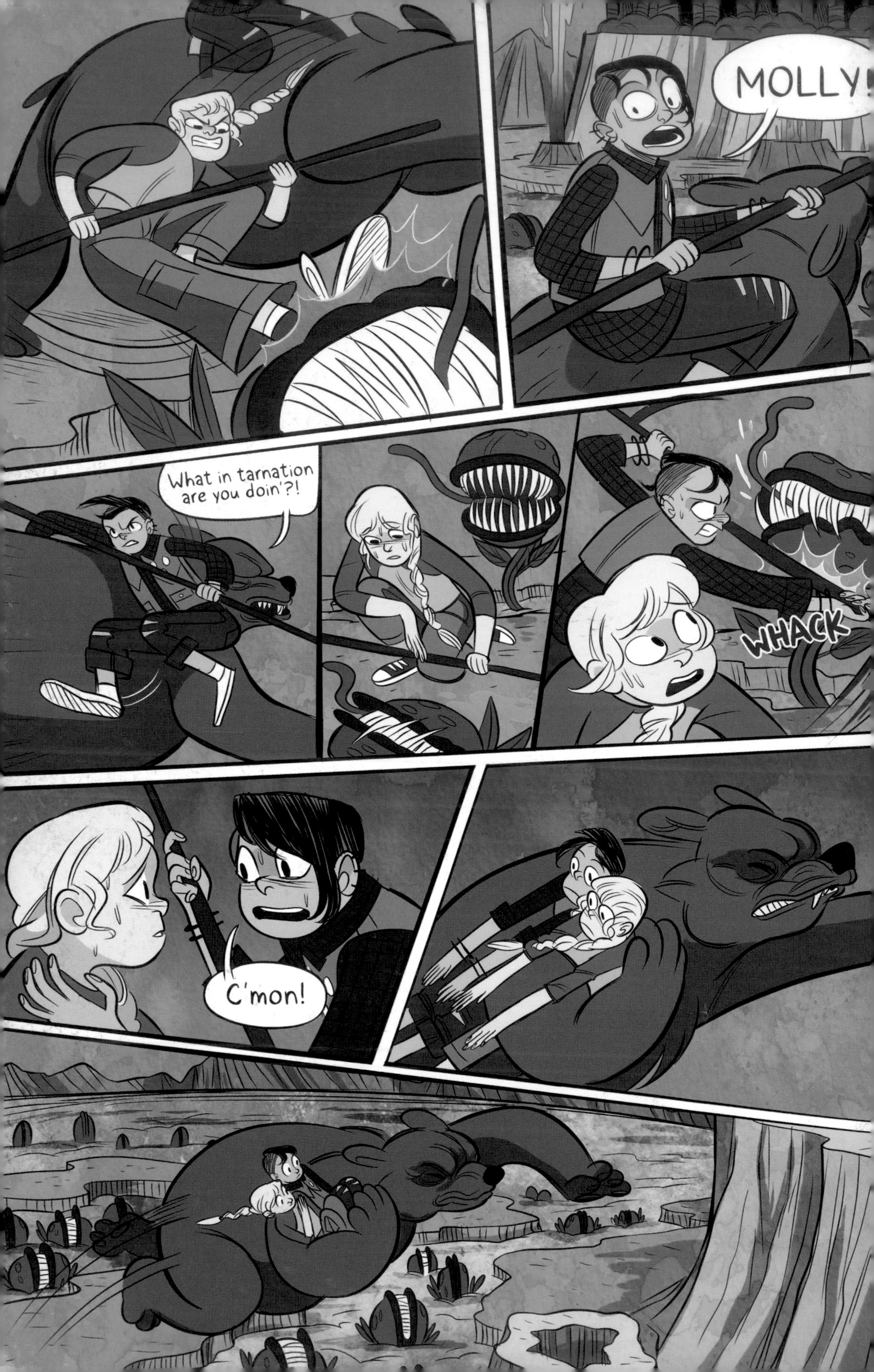
MOLLY!
What in tarnation are you doin'?!
WHACK
C'mon!

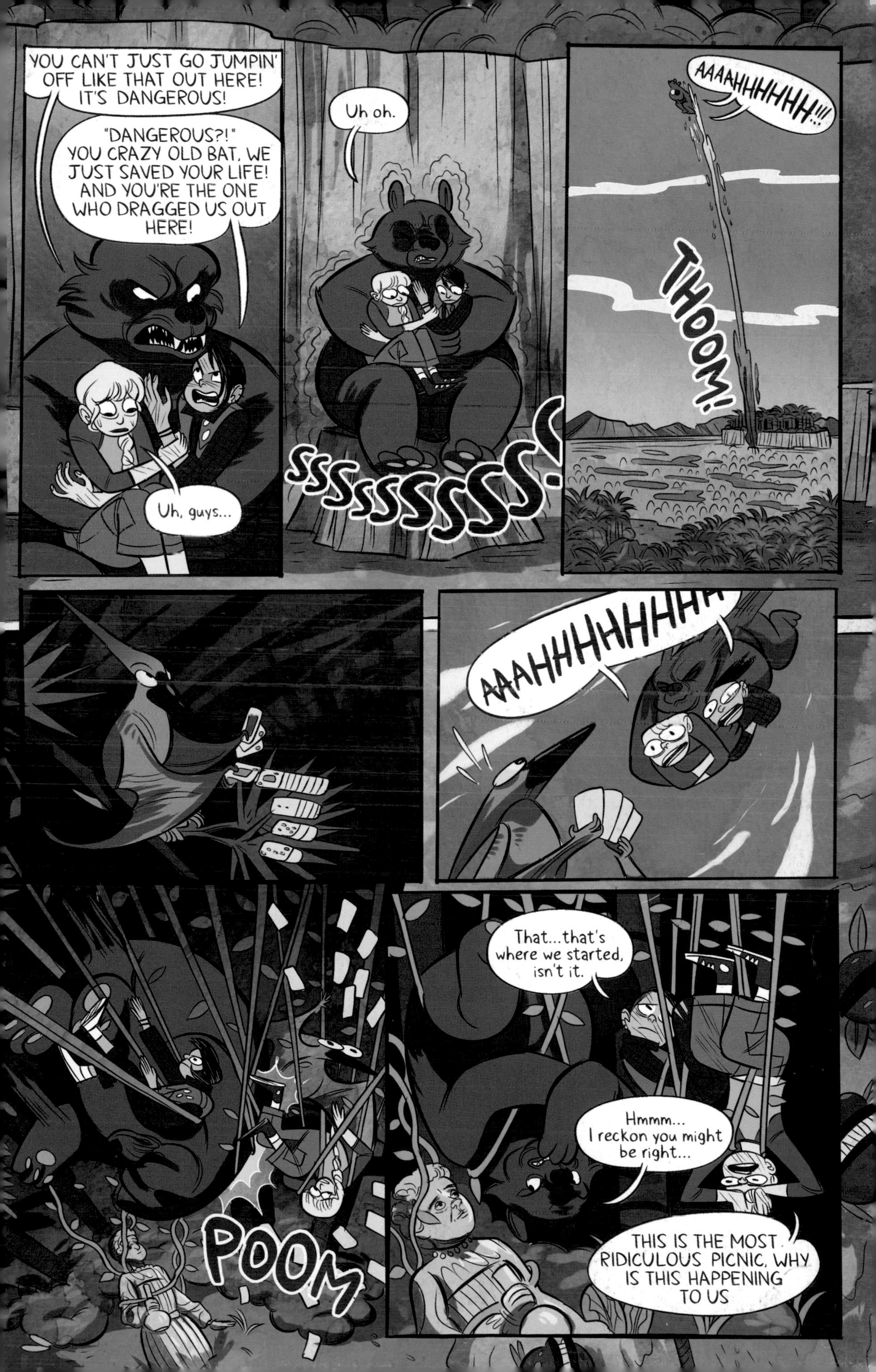

YOU CAN'T JUST GO JUMPIN' OFF LIKE THAT OUT HERE! IT'S DANGEROUS!
"DANGEROUS?!" YOU CRAZY OLD BAT, WE JUST SAVED YOUR LIFE! AND YOU'RE THE ONE WHO DRAGGED US OUT HERE!
Uh, guys...
Uh oh.
SSSSSSSSS!
AAAAHHHHHH!!!
THOOM!
AAAHHHHHHHHH
POOM
That...that's where we started, isn't it.
Hmmm... I reckon you might be right...
THIS IS THE MOST RIDICULOUS PICNIC, WHY IS THIS HAPPENING TO US

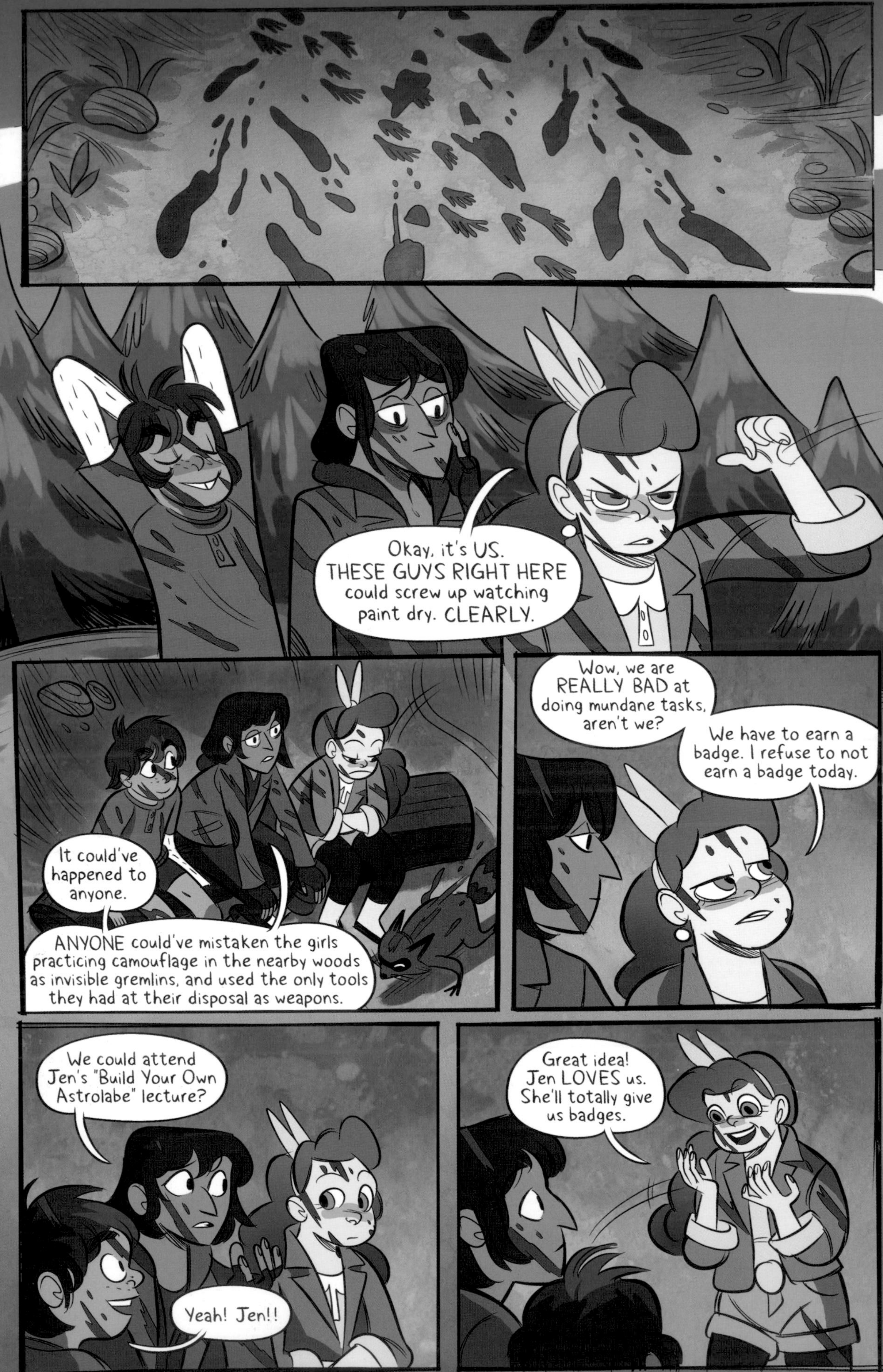
Okay, it's US. THESE GUYS RIGHT HERE could screw up watching paint dry. CLEARLY.
It could've happened to anyone.
ANYONE could've mistaken the girls practicing camouflage in the nearby woods as invisible gremlins, and used the only tools they had at their disposal as weapons.
Wow, we are REALLY BAD at doing mundane tasks, aren't we?
We have to earn a badge. I refuse to not earn a badge today.
We could attend Jen's "Build Your Own Astrolabe" lecture?
Yeah! Jen!!
Great idea! Jen LOVES us. She'll totally give us badges.

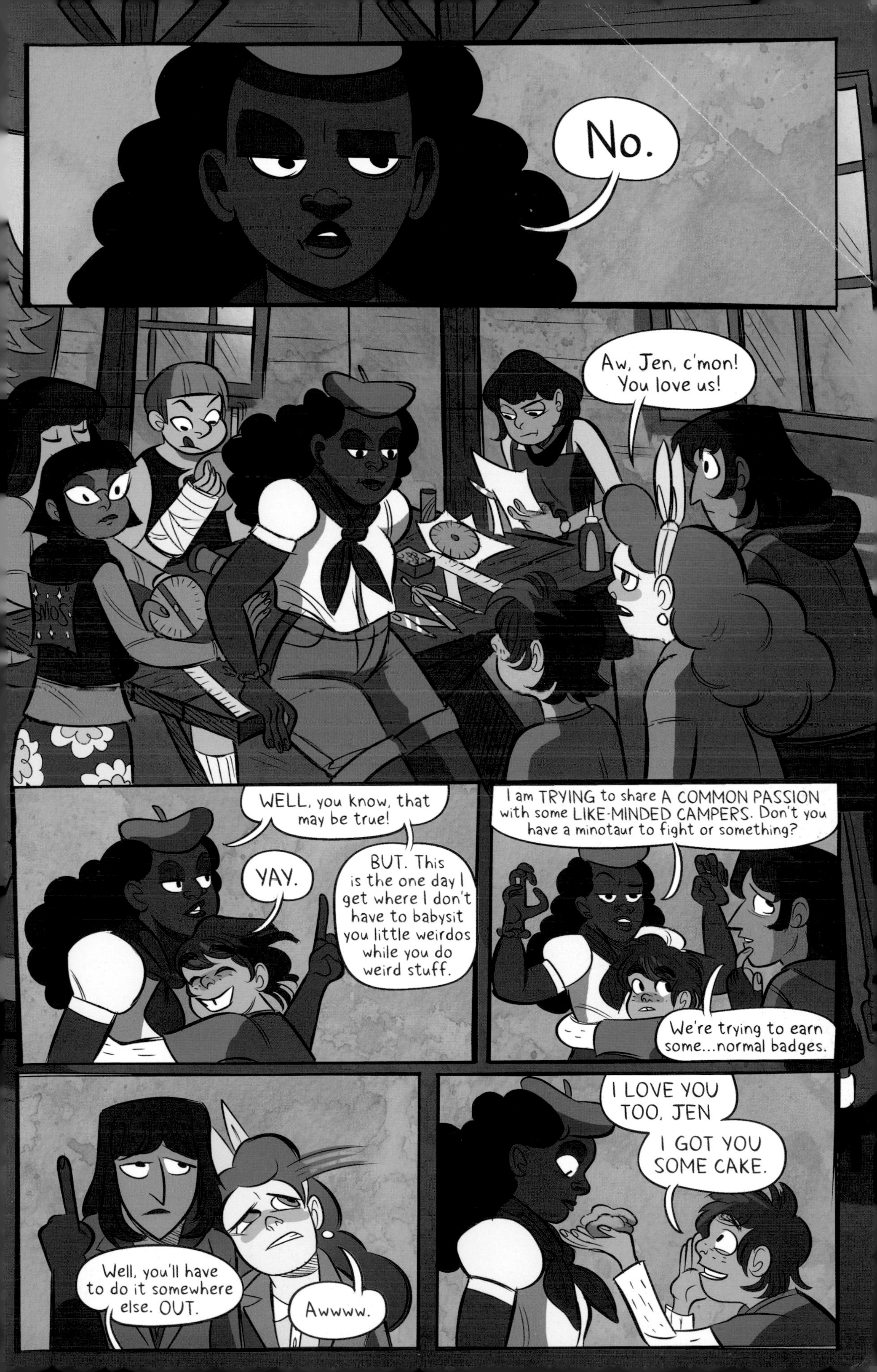
No.
Aw, Jen, c'mon! You love us!
SMOS
WELL, you know, that may be true!
YAY.
BUT. This is the one day I get where I don't have to babysit you little weirdos while you do weird stuff.
I am TRYING to share A COMMON PASSION with some LIKE-MINDED CAMPERS. Don't you have a minotaur to fight or something?
We're trying to earn some...normal badges.
Well, you'll have to do it somewhere else. OUT.
Awwww.
I LOVE YOU TOO, JEN
I GOT YOU SOME CAKE.

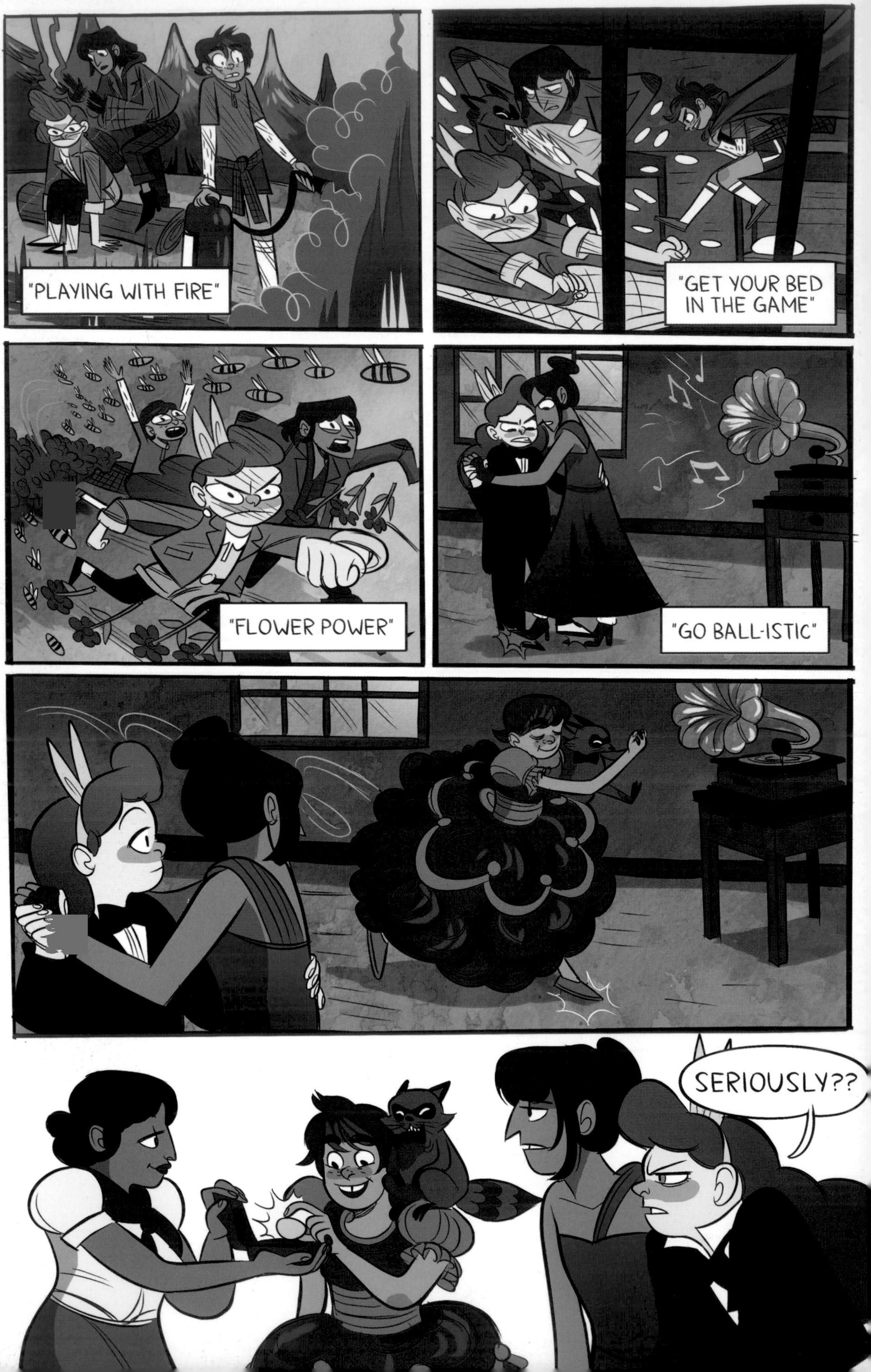
"PLAYING WITH FIRE"
"GET YOUR BED IN THE GAME"
"FLOWER POWER"
"GO BALL-ISTIC"
SERIOUSLY??

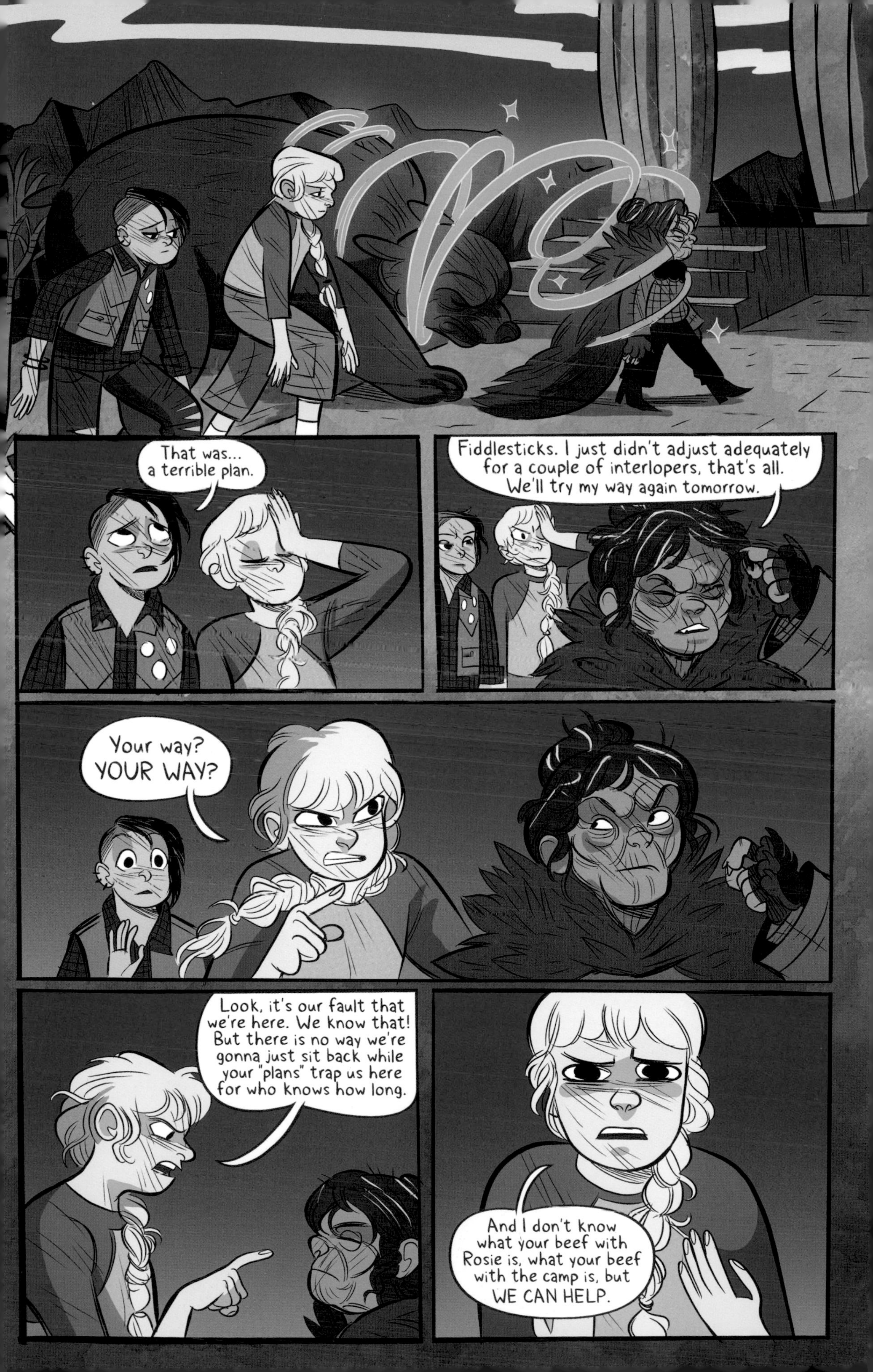
That was... a terrible plan.
Fiddlesticks. I just didn't adjust adequately for a couple of interlopers, that's all. We'll try my way again tomorrow.
Your way? YOUR WAY?
Look, it's our fault that we're here. We know that! But there is no way we're gonna just sit back while your "plans" trap us here for who knows how long.
And I don't know what your beef with Rosie is, what your beef with the camp is, but WE CAN HELP.

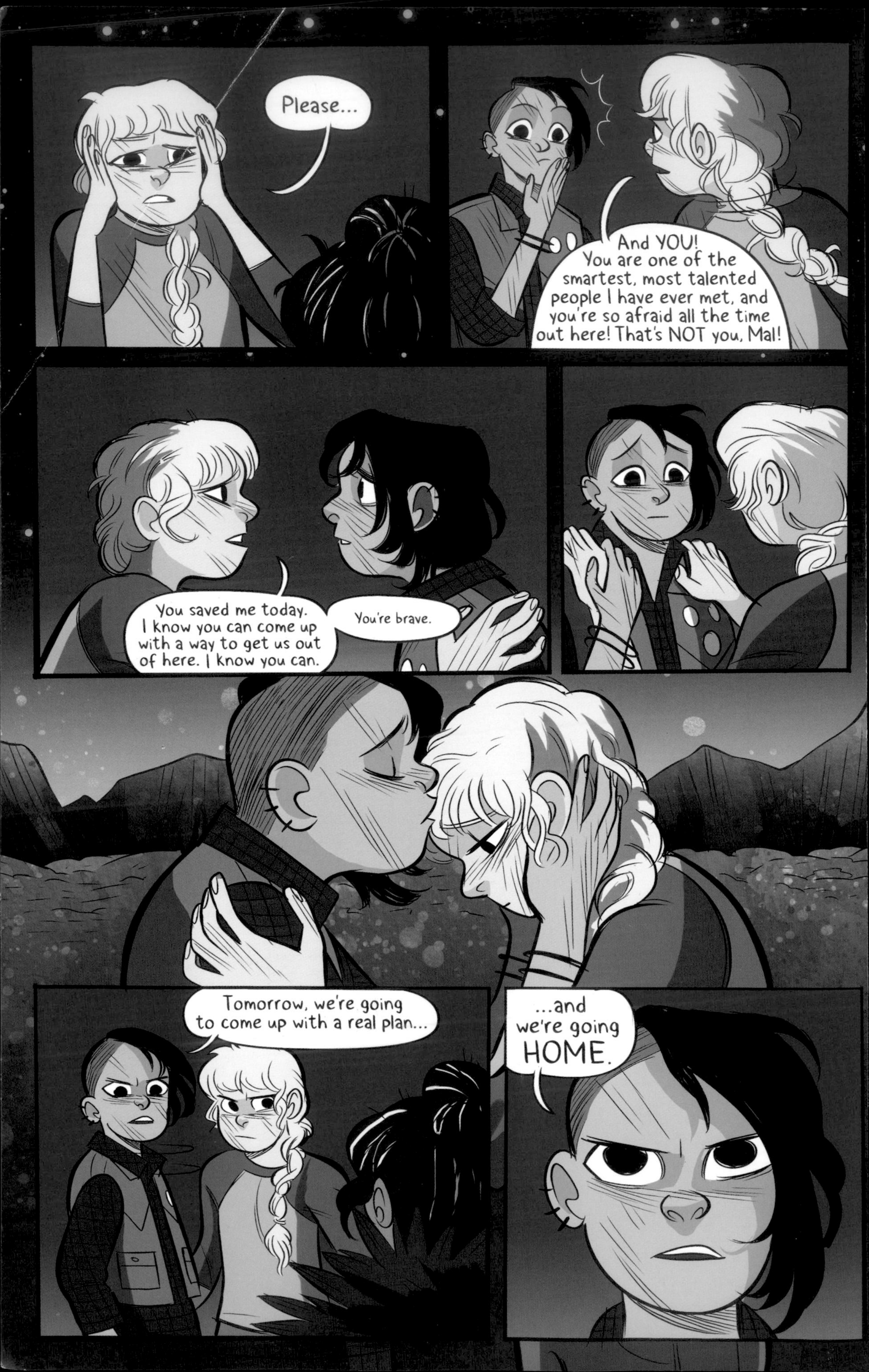
Please...
And YOU! You are one of the smartest, most talented people I have ever met, and you're so afraid all the time out here! That's NOT you, Mal!
You saved me today. I know you can come up with a way to get us out of here. I know you can.
You're brave.
Tomorrow, we're going to come up with a real plan...
...and we're going HOME.

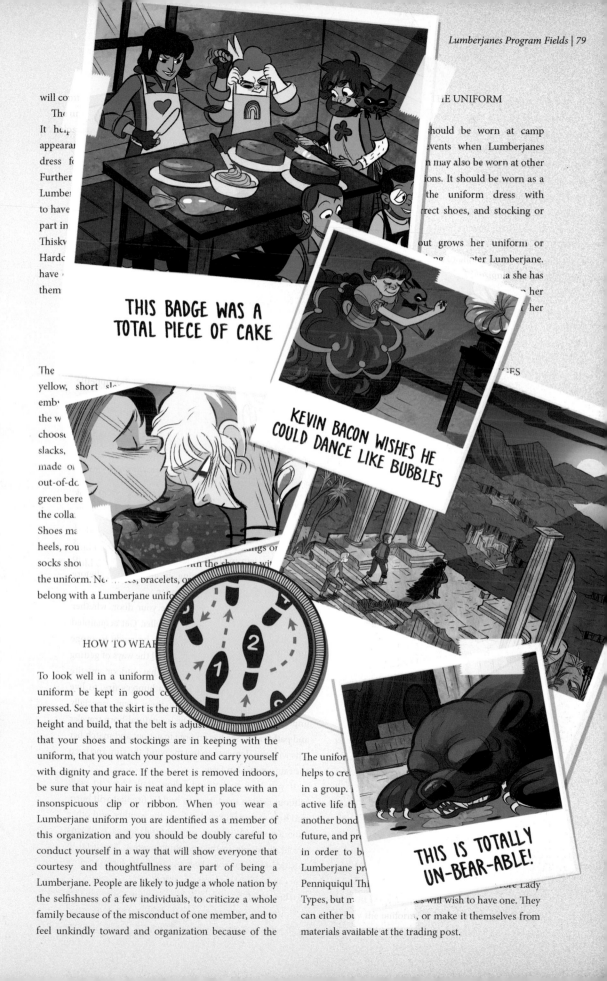

will co

The

It he

appeara

dress f

Further

Lumbe

to have

part in

Thisk

Hard

have

them

HE UNIFORM

should be worn at camp
events when Lumberjanes
n may also be worn at other
ions. It should be worn as a
the uniform dress with
rrect shoes, and stocking or

out grows her uniform or
ter Lumberjane.
a she has
her
her

The
yellow, short sl
emb
the w
choos
slacks,
made o
out-of-d
green bere
the colla
Shoes m
heels, rou
socks sho
the uniform. Ne
belong with a Lumberjane unif

HOW TO WEA

To look well in a uniform
uniform be kept in good c
pressed. See that the skirt is the ri
height and build, that the belt is adju
that your shoes and stockings are in keeping with the uniform, that you watch your posture and carry yourself with dignity and grace. If the beret is removed indoors, be sure that your hair is neat and kept in place with an insonspicuous clip or ribbon. When you wear a Lumberjane uniform you are identified as a member of this organization and you should be doubly careful to conduct yourself in a way that will show everyone that courtesy and thoughtfullness are part of being a Lumberjane. People are likely to judge a whole nation by the selfishness of a few individuals, to criticize a whole family because of the misconduct of one member, and to feel unkindly toward and organization because of the

The unifor
helps to cre
in a group.
active life th
another bond
future, and pr
in order to b
Lumberjane pr
Penniquiqul Thi
Types, but m
can either bu
materials available at the trading post.

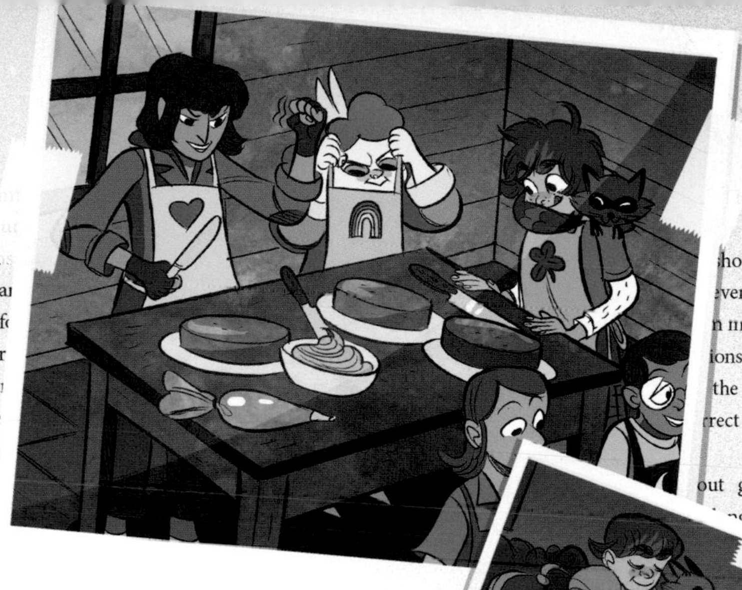

THIS BADGE WAS A TOTAL PIECE OF CAKE

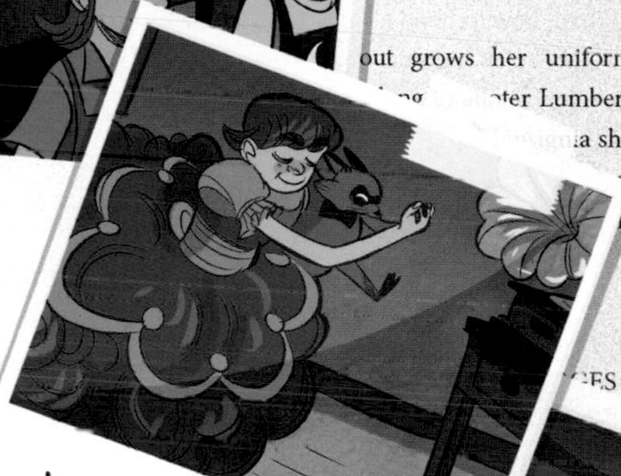

KEVIN BACON WISHES HE COULD DANCE LIKE BUBBLES

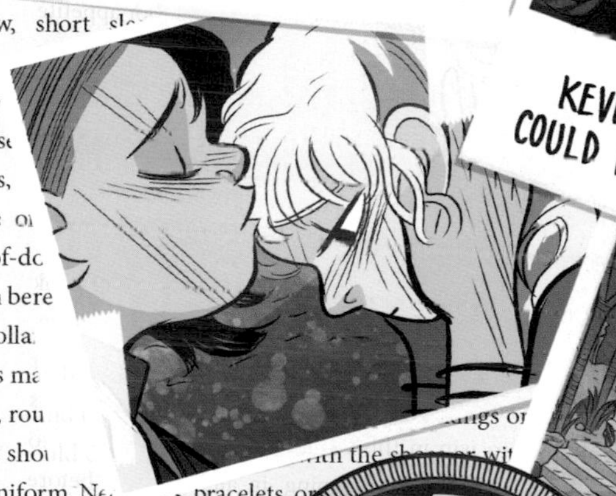

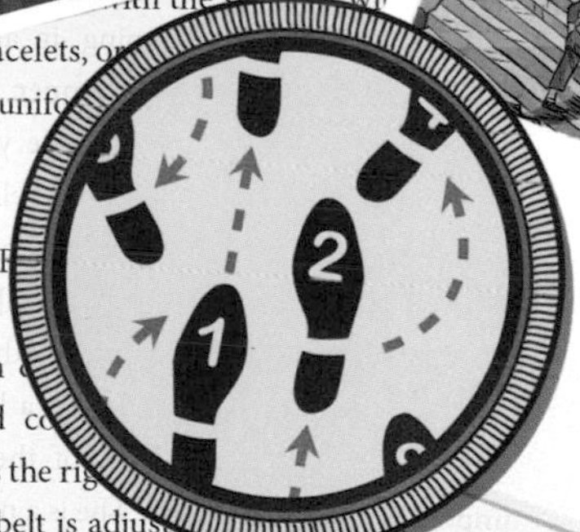

1
2

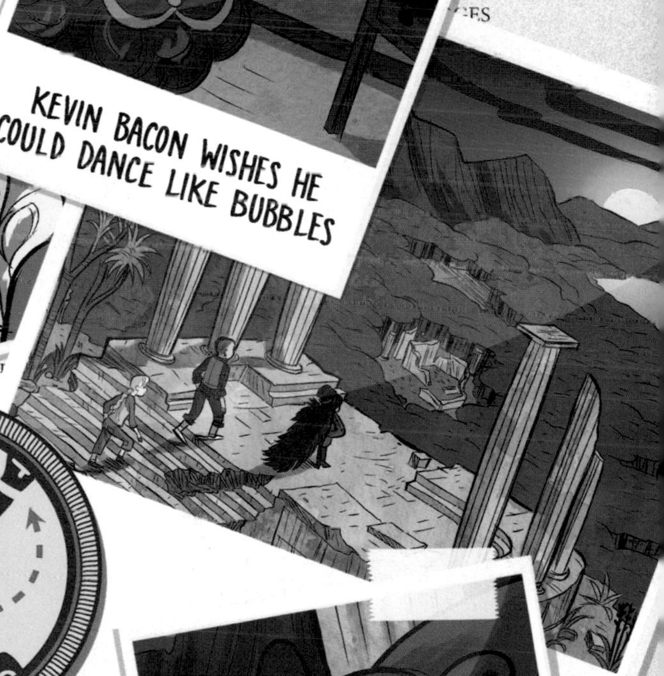

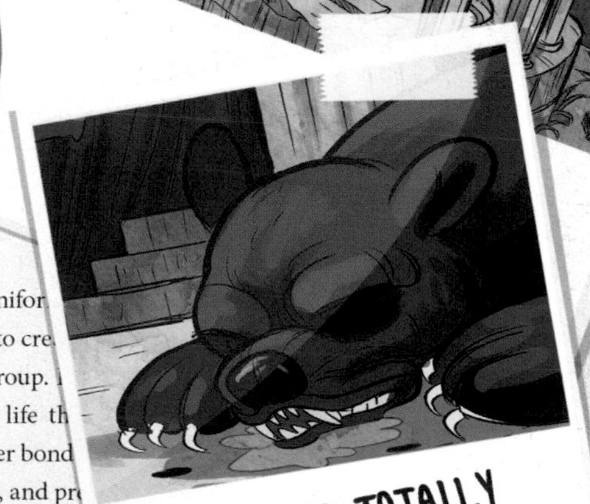

THIS IS TOTALLY UN-BEAR-ABLE!

LUMBERJANES FIELD MANUAL

CHAPTER TWELVE

Lumberjanes "Arts and Crafts" Program Field

OLDIE BUT GOODIE BADGE

"Helping history stay alive."

Every year we grow older and mature as women. Like any well rounded Lumberjane, we will understand that the experiences of those older than ourselves are meant to help guide us on our path. They are the ropes on the walkway of our journey, hinting at directions that should be taken while not forcing us to stay on just one path. Being a Lumberjane is more than learning skills for the great outdoors, it is also a chance to learn from this community of unique individuals. 'Respect your elders' is not a term that is taken lightly at Lumberjane camp and it never will be. All women learn from the follies of their youth, just as each young woman could learn a different lesson from the same problem it is up to all the Lumberjanes to seek guidance in their counselors, their peers, and their elders.

The importance of the *Oldie But Goodie* badge is that it teaches respect, and how to value all the lives around

you, even if they don't visibly affect your own. We are all connected under the same sky and one decision from a young scout fifty years in the past can still affect the decisions of young Lumberjanes attending camp this day. History is important, it is a chance for us to learn from the actions of others, to see the courses that were already taken and to take a step in an all-new direction. Even our own personal histories are used as guides in every decision we make as we continue on our personal journeys.

To obtain the *Oldie But Goodie* badge a Lumberjane must help an elder in the camp. In this performance they will be able to see what is needed to assist and will do all that they can to make sure that they are able to help. They are not required to perform on their own as to be a Lumberjane means to be constantly surrounded by friends, and in this badge, all who help out will each earn their own *Oldie But Goodie* badge. It is

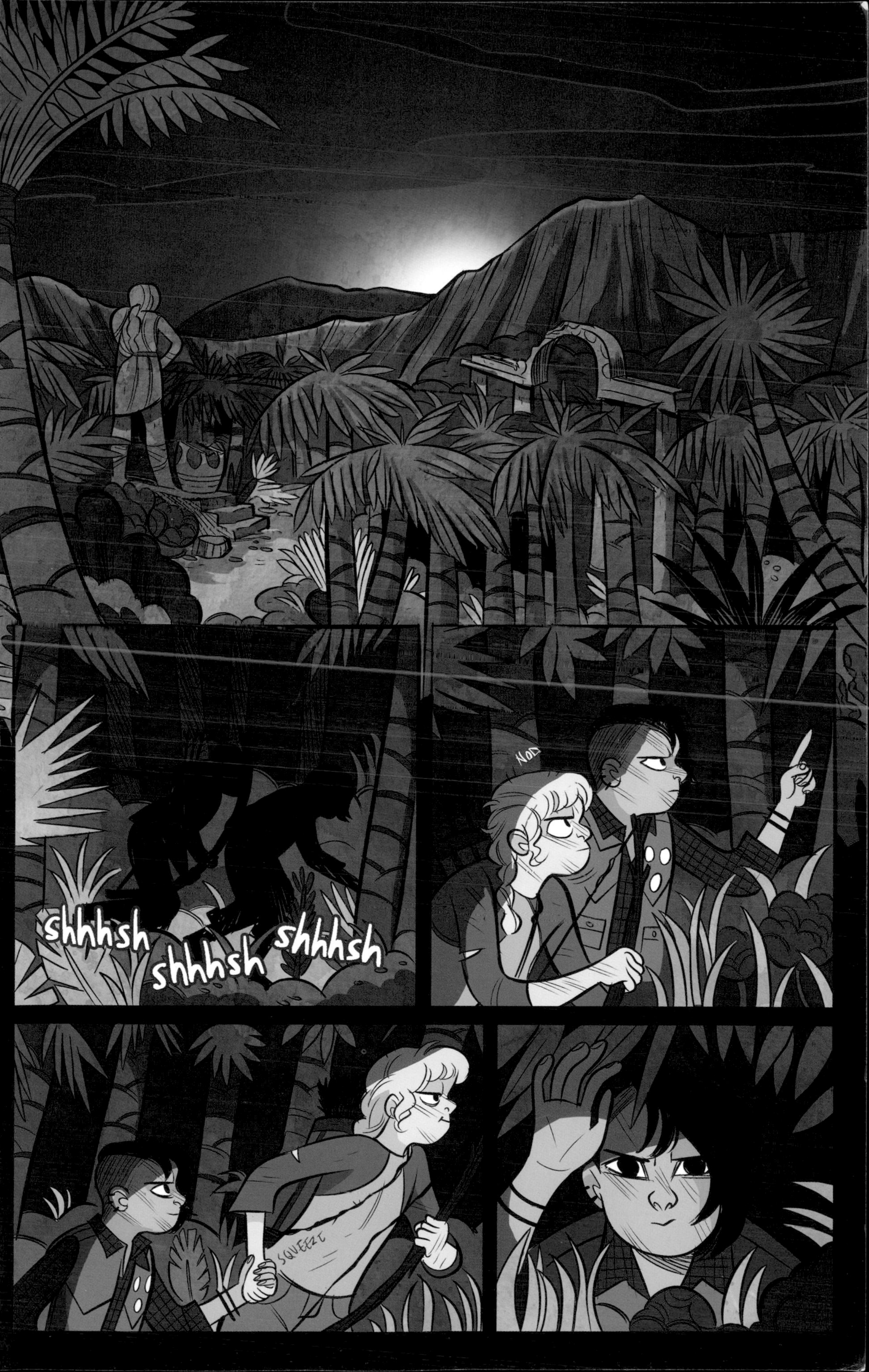
shhhsh
shhhsh
shhhsh
NOD
SQUEEZE

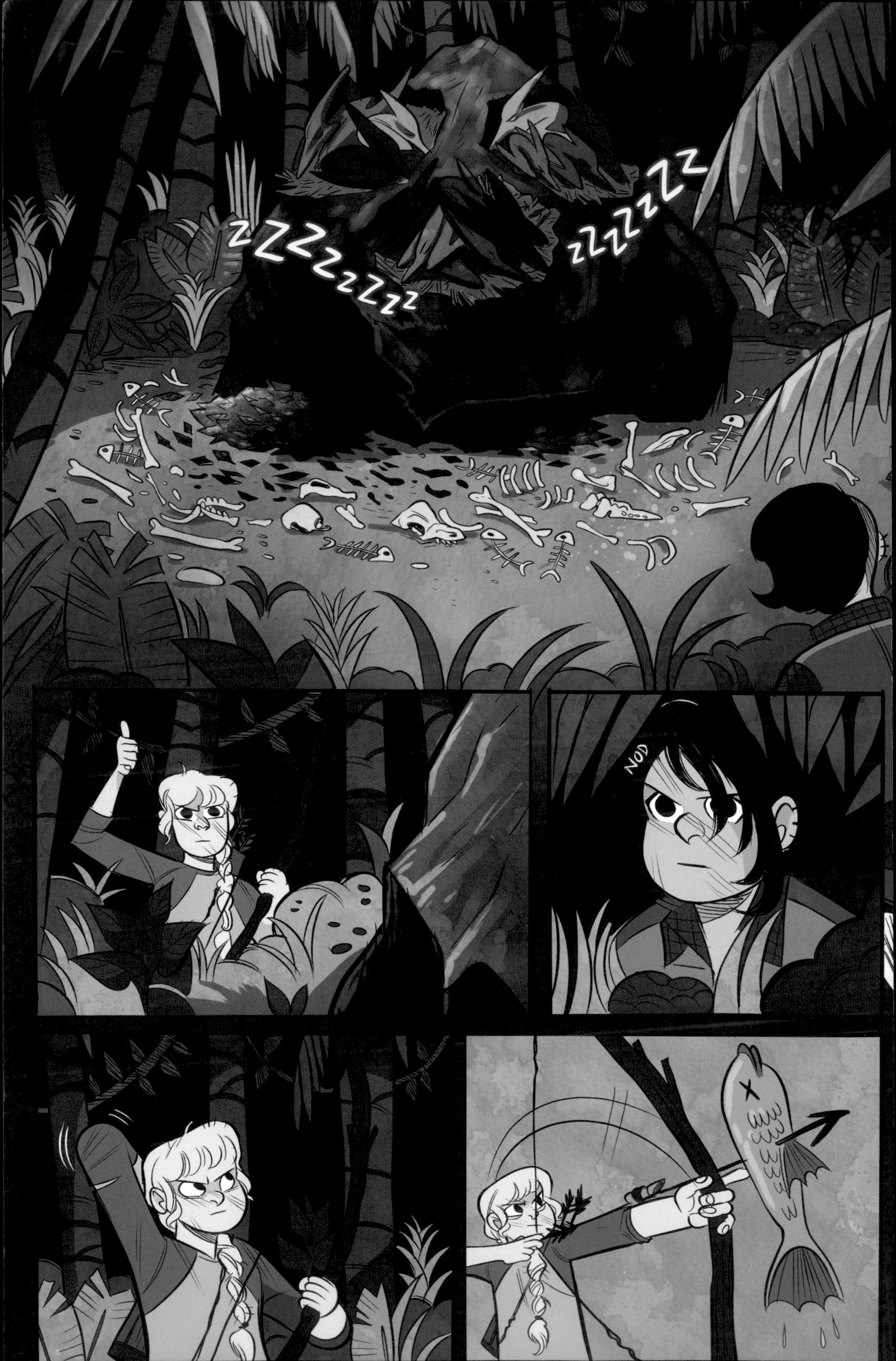
zZZZzzZzz
zzzZzZZZ
NOD

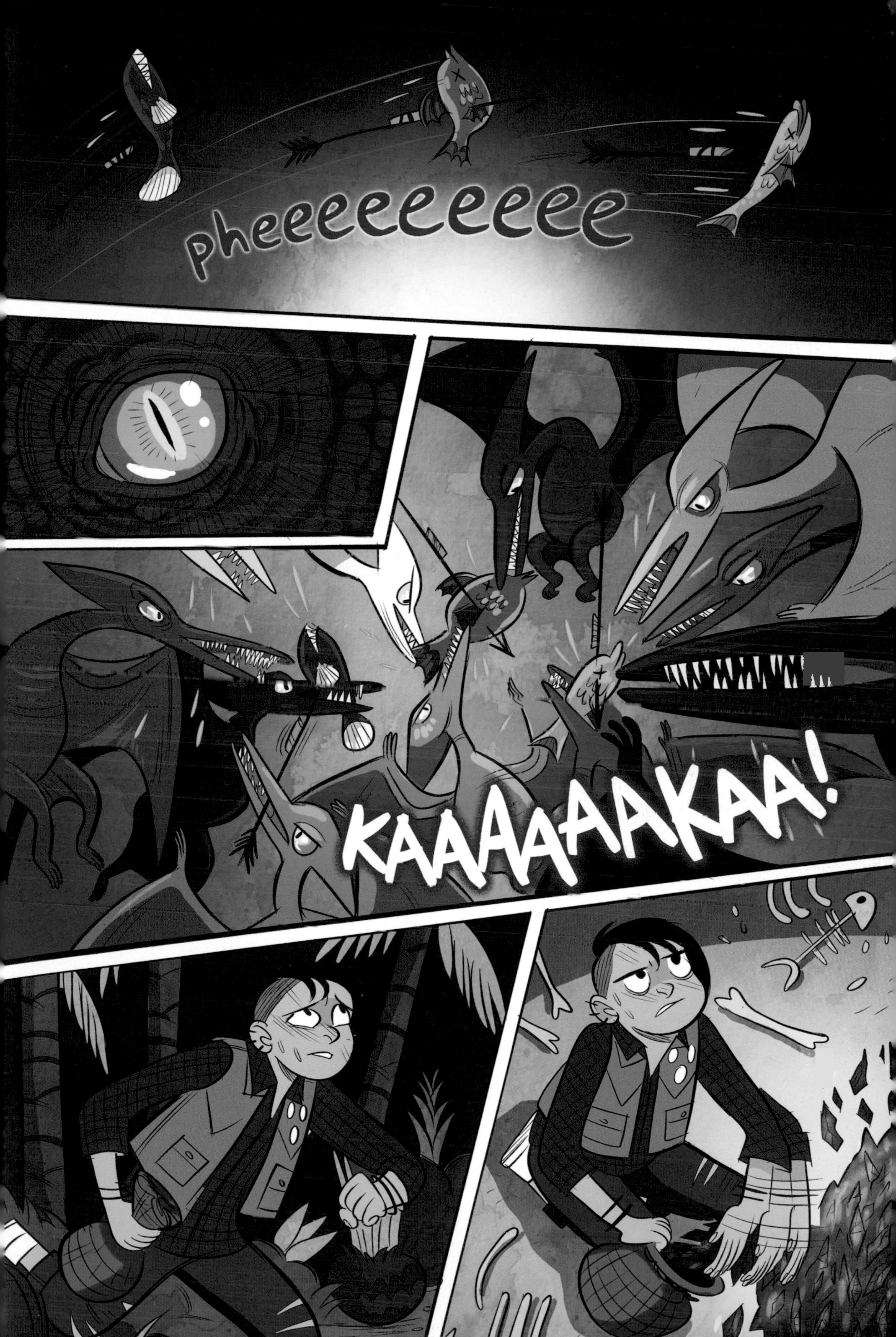
pheeeeeeeee
KAAAAAAKAA!

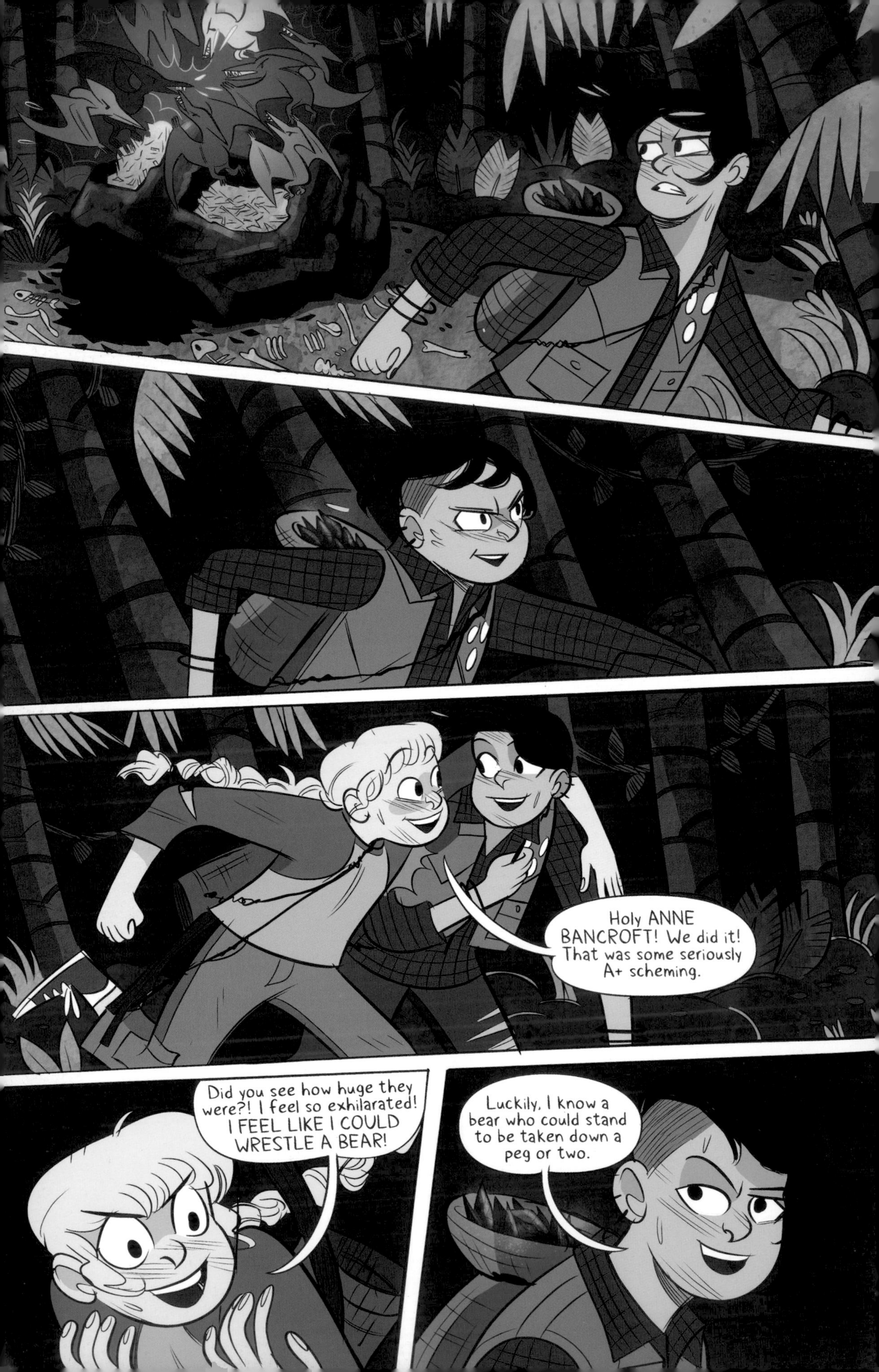

Holy ANNE BANCROFT! We did it! That was some seriously A+ scheming.
Did you see how huge they were?! I feel so exhilarated! I FEEL LIKE I COULD WRESTLE A BEAR!
Luckily, I know a bear who could stand to be taken down a peg or two.

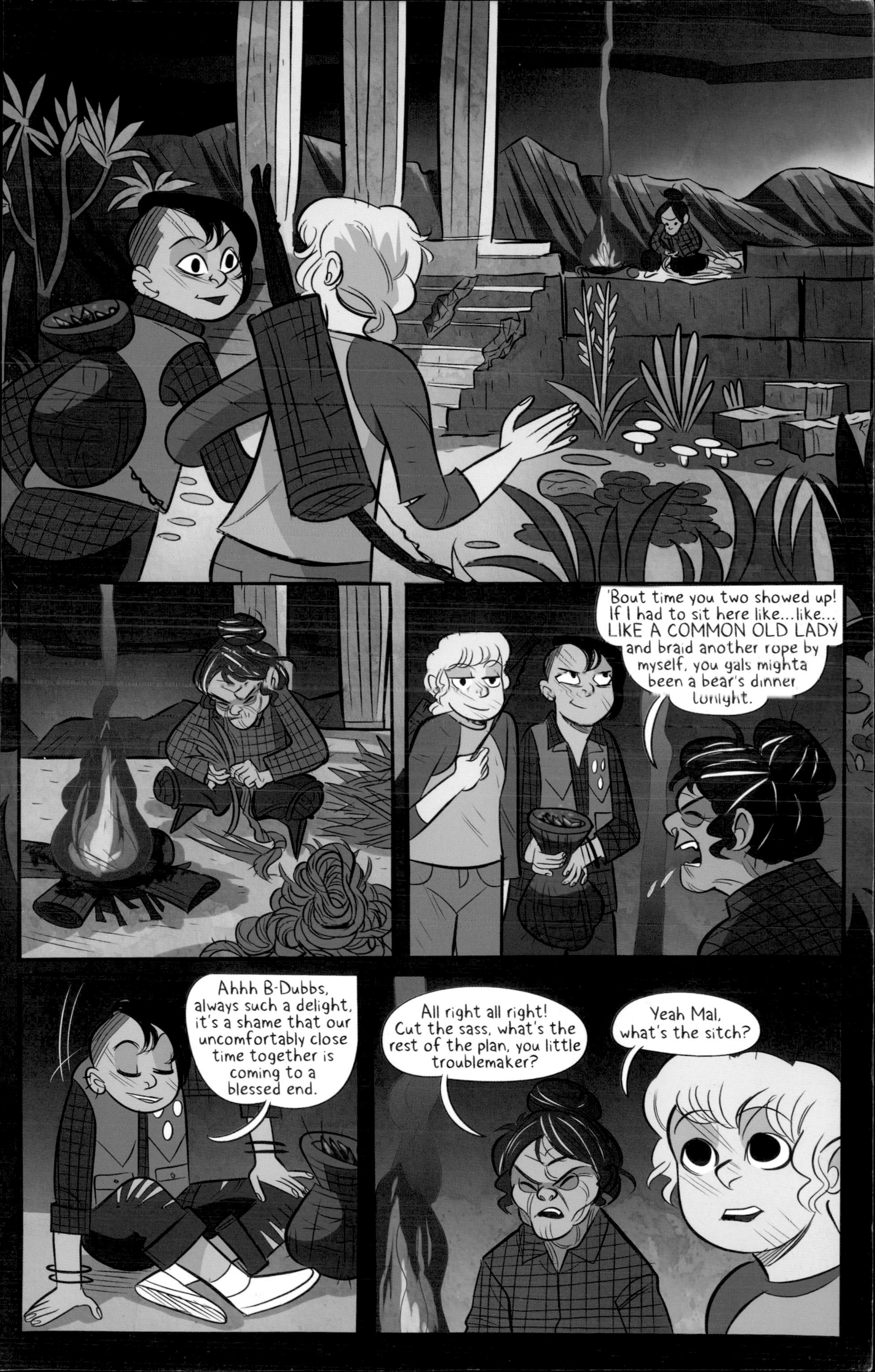
'Bout time you two showed up! If I had to sit here like... like... LIKE A COMMON OLD LADY and braid another rope by myself, you gals mighta been a bear's dinner tonight.
Ahhh B-Dubbs, always such a delight, it's a shame that our uncomfortably close time together is coming to a blessed end.
All right all right! Cut the sass, what's the rest of the plan, you little troublemaker?
Yeah Mal, what's the sitch?

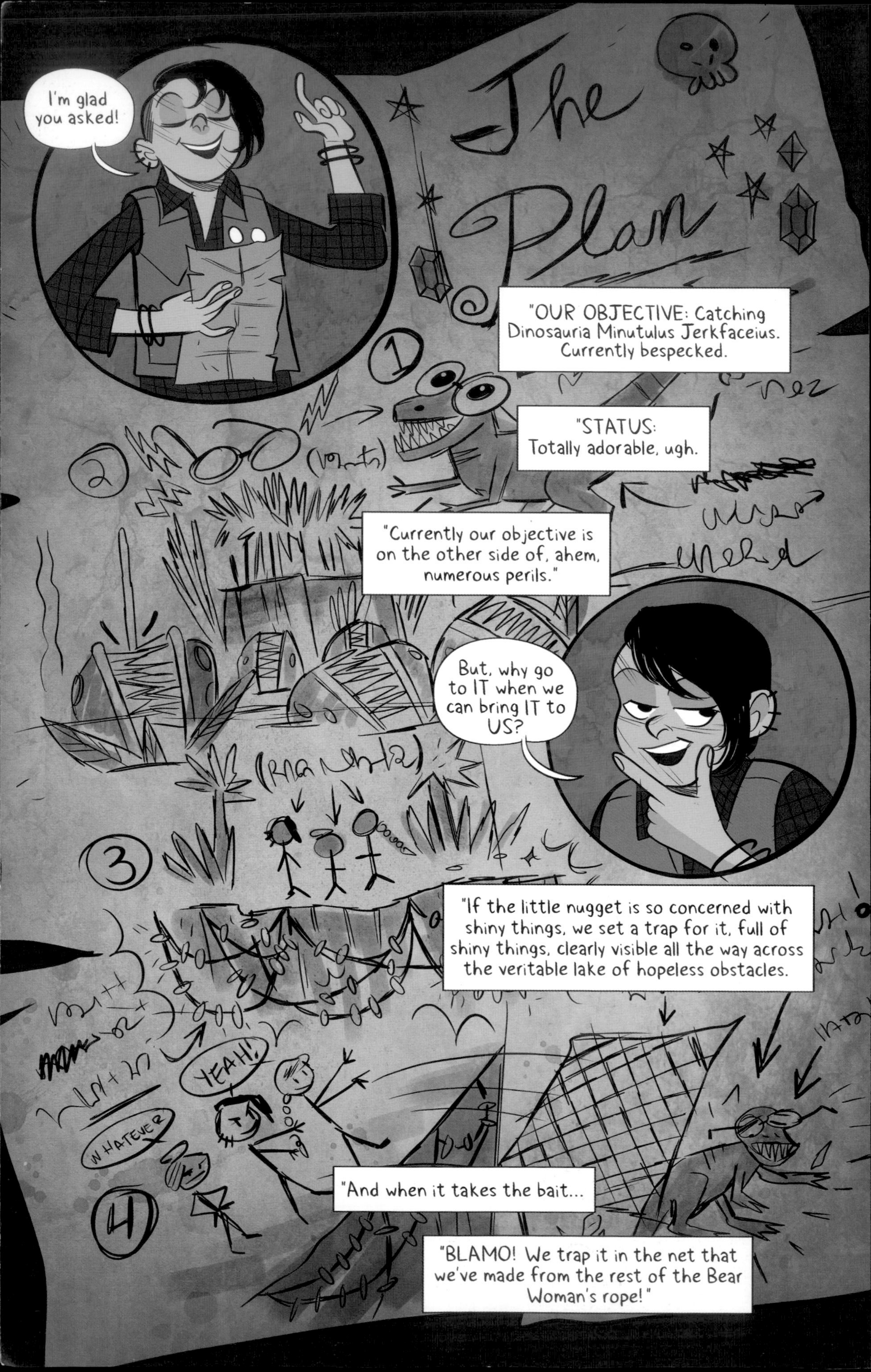

I'm glad you asked!
The Plan
"OUR OBJECTIVE: Catching Dinosauria Minutulus Jerkfaceius. Currently bespecked.
"STATUS: Totally adorable, ugh.
"Currently our objective is on the other side of, ahem, numerous perils."
But, why go to IT when we can bring IT to US?
"If the little nugget is so concerned with shiny things, we set a trap for it, full of shiny things, clearly visible all the way across the veritable lake of hopeless obstacles.
YEAH!
WHATEVER
"And when it takes the bait...
"BLAMO! We trap it in the net that we've made from the rest of the Bear Woman's rope!"

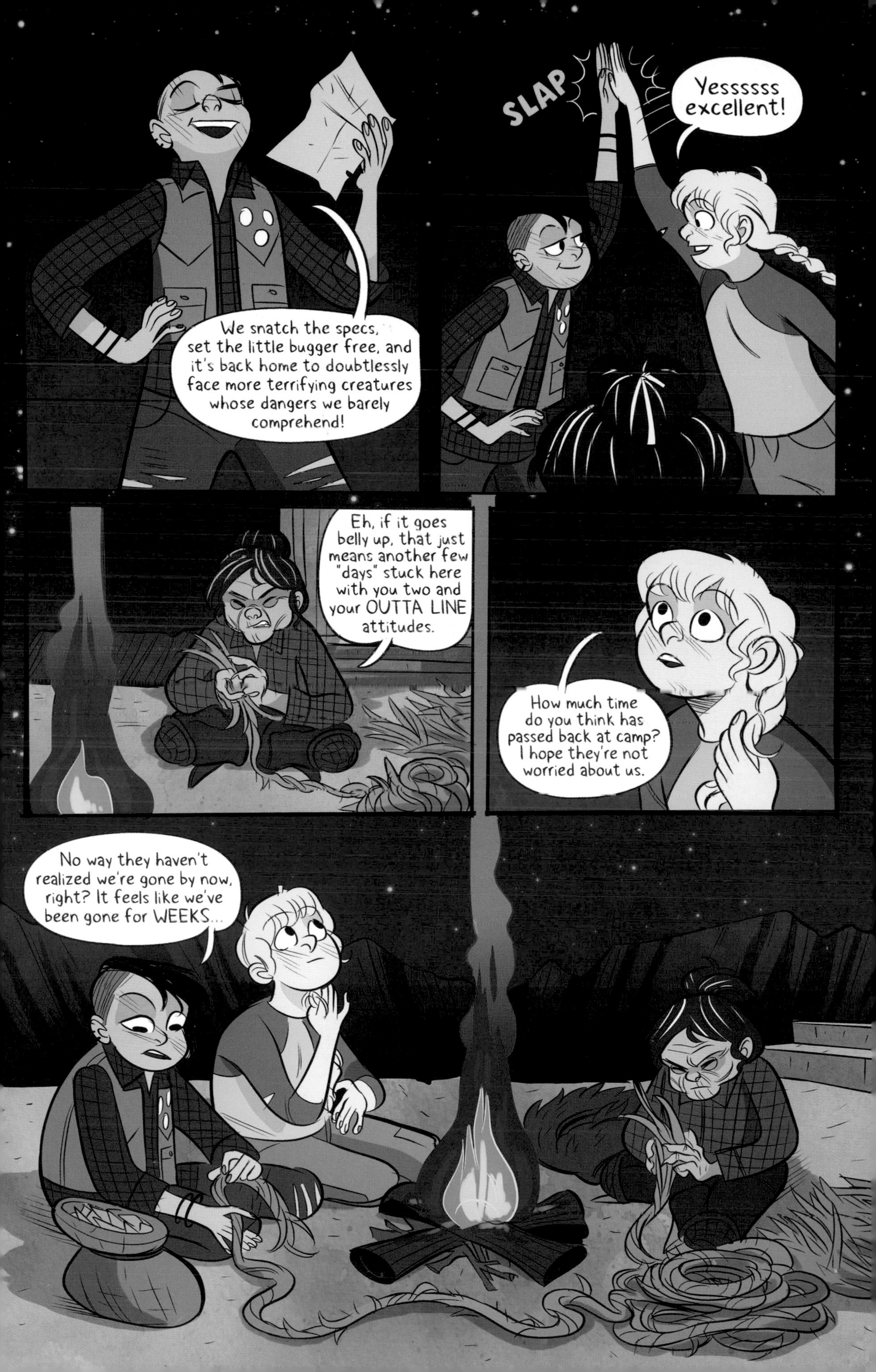
We snatch the specs, set the little bugger free, and it's back home to doubtlessly face more terrifying creatures whose dangers we barely comprehend!
SLAP
Yessssss excellent!
Eh, if it goes belly up, that just means another few "days" stuck here with you two and your OUTTA LINE attitudes.
How much time do you think has passed back at camp? I hope they're not worried about us.
No way they haven't realized we're gone by now, right? It feels like we've been gone for WEEKS...

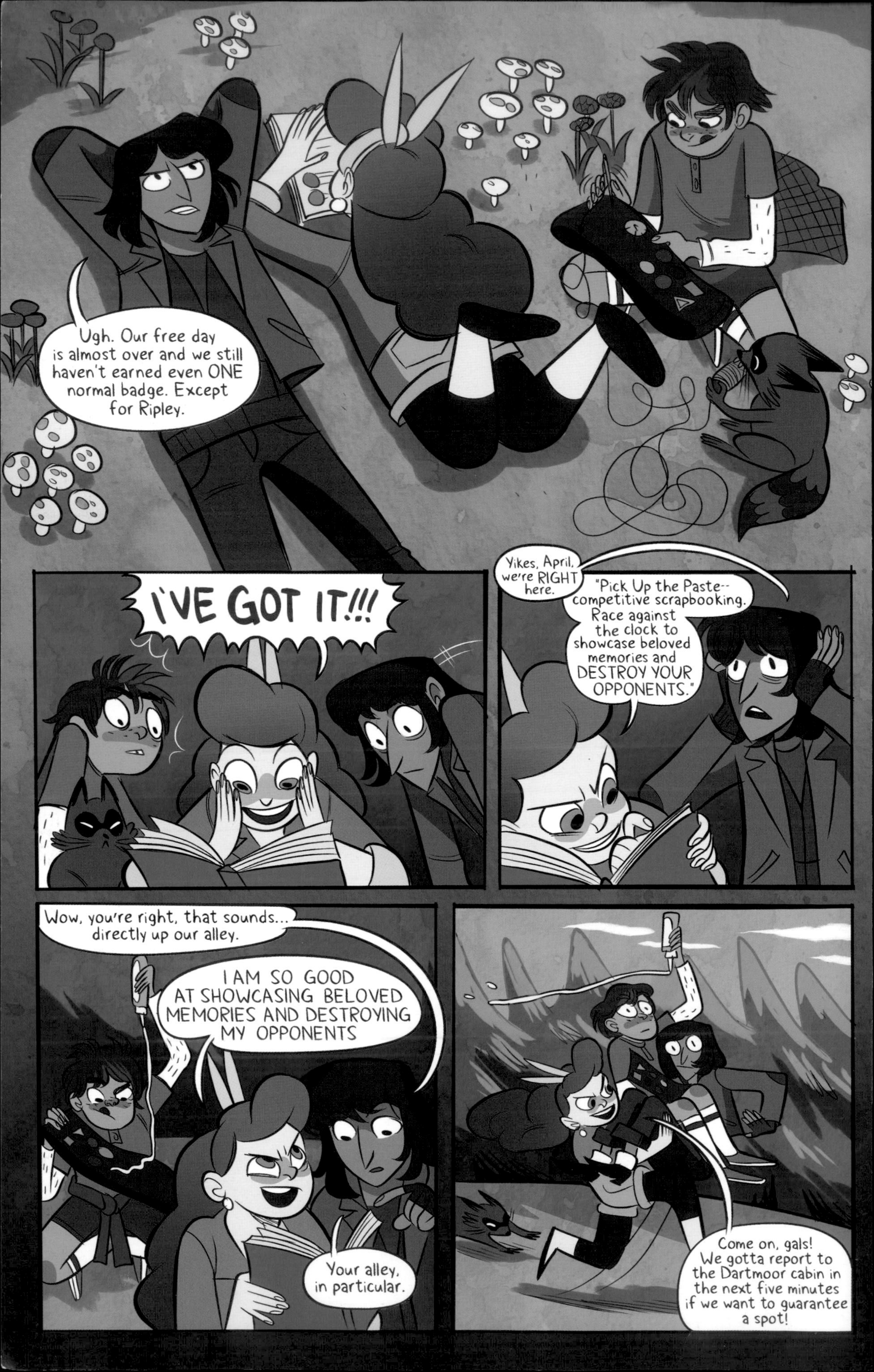
Ugh. Our free day is almost over and we still haven't earned even ONE normal badge. Except for Ripley.
I'VE GOT IT!!!
Yikes, April, we're RIGHT here.
"Pick Up the Paste--competitive scrapbooking. Race against the clock to showcase beloved memories and DESTROY YOUR OPPONENTS."
Wow, you're right, that sounds... directly up our alley.
I AM SO GOOD AT SHOWCASING BELOVED MEMORIES AND DESTROYING MY OPPONENTS
Your alley, in particular.
Come on, gals! We gotta report to the Dartmoor cabin in the next five minutes if we want to guarantee a spot!

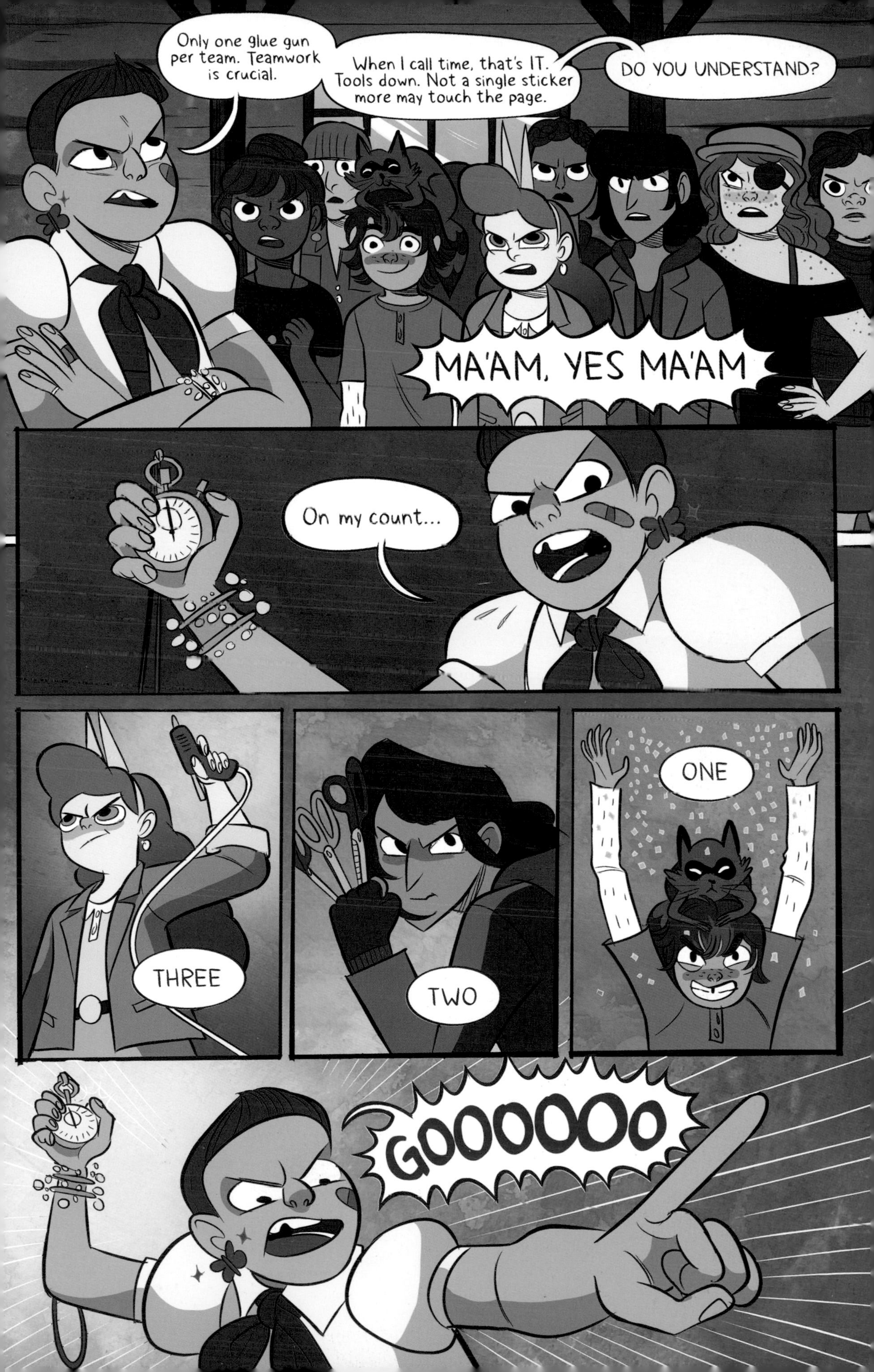

Only one glue gun per team. Teamwork is crucial.
When I call time, that's IT. Tools down. Not a single sticker more may touch the page.
DO YOU UNDERSTAND?
MA'AM, YES MA'AM
On my count...
THREE
TWO
ONE
GOOOOOO

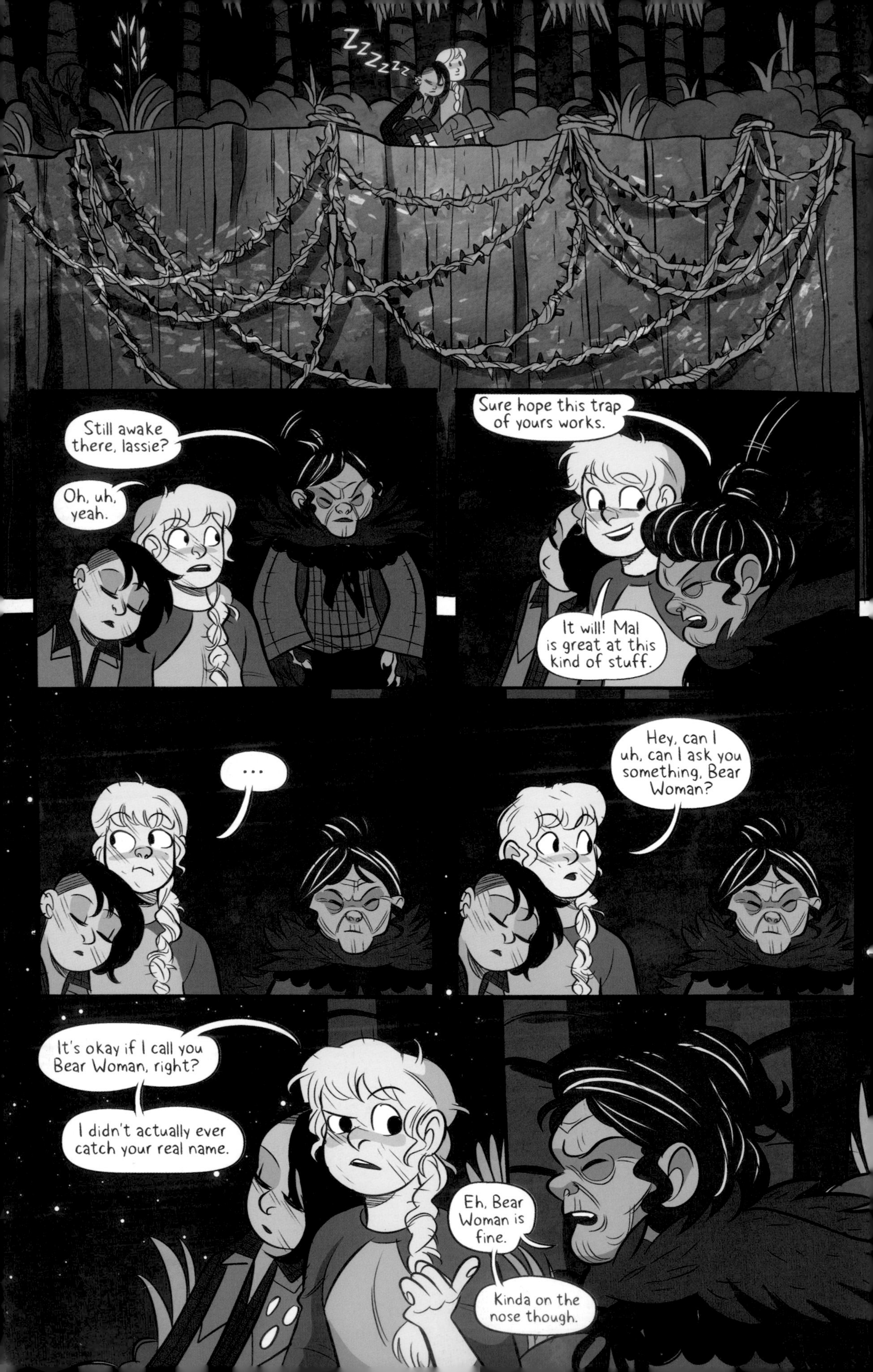

ZZZZZZ
Still awake there, lassie?
Oh, uh, yeah.
Sure hope this trap of yours works.
It will! Mal is great at this kind of stuff.
...
Hey, can I uh, can I ask you something, Bear Woman?
It's okay if I call you Bear Woman, right?
I didn't actually ever catch your real name.
Eh, Bear Woman is fine.
Kinda on the nose though.

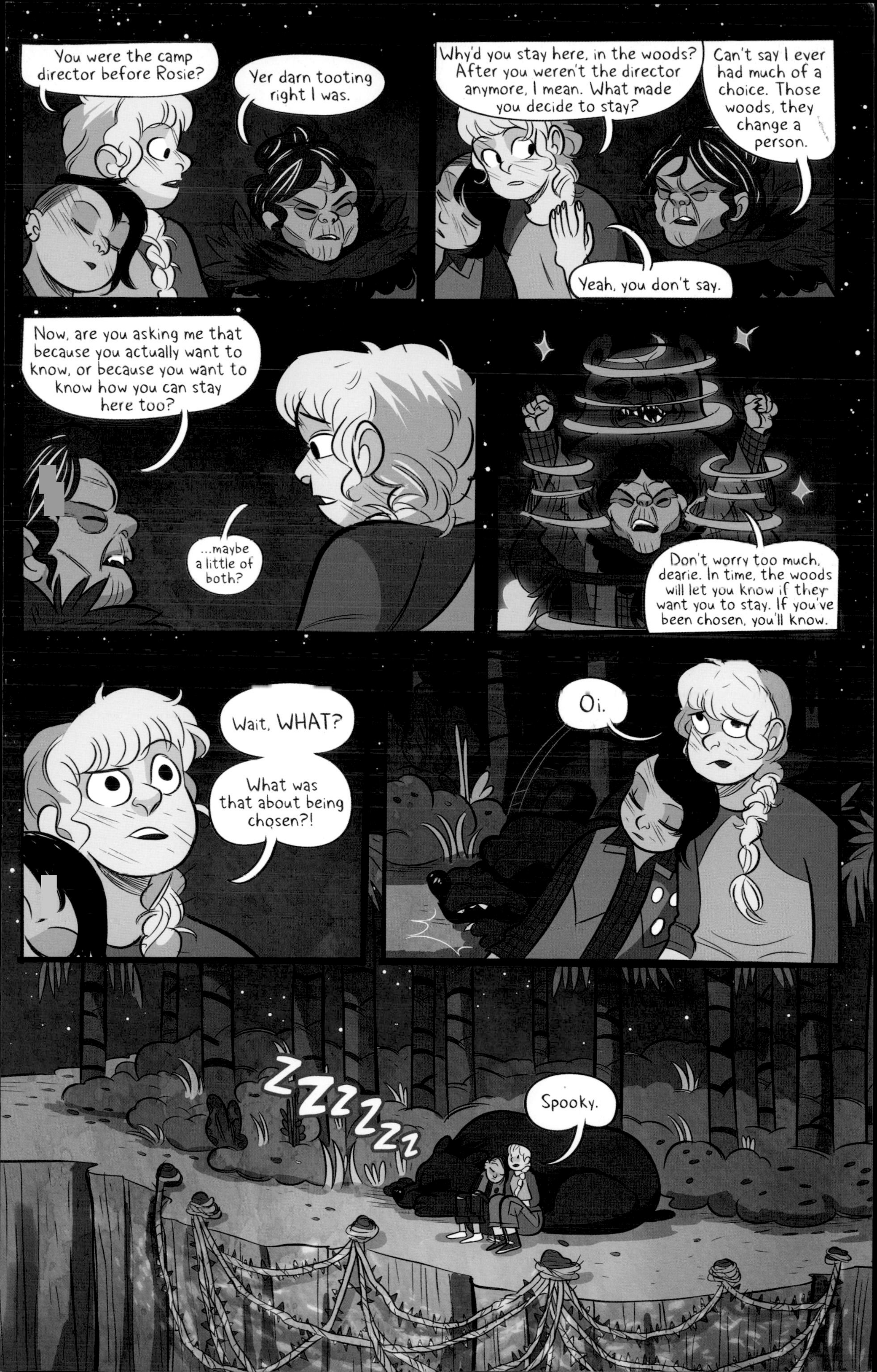
You were the camp director before Rosie?
Yer darn tooting right I was.
Why'd you stay here, in the woods? After you weren't the director anymore, I mean. What made you decide to stay?
Can't say I ever had much of a choice. Those woods, they change a person.
Yeah, you don't say.
Now, are you asking me that because you actually want to know, or because you want to know how you can stay here too?
...maybe a little of both?
Don't worry too much, dearie. In time, the woods will let you know if they want you to stay. If you've been chosen, you'll know.
Wait, WHAT?
What was that about being chosen?!
Oi.
ZZZZZZZ
Spooky.

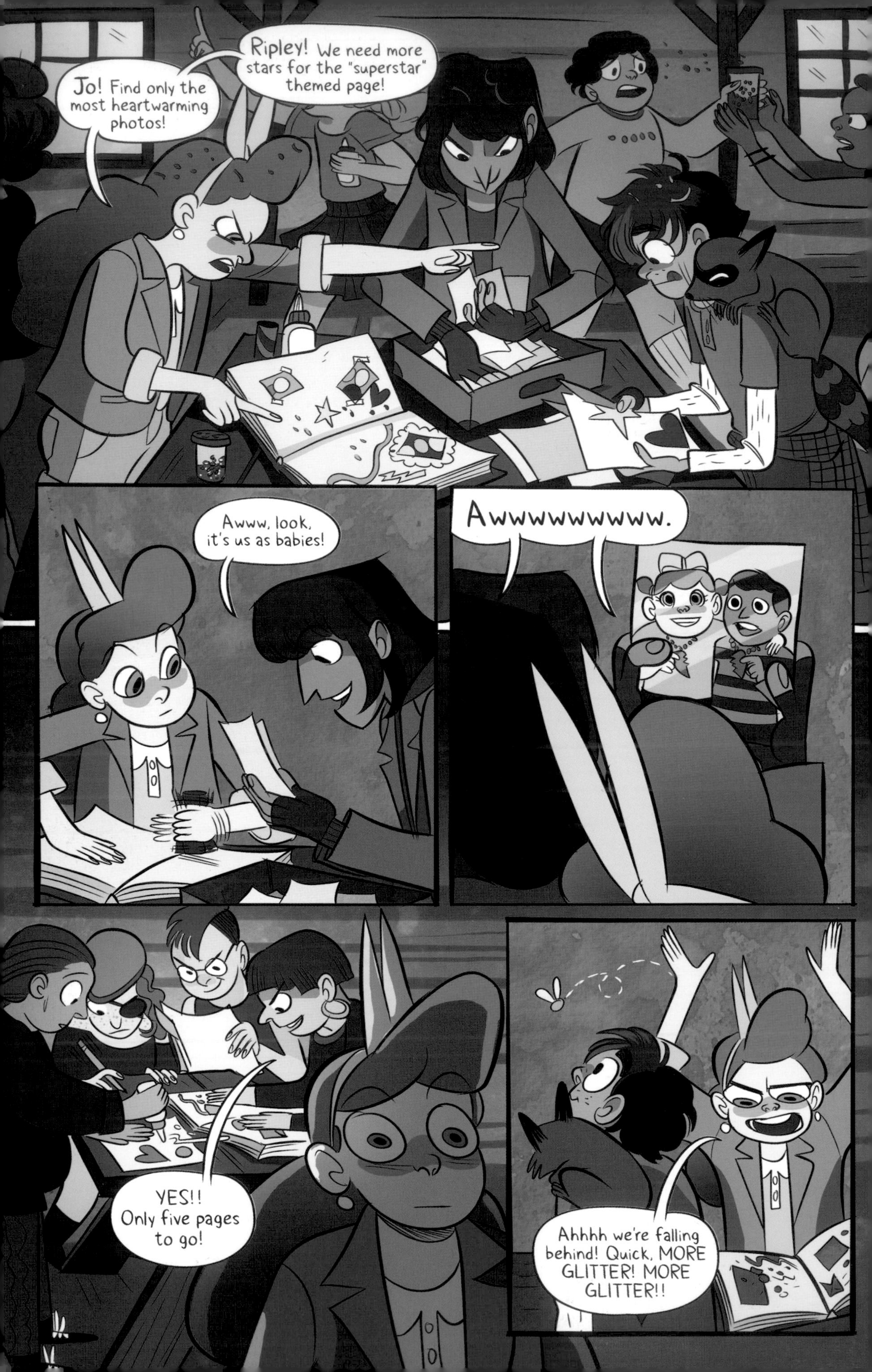
Jo! Find only the most heartwarming photos!
Ripley! We need more stars for the "superstar" themed page!
Awww, look, it's us as babies!
Awwwwwwwww.
YES!! Only five pages to go!
Ahhhh we're falling behind! Quick, MORE GLITTER! MORE GLITTER!!

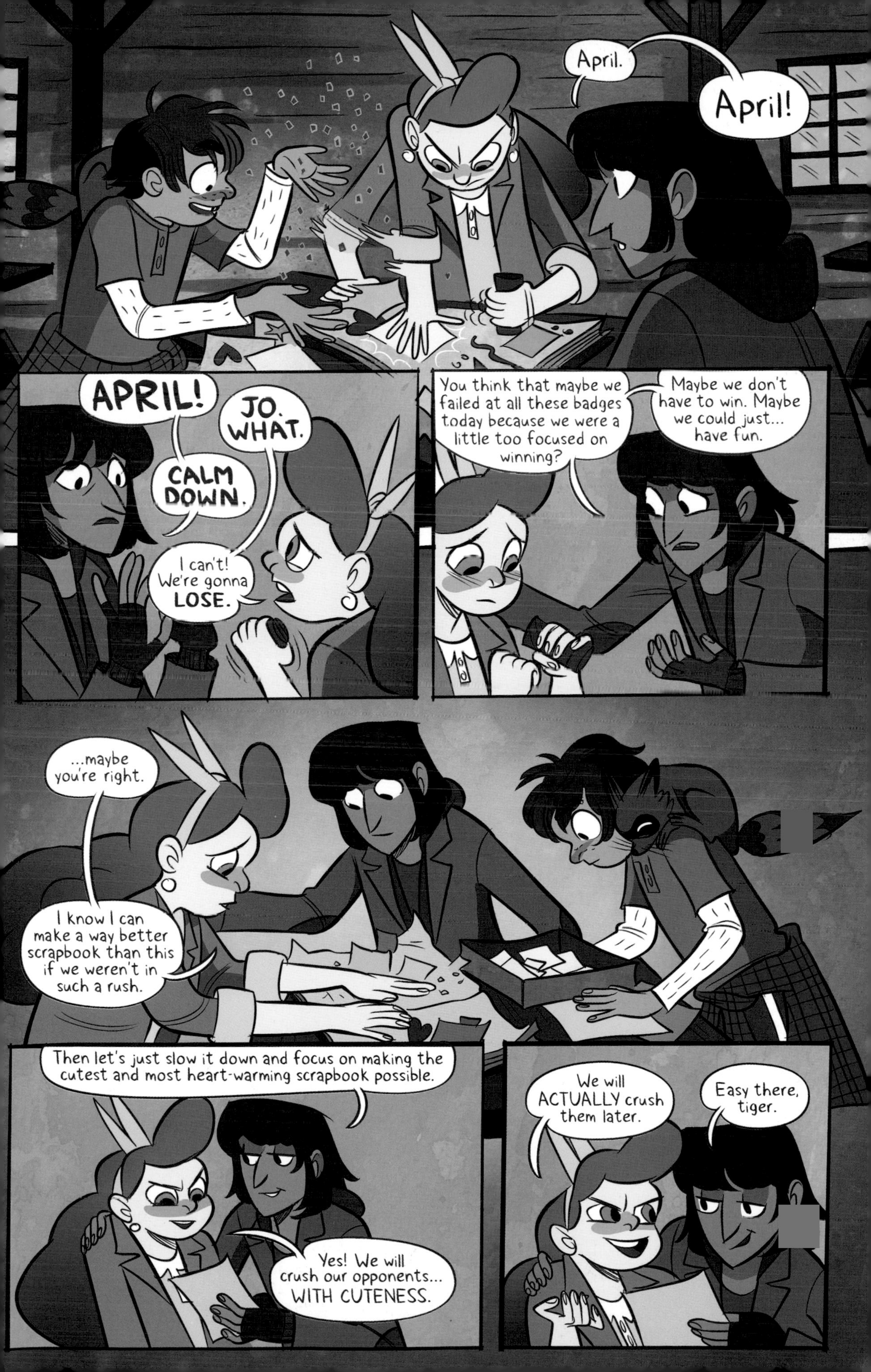
April.
April!
APRIL!
CALM DOWN.
JO. WHAT.
I can't! We're gonna LOSE.
You think that maybe we failed at all these badges today because we were a little too focused on winning?
Maybe we don't have to win. Maybe we could just... have fun.
...maybe you're right.
I know I can make a way better scrapbook than this if we weren't in such a rush.
Then let's just slow it down and focus on making the cutest and most heart-warming scrapbook possible.
Yes! We will crush our opponents... WITH CUTENESS.
We will ACTUALLY crush them later.
Easy there, tiger.

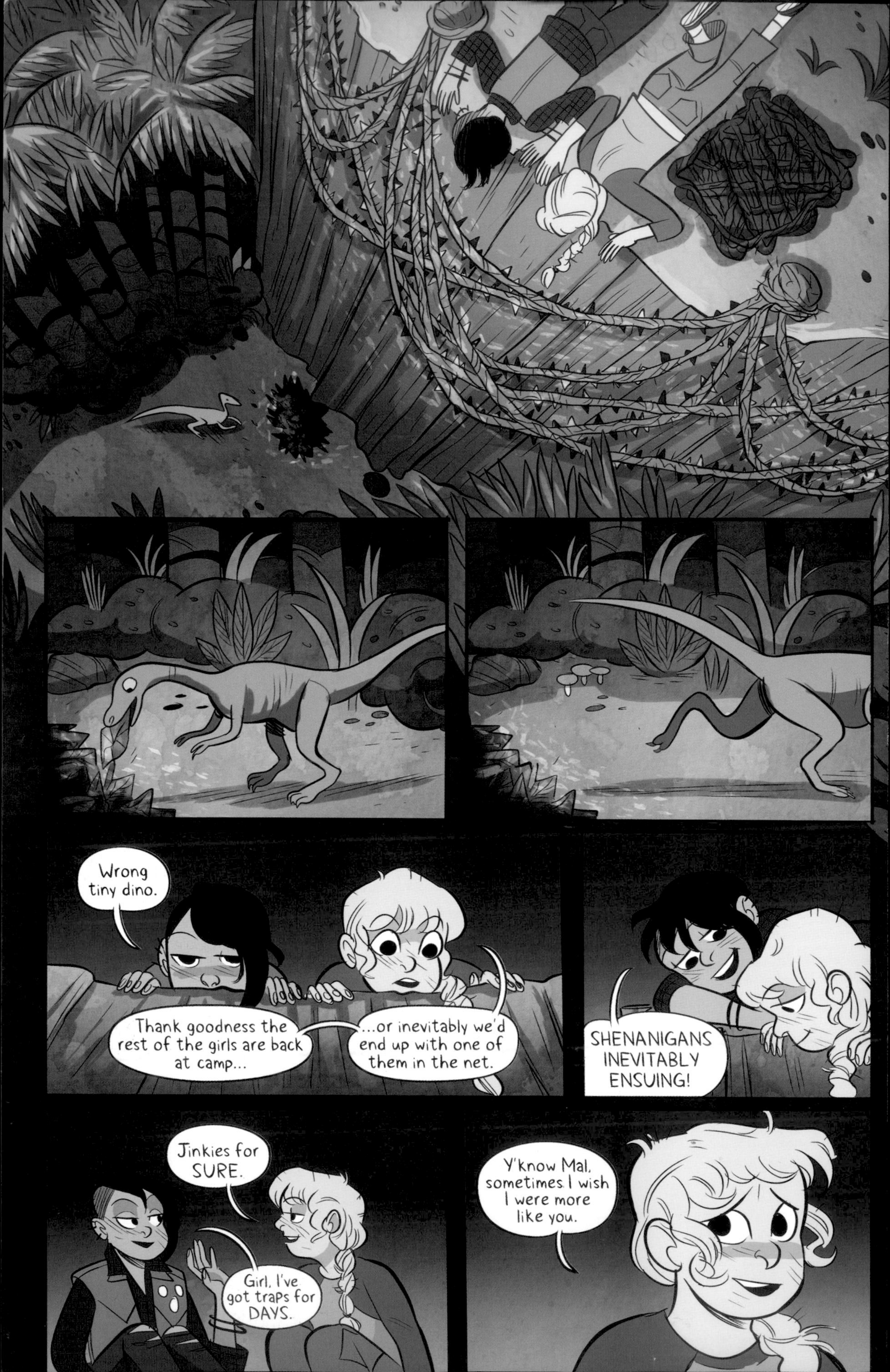
Wrong tiny dino.
Thank goodness the rest of the girls are back at camp...
...or inevitably we'd end up with one of them in the net.
SHENANIGANS INEVITABLY ENSUING!
Jinkies for SURE.
Girl, I've got traps for DAYS.
Y'know Mal, sometimes I wish I were more like you.

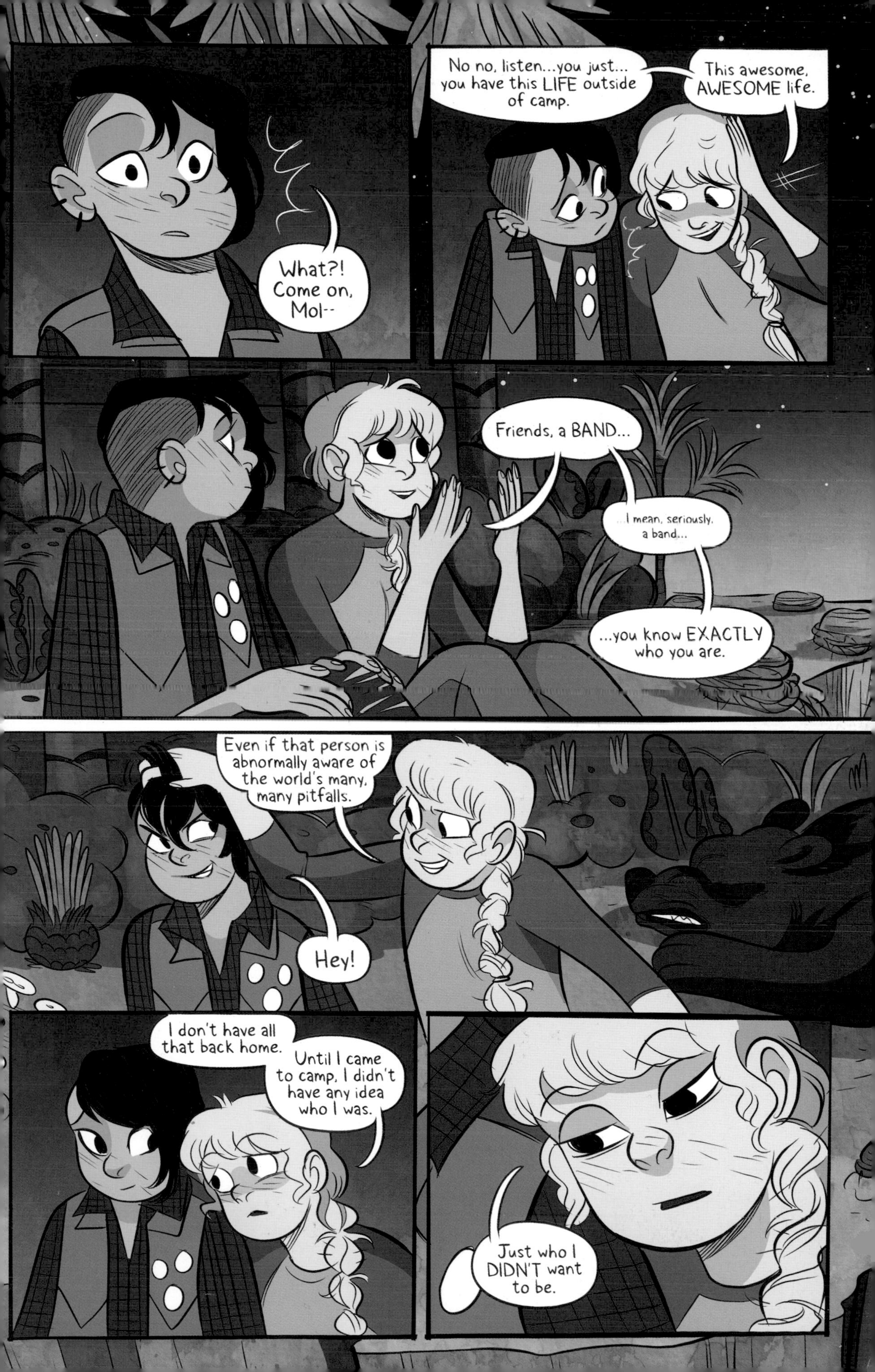
What?! Come on, Mol--
No no, listen...you just... you have this LIFE outside of camp.
This awesome, AWESOME life.
Friends, a BAND...
...I mean, seriously, a band...
...you know EXACTLY who you are.
Even if that person is abnormally aware of the world's many, many pitfalls.
Hey!
I don't have all that back home.
Until I came to camp, I didn't have any idea who I was.
Just who I DIDN'T want to be.

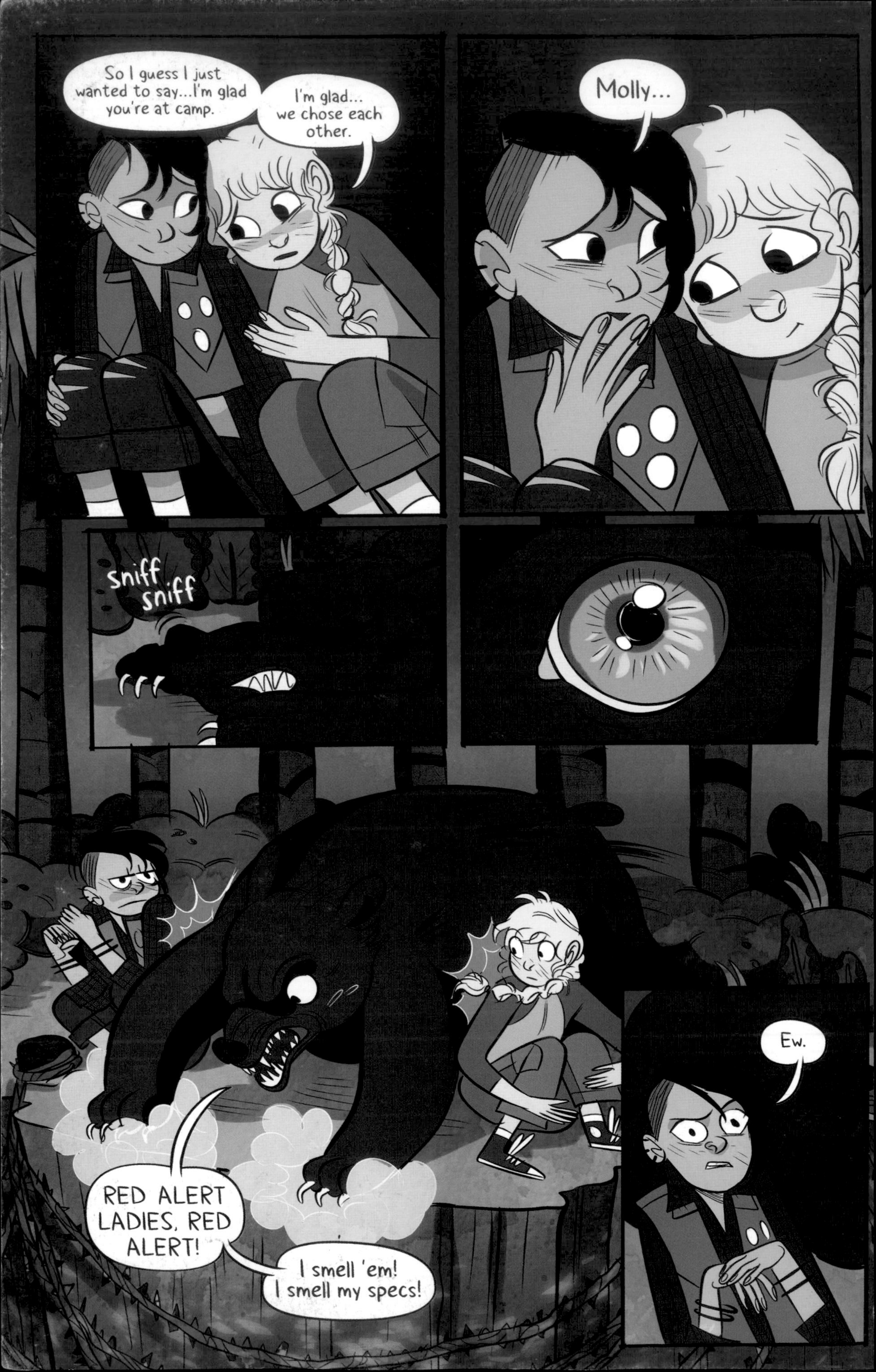
So I guess I just wanted to say...I'm glad you're at camp.
I'm glad... we chose each other.
Molly...
sniff sniff
Ew.
RED ALERT LADIES, RED ALERT!
I smell 'em! I smell my specs!

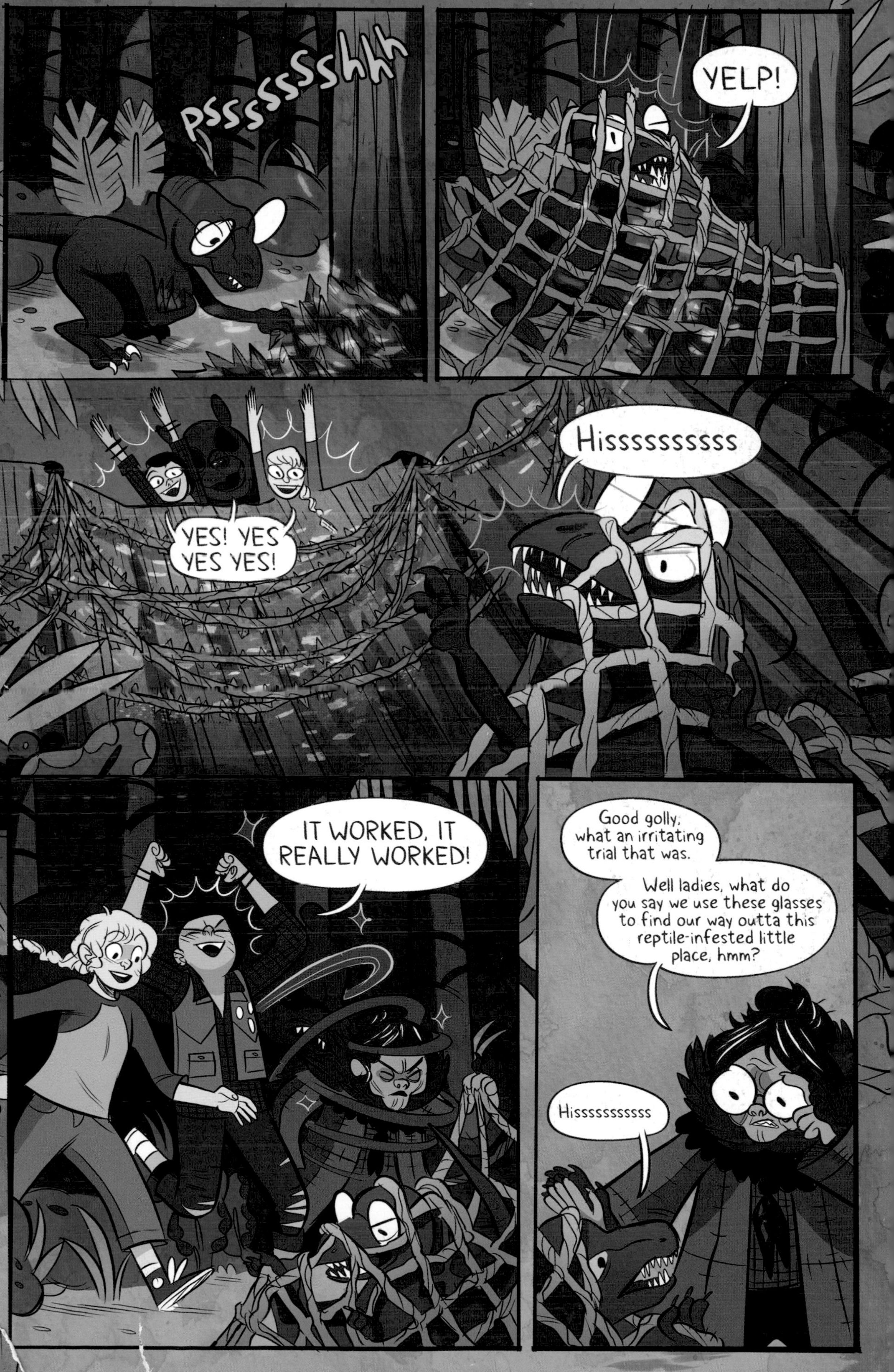
PSSSSSSShhh
YELP!
Hissssssssss
YES! YES YES YES!
IT WORKED, IT REALLY WORKED!
Good golly, what an irritating trial that was.
Well ladies, what do you say we use these glasses to find our way outta this reptile-infested little place, hmm?
Hissssssssssss

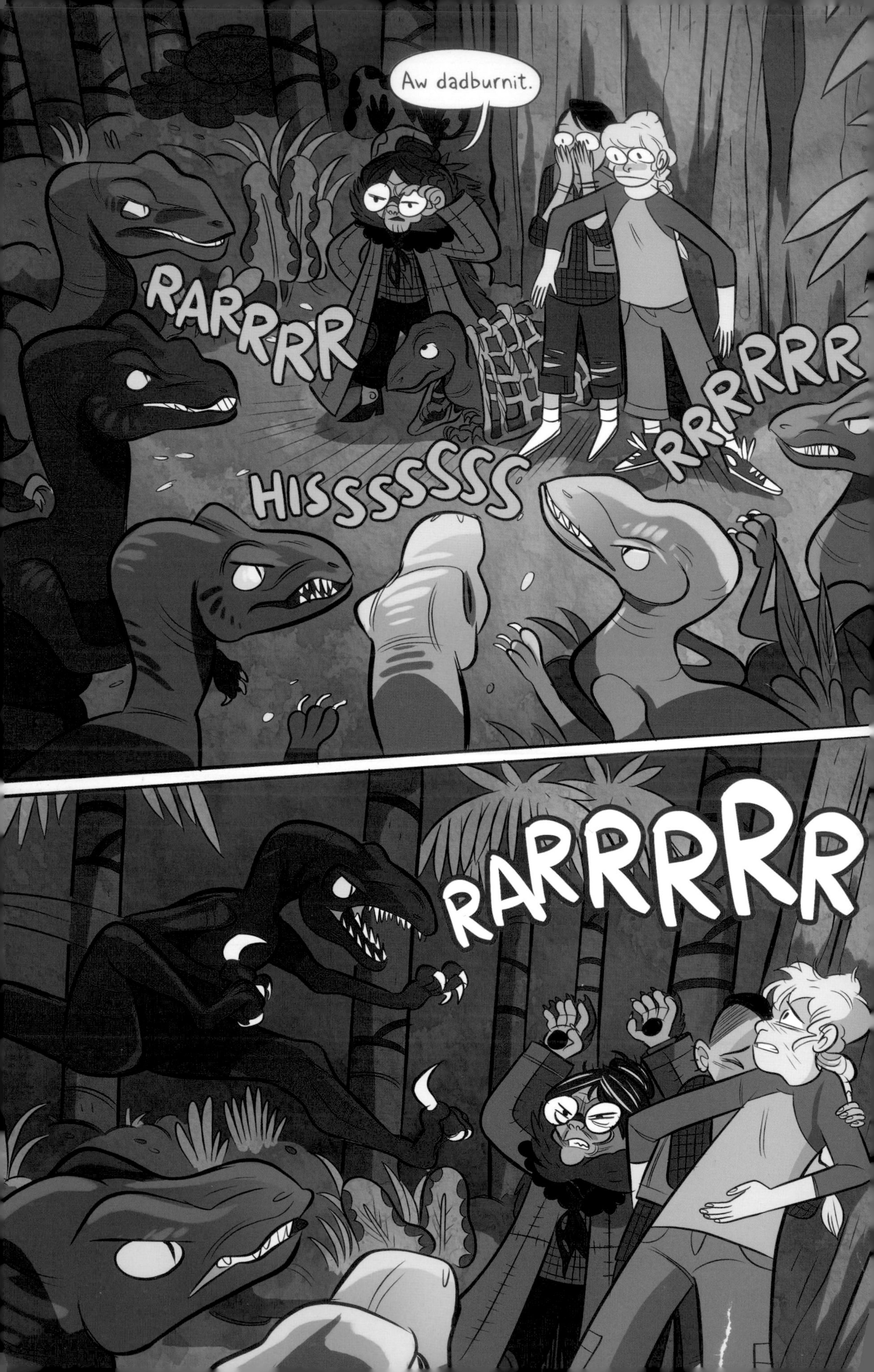
Aw dadburnit.
RARRRR
RRRRRRR
HISSSSSS
RARRRRR

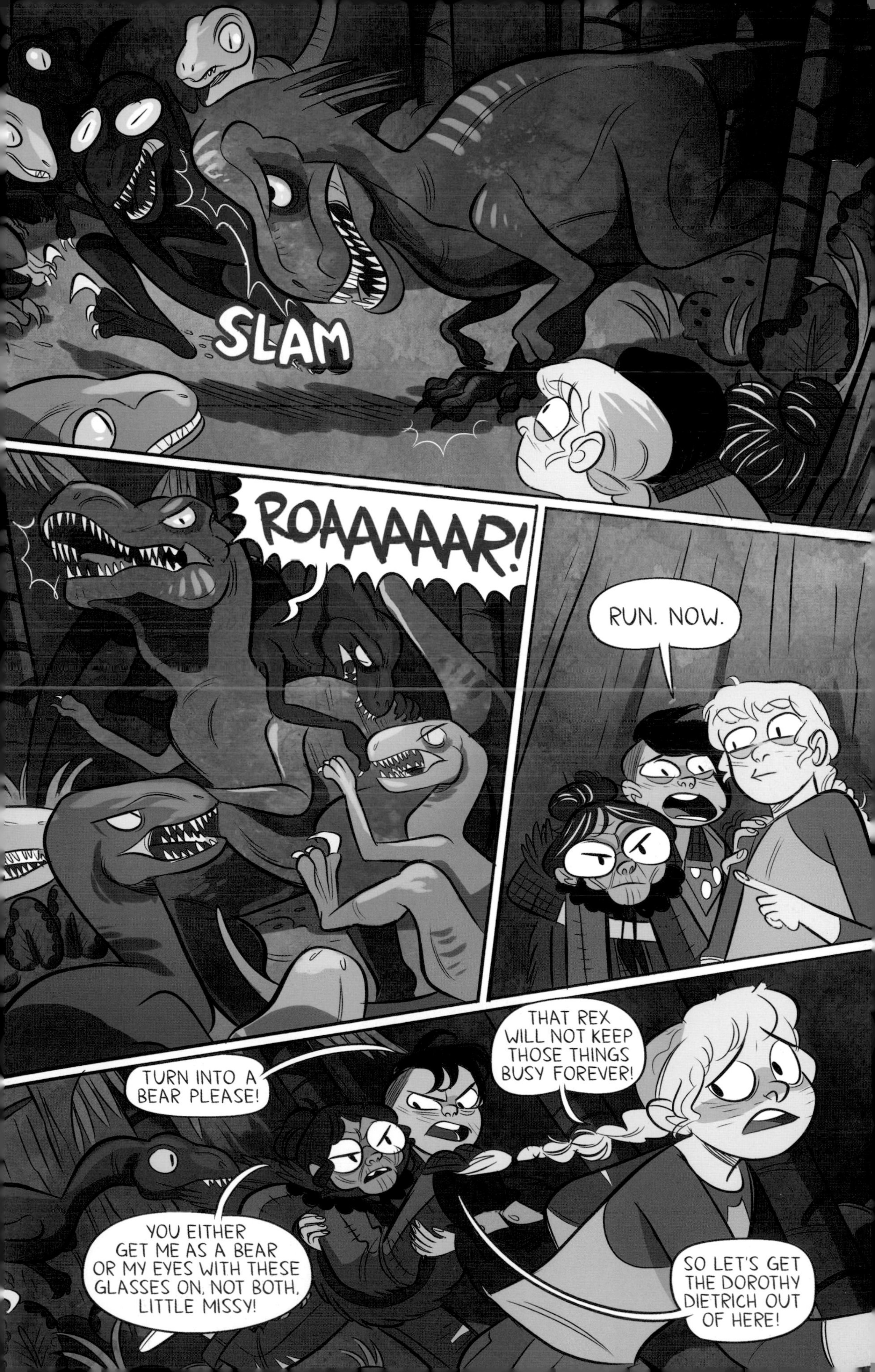
SLAM
ROAAAAAR!
RUN. NOW.
TURN INTO A BEAR PLEASE!
THAT REX WILL NOT KEEP THOSE THINGS BUSY FOREVER!
YOU EITHER GET ME AS A BEAR OR MY EYES WITH THESE GLASSES ON, NOT BOTH, LITTLE MISSY!
SO LET'S GET THE DOROTHY DIETRICH OUT OF HERE!

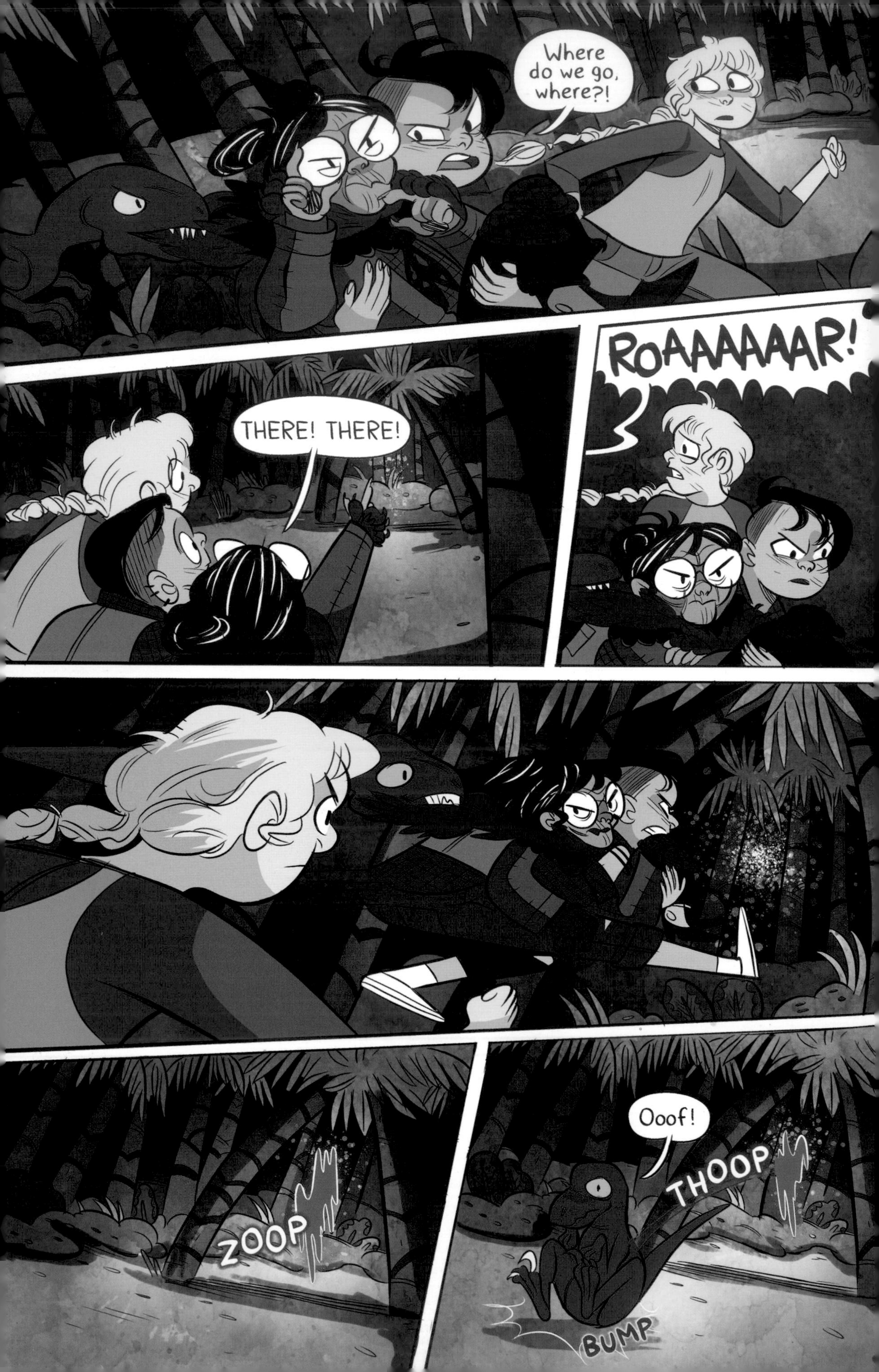
Where do we go, where?!
THERE! THERE!
ROAAAAAAR!
ZOOP
Ooof!
THOOP
BUMP

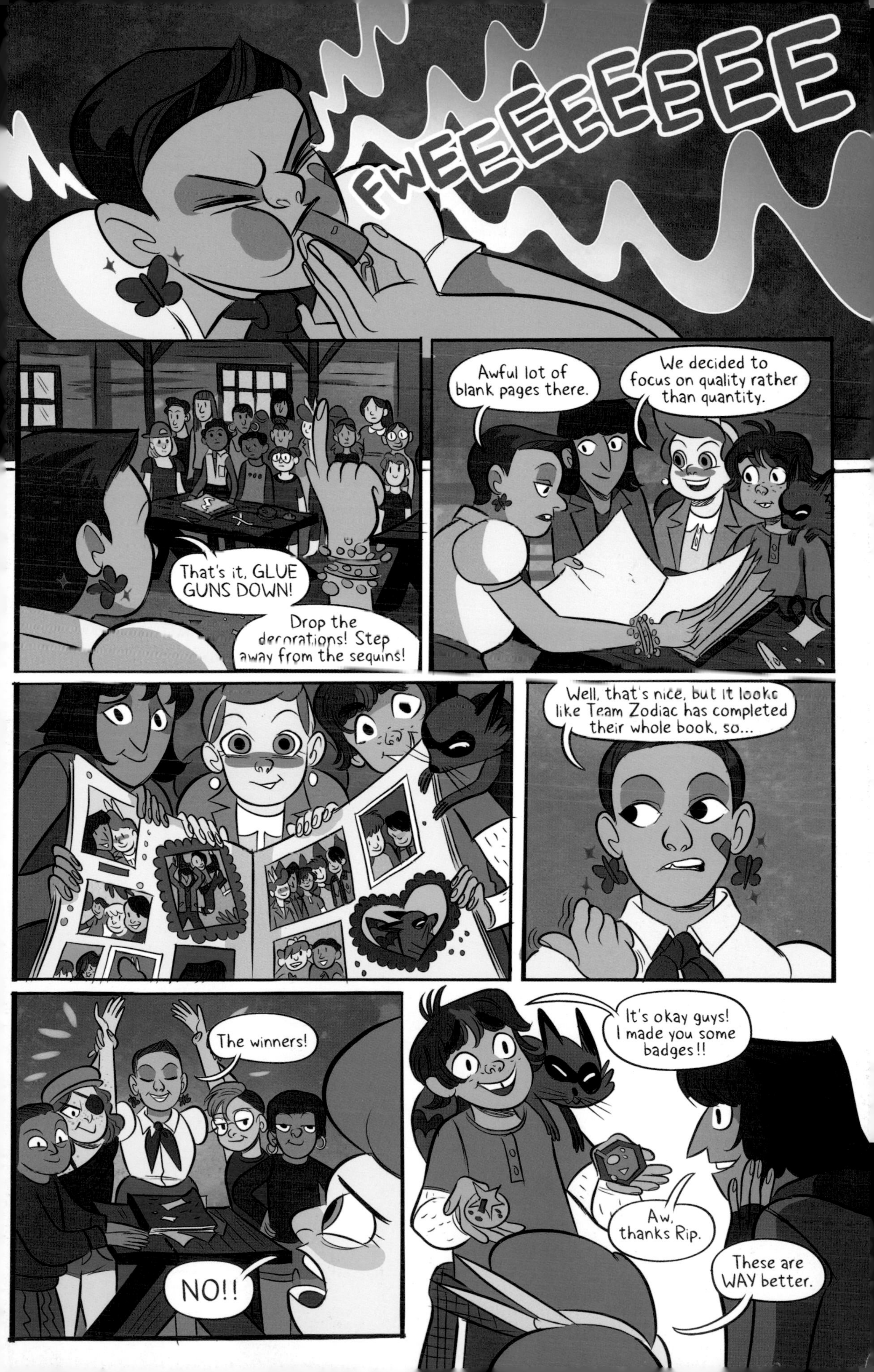
FWEEEEEEEEE
That's it, GLUE GUNS DOWN!
Drop the decorations! Step away from the sequins!
Awful lot of blank pages there.
We decided to focus on quality rather than quantity.
Well, that's nice, but it looks like Team Zodiac has completed their whole book, so...
The winners!
NO!!
It's okay guys! I made you some badges!!
Aw, thanks Rip.
These are WAY better.

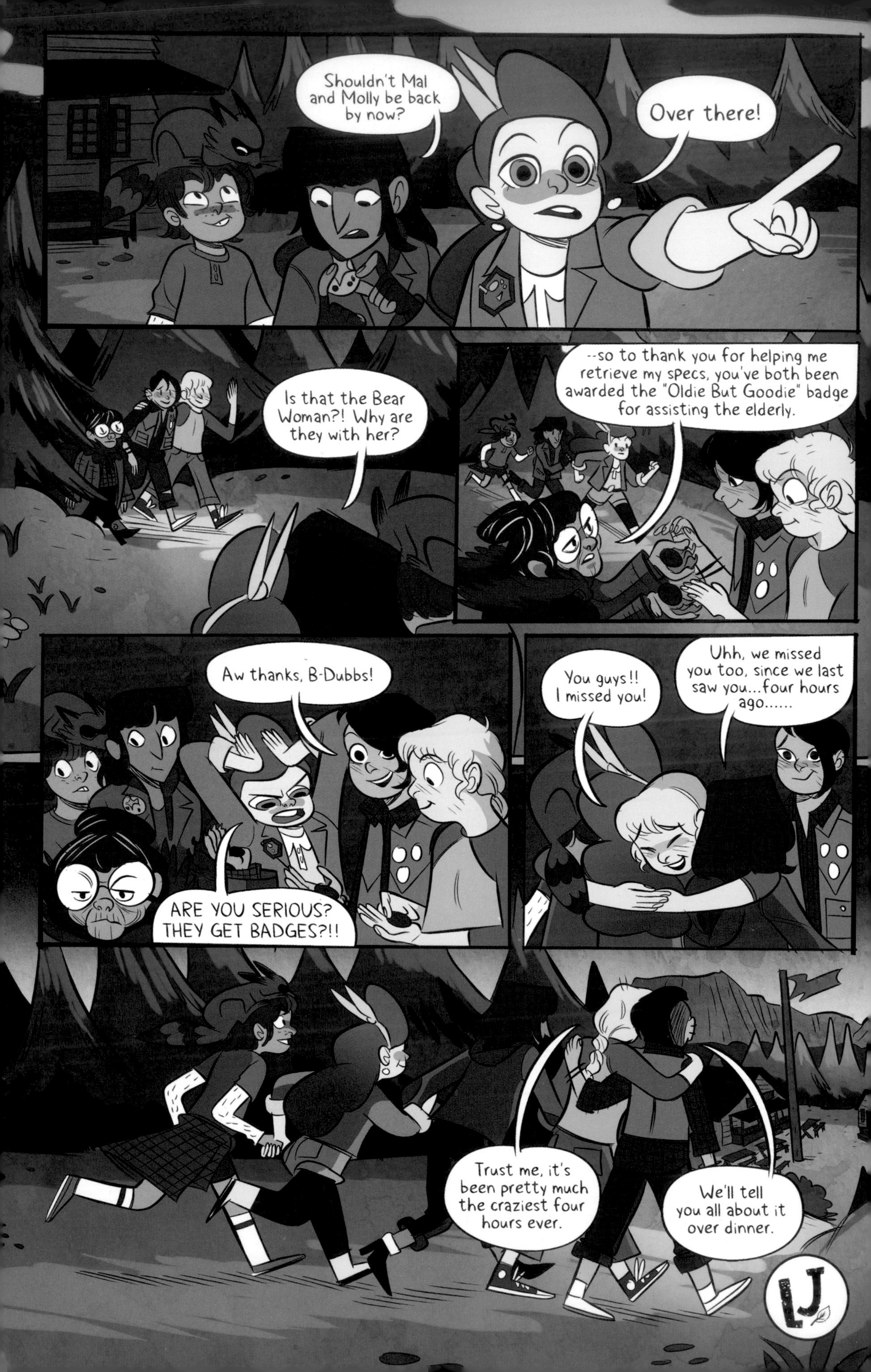
Shouldn't Mal and Molly be back by now?
Over there!
Is that the Bear Woman?! Why are they with her?
--so to thank you for helping me retrieve my specs, you've both been awarded the "Oldie But Goodie" badge for assisting the elderly.
Aw thanks, B-Dubbs!
ARE YOU SERIOUS? THEY GET BADGES?!!
You guys!! I missed you!
Uhh, we missed you too, since we last saw you...four hours ago......
Trust me, it's been pretty much the craziest four hours ever.
We'll tell you all about it over dinner.

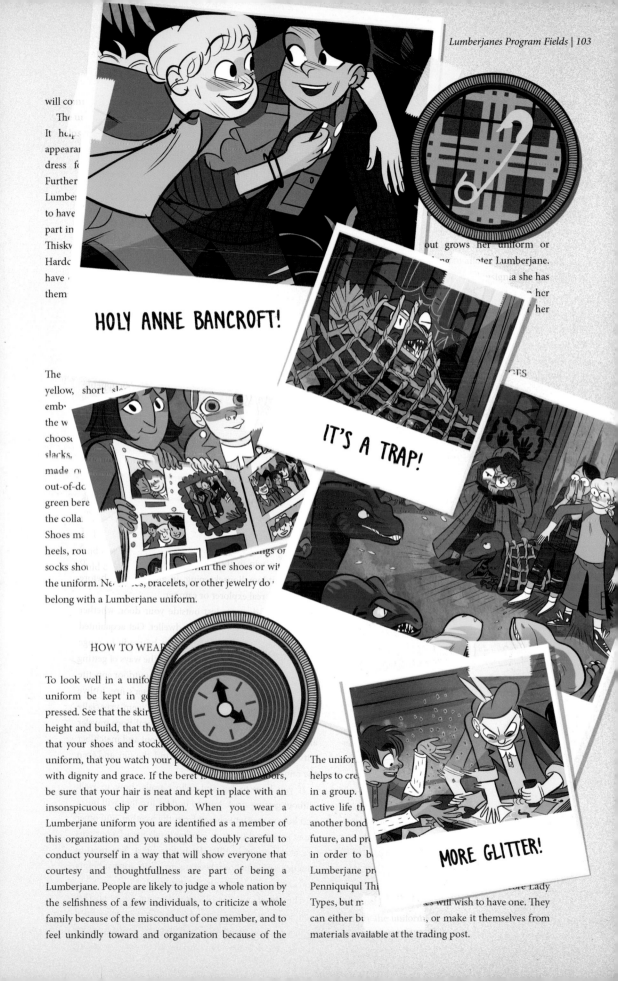

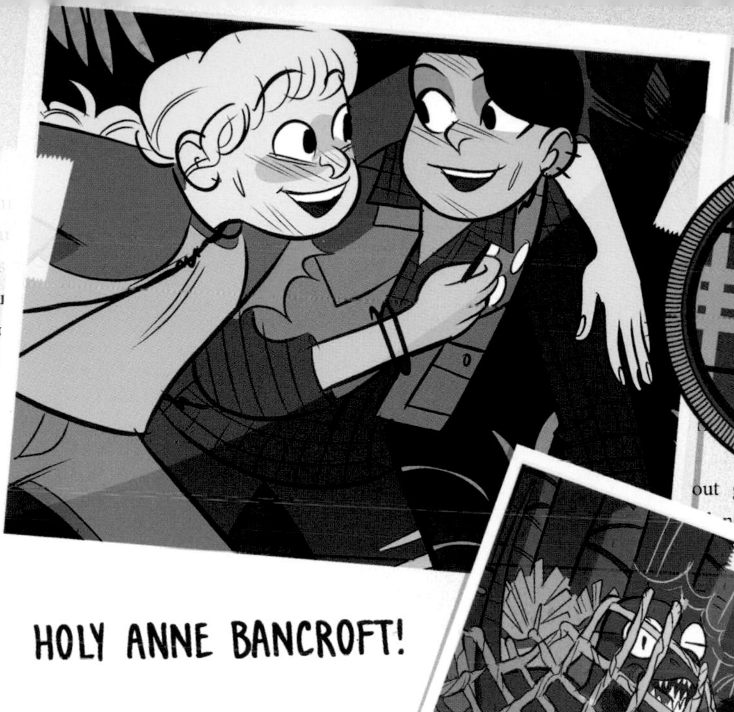
HOLY ANNE BANCROFT!

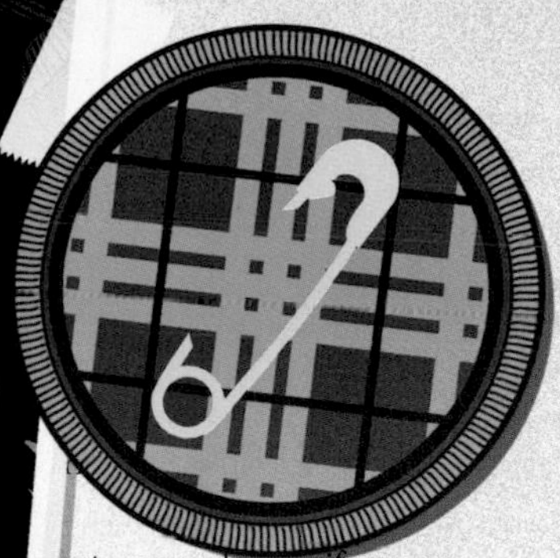

will com

The u

It helps

appeara

dress fo

Further

Lumbe

to have

part in

Thiskv

Hardc

have

them

out grows her uniform or

...ter Lumberjane.

...ia she has

... her

... her

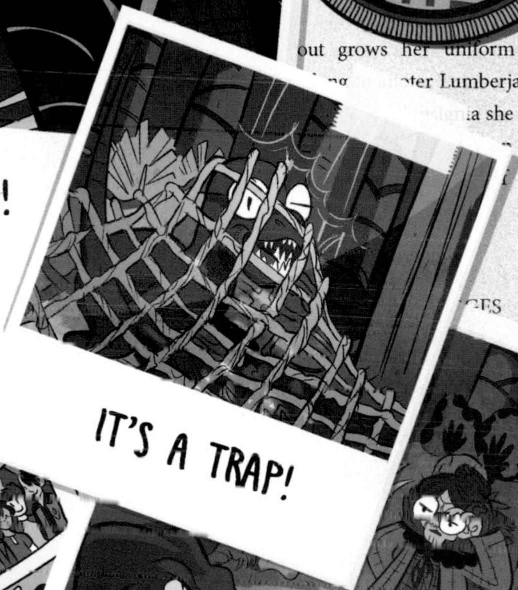
IT'S A TRAP!

The ... ICES

yellow, short sl...

emb...

the w...

choose

slacks,

made o...

out-of-do...

green bere...

the colla...

Shoes ma...

heels, rou... ...ings or

socks shou... with the shoes or wi...

the uniform. Ne...es, bracelets, or other jewelry do...

belong with a Lumberjane uniform.

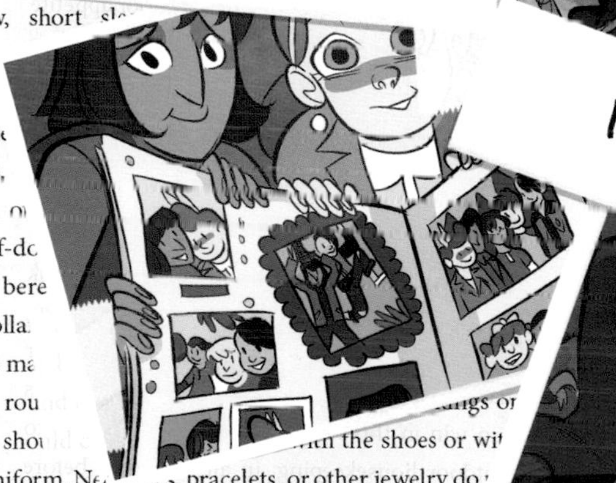

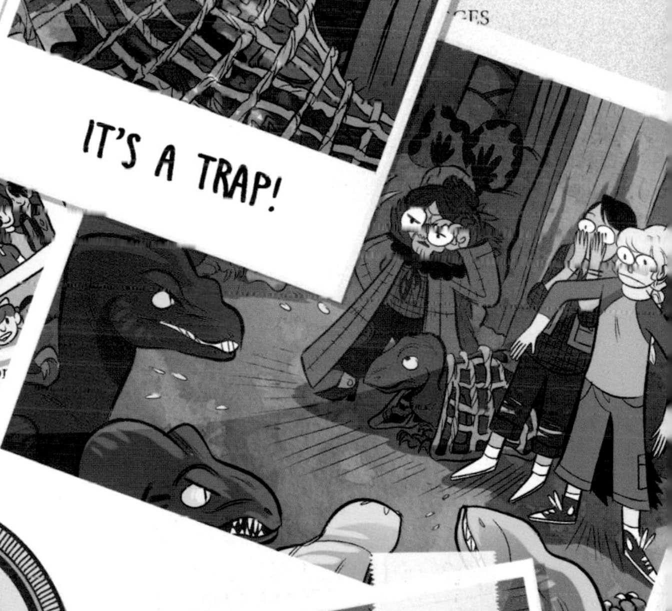

HOW TO WEAR

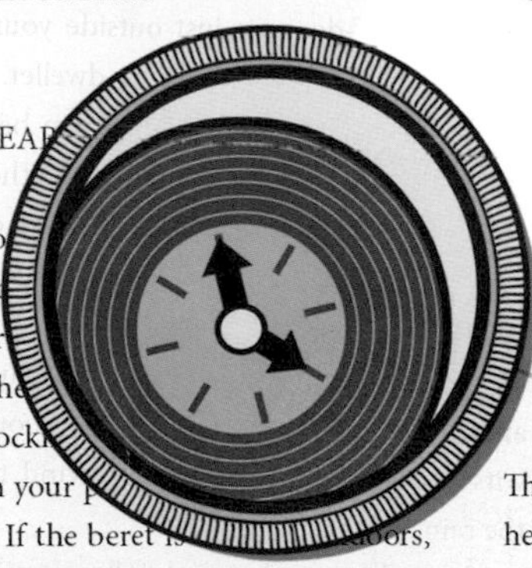

To look well in a unifo... uniform be kept in go... pressed. See that the skir... height and build, that the... that your shoes and stock... uniform, that you watch your p... with dignity and grace. If the beret ...doors, be sure that your hair is neat and kept in place with an insonspicuous clip or ribbon. When you wear a Lumberjane uniform you are identified as a member of this organization and you should be doubly careful to conduct yourself in a way that will show everyone that courtesy and thoughtfullness are part of being a Lumberjane. People are likely to judge a whole nation by the selfishness of a few individuals, to criticize a whole family because of the misconduct of one member, and to feel unkindly toward and organization because of the

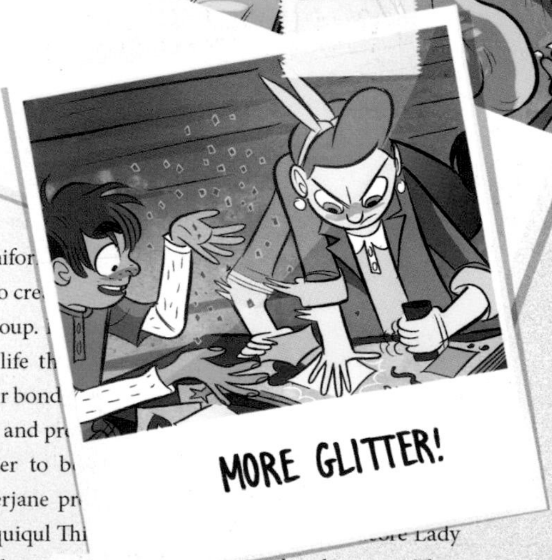
MORE GLITTER!

The unifor... helps to cre... in a group. ... active life th... another bond... future, and pr... in order to b... Lumberjane pr... Penniquiql Thi... ...ore Lady Types, but m... ...es will wish to have one. They can either bu... ...uniform, or make it themselves from materials available at the trading post.

LUMBERJANES FIELD MANUAL

CHAPTER THIRTEEN

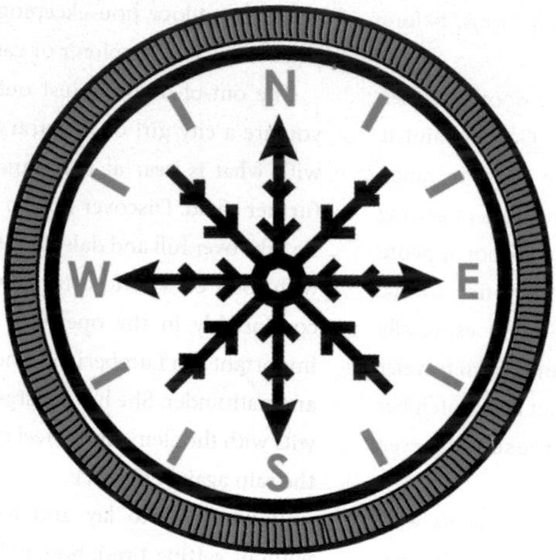
N
E
S
W

Lumberjanes "Out-of-Doors" Program Field

SNOW-GLOBE TROTTER BADGE

"There's snow stopping us now!"

Traveling the world is just one of the many enjoyments of life, and being a Lumberjane is, for a large part, about enjoyment. Every Lumberjane should leave camp with the basic understanding of survival when it comes to any form of travel. Whether it be a sleeping party with just a blanket and the stars for company or a grand excursion through the tallest mountains she is able to find. A Lumberjane encounters many problems through life, but she will survive and thrive through them all. One of the many goals of the Lumberjanes is to make sure every young lady leaves with the tools to succeed. And some of these tools are taught as the Lumberjanes earns her *Snow-Globe Trotter* badge.

Traveling is a fine pass time, as well as a great career that any Lumberjane could find herself enjoying. It is the tendency for a Lumberjane to want to learn everything there is to know about the world at large. She will want to learn, and she will want to discover and explore all the places that haven't yet been touched by civilization. There are so many amazing worlds out there and this camp is only the beginning. There are many exercises the Lumberjanes will find at this camp that will help them find the tools and training they need to make all of this possible for them.

To obtain the *Snow-Globe Trotter* badge, a Lumberjane must keep a journal of her discoveries as she travels through the camp. With the help of her cabin, she will connect with the nature around her and create a map of the area. She will gain basic survival skills of what to do in the wilderness, and she will learn the amazing art of mapmaking. She will be able to be identify plants from all over the globe, as well as know the traits of poisonous plants, so that she should come across something unknown she will be able to ensure that none of her

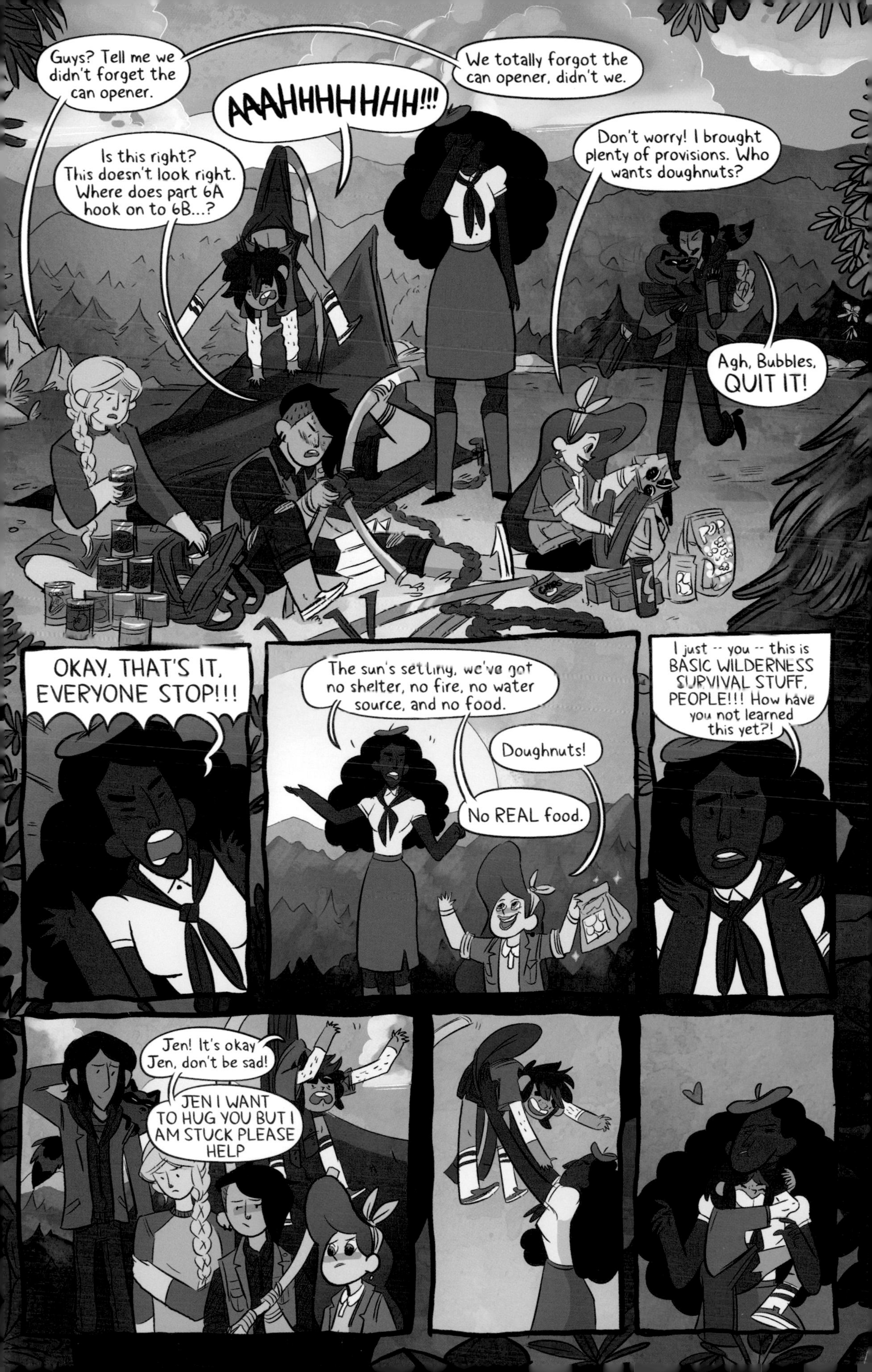
Guys? Tell me we didn't forget the can opener.
We totally forgot the can opener, didn't we.
AAAHHHHHHH!!!
Is this right? This doesn't look right. Where does part 6A hook on to 6B...?
Don't worry! I brought plenty of provisions. Who wants doughnuts?
Agh, Bubbles, QUIT IT!
OKAY, THAT'S IT, EVERYONE STOP!!!
The sun's setting, we've got no shelter, no fire, no water source, and no food.
Doughnuts!
No REAL food.
I just -- you -- this is BASIC WILDERNESS SURVIVAL STUFF, PEOPLE!!! How have you not learned this yet?!
Jen! It's okay Jen, don't be sad!
JEN I WANT TO HUG YOU BUT I AM STUCK PLEASE HELP

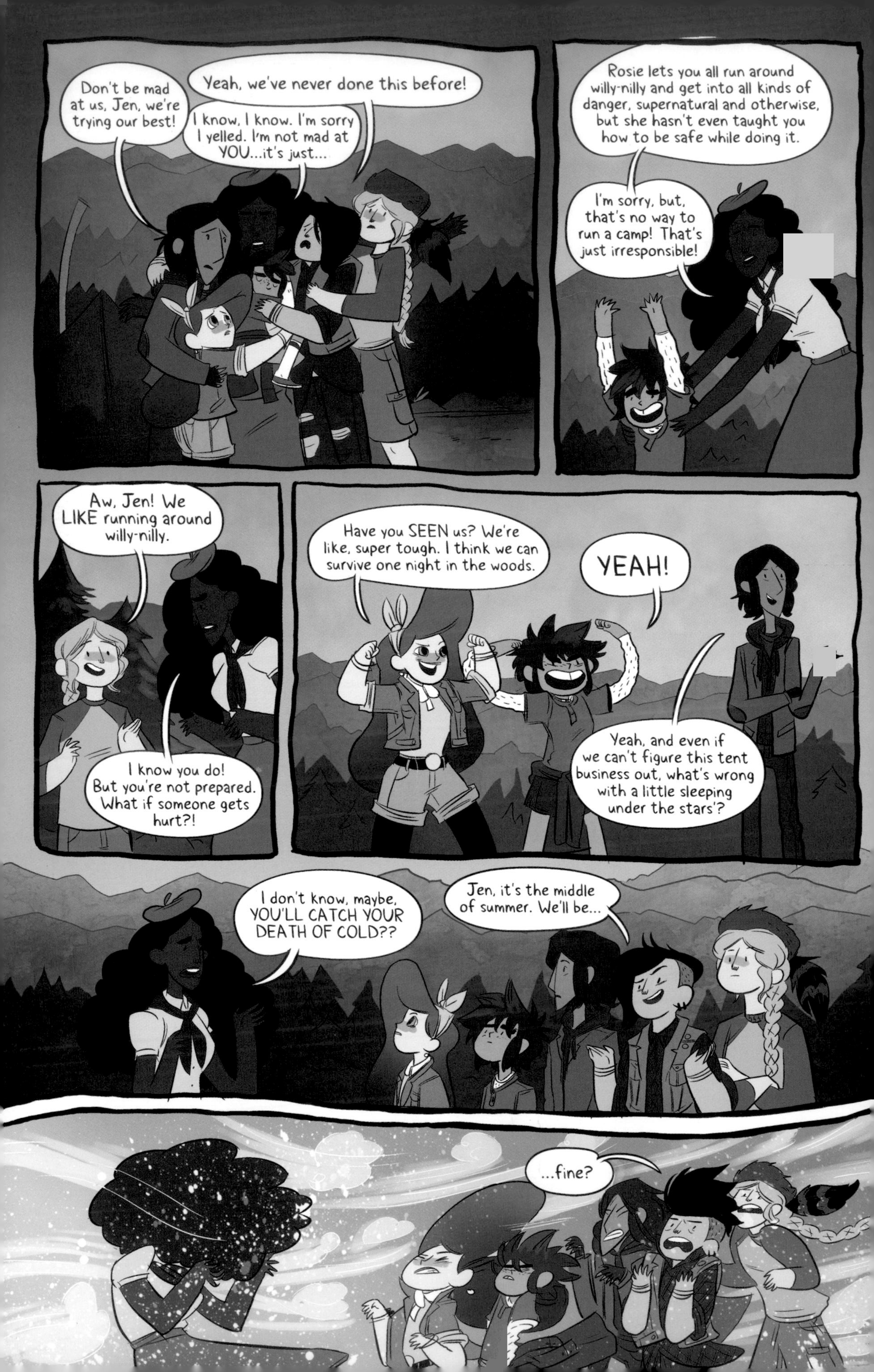
Don't be mad at us, Jen, we're trying our best!
Yeah, we've never done this before!
I know, I know. I'm sorry I yelled. I'm not mad at YOU...it's just...
Rosie lets you all run around willy-nilly and get into all kinds of danger, supernatural and otherwise, but she hasn't even taught you how to be safe while doing it.
I'm sorry, but, that's no way to run a camp! That's just irresponsible!
Aw, Jen! We LIKE running around willy-nilly.
I know you do! But you're not prepared. What if someone gets hurt?!
Have you SEEN us? We're like, super tough. I think we can survive one night in the woods.
YEAH!
Yeah, and even if we can't figure this tent business out, what's wrong with a little sleeping under the stars'?
I don't know, maybe, YOU'LL CATCH YOUR DEATH OF COLD??
Jen, it's the middle of summer. We'll be...
...fine?

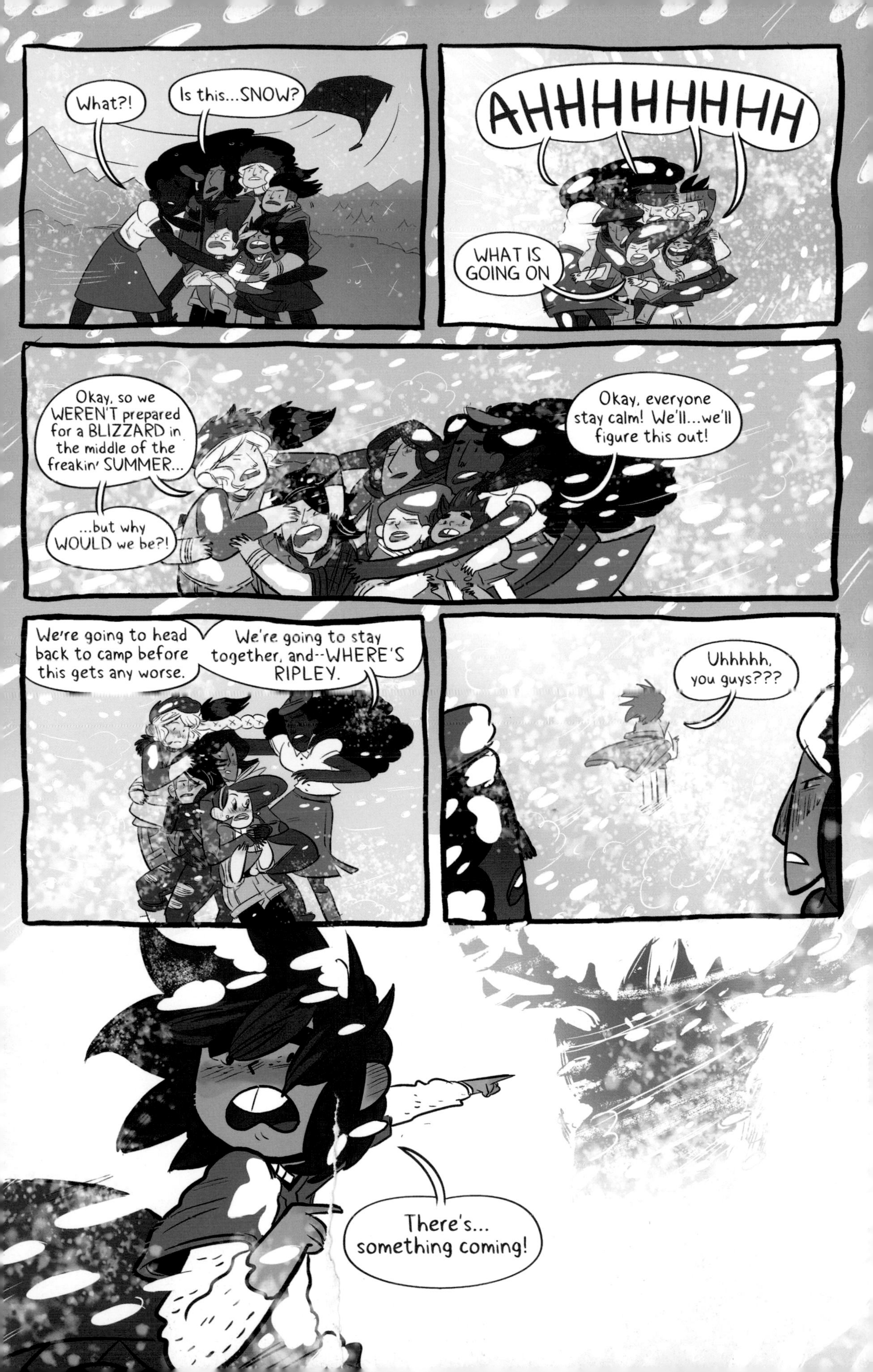
What?!
Is this...SNOW?
AHHHHHHHH
WHAT IS GOING ON
Okay, so we WEREN'T prepared for a BLIZZARD in the middle of the freakin' SUMMER...
...but why WOULD we be?!
Okay, everyone stay calm! We'll...we'll figure this out!
We're going to head back to camp before this gets any worse.
We're going to stay together, and--WHERE'S RIPLEY.
Uhhhhh, you guys???
There's... something coming!

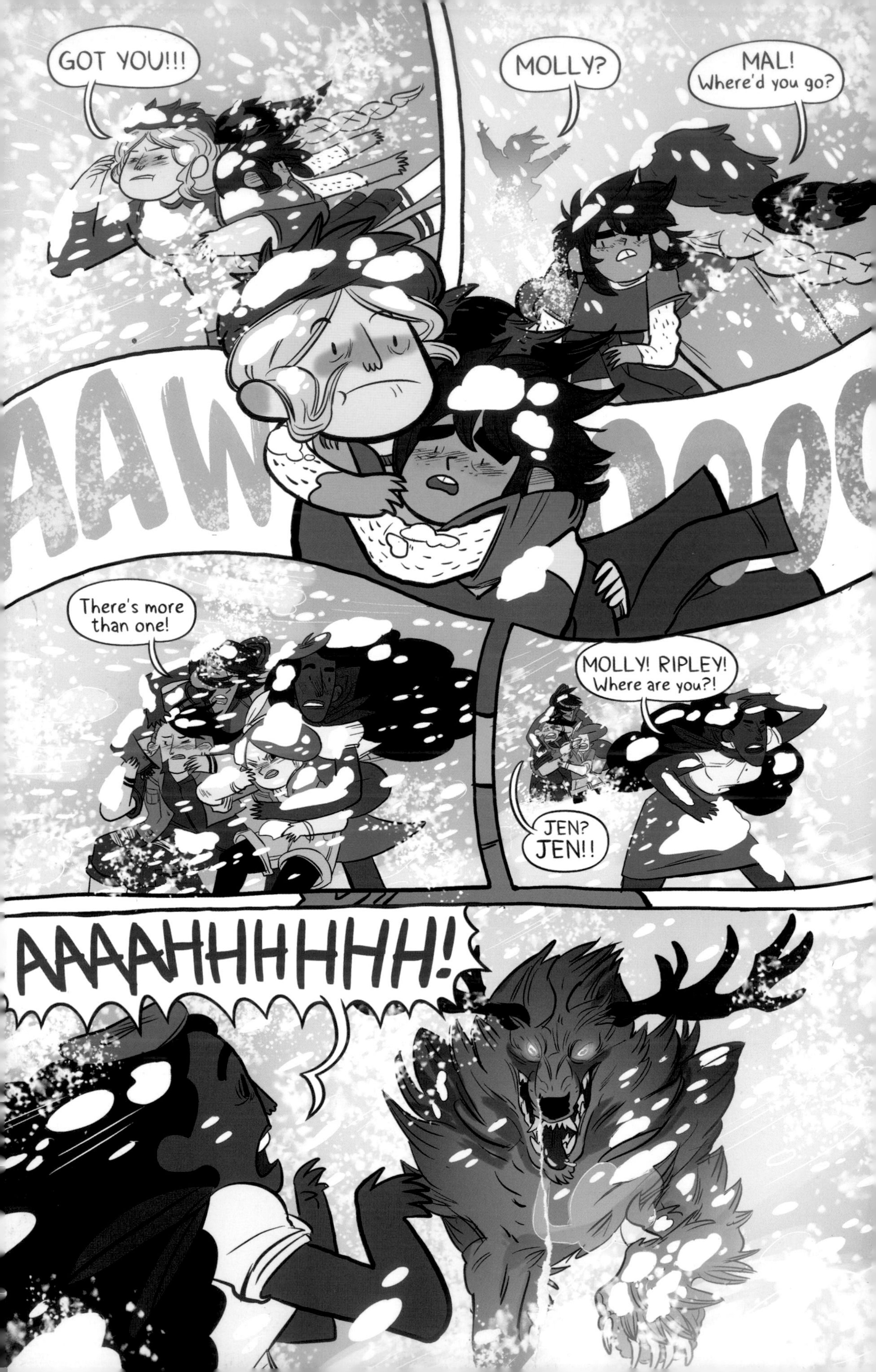
GOT YOU!!!
MOLLY?
MAL!
Where'd you go?
AAWOOOO
There's more than one!
MOLLY! RIPLEY!
Where are you?!
JEN?
JEN!!
AAAAHHHHHH!

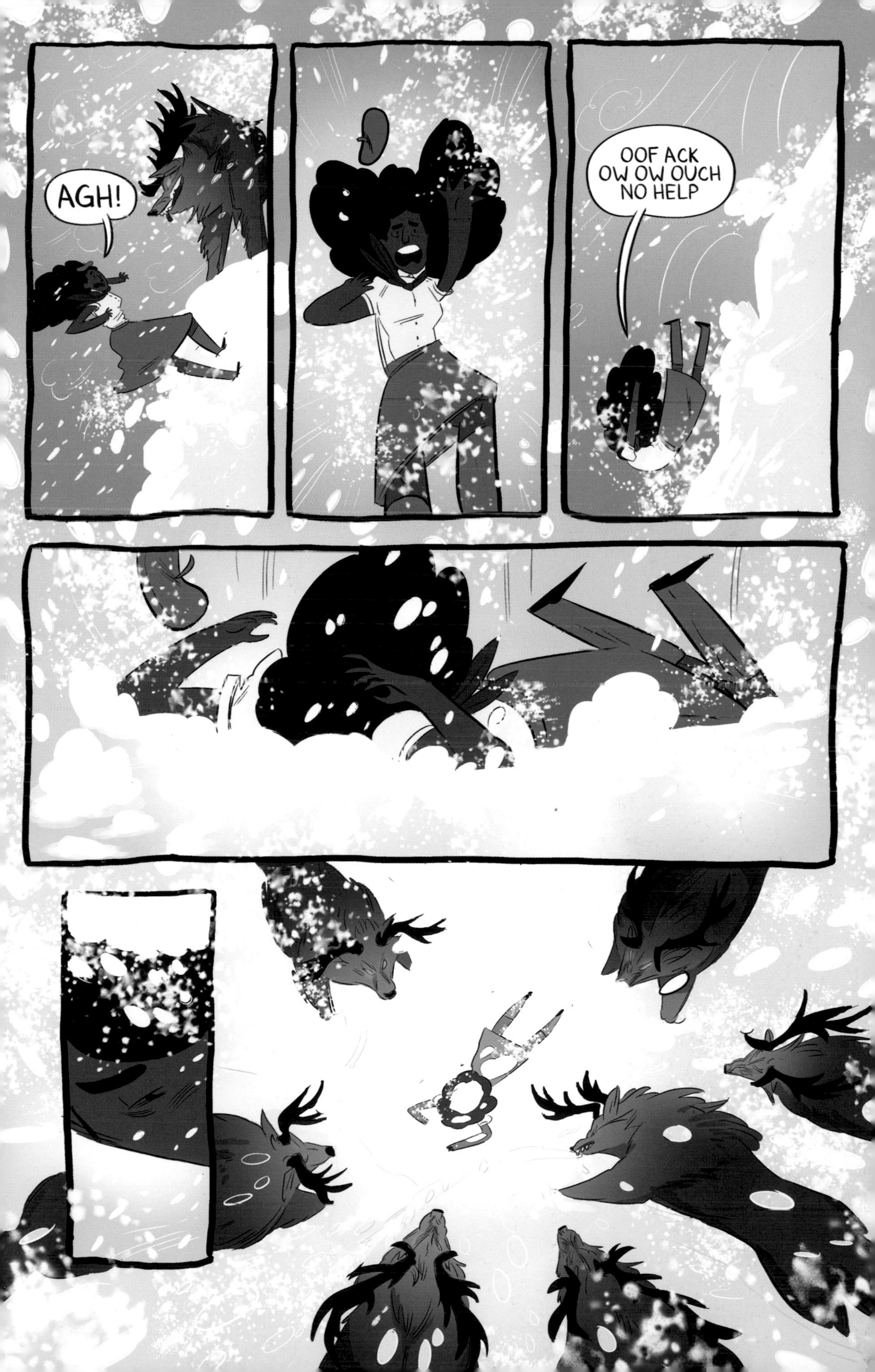
AGH!
OOF ACK OW OW OUCH NO HELP

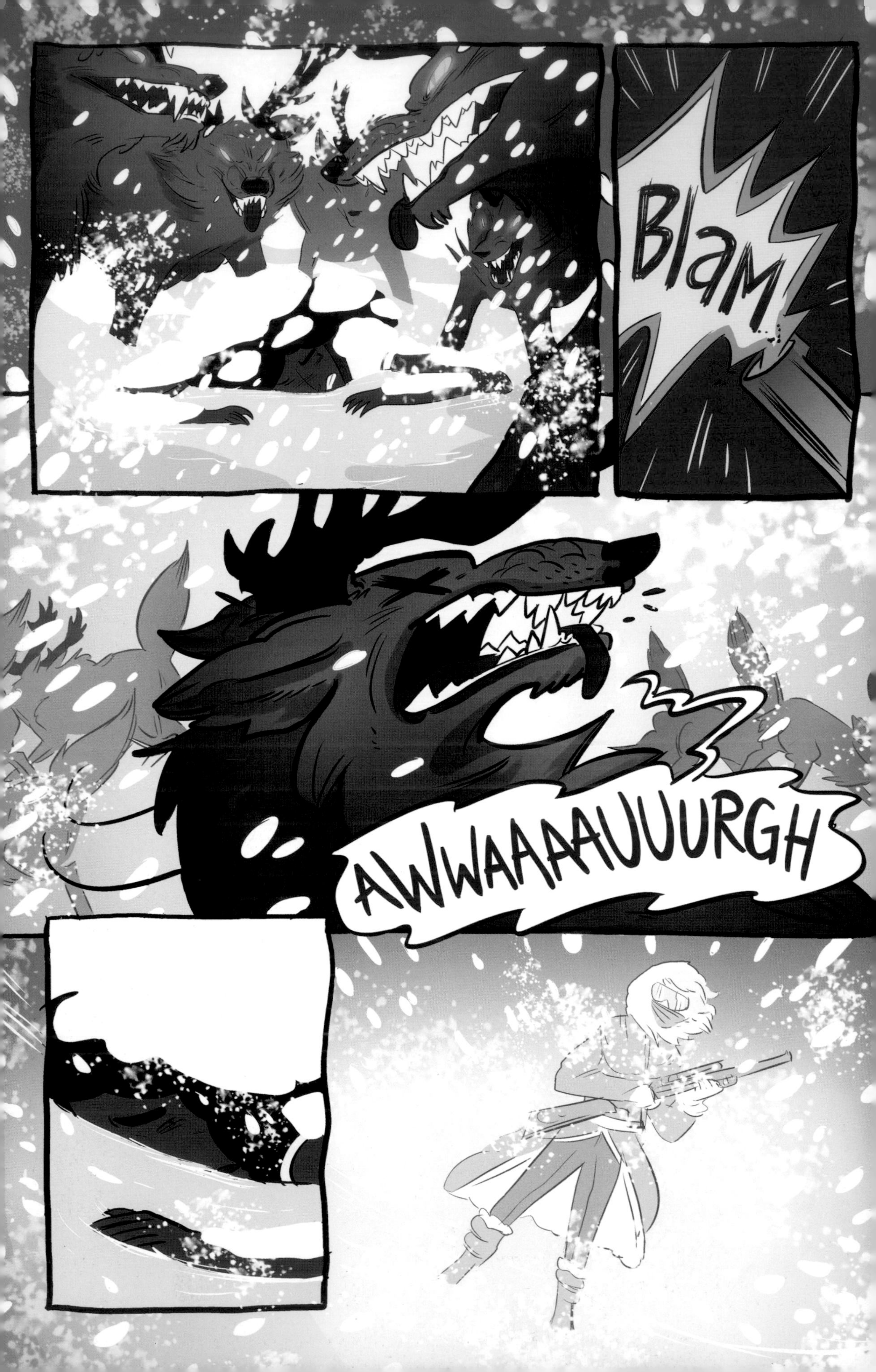
BLAM
AWWAAAAUUURGH

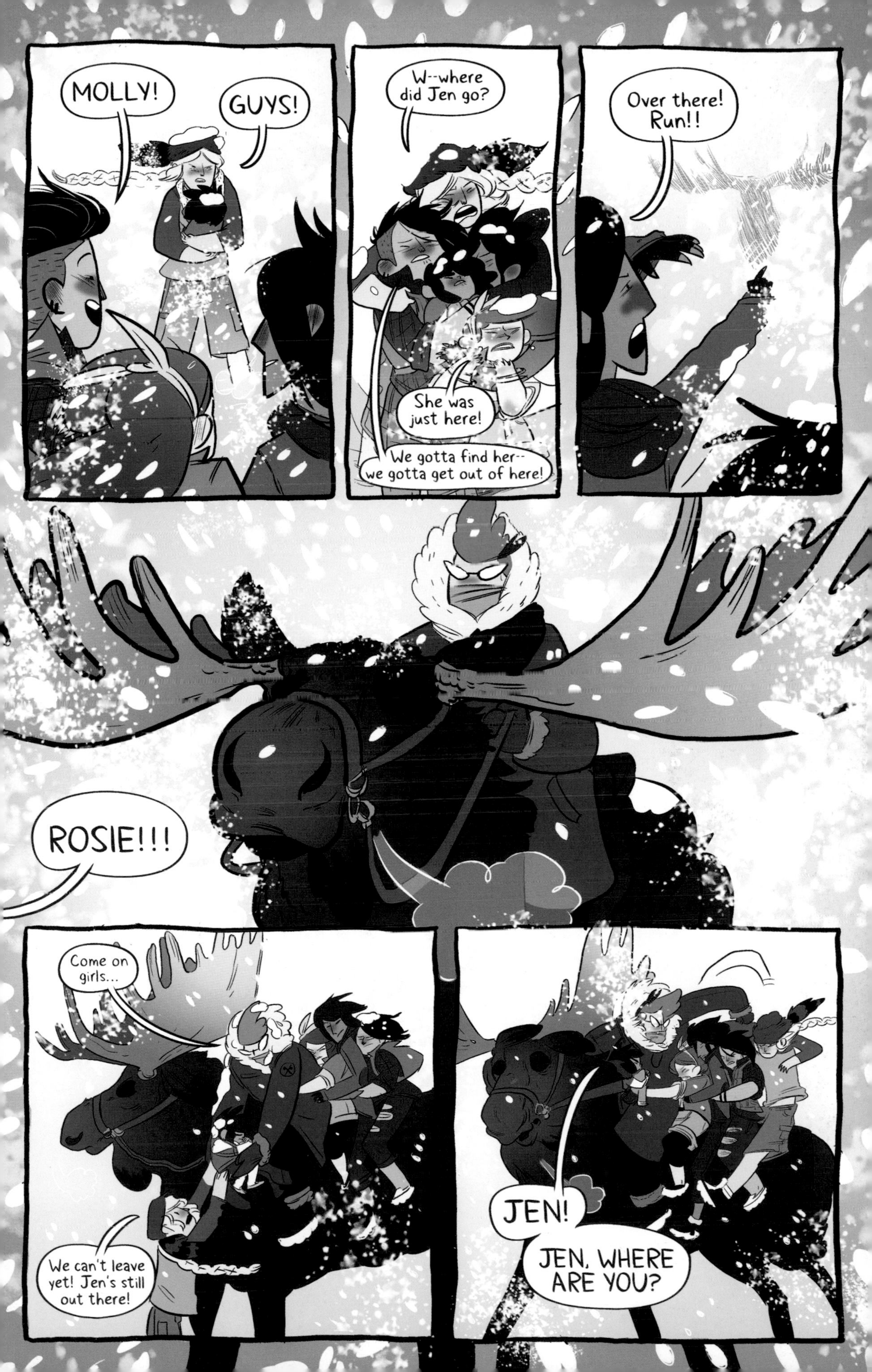
MOLLY!
GUYS!
W--where did Jen go?
She was just here!
We gotta find her-- we gotta get out of here!
Over there! Run!!
ROSIE!!!
Come on girls...
We can't leave yet! Jen's still out there!
JEN!
JEN, WHERE ARE YOU?

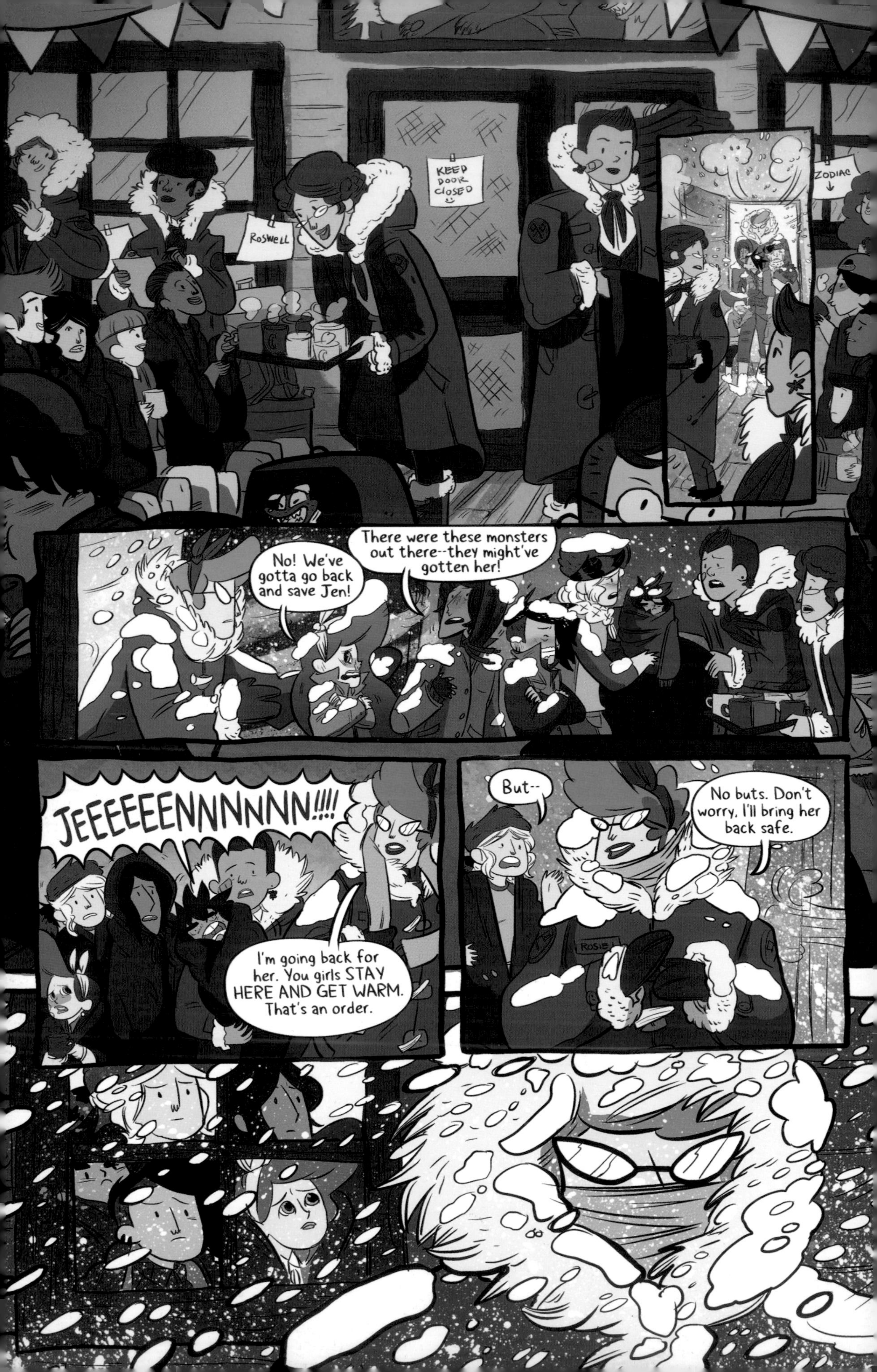

ROSWELL
KEEP DOOR CLOSED
ZODIAC
No! We've gotta go back and save Jen!
There were these monsters out there--they might've gotten her!
JEEEEEENNNNNN!!!!
I'm going back for her. You girls STAY HERE AND GET WARM. That's an order.
But--
No buts. Don't worry, I'll bring her back safe.
ROSIE

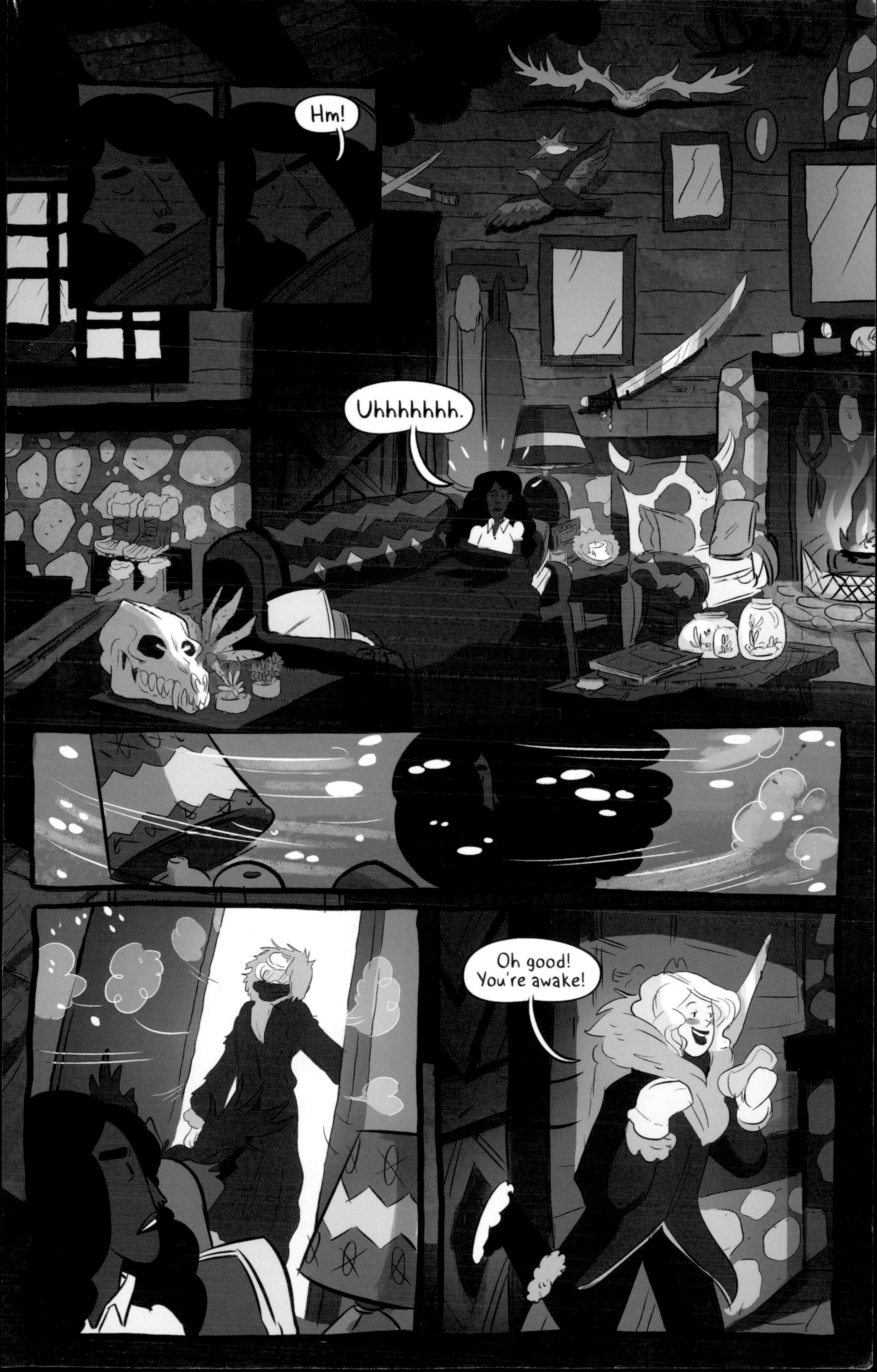
Hm!
Uhhhhhhh.
Oh good! You're awake!

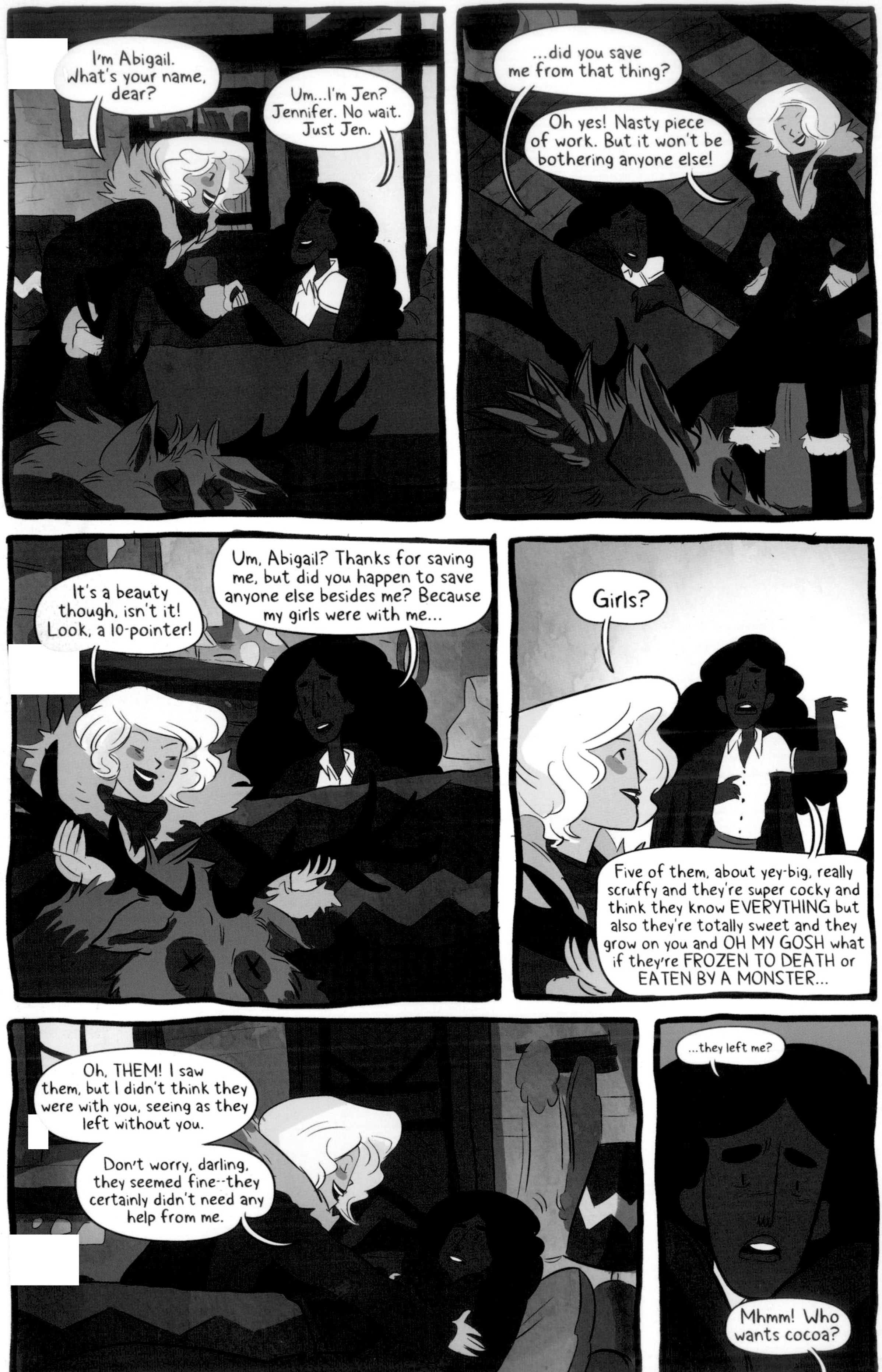
I'm Abigail. What's your name, dear?
Um...I'm Jen? Jennifer. No wait. Just Jen.
...did you save me from that thing?
Oh yes! Nasty piece of work. But it won't be bothering anyone else!
It's a beauty though, isn't it! Look, a 10-pointer!
Um, Abigail? Thanks for saving me, but did you happen to save anyone else besides me? Because my girls were with me...
Girls?
Five of them, about yey-big, really scruffy and they're super cocky and think they know EVERYTHING but also they're totally sweet and they grow on you and OH MY GOSH what if they're FROZEN TO DEATH or EATEN BY A MONSTER...
Oh, THEM! I saw them, but I didn't think they were with you, seeing as they left without you.
Don't worry, darling, they seemed fine--they certainly didn't need any help from me.
...they left me?
Mhmm! Who wants cocoa?

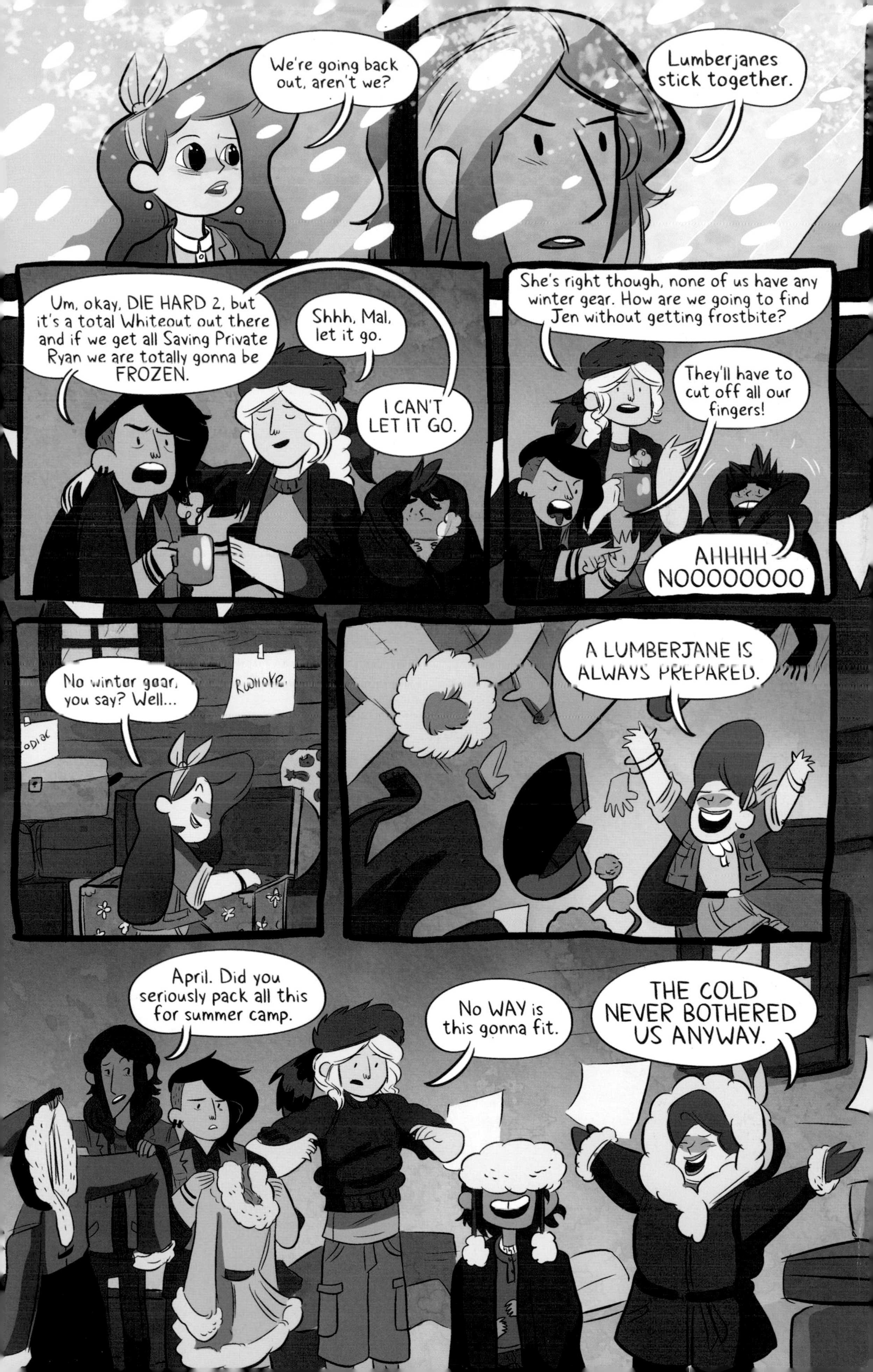
We're going back out, aren't we?
Lumberjanes stick together.
Um, okay, DIE HARD 2, but it's a total Whiteout out there and if we get all Saving Private Ryan we are totally gonna be FROZEN.
Shhh, Mal, let it go.
I CAN'T LET IT GO.
She's right though, none of us have any winter gear. How are we going to find Jen without getting frostbite?
They'll have to cut off all our fingers!
AHHHH NOOOOOOOOO
No winter gear, you say? Well...
A LUMBERJANE IS ALWAYS PREPARED.
April. Did you seriously pack all this for summer camp.
No WAY is this gonna fit.
THE COLD NEVER BOTHERED US ANYWAY.

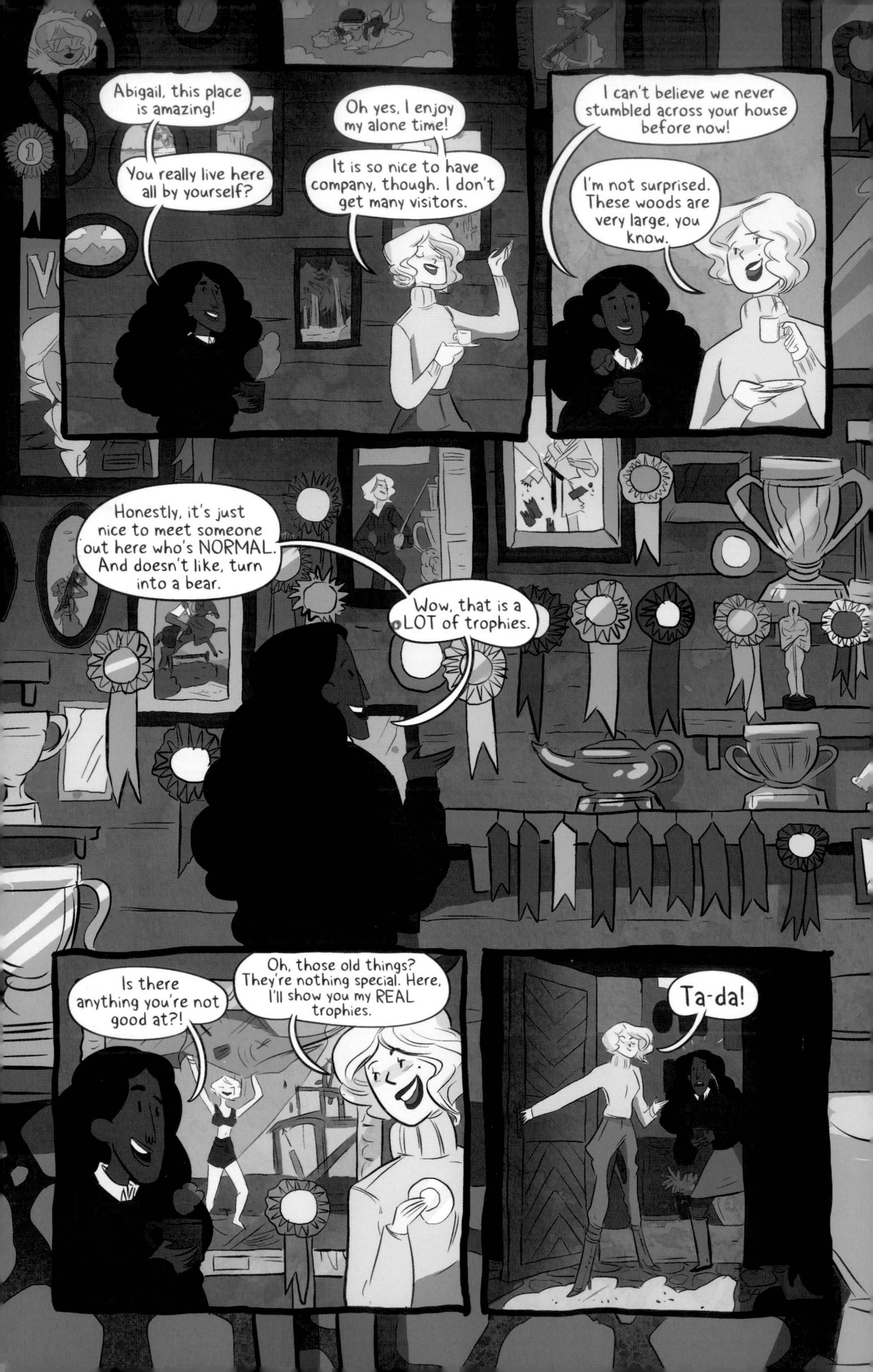

Abigail, this place is amazing!
You really live here all by yourself?
Oh yes, I enjoy my alone time!
It is so nice to have company, though. I don't get many visitors.
I can't believe we never stumbled across your house before now!
I'm not surprised. These woods are very large, you know.
Honestly, it's just nice to meet someone out here who's NORMAL. And doesn't like, turn into a bear.
Wow, that is a LOT of trophies.
Is there anything you're not good at?!
Oh, those old things? They're nothing special. Here, I'll show you my REAL trophies.
Ta-da!

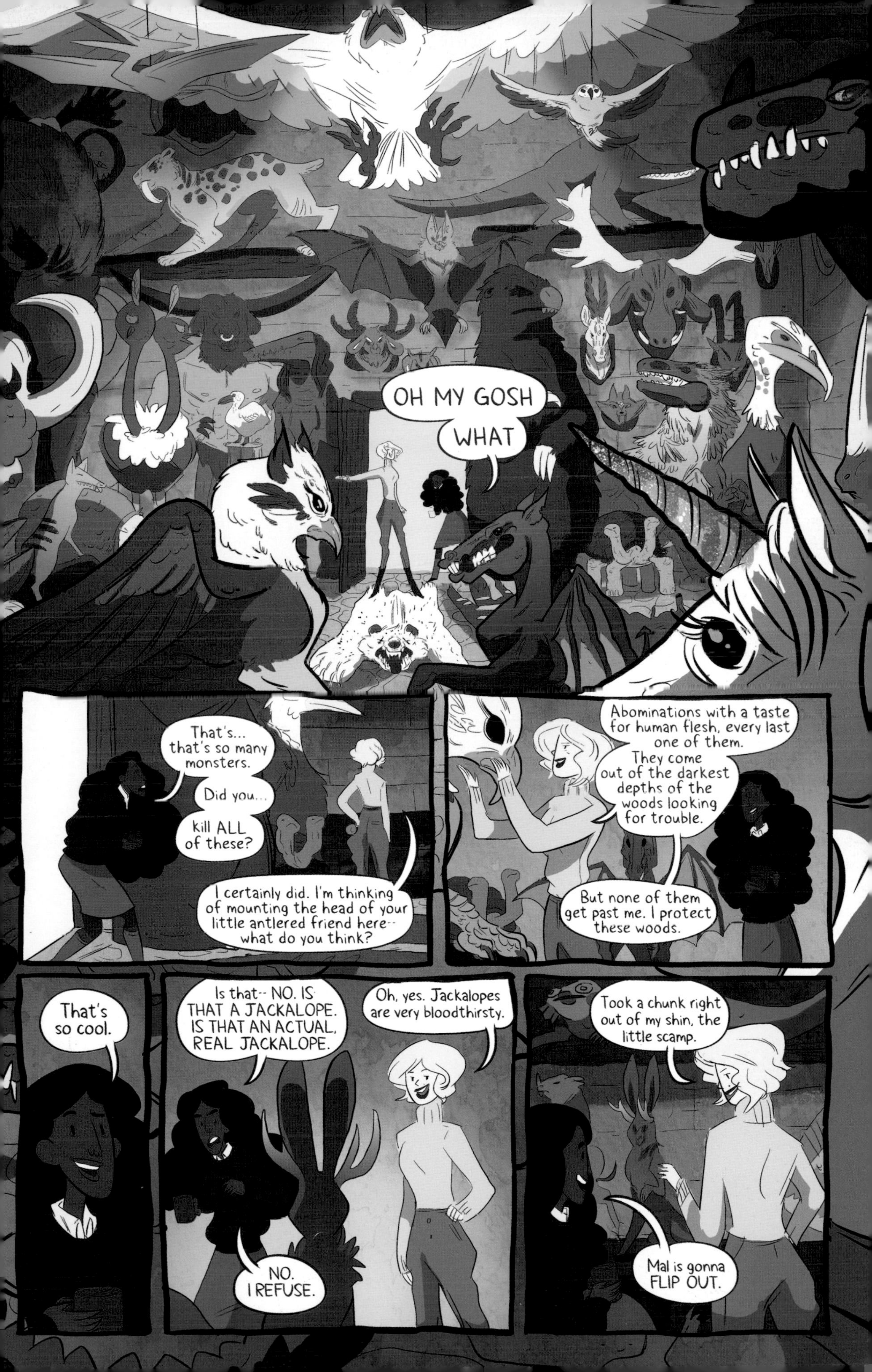

OH MY GOSH
WHAT
That's... that's so many monsters.
Did you...
kill ALL of these?
I certainly did. I'm thinking of mounting the head of your little antlered friend here-- what do you think?
Abominations with a taste for human flesh, every last one of them.
They come out of the darkest depths of the woods looking for trouble.
But none of them get past me. I protect these woods.
That's so cool.
Is that-- NO. IS THAT A JACKALOPE. IS THAT AN ACTUAL, REAL JACKALOPE.
Oh, yes. Jackalopes are very bloodthirsty.
NO. I REFUSE.
Took a chunk right out of my shin, the little scamp.
Mal is gonna FLIP OUT.

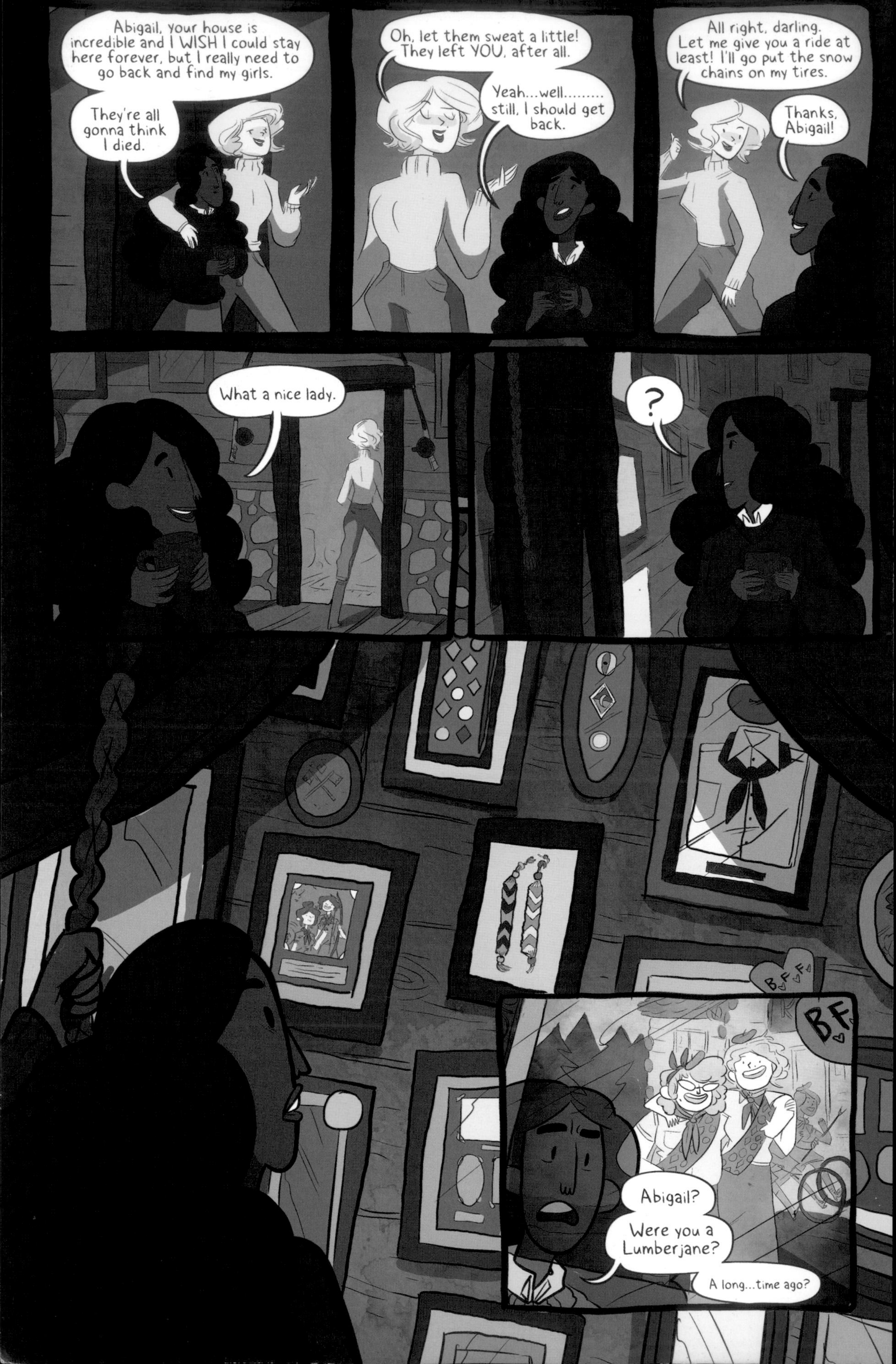

Abigail, your house is incredible and I WISH I could stay here forever, but I really need to go back and find my girls.
They're all gonna think I died.
Oh, let them sweat a little! They left YOU, after all.
Yeah...well......... still, I should get back.
All right, darling. Let me give you a ride at least! I'll go put the snow chains on my tires.
Thanks, Abigail!
What a nice lady.
?
B.F.F.
B.F.
Abigail?
Were you a Lumberjane?
A long...time ago?

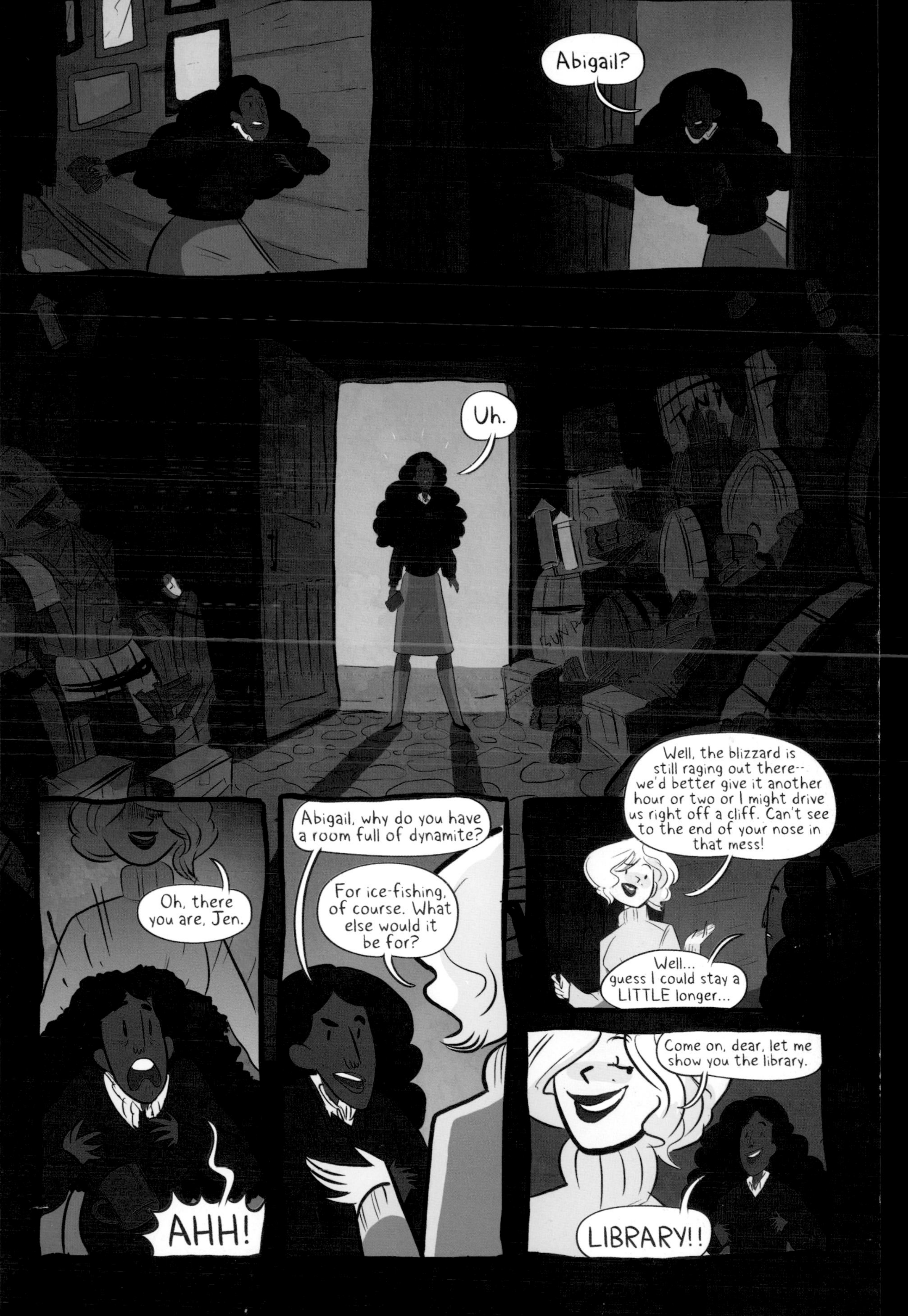
Abigail?
Uh.
Oh, there you are, Jen.
AHH!
Abigail, why do you have a room full of dynamite?
For ice-fishing, of course. What else would it be for?
Well, the blizzard is still raging out there-- we'd better give it another hour or two or I might drive us right off a cliff. Can't see to the end of your nose in that mess!
Well... guess I could stay a LITTLE longer...
Come on, dear, let me show you the library.
LIBRARY!!

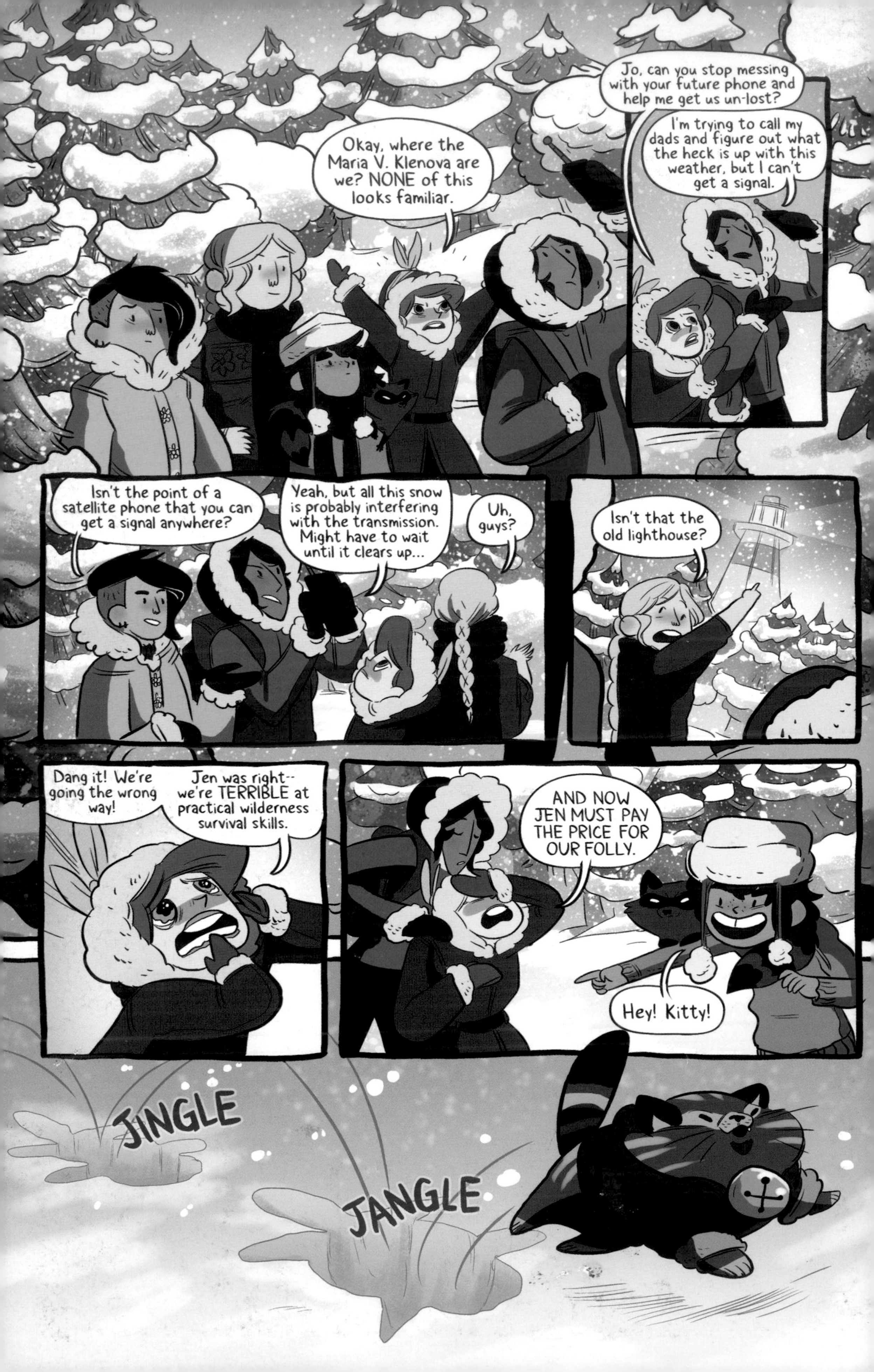

Okay, where the Maria V. Klenova are we? NONE of this looks familiar.
Jo, can you stop messing with your future phone and help me get us un-lost?
I'm trying to call my dads and figure out what the heck is up with this weather, but I can't get a signal.
Isn't the point of a satellite phone that you can get a signal anywhere?
Yeah, but all this snow is probably interfering with the transmission. Might have to wait until it clears up...
Uh, guys?
Isn't that the old lighthouse?
Dang it! We're going the wrong way!
Jen was right-- we're TERRIBLE at practical wilderness survival skills.
AND NOW JEN MUST PAY THE PRICE FOR OUR FOLLY.
Hey! Kitty!
JINGLE
JANGLE

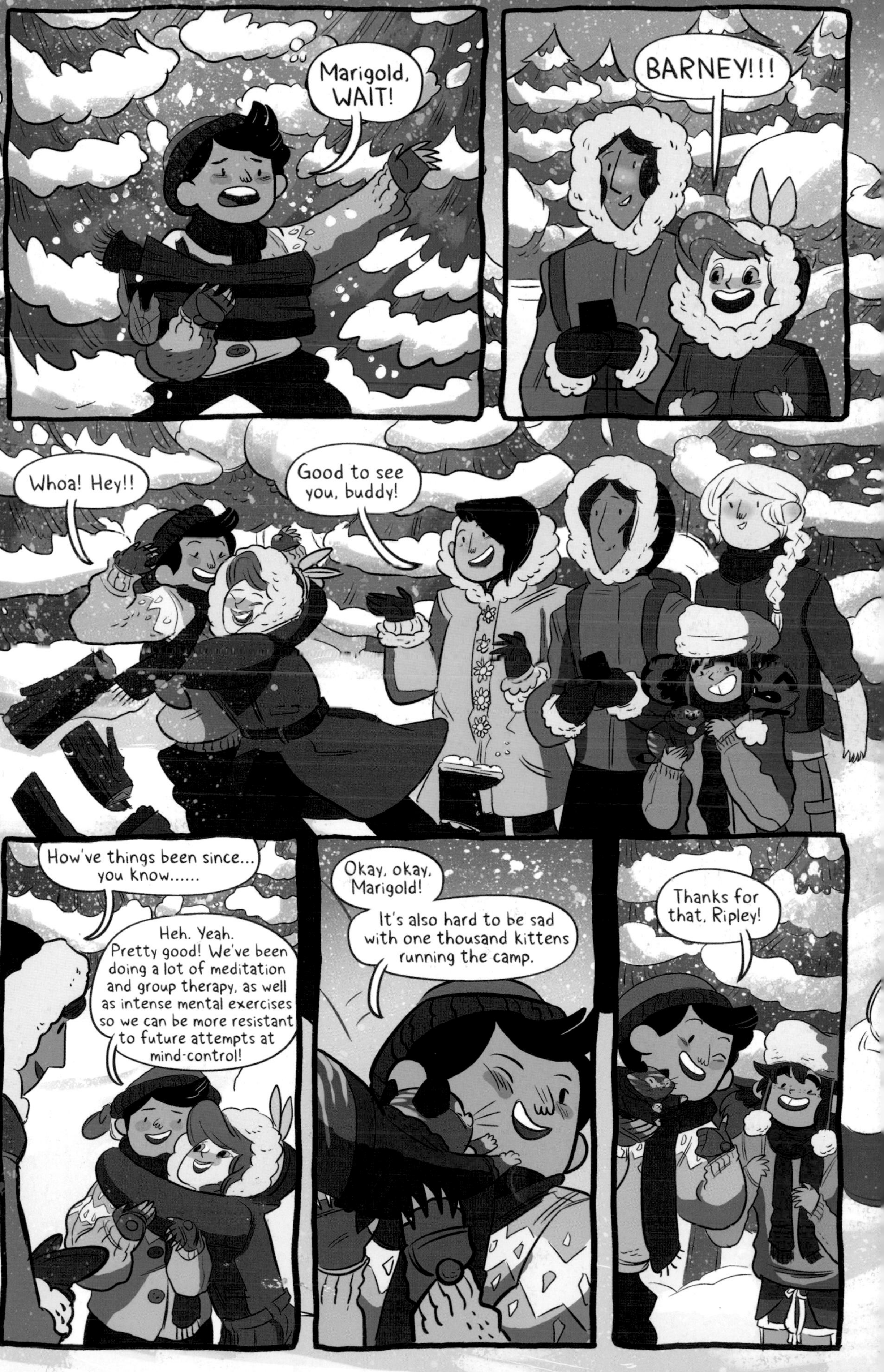
Marigold, WAIT!
BARNEY!!!
Whoa! Hey!!
Good to see you, buddy!
How've things been since... you know......
Heh. Yeah. Pretty good! We've been doing a lot of meditation and group therapy, as well as intense mental exercises so we can be more resistant to future attempts at mind-control!
Okay, okay, Marigold!
It's also hard to be sad with one thousand kittens running the camp.
Thanks for that, Ripley!

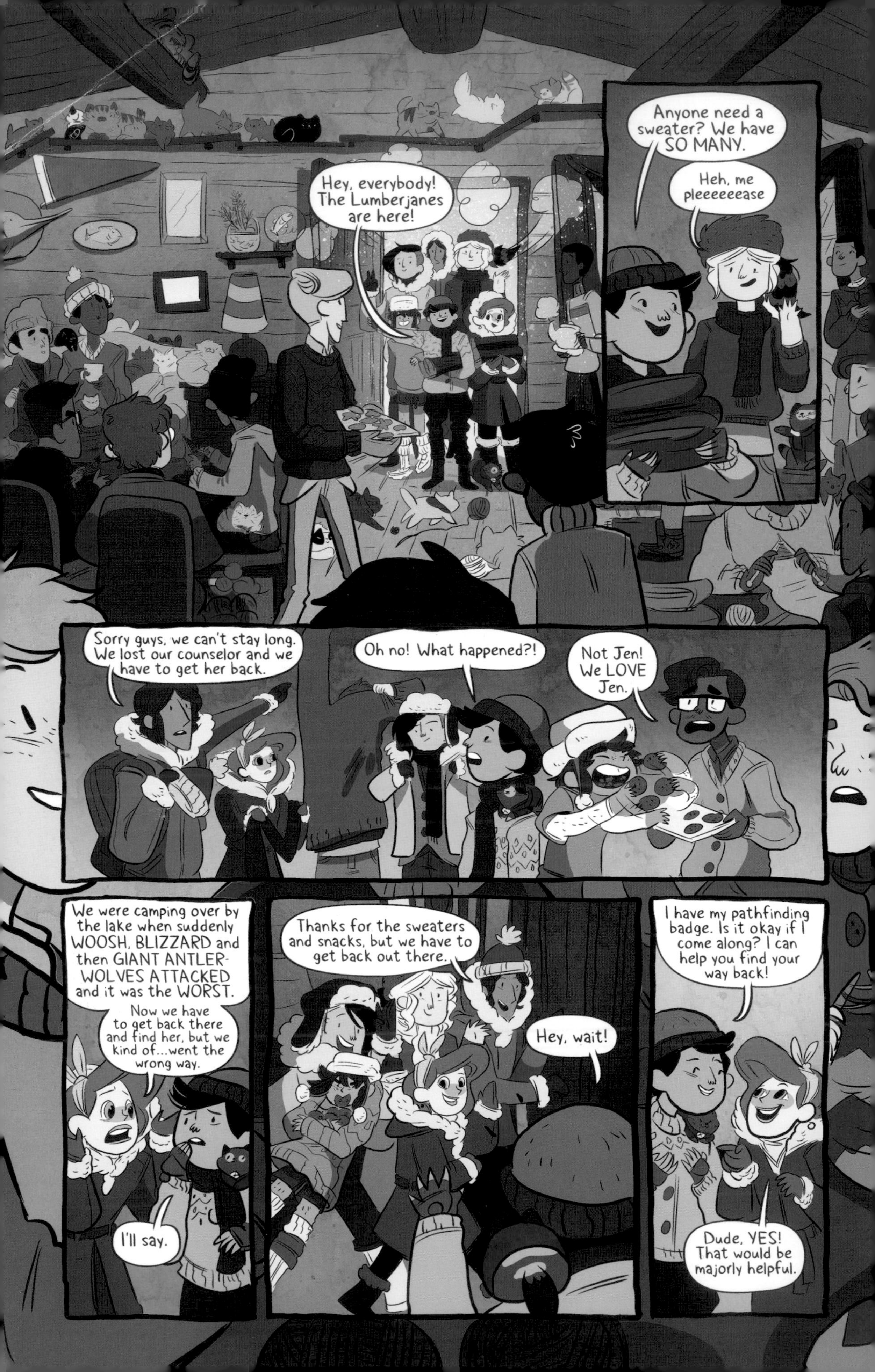
Hey, everybody! The Lumberjanes are here!
Anyone need a sweater? We have SO MANY.
Heh, me pleeeeeease
Sorry guys, we can't stay long. We lost our counselor and we have to get her back.
Oh no! What happened?!
Not Jen! We LOVE Jen.
We were camping over by the lake when suddenly WOOSH, BLIZZARD and then GIANT ANTLER-WOLVES ATTACKED and it was the WORST.
Now we have to get back there and find her, but we kind of...went the wrong way.
I'll say.
Thanks for the sweaters and snacks, but we have to get back out there.
Hey, wait!
I have my pathfinding badge. Is it okay if I come along? I can help you find your way back!
Dude, YES! That would be majorly helpful.

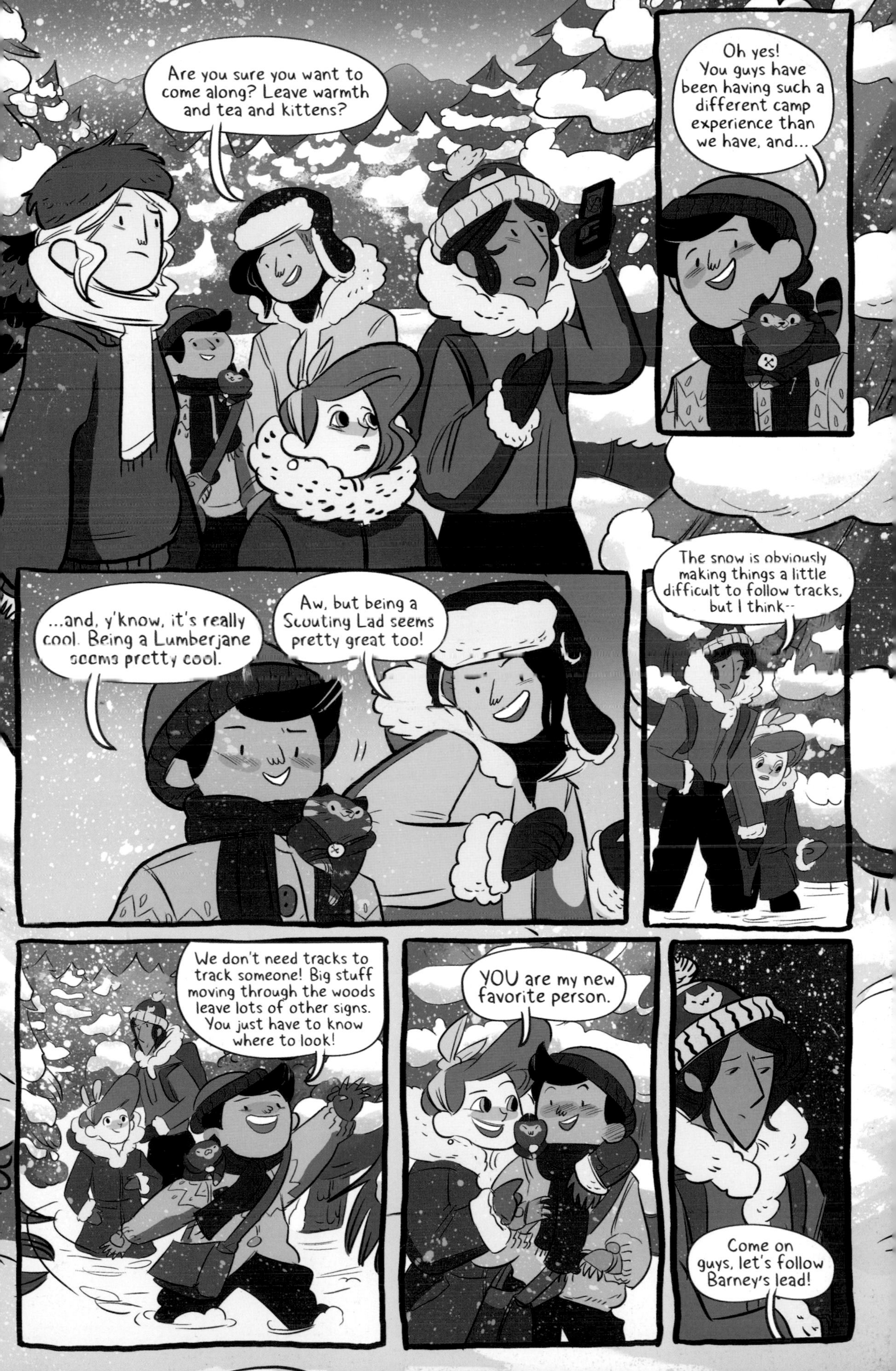
Are you sure you want to come along? Leave warmth and tea and kittens?
Oh yes! You guys have been having such a different camp experience than we have, and...
...and, y'know, it's really cool. Being a Lumberjane seems pretty cool.
Aw, but being a Scouting Lad seems pretty great too!
The snow is obviously making things a little difficult to follow tracks, but I think--
We don't need tracks to track someone! Big stuff moving through the woods leave lots of other signs. You just have to know where to look!
YOU are my new favorite person.
Come on guys, let's follow Barney's lead!

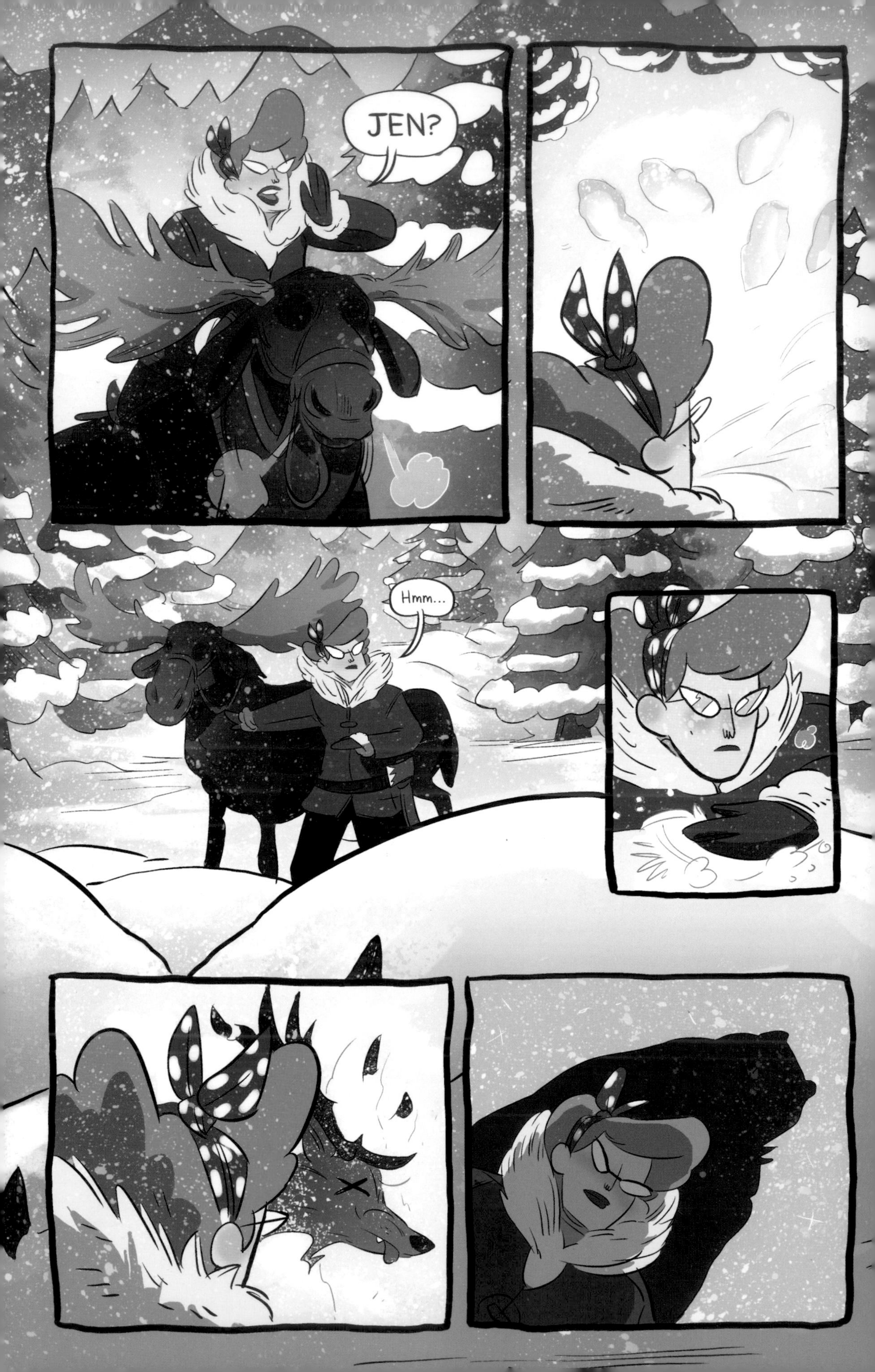
JEN?
Hmm...

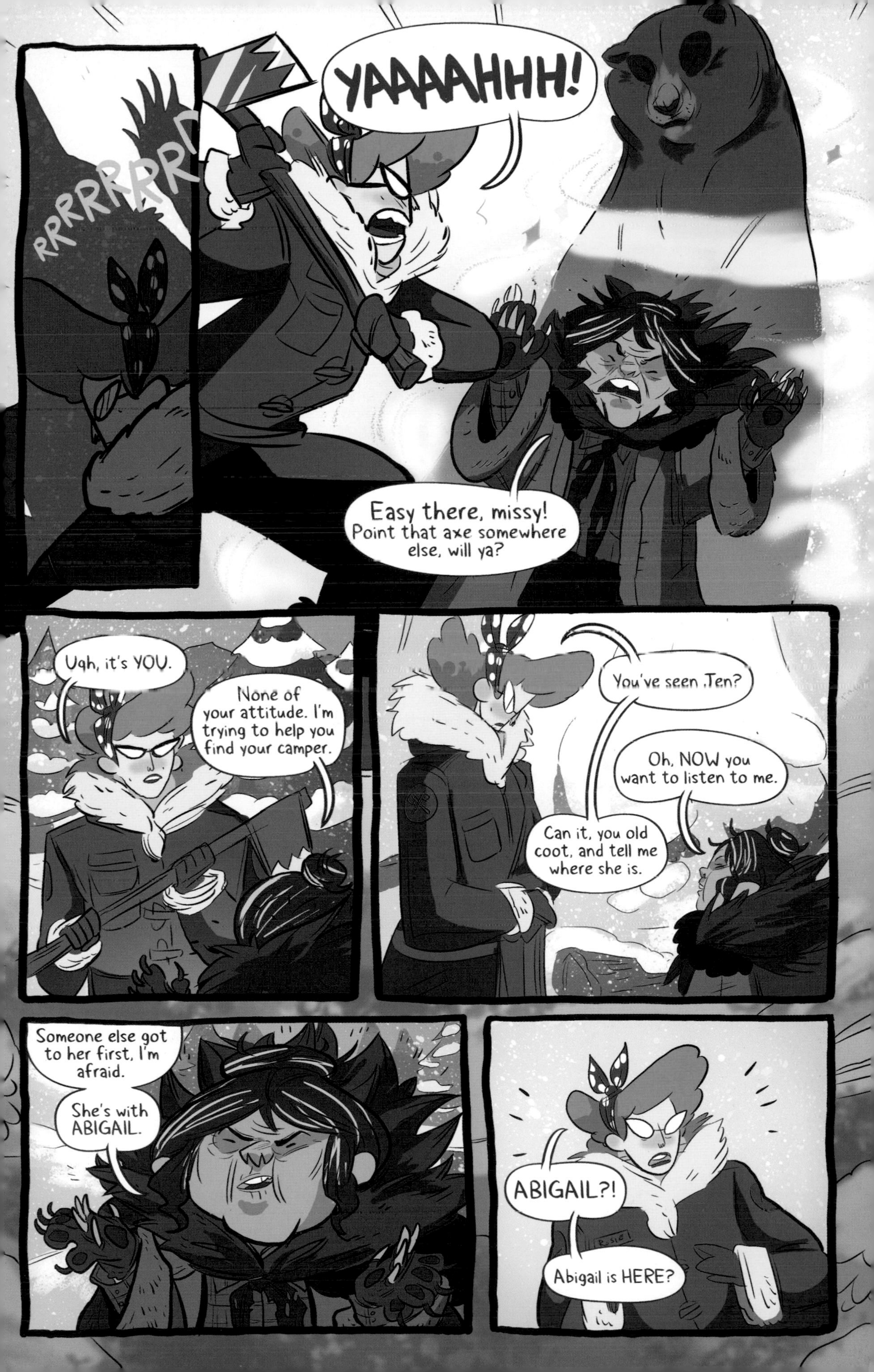
RRRRRRRD
YAAAAHHH!
Easy there, missy! Point that axe somewhere else, will ya?
Ugh, it's YOU.
None of your attitude. I'm trying to help you find your camper.
You've seen Jen?
Oh, NOW you want to listen to me.
Can it, you old coot, and tell me where she is.
Someone else got to her first, I'm afraid.
She's with ABIGAIL.
ABIGAIL?!
Abigail is HERE?

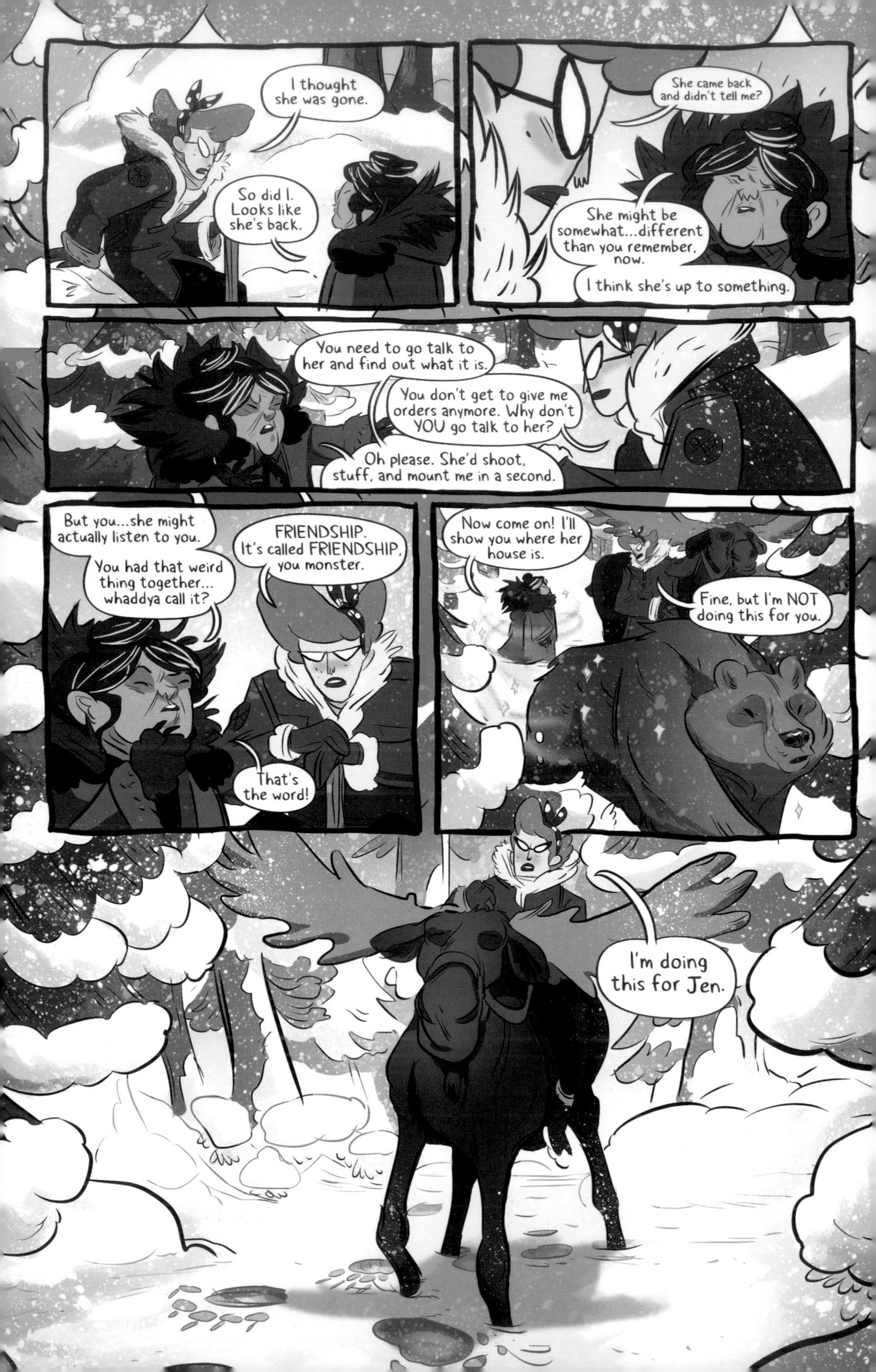
I thought she was gone.
So did I. Looks like she's back.
She came back and didn't tell me?
She might be somewhat...different than you remember, now.
I think she's up to something.
You need to go talk to her and find out what it is.
You don't get to give me orders anymore. Why don't YOU go talk to her?
Oh please. She'd shoot, stuff, and mount me in a second.
But you...she might actually listen to you.
You had that weird thing together... whaddya call it?
FRIENDSHIP. It's called FRIENDSHIP, you monster.
That's the word!
Now come on! I'll show you where her house is.
Fine, but I'm NOT doing this for you.
I'm doing this for Jen.

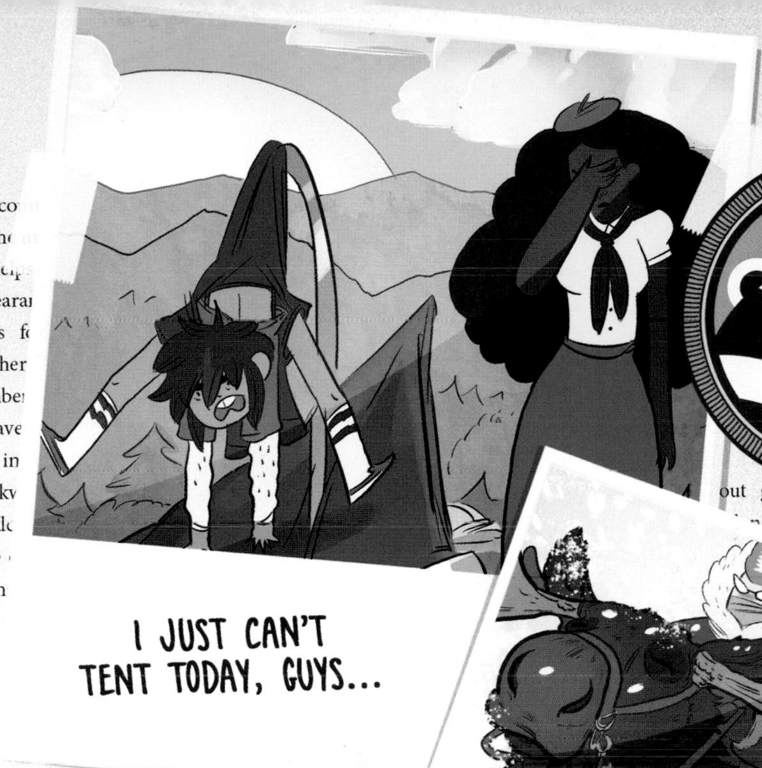
I JUST CAN'T
TENT TODAY, GUYS...

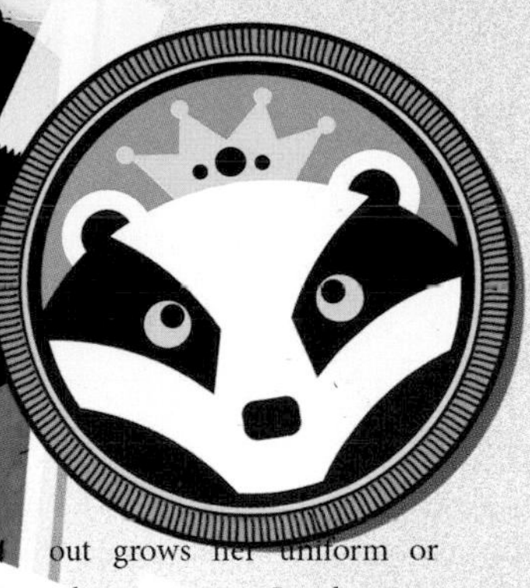

will co

The

It help

appeara

dress f

Further

Lumbe

to have

part in

Thiskw

Hard

have

them

out grows her uniform or

ter Lumberjane.

ia she has

her

her

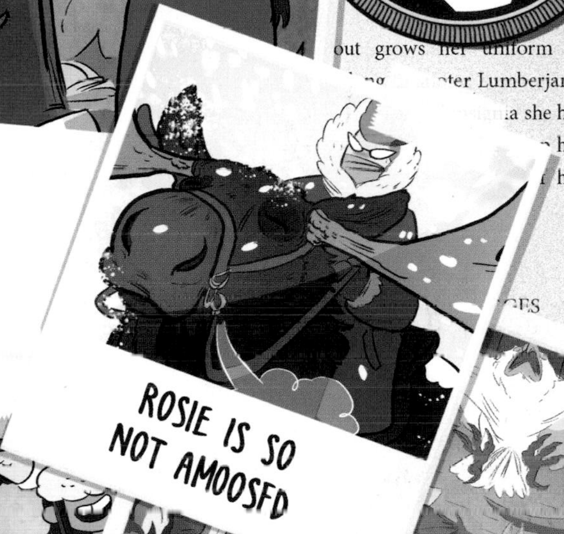
ROSIE IS SO
NOT AMOOSED

GES

The

yellow, short sl

emb

the w

choose

slacks,

made o

out-of-do

green bere

the colla

Shoes ma

heels, rou

ings or

socks shou

with the sh

wit

the uniform. Ne es, bracelets, or

belong with a Lumberjane unifo

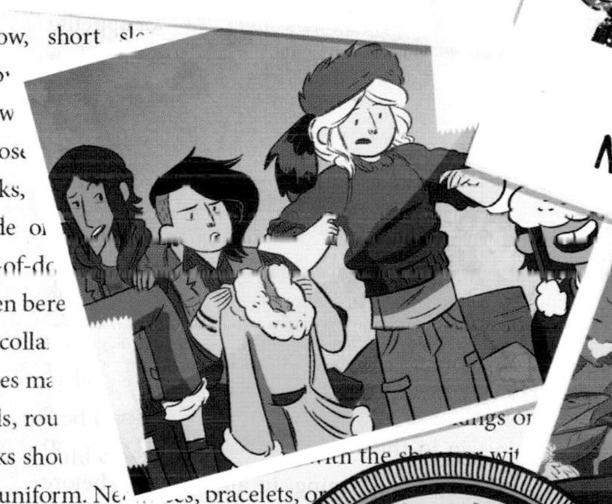

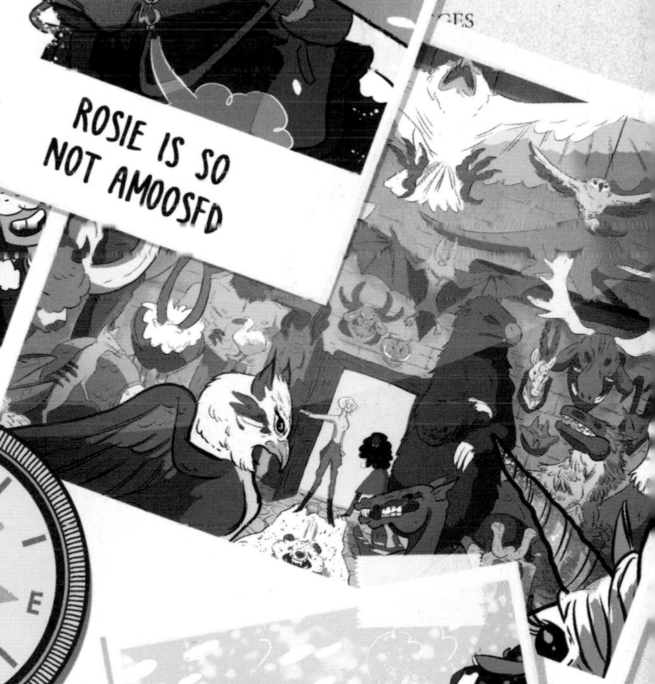

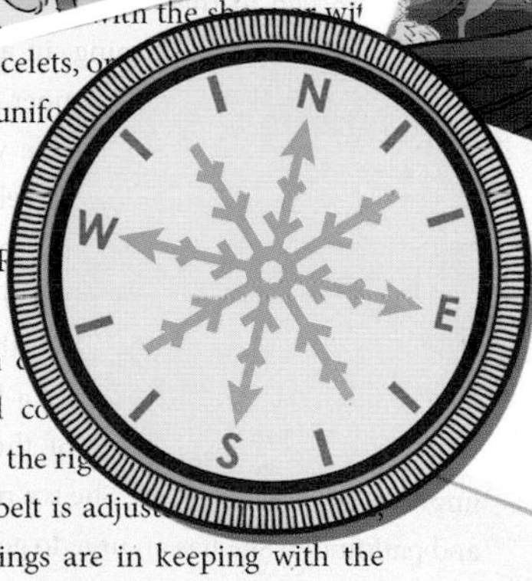
N
W
E
S

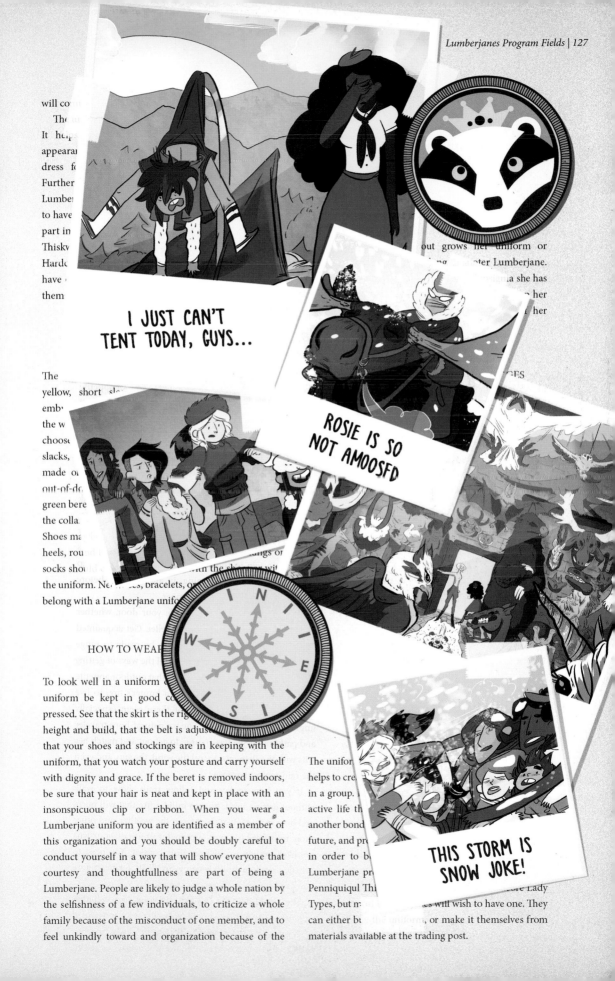

HOW TO WEAR

To look well in a uniform

uniform be kept in good co

pressed. See that the skirt is the rig

height and build, that the belt is adjust

that your shoes and stockings are in keeping with the uniform, that you watch your posture and carry yourself with dignity and grace. If the beret is removed indoors, be sure that your hair is neat and kept in place with an insonspicuous clip or ribbon. When you wear a Lumberjane uniform you are identified as a member of this organization and you should be doubly careful to conduct yourself in a way that will show everyone that courtesy and thoughtfullness are part of being a Lumberjane. People are likely to judge a whole nation by the selfishness of a few individuals, to criticize a whole family because of the misconduct of one member, and to feel unkindly toward and organization because of the

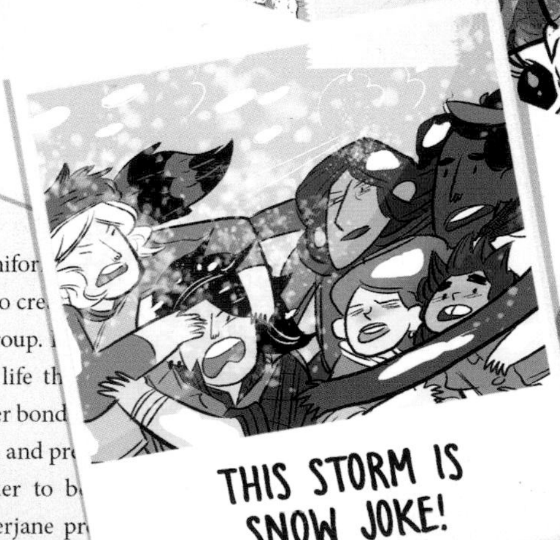
THIS STORM IS
SNOW JOKE!

The unifor

helps to cre

in a group.

active life th

another bond

future, and pr

in order to b

Lumberjane pr

Penniquiqul Thi ore Lady

Types, but m es will wish to have one. They

can either b uniform, or make it themselves from

materials available at the trading post.

LUMBERJANES FIELD MANUAL
CHAPTER FOURTEEN

Lumberjanes "Literature" Program Field

THE MYSTERY OF HISTORY BADGE

"It's not about what's remembered, it's about why."

The amazing thing about memory is that it can be tricked. You can go through life knowing one thing as a fact but still be proven wrong at a later date. This is because if someone believes in something strong enough, they can make it feel like a fact for them. They can make something the truth, even though it wasn't. Which is why history is important, but might not always be reliable. As a Lumberjane, it will be important to not only keep an open mind to the occurrences around you but to stay on top of all the changes that happen around you. Everyone has their own unique experience, even if it's all the same event, because we are all unique individuals with our own unique backgrounds. This is what makes us great, what makes us human, what makes us Lumberjanes. All Lumberjanes must have a journal that they keep on themselves and use these journals to keep track of the events that happen to them at this camp, and hopefully the events that happen outside of the camp as well.

The Mystery of History badge is a badge that can only be earned in the library. Every scout will go to the camp's library and pick out a book. It can be any book, from humor to non-fiction, and they will research everything that went into the creation of the book. They will learn about the authors, about their life, about what inspired them to create the book and find all the information that they wouldn't be able to find in the book they chose by itself. One of the many fun opportunities with this badge is the chance to get a better knowledge of how things change from what actually happened to what ends up on paper. Capture the flag will be and will always be the biggest battle of the summer, but the real challenge to the game actually isn't getting the flag. It's breaking out of your enemies prison.

To obtain *The Mystery of History* badge a Lumberjane

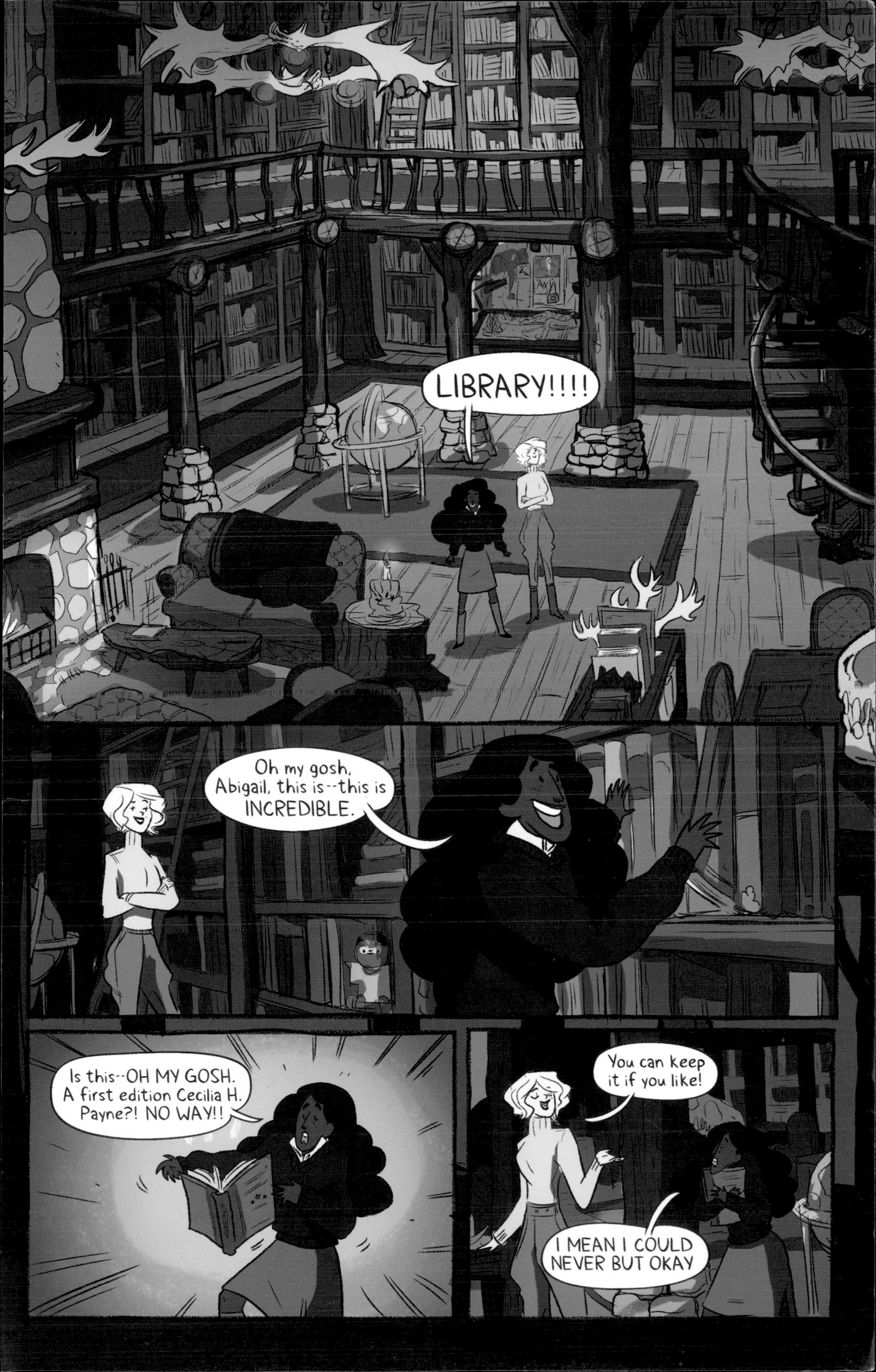
LIBRARY!!!!
Oh my gosh, Abigail, this is--this is INCREDIBLE.
Is this--OH MY GOSH. A first edition Cecilia H. Payne?! NO WAY!!
You can keep it if you like!
I MEAN I COULD NEVER BUT OKAY

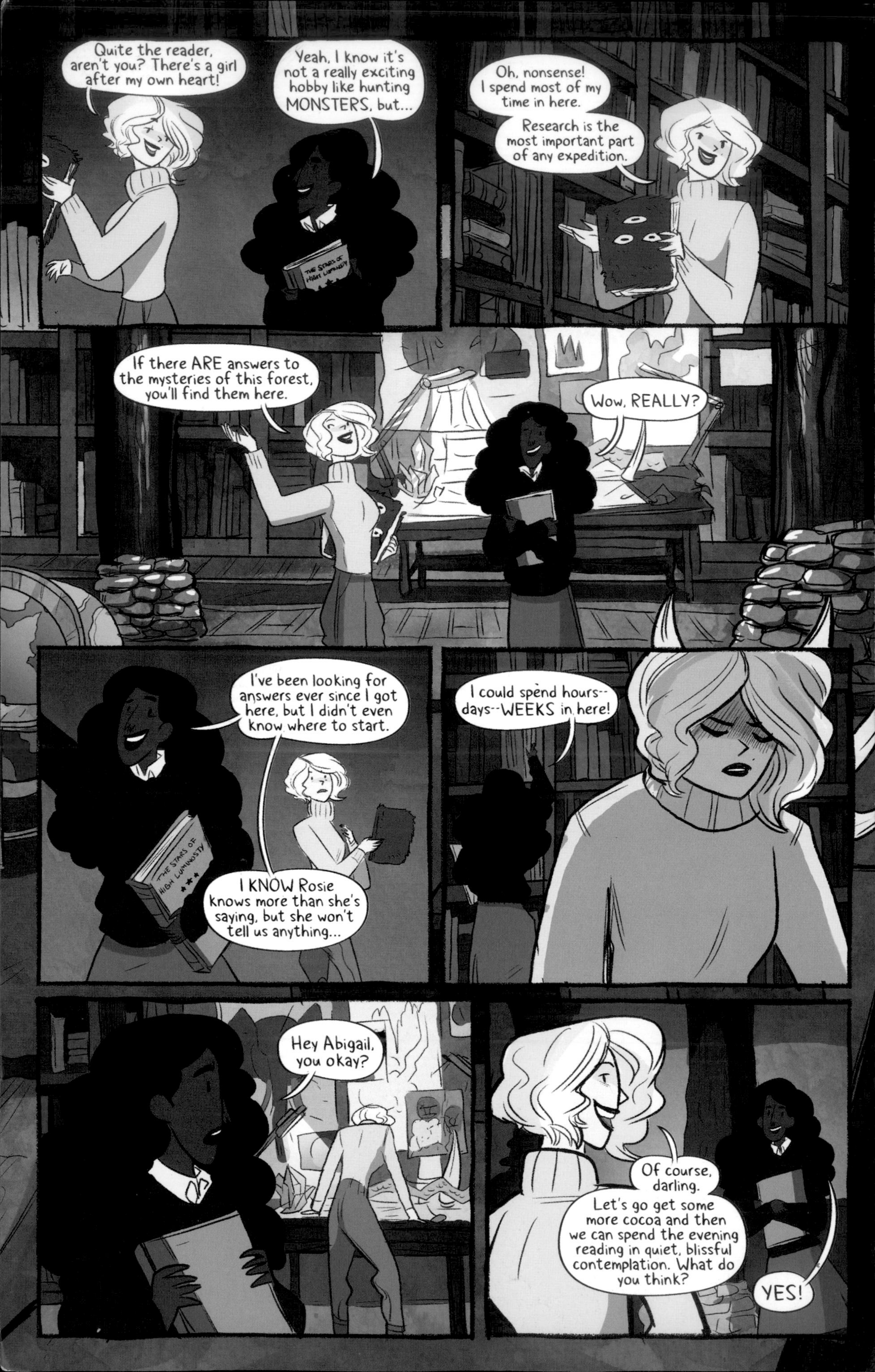
Quite the reader, aren't you? There's a girl after my own heart!
Yeah, I know it's not a really exciting hobby like hunting MONSTERS, but...
THE STARS OF HIGH LUMINOSITY
Oh, nonsense! I spend most of my time in here.
Research is the most important part of any expedition.
If there ARE answers to the mysteries of this forest, you'll find them here.
Wow, REALLY?
I've been looking for answers ever since I got here, but I didn't even know where to start.
THE STARS OF HIGH LUMINOSITY
I KNOW Rosie knows more than she's saying, but she won't tell us anything...
I could spend hours--days--WEEKS in here!
Hey Abigail, you okay?
Of course, darling.
Let's go get some more cocoa and then we can spend the evening reading in quiet, blissful contemplation. What do you think?
YES!

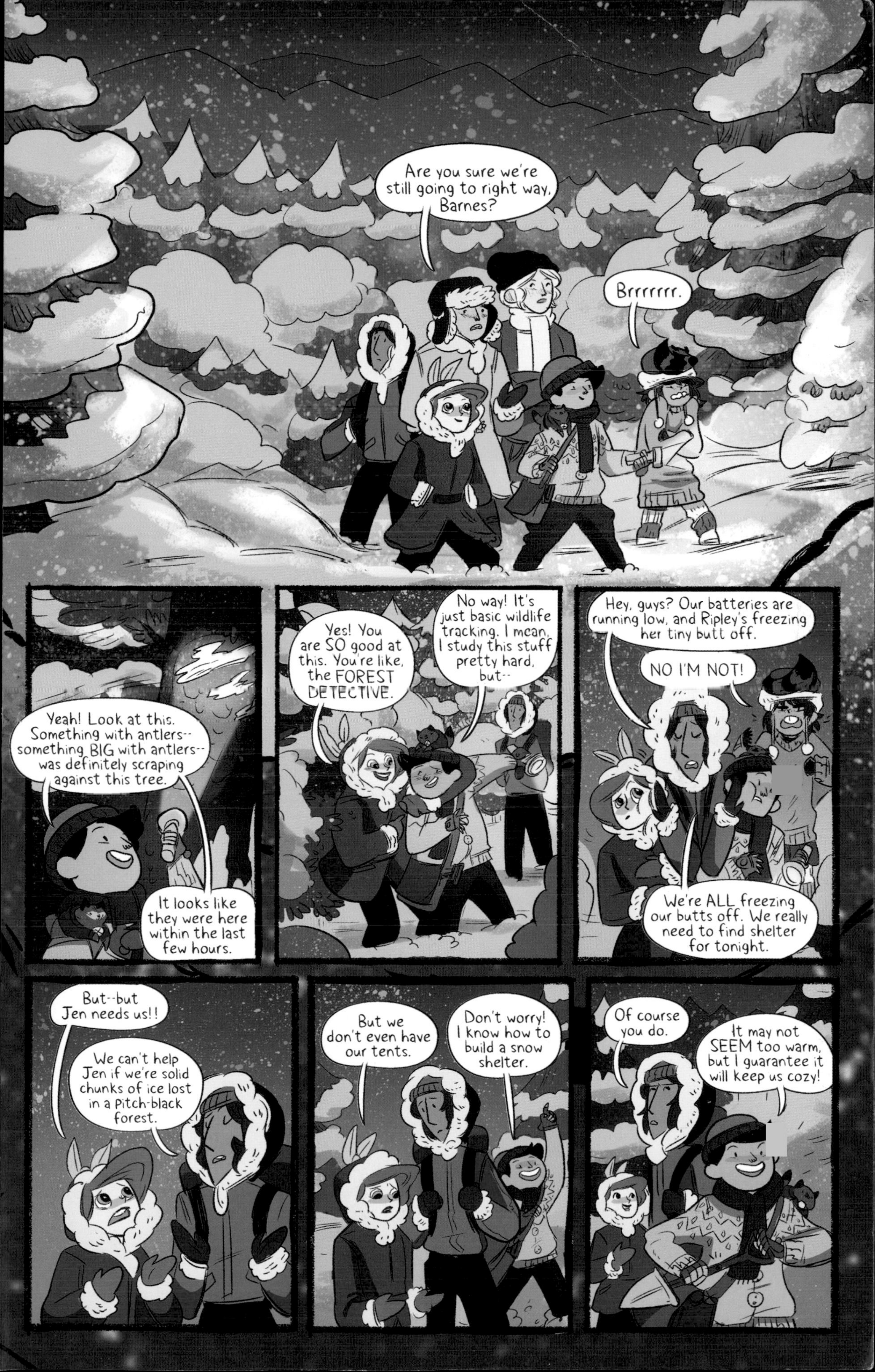
Are you sure we're still going to right way, Barnes?
Brrrrrrr.
Yeah! Look at this. Something with antlers-- something BIG with antlers-- was definitely scraping against this tree.
It looks like they were here within the last few hours.
Yes! You are SO good at this. You're like, the FOREST DETECTIVE.
No way! It's just basic wildlife tracking. I mean, I study this stuff pretty hard, but--
Hey, guys? Our batteries are running low, and Ripley's freezing her tiny butt off.
NO I'M NOT!
We're ALL freezing our butts off. We really need to find shelter for tonight.
But--but Jen needs us!!
We can't help Jen if we're solid chunks of ice lost in a pitch-black forest.
But we don't even have our tents.
Don't worry! I know how to build a snow shelter.
Of course you do.
It may not SEEM too warm, but I guarantee it will keep us cozy!

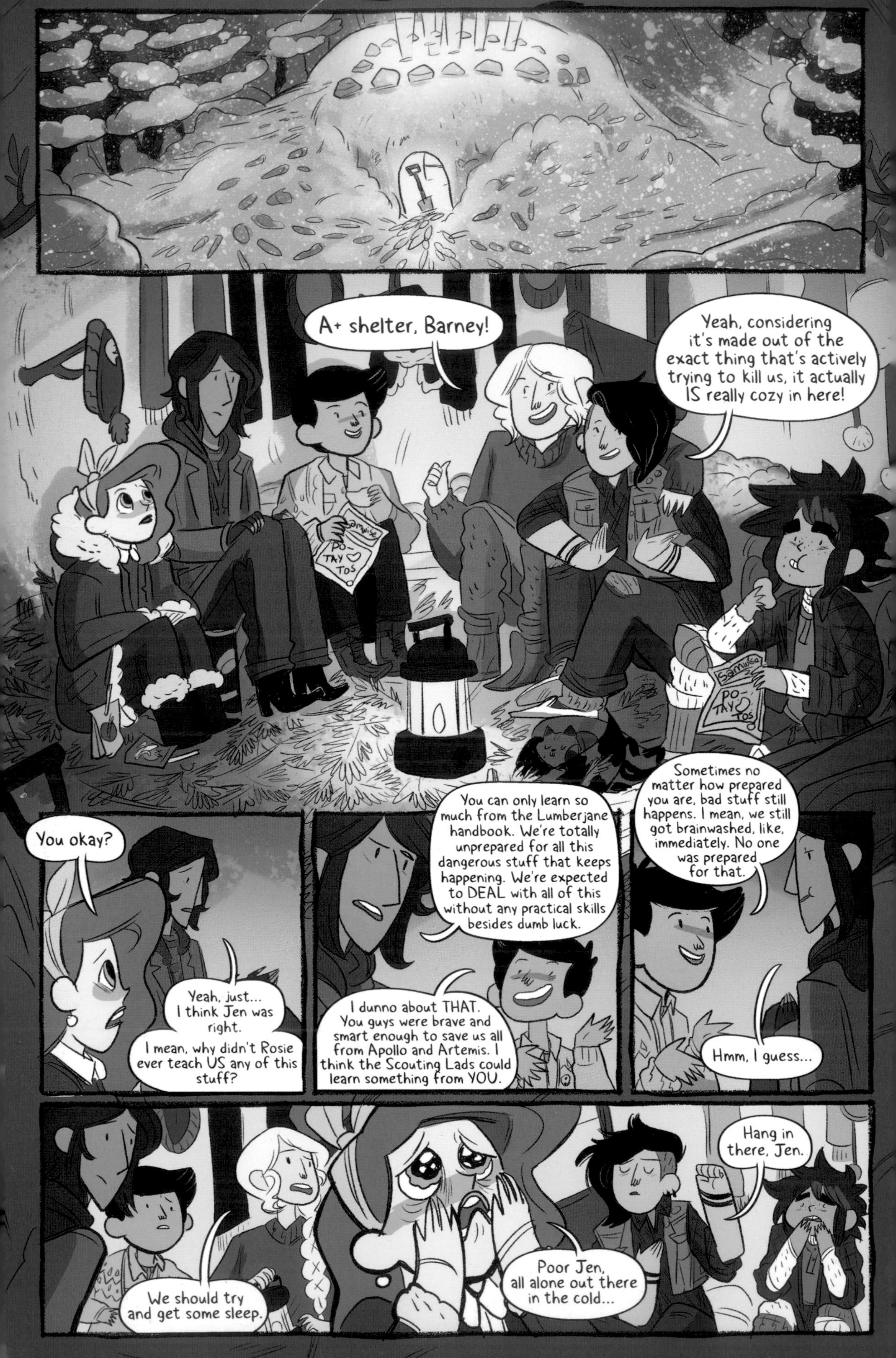

A+ shelter, Barney!
Yeah, considering it's made out of the exact thing that's actively trying to kill us, it actually IS really cozy in here!
Samwise PO-TAY-TOS
You okay?
Yeah, just... I think Jen was right.
I mean, why didn't Rosie ever teach US any of this stuff?
You can only learn so much from the Lumberjane handbook. We're totally unprepared for all this dangerous stuff that keeps happening. We're expected to DEAL with all of this without any practical skills besides dumb luck.
I dunno about THAT. You guys were brave and smart enough to save us all from Apollo and Artemis. I think the Scouting Lads could learn something from YOU.
Sometimes no matter how prepared you are, bad stuff still happens. I mean, we still got brainwashed, like, immediately. No one was prepared for that.
Hmm, I guess...
We should try and get some sleep.
Poor Jen, all alone out there in the cold...
Hang in there, Jen.

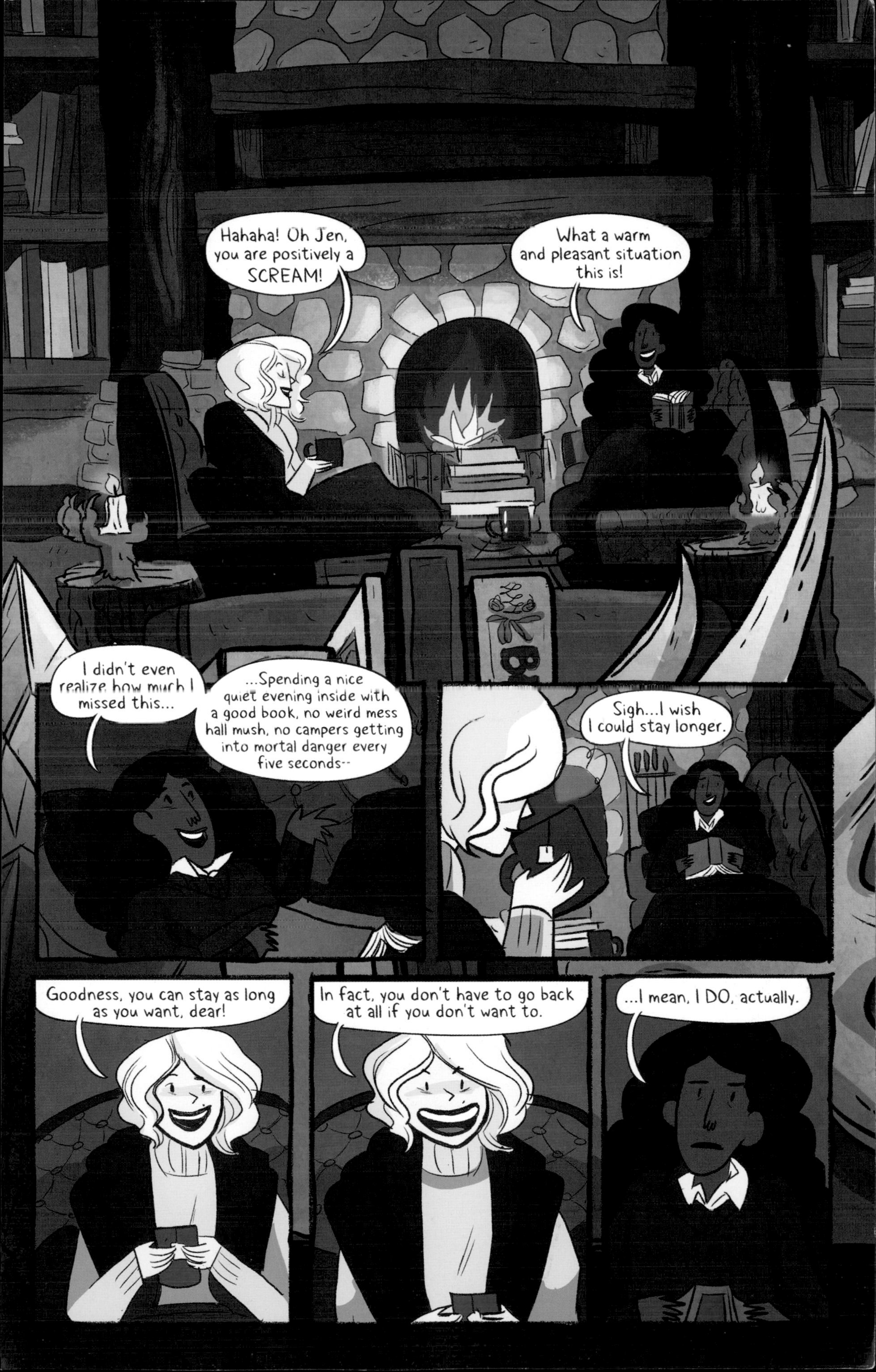
Hahaha! Oh Jen, you are positively a SCREAM!
What a warm and pleasant situation this is!
I didn't even realize how much I missed this...
...Spending a nice quiet evening inside with a good book, no weird mess hall mush, no campers getting into mortal danger every five seconds--
Sigh...I wish I could stay longer.
Goodness, you can stay as long as you want, dear!
In fact, you don't have to go back at all if you don't want to.
...I mean, I DO, actually.

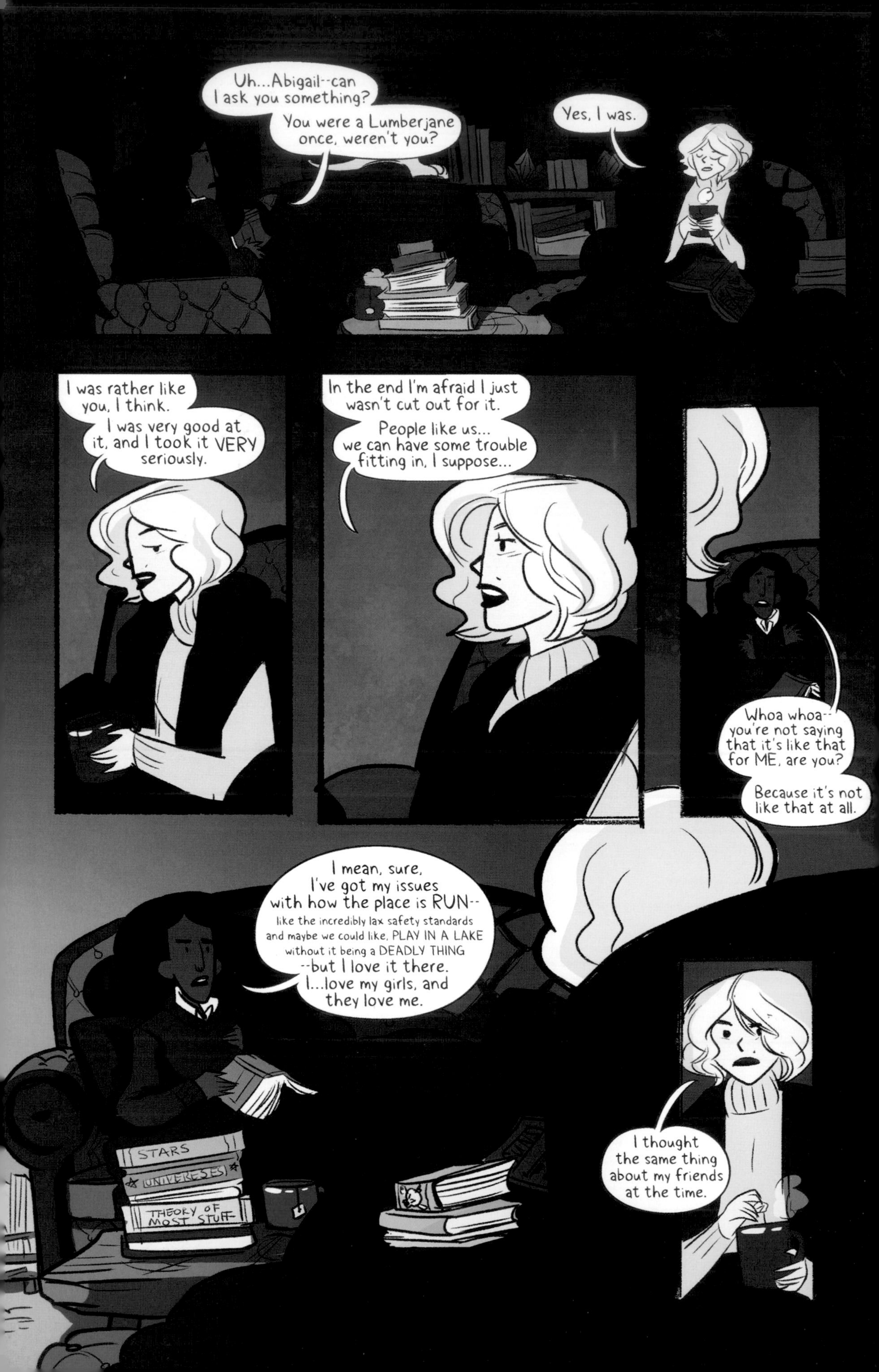
Uh...Abigail--can I ask you something?
You were a Lumberjane once, weren't you?
Yes, I was.
I was rather like you, I think.
I was very good at it, and I took it VERY seriously.
In the end I'm afraid I just wasn't cut out for it.
People like us... we can have some trouble fitting in, I suppose...
Whoa whoa--you're not saying that it's like that for ME, are you?
Because it's not like that at all.
I mean, sure, I've got my issues with how the place is RUN--like the incredibly lax safety standards and maybe we could like, PLAY IN A LAKE without it being a DEADLY THING--but I love it there. I...love my girls, and they love me.
STARS
UNIVERESES
THEORY OF MOST STUFF
I thought the same thing about my friends at the time.

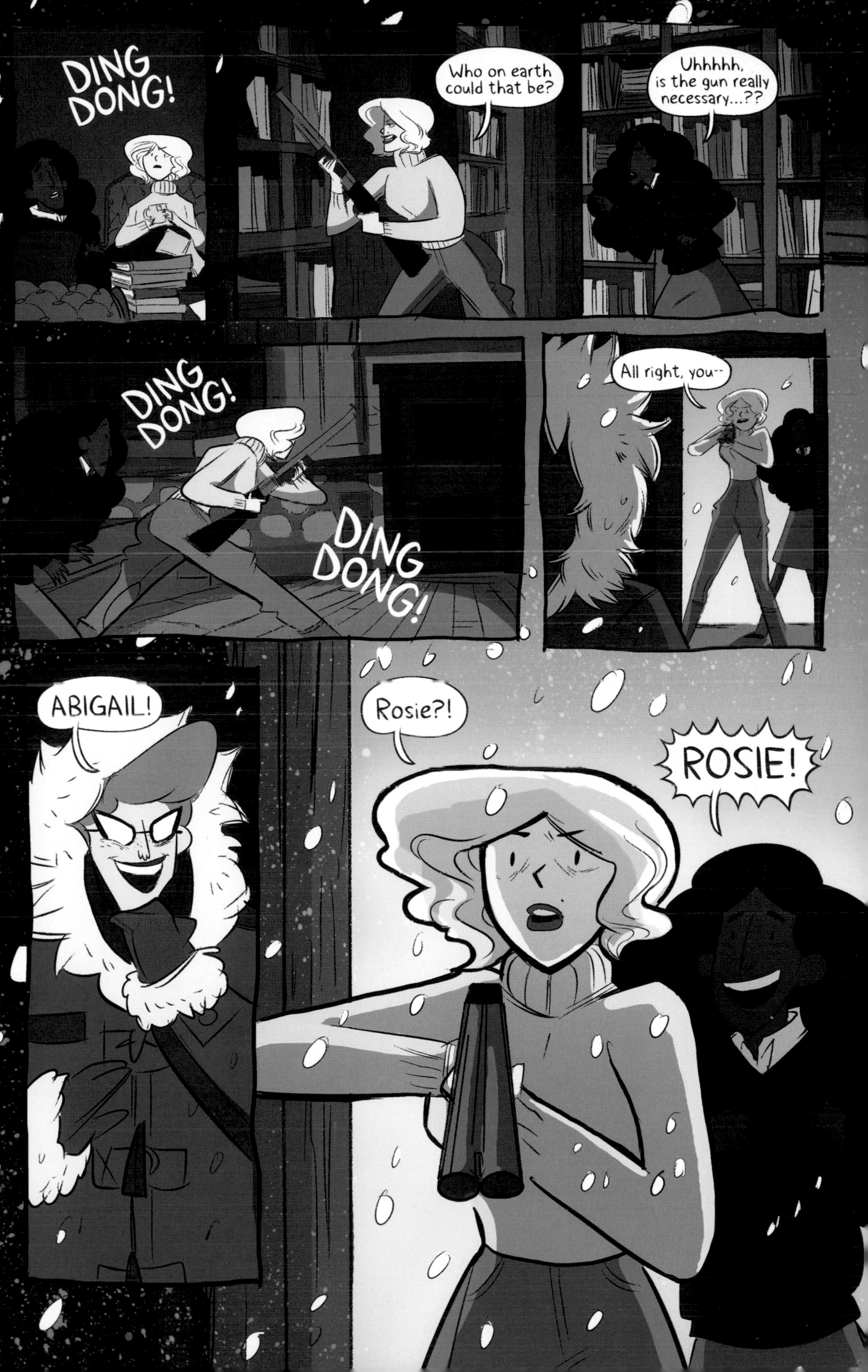
DING DONG!
Who on earth could that be?
Uhhhhh, is the gun really necessary...??
DING DONG!
DING DONG!
All right, you--
ABIGAIL!
Rosie?!
ROSIE!

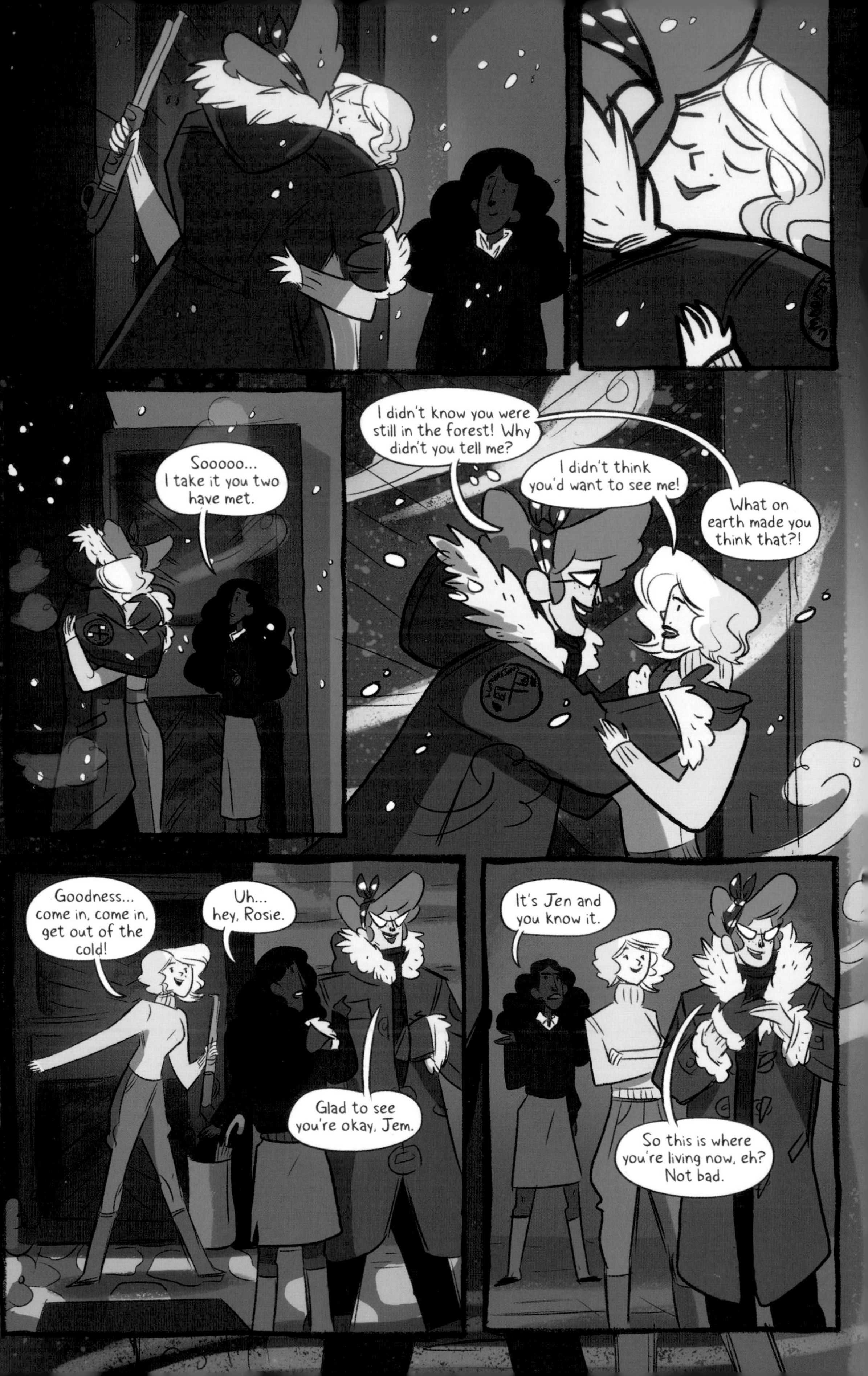

Sooooo... I take it you two have met.
I didn't know you were still in the forest! Why didn't you tell me?
I didn't think you'd want to see me!
What on earth made you think that?!
Goodness... come in, come in, get out of the cold!
Uh... hey, Rosie.
Glad to see you're okay, Jem.
It's Jen and you know it.
So this is where you're living now, eh? Not bad.

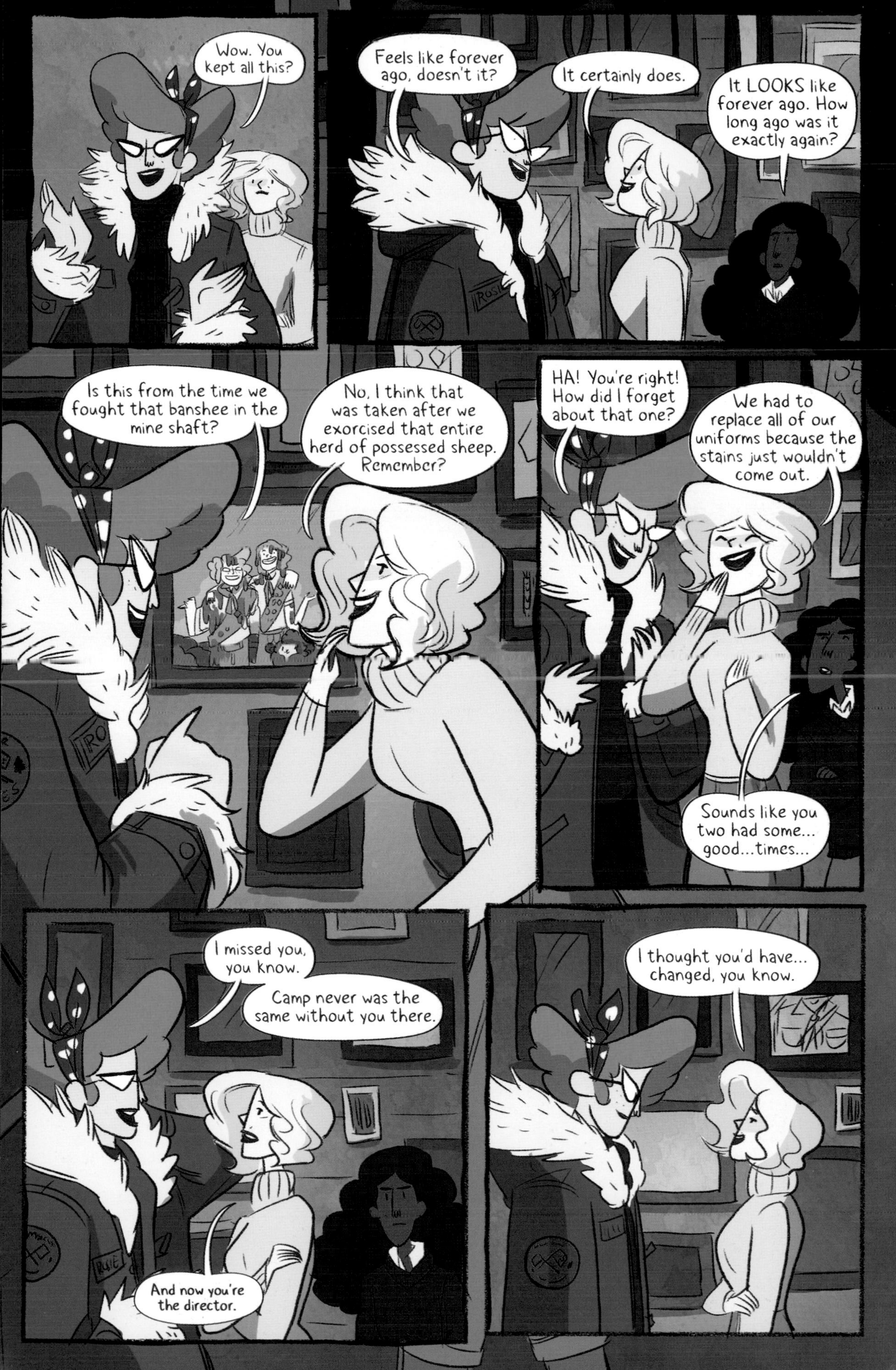
Wow. You kept all this?
Feels like forever ago, doesn't it?
It certainly does.
It LOOKS like forever ago. How long ago was it exactly again?
Is this from the time we fought that banshee in the mine shaft?
No, I think that was taken after we exorcised that entire herd of possessed sheep. Remember?
HA! You're right! How did I forget about that one?
We had to replace all of our uniforms because the stains just wouldn't come out.
Sounds like you two had some... good...times...
I missed you, you know.
Camp never was the same without you there.
And now you're the director.
I thought you'd have... changed, you know.

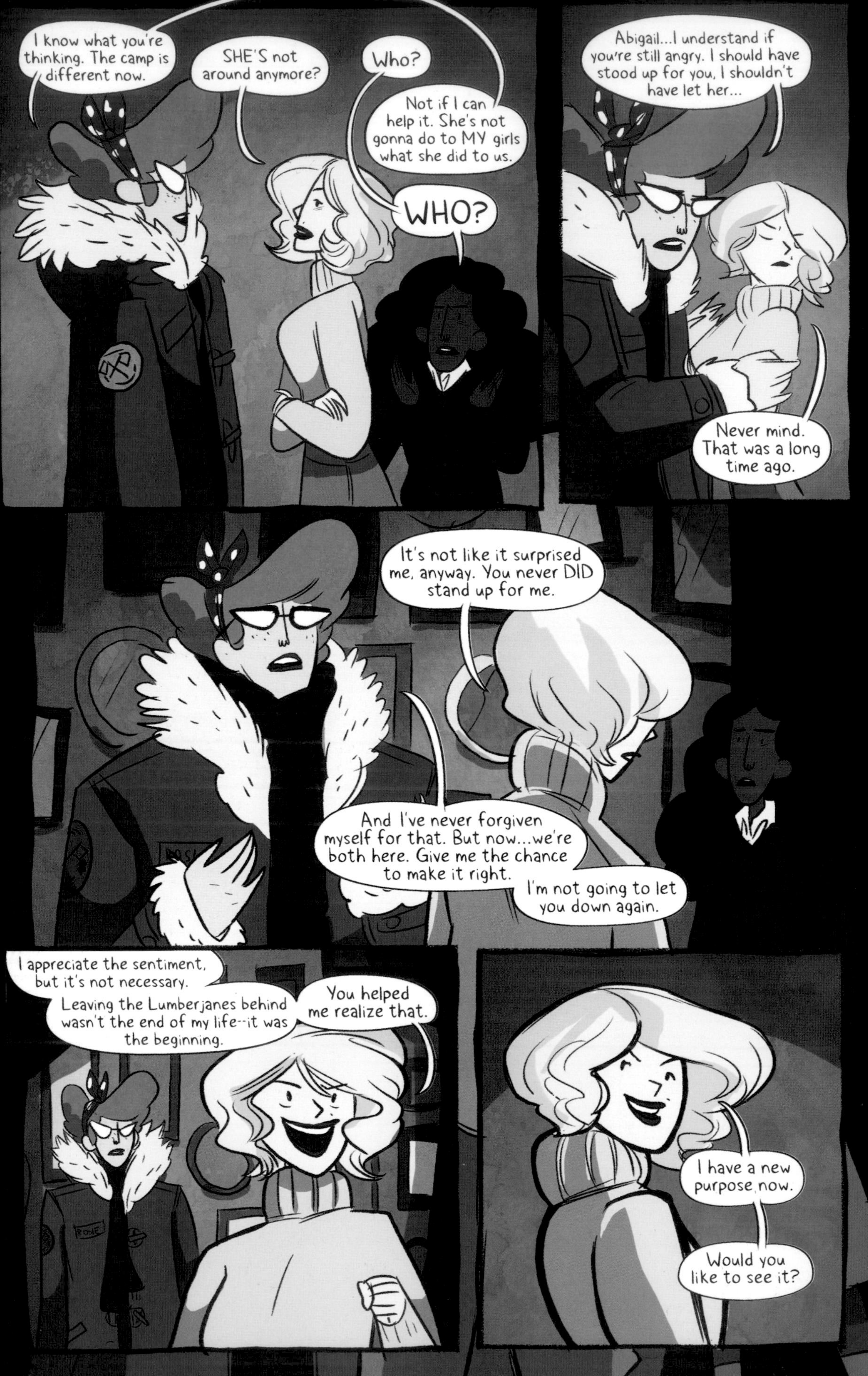
I know what you're thinking. The camp is different now.
SHE'S not around anymore?
Who?
Not if I can help it. She's not gonna do to MY girls what she did to us.
WHO?
Abigail...I understand if you're still angry. I should have stood up for you, I shouldn't have let her...
Never mind. That was a long time ago.
It's not like it surprised me, anyway. You never DID stand up for me.
And I've never forgiven myself for that. But now...we're both here. Give me the chance to make it right.
I'm not going to let you down again.
I appreciate the sentiment, but it's not necessary.
Leaving the Lumberjanes behind wasn't the end of my life--it was the beginning.
You helped me realize that.
I have a new purpose now.
Would you like to see it?

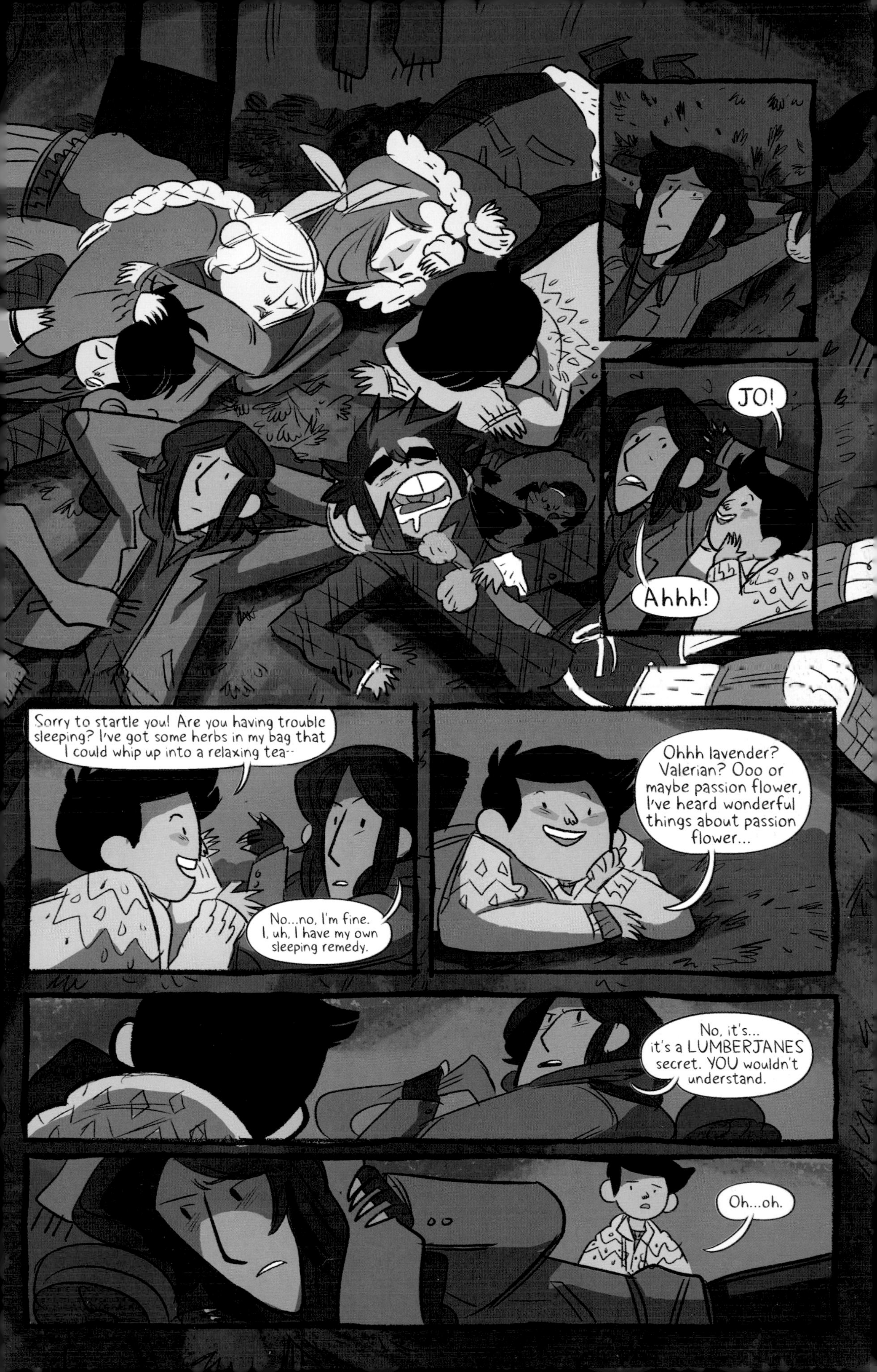
JO!
Ahhh!
Sorry to startle you! Are you having trouble sleeping? I've got some herbs in my bag that I could whip up into a relaxing tea--
No...no, I'm fine. I, uh, I have my own sleeping remedy.
Ohhh lavender? Valerian? Ooo or maybe passion flower, I've heard wonderful things about passion flower...
No, it's... it's a LUMBERJANES secret. YOU wouldn't understand.
Oh...oh.

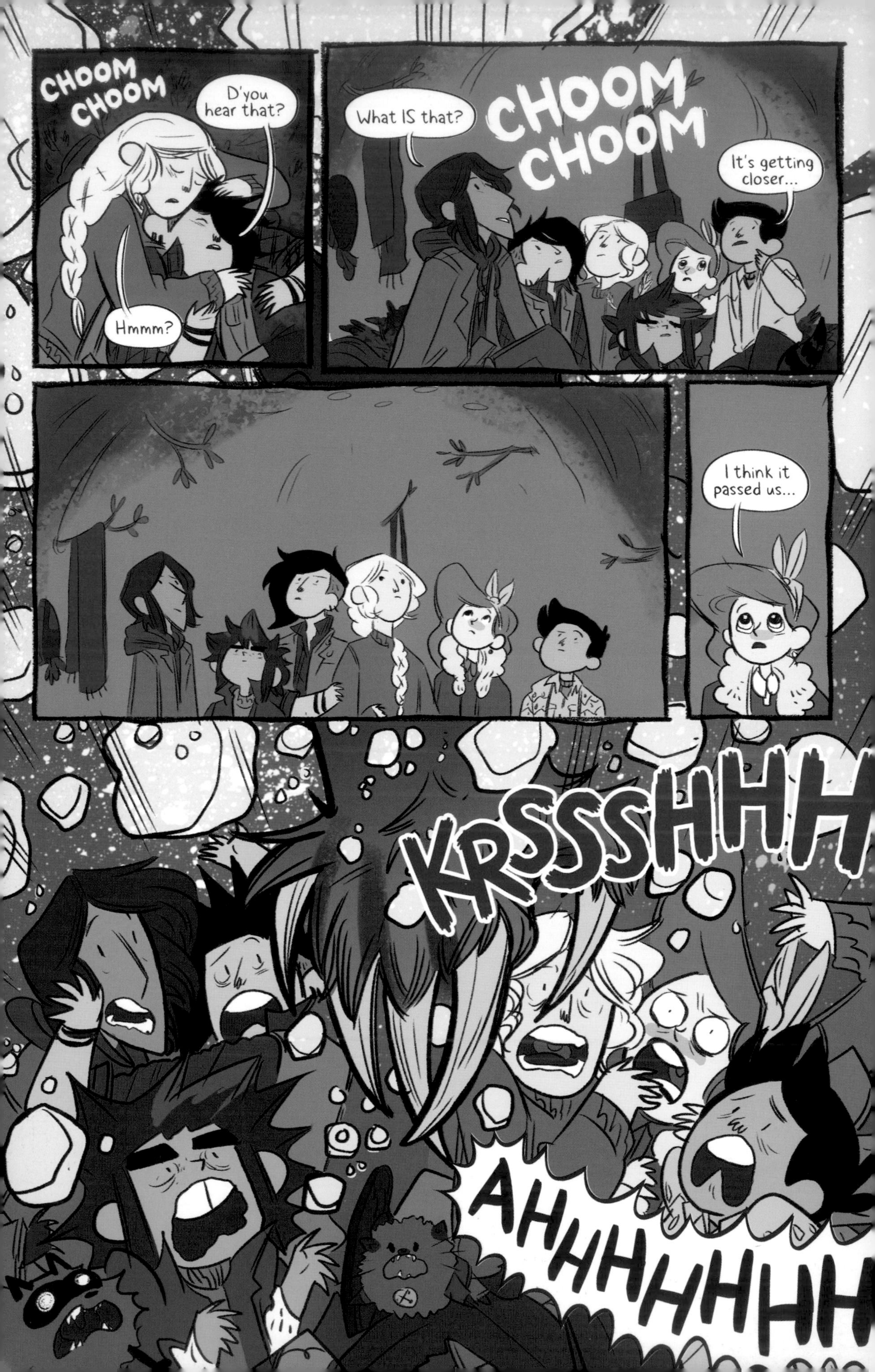
CHOOM CHOOM
D'you hear that?
Hmmm?
What IS that?
CHOOM CHOOM
It's getting closer...
I think it passed us...
KRSSSHHH
AHHHHHHHH

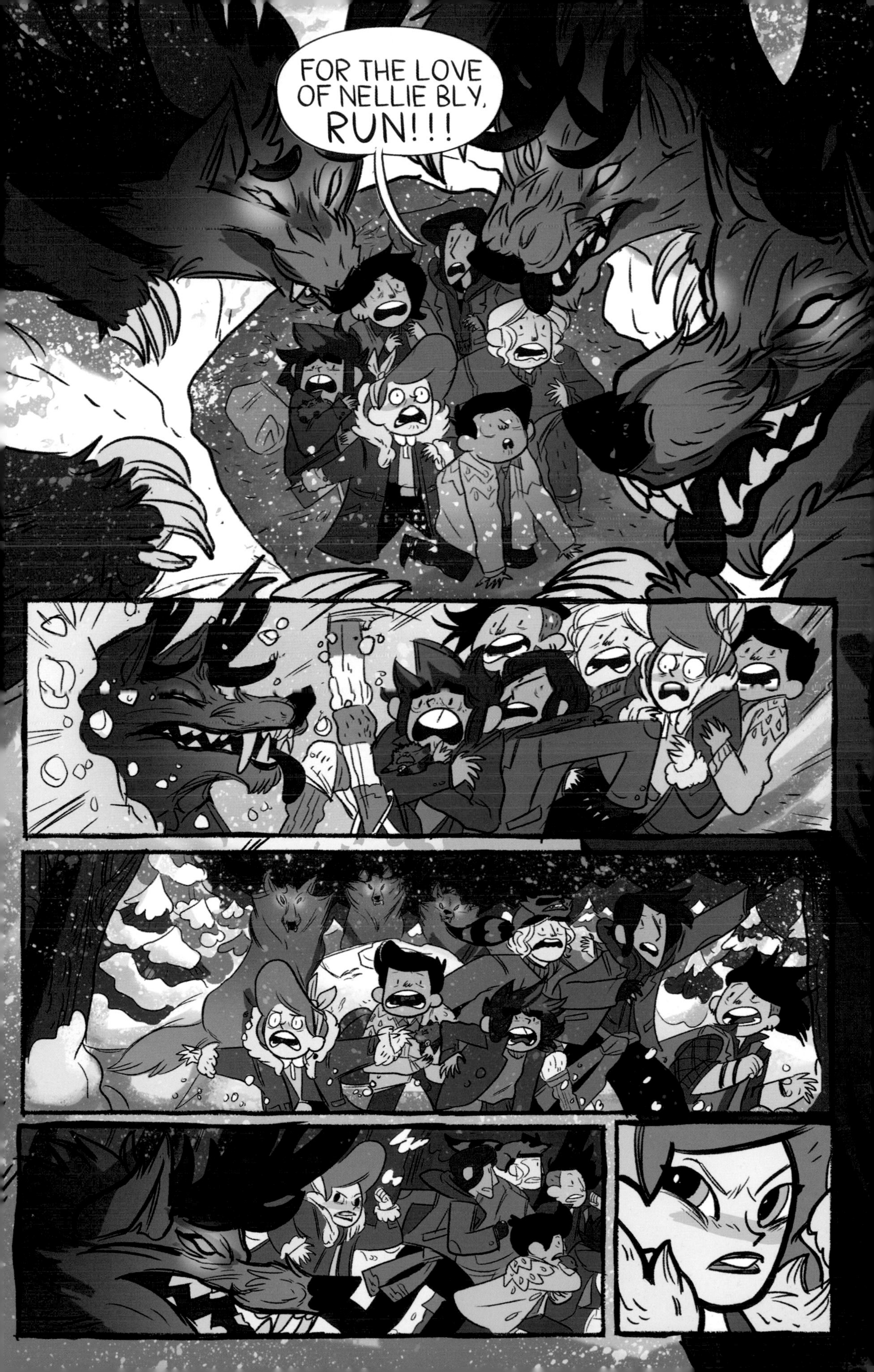
FOR THE LOVE OF NELLIE BLY, RUN!!!

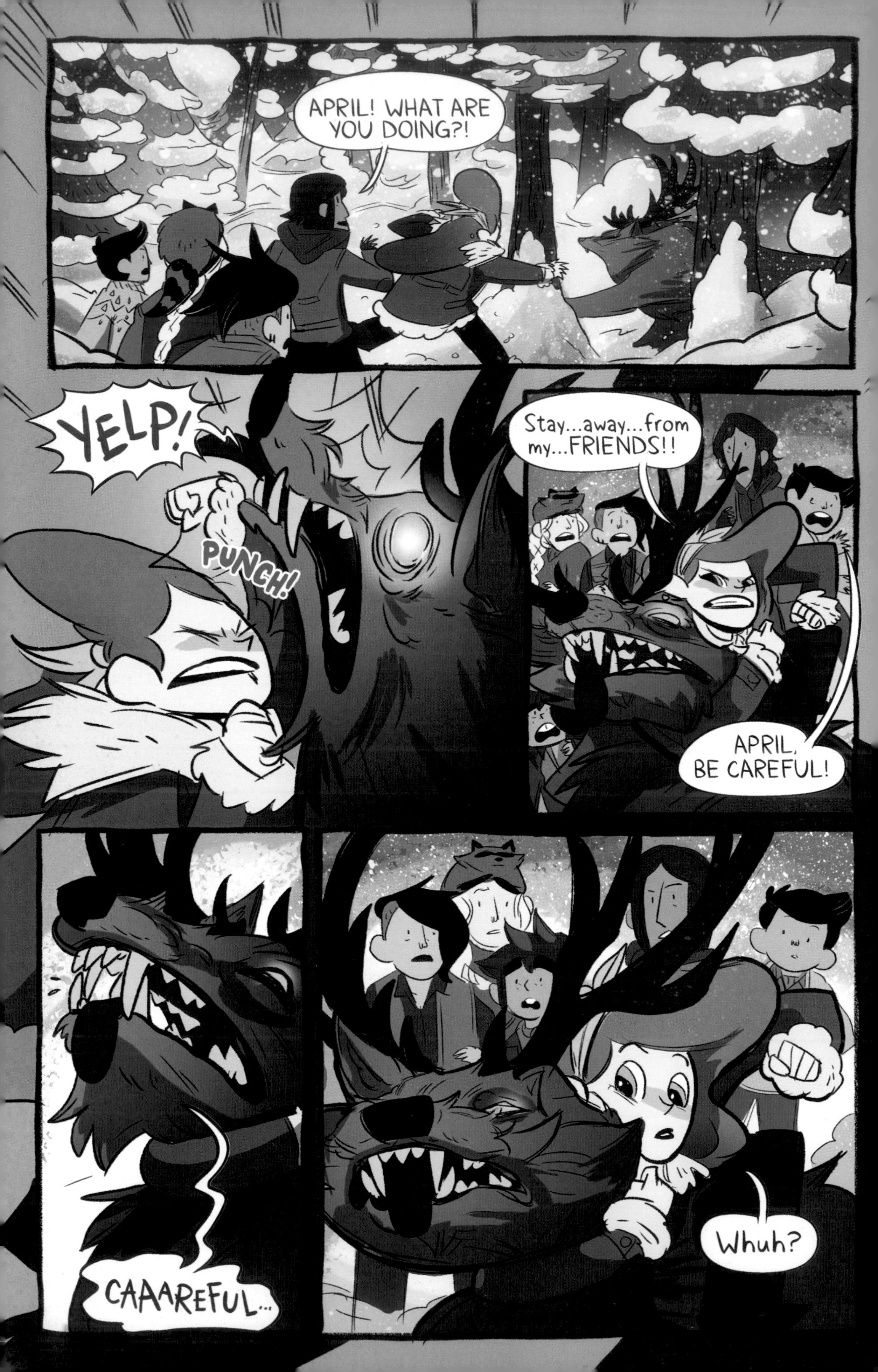
APRIL! WHAT ARE YOU DOING?!
YELP!
PUNCH!
Stay...away...from my...FRIENDS!!
APRIL, BE CAREFUL!
CAAAREFUL...
Whuh?

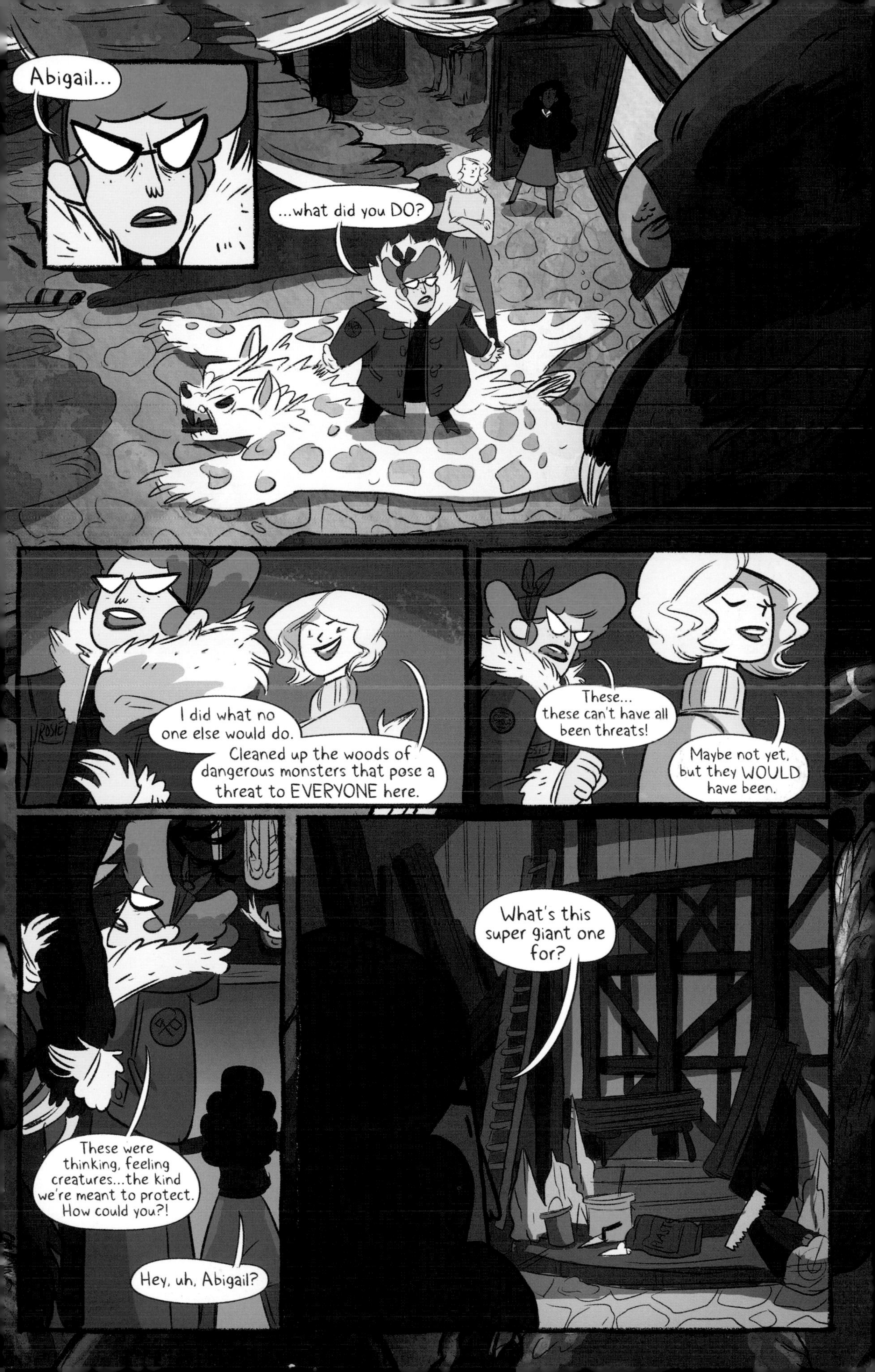
Abigail...
...what did you DO?
I did what no one else would do.
Cleaned up the woods of dangerous monsters that pose a threat to EVERYONE here.
These... these can't have all been threats!
Maybe not yet, but they WOULD have been.
These were thinking, feeling creatures...the kind we're meant to protect. How could you?!
Hey, uh, Abigail?
What's this super giant one for?

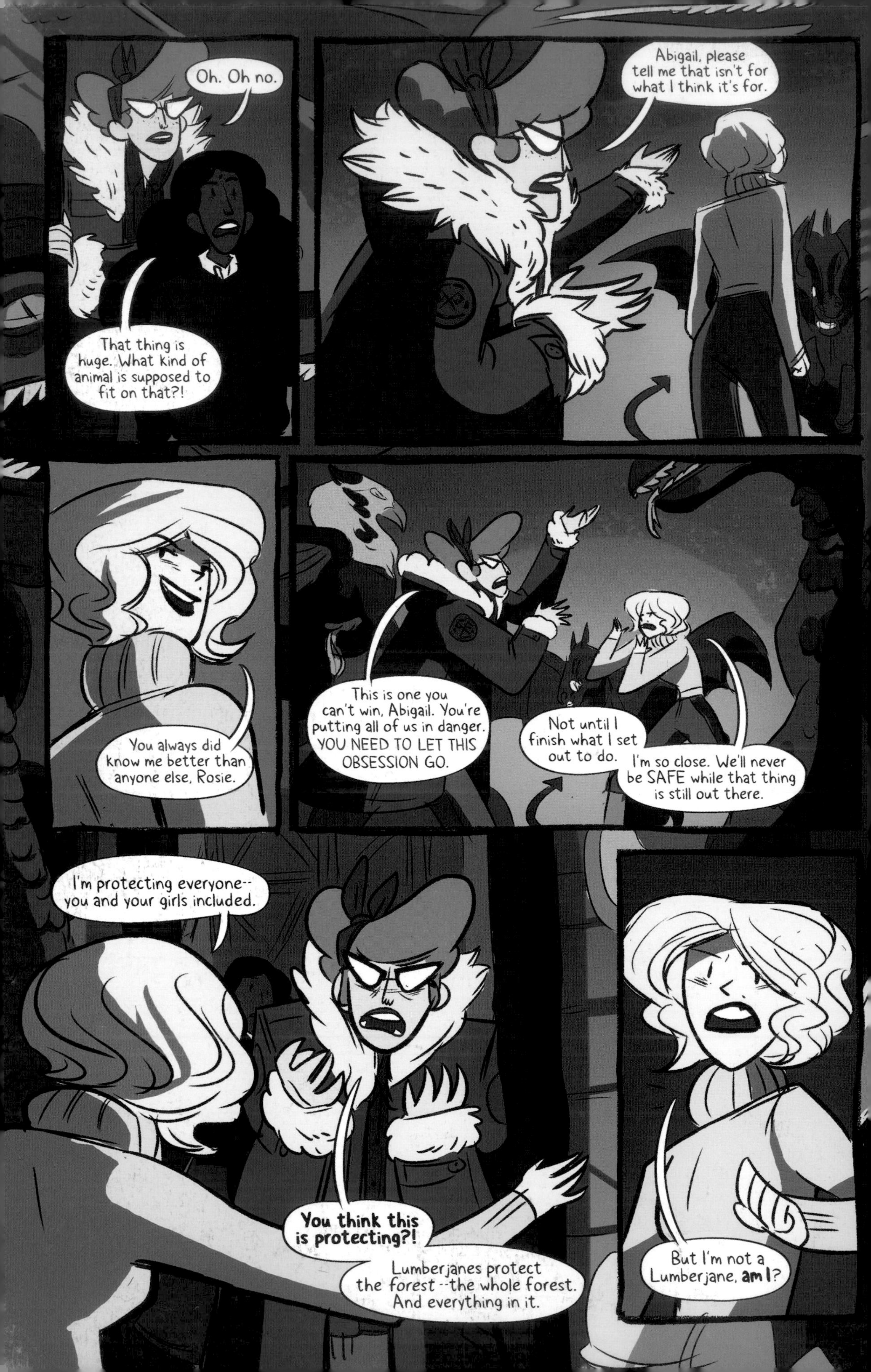

Oh. Oh no.
That thing is huge. What kind of animal is supposed to fit on that?!
Abigail, please tell me that isn't for what I think it's for.
You always did know me better than anyone else, Rosie.
This is one you can't win, Abigail. You're putting all of us in danger. YOU NEED TO LET THIS OBSESSION GO.
Not until I finish what I set out to do.
I'm so close. We'll never be SAFE while that thing is still out there.
I'm protecting everyone-- you and your girls included.
You think this is protecting?!
Lumberjanes protect the *forest*--the whole forest. And everything in it.
But I'm not a Lumberjane, **am I**?

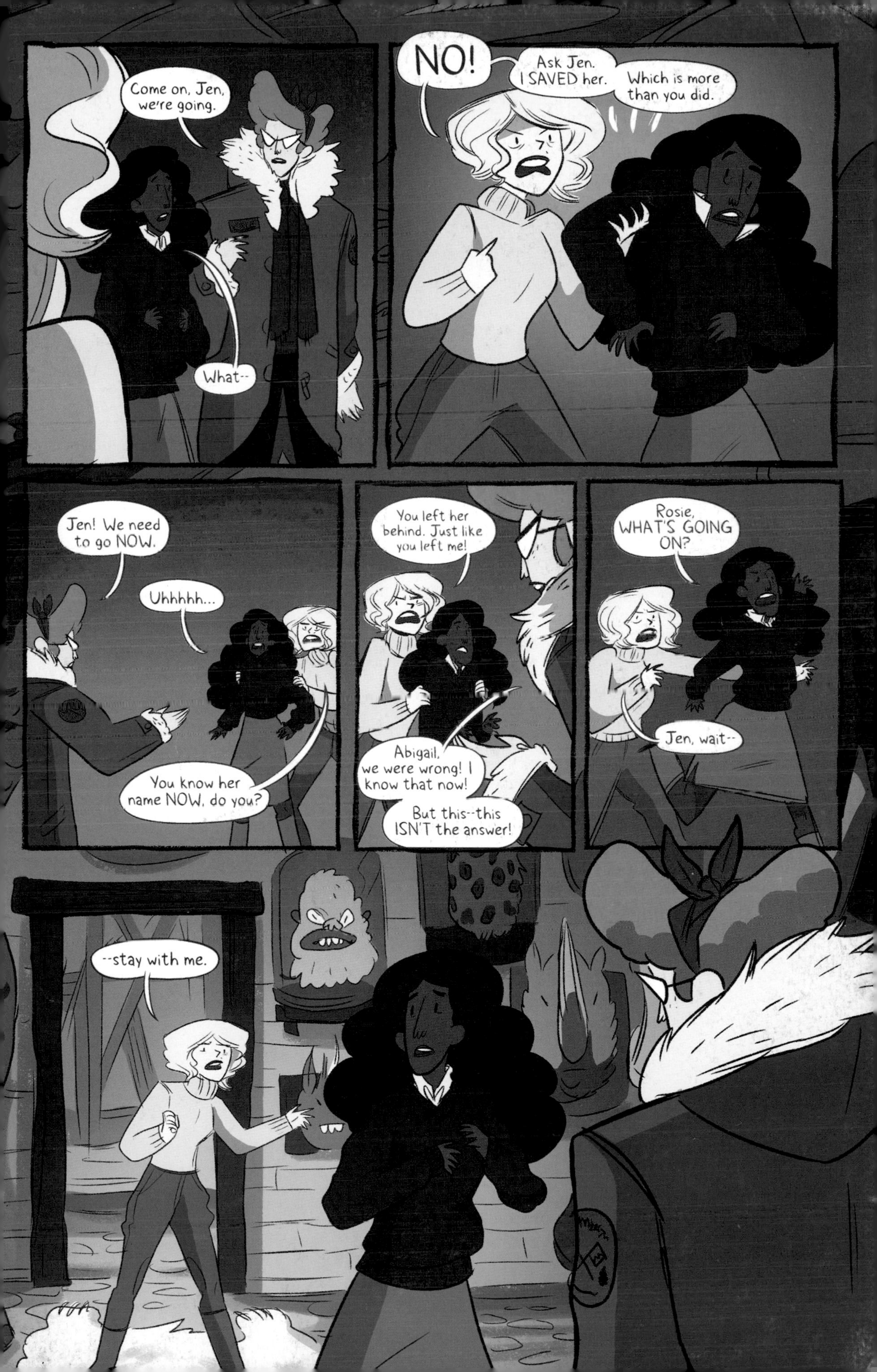
Come on, Jen, we're going.
What--
NO!
Ask Jen. I SAVED her.
Which is more than you did.
Jen! We need to go NOW.
Uhhhhh...
You know her name NOW, do you?
You left her behind. Just like you left me!
Abigail, we were wrong! I know that now!
But this--this ISN'T the answer!
Rosie, WHAT'S GOING ON?
Jen, wait--
--stay with me.

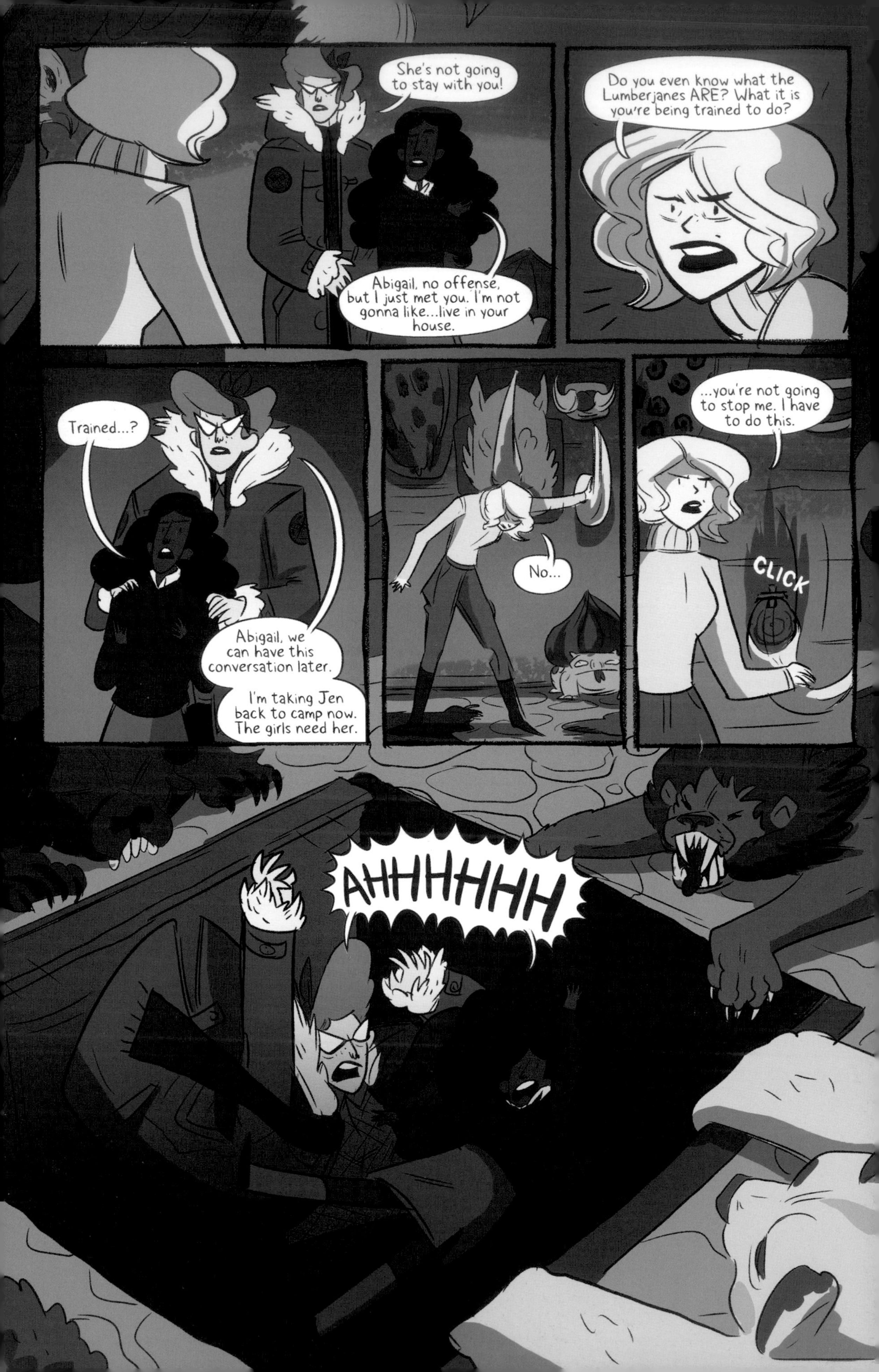

She's not going to stay with you!
Abigail, no offense, but I just met you. I'm not gonna like...live in your house.
Do you even know what the Lumberjanes ARE? What it is you're being trained to do?
Trained...?
Abigail, we can have this conversation later.
I'm taking Jen back to camp now. The girls need her.
No...
...you're not going to stop me. I have to do this.
CLICK
AHHHHHH

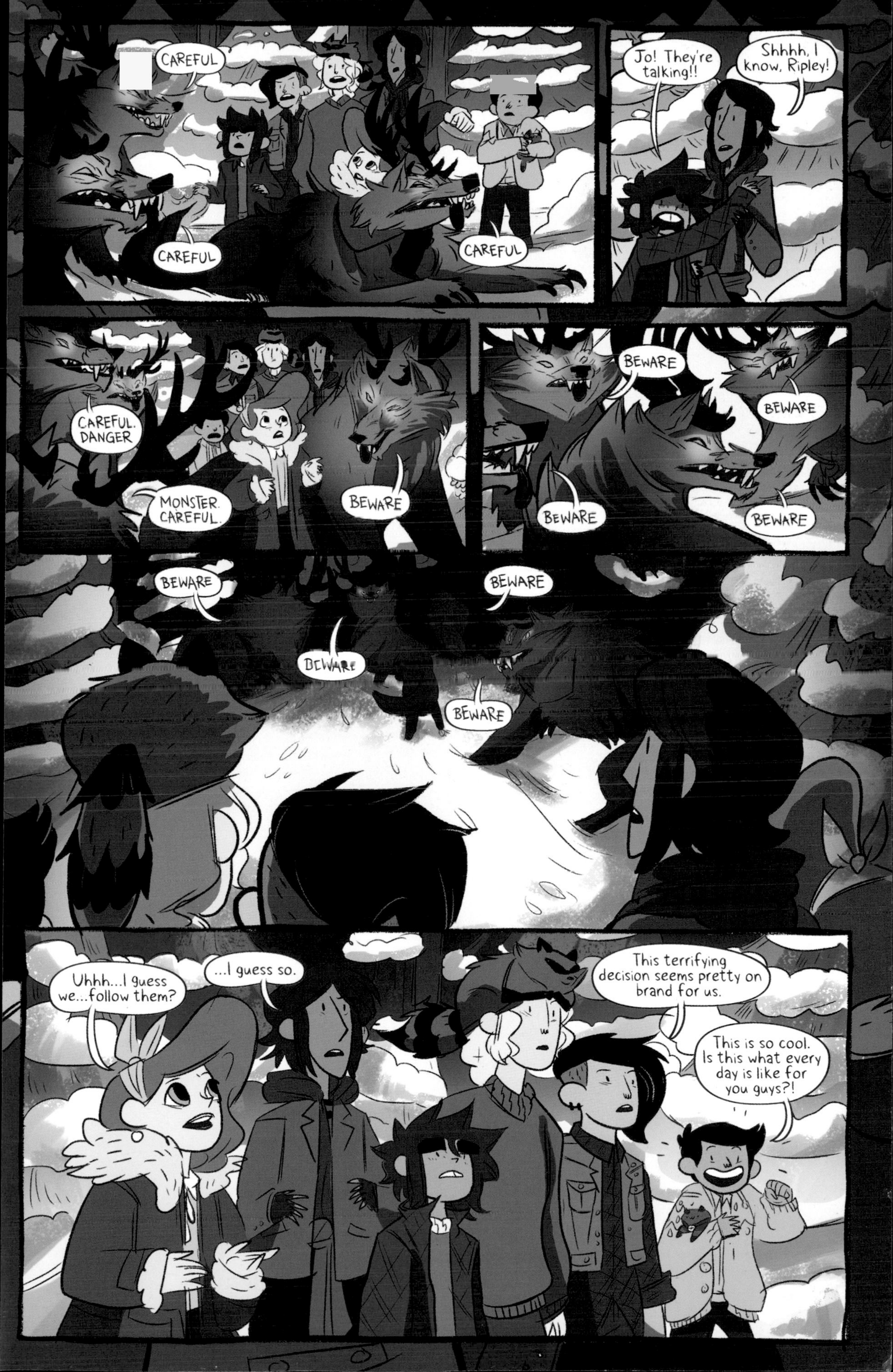
CAREFUL
CAREFUL
CAREFUL
Jo! They're talking!!
Shhhh, I know, Ripley!
CAREFUL. DANGER
MONSTER. CAREFUL.
BEWARE
BEWARE
BEWARE
BEWARE
BEWARE
BEWARE
BEWARE
BEWARE
Uhhh...I guess we...follow them?
...I guess so.
This terrifying decision seems pretty on brand for us.
This is so cool. Is this what every day is like for you guys?!

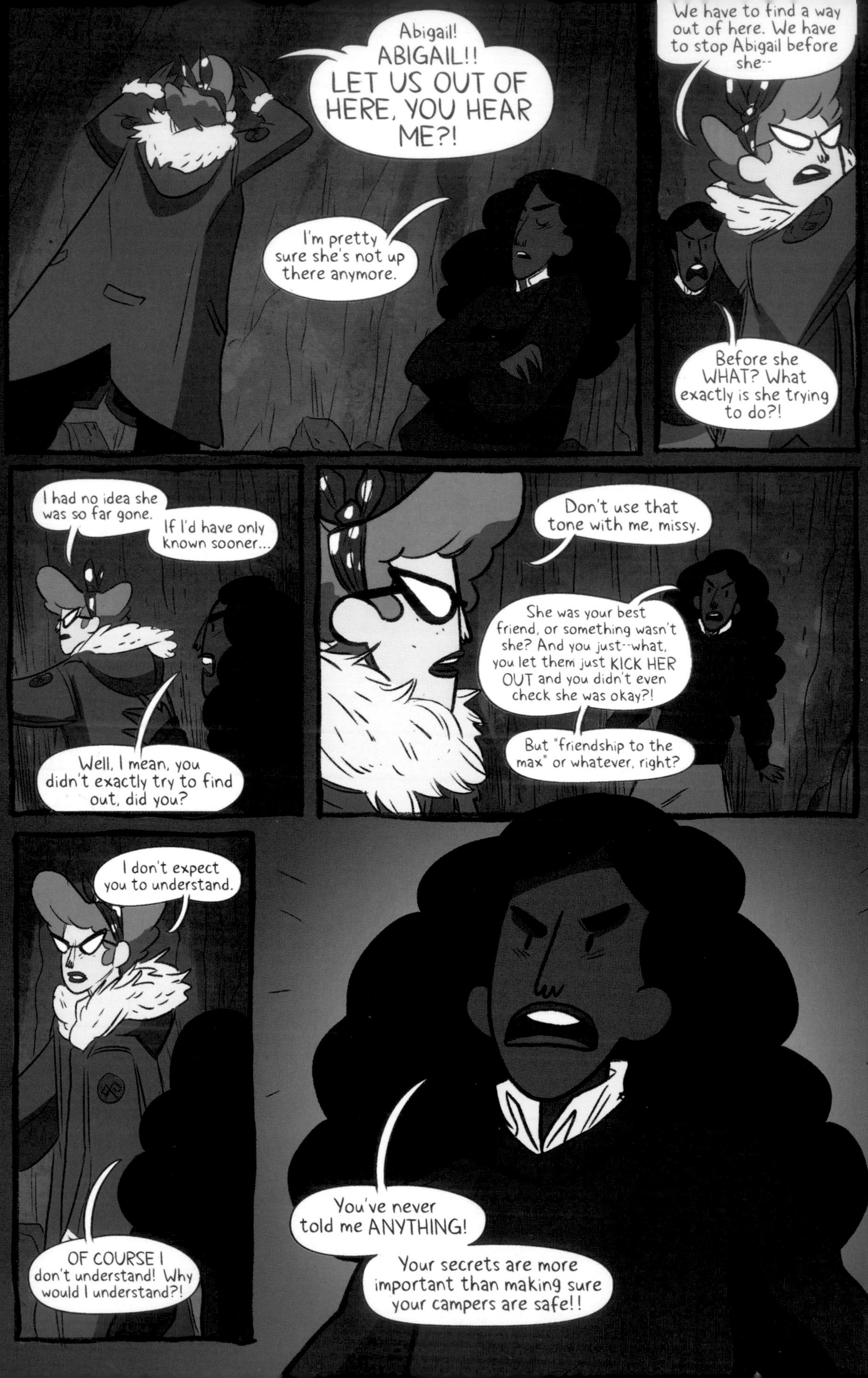
Abigail! ABIGAIL!! LET US OUT OF HERE, YOU HEAR ME?!
I'm pretty sure she's not up there anymore.
We have to find a way out of here. We have to stop Abigail before she--
Before she WHAT? What exactly is she trying to do?!
I had no idea she was so far gone.
If I'd have only known sooner...
Well, I mean, you didn't exactly try to find out, did you?
Don't use that tone with me, missy.
She was your best friend, or something wasn't she? And you just--what, you let them just KICK HER OUT and you didn't even check she was okay?!
But "friendship to the max" or whatever, right?
I don't expect you to understand.
OF COURSE I don't understand! Why would I understand?!
You've never told me ANYTHING!
Your secrets are more important than making sure your campers are safe!!

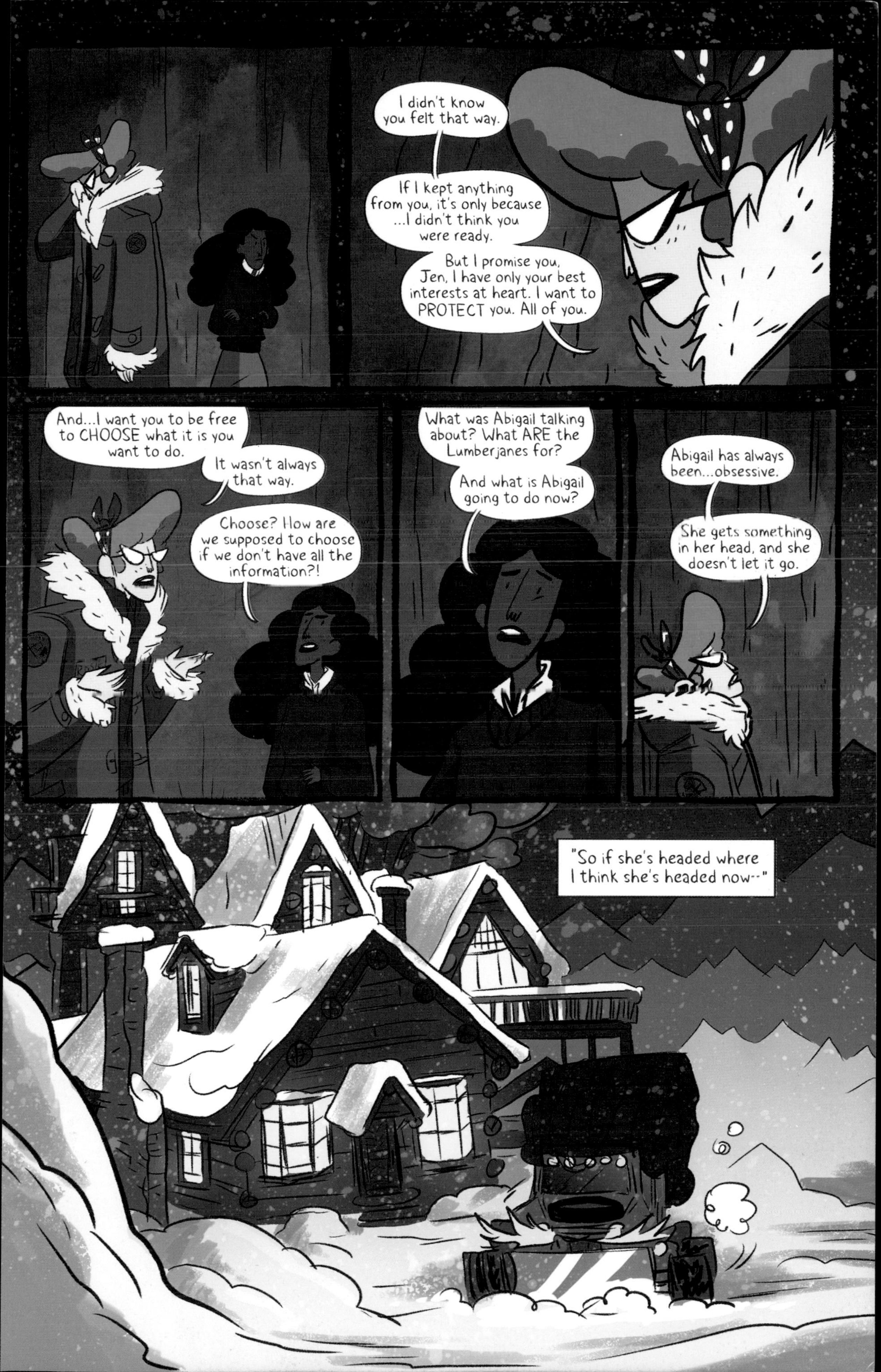

I didn't know you felt that way.
If I kept anything from you, it's only because ...I didn't think you were ready.
But I promise you, Jen, I have only your best interests at heart. I want to PROTECT you. All of you.
And...I want you to be free to CHOOSE what it is you want to do.
It wasn't always that way.
Choose? How are we supposed to choose if we don't have all the information?!
What was Abigail talking about? What ARE the Lumberjanes for?
And what is Abigail going to do now?
Abigail has always been...obsessive.
She gets something in her head, and she doesn't let it go.
"So if she's headed where I think she's headed now--"

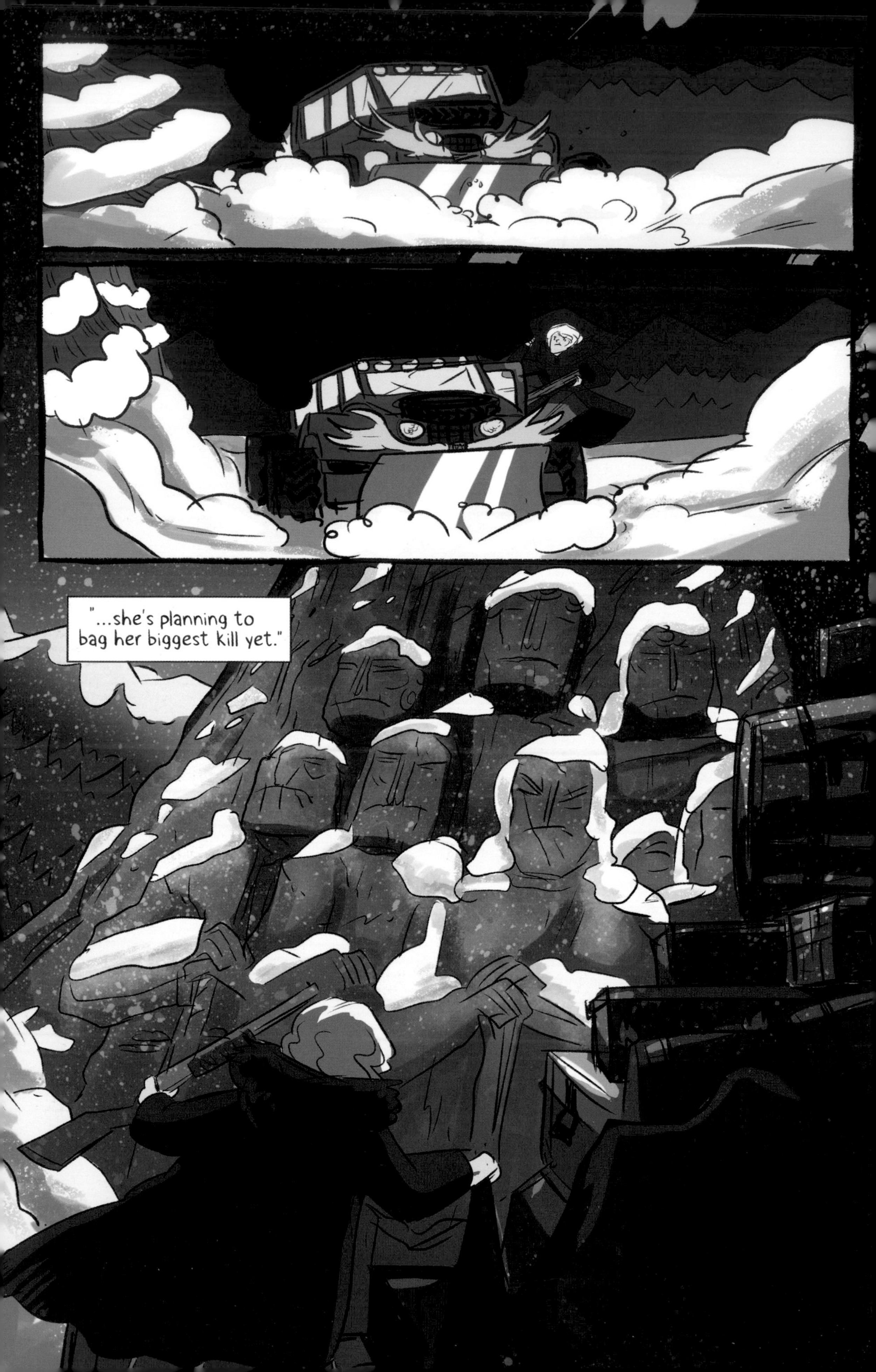
"...she's planning to bag her biggest kill yet."

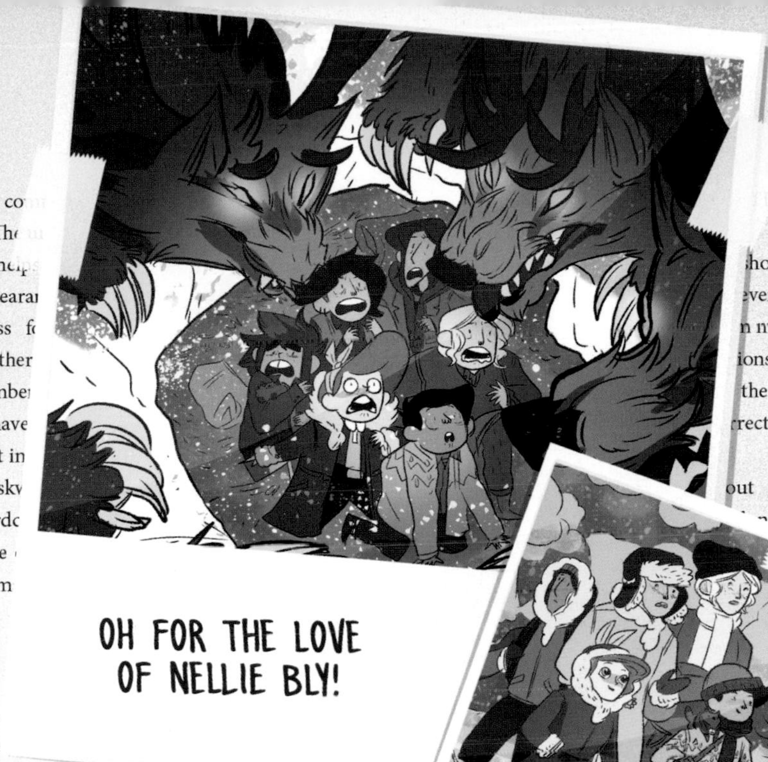
OH FOR THE LOVE
OF NELLIE BLY!

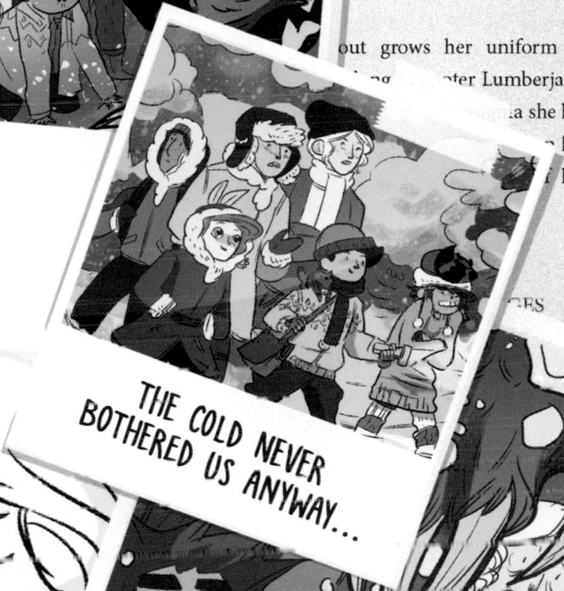
THE COLD NEVER
BOTHERED US ANYWAY...

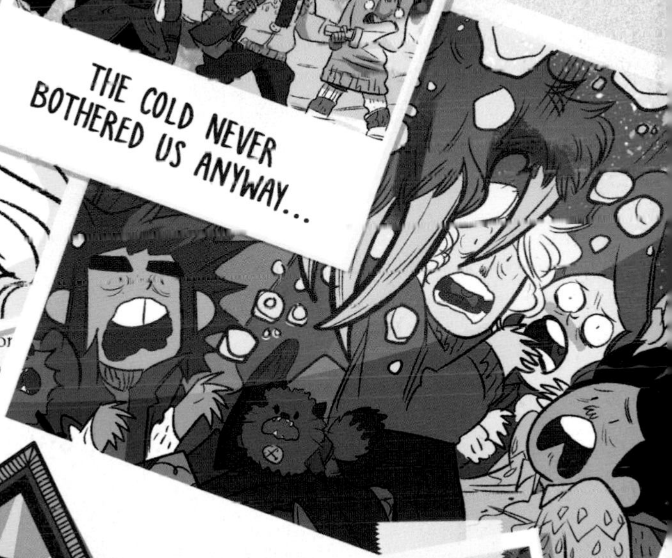

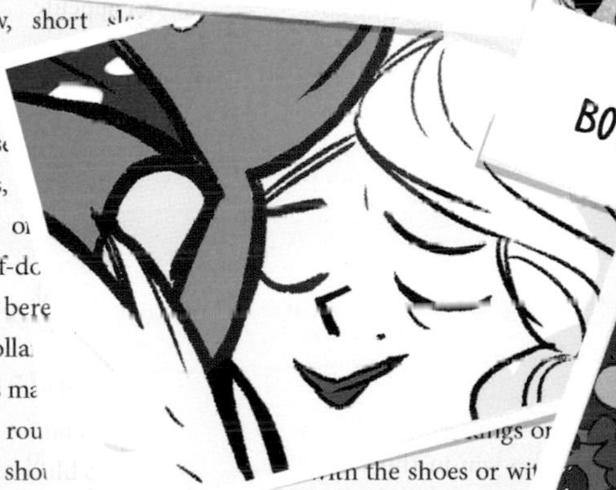

will co

The u

It helps

appearan

dress fo

Further

Lumbe

to have

part in

Thiskw

Hardc

have

them

...HE UNIFORM

...should be worn at camp
...events when Lumberjanes
...n may also be worn at other
...ions. It should be worn as a
...the uniform dress with
...rrect shoes, and stocking or

...out grows her uniform or
...ter Lumberjane.
...a she has
...her
...her

The
yellow, short sl
emb
the w
choos
slacks,
made o
out-of-do
green bere
the colla
Shoes ma
heels, rou ... ings or
socks shou ... with the shoes or wi
the uniform. Ne... es, bracelets, or other jewelry do
belong with a Lumberjane uniform.

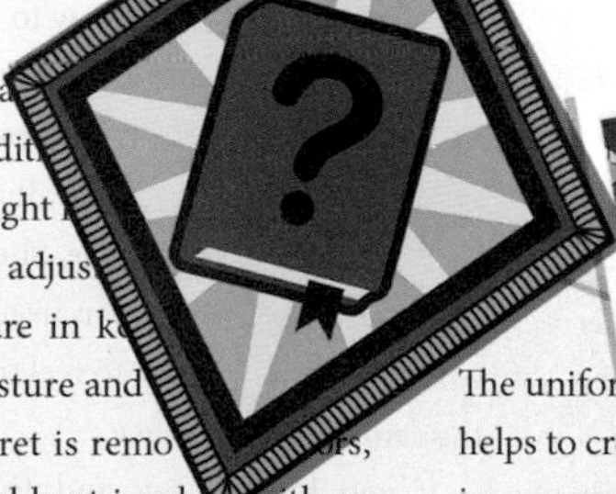

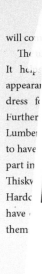

HOW TO WEAR THE UNIFO...

To look well in a uniform dema... uniform be kept in good conditi... pressed. See that the skirt is the right ... height and build, that the belt is adjus... that your shoes and stockings are in k... uniform, that you watch your posture and ... with dignity and grace. If the beret is remo... rs, be sure that your hair is neat and kept in pla... with an insonspicuous clip or ribbon. When you wear a Lumberjane uniform you are identified as a member of this organization and you should be doubly careful to conduct yourself in a way that will show everyone that courtesy and thoughtfullness are part of being a Lumberjane. People are likely to judge a whole nation by the selfishness of a few individuals, to criticize a whole family because of the misconduct of one member, and to feel unkindly toward and organization because of the

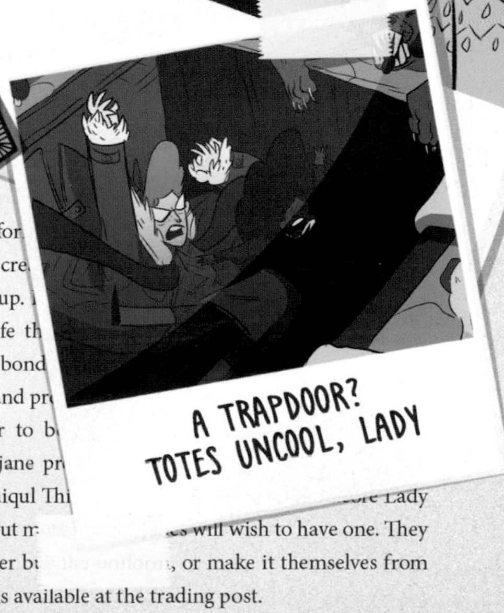
A TRAPDOOR?
TOTES UNCOOL, LADY

The unifor...
helps to cre...
in a group. ...
active life th...
another bond...
future, and pr...
in order to b...
Lumberjane pr...
Penniquiqul Thi... ...ore Lady
Types, but m... ...s will wish to have one. They
can either bu... ...uniform, or make it themselves from
materials available at the trading post.

LUMBERJANES FIELD MANUAL

CHAPTER FIFTEEN

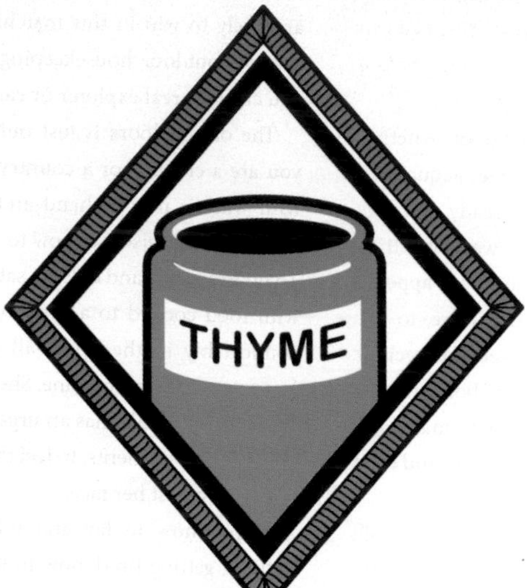
THYME

Lumberjanes "Cooking" Program Field

OUT OF THYME BADGE

"Sometimes expediency is necessary."

Timeliness is next to godliness, or so the saying goes. For a Lumberjane, timeliness is an essential part of everyday life. There are many things that a Lumberjane will learn while at camp, she will learn how to care for the wildlife around her and how to use it to better her life and those around her. She will learn the importance of social customs and manners while at the same time enjoying the chance to break the boundaries that society might place upon her. And above all else, a Lumberjane will learn the importance of being on time.

The *Out of Thyme* badge is not just another badge that helps a Lumberjane understand the importance of seasoning, but it is a badge that helps teach the importance of knowing what time it is and constantly using that to her advantage. Need to slow cook a beef brisket, carve additional chairs for your guests and feed the bees that your neighbor left in your care while they went on their annual Everest hike? Understanding how to use time is the key solution to ensuring that a Lumberjane is not only able to get all of that done, but is able to do it with enough time to spare that they'll be able to handle anything else life might throw her way.

To obtain the *Out of Thyme* badge, a Lumberjanes must show her understanding of spices in the kitchen. On top of that, a Lumberjane must also prove her time management skills through various timed courses. On top of that, she will have to complete several balanced meals in which she will have to feed her cabin. If the cabin decides to earn this badge as a team, which is encouraged, then the cabin will be asked to serve a meal for the entire class. They will have to gather the ingredients themselves, and with the help of their counselor, they will use the kitchens. It is also important that the Lumberjane cleans up after themselves as they

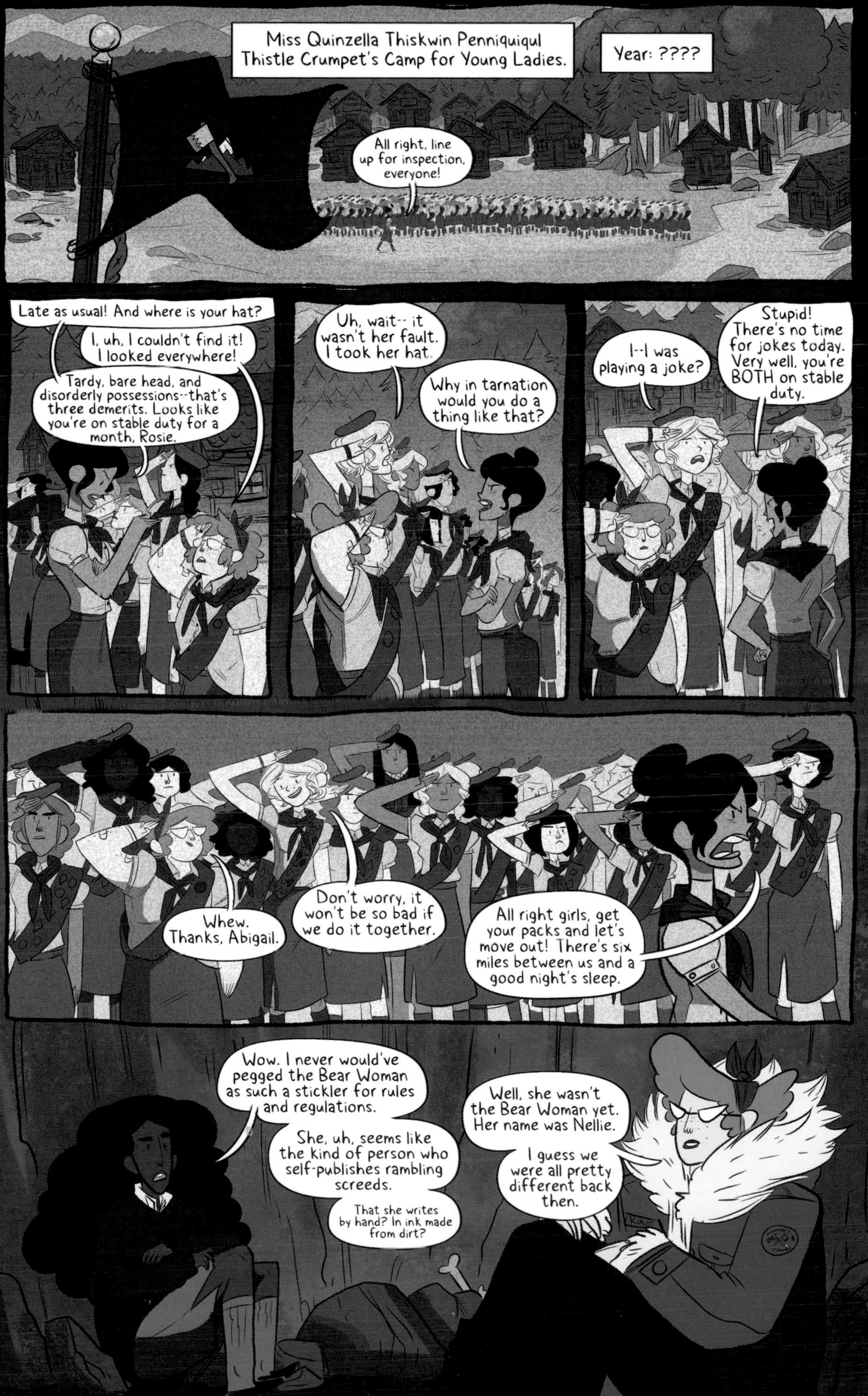
Miss Quinzella Thiskwin Penniquiqul Thistle Crumpet's Camp for Young Ladies.
Year: ????
All right, line up for inspection, everyone!
Late as usual! And where is your hat?
I, uh, I couldn't find it! I looked everywhere!
Tardy, bare head, and disorderly possessions--that's three demerits. Looks like you're on stable duty for a month, Rosie.
Uh, wait-- it wasn't her fault. I took her hat.
Why in tarnation would you do a thing like that?
I--I was playing a joke?
Stupid! There's no time for jokes today. Very well, you're BOTH on stable duty.
Whew. Thanks, Abigail.
Don't worry, it won't be so bad if we do it together.
All right girls, get your packs and let's move out! There's six miles between us and a good night's sleep.
Wow. I never would've pegged the Bear Woman as such a stickler for rules and regulations.
She, uh, seems like the kind of person who self-publishes rambling screeds.
That she writes by hand? In ink made from dirt?
Well, she wasn't the Bear Woman yet. Her name was Nellie.
I guess we were all pretty different back then.

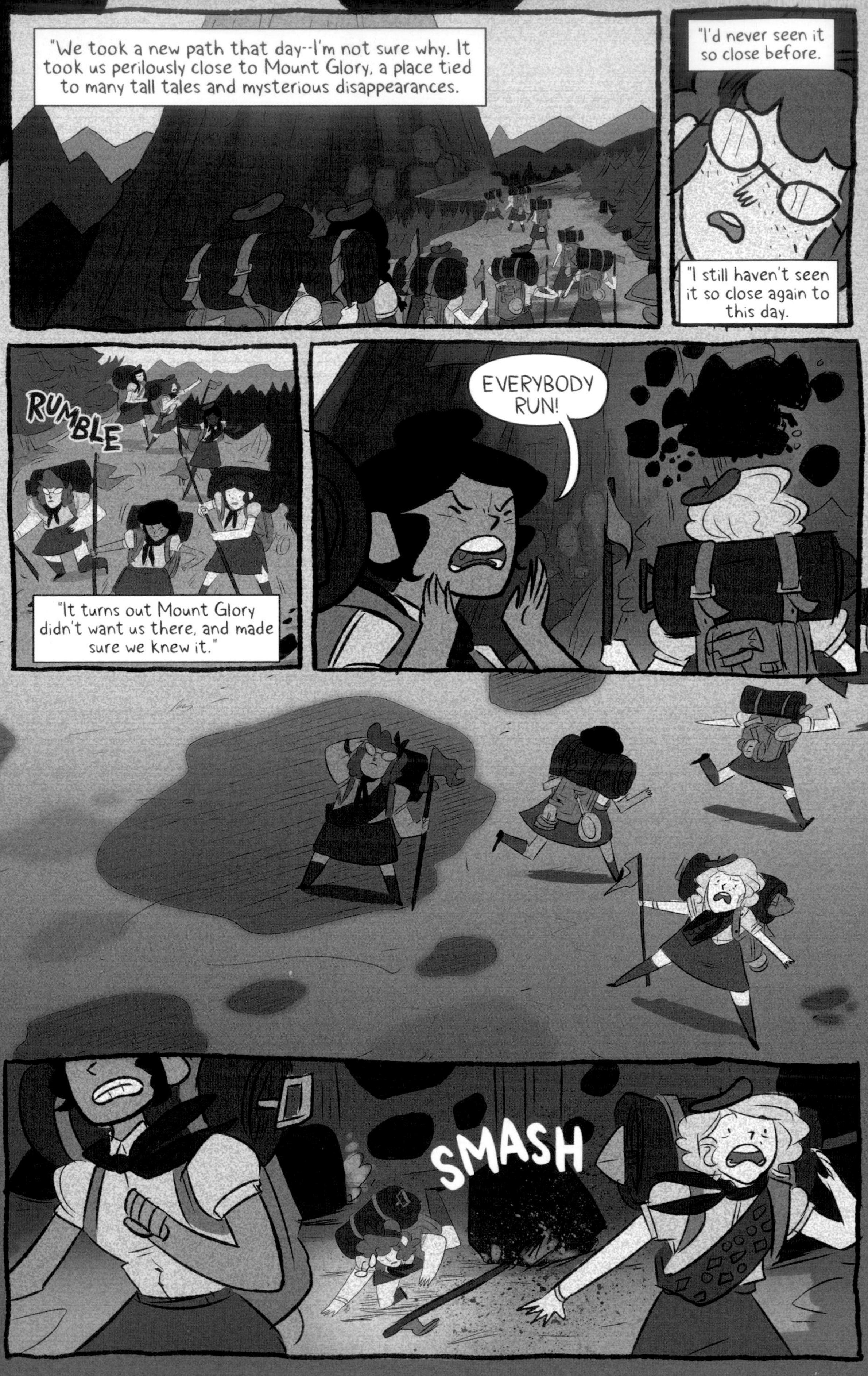
"We took a new path that day--I'm not sure why. It took us perilously close to Mount Glory, a place tied to many tall tales and mysterious disappearances.
"I'd never seen it so close before.
"I still haven't seen it so close again to this day.
RUMBLE
"It turns out Mount Glory didn't want us there, and made sure we knew it."
EVERYBODY RUN!
SMASH

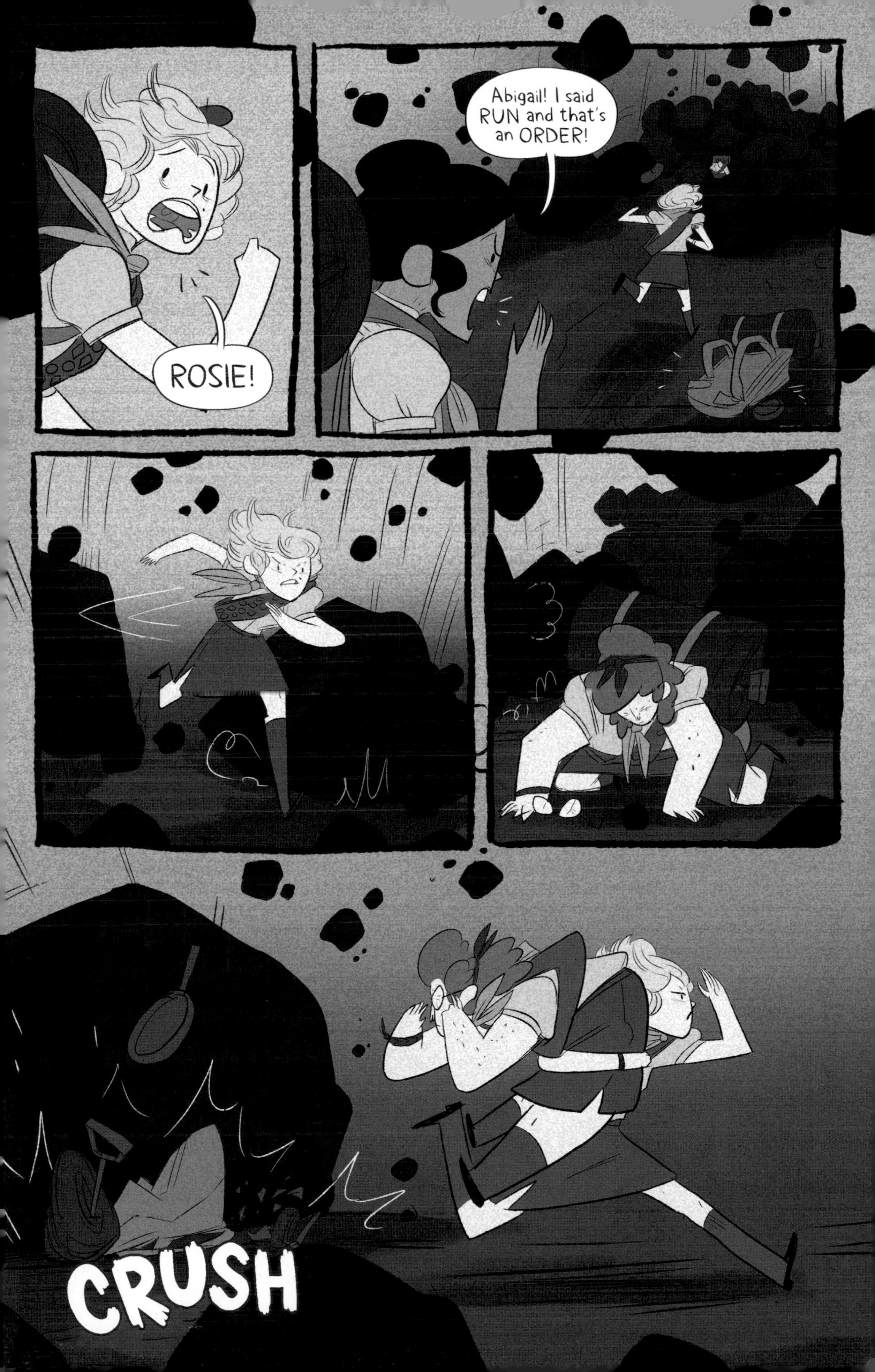
ROSIE!
Abigail! I said RUN and that's an ORDER!
CRUSH

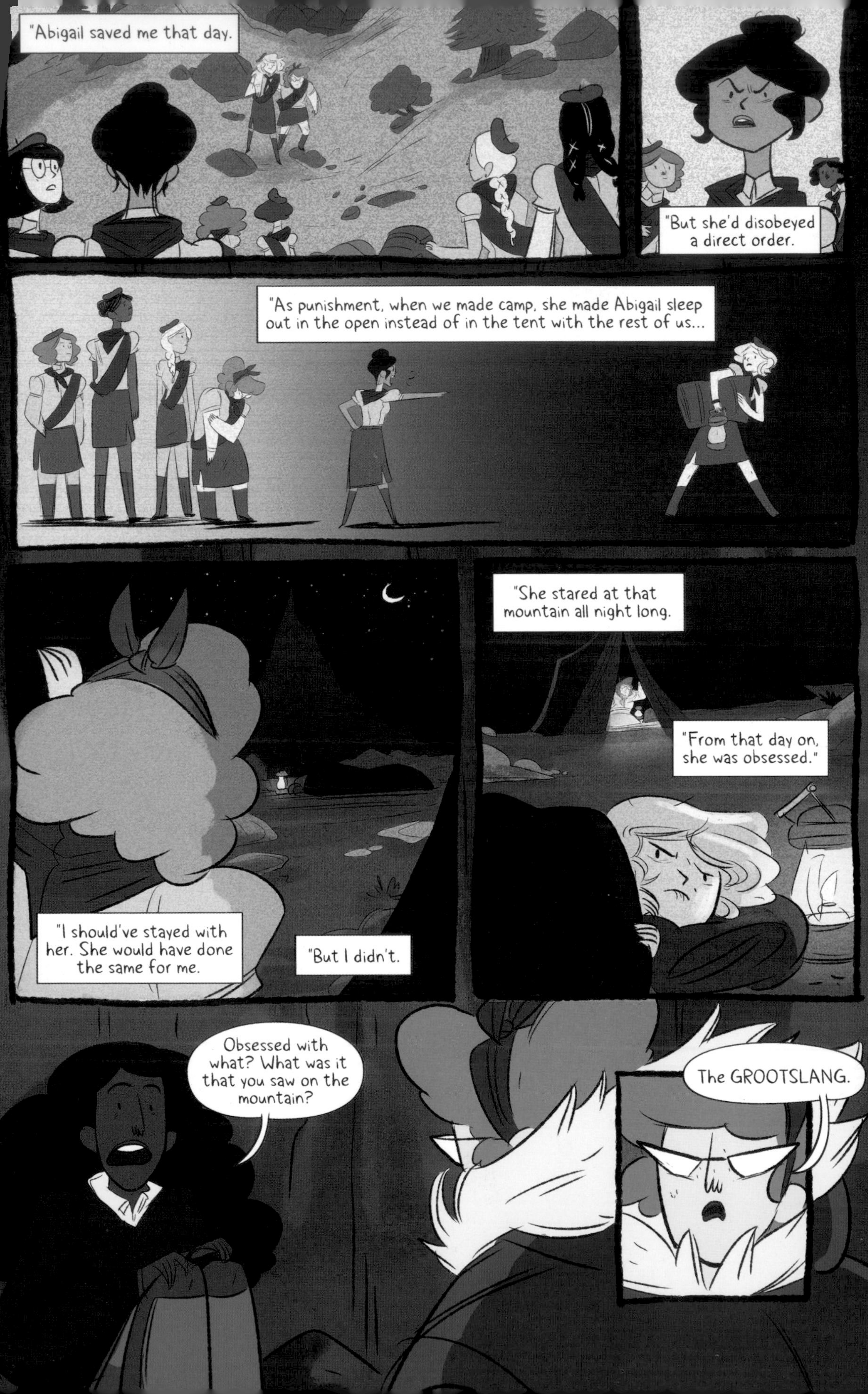
"Abigail saved me that day.
"But she'd disobeyed a direct order.
"As punishment, when we made camp, she made Abigail sleep out in the open instead of in the tent with the rest of us...
"I should've stayed with her. She would have done the same for me.
"But I didn't.
"She stared at that mountain all night long.
"From that day on, she was obsessed."
Obsessed with what? What was it that you saw on the mountain?
The GROOTSLANG.

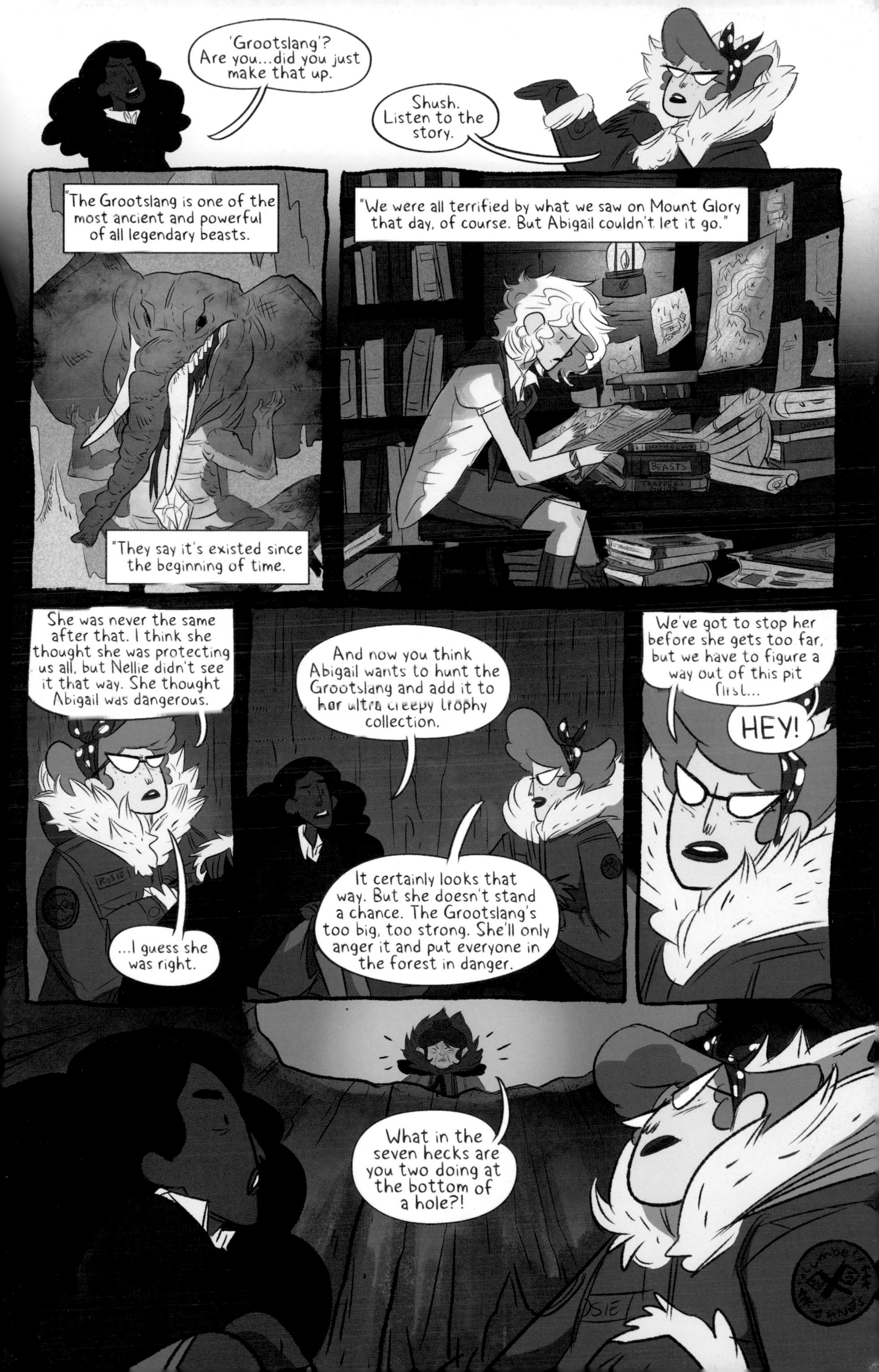
'Grootslang'? Are you...did you just make that up.
Shush. Listen to the story.
"The Grootslang is one of the most ancient and powerful of all legendary beasts.
"They say it's existed since the beginning of time.
"We were all terrified by what we saw on Mount Glory that day, of course. But Abigail couldn't let it go."
MYTHOLOGY
BEASTS
TRAPPERS GUIDE
She was never the same after that. I think she thought she was protecting us all, but Nellie didn't see it that way. She thought Abigail was dangerous.
ROSIE
...I guess she was right.
And now you think Abigail wants to hunt the Grootslang and add it to her ultra creepy trophy collection.
It certainly looks that way. But she doesn't stand a chance. The Grootslang's too big, too strong. She'll only anger it and put everyone in the forest in danger.
We've got to stop her before she gets too far, but we have to figure a way out of this pit first...
HEY!
What in the seven hecks are you two doing at the bottom of a hole?!

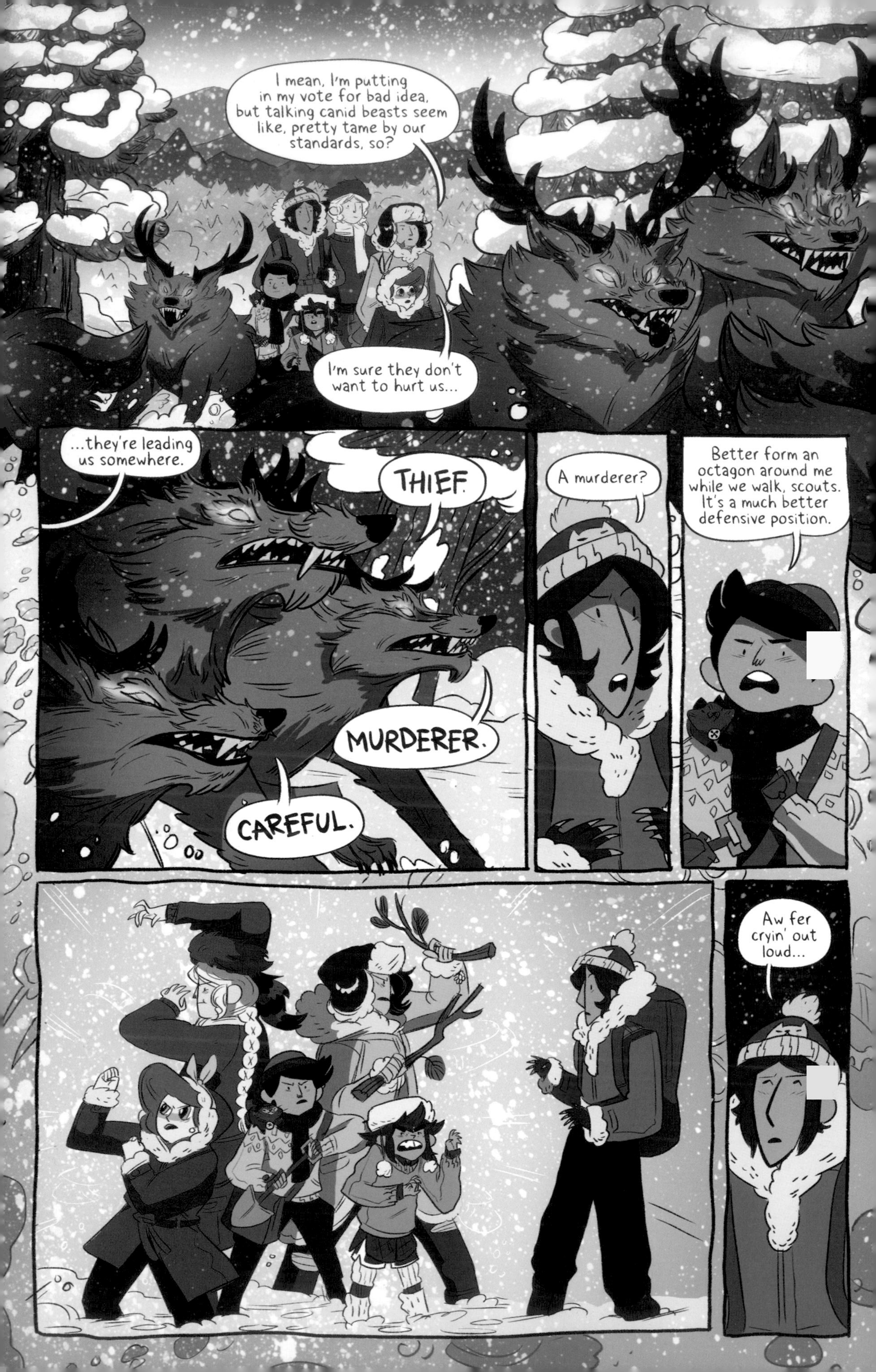
I mean, I'm putting in my vote for bad idea, but talking canid beasts seem like, pretty tame by our standards, so?
I'm sure they don't want to hurt us...
...they're leading us somewhere.
THIEF.
MURDERER.
CAREFUL.
A murderer?
Better form an octagon around me while we walk, scouts. It's a much better defensive position.
Aw fer cryin' out loud...

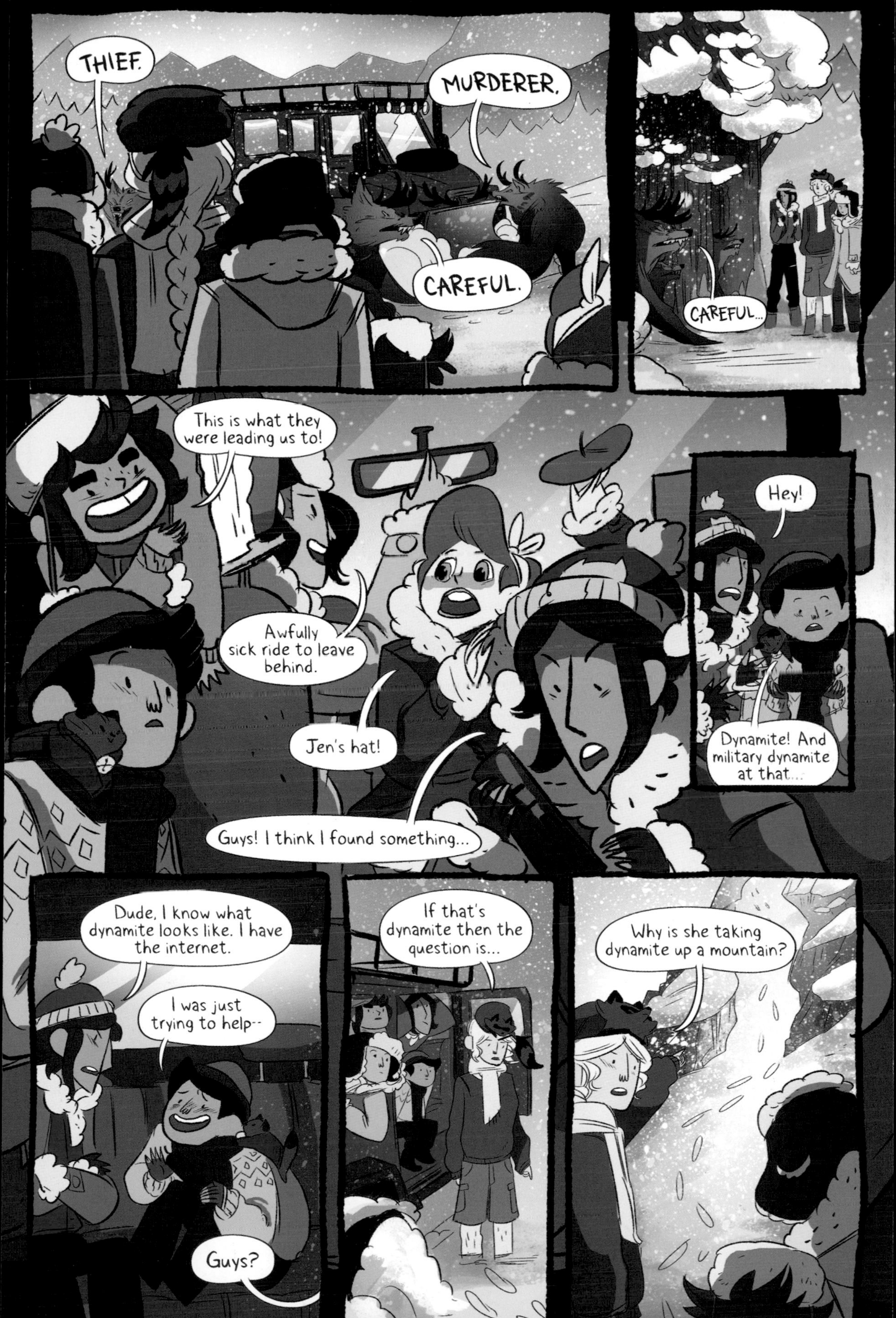
THIEF.
MURDERER.
CAREFUL.
CAREFUL...
This is what they were leading us to!
Awfully sick ride to leave behind.
Jen's hat!
Guys! I think I found something...
Hey!
Dynamite! And military dynamite at that...
Dude, I know what dynamite looks like. I have the internet.
I was just trying to help--
Guys?
If that's dynamite then the question is...
Why is she taking dynamite up a mountain?

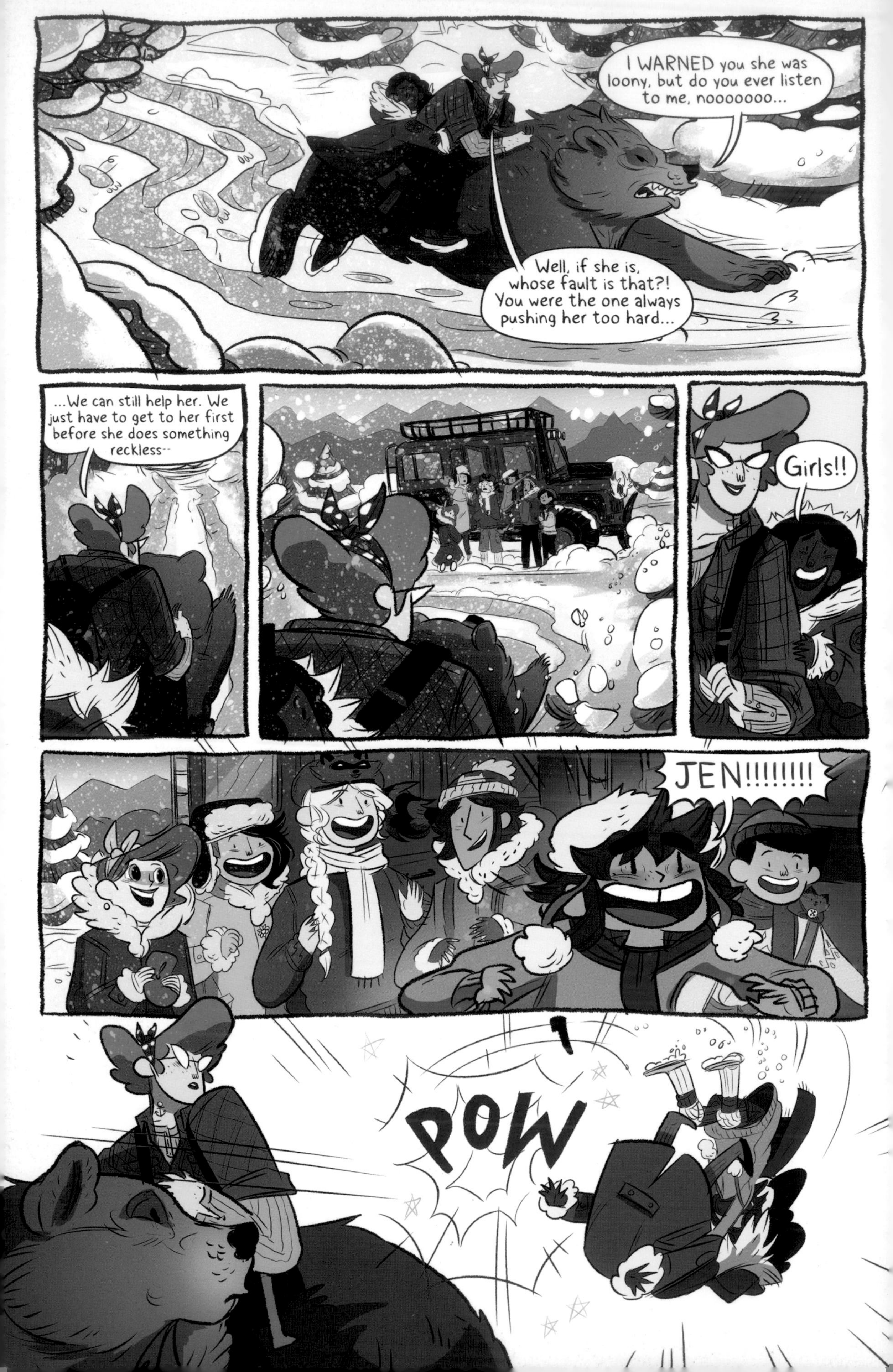

I WARNED you she was loony, but do you ever listen to me, noooooo...
Well, if she is, whose fault is that?! You were the one always pushing her too hard...
...We can still help her. We just have to get to her first before she does something reckless--
Girls!!
JEN!!!!!!!!!
POW

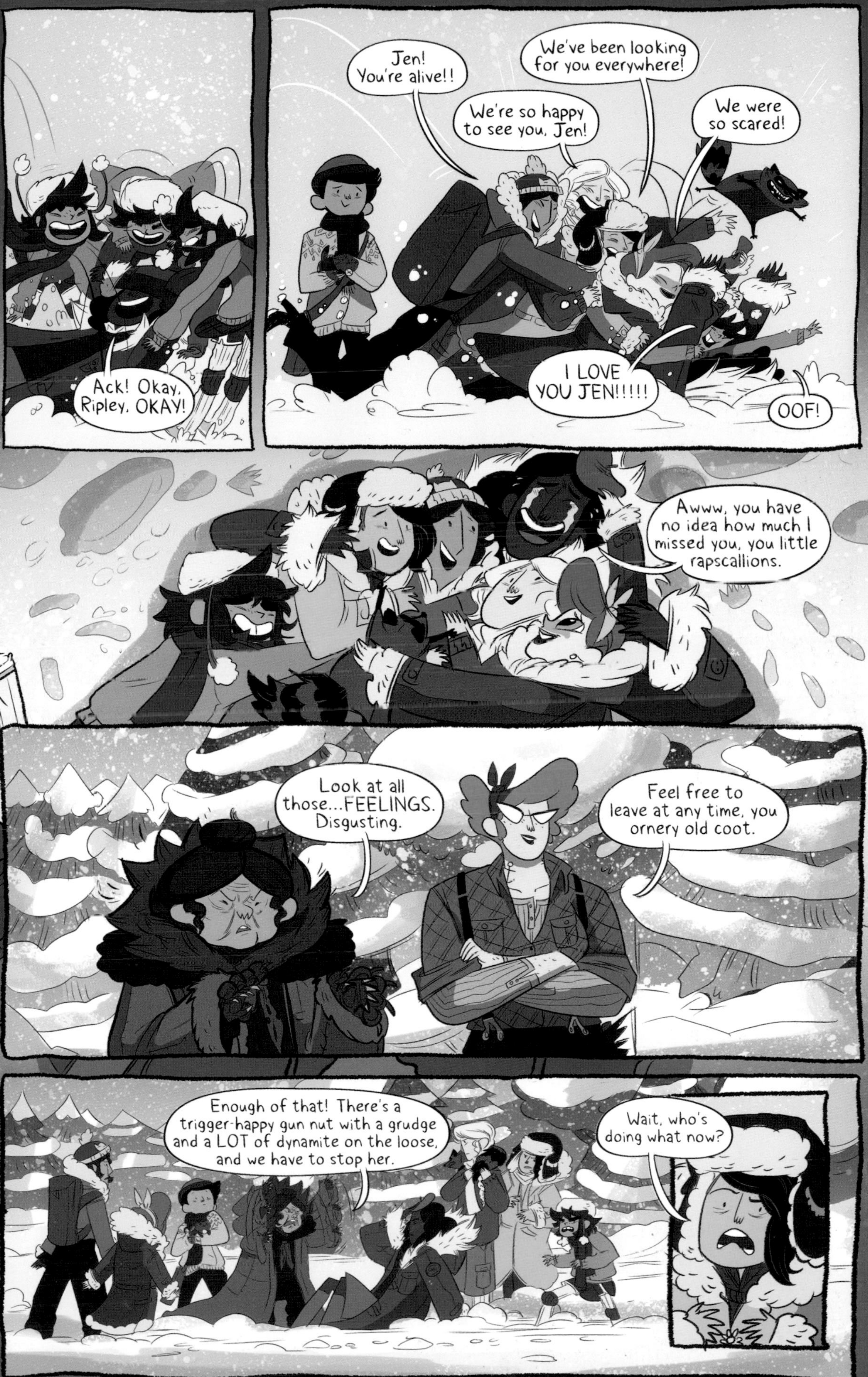
Ack! Okay, Ripley, OKAY!
Jen! You're alive!!
We're so happy to see you, Jen!
We've been looking for you everywhere!
We were so scared!
I LOVE YOU JEN!!!!!
OOF!
Awww, you have no idea how much I missed you, you little rapscallions.
Look at all those...FEELINGS. Disgusting.
Feel free to leave at any time, you ornery old coot.
Enough of that! There's a trigger-happy gun nut with a grudge and a LOT of dynamite on the loose, and we have to stop her.
Wait, who's doing what now?

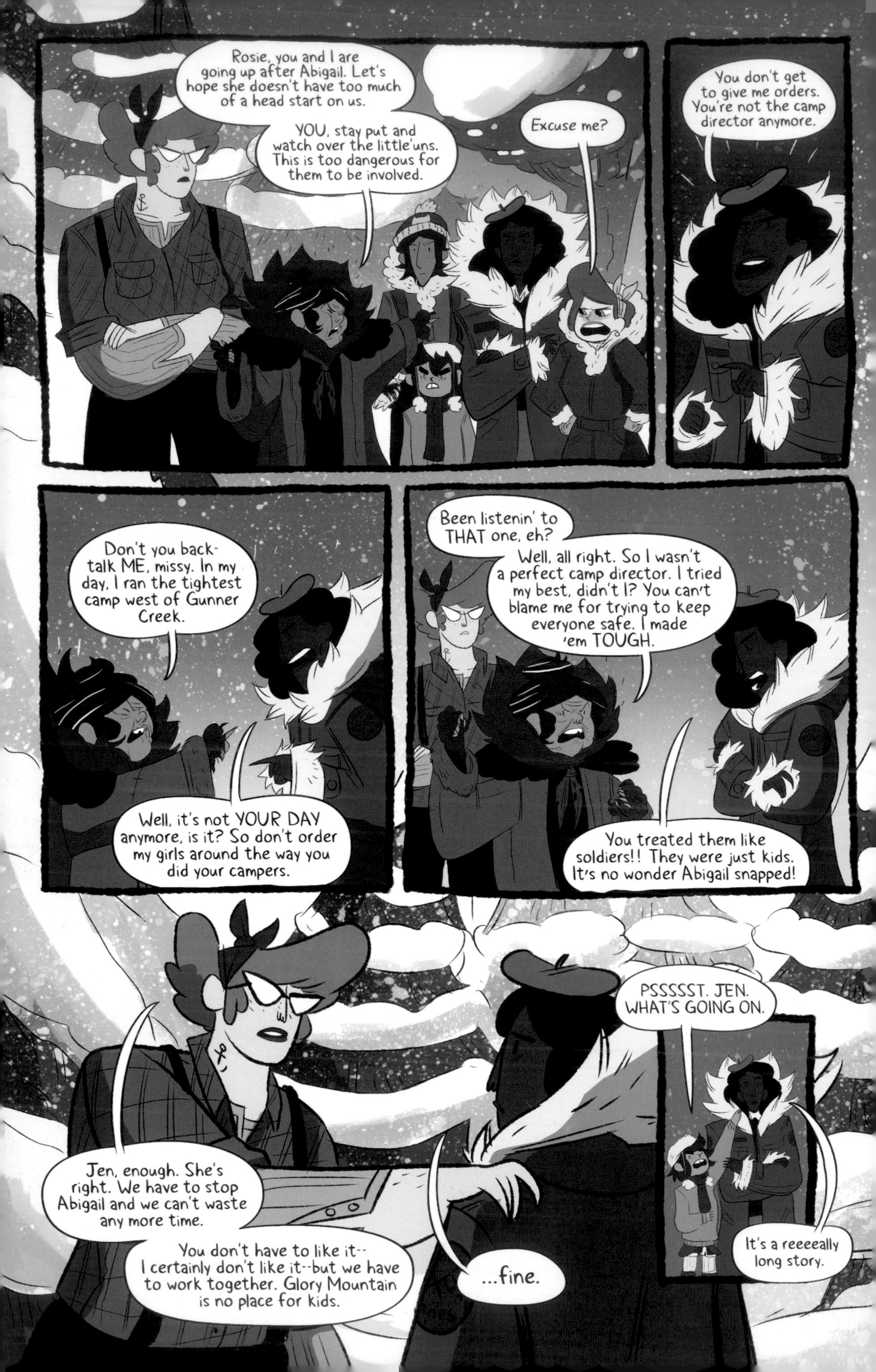

Rosie, you and I are going up after Abigail. Let's hope she doesn't have too much of a head start on us.
YOU, stay put and watch over the little'uns. This is too dangerous for them to be involved.
Excuse me?
You don't get to give me orders. You're not the camp director anymore.
Don't you back-talk ME, missy. In my day, I ran the tightest camp west of Gunner Creek.
Well, it's not YOUR DAY anymore, is it? So don't order my girls around the way you did your campers.
Been listenin' to THAT one, eh?
Well, all right. So I wasn't a perfect camp director. I tried my best, didn't I? You can't blame me for trying to keep everyone safe. I made 'em TOUGH.
You treated them like soldiers!! They were just kids. It's no wonder Abigail snapped!
Jen, enough. She's right. We have to stop Abigail and we can't waste any more time.
You don't have to like it-- I certainly don't like it--but we have to work together. Glory Mountain is no place for kids.
...fine.
PSSSSST. JEN. WHAT'S GOING ON.
It's a reeeeally long story.

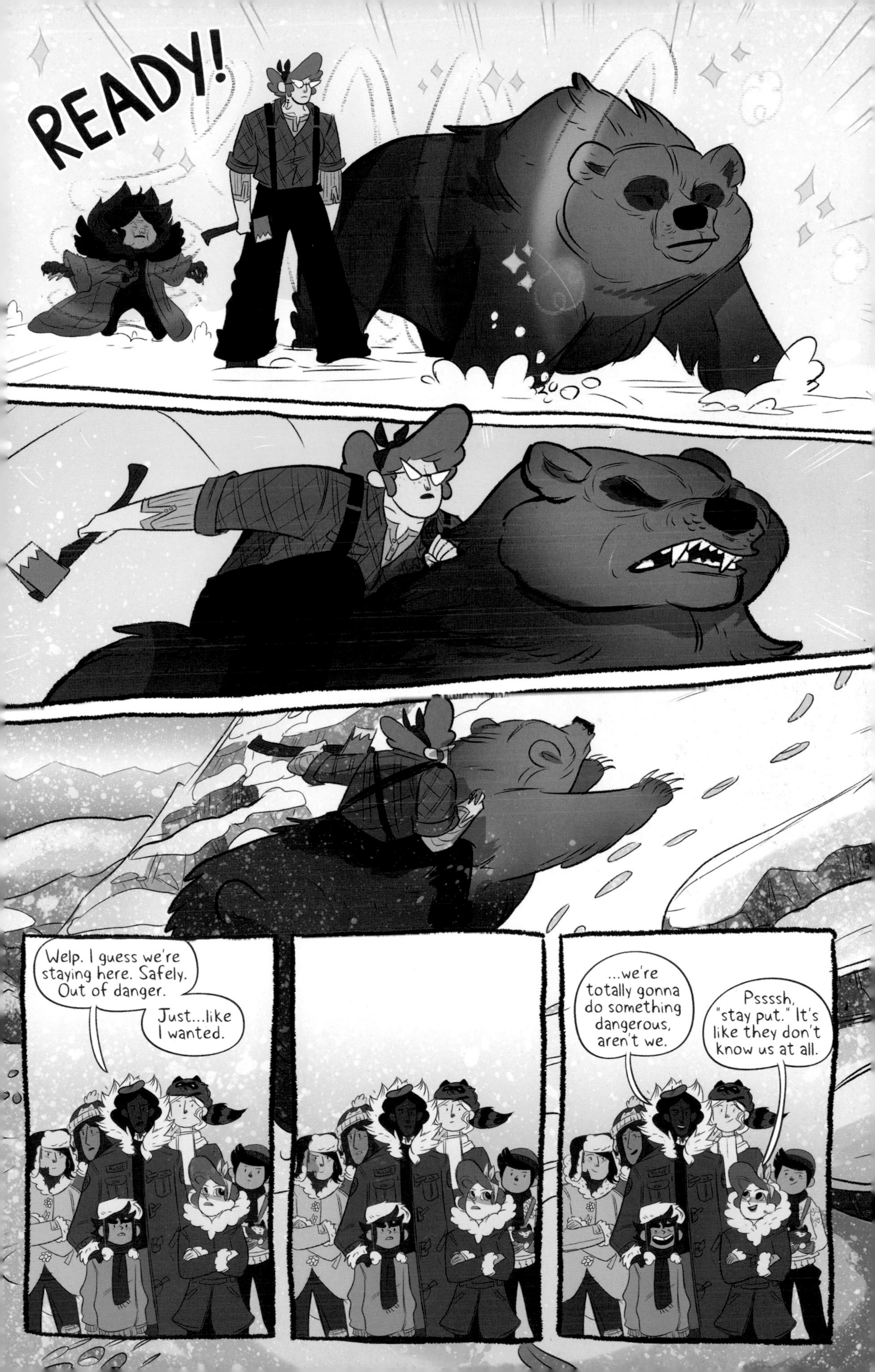
READY!
Welp. I guess we're staying here. Safely. Out of danger.
Just...like I wanted.
...we're totally gonna do something dangerous, aren't we.
Pssssh, "stay put." It's like they don't know us at all.

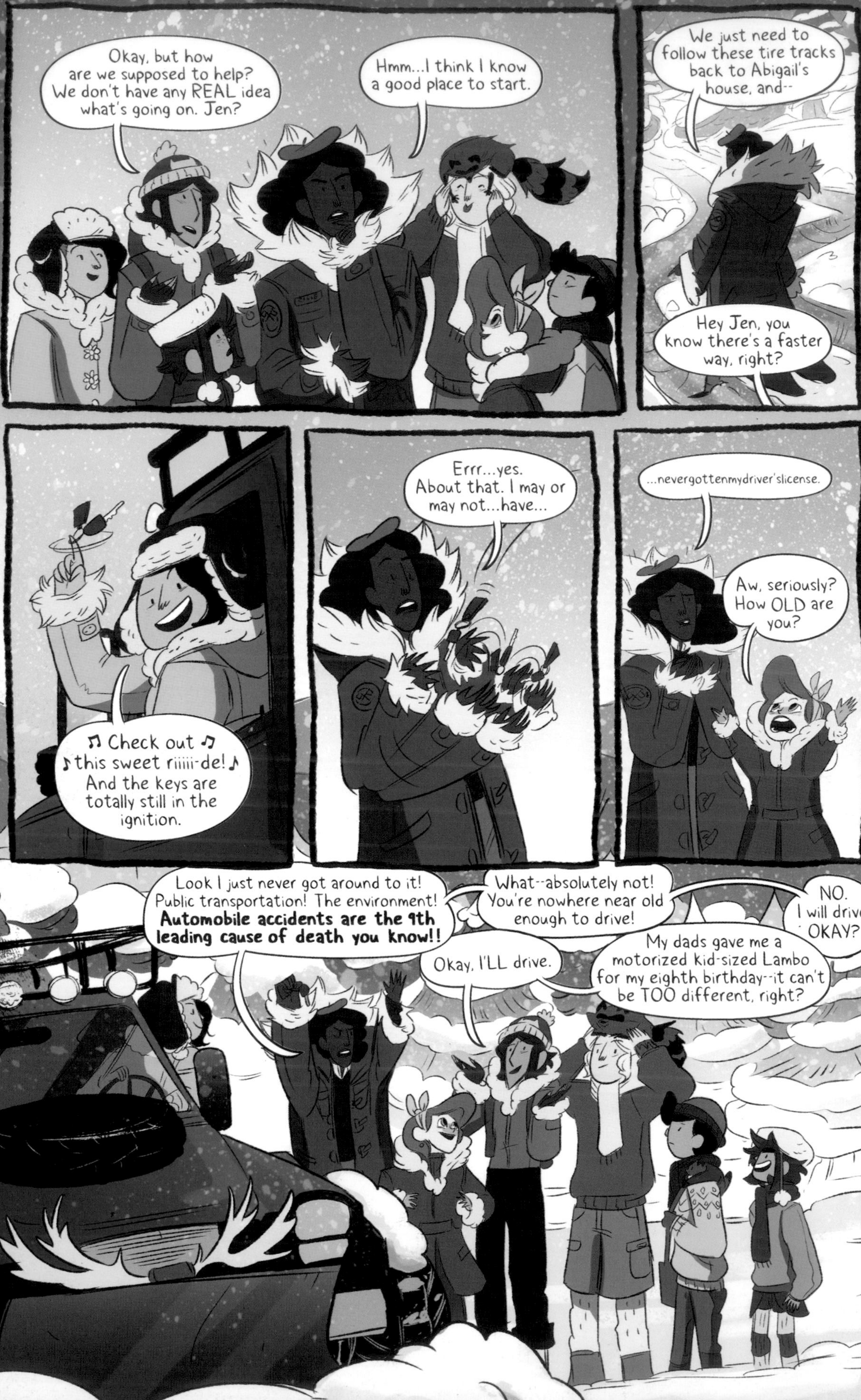

Okay, but how are we supposed to help? We don't have any REAL idea what's going on. Jen?
Hmm...I think I know a good place to start.
We just need to follow these tire tracks back to Abigail's house, and--
Hey Jen, you know there's a faster way, right?
♫ Check out ♫ ♪ this sweet riiiii-de! ♪ And the keys are totally still in the ignition.
Errr...yes. About that. I may or may not...have...
...nevergottenmydriver'slicense.
Aw, seriously? How OLD are you?
Look I just never got around to it! Public transportation! The environment! **Automobile accidents are the 9th leading cause of death you know!!**
What--absolutely not! You're nowhere near old enough to drive!
NO. I will drive, OKAY?
Okay, I'LL drive.
My dads gave me a motorized kid-sized Lambo for my eighth birthday--it can't be TOO different, right?

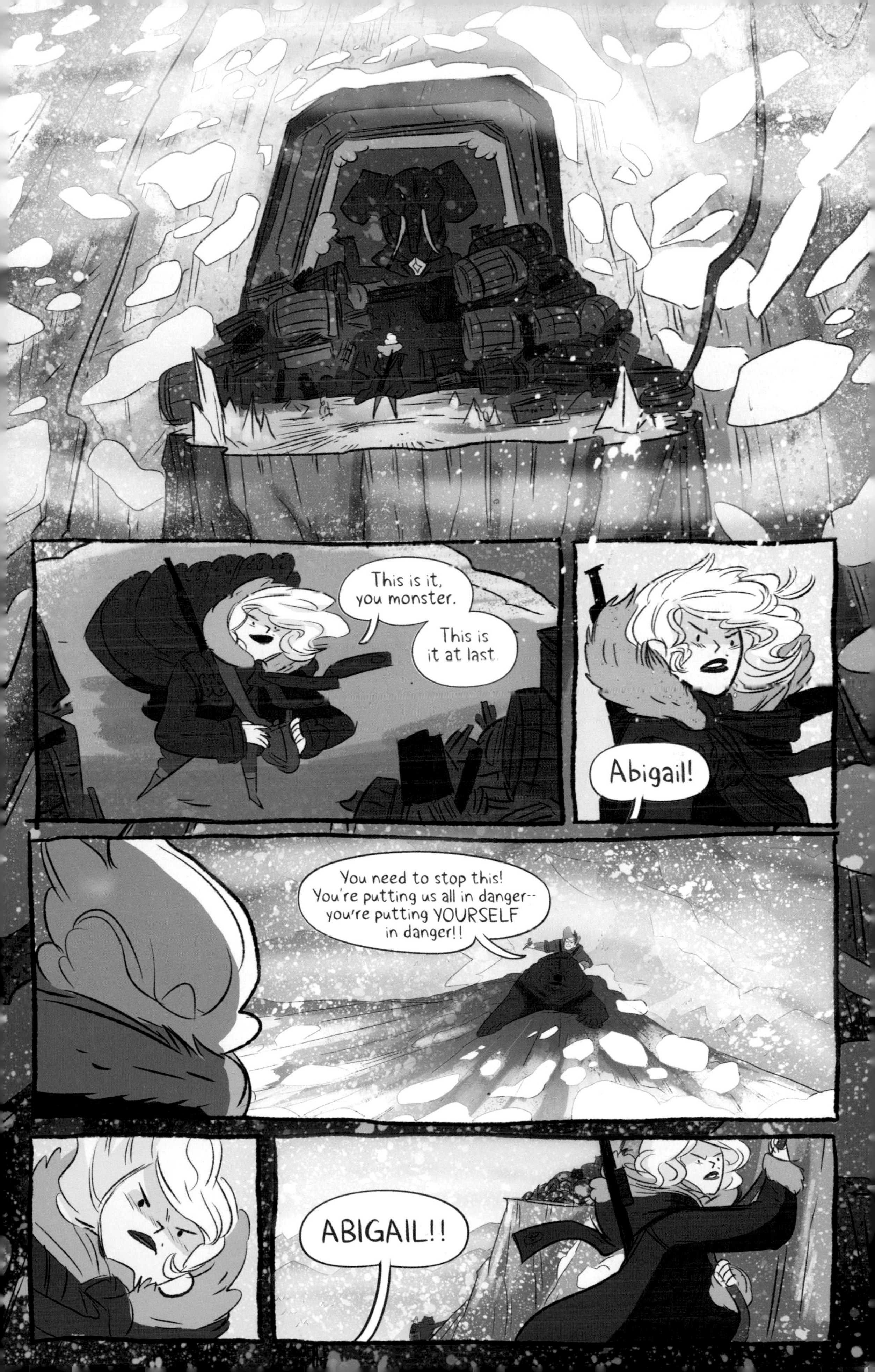
This is it, you monster.
This is it at last.
Abigail!
You need to stop this! You're putting us all in danger-- you're putting YOURSELF in danger!!
ABIGAIL!!

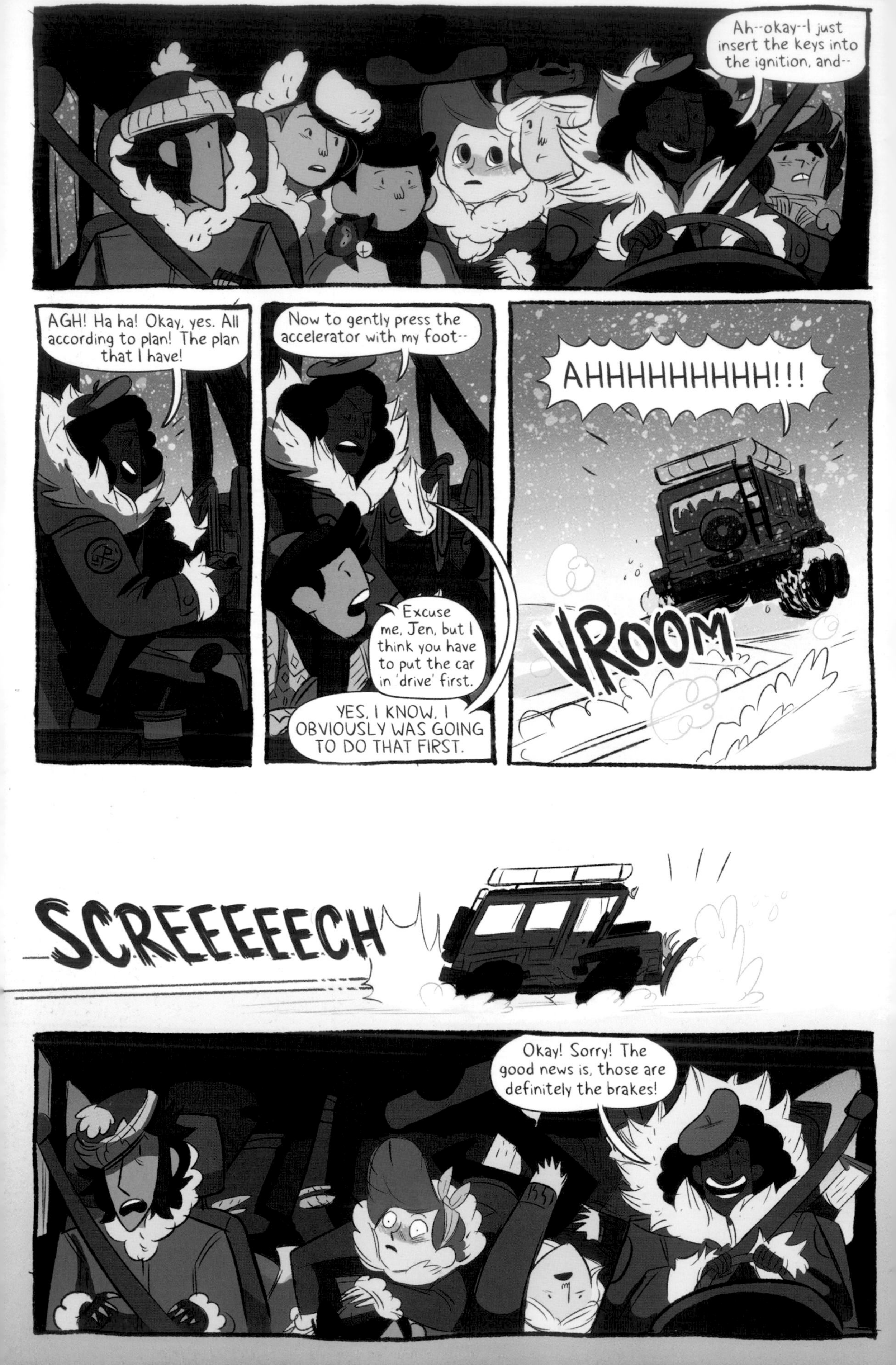
Ah--okay--I just insert the keys into the ignition, and--
AGH! Ha ha! Okay, yes. All according to plan! The plan that I have!
Now to gently press the accelerator with my foot--
Excuse me, Jen, but I think you have to put the car in 'drive' first.
YES, I KNOW, I OBVIOUSLY WAS GOING TO DO THAT FIRST.
AHHHHHHHHHH!!!
VROOM
SCREEEEECH
Okay! Sorry! The good news is, those are definitely the brakes!

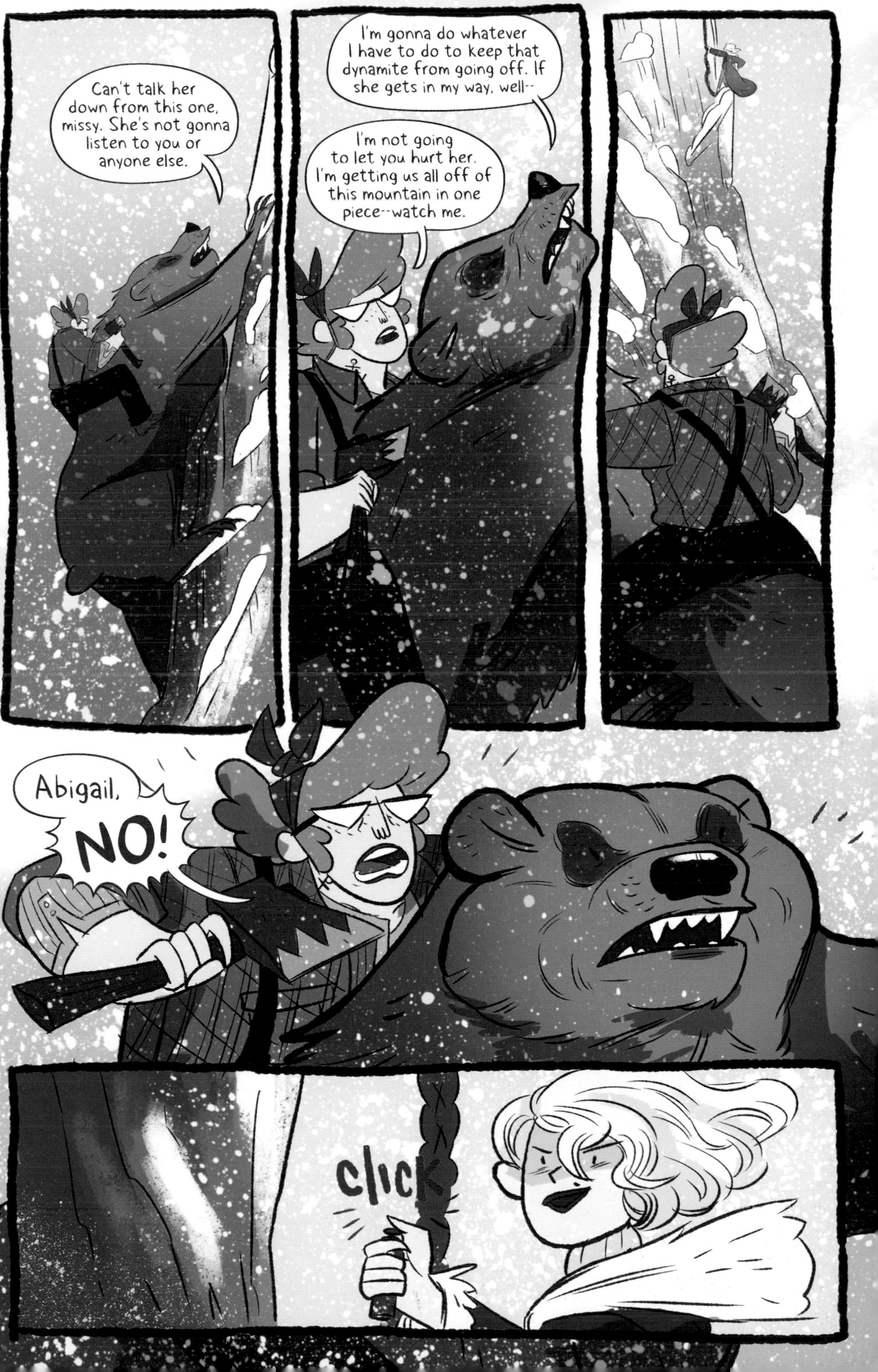

Can't talk her down from this one, missy. She's not gonna listen to you or anyone else.
I'm gonna do whatever I have to do to keep that dynamite from going off. If she gets in my way, well--
I'm not going to let you hurt her. I'm getting us all off of this mountain in one piece--watch me.
Abigail, NO!
CLICK

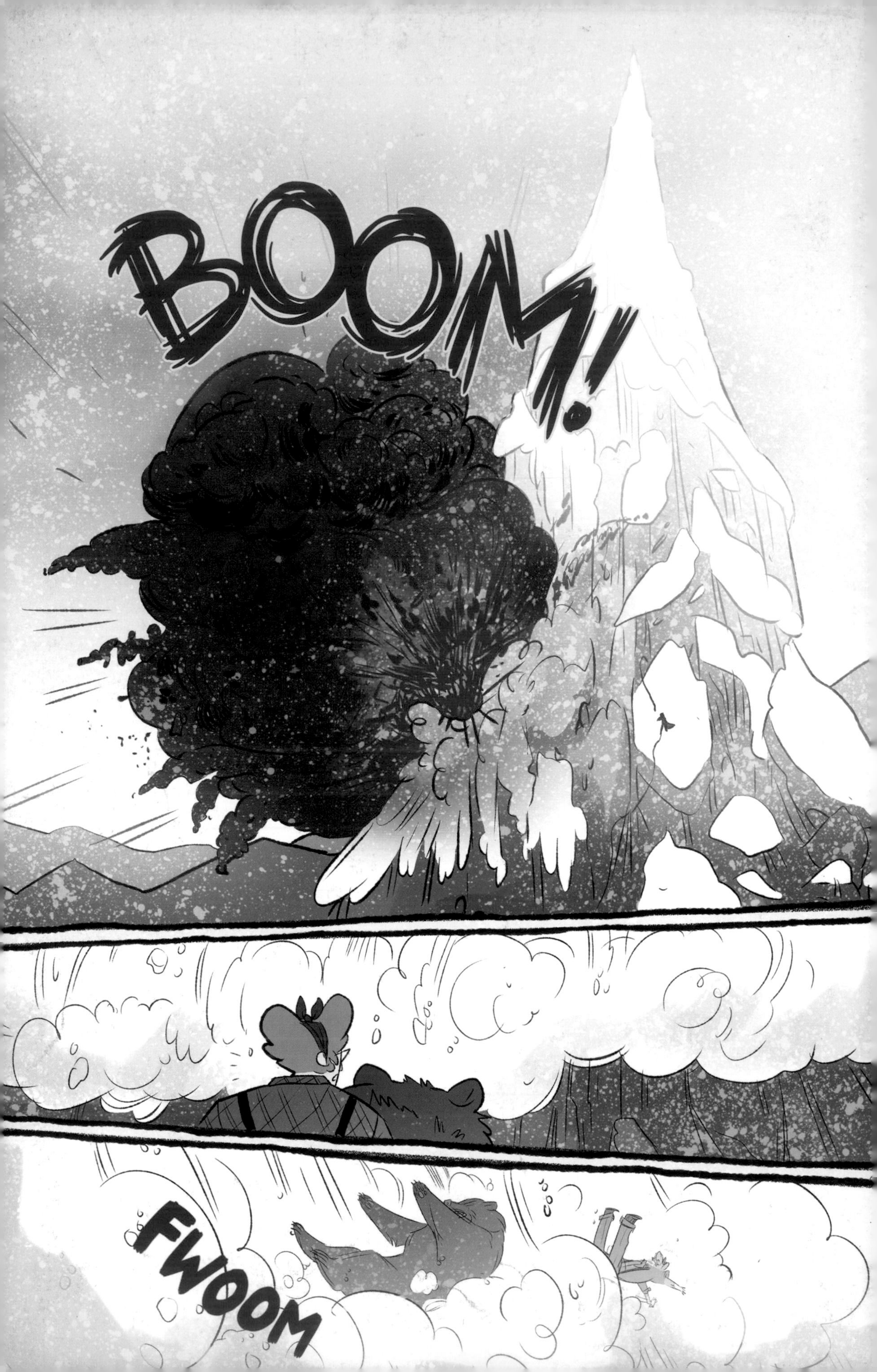
BOOM!
FWOOM

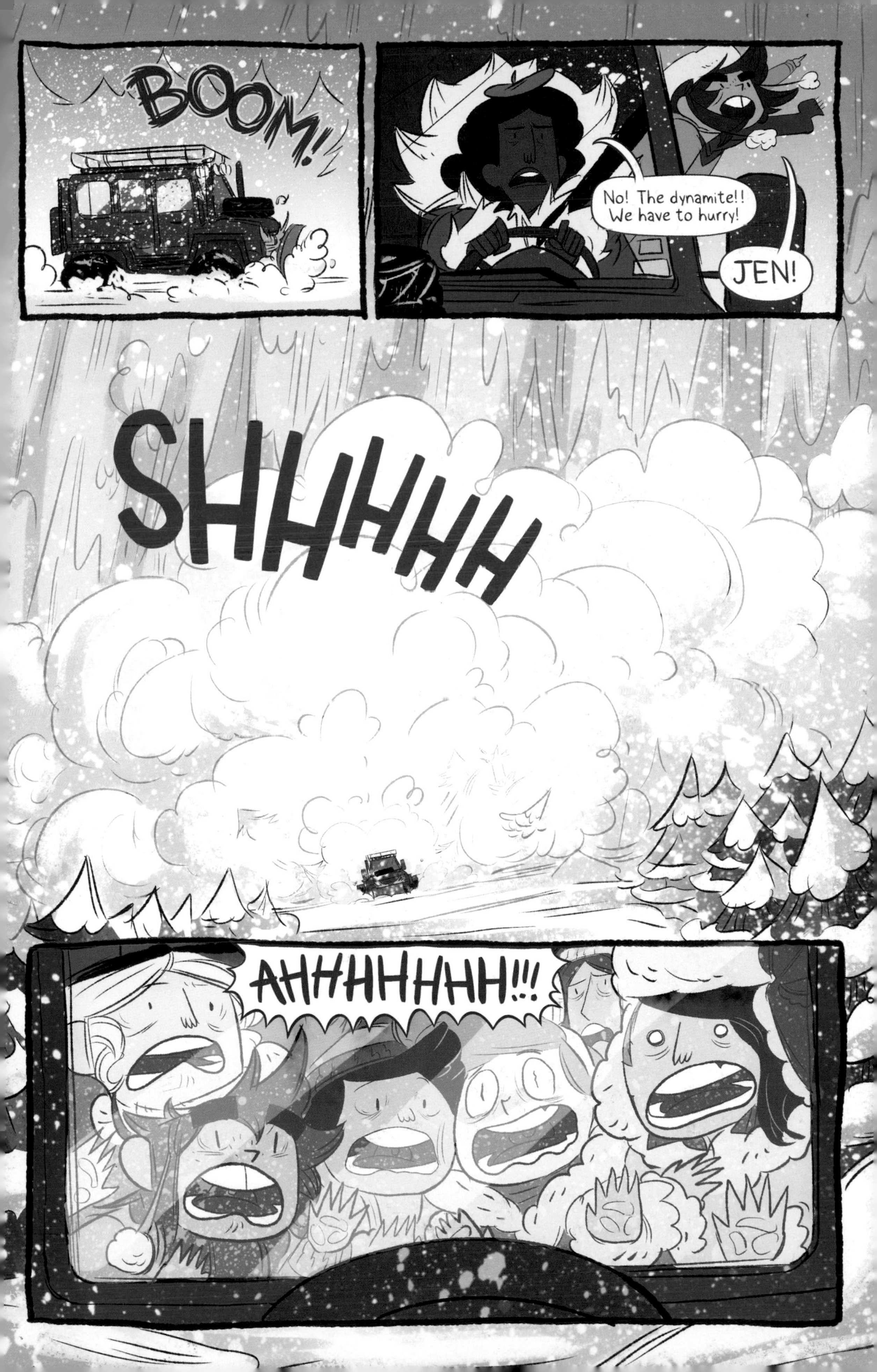
BOOM!
No! The dynamite!! We have to hurry!
JEN!
SHHHHHH
AHHHHHHH!!!

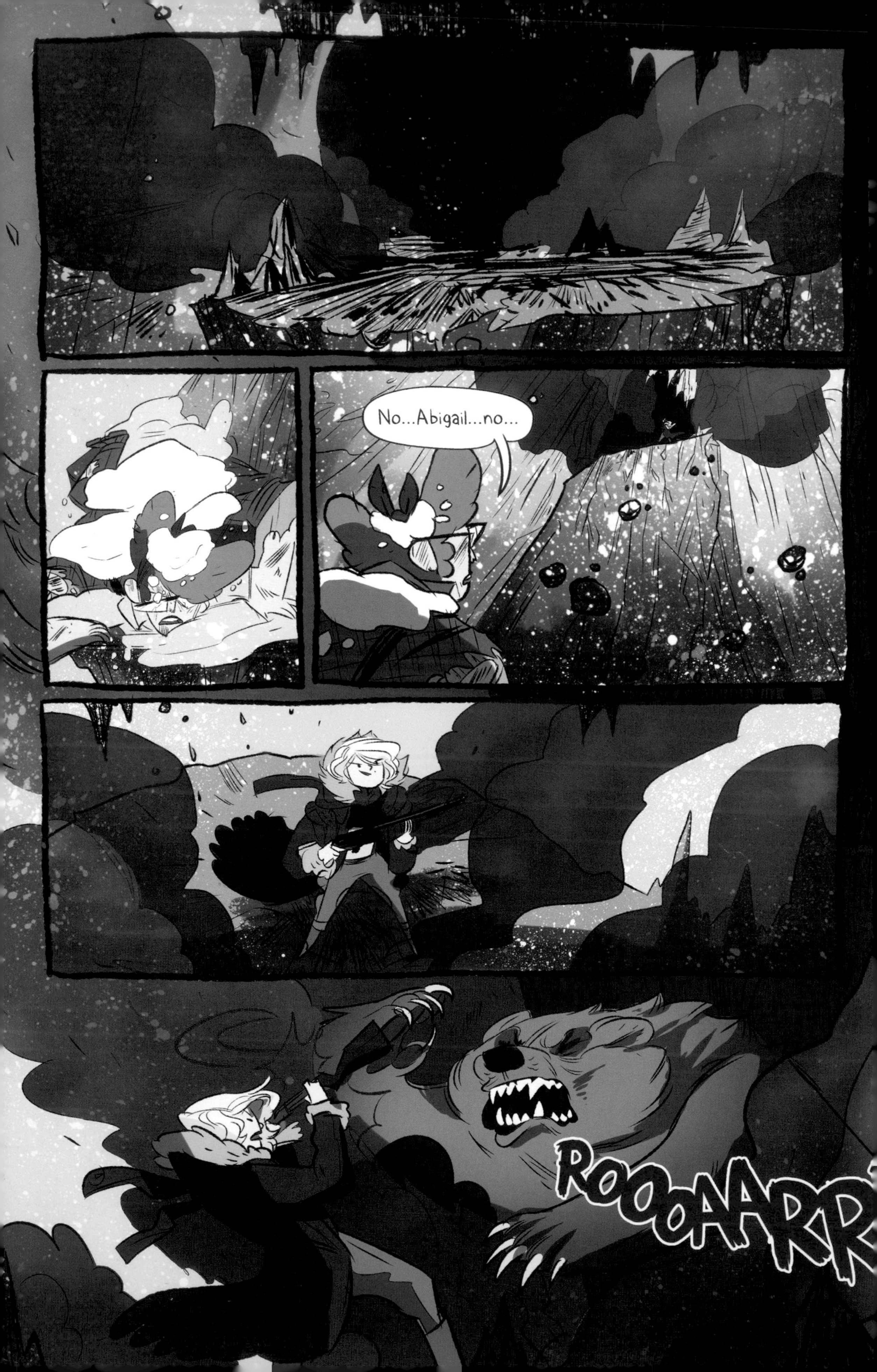
No...Abigail...no...
ROOOAARR

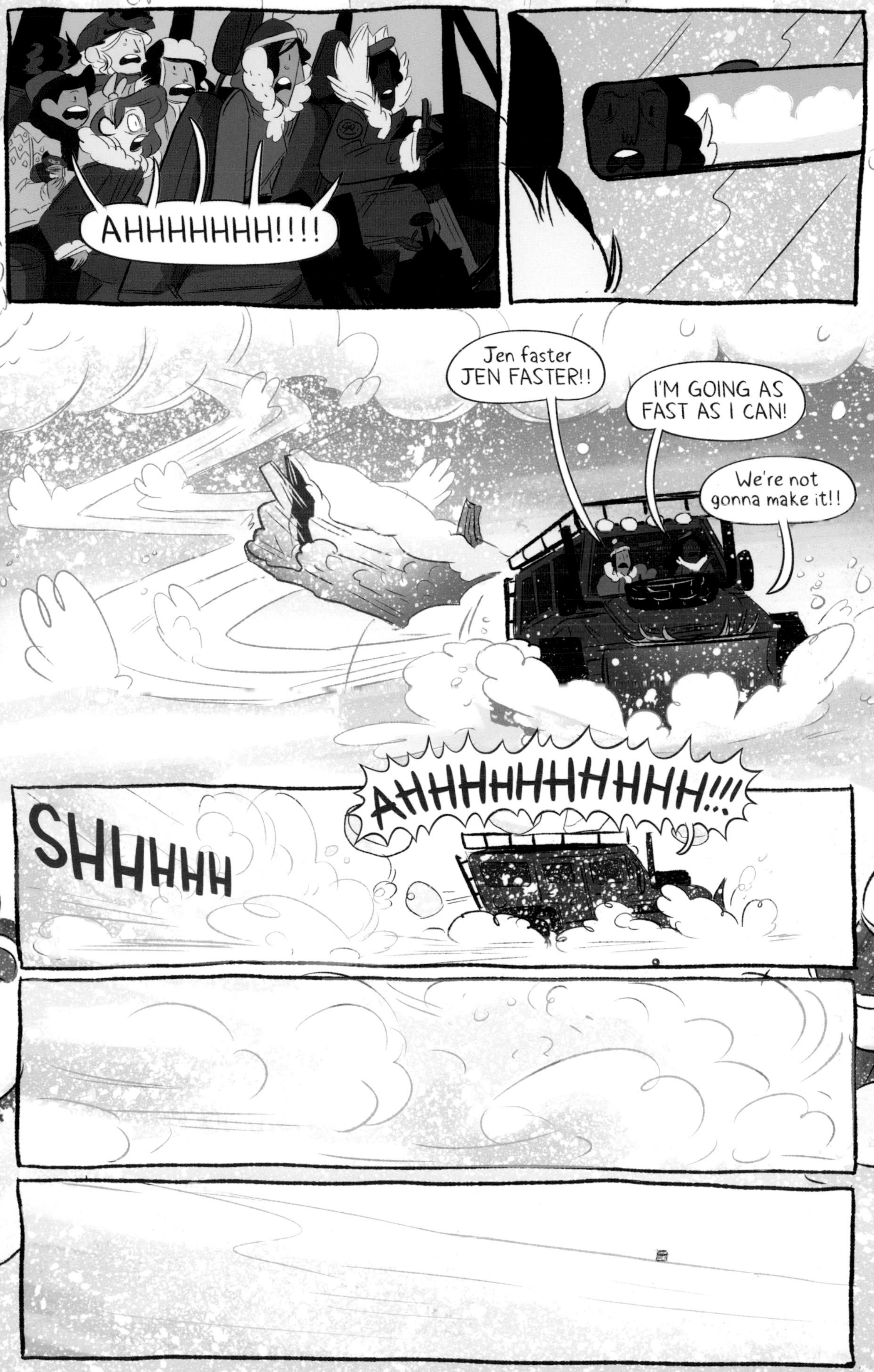
AHHHHHHHH!!!!
Jen faster JEN FASTER!!
I'M GOING AS FAST AS I CAN!
We're not gonna make it!!
AHHHHHHHHHHH!!!
SHHHHH

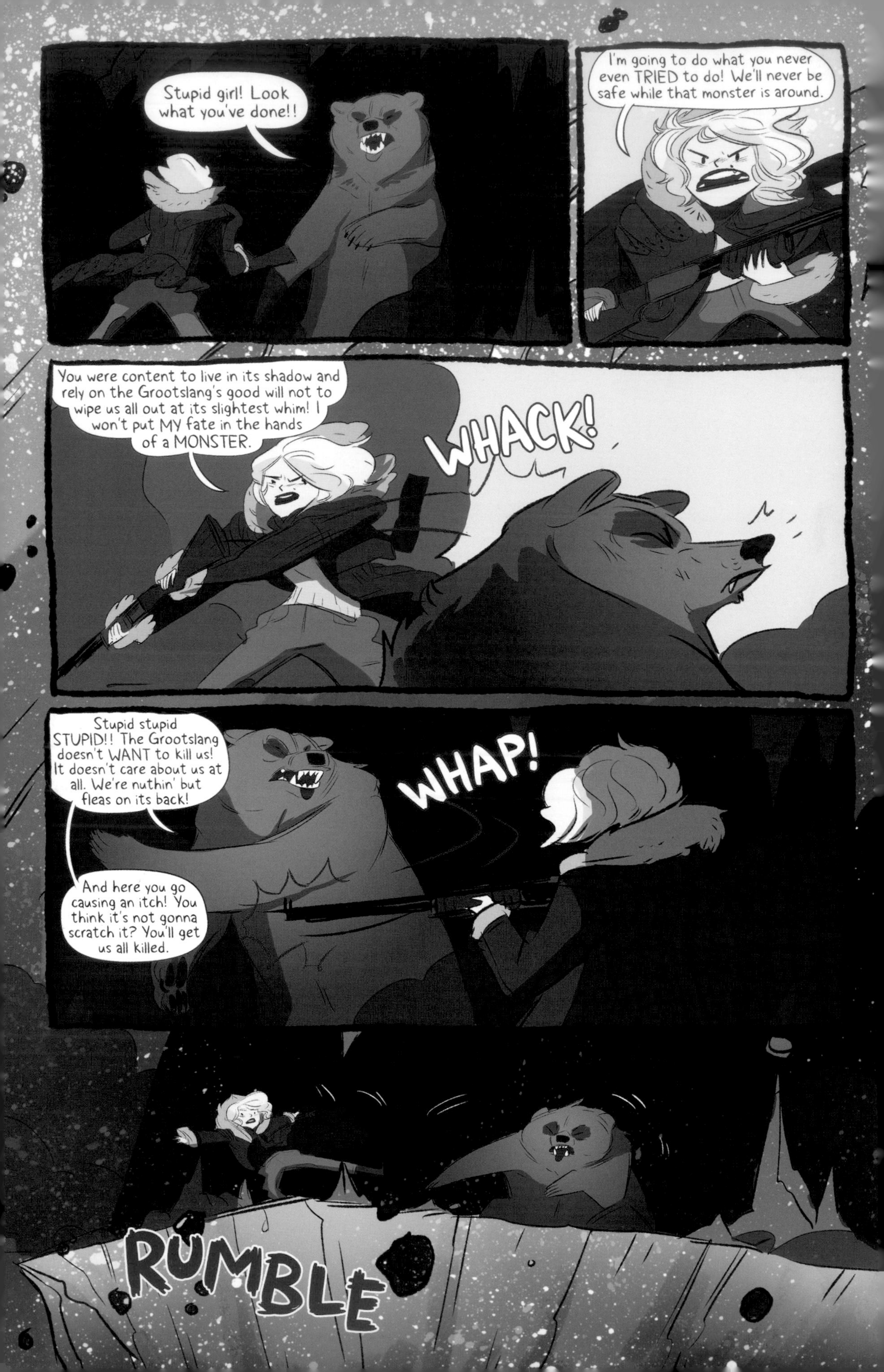
Stupid girl! Look what you've done!!
I'm going to do what you never even TRIED to do! We'll never be safe while that monster is around.
You were content to live in its shadow and rely on the Grootslang's good will not to wipe us all out at its slightest whim! I won't put MY fate in the hands of a MONSTER.
WHACK!
Stupid stupid STUPID!! The Grootslang doesn't WANT to kill us! It doesn't care about us at all. We're nuthin' but fleas on its back!
WHAP!
And here you go causing an itch! You think it's not gonna scratch it? You'll get us all killed.
RUMBLE

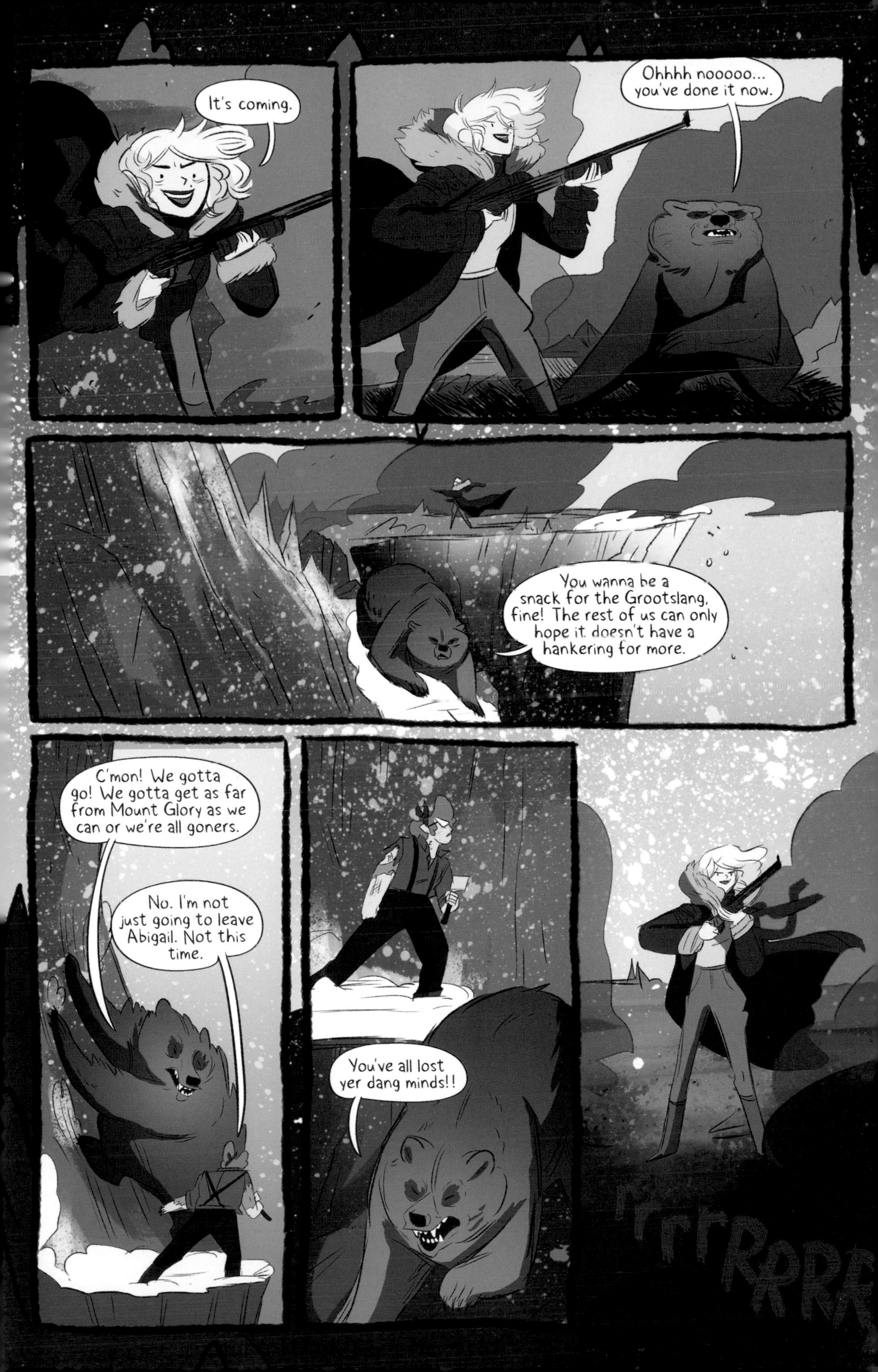
It's coming.
Ohhhh nooooo... you've done it now.
You wanna be a snack for the Grootslang, fine! The rest of us can only hope it doesn't have a hankering for more.
C'mon! We gotta go! We gotta get as far from Mount Glory as we can or we're all goners.
No. I'm not just going to leave Abigail. Not this time.
You've all lost yer dang minds!!
rrrrRRRR

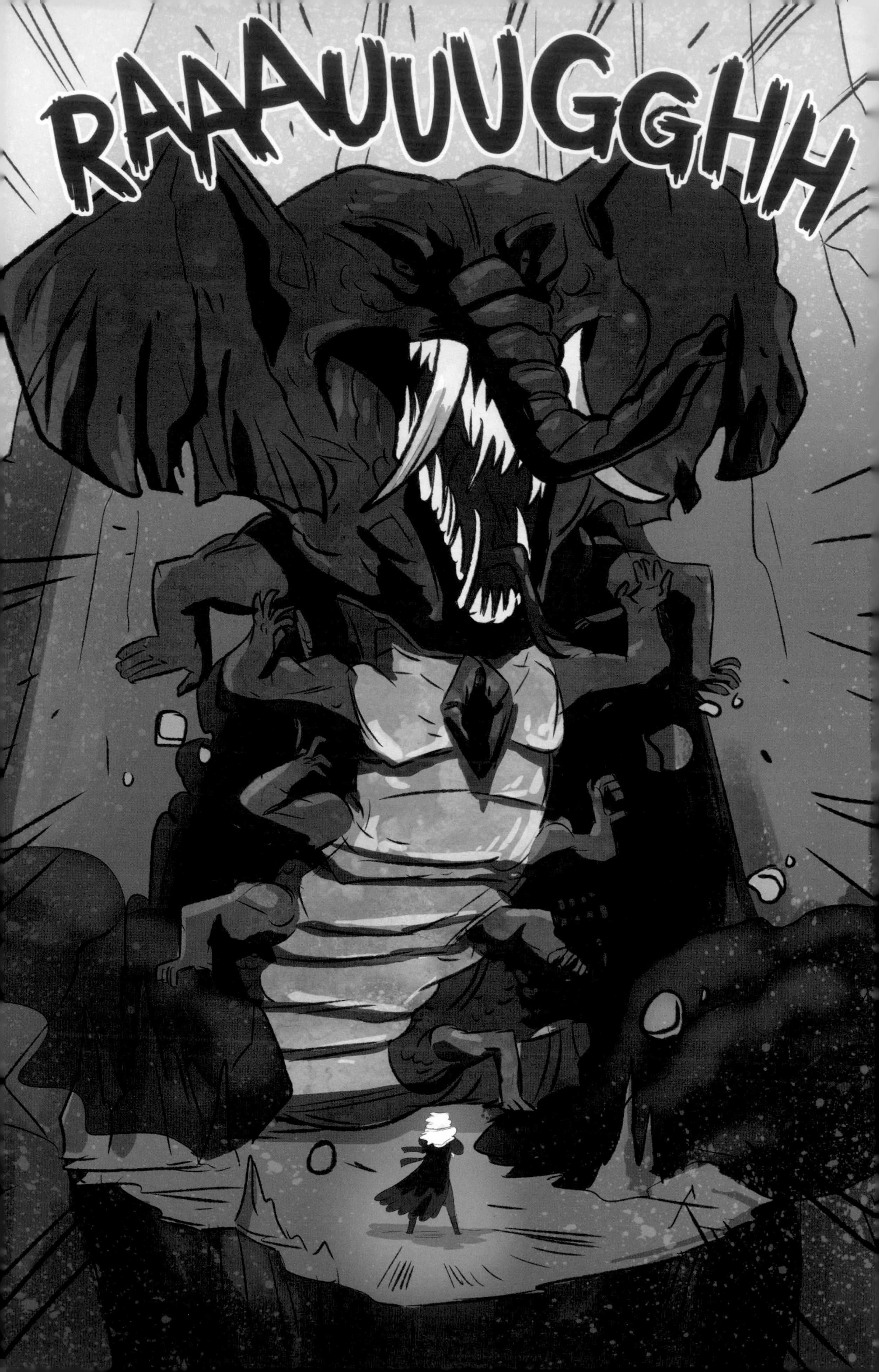
RAAAUUUGGHH

will co
The
It he
appearar
dress fo
Further
Lumber
to have
part in
Thiskv
Hardc
have
them

E UNIFORM

should be worn at camp
events when Lumberjanes
may also be worn at other
ions. It should be worn as a
the uniform dress with
rect shoes, and stocking or

out grows her uniform or
ter Lumberjane.
a she has
her
her

The
yellow, short sl
emb
the w
choose
slacks,
made o
out-of-dc
green bere
the colla
Shoes ma
heels, rou
socks sho   with the shoes or wi
the uniform. Ne   es, bracelets, or other jewelry do
belong with a Lumberjane uniform.

HOW TO WEAR THE UNIFO

To look well in a uniform demans fi
uniform be kept in good conditio
pressed. See that the skirt is the right
height and build, that the belt is adjusted
that your shoes and stockings are in keeping
uniform, that you watch your posture and carry you
with dignity and grace. If the beret is removed indoors,
be sure that your hair is neat and kept in place with an
insonspicuous clip or ribbon. When you wear a
Lumberjane uniform you are identified as a member of
this organization and you should be doubly careful to
conduct yourself in a way that will show everyone that
courtesy and thoughtfullness are part of being a
Lumberjane. People are likely to judge a whole nation by
the selfishness of a few individuals, to criticize a whole
family because of the misconduct of one member, and to
feel unkindly toward and organization because of the

GES

e unifor
elps to cre
in a group.
active life th
another bond
future, and pr
in order to b
Lumberjane pr
Penniquiqul Thi   ore Lady
Types, but m   es will wish to have one. They
can either b   e uniform, or make it themselves from
materials available at the trading post.

LUMBERJANES FIELD MANUAL

CHAPTER SIXTEEN

Lumberjanes "Automotive" Program Field

SPARE ME BADGE

"Automobile safety saves."

Like any well rounded young woman, a Lumberjane will understand the importance of automobile safety. The key to this knowledge is understanding the vehicle inside and out. The Lumberjanes will be responsible for the care and upkeep of the camp vehicle in the summer that they are at the camp. The counselor in charge of the auto shop will educate each Lumberjane on how to identify parts of the engine, understand the common problems that are faced on the road, as well as the way to solve those problems with the tools available to them.

Life on the open road will be an experience that most will go through as they transition through their life, and even if it's an experience that not everyone will enjoy, it's definitely something a Lumberjane should be prepared for. From safety features like seat belts to how to change a tire, the *Spare Me* badge is about understanding practical knowledge of automobiles. As a Lumberjane,

our campers will understand the importance of keeping their property in tip top shape. They will have experience in taking care of their own belongings as well as helping others with their own, and they will be able see the benefit of taking the time to ensure their property is in great quality so that it will last for a long time.

To obtain the *Spare Me* badge a Lumberjane must choose the camp vehicle they will want to work on. They will learn all practical knowledge there is about the vehicle and will learn safety guidelines and laws from their home state. They will change the oil in the car, and they will learn how to change a flat tire. If they are of age, they will learn how to drive the vehicle without supervision and will be used to help transport campers or run other errands that might be needed. They will meet with the park ranger to talk about the dangers of driving in the mountains, what to look out for if off

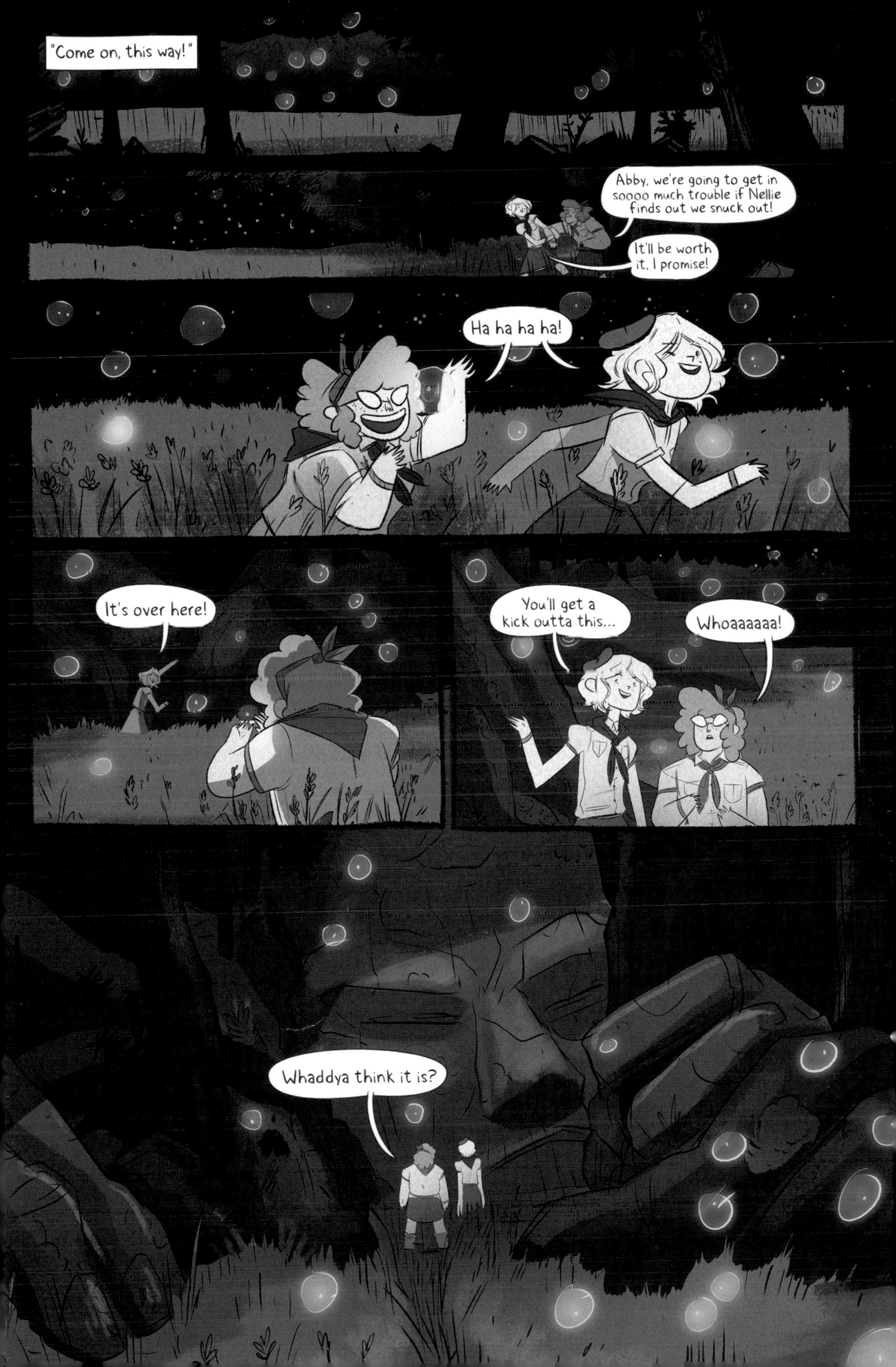
"Come on, this way!"
Abby, we're going to get in soooo much trouble if Nellie finds out we snuck out!
It'll be worth it, I promise!
Ha ha ha ha!
It's over here!
You'll get a kick outta this...
Whoaaaaaa!
Whaddya think it is?

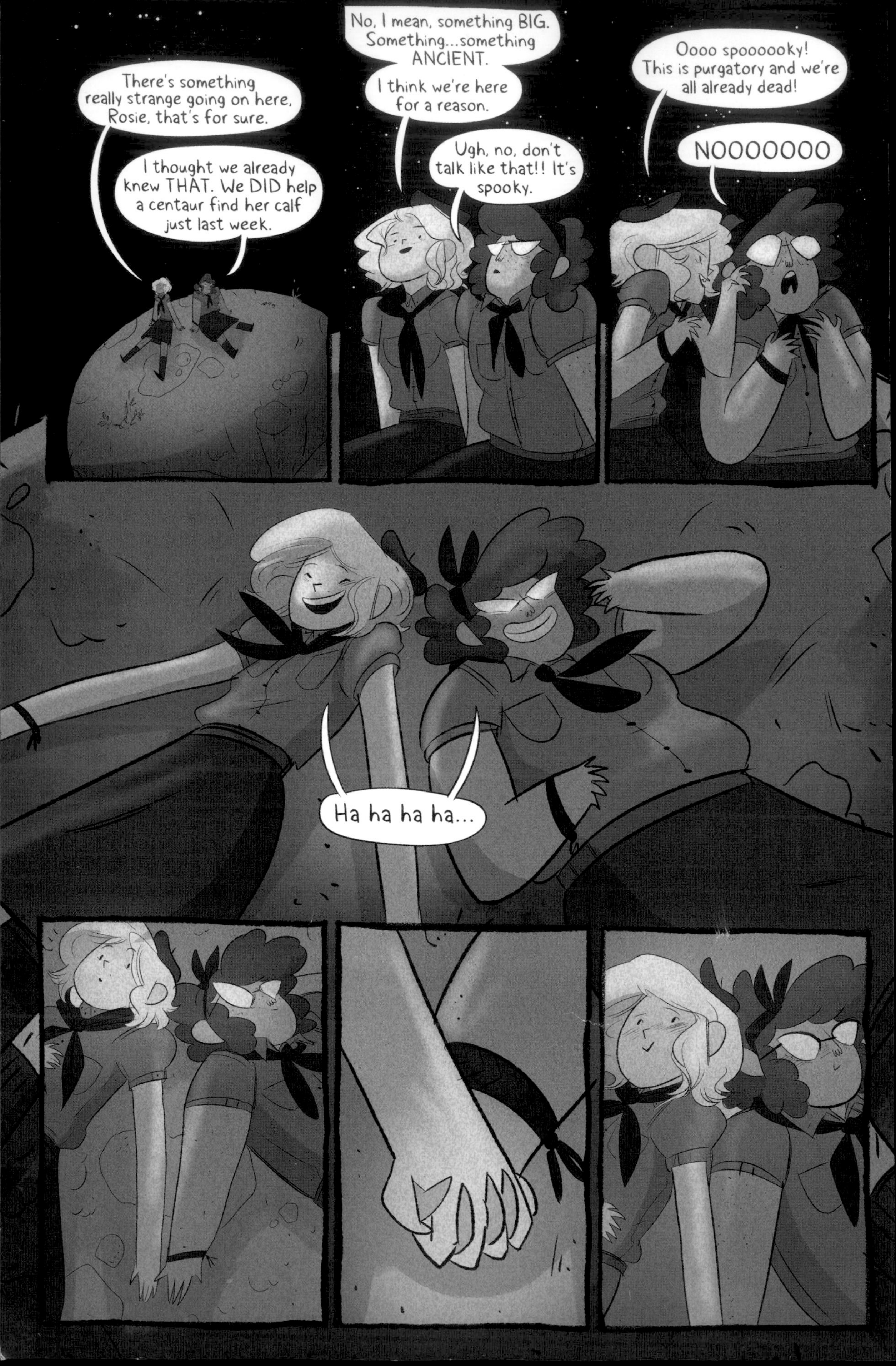
There's something really strange going on here, Rosie, that's for sure.
I thought we already knew THAT. We DID help a centaur find her calf just last week.
No, I mean, something BIG. Something...something ANCIENT.
I think we're here for a reason.
Ugh, no, don't talk like that!! It's spooky.
Oooo spoooooky! This is purgatory and we're all already dead!
NOOOOOOO
Ha ha ha ha...

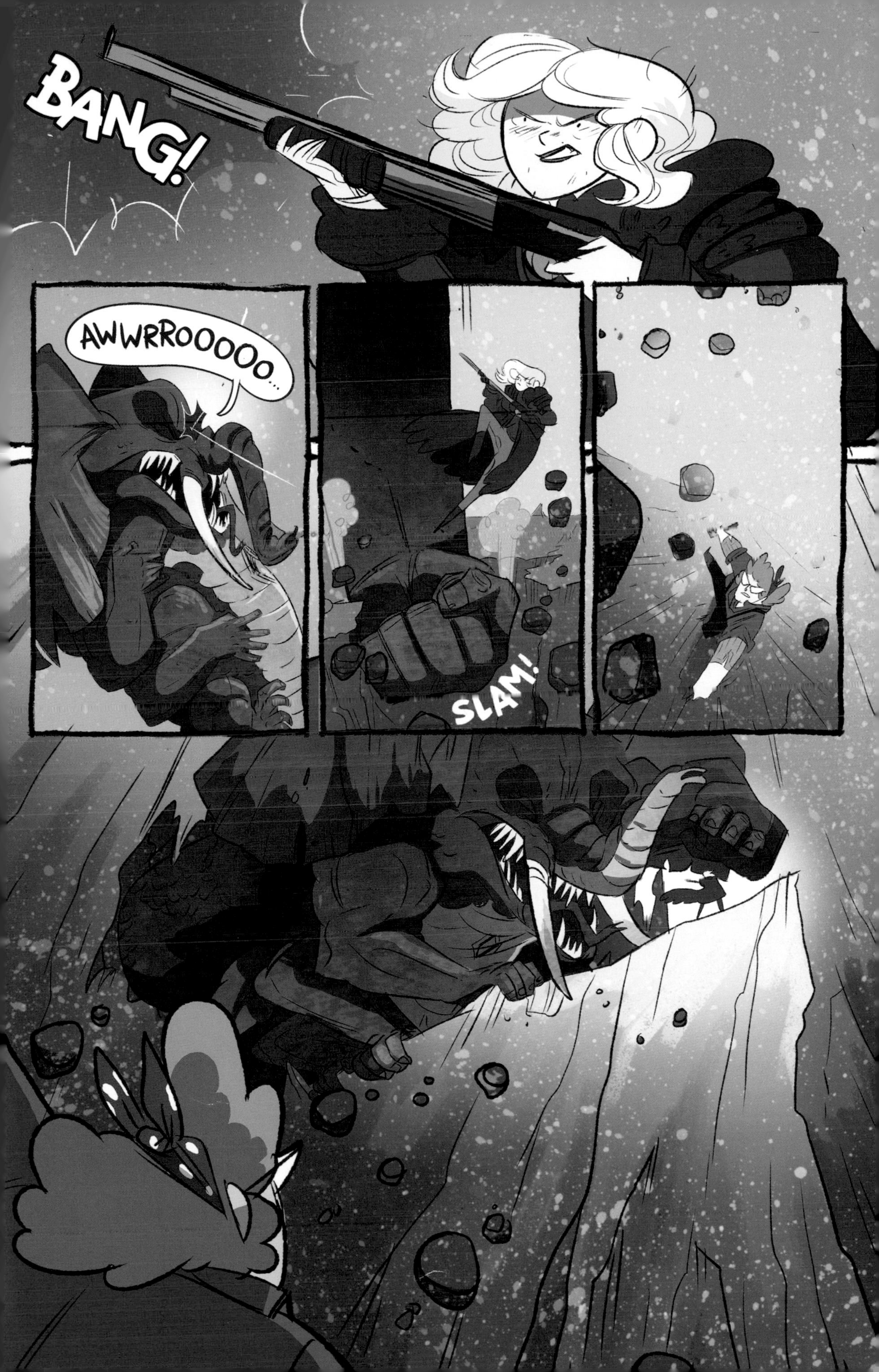
BANG!
AWWRROOOOO...
SLAM!

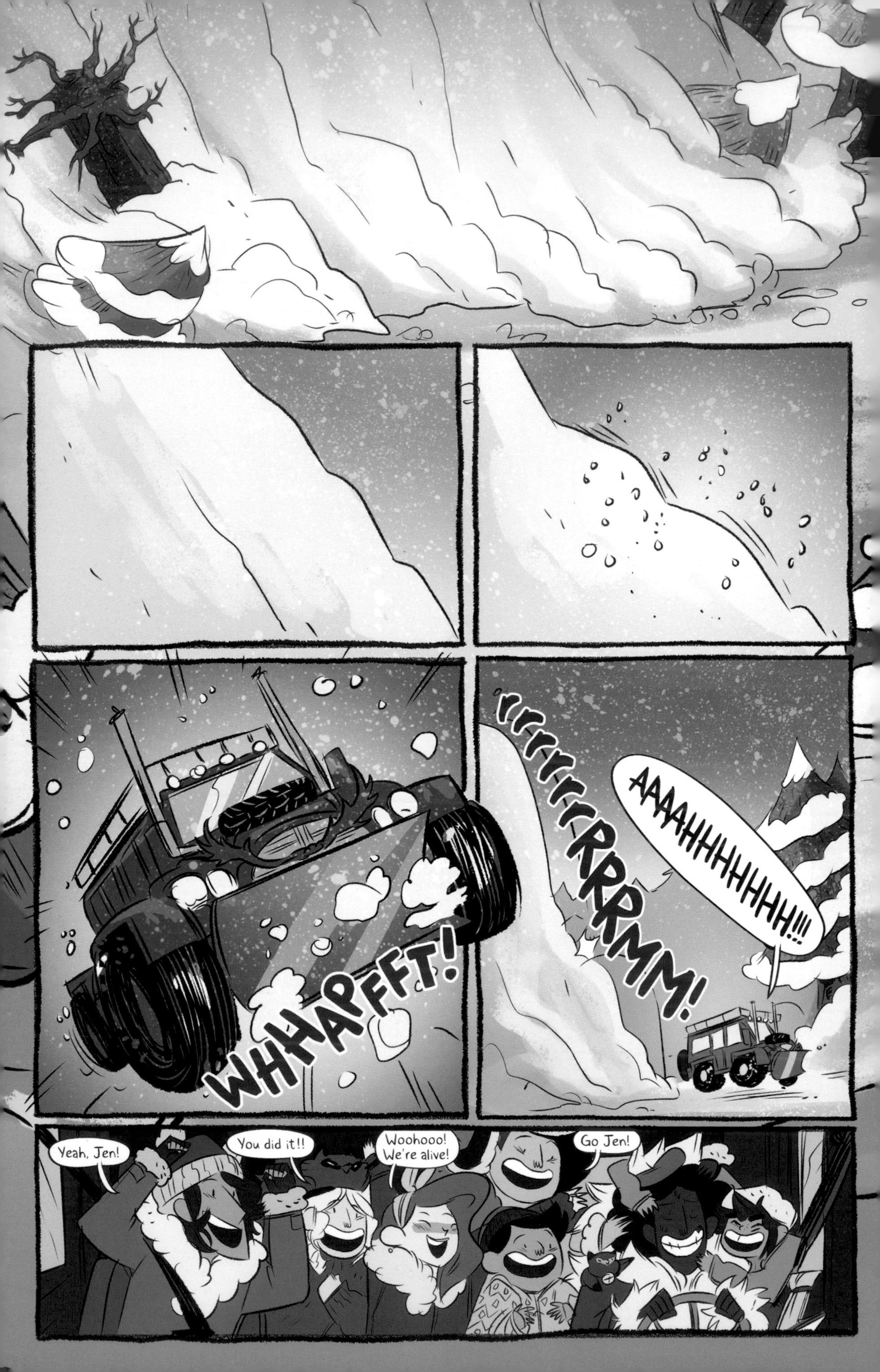

WHHAPFFT!
rrrrrrrrrRRRMM!
AAAAHHHHHHHH!!!
Yeah, Jen!
You did it!!
Woohooo! We're alive!
Go Jen!

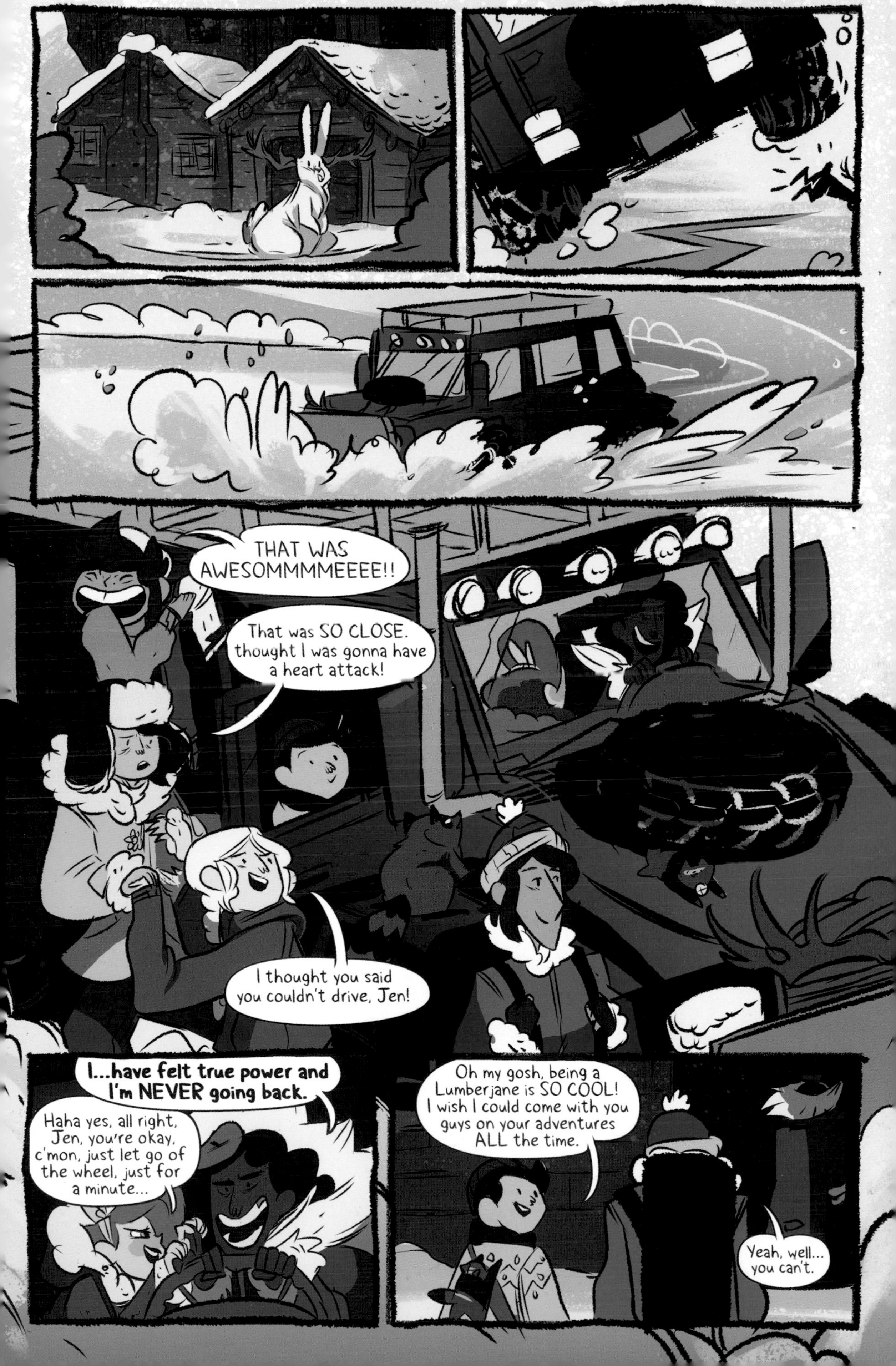

THAT WAS AWESOMMMMEEEE!!
That was SO CLOSE. thought I was gonna have a heart attack!
I thought you said you couldn't drive, Jen!
I...have felt true power and I'm NEVER going back.
Haha yes, all right, Jen, you're okay, c'mon, just let go of the wheel, just for a minute...
Oh my gosh, being a Lumberjane is SO COOL! I wish I could come with you guys on your adventures ALL the time.
Yeah, well... you can't.

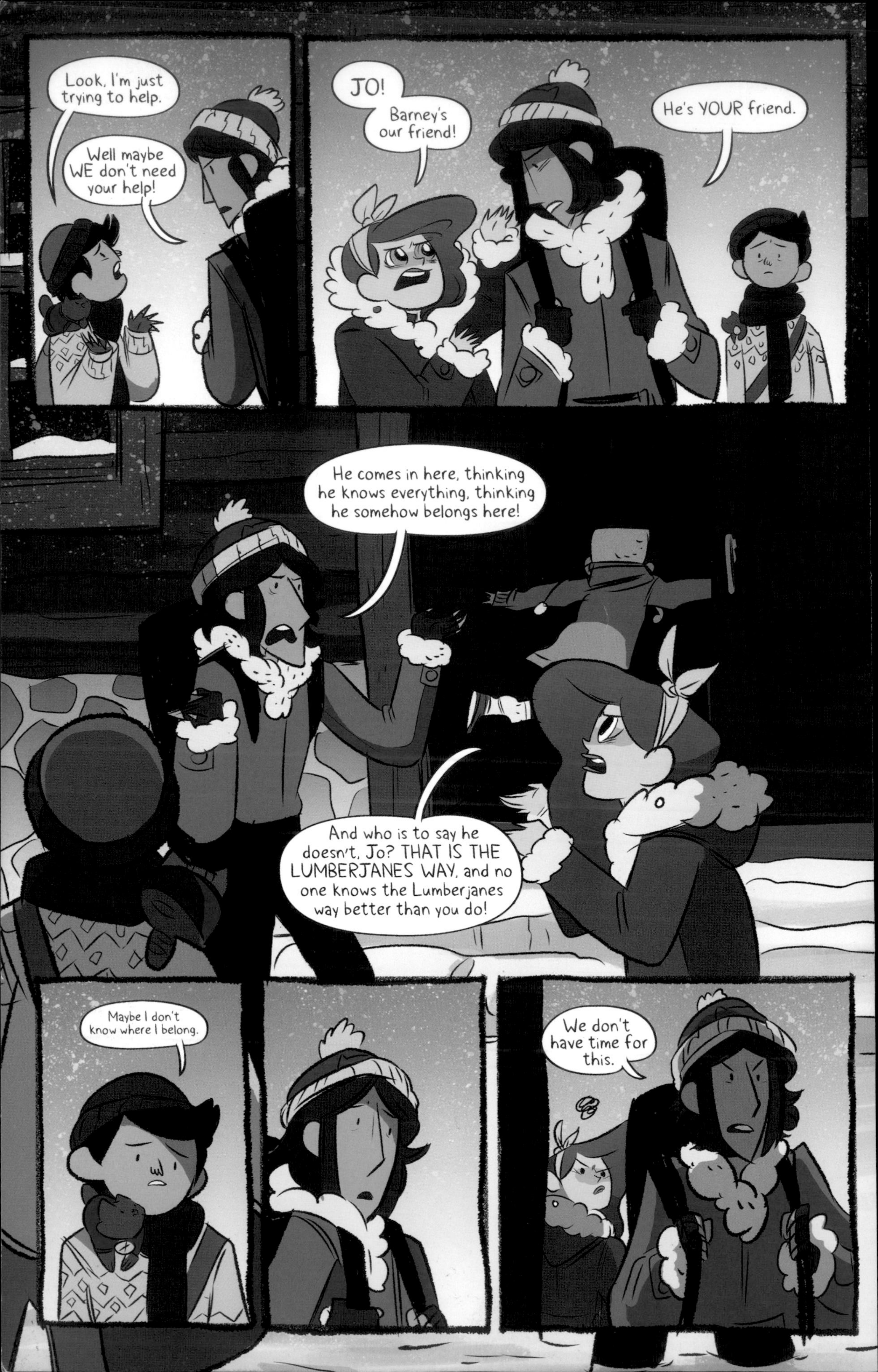
Look, I'm just trying to help.
Well maybe WE don't need your help!
JO!
Barney's our friend!
He's YOUR friend.
He comes in here, thinking he knows everything, thinking he somehow belongs here!
And who is to say he doesn't, Jo? THAT IS THE LUMBERJANES WAY, and no one knows the Lumberjanes way better than you do!
Maybe I don't know where I belong.
We don't have time for this.

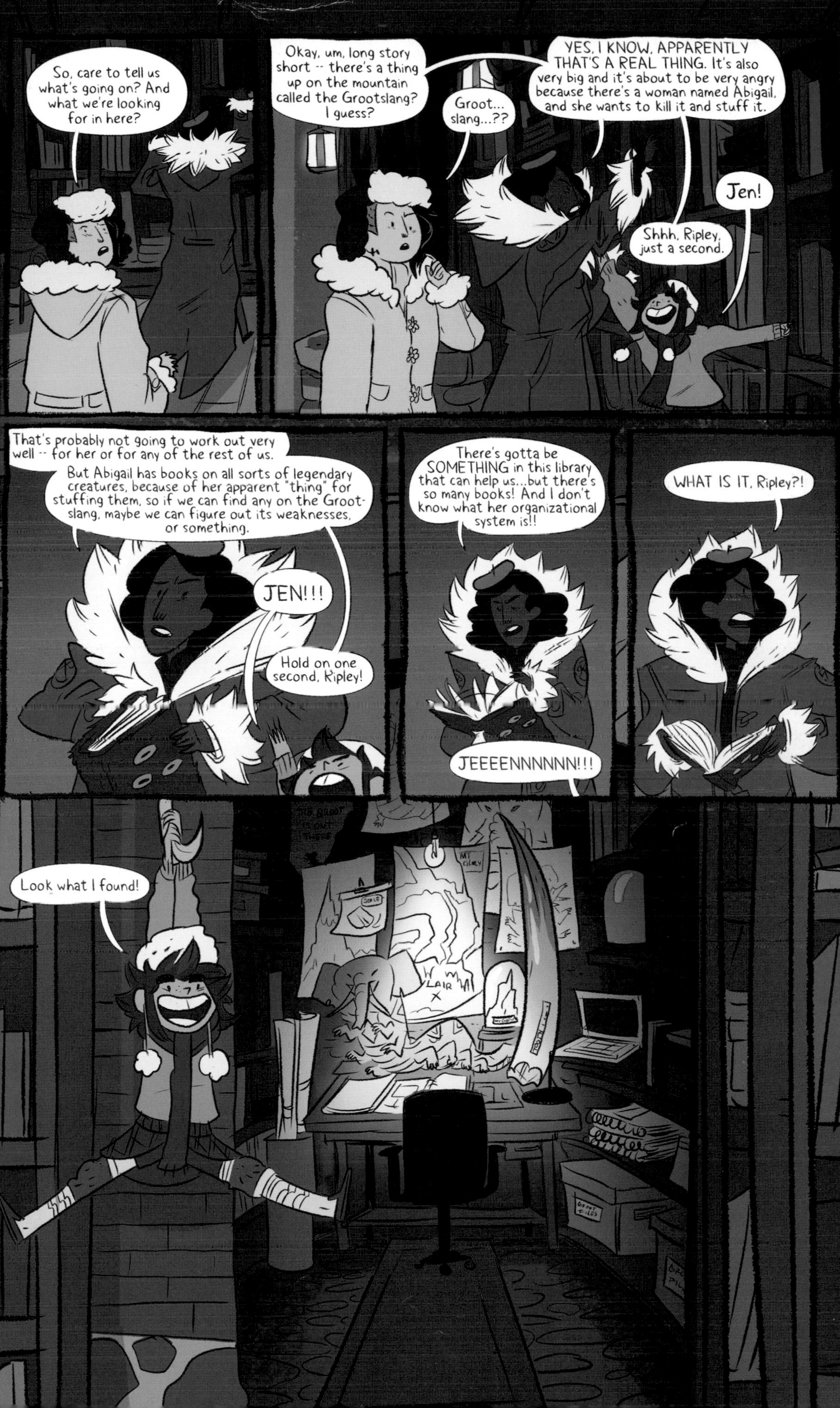

So, care to tell us what's going on? And what we're looking for in here?
Okay, um, long story short -- there's a thing up on the mountain called the Grootslang? I guess?
Groot... slang...??
YES, I KNOW, APPARENTLY THAT'S A REAL THING. It's also very big and it's about to be very angry because there's a woman named Abigail, and she wants to kill it and stuff it.
Jen!
Shhh, Ripley, just a second.
That's probably not going to work out very well -- for her or for any of the rest of us.
But Abigail has books on all sorts of legendary creatures, because of her apparent "thing" for stuffing them, so if we can find any on the Grootslang, maybe we can figure out its weaknesses, or something.
JEN!!!
Hold on one second, Ripley!
There's gotta be SOMETHING in this library that can help us...but there's so many books! And I don't know what her organizational system is!!
JEEEENNNNNN!!!
WHAT IS IT, Ripley?!
Look what I found!
LAIR

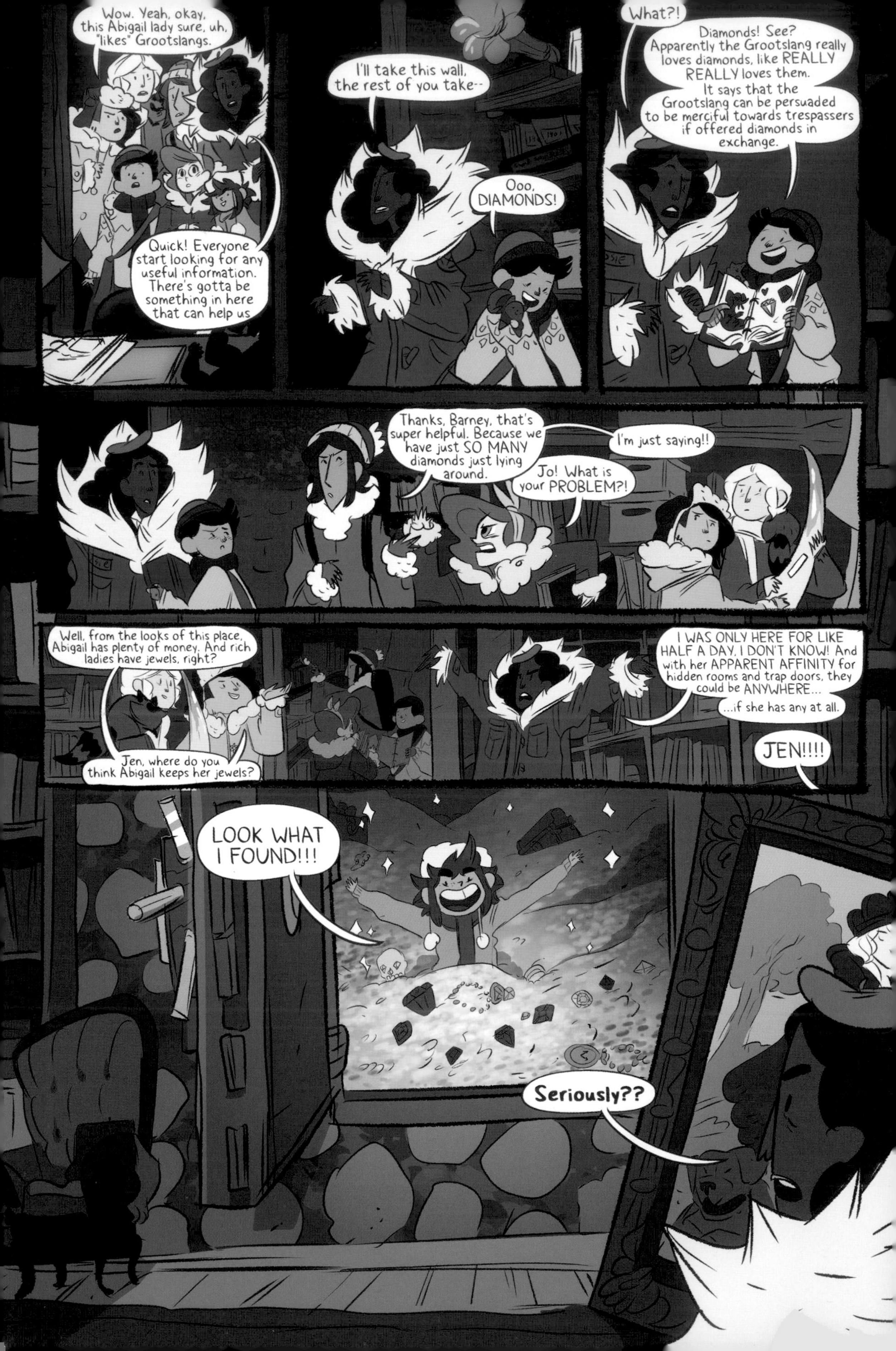

Wow. Yeah, okay, this Abigail lady sure, uh, "likes" Grootslangs.
Quick! Everyone start looking for any useful information. There's gotta be something in here that can help us
I'll take this wall, the rest of you take--
Ooo, DIAMONDS!
What?!
Diamonds! See? Apparently the Grootslang really loves diamonds, like REALLY REALLY loves them.
It says that the Grootslang can be persuaded to be merciful towards trespassers if offered diamonds in exchange.
Thanks, Barney, that's super helpful. Because we have just SO MANY diamonds just lying around.
I'm just saying!!
Jo! What is your PROBLEM?!
Well, from the looks of this place, Abigail has plenty of money. And rich ladies have jewels, right?
Jen, where do you think Abigail keeps her jewels?
I WAS ONLY HERE FOR LIKE HALF A DAY, I DON'T KNOW! And with her APPARENT AFFINITY for hidden rooms and trap doors, they could be ANYWHERE...
...if she has any at all.
JEN!!!!
LOOK WHAT I FOUND!!!
Seriously??

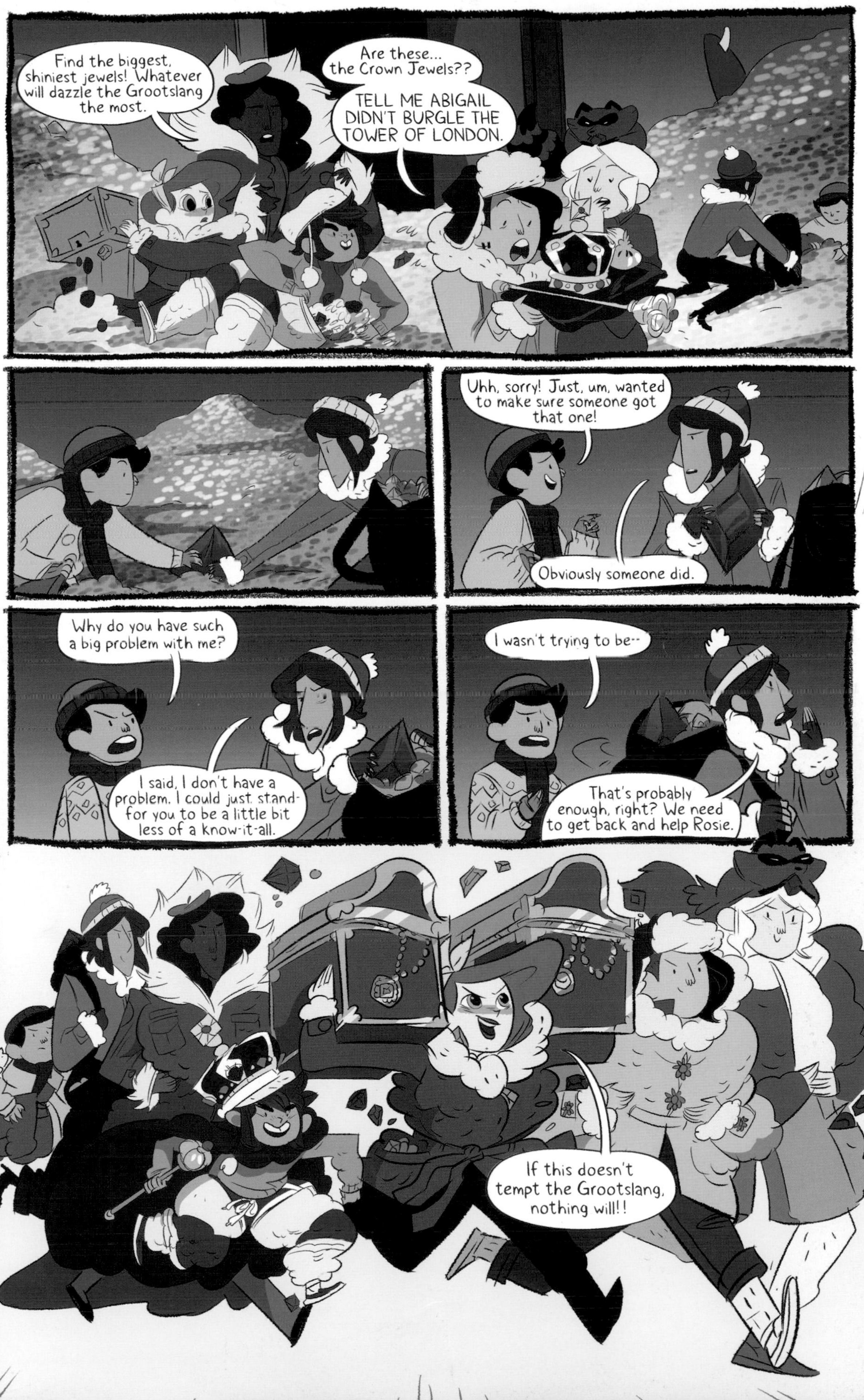

Find the biggest, shiniest jewels! Whatever will dazzle the Grootslang the most.
Are these... the Crown Jewels??
TELL ME ABIGAIL DIDN'T BURGLE THE TOWER OF LONDON.
Uhh, sorry! Just, um, wanted to make sure someone got that one!
Obviously someone did.
Why do you have such a big problem with me?
I said, I don't have a problem. I could just stand for you to be a little bit less of a know-it-all.
I wasn't trying to be--
That's probably enough, right? We need to get back and help Rosie.
If this doesn't tempt the Grootslang, nothing will!!

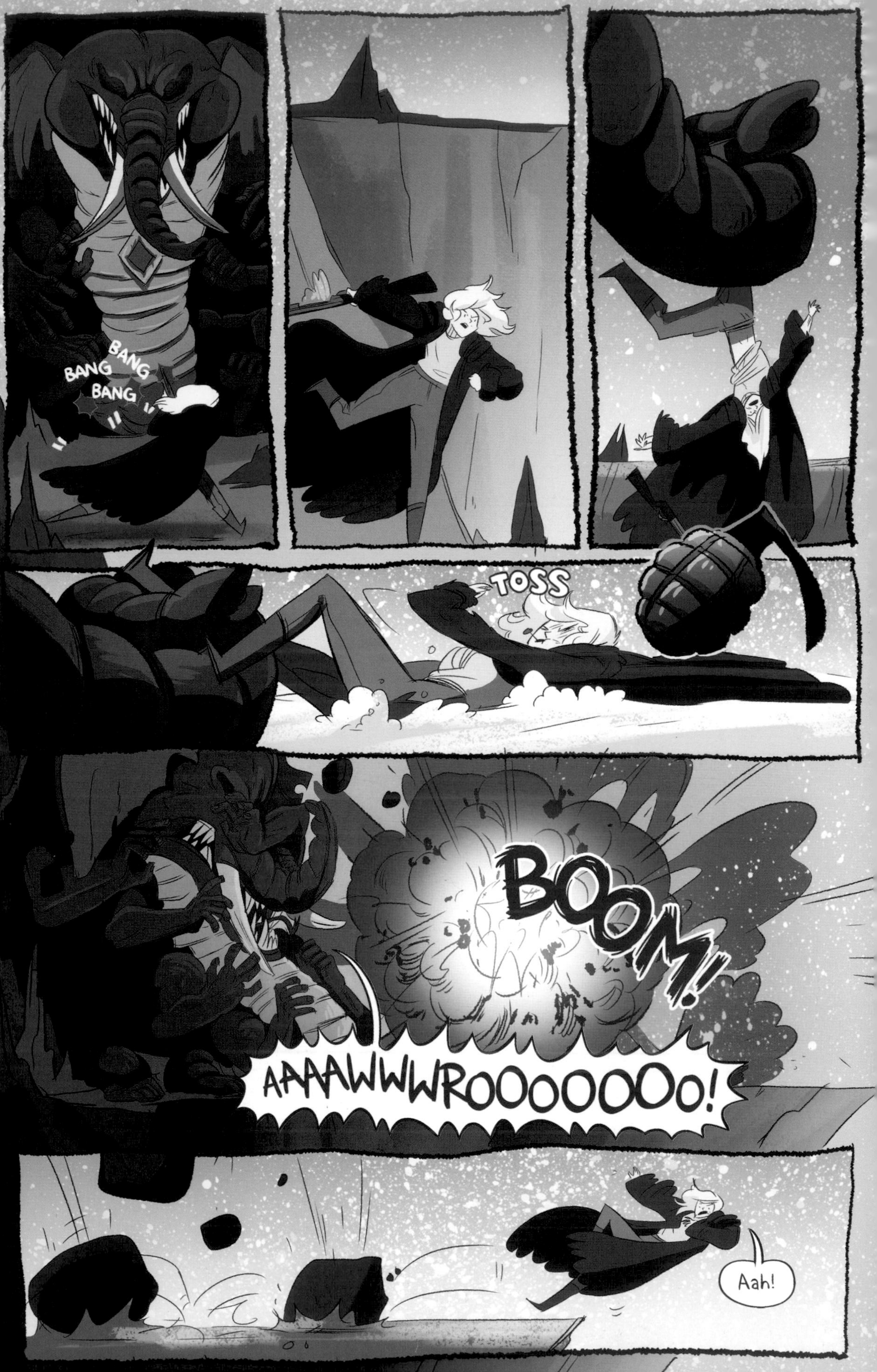
BANG
BANG
BANG
TOSS
BOOM!
AAAAWWWROOOOOOOo!
Aah!

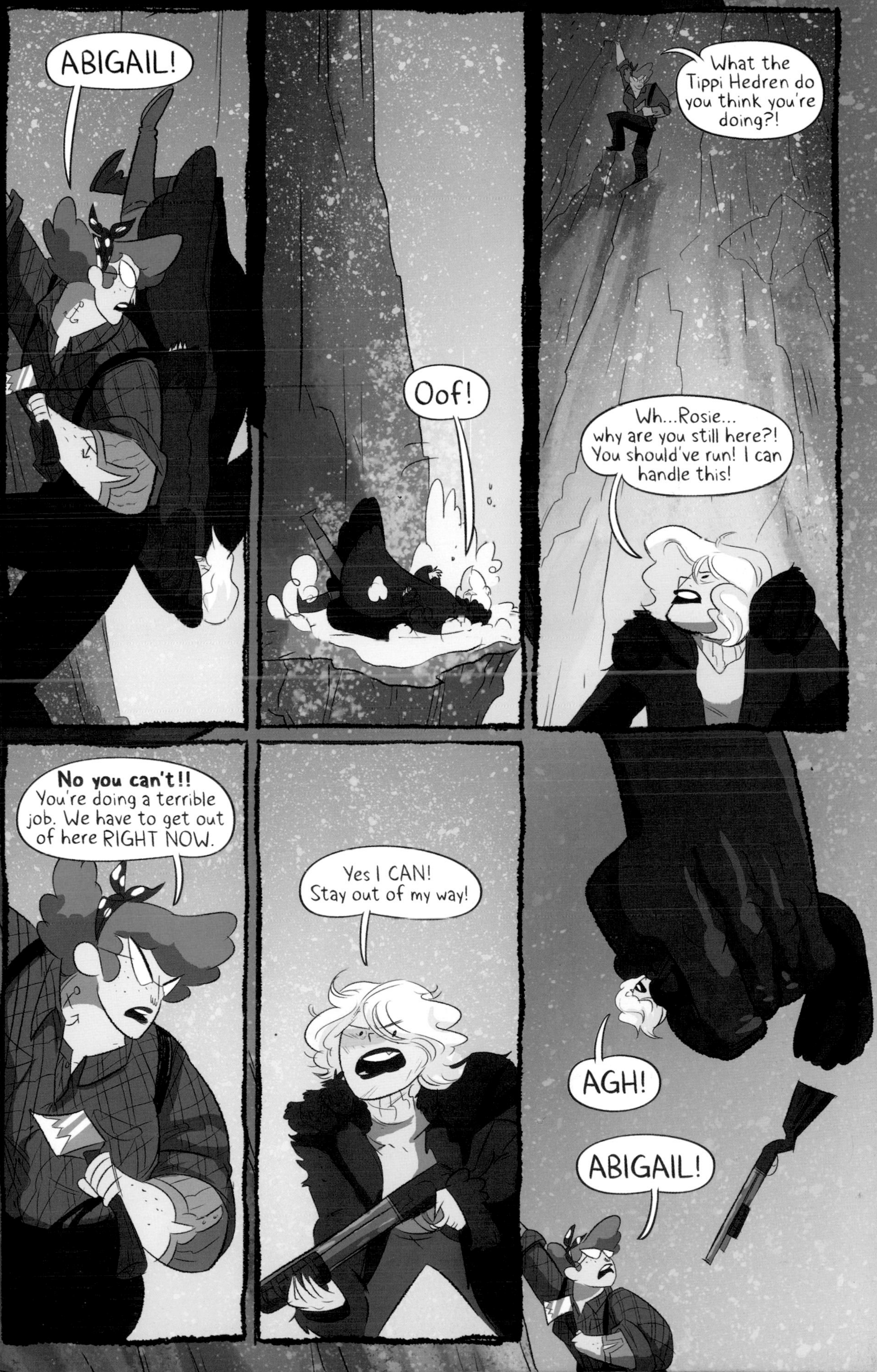
ABIGAIL!
Oof!
What the Tippi Hedren do you think you're doing?!
Wh...Rosie... why are you still here?! You should've run! I can handle this!
No you can't!! You're doing a terrible job. We have to get out of here RIGHT NOW.
Yes I CAN! Stay out of my way!
AGH!
ABIGAIL!

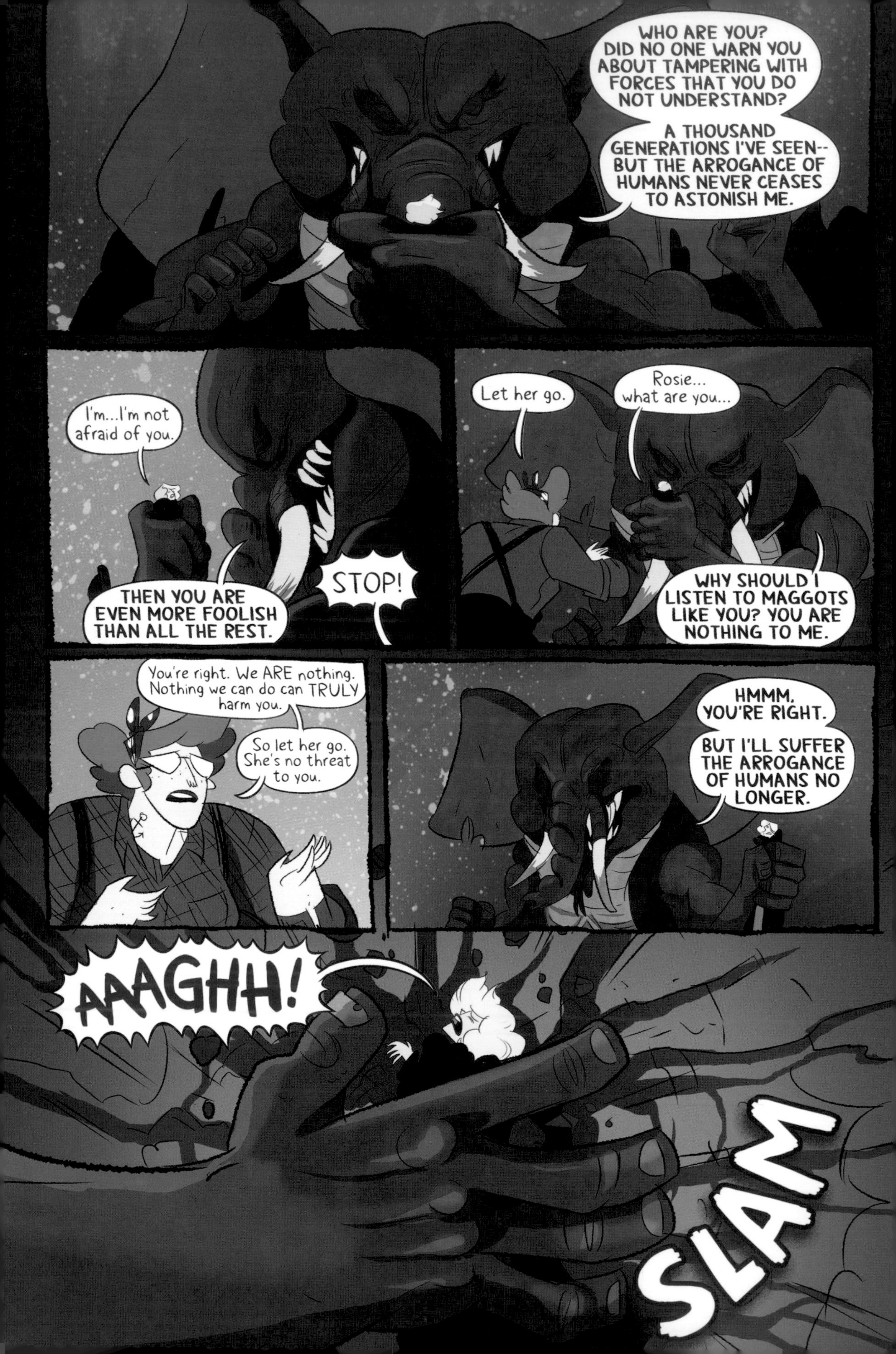
WHO ARE YOU? DID NO ONE WARN YOU ABOUT TAMPERING WITH FORCES THAT YOU DO NOT UNDERSTAND?
A THOUSAND GENERATIONS I'VE SEEN-- BUT THE ARROGANCE OF HUMANS NEVER CEASES TO ASTONISH ME.
I'm...I'm not afraid of you.
THEN YOU ARE EVEN MORE FOOLISH THAN ALL THE REST.
STOP!
Let her go.
Rosie... what are you...
WHY SHOULD I LISTEN TO MAGGOTS LIKE YOU? YOU ARE NOTHING TO ME.
You're right. We ARE nothing. Nothing we can do can TRULY harm you.
So let her go. She's no threat to you.
HMMM, YOU'RE RIGHT.
BUT I'LL SUFFER THE ARROGANCE OF HUMANS NO LONGER.
AAAGHH!
SLAM

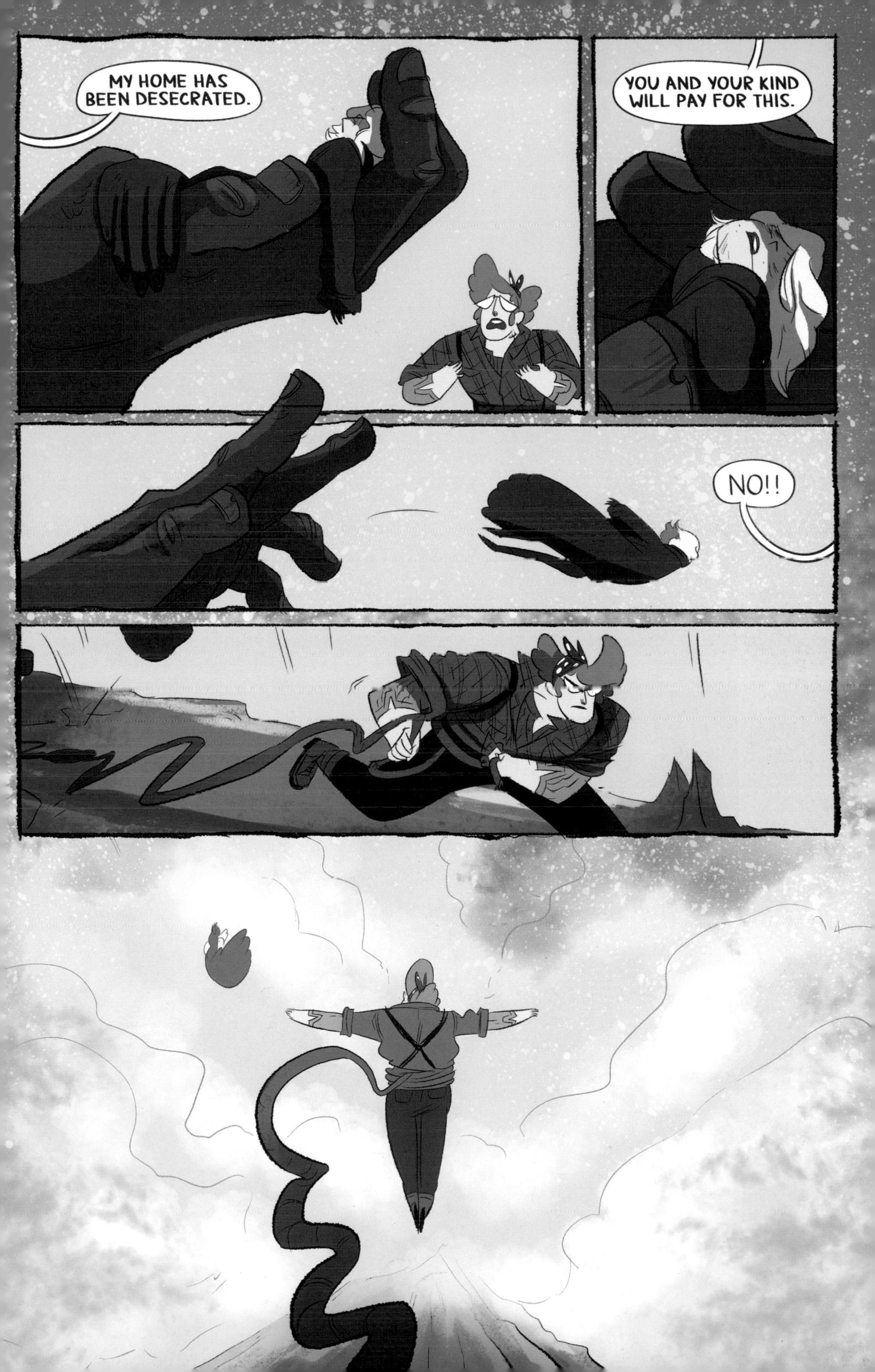
MY HOME HAS BEEN DESECRATED.
YOU AND YOUR KIND WILL PAY FOR THIS.
NO!!

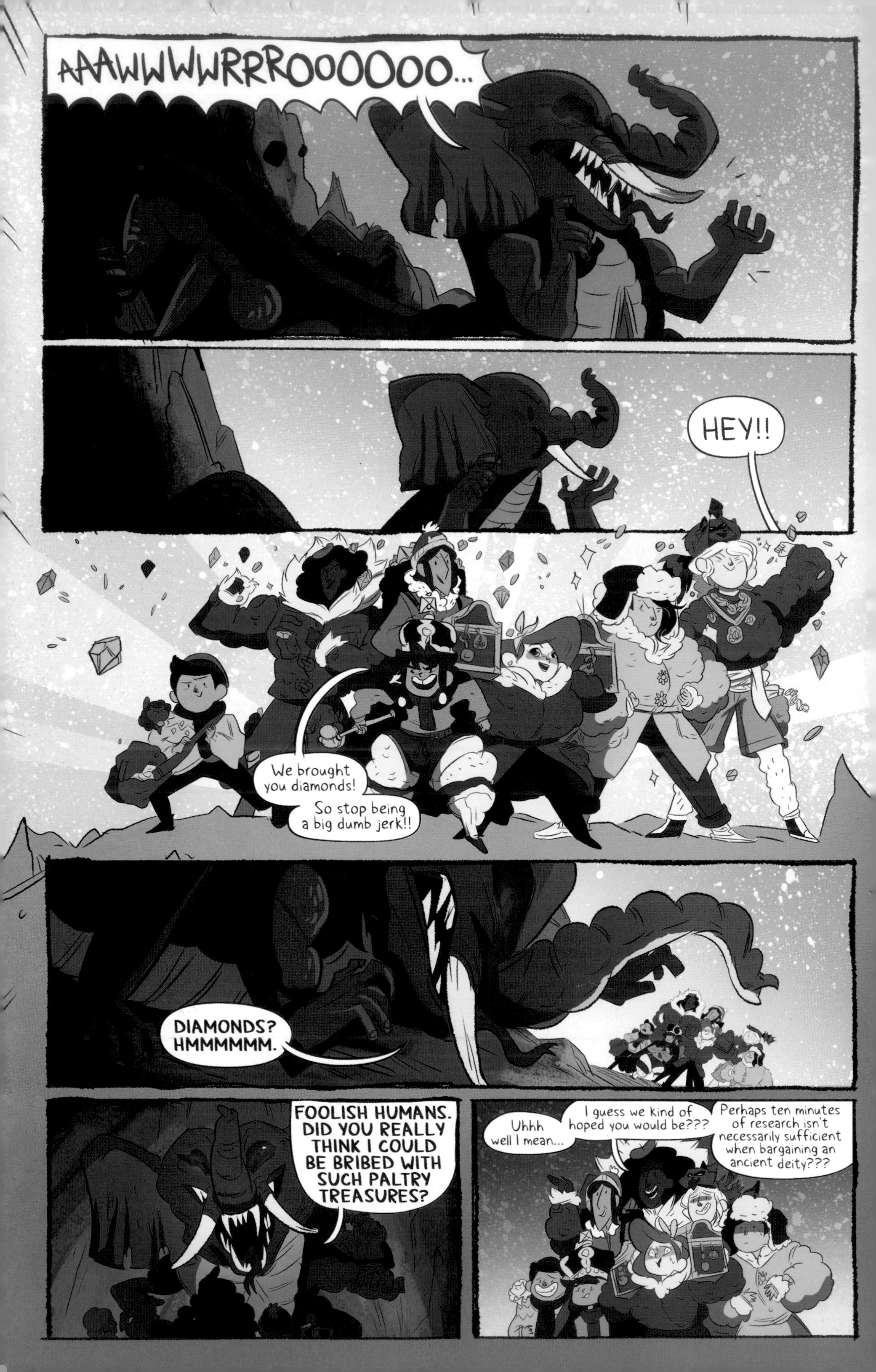
AAAWWWWRRROOOOOO...
HEY!!
We brought you diamonds!
So stop being a big dumb jerk!!
DIAMONDS? HMMMMMM.
FOOLISH HUMANS. DID YOU REALLY THINK I COULD BE BRIBED WITH SUCH PALTRY TREASURES?
Uhhh well I mean...
I guess we kind of hoped you would be???
Perhaps ten minutes of research isn't necessarily sufficient when bargaining an ancient deity???

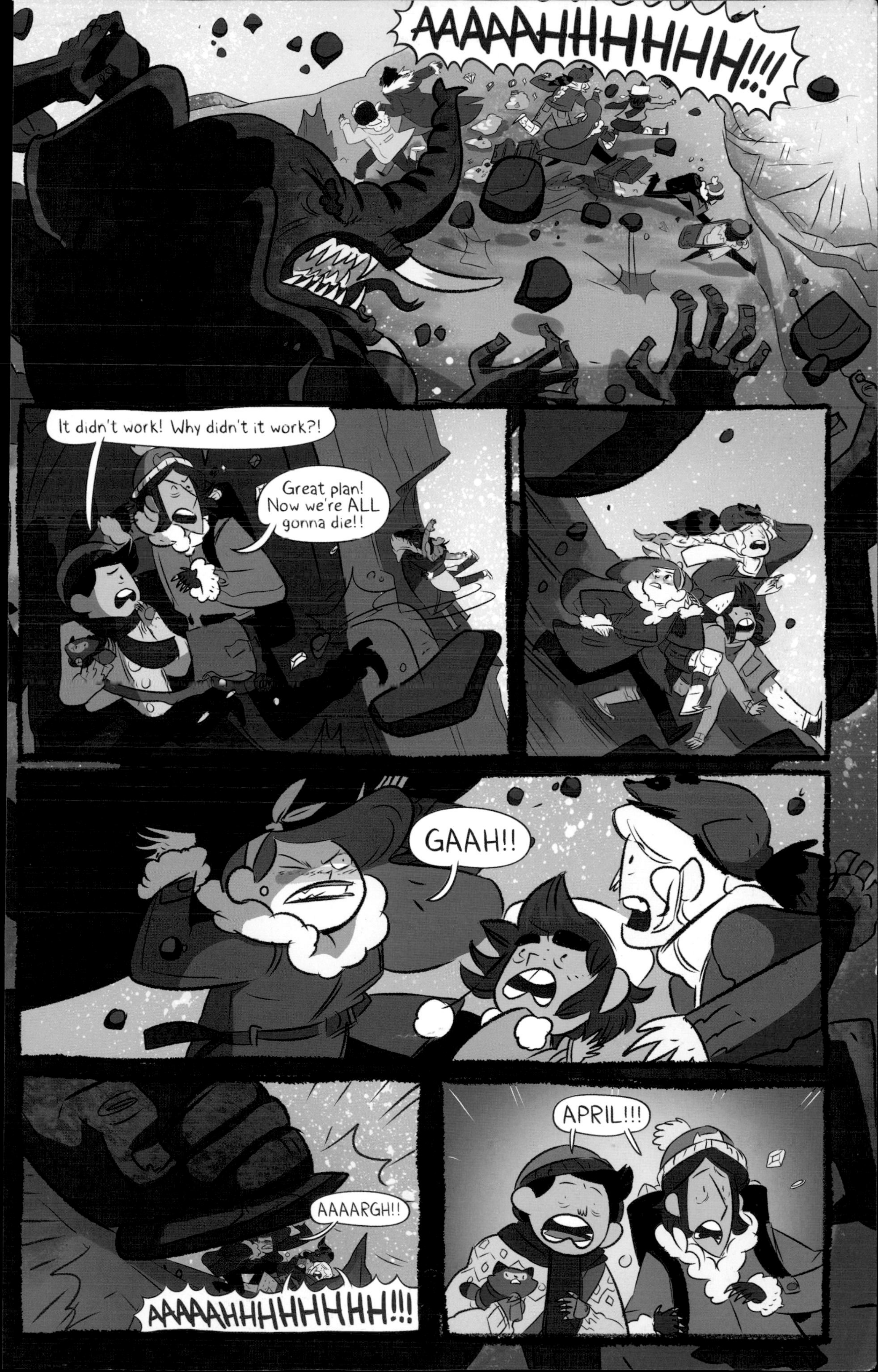
AAAAAHHHHHH!!!
It didn't work! Why didn't it work?!
Great plan! Now we're ALL gonna die!!
GAAH!!
AAAARGH!!
AAAAAHHHHHHHHH!!!
APRIL!!!

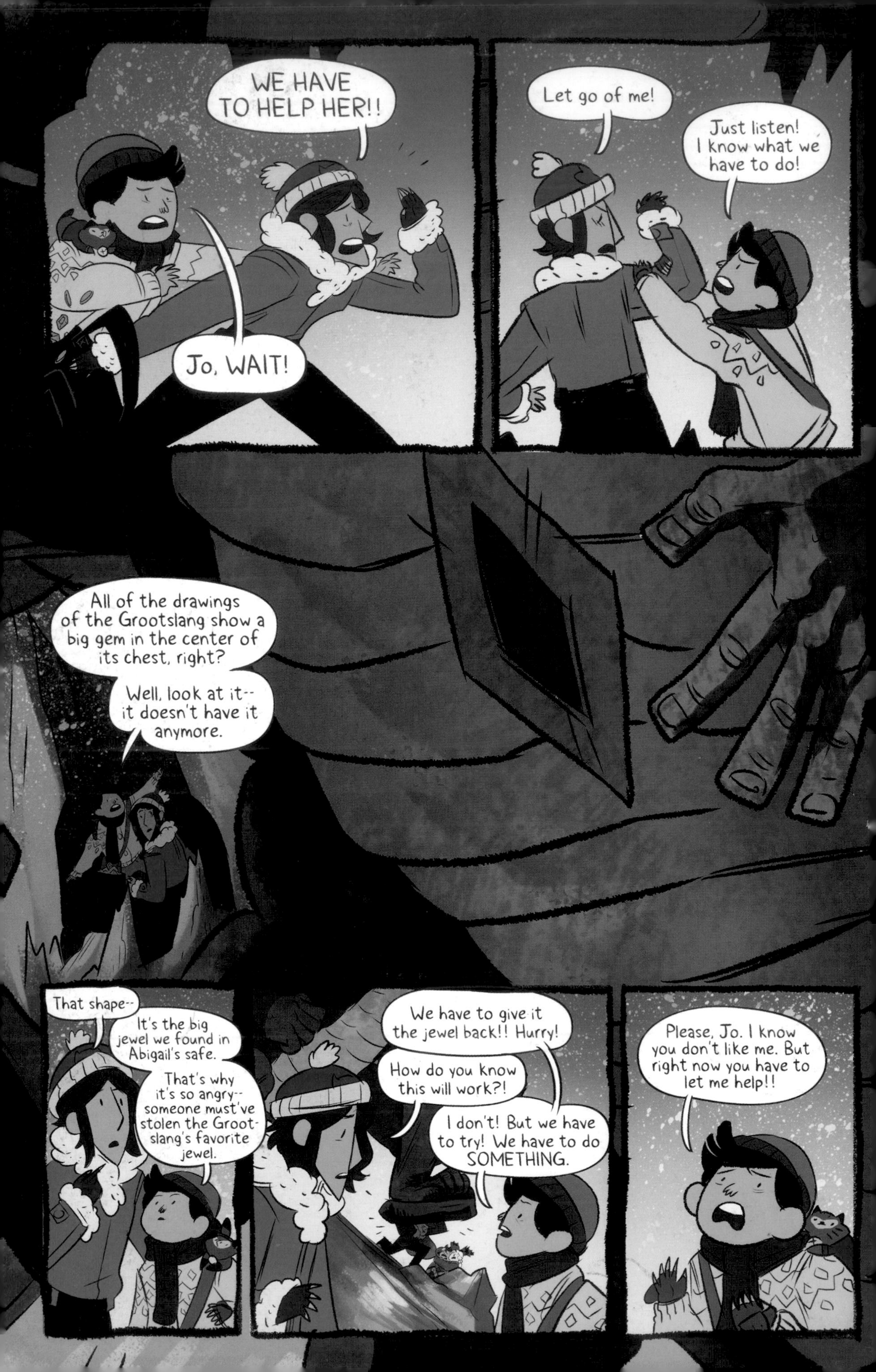
WE HAVE TO HELP HER!!
Jo, WAIT!
Let go of me!
Just listen! I know what we have to do!
All of the drawings of the Grootslang show a big gem in the center of its chest, right?
Well, look at it-- it doesn't have it anymore.
That shape--
It's the big jewel we found in Abigail's safe.
That's why it's so angry-- someone must've stolen the Grootslang's favorite jewel.
We have to give it the jewel back!! Hurry!
How do you know this will work?!
I don't! But we have to try! We have to do SOMETHING.
Please, Jo. I know you don't like me. But right now you have to let me help!!

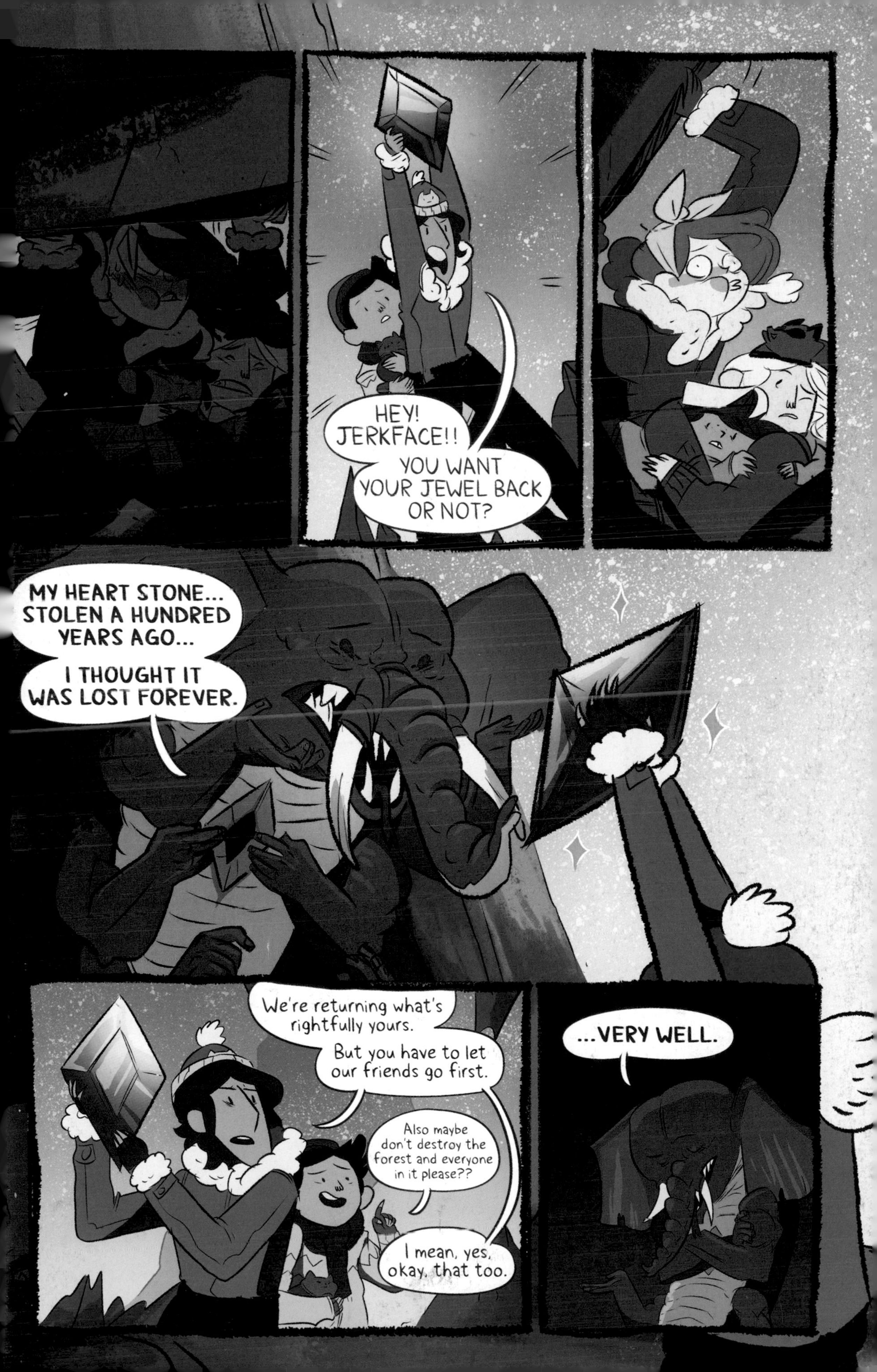
HEY! JERKFACE!!
YOU WANT YOUR JEWEL BACK OR NOT?
MY HEART STONE... STOLEN A HUNDRED YEARS AGO...
I THOUGHT IT WAS LOST FOREVER.
We're returning what's rightfully yours.
But you have to let our friends go first.
Also maybe don't destroy the forest and everyone in it please??
I mean, yes, okay, that too.
...VERY WELL.

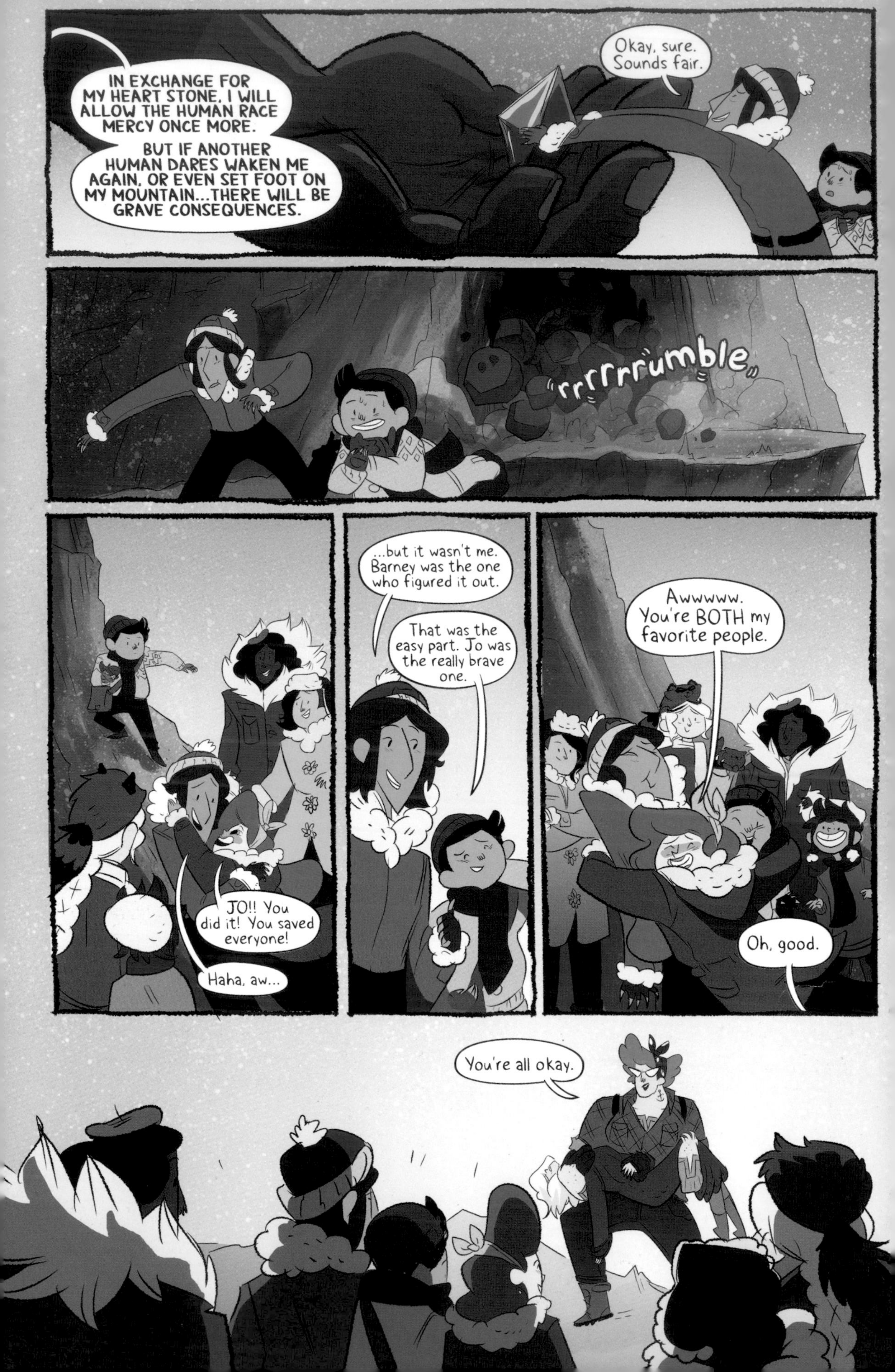
IN EXCHANGE FOR MY HEART STONE, I WILL ALLOW THE HUMAN RACE MERCY ONCE MORE.
BUT IF ANOTHER HUMAN DARES WAKEN ME AGAIN, OR EVEN SET FOOT ON MY MOUNTAIN...THERE WILL BE GRAVE CONSEQUENCES.
Okay, sure. Sounds fair.
"rrrrrrumble"
JO!! You did it! You saved everyone!
Haha, aw...
...but it wasn't me. Barney was the one who figured it out.
That was the easy part. Jo was the really brave one.
Awwwww. You're BOTH my favorite people.
Oh, good.
You're all okay.

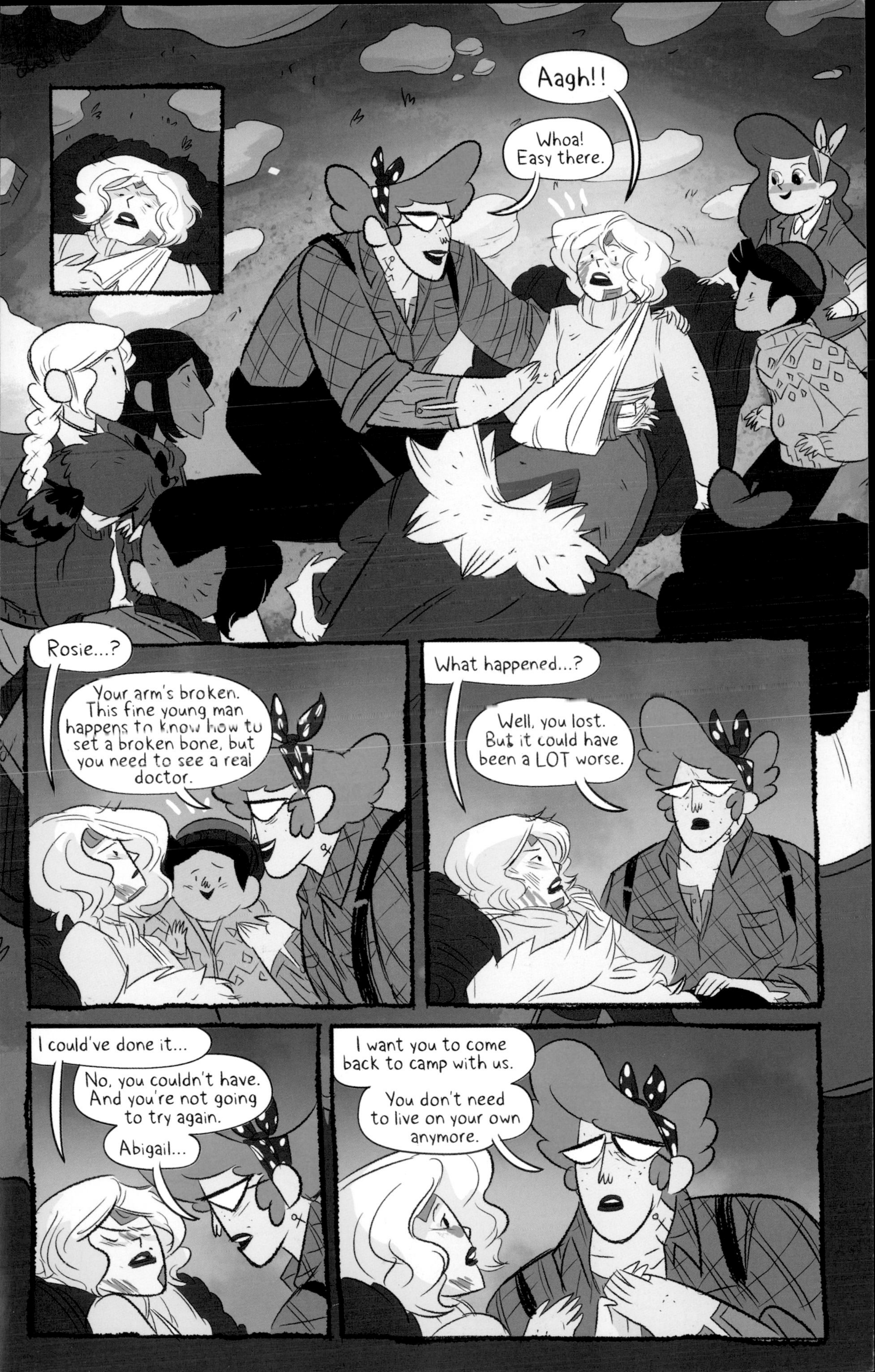

Aagh!!
Whoa! Easy there.
Rosie...?
Your arm's broken. This fine young man happens to know how to set a broken bone, but you need to see a real doctor.
What happened...?
Well, you lost. But it could have been a LOT worse.
I could've done it...
No, you couldn't have. And you're not going to try again.
Abigail...
I want you to come back to camp with us.
You don't need to live on your own anymore.

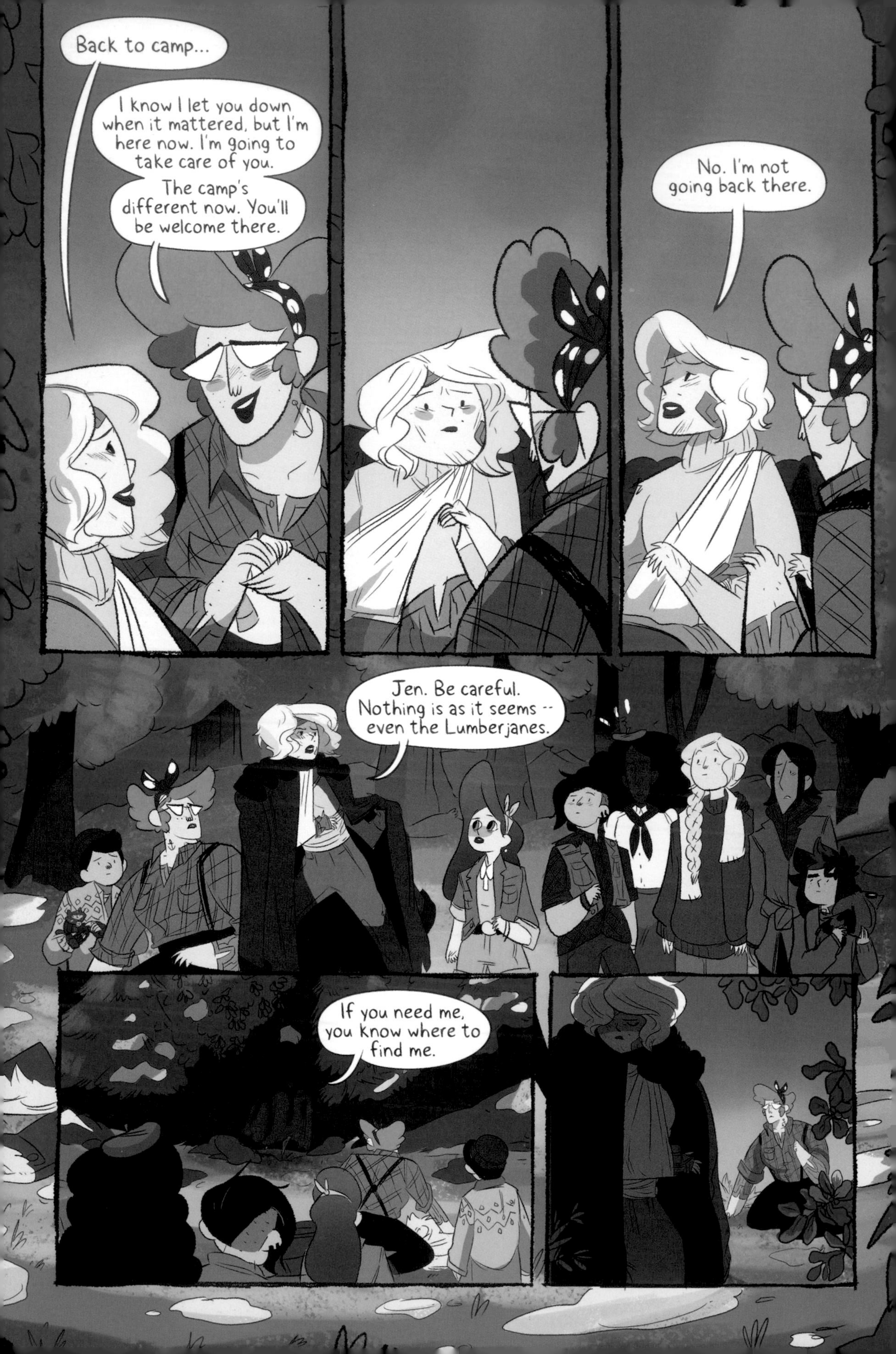
Back to camp...
I know I let you down when it mattered, but I'm here now. I'm going to take care of you.
The camp's different now. You'll be welcome there.
No. I'm not going back there.
Jen. Be careful. Nothing is as it seems -- even the Lumberjanes.
If you need me, you know where to find me.

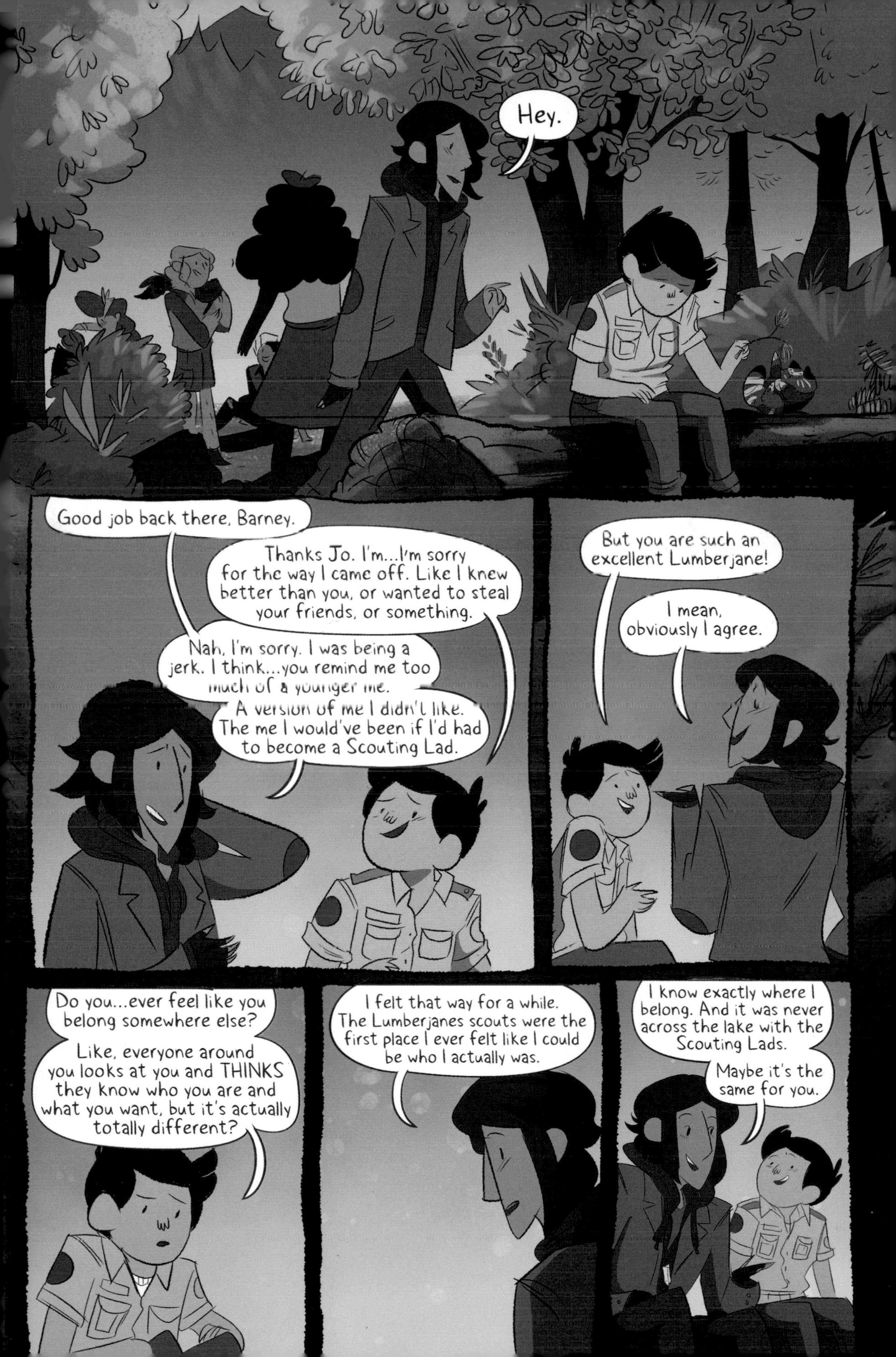
Hey.
Good job back there, Barney.
Thanks Jo. I'm...I'm sorry for the way I came off. Like I knew better than you, or wanted to steal your friends, or something.
Nah, I'm sorry. I was being a jerk. I think...you remind me too much of a younger me.
A version of me I didn't like. The me I would've been if I'd had to become a Scouting Lad.
But you are such an excellent Lumberjane!
I mean, obviously I agree.
Do you...ever feel like you belong somewhere else?
Like, everyone around you looks at you and THINKS they know who you are and what you want, but it's actually totally different?
I felt that way for a while. The Lumberjanes scouts were the first place I ever felt like I could be who I actually was.
I know exactly where I belong. And it was never across the lake with the Scouting Lads.
Maybe it's the same for you.

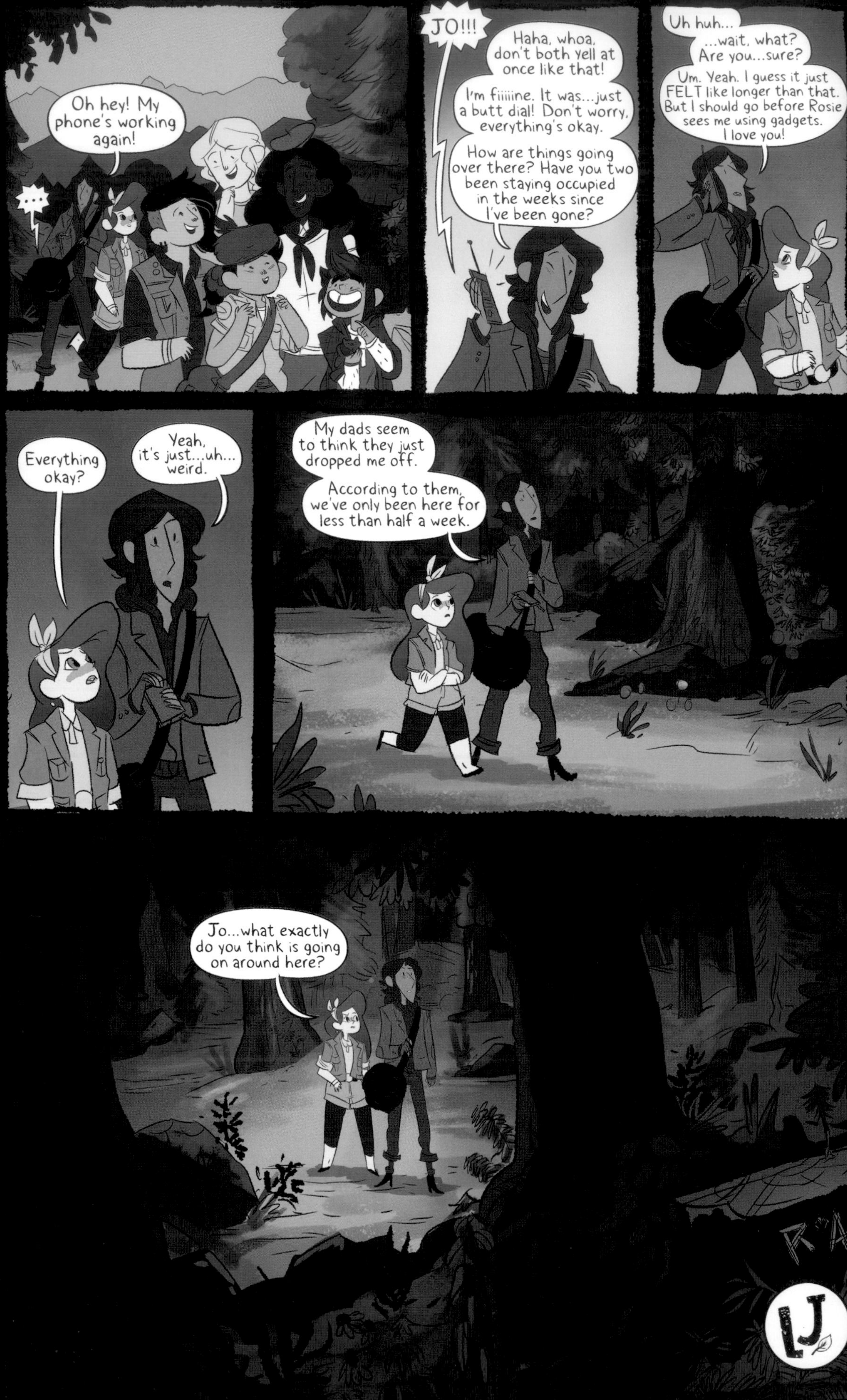

Oh hey! My phone's working again!
...
JO!!!
Haha, whoa, don't both yell at once like that!
I'm fiiiiine. It was...just a butt dial! Don't worry, everything's okay.
How are things going over there? Have you two been staying occupied in the weeks since I've been gone?
Uh huh...
...wait, what? Are you...sure?
Um. Yeah. I guess it just FELT like longer than that. But I should go before Rosie sees me using gadgets. I love you!
Everything okay?
Yeah, it's just...uh... weird.
My dads seem to think they just dropped me off.
According to them, we've only been here for less than half a week.
Jo...what exactly do you think is going on around here?

will co...
The ...
It he...
appearan...
dress f...
Further...
Lumber...
to have...
part in...
Thiskv...
Hardc...
have ...
them ...

MO MONEY, MO PROBLEMS...

The ...
yellow, short sl...
emb...
the w...
choose...
slacks, ...
made o...
out-of-dc...
green bere...
the colla...
Shoes ma...
heels, rou...
socks sho...
the uniform. Ne... ...es, bracelets, or other jewelry do ...
belong with a Lumberjane uniform.

HOW TO WEAR ...

To look well in a uniform ...
uniform be kept in goc...
pressed. See that the skirt i...
height and build, that the b...
that your shoes and stocking...
uniform, that you watch your post...
with dignity and grace. If the beret is removed indoors,
be sure that your hair is neat and kept in place with an
insconspicuous clip or ribbon. When you wear a
Lumberjane uniform you are identified as a member of
this organization and you should be doubly careful to
conduct yourself in a way that will show everyone that
courtesy and thoughtfullness are part of being a
Lumberjane. People are likely to judge a whole nation by
the selfishness of a few individuals, to criticize a whole
family because of the misconduct of one member, and to
feel unkindly toward and organization because of the

...IE UNIFORM

...should be worn at camp
...events when Lumberjanes
...n may also be worn at other
...ions. It should be worn as a
...the uniform dress with
...rect shoes, and stocking or

...out grows her uniform or
...ter Lumberjane.
...a she has
...her
...her

...ES

The unifor...
helps to cre...
in a group. ...
active life th...
another bond...
future, and pr...
in order to b...
Lumberjane pr...
Penniquiqul Thi...
Types, but m... ...es will wish to have one. They
can either b... ...uniform, or make it themselves from
materials available at the trading post.

FOR ONCE, JEN DROVE US CRAZY!

TEAMWORK TO THE MAX!

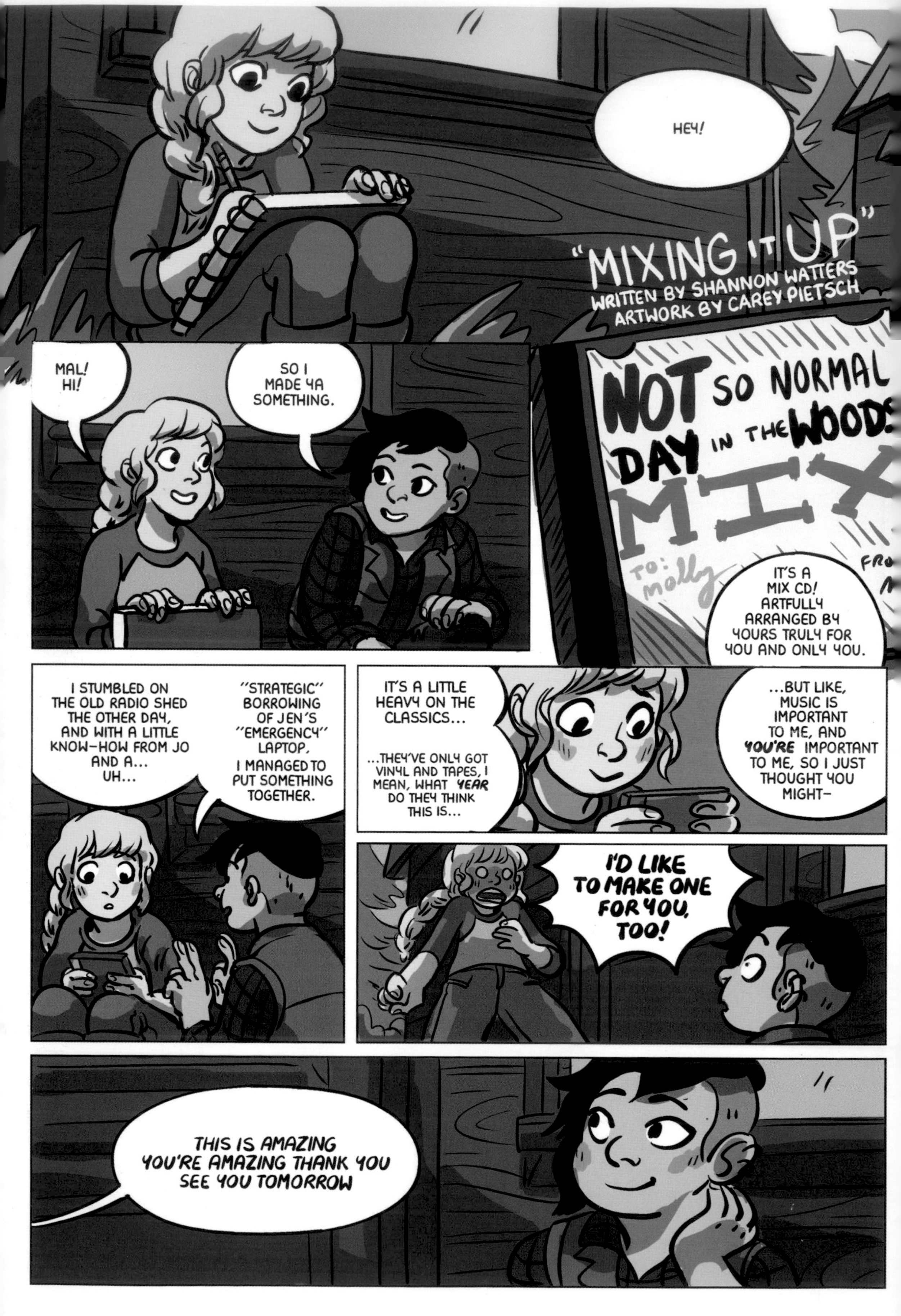
HEY!
"MIXING IT UP"
WRITTEN BY SHANNON WATTERS
ARTWORK BY CAREY PIETSCH
MAL! HI!
SO I MADE YA SOMETHING.
NOT SO NORMAL DAY IN THE WOODS MIX
TO: molly
IT'S A MIX CD! ARTFULLY ARRANGED BY YOURS TRULY FOR YOU AND ONLY YOU.
I STUMBLED ON THE OLD RADIO SHED THE OTHER DAY, AND WITH A LITTLE KNOW-HOW FROM JO AND A... UH...
"STRATEGIC" BORROWING OF JEN'S "EMERGENCY" LAPTOP, I MANAGED TO PUT SOMETHING TOGETHER.
IT'S A LITTLE HEAVY ON THE CLASSICS...
...THEY'VE ONLY GOT VINYL AND TAPES, I MEAN, WHAT YEAR DO THEY THINK THIS IS...
...BUT LIKE, MUSIC IS IMPORTANT TO ME, AND YOU'RE IMPORTANT TO ME, SO I JUST THOUGHT YOU MIGHT-
I'D LIKE TO MAKE ONE FOR YOU, TOO!
THIS IS AMAZING YOU'RE AMAZING THANK YOU SEE YOU TOMORROW

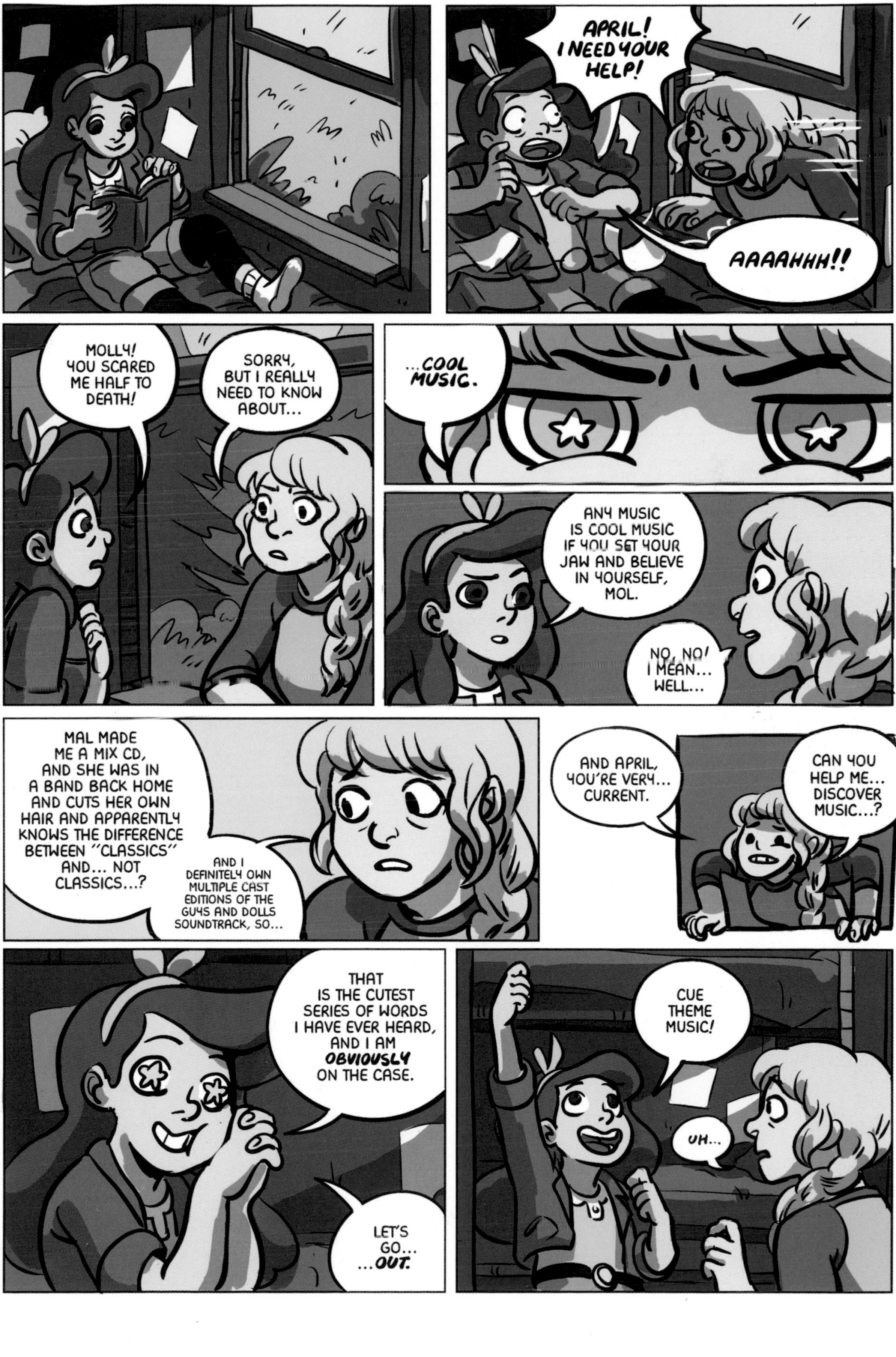
APRIL! I NEED YOUR HELP!
AAAAHHH!!
MOLLY! YOU SCARED ME HALF TO DEATH!
SORRY, BUT I REALLY NEED TO KNOW ABOUT...
...COOL MUSIC.
ANY MUSIC IS COOL MUSIC IF YOU SET YOUR JAW AND BELIEVE IN YOURSELF, MOL.
NO, NO! I MEAN... WELL...
MAL MADE ME A MIX CD, AND SHE WAS IN A BAND BACK HOME AND CUTS HER OWN HAIR AND APPARENTLY KNOWS THE DIFFERENCE BETWEEN "CLASSICS" AND... NOT CLASSICS...?
AND I DEFINITELY OWN MULTIPLE CAST EDITIONS OF THE GUYS AND DOLLS SOUNDTRACK, SO...
AND APRIL, YOU'RE VERY... CURRENT.
CAN YOU HELP ME... DISCOVER MUSIC...?
THAT IS THE CUTEST SERIES OF WORDS I HAVE EVER HEARD, AND I AM OBVIOUSLY ON THE CASE.
LET'S GO... ...OUT.
CUE THEME MUSIC!
UH...

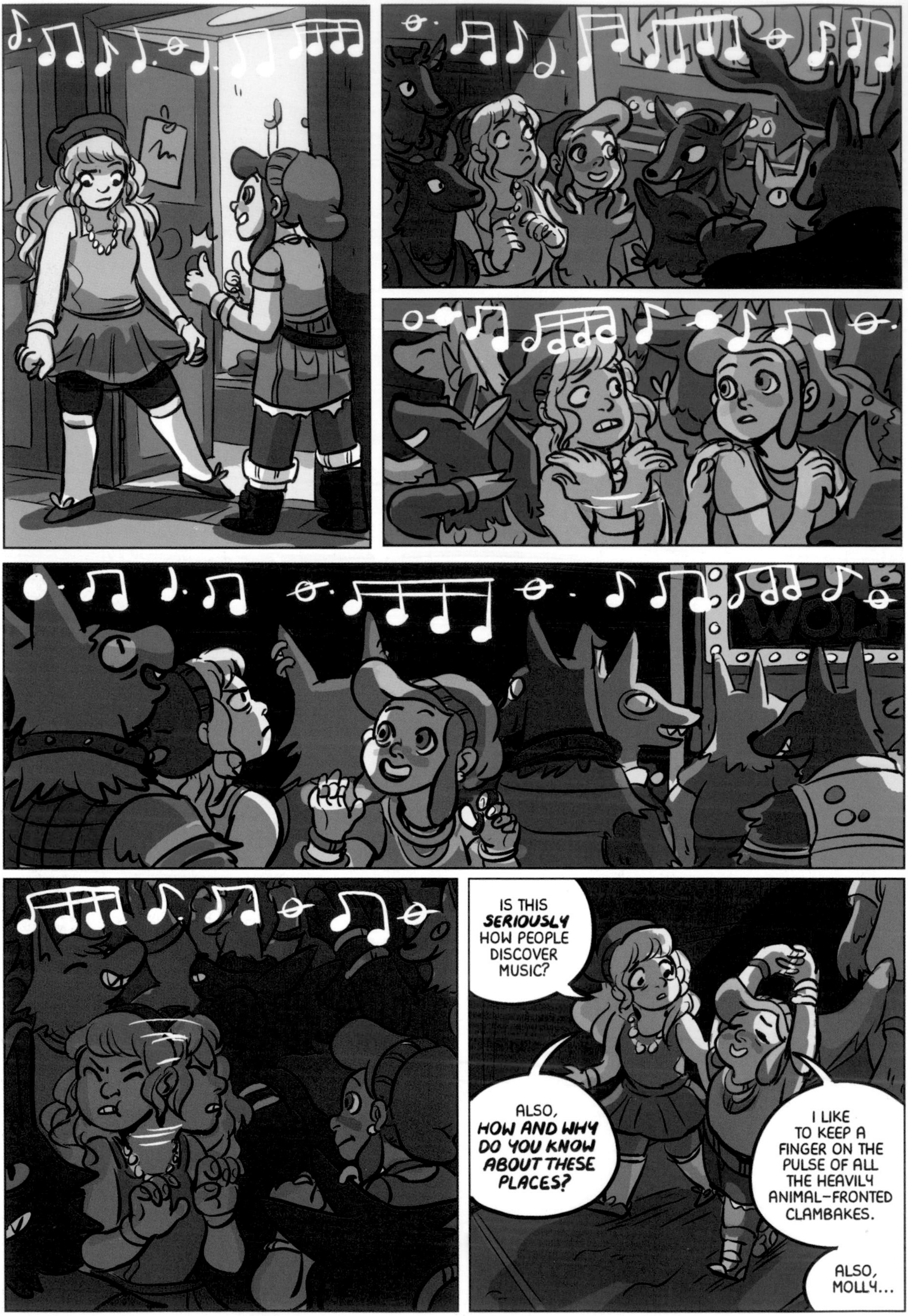
IS THIS SERIOUSLY HOW PEOPLE DISCOVER MUSIC?
ALSO, HOW AND WHY DO YOU KNOW ABOUT THESE PLACES?
I LIKE TO KEEP A FINGER ON THE PULSE OF ALL THE HEAVILY ANIMAL-FRONTED CLAMBAKES.
ALSO, MOLLY...

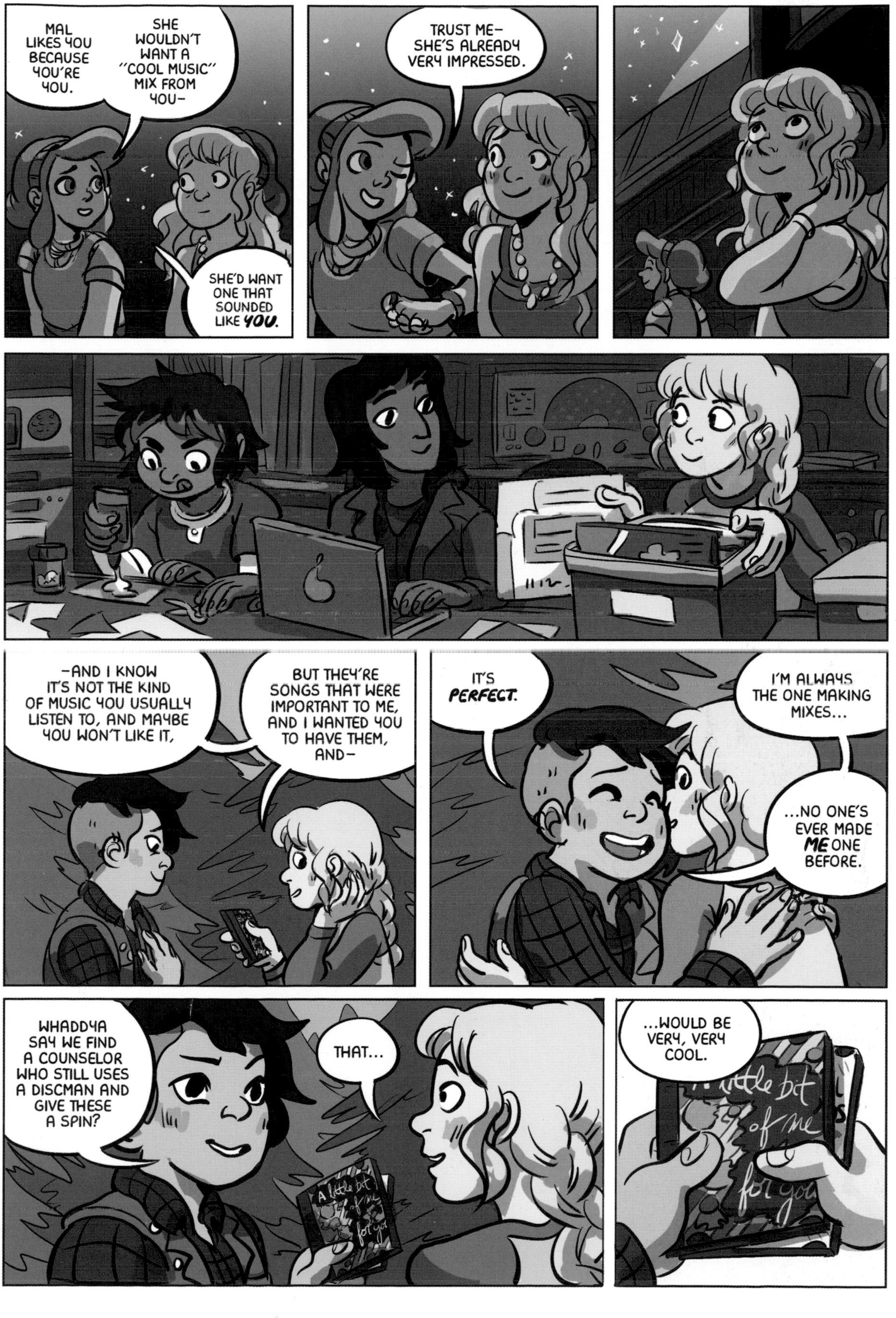
MAL LIKES YOU BECAUSE YOU'RE YOU.
SHE WOULDN'T WANT A "COOL MUSIC" MIX FROM YOU–
SHE'D WANT ONE THAT SOUNDED LIKE *YOU*.
TRUST ME– SHE'S ALREADY VERY IMPRESSED.
–AND I KNOW IT'S NOT THE KIND OF MUSIC YOU USUALLY LISTEN TO, AND MAYBE YOU WON'T LIKE IT,
BUT THEY'RE SONGS THAT WERE IMPORTANT TO ME, AND I WANTED YOU TO HAVE THEM, AND–
IT'S *PERFECT*.
I'M ALWAYS THE ONE MAKING MIXES...
...NO ONE'S EVER MADE **ME** ONE BEFORE.
WHADDYA SAY WE FIND A COUNSELOR WHO STILL USES A DISCMAN AND GIVE THESE A SPIN?
THAT...
...WOULD BE VERY, VERY COOL.
A little bit of me for you

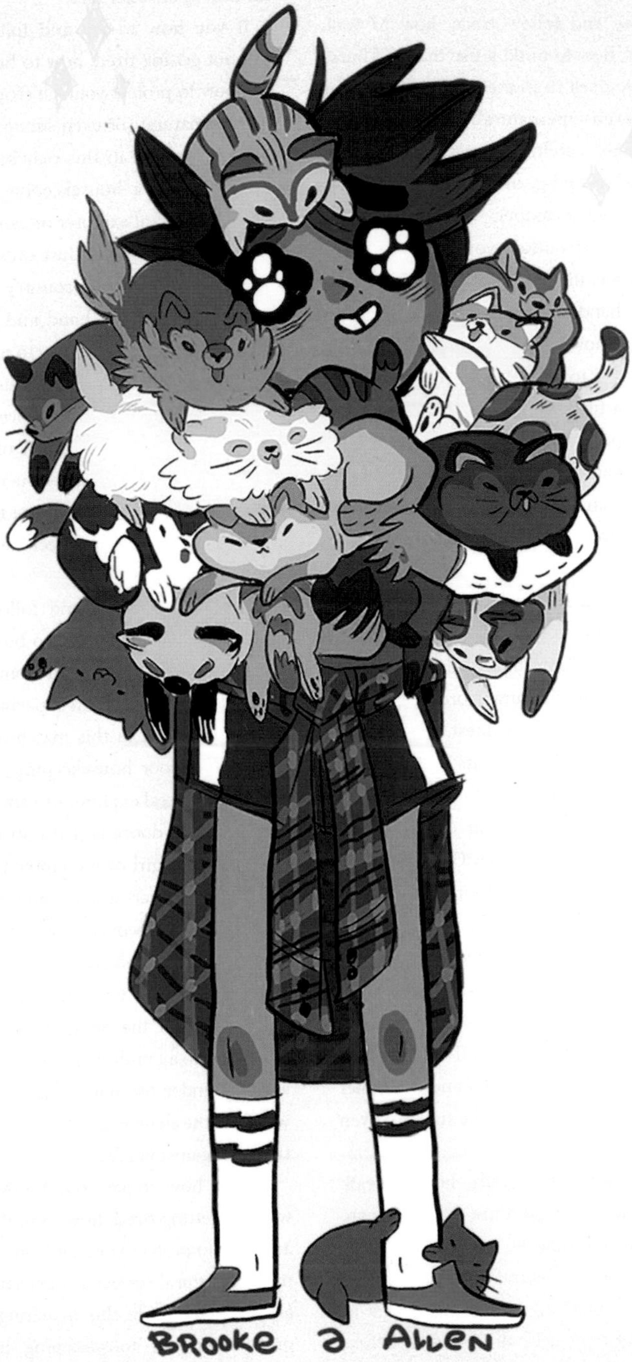
BROOKE A ALLEN

LUMBERJANES FIELD MANUAL
AFTERWORD

When I got the email from Shannon asking if I could take a look at the issues of *Lumberjanes* where Jo comes out as trans, I tweeted that I had just received "one of the best emails of my life, on the same level as confirming my first (Hormone Replacement Therapy) appointment." And I wasn't exaggerating. Trans representation, especially when it comes to trans kids, is tremendously important to me, and when I learned that the *Lumberjanes* team was asking for advice from a trans woman and taking every step they could to make sure they got this storyline right, I knew that the same was true for them. They knew how important it was to get this moment right because they knew that somewhere, a young trans girl would pick up *Lumberjanes* #17, read those words that Jo says, and finally feel good about who they are.

So often society tells girls that who they are, how they are, is wrong. They're told that they're too fat or too short or too ugly. They're too smart or too pushy or too loud. They're too brown or too Black or too gay. Things about themselves that they can't change, that they shouldn't change, that they don't want to change, are things that are used against them and that are used to make them feel small and weak and wrong. This is especially true for queer and trans girls, who, from a young age, are taught that they should be ashamed of who they are and that they should take that part of themselves and shove it deep down until it's no longer visible.

While society is so often telling girls that they're wrong, *Lumberjanes* is doing the exact opposite. It's not just saying that girls of all kinds are right for being who they are, but that they are spectacularly and brilliantly right.

That's what *Lumberjanes* means to me, and to many more of its fans. It's more than just a comic, it's a reminder to girls everywhere that they are wonderful and smart and strong and brave and clever. And when it was able to expand beyond it's original intended run, it was able to soar to new heights of empowering female readers everywhere. This extension of the series allowed for character growth, more sweet moments between Mal and Molly, and in a case that's especially meaningful to me, it allowed for Jo, one of the main characters and, the heroes, of the book, to come out as a trans girl.

When I was Jo's age, I desperately wished I could be a girl (my understanding of gender and identity didn't allow me to realize that I already was one) but didn't see any way that that could happen. My only points of reference for trans girls were fairy tales and fantasies with magical spells or, usually, curses. It seemed impossible that a person like me could ever be a girl. But things aren't the same for young trans girls anymore. They can pick up this book, *Lumberjanes*, and they can see Jo talking about how everyone thought she should've been a Scouting Lad, but she knew that that wasn't right. She's always been a Lumberjane.

If we measure a work of art's worth by the amount of good it does, the amount of lives it changes, then *Lumberjanes* is truly a masterpiece. If just one trans girl reads the conversation that Jo and Barney have and feels better about herself or finally understands who she is or decides that it's the right time to share who she is with the world, this book will have been so much more than worth it. *Lumberjanes* gives girls everywhere, all kinds of girls, a chance to feel like they belong, to feel like they deserve love, adventure, happiness and, above all, friendship to the max.

MEY RUDE
Editor & Writer for *Autostraddle*

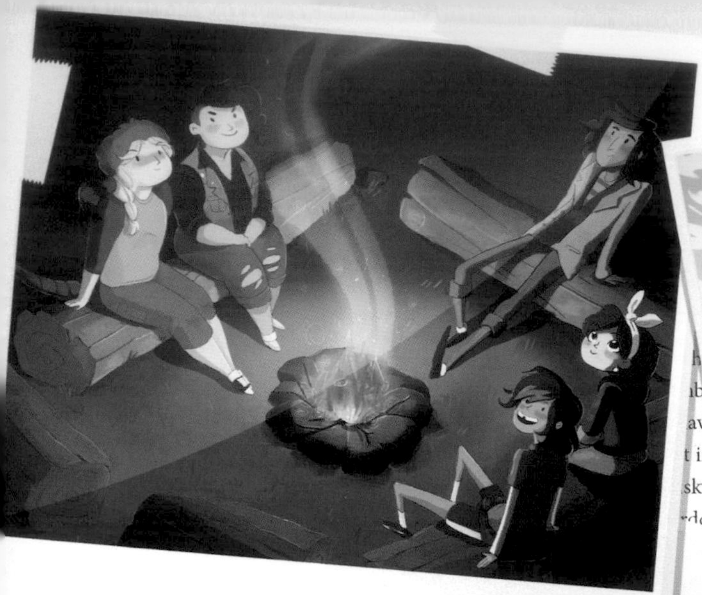

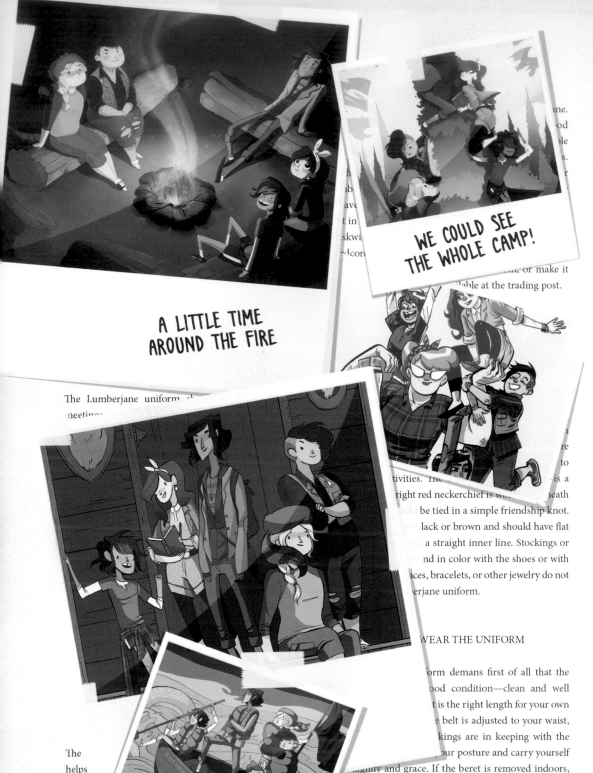

A LITTLE TIME AROUND THE FIRE

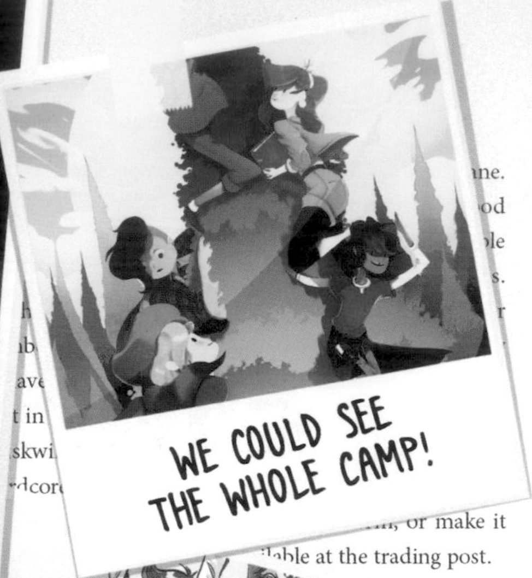

WE COULD SEE THE WHOLE CAMP!

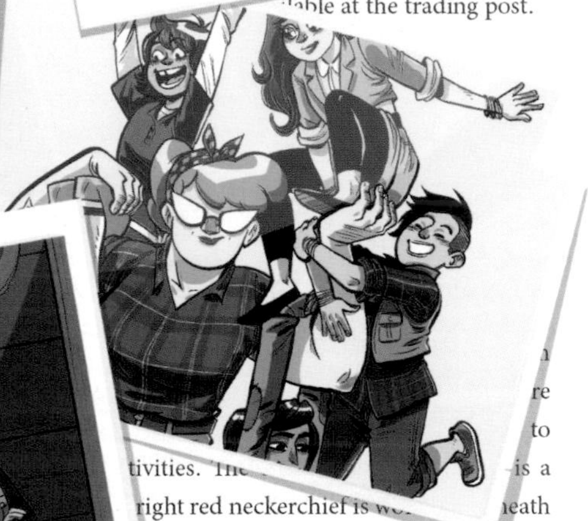

The Lumberjane uniform ...

meeting...

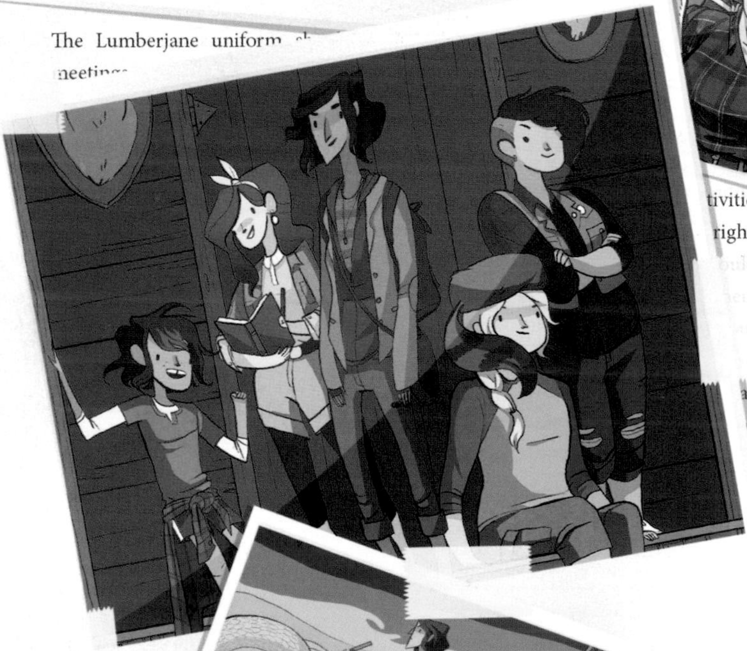

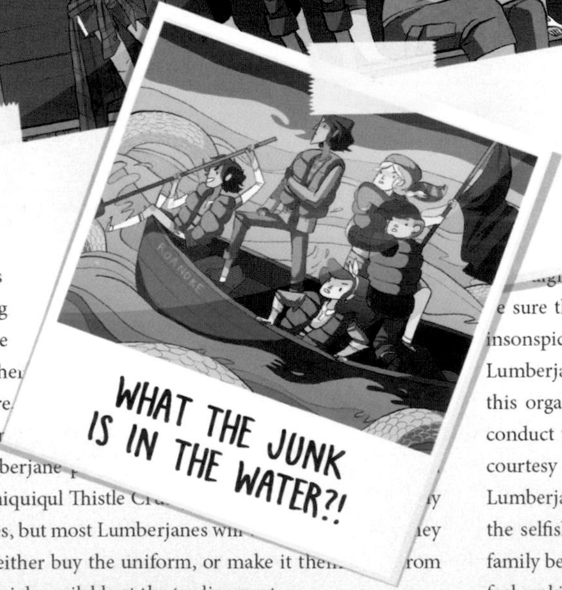

WHAT THE JUNK IS IN THE WATER?!

The ... helps ... in a g... active ... another ... future ... in or... Lumberjane p... Penniquiqul Thistle Cr... ...y Types, but most Lumberjanes wi... ...ey can either buy the uniform, or make it them... ...rom materials available at the trading post.

...ane. ...od ...ble ...s. ...r ...m, or make it ...ilable at the trading post.

...a ...re ...to ...tivities. The ... is a ...right red neckerchief is wo... ...neath ...be tied in a simple friendship knot. ...lack or brown and should have flat ...a straight inner line. Stockings or ...nd in color with the shoes or with ...aces, bracelets, or other jewelry do not ...erjane uniform.

...WEAR THE UNIFORM

...orm demans first of all that the ...ood condition—clean and well ...t is the right length for your own ...e belt is adjusted to your waist, ...kings are in keeping with the ...our posture and carry yourself ...ignity and grace. If the beret is removed indoors, ...e sure that your hair is neat and kept in place with an insonspicuous clip or ribbon. When you wear a Lumberjane uniform you are identified as a member of this organization and you should be doubly careful to conduct yourself in a way that will show everyone that courtesy and thoughtfullness are part of being a Lumberjane. People are likely to judge a whole nation by the selfishness of a few individuals, to criticize a whole family because of the misconduct of one member, and to feel unkindly toward and organization because of the

COVER GALLERY

Lumberjanes "Wildlife" Program Field

BADGER OF HONOR BADGE

"The more the merrier."

A Lumberjanes success is not based solely on the badges that she earns, but it can be a lot of fun to collect them all. There are hundreds of badges that a Lumberjane is able to earn, from the *Pungeon Master* badge to the beloved *Dye Hard* badge, in which Lumberjanes learn how to create dye from nature around them. In our Lumberjanes camp, we want all the Lumberjanes to only take on the badges that they are able to fit into their time at the camp, and if that means someone is able to tackle the whole handbook and it's several other volumes, then we applaud this individual. It is up to the camper to find every counselor, every possible teacher, to find out what badges she can earn in the time frame she has allotted.

If a Lumberjane scout is able to collect all the badges available to them at the time that this badge becomes available, then they will get the *Badger of Honor* badge, as well as a lesson in how to extend their sash in a tasteful

fashion. Though if they are already earning this badge then there is a good chance they they've already decides to extend their sash several times over. To the Lumberjane who decided to take on this challenge, keep in mind that competition is encouraged, as long as it remains happy, healthy, and non-detrimental to anyone else at the camp. The *Badger of Honor* badge is a badge earned because Lumberjanes never quit. Lumberjanes want to excel at everything they have the chance to. This is a badge earned by those who know what they want to accomplish and will be able to take on the challenge while most likely bringing their friends along for the ride.

To obtain the *Badger of Honor* badge, a Lumberjane must be persistent, she must keep her head up and tackle every obstacle that is thrown at her. She will go out of her way to find more badges for her to earn, and with the help of her friends, accomplish every task she sets forth

Issue Nine
CHYNNA CLUGSTON FLORES

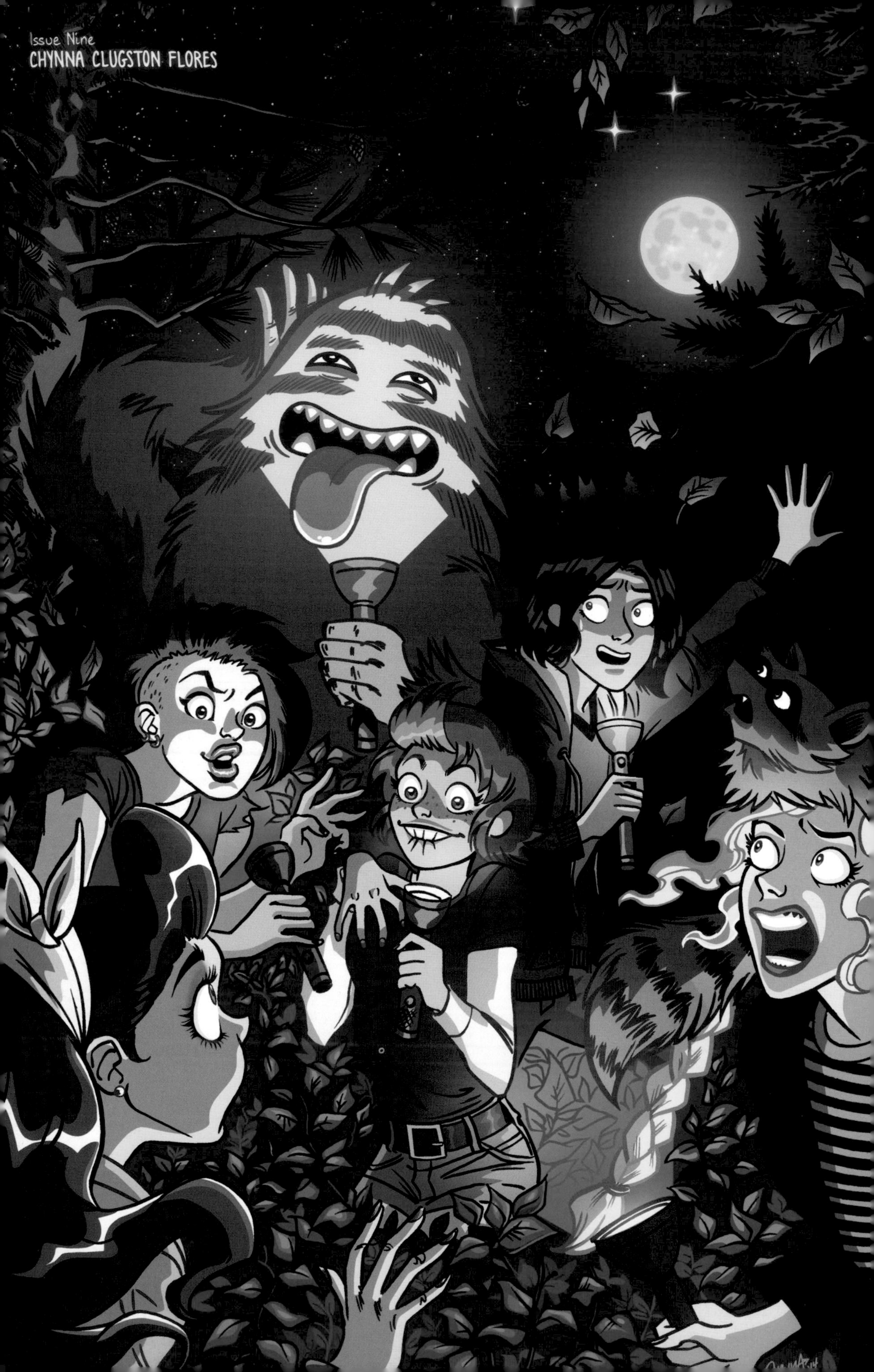

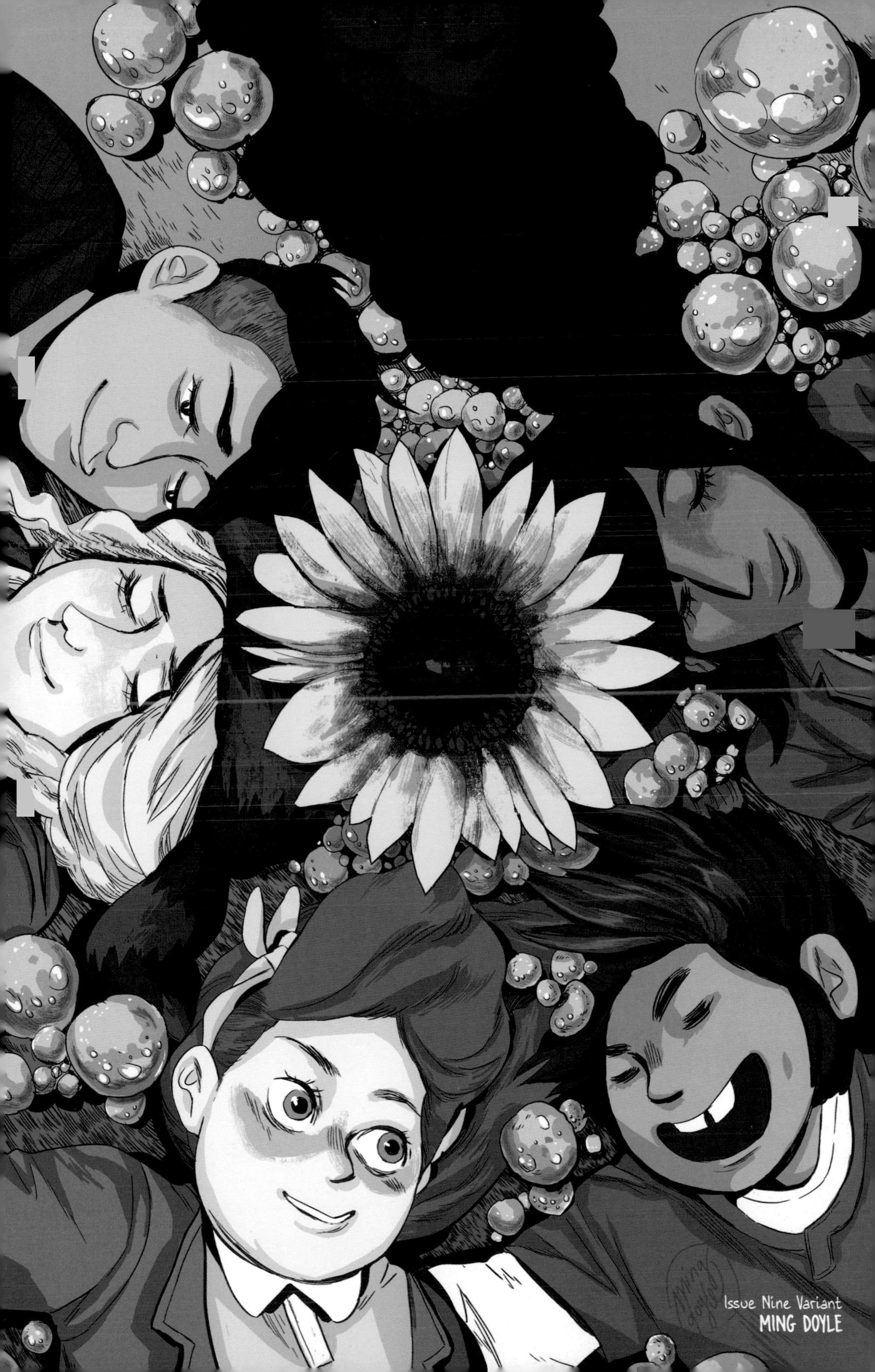
ming doyle

Issue Nine Variant
MING DOYLE

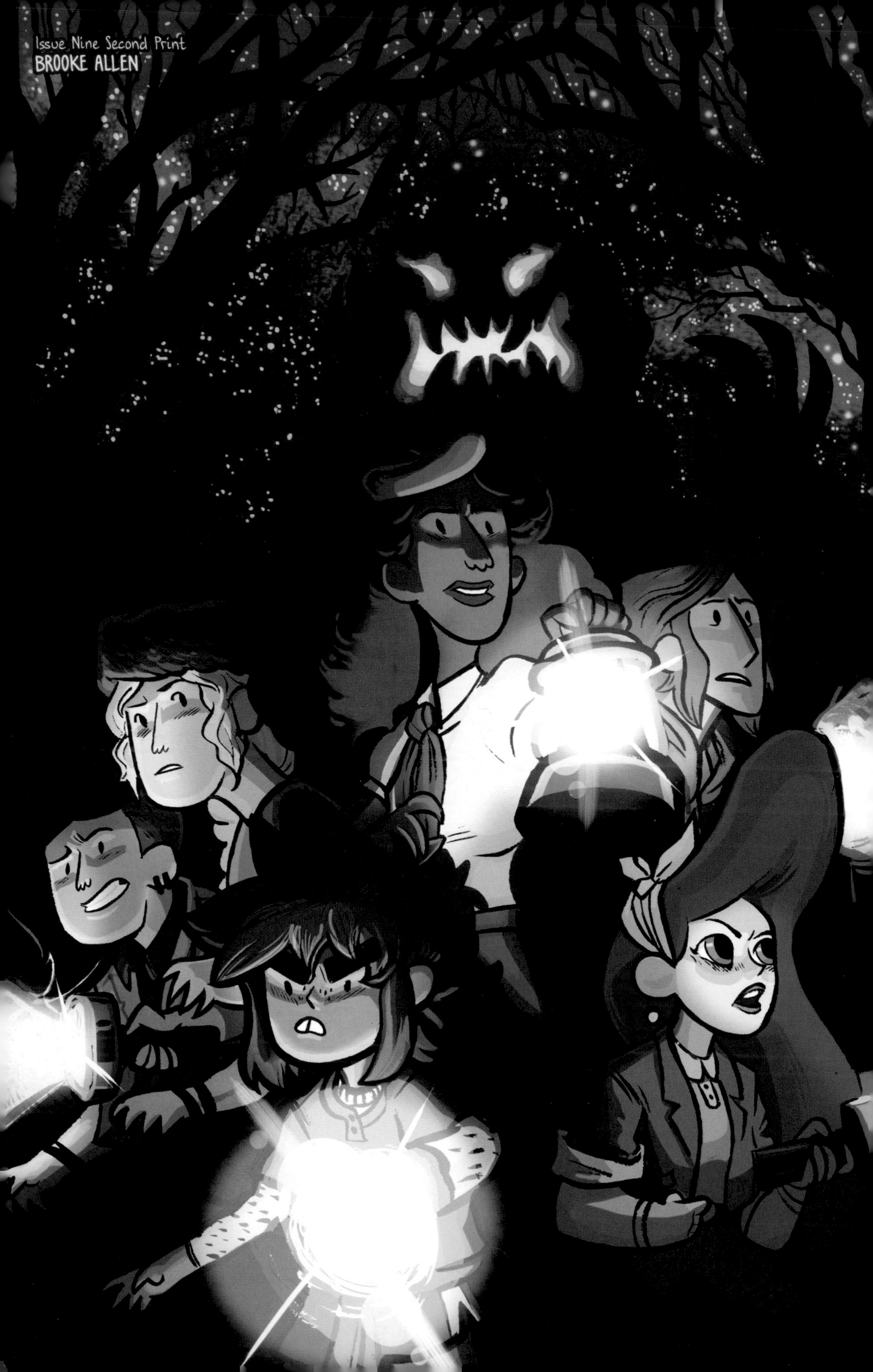
Issue Nine Second Print
BROOKE ALLEN

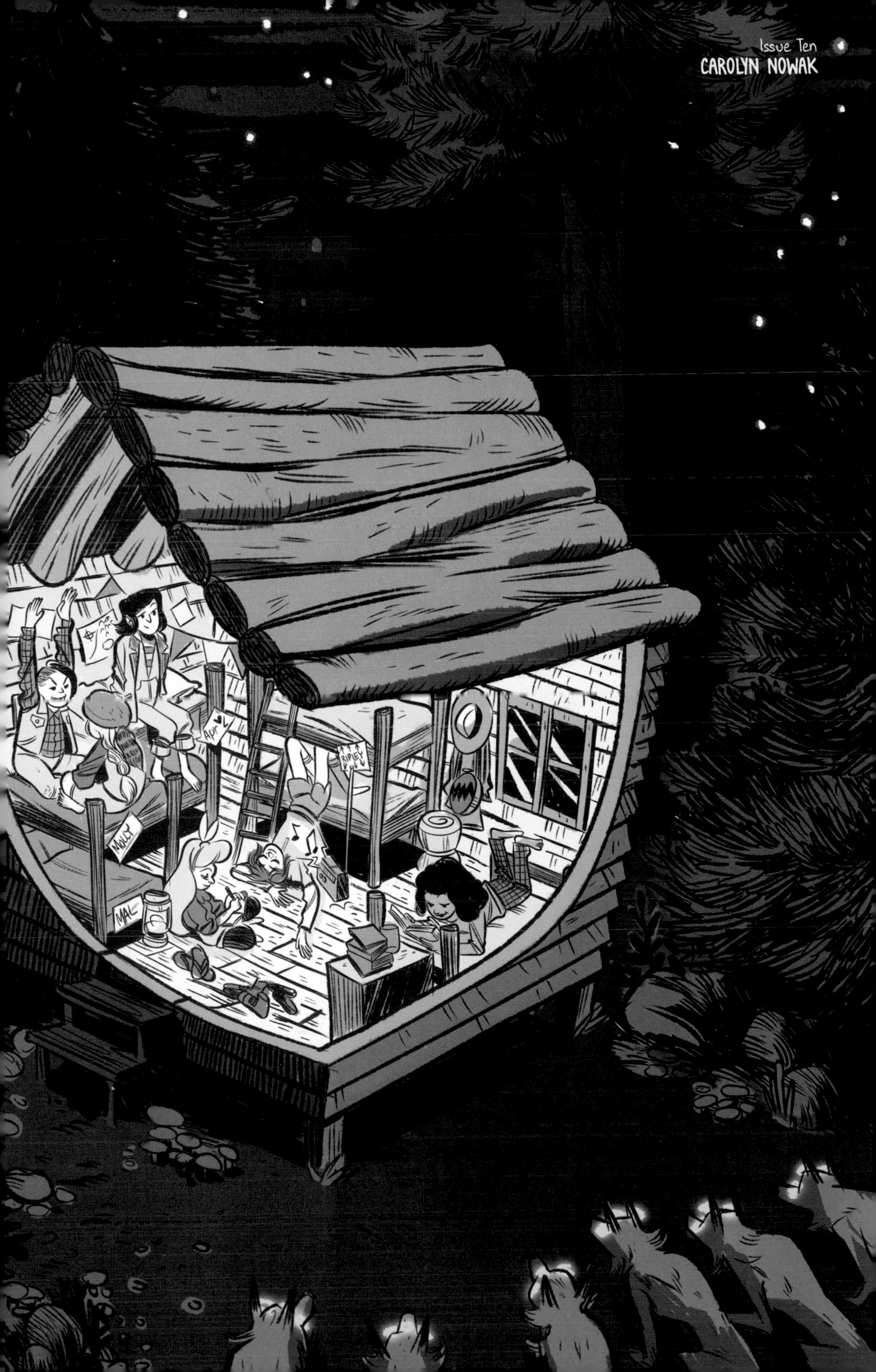
Issue Ten
CAROLYN NOWAK
RIPLEY
MOLLY
MAL

Issue Ten Variant
KAT LEYH

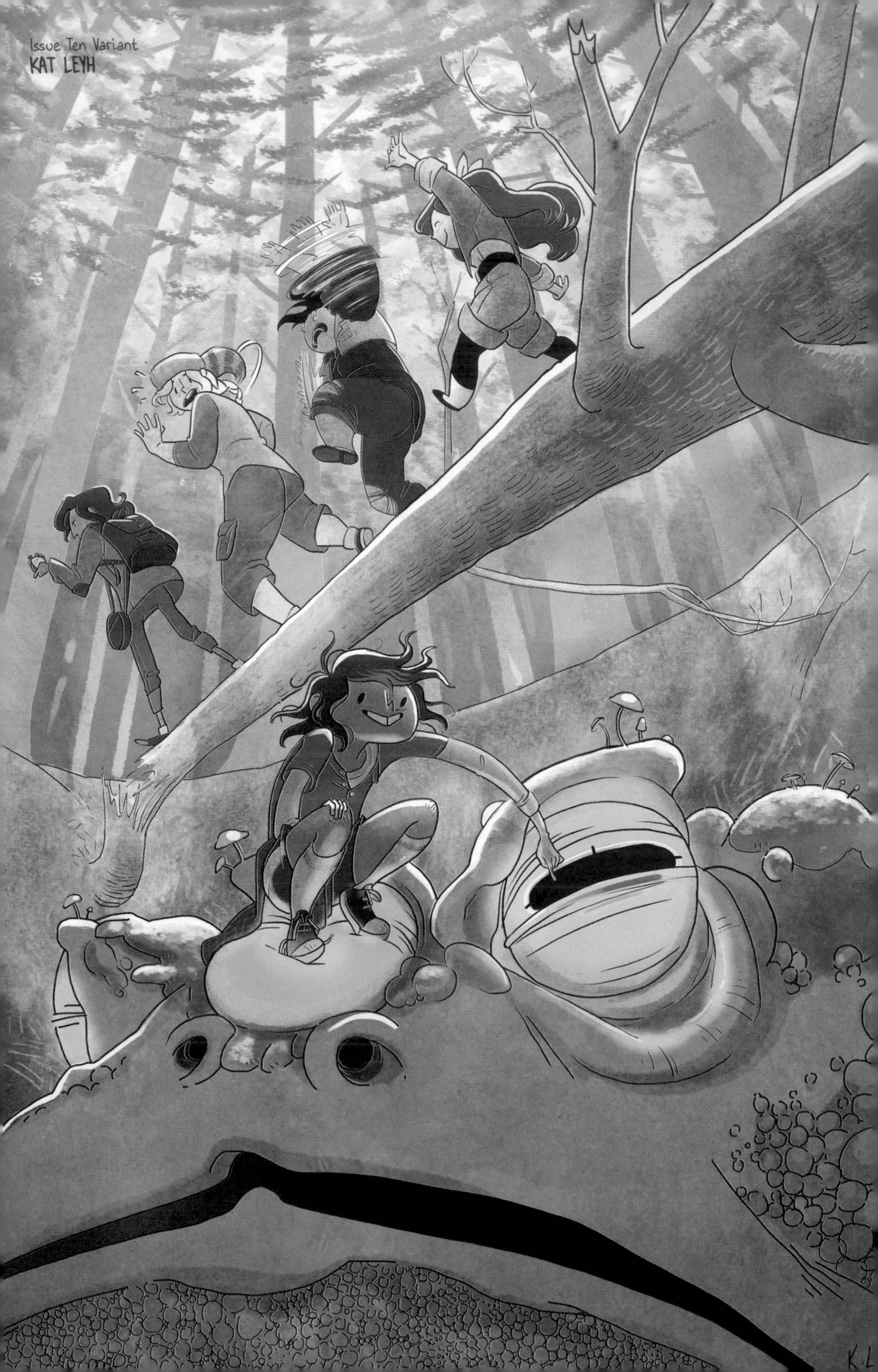

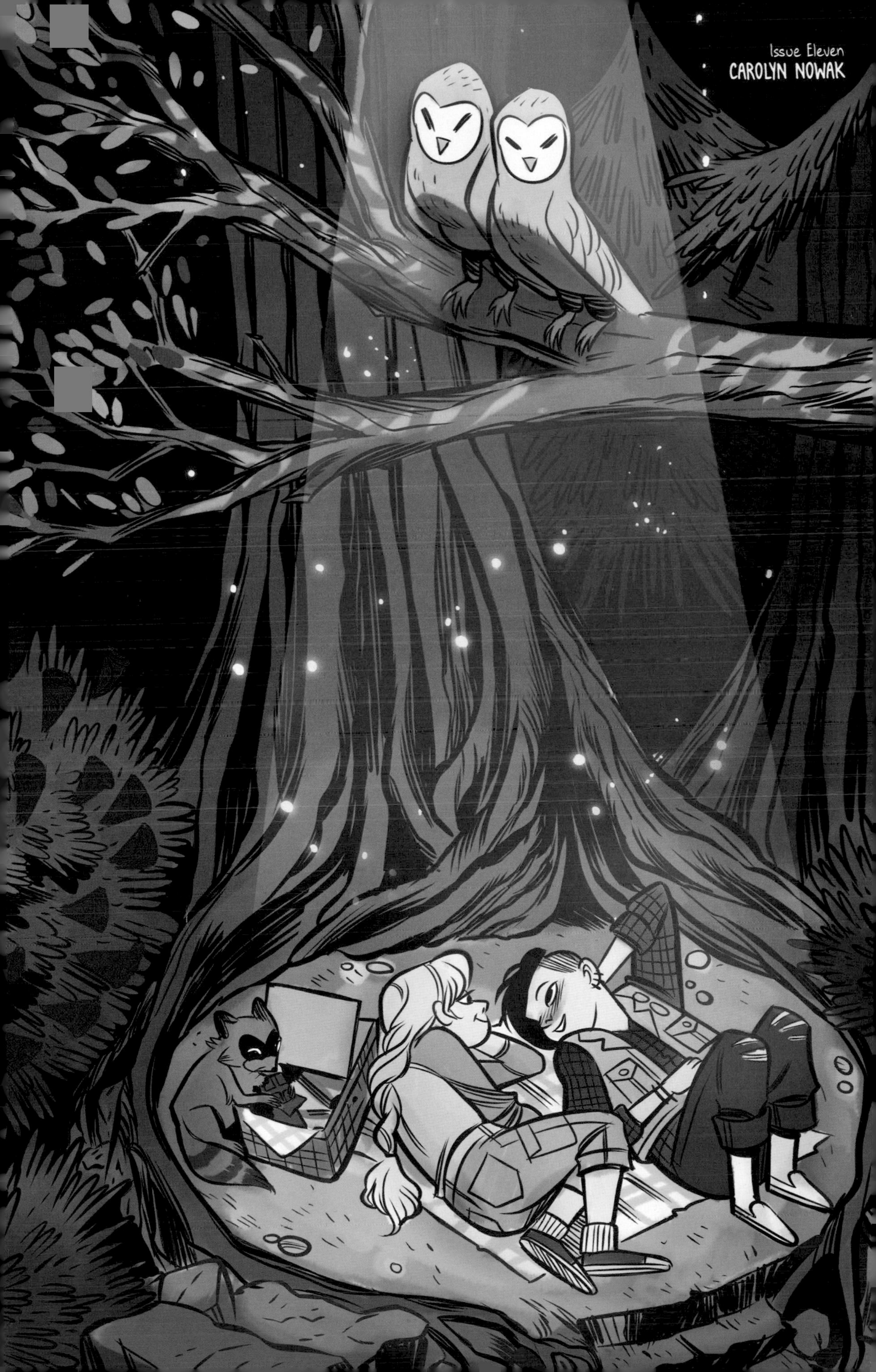
Issue Eleven
CAROLYN NOWAK

Issue Eleven Variant
EMILY HU

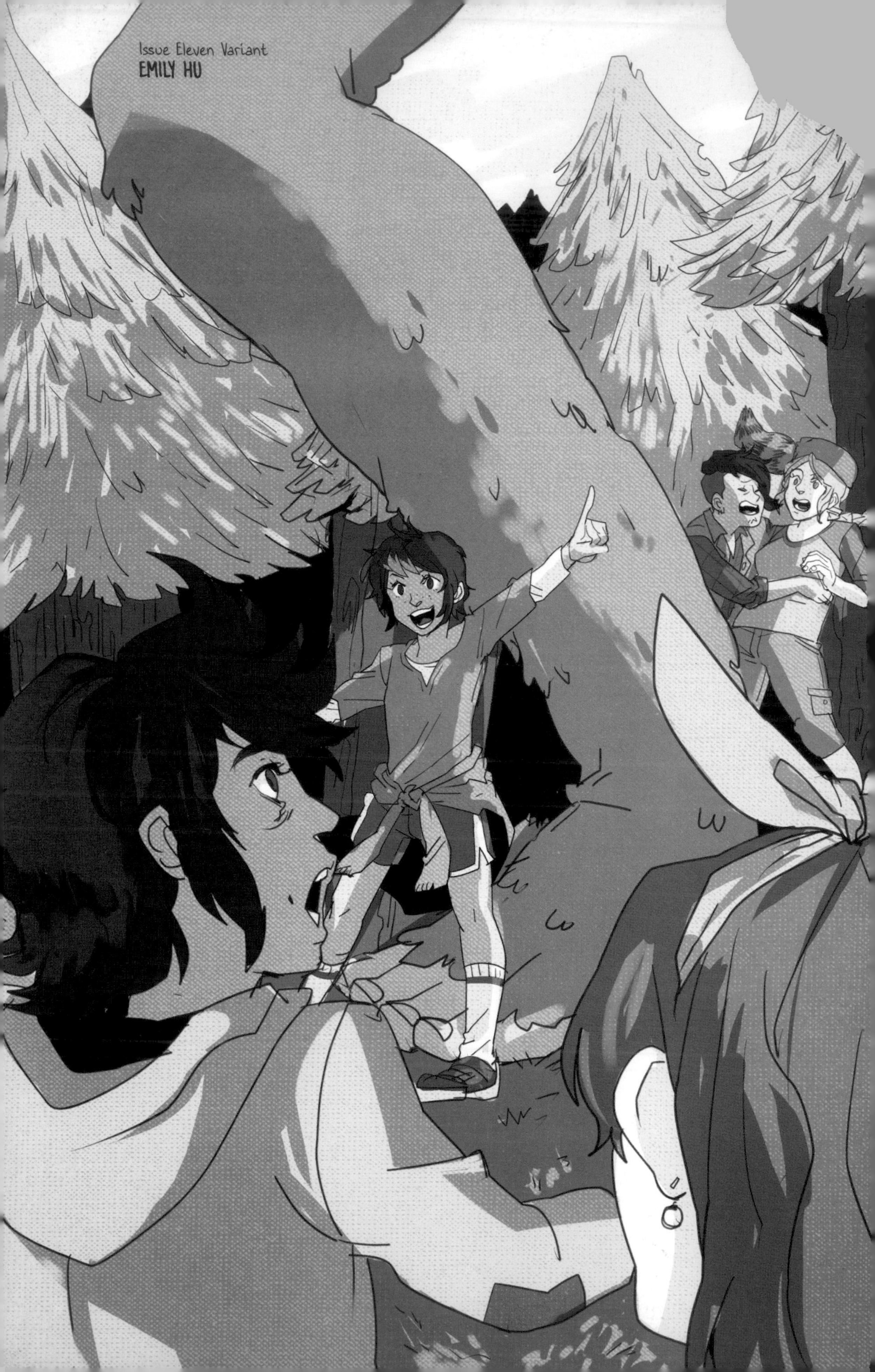

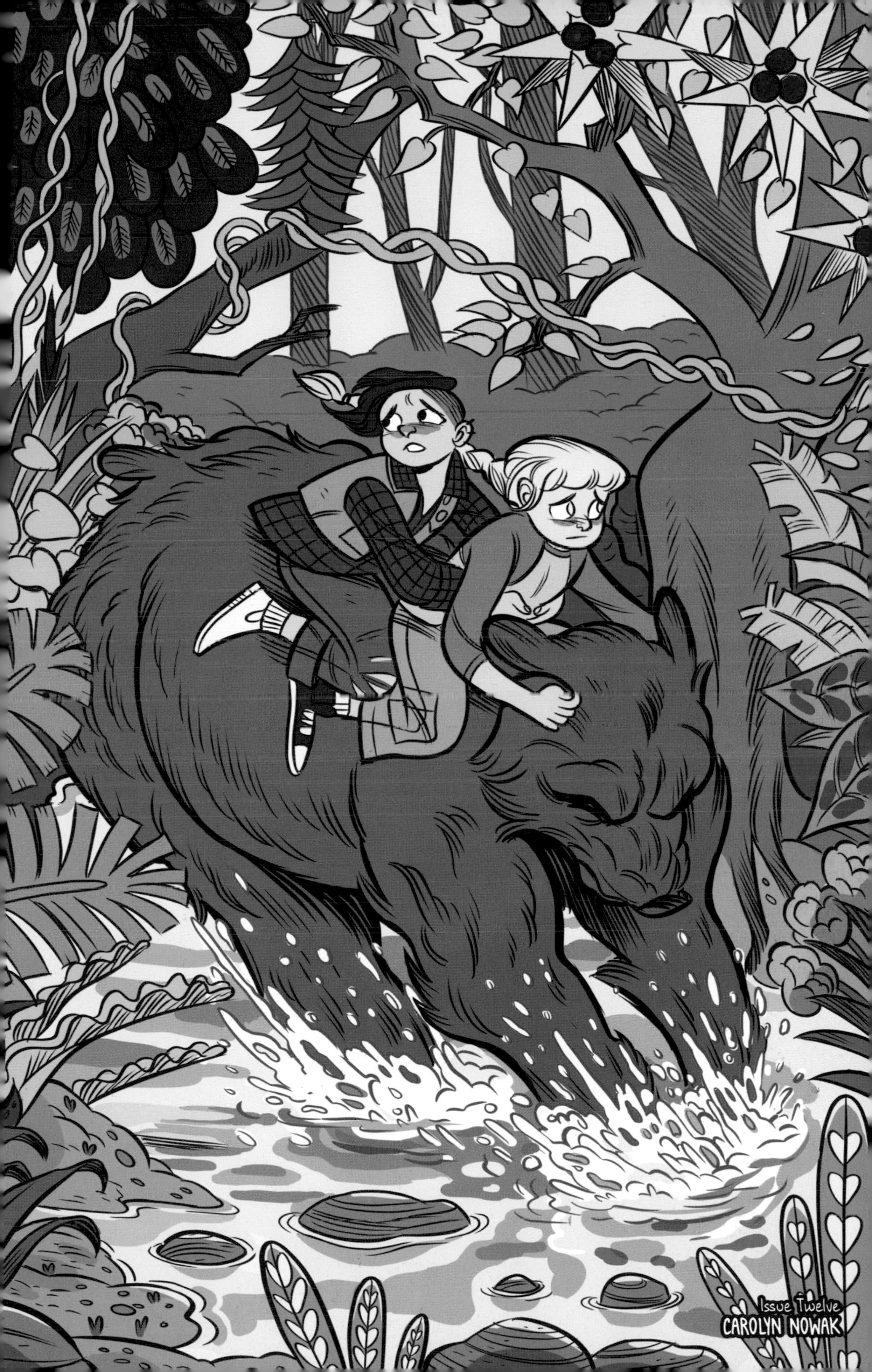
Issue Twelve
CAROLYN NOWAK

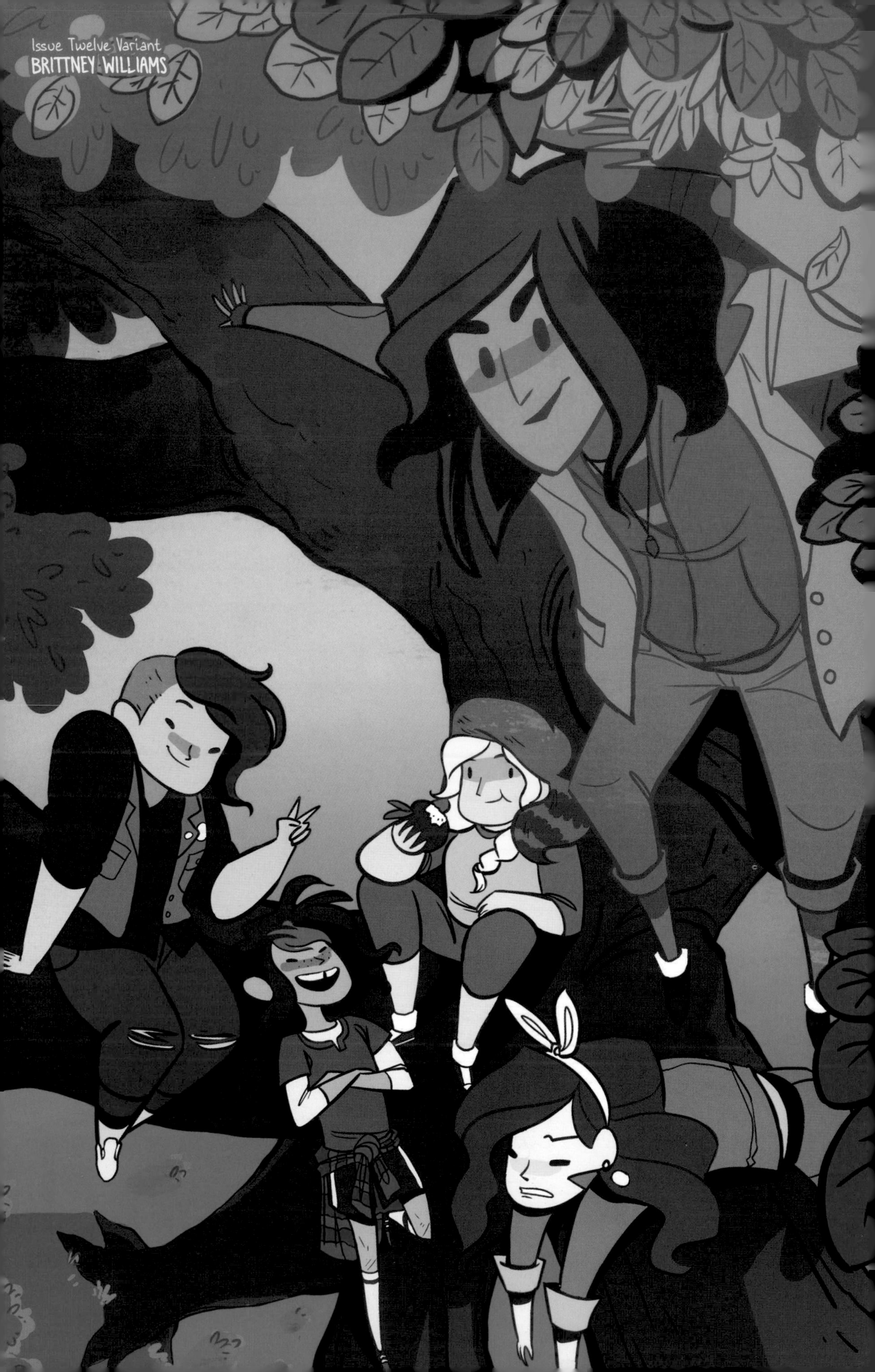
Issue Twelve Variant
BRITTNEY WILLIAMS

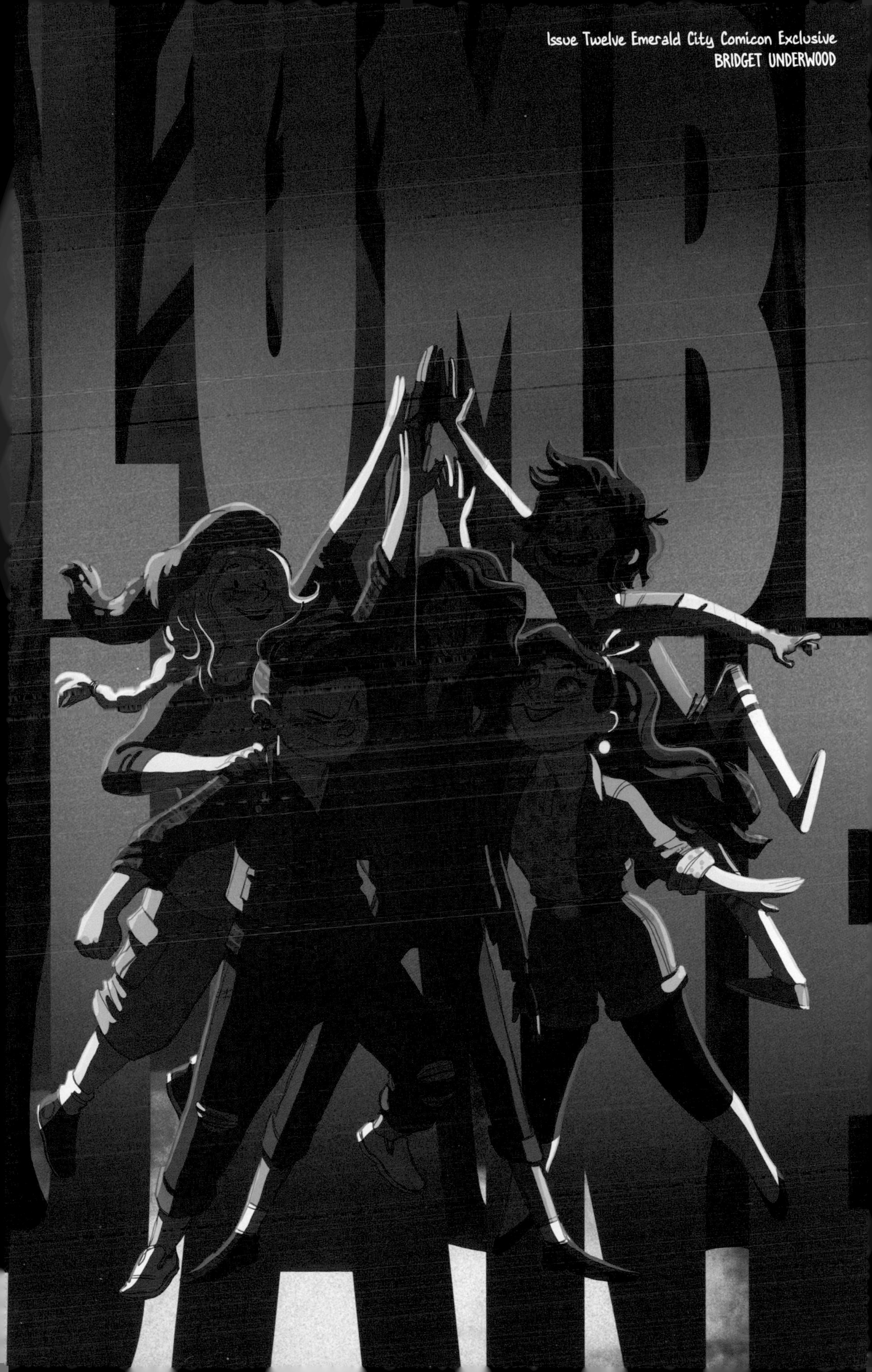
Issue Twelve Emerald City Comicon Exclusive
BRIDGET UNDERWOOD

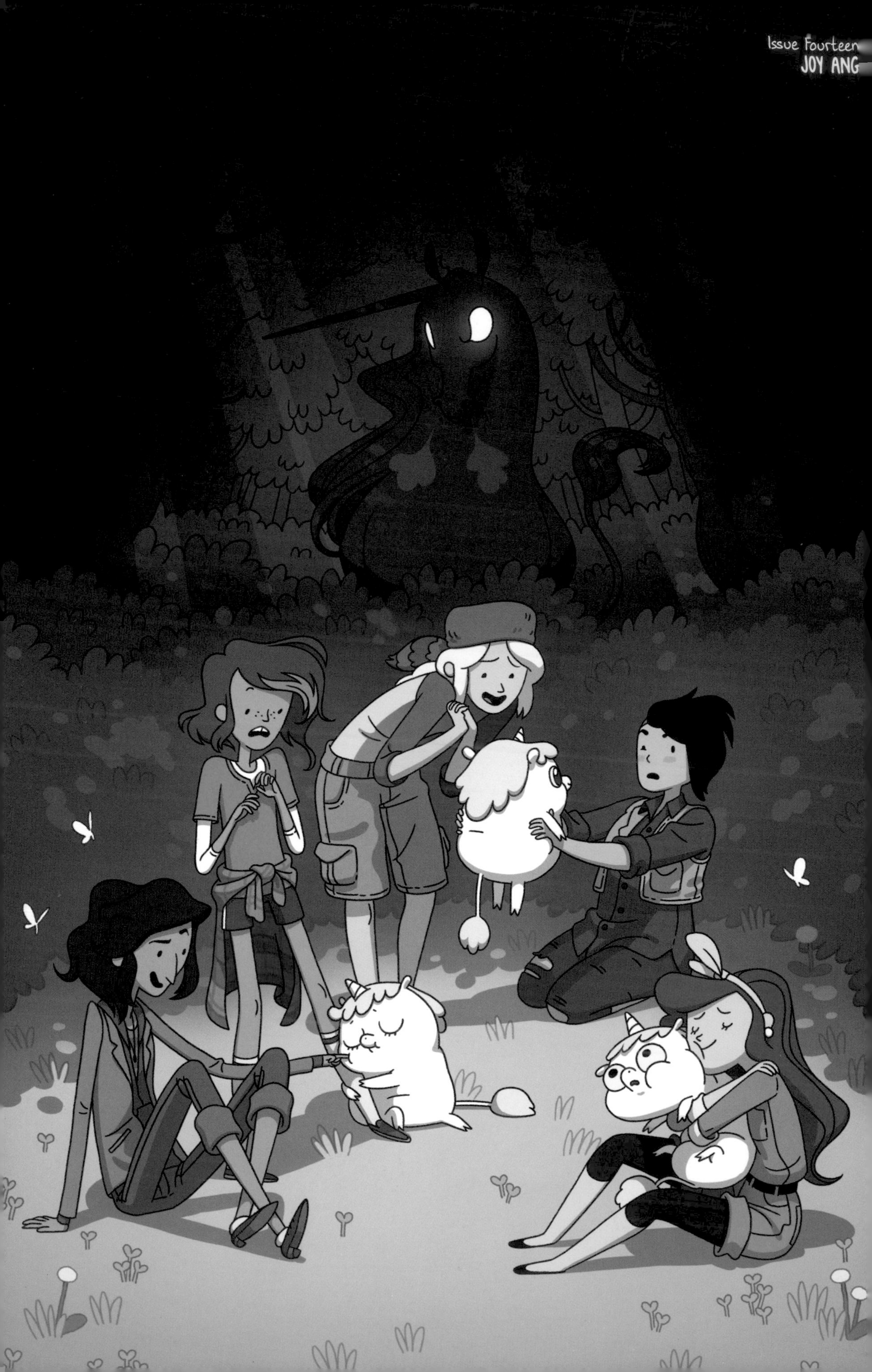
Issue Fourteen
JOY ANG

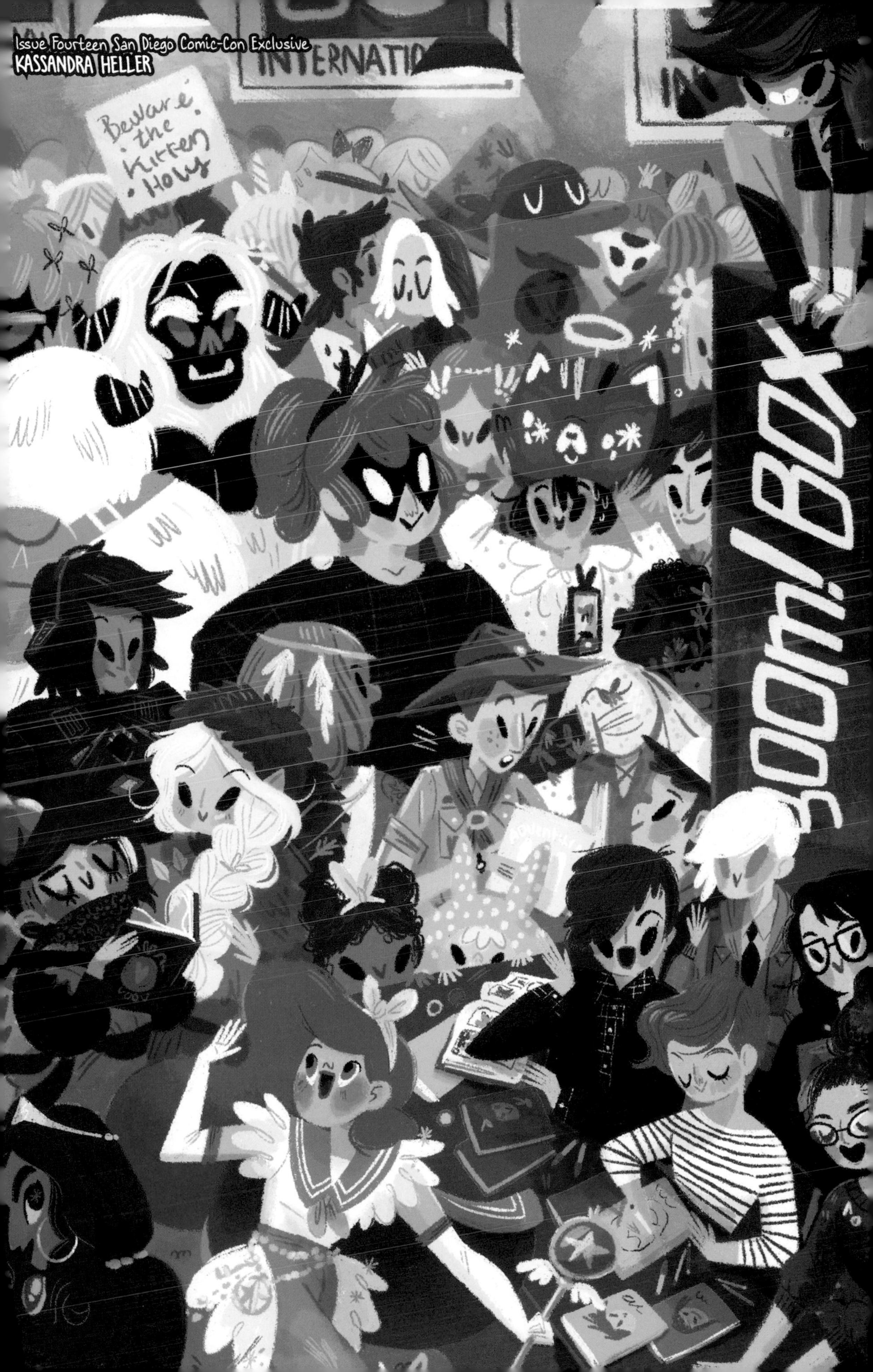
Issue Fourteen San Diego Comic-Con Exclusive
KASSANDRA HELLER
INTERNATI
Beware the Kitten Holy
BOOM! BOX

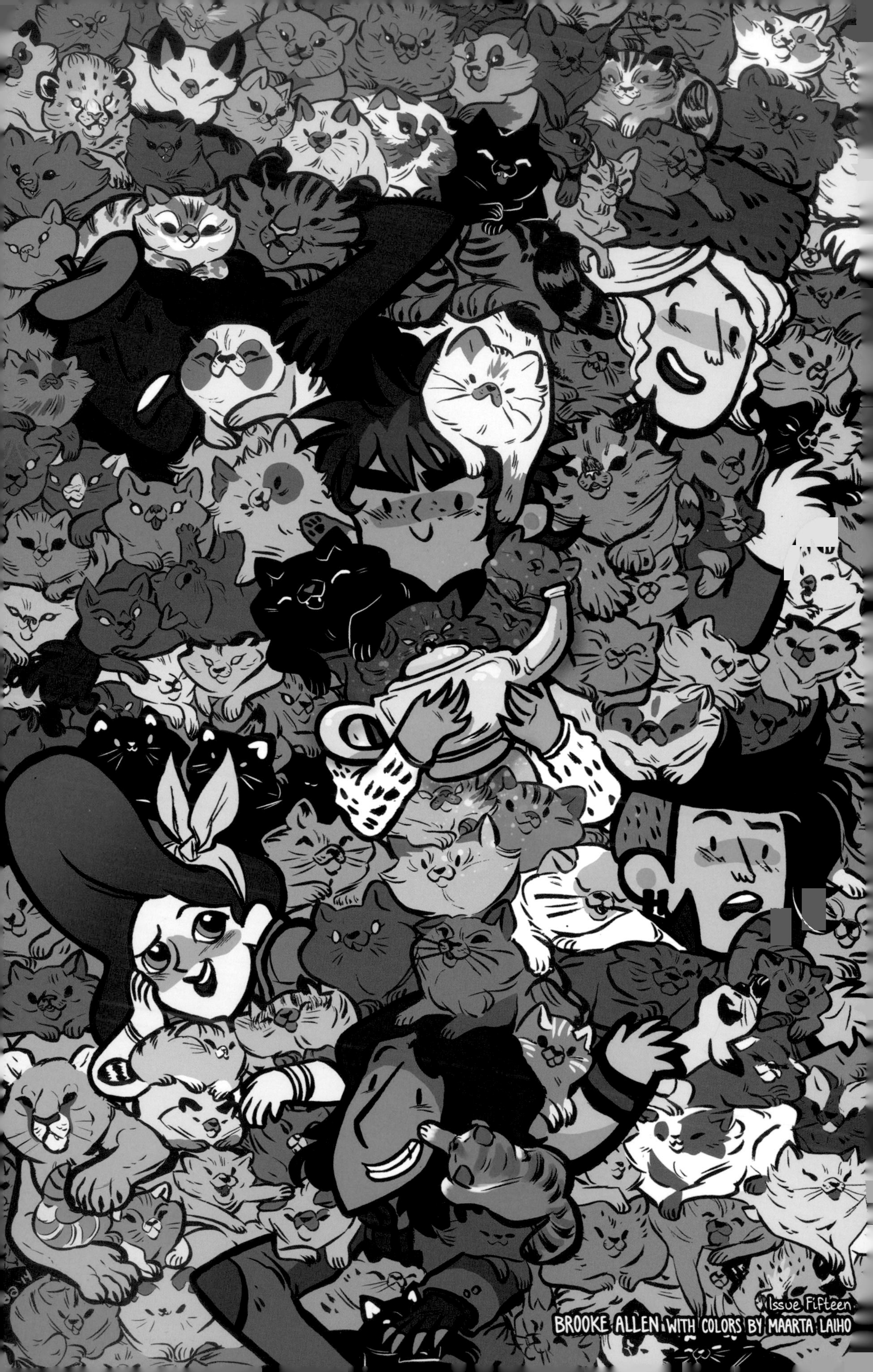
Issue Fifteen
BROOKE ALLEN WITH COLORS BY MAARTA LAIHO

Issue Fifteen Variant
RICARDO BESSA

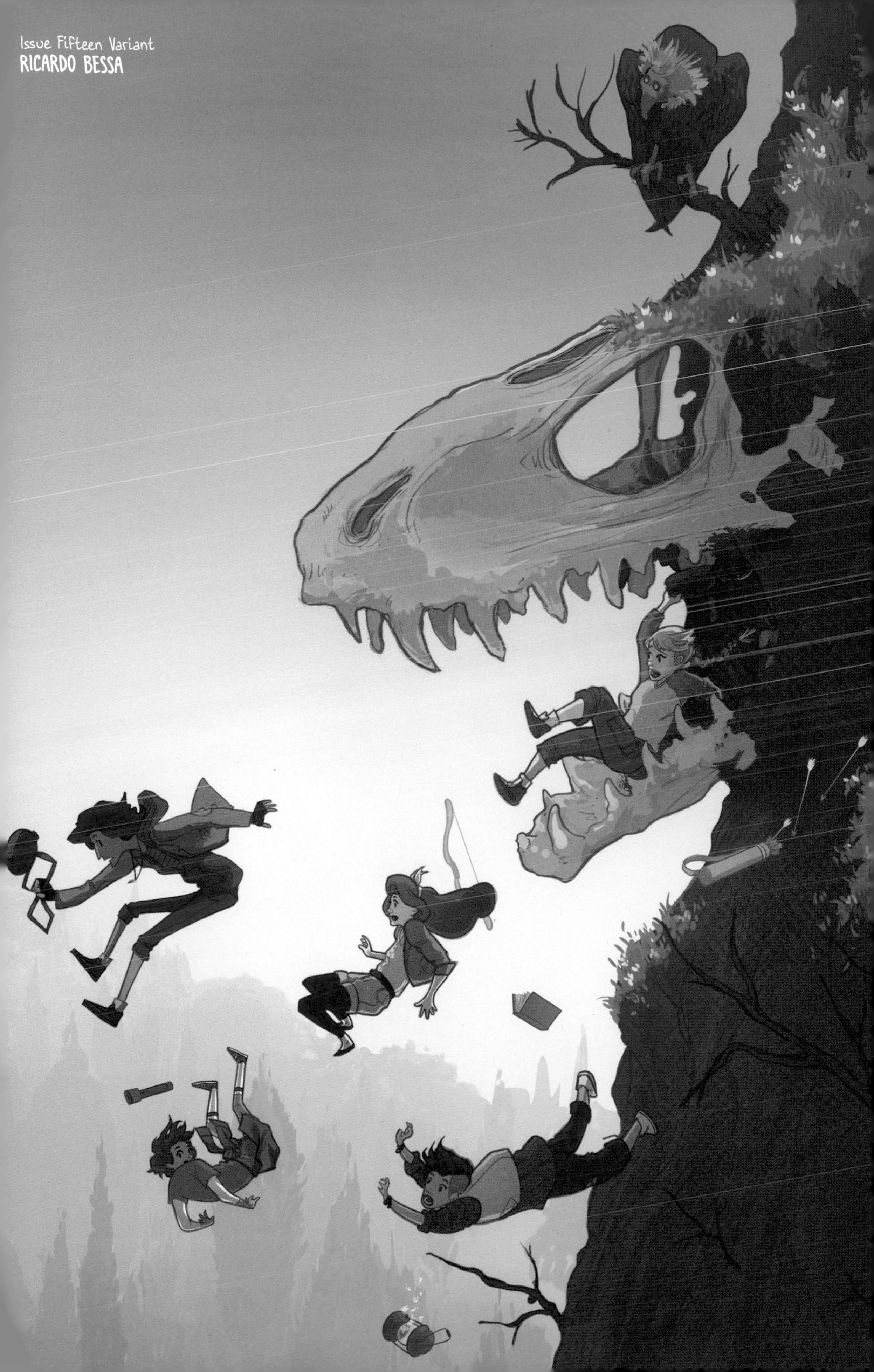

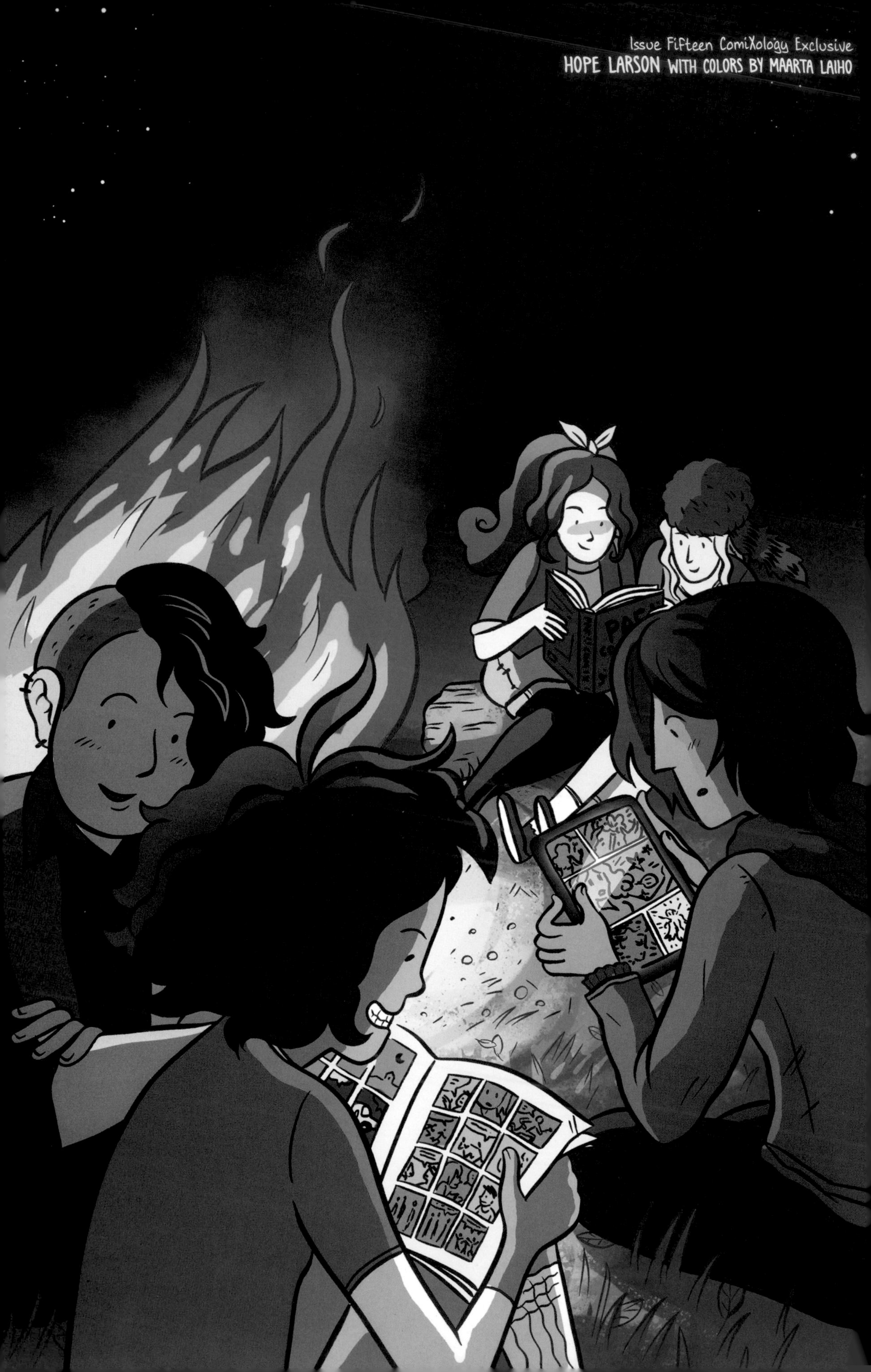
Issue Fifteen ComiXology Exclusive
HOPE LARSON WITH COLORS BY MAARTA LAIHO

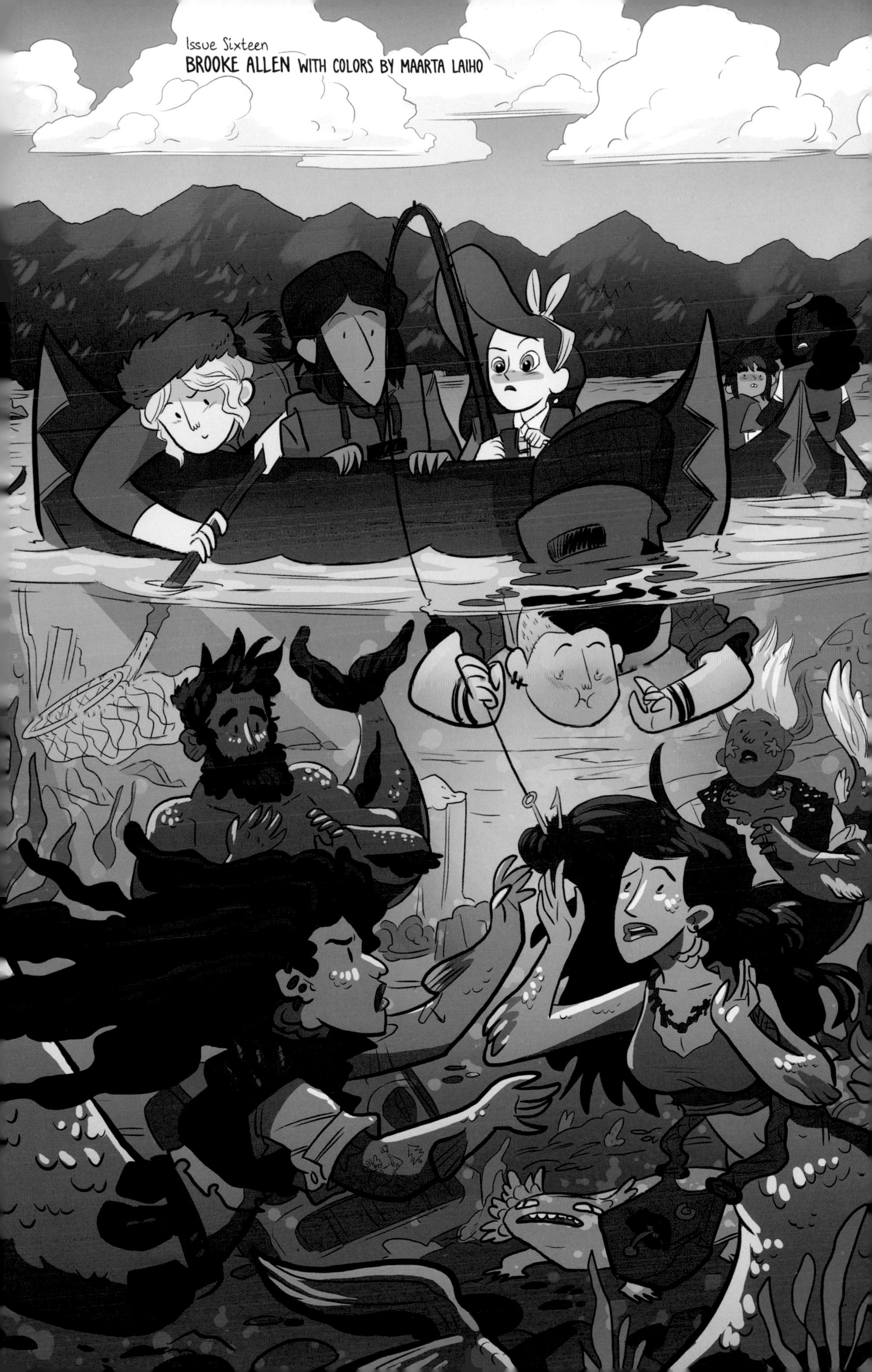
Issue Sixteen
BROOKE ALLEN WITH COLORS BY MAARTA LAIHO

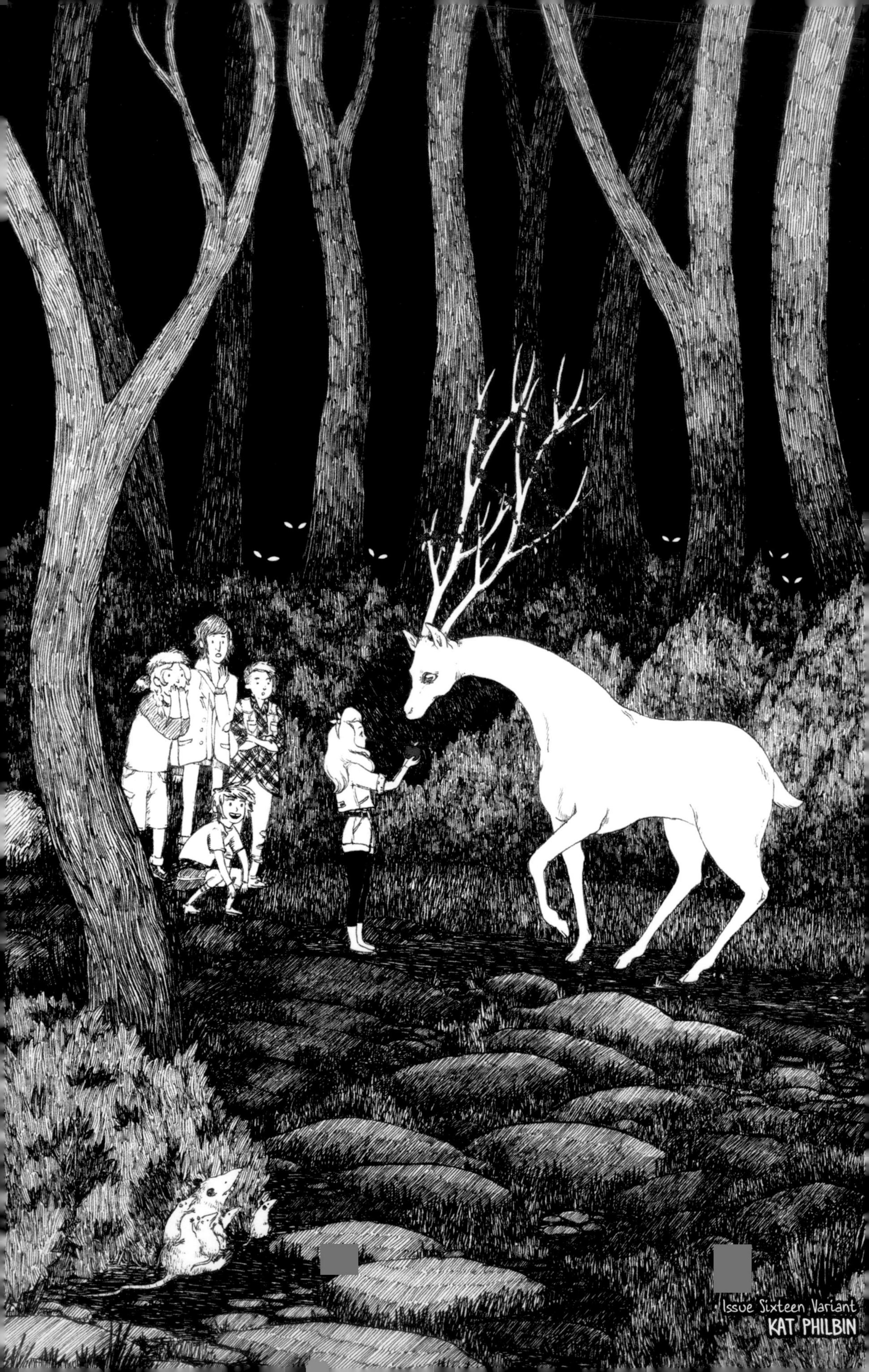
Issue Sixteen Variant
KAT PHILBIN

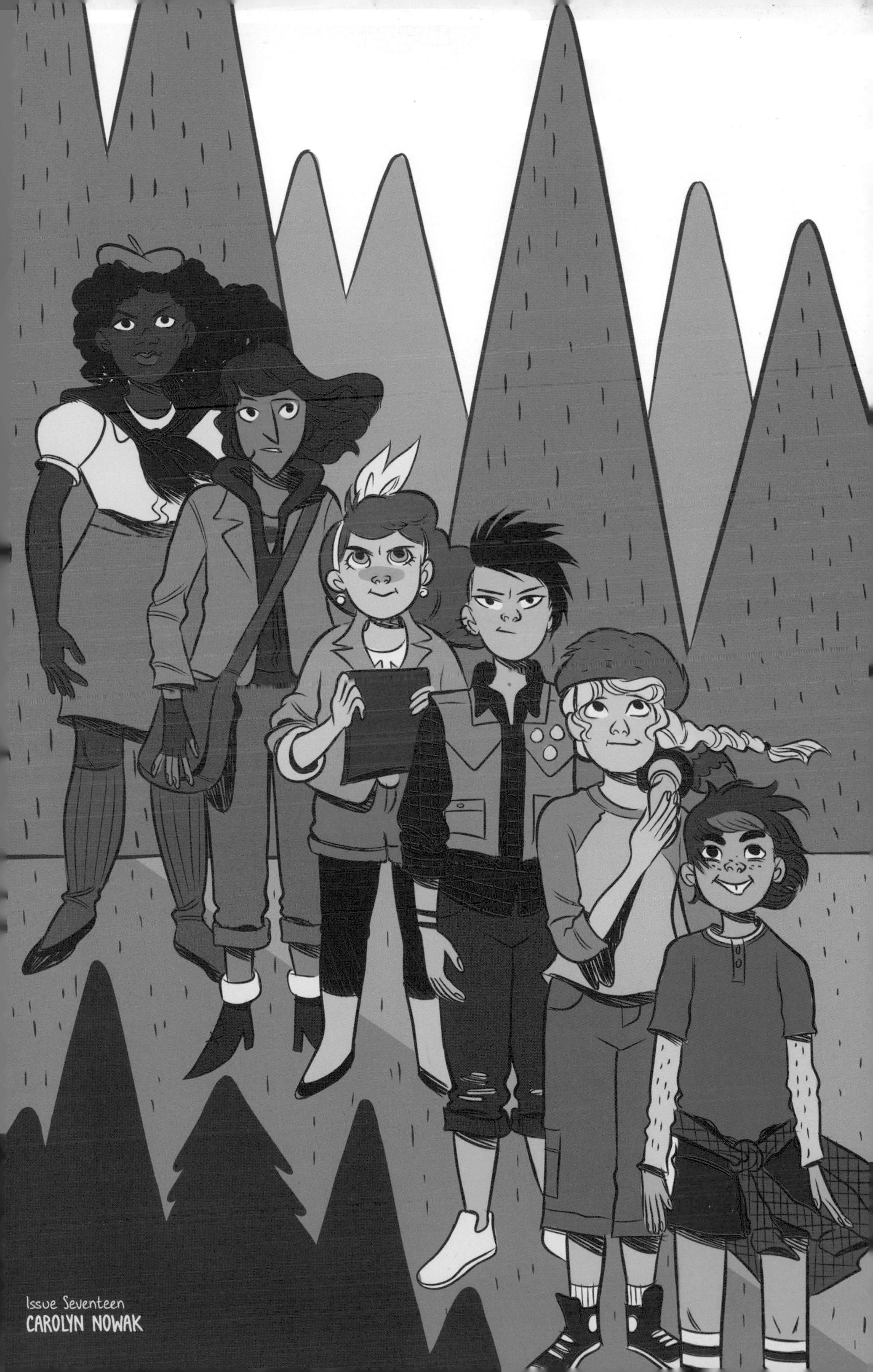
Issue Seventeen
CAROLYN NOWAK

Issue Seventeen Variant
JEN WANG

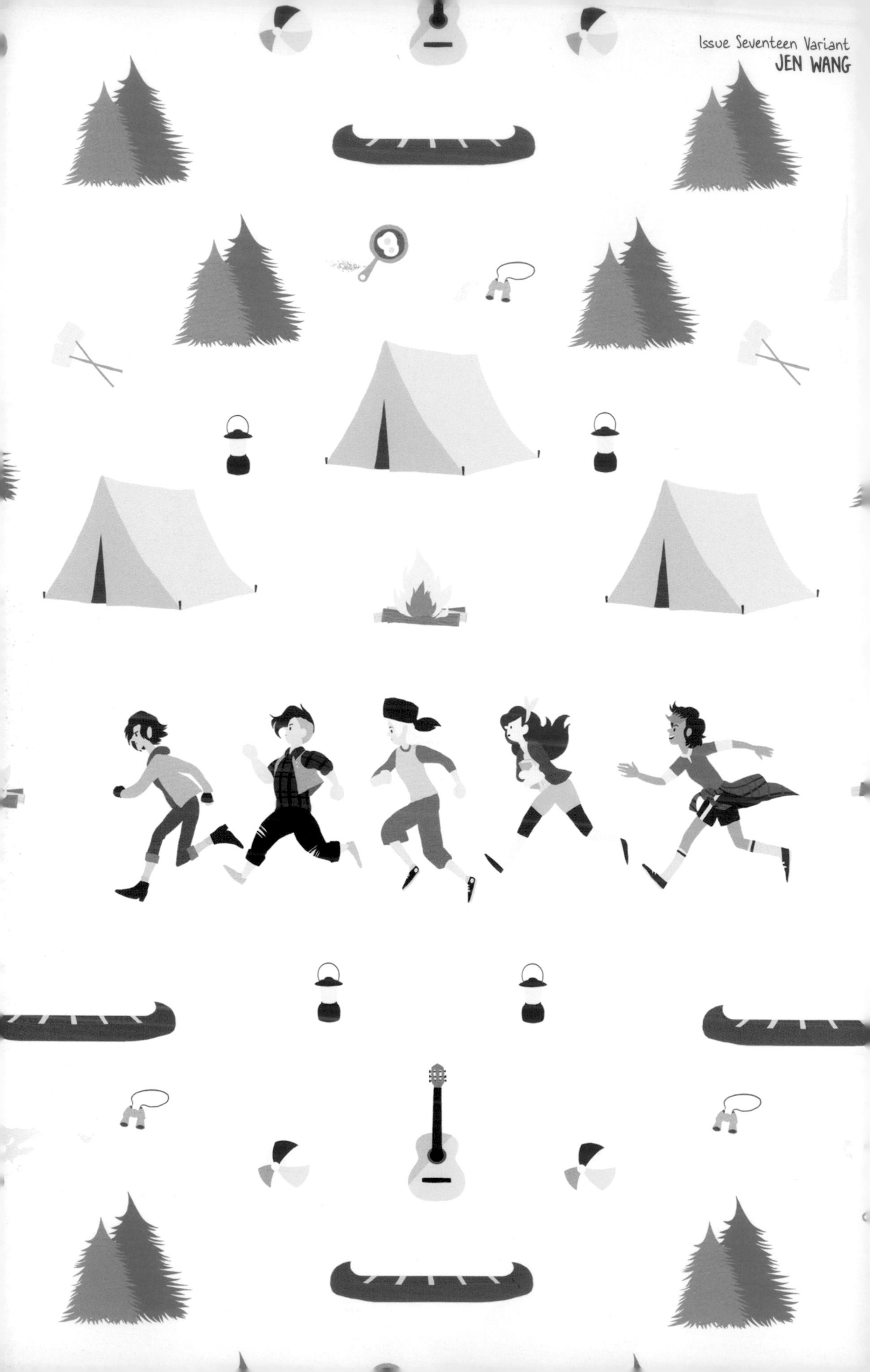

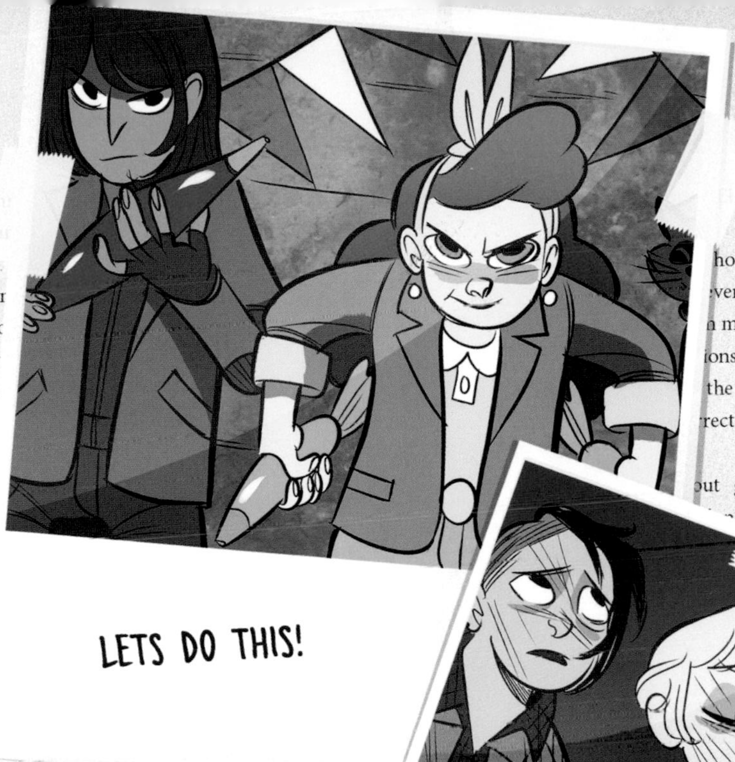
LETS DO THIS!

will co
The u
It he
appearar
dress f
Further
Lumbe
to have
part in
Thisk
Hardc
have
thems

E UNIFORM

hould be worn at camp
events when Lumberjanes
may also be worn at other
ions. It should be worn as a
the uniform dress with
rect shoes, and stocking or

out grows her uniform or
ter Lumberjane.
a she has
her
her

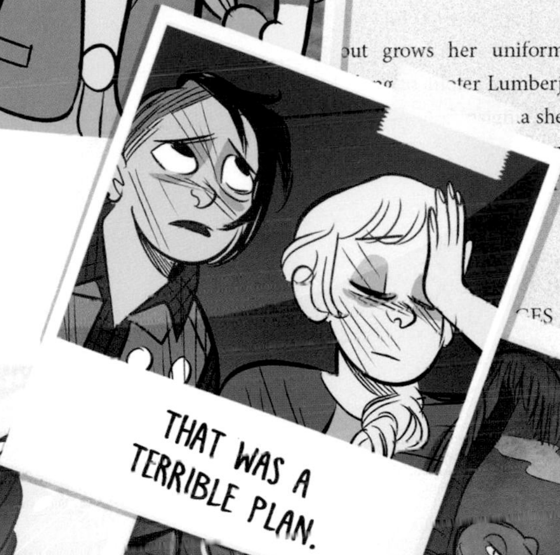
THAT WAS A
TERRIBLE PLAN.

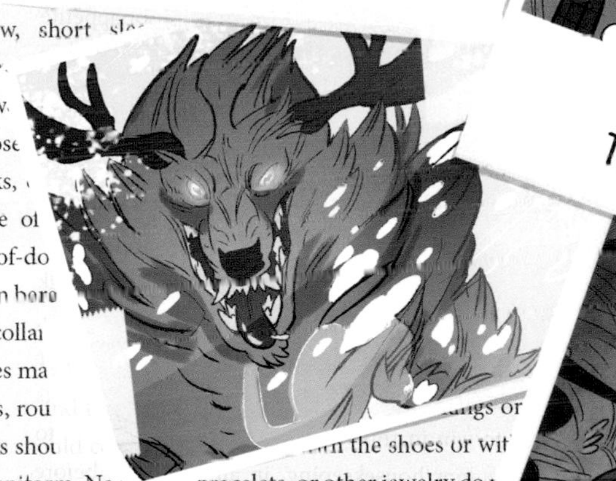

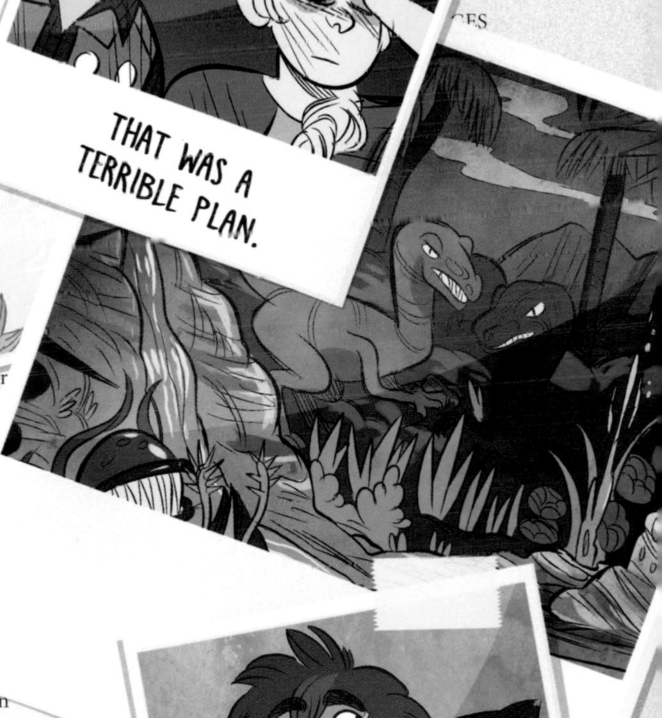

The
yellow, short sle
emb
the w
choose
slacks,
made o
out-of-do
green bere
the collar
Shoes ma
heels, rou ings or
socks shou th the shoes or wit
the uniform. Ne es, bracelets, or other jewelry do
belong with a Lumberjane uniform.

HOW TO WEAR THE UNIFORM

To look well in a uniform demans first of
uniform be kept in good condition—clean
pressed. See that the skirt is the right length for your own height and build, that the belt is adjusted to your waist, that your shoes and stockings are in keeping with the uniform, that you watch your posture and carry yourself with dignity and grace. If the beret is removed indoors, be sure that your hair is neat and kept in place with an insonspicuous clip or ribbon. When you wear a Lumberjane uniform you are identified as a member of this organization and you should be doubly careful to conduct yourself in a way that will show everyone that courtesy and thoughtfullness are part of being a Lumberjane. People are likely to judge a whole nation by the selfishness of a few individuals, to criticize a whole family because of the misconduct of one member, and to feel unkindly toward and organization because of the

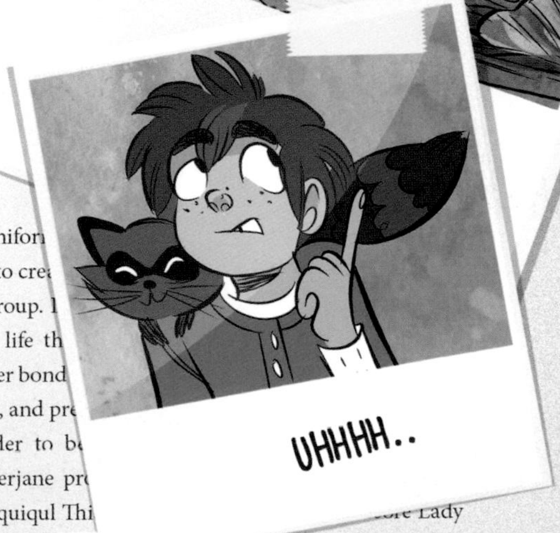
UHHHH..

The unifor
helps to cre
in a group.
active life th
another bond
future, and pre
in order to b
Lumberjane pr
Penniquiqul Thi
Types, but m es will wish to have one. They
can either bu , or make it themselves from
materials available at the trading post.

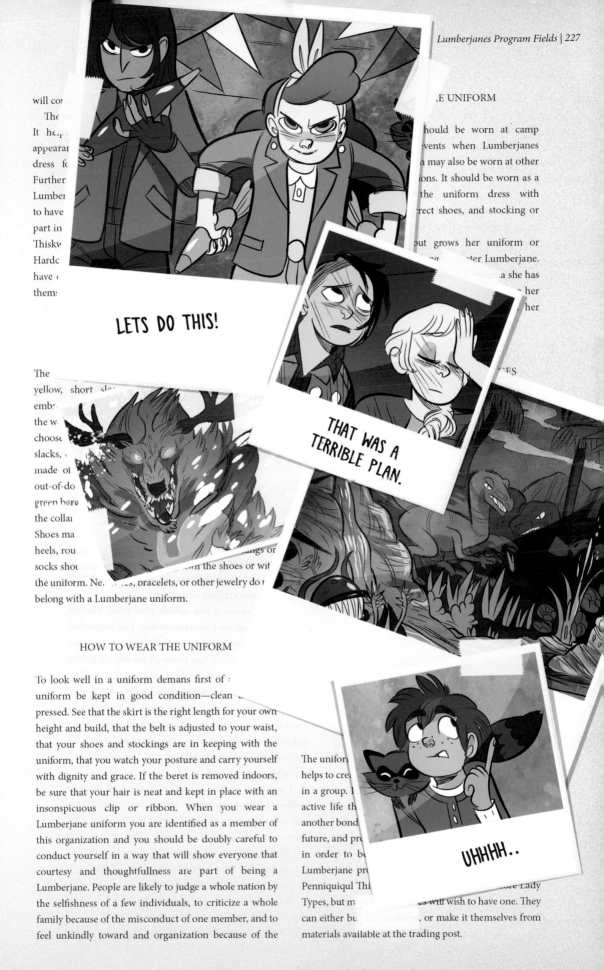

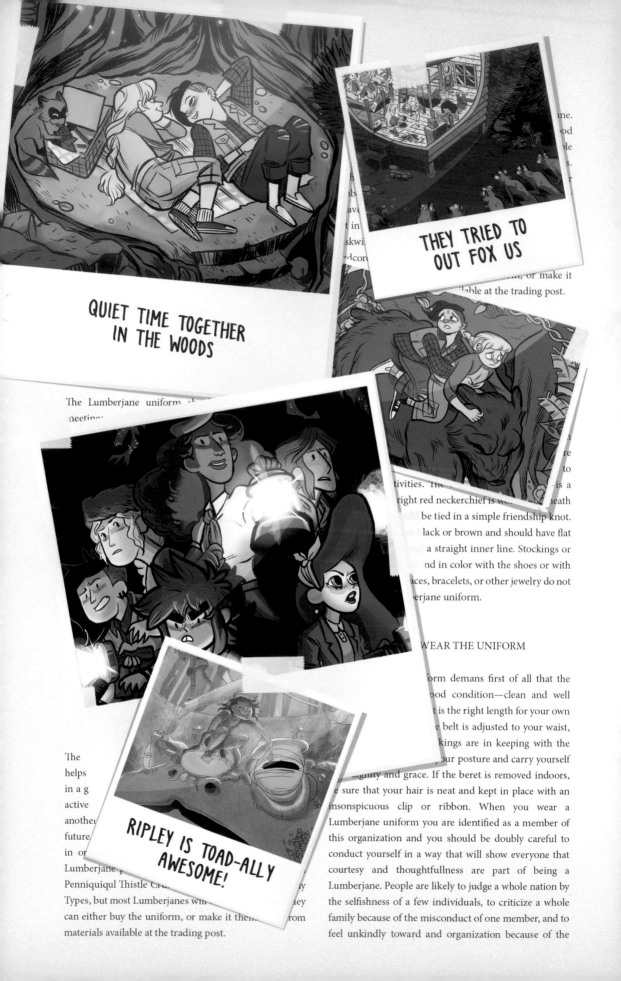

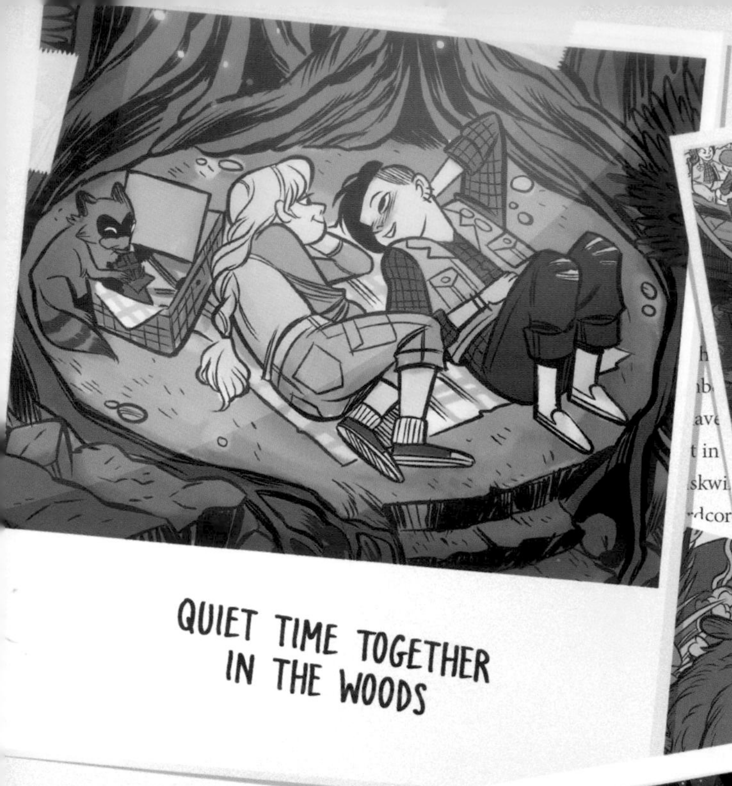
QUIET TIME TOGETHER
IN THE WOODS

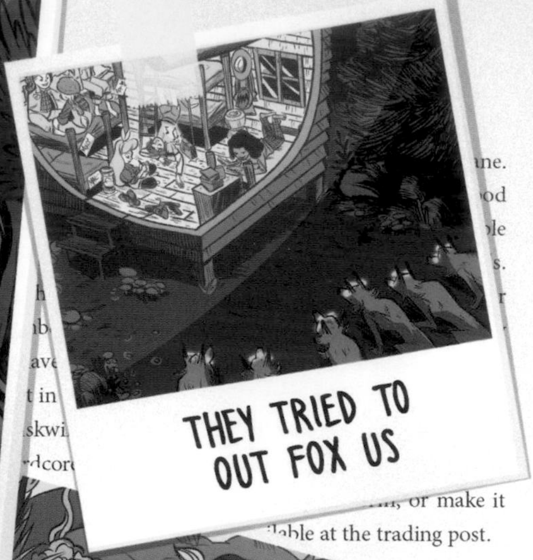
THEY TRIED TO
OUT FOX US

...ne.
...od
...le
...s.
h... ...r
nb...
ave...
t in...
skwi...
rdcor...
..., or make it
...lable at the trading post.

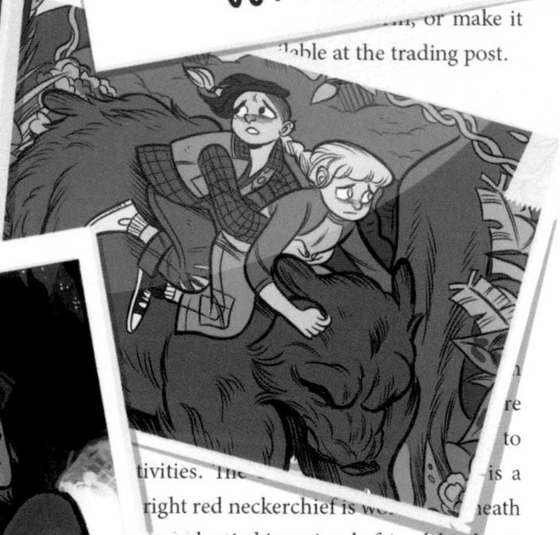

The Lumberjane uniform sh...
meetings...

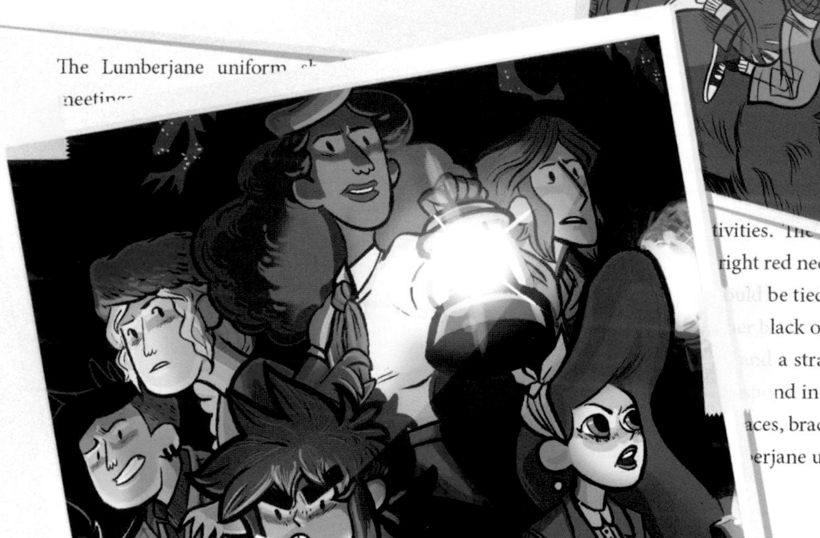

...tivities. The ... is a
...right red neckerchief is wo... ...eath
...uld be tied in a simple friendship knot.
...er black or brown and should have flat
...and a straight inner line. Stockings or
...spond in color with the shoes or with
...aces, bracelets, or other jewelry do not
...erjane uniform.

...WEAR THE UNIFORM

...form demans first of all that the ...ood condition—clean and well ...t is the right length for your own ...e belt is adjusted to your waist, ...kings are in keeping with the ...our posture and carry yourself ...dignity and grace. If the beret is removed indoors, ...e sure that your hair is neat and kept in place with an inconspicuous clip or ribbon. When you wear a Lumberjane uniform you are identified as a member of this organization and you should be doubly careful to conduct yourself in a way that will show everyone that courtesy and thoughtfullness are part of being a Lumberjane. People are likely to judge a whole nation by the selfishness of a few individuals, to criticize a whole family because of the misconduct of one member, and to feel unkindly toward and organization because of the

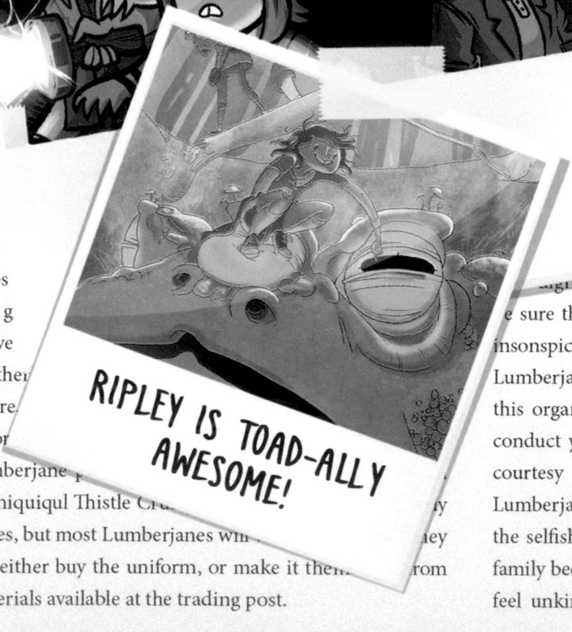
RIPLEY IS TOAD-ALLY
AWESOME!

The ...
helps ...
in a g...
active ...
another...
future...
in or...
Lumberjane p...
Penniquiqul Thistle Cru... ...y
Types, but most Lumberjanes wi... ...hey
can either buy the uniform, or make it them... ...rom
materials available at the trading post.

SKETCHBOOK

Lumberjanes "Out-of-Doors" Program Field

GRUNGEON MASTER BADGE

"Put a pin in it."

There can only be one. Not really, but one day there might be a class where that is the case and it's important to remain vigilant as the lessons taught at this camp adapt and evolve with the times. At camp there will be many obstacles and challenges that the Lumberjanes will face as a team and just as many that they will face on their own. Grunge does not represent the ultimate movement within rock'n roll as every Lumberjane will learn, it is however, it was a great movement of music. Grunge was the last sort of unifying force that brought together a generation and it brought together a variety of people and creatures from any gender, age, or race. It was passionate, exciting, and those are just some of the qualities that we feel it is important for a Lumberjane to understand.

In the practice for the *Grungeon Master* badge, a Lumberjane understands what it means to go underground,

the importance of finding something that will separate her from her peers but will at the same time offer unifying aspect that will show her fellow scouts that while every member of this camp is unique and different, we are also all united in our differences. She will bring out the best of everyone she works with and will strive to bring out the best in herself as well.

To obtain the *Grungeon Master* badge, the Lumberjanes must display their knowledge in the art of plaid. They must be able to look at their challenge and understand where to place a pin and a patch. They must be able to understand what they are capable of and how their actions will affect those around them. This badge is meant to both unify the camp and help each scout show off their uniqueness and their independence. Every creature in this plane must enjoy what makes them different, embrace what separates them from the

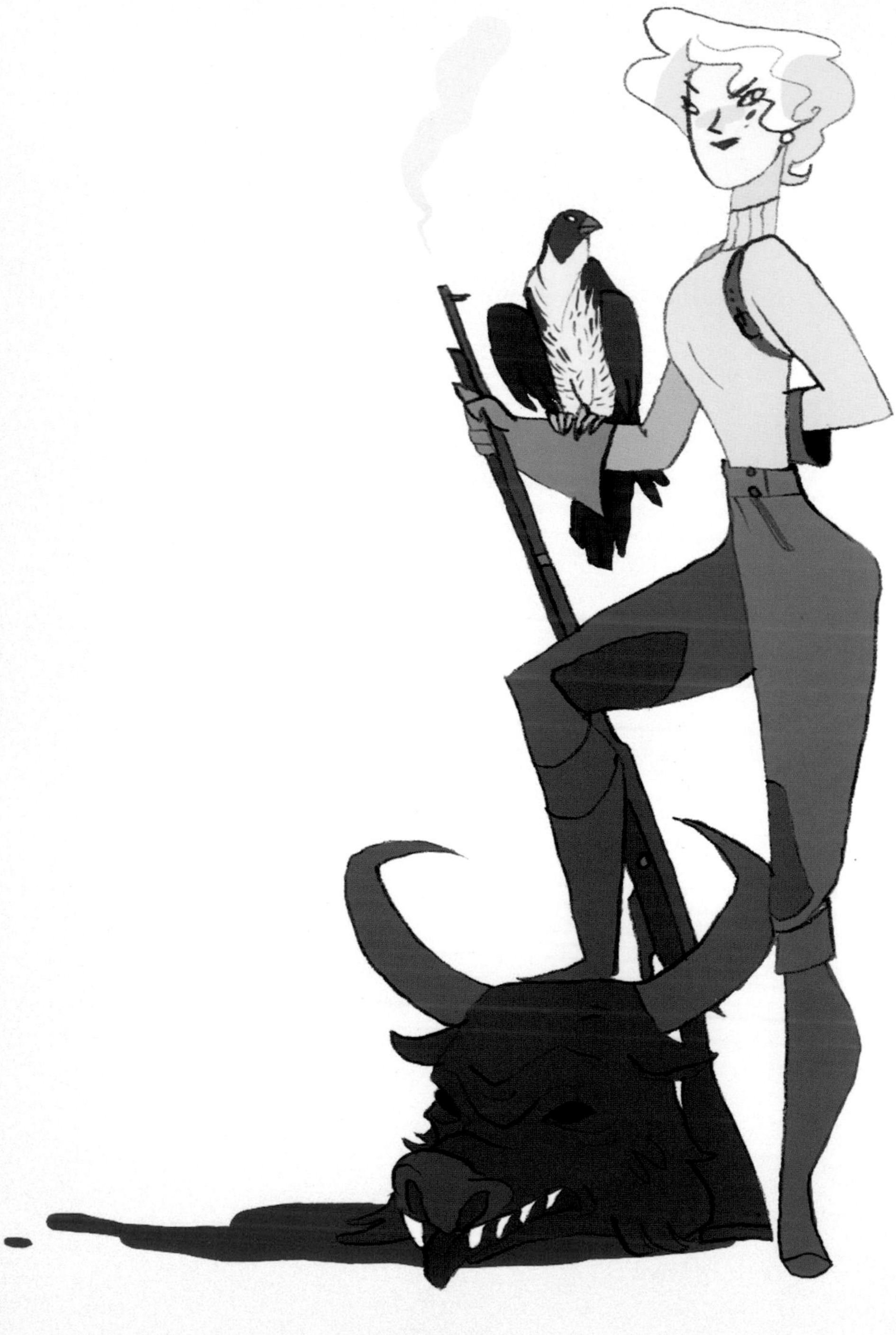

ILLUSTRATIONS BY **NOELLE STEVENSON**

ILLUSTRATIONS BY **BROOKE ALLEN**

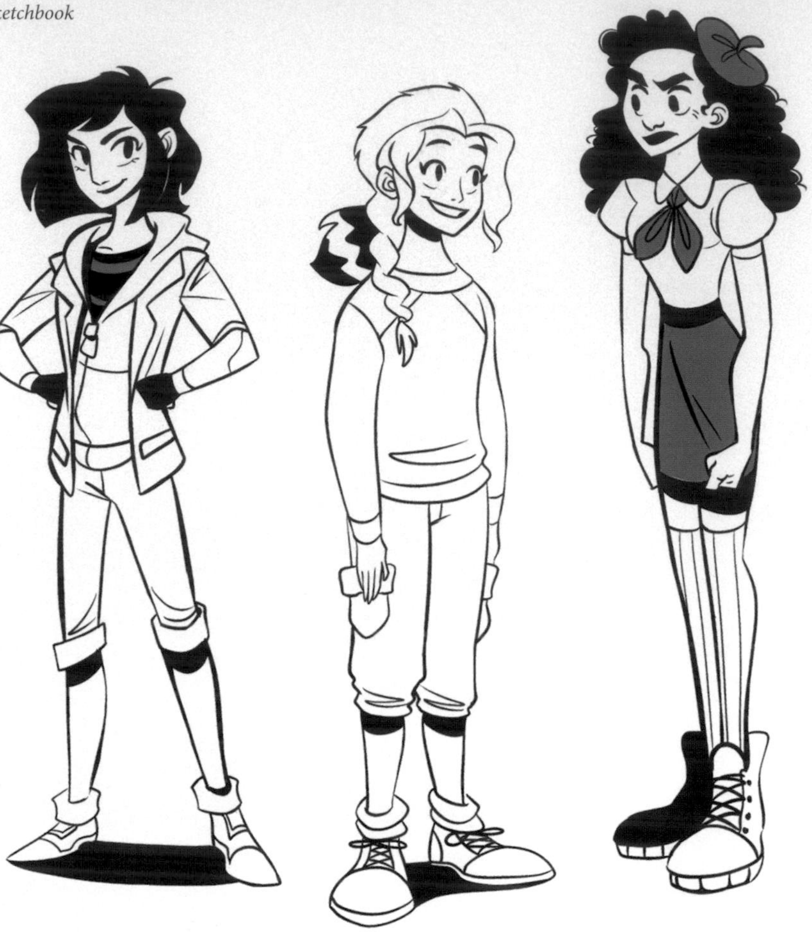

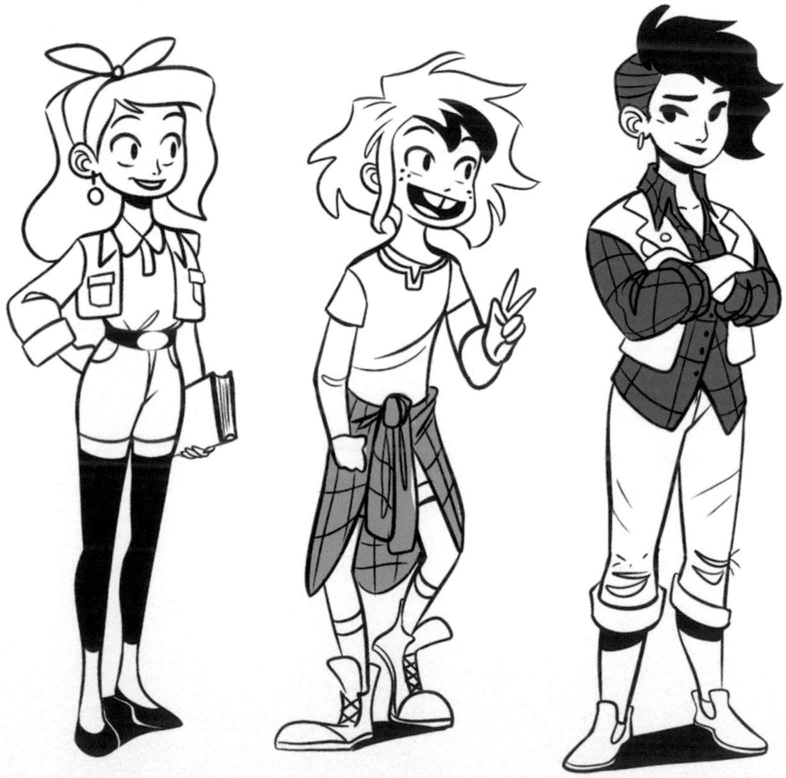

ILLUSTRATIONS BY **BRITTANY WILLIAMS**

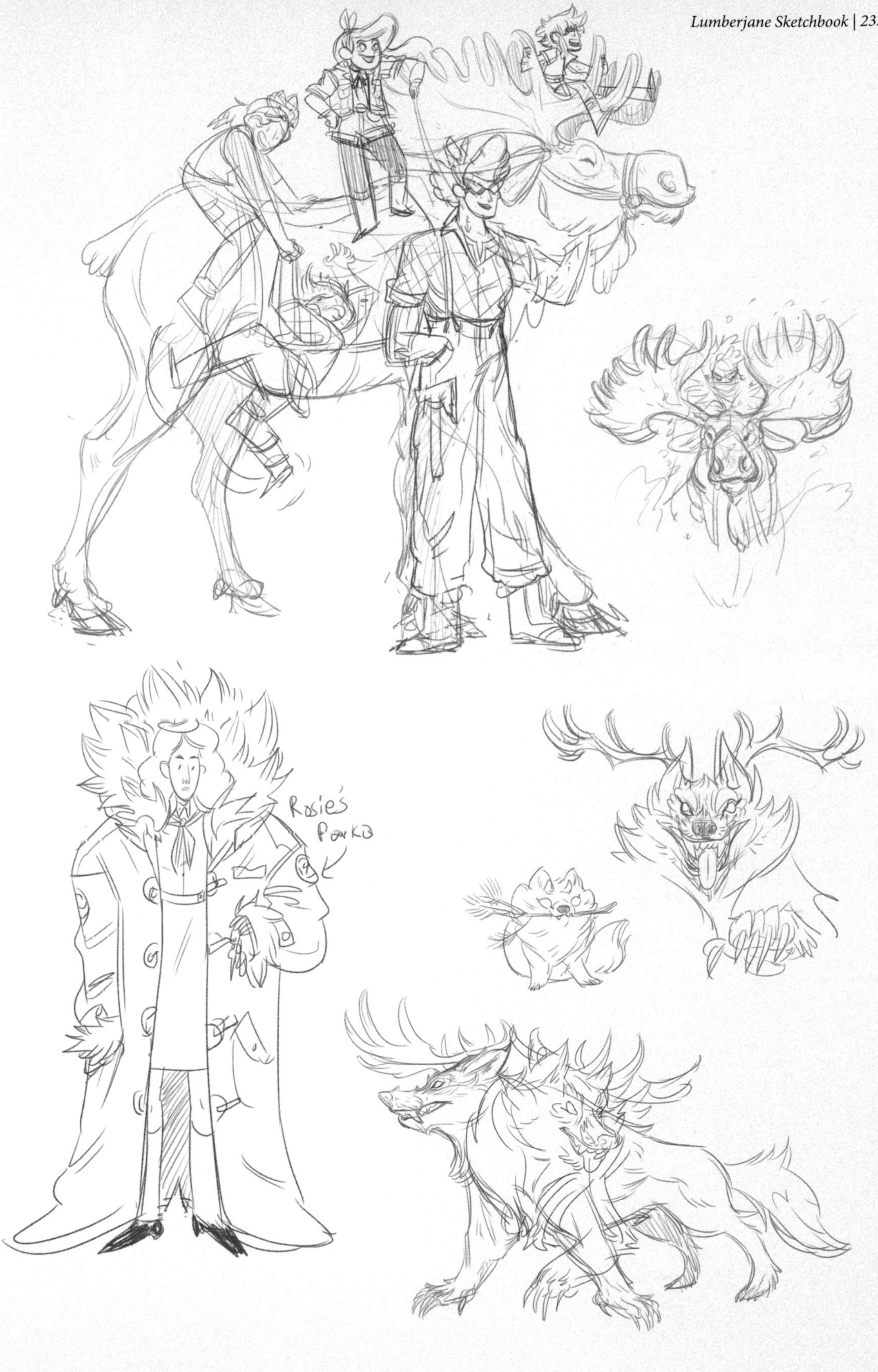
Rosie's Parka

ILLUSTRATIONS BY **BROOKE ALLEN**

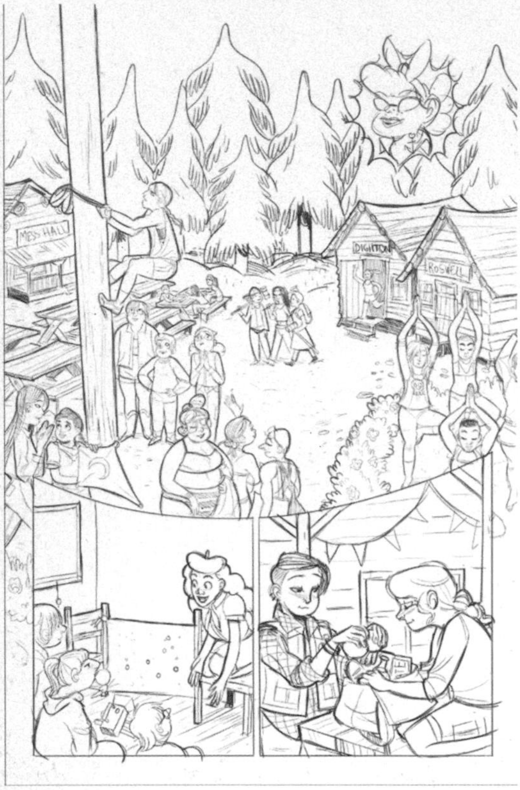
MESS HALL
DIGHTON
ROSWELL

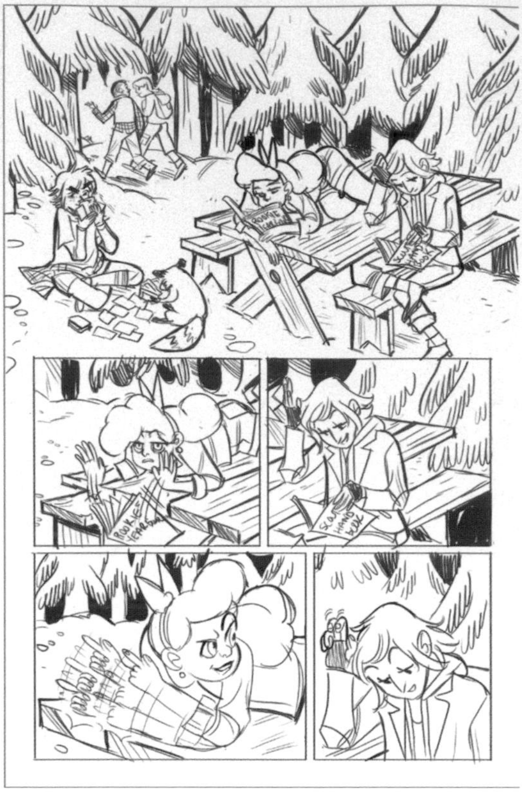
SCOUT HAND BOOK

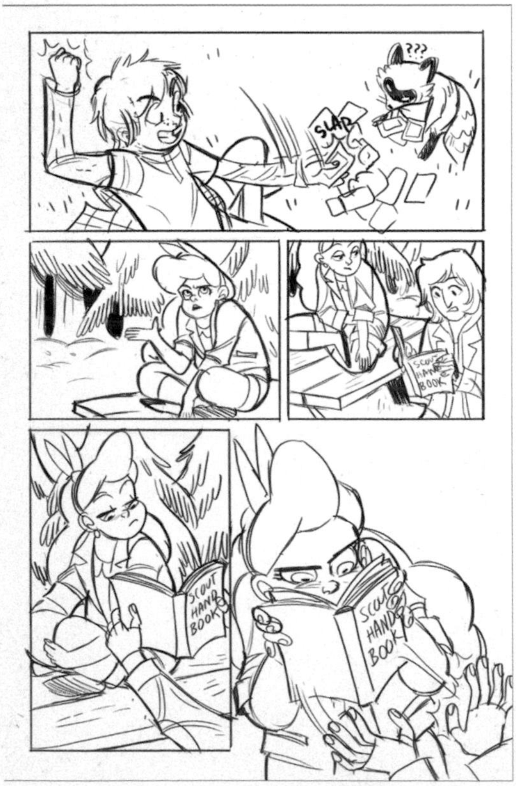
???
SLAP
SCOUT HAND BOOK
SCOUT HAND BOOK
SCOUT HAND BOOK

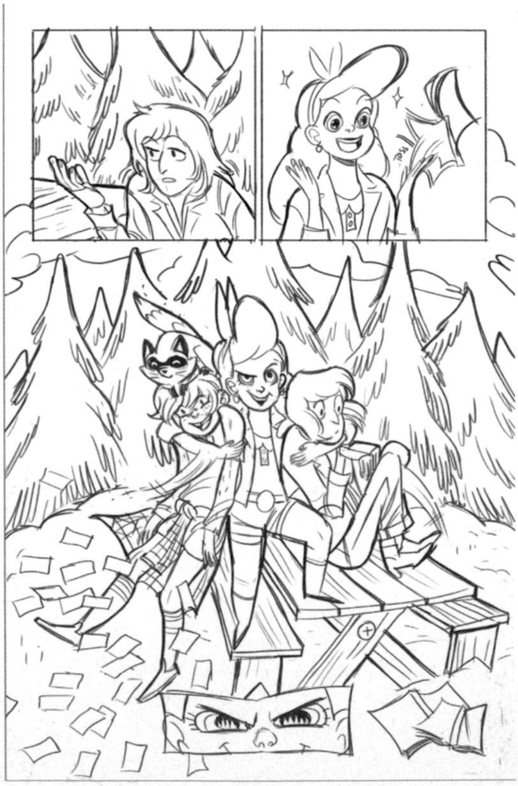

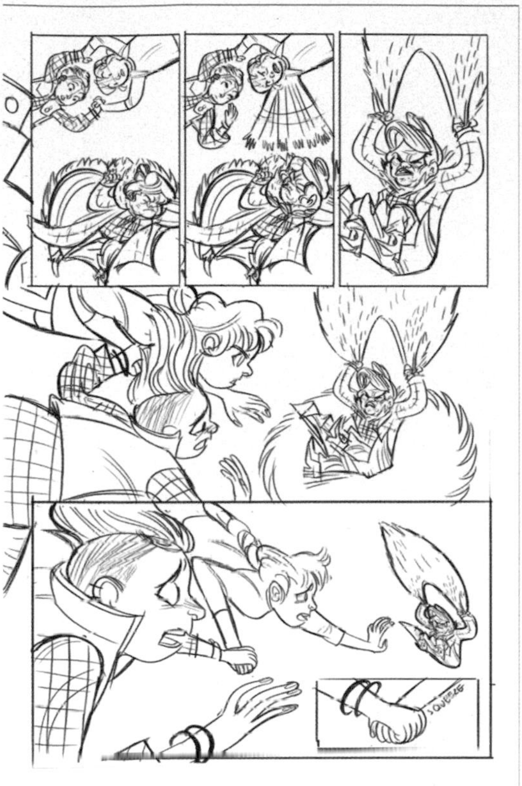

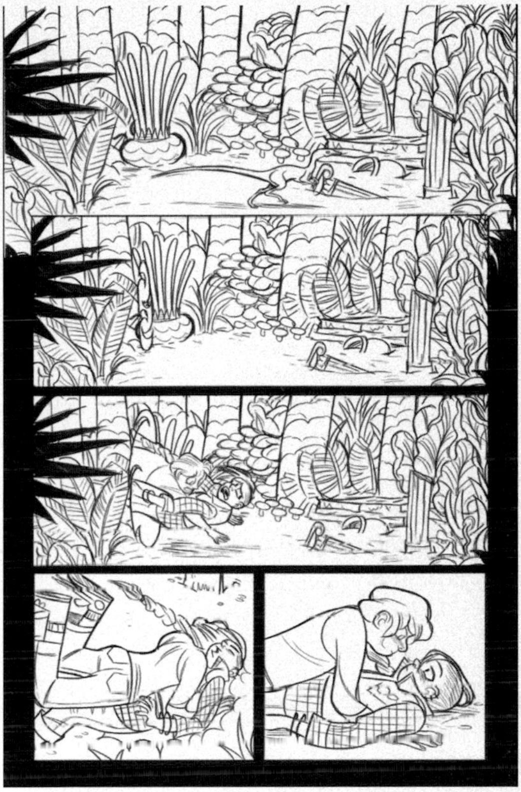

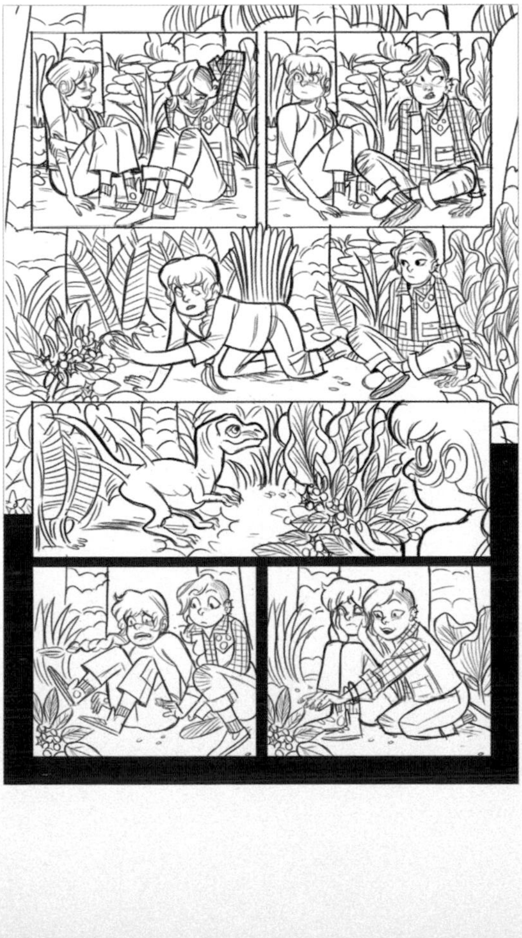

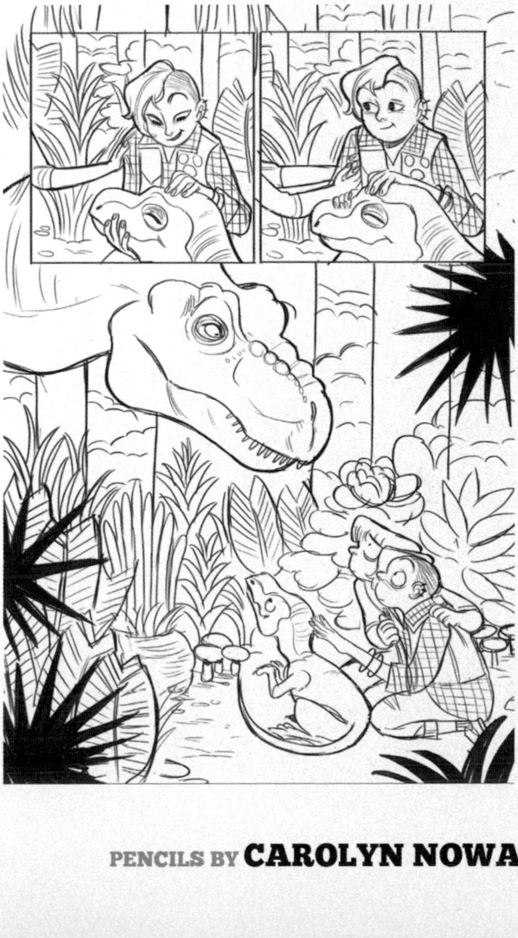

PENCILS BY CAROLYN NOWAK

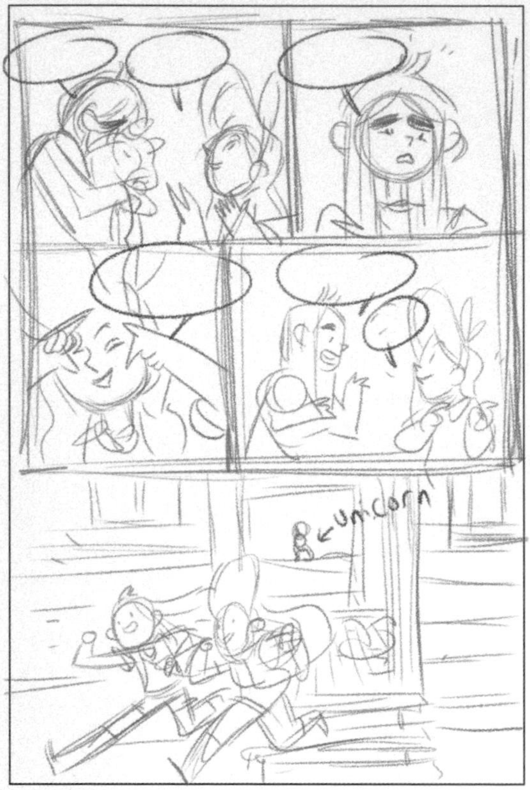
unicorn

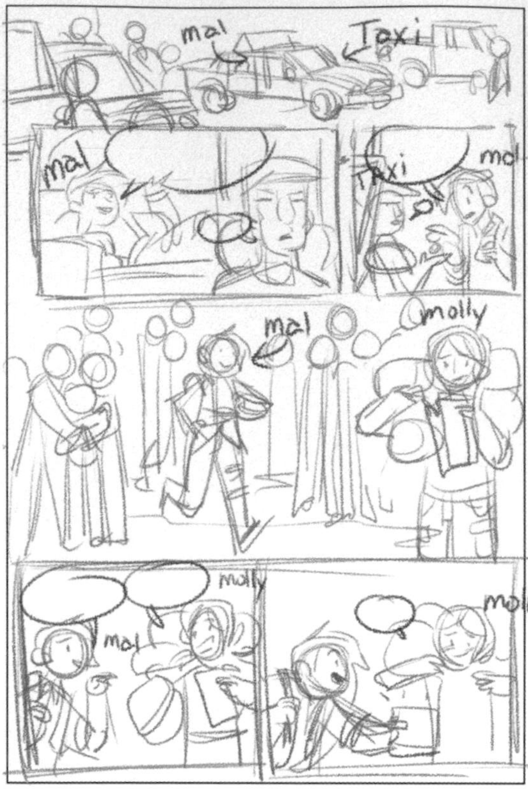
mal
Taxi
mal
Taxi
mol
mal
molly
molly
mal
molly

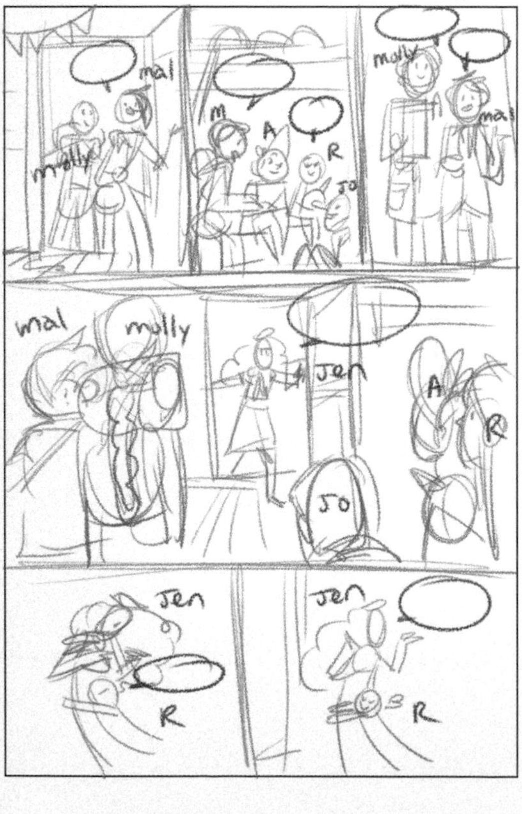
mal
molly
M
A
R
Jo
molly
mal
mal
molly
Jen
A
R
Jo
Jen
R
Jen
R

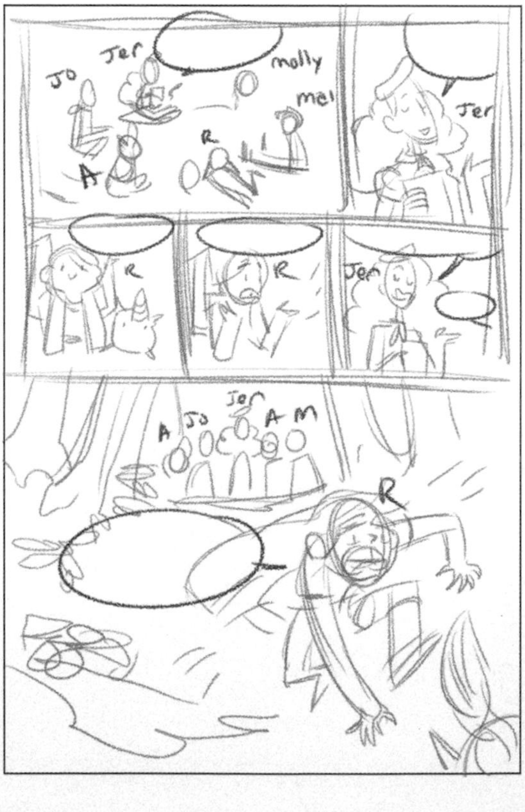
Jo
Jen
molly
mal
R
A
Jen
R
R
Jen
A Jo Jen A M
R

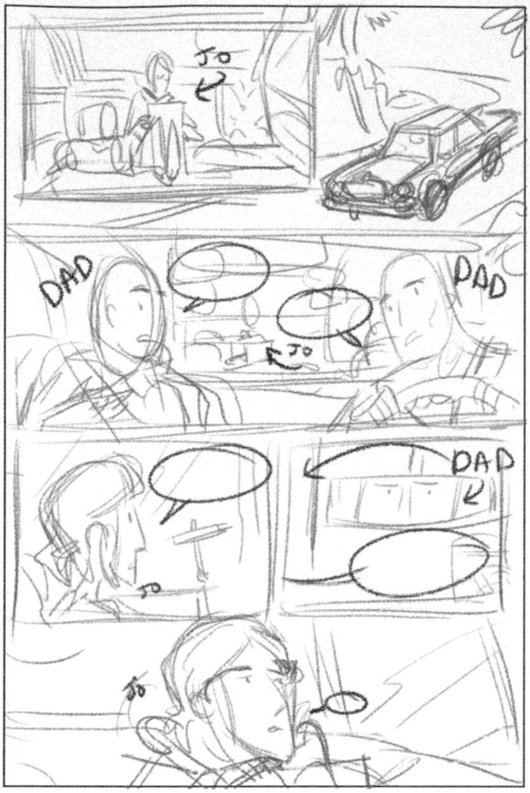
JO
DAD
DAD
JO
DAD
JO
JO

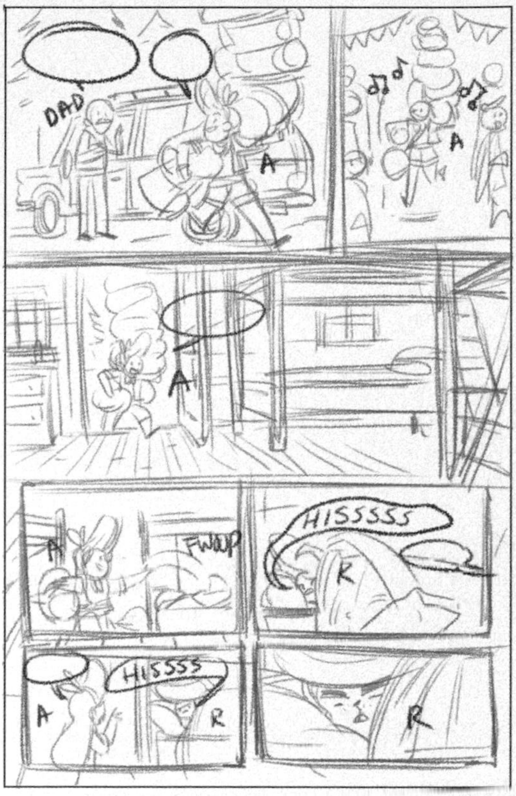
DAD
A
A
A
A
FWOOP
HISSSSS
R
A
HISSSS
R
R

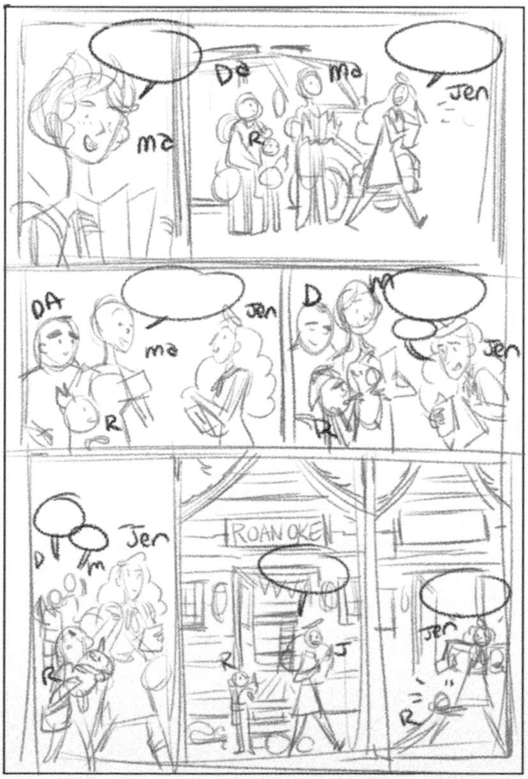
ma
Da
ma
Jen
R
DA
ma
Jen
R
D
M
Jen
R
Jen
R
ROANOKE
R
J
Jen
R

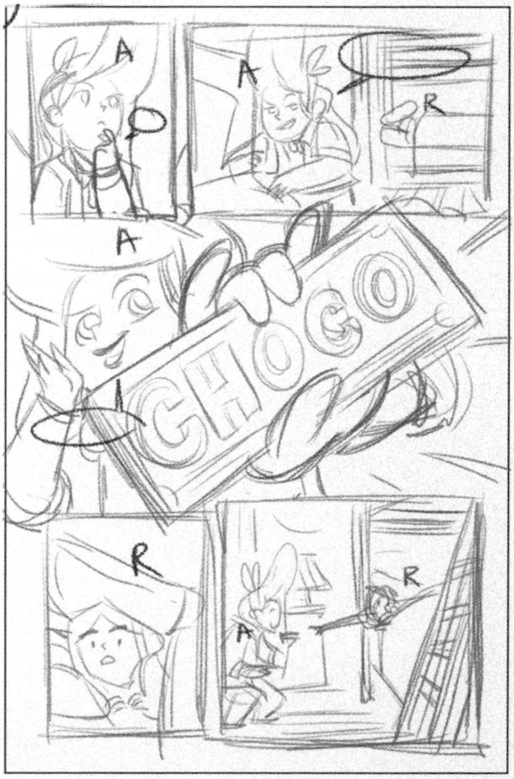
A
A
R
A
CHOCO
R
R
A

PENCILS BY **BROOKE ALLEN**

Issue Nine, Page Seven

PANEL ONE: We're back around the fire. Jo is grinning with the flashlight on her face. April is clapping next to her. The atmosphere is darker now, though. The fire is starting to go down and the night is spookier.

    APRIL: Truly, a tale of terror for our troubled times!

PANEL TWO: Mal and Molly. Molly is looking nervous, and Bubbles is asleep on her head, looking like a hat. She's cuddled closer to Mal, who looks concerned and is patting her shoulder.

    MOLLY (small): Is it darker suddenly, or…?

PANEL THREE: Ripley jumps up, startling Jen.

    JEN: AAAGH

    RIPLEY: I WANNA TELL ONE, CAN I TELL ONE?!

PANEL FOUR: April, leaning forward and grinning. She LIVES FOR THIS.

APRIL: Take us to scare town, Ripley!

PANEL FIVE: Ripley is assuming a scary monster pose. Again, this shot is super dramatic as it leads into her story.

RIPLEY: Once, there was a little girl...

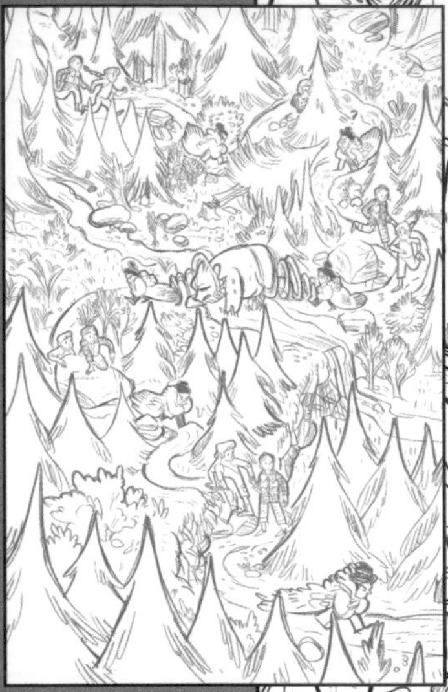

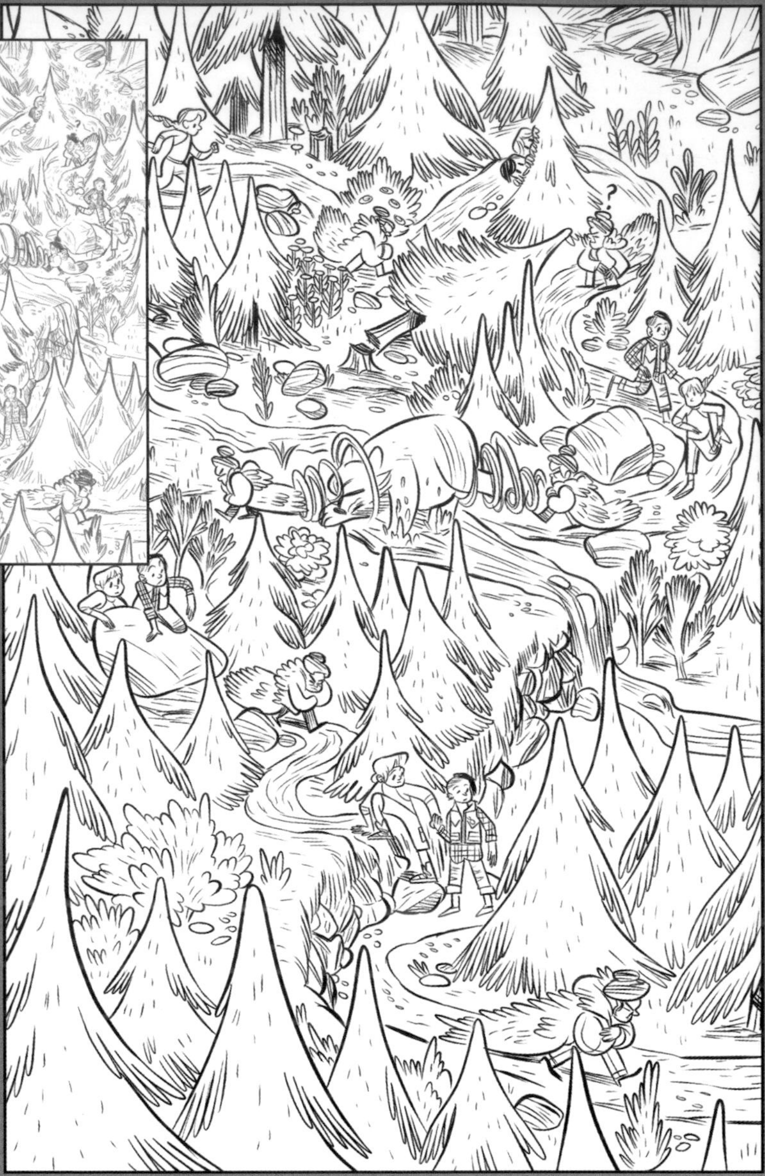

Issue Ten, Page Ten

PANEL ONE: This looks a little like a map…the girls and the bear women are traveling through the woods, which we're observing from above. They're doing different things as they travel through the woods…crossing streams, helping each other off of ledges, jumping across tall rocks, hiding when the Bear Woman turns around, etc. The Bear Woman is turning back and forth from a bear and lady as the situation necessitates.

Issue Twelve, Page Fifteen

Panel 1: Mal, looking a little stunned.

    MAL: What?! Come on, Mol--

Panel 2: Molly nudging Mal with her shoulder. Mal is looking concerned.

    MOLLY: No no, listen…you just…you have this LIFE outside of camp.

    MOLLY: This awesome, AWESOME life.

Panel 3: Molly looking up, wistfully.

    MOLLY: Friends, a BAND...

    MOLLY (small): …I mean, seriously, a band…

    MOLLY…you know EXACTLY who you are.

PANEL FOUR: Molly ruffling Mal's hair.

MOLLY: Even if that person is abnormally aware of the world's many, many pitfalls.

MAL: Hey!

PANEL FIVE: Molly is leaning against Mal a little.

MOLLY: I don't have all that back home.

MOLLY: Until I came to camp, I didn't have any idea who I was.

PANEL SIX: Molly, extreme close-up, narrowed eyes.

MOLLY: Just who I DIDN'T want to be.

Issue Fourteen, Page Three

PANEL 1: Gale-force winds hit them, blowing the tent away in the background—they huddle together for warmth, looking around in confusion. A flurry of flakes is beginning to fall.

    JEN: What?!

    JO: Is this…SNOW?

PANEL 2: The winds pick up even more, and they're hit with the full force of the blizzard. They all scream.

    EVERYONE: AHHHHHHHHH

    APRIL: WHAT IS GOING ON

PANEL 3: Molly shields Mal from the snow.

    MOLLY: Okay, so we WEREN'T prepared for a BLIZZARD in the middle of the freakin' SUMMER…

    MOLLY: …but why WOULD we be?!

JEN: Okay, everyone stay calm! We'll…we'll figure this out!

PANEL FOUR:

JEN: We're going to head back to camp before this gets any worse.

JEN: We're going to stay together, and—WHERE'S RIPLEY.

PANEL 5: Ripley is standing off from the rest, almost obscured by the whiteout. Squinting into the snow.

RIPLEY: Uhhhhh, you guys???

PANEL 6: She points—a huge, hulking silhouette is moving through the whiteness. It's a DARTMOOR BEAST—think like, a giant wolf/lion/boar. With glowing eyes. And a skeleton head, maybe. With antlers. Yeah just so much shit on it. It's really freaky.

RIPLEY: There's…something coming!

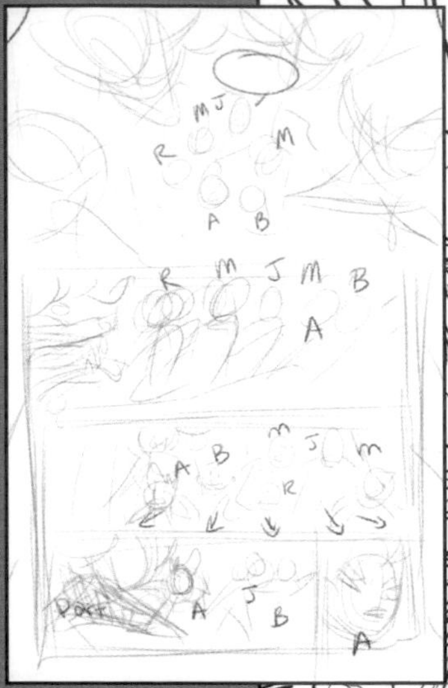

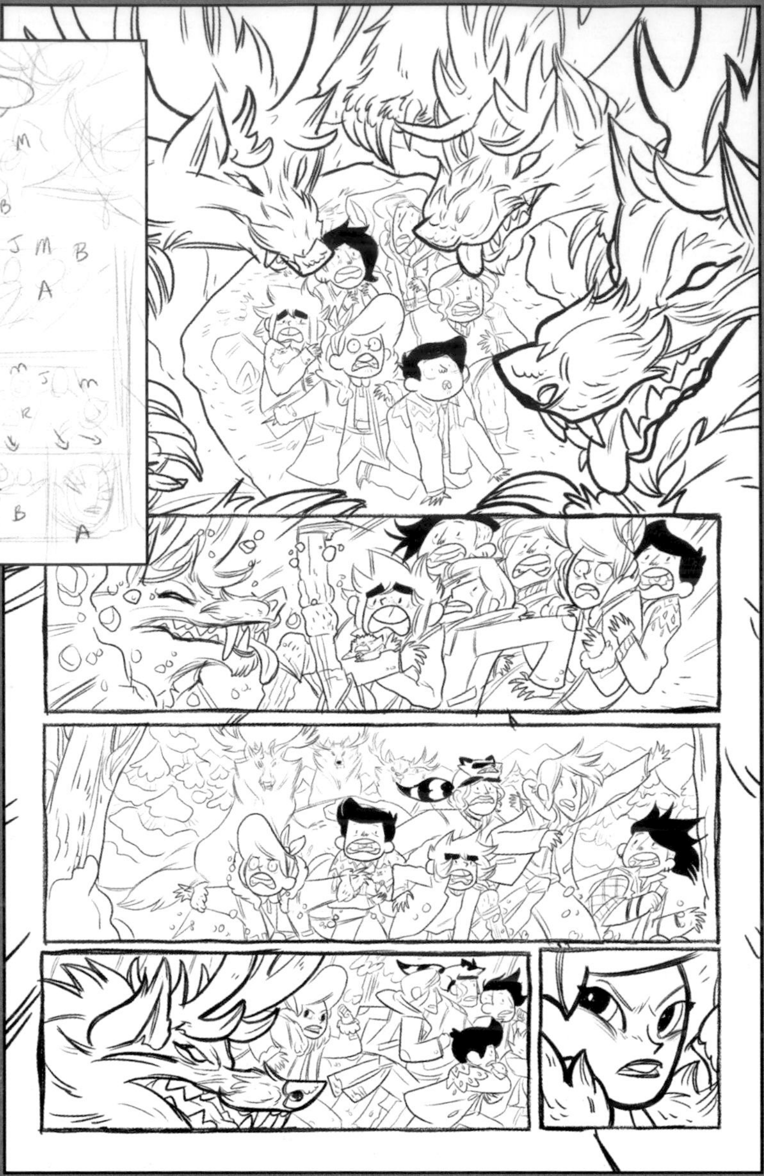

Issue Fifteen, Page Thirteen

PANEL ONE: Show the collapsed shelter from the outside—the kids huddle together at the bottom of what WAS a shelter and now is little more than a hole. They cling to each other, terrified—they're surrounded by four Dartmoor beasts.

JO: FOR THE LOVE OF NELLIE BLY, RUN!!!

PANEL TWO: One of the beasts' face pushes in close to them, teeth bared, as they scramble out of the collapsed shelter.

PANEL THREE: They take off into the woods, the beasts on their tail.

PANEL FOUR: They run blindly through the wood, stumbling in drifts—April looks over to see one of them running beside them, its eyes glowing in the darkness.

PANEL FIVE: April's eyes narrow.

Issue Sixteen, Page Three

PANEL ONE: Abigail stops and looks back.

    ABIGAIL: ROSIE!

PANEL TWO: Abigail runs back towards the mountain.

    BW: Abigail! I said RUN and that's an ORDER!

PANEL THREE: Abigail ignores her, dodging a barrage of smaller rocks that smash to the ground all around her.

PANEL FOUR: She finds Rosie, staggering blindly forward with scraped knees, retrieving her shattered specs from the ground.

PANEL FIVE: Abigail grabs Rosie and hauls her to safety as another huge boulder smashes down where they were just standing.

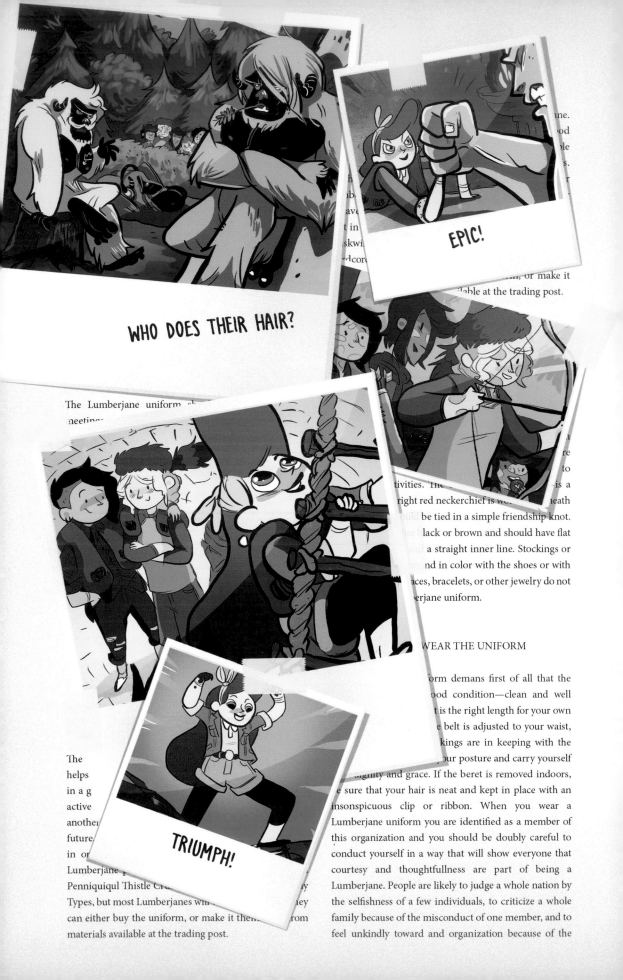

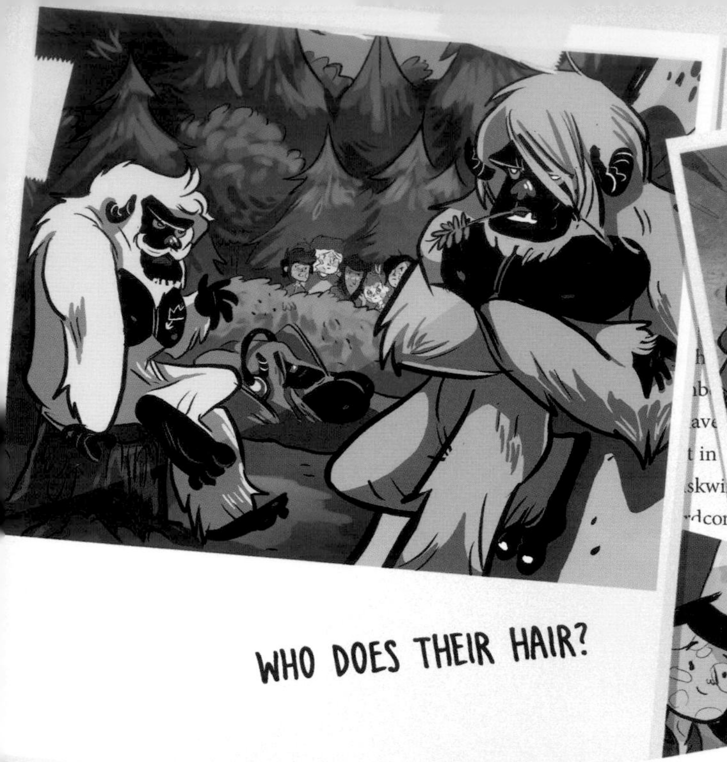
WHO DOES THEIR HAIR?

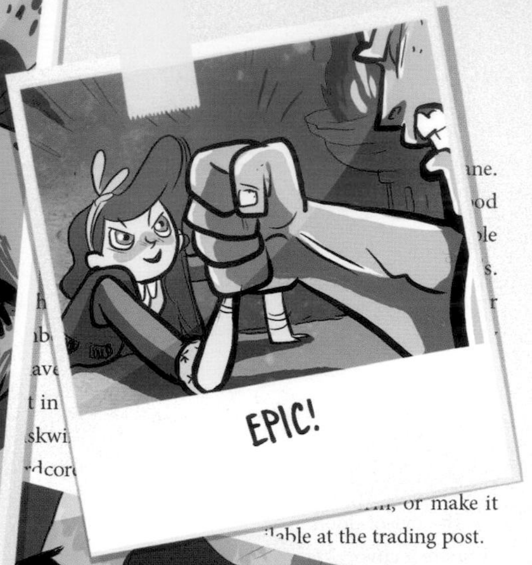
EPIC!

...ne.
...od
...le
...s.
...r
h...
nb...
ave...
t in...
skwi...
dcor...
...m, or make it
...ilable at the trading post.

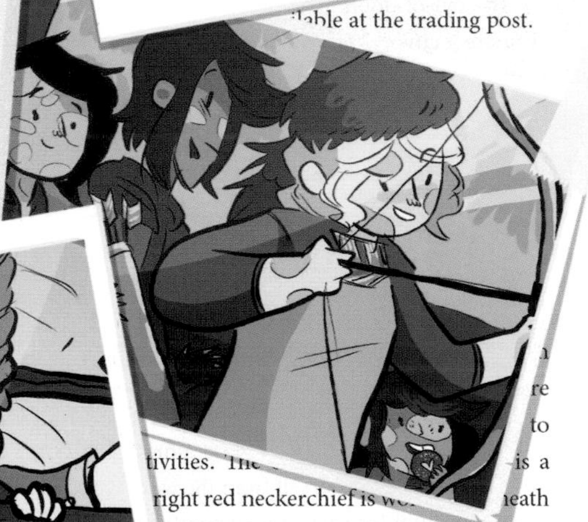

The Lumberjane uniform sh...
meetin...

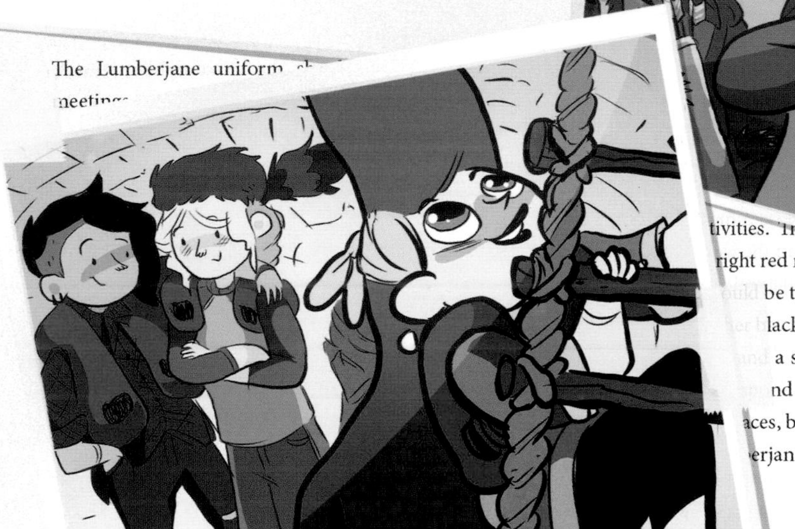

...n
...re
...to
...tivities. The ... is a
...right red neckerchief is wo... ...neath
...ould be tied in a simple friendship knot.
...er black or brown and should have flat
...and a straight inner line. Stockings or
...nd in color with the shoes or with
...aces, bracelets, or other jewelry do not
...erjane uniform.

...WEAR THE UNIFORM

...form demans first of all that the
...ood condition—clean and well
...t is the right length for your own
...e belt is adjusted to your waist,
...kings are in keeping with the
...our posture and carry yourself
...dignity and grace. If the beret is removed indoors,
...e sure that your hair is neat and kept in place with an insonspicuous clip or ribbon. When you wear a Lumberjane uniform you are identified as a member of this organization and you should be doubly careful to conduct yourself in a way that will show everyone that courtesy and thoughtfullness are part of being a Lumberjane. People are likely to judge a whole nation by the selfishness of a few individuals, to criticize a whole family because of the misconduct of one member, and to feel unkindly toward and organization because of the

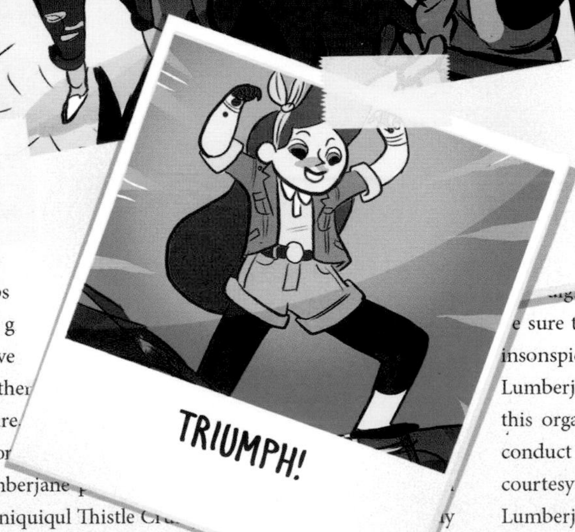
TRIUMPH!

The...
helps...
in a g...
active...
another...
future...
in or...
Lumberjane p...
Penniquiql Thistle Cr... ...y
Types, but most Lumberjanes wi... ...ey
can either buy the uniform, or make it the... ...rom
materials available at the trading post.

LUMBERJANES FIELD MANUAL

ABOUT THE AUTHORS

SHANNON WATTERS

Shannon Watters is an editor lady by day and the co-creator of *Lumberjanes*...also by day. She helped guide KaBOOM!—BOOM! Studios' all-ages imprint—to commercial and critical success, and oversees BOOM! Box, an experimental imprint created "for the love of it." She has a great love for all things indie and comics, which is something she's been passionate about since growing up in the wilds of Arizona. When she's not working on comics she can be found watching classic films and enjoying the local cuisine.

ART BY **BROOKE ALLEN**

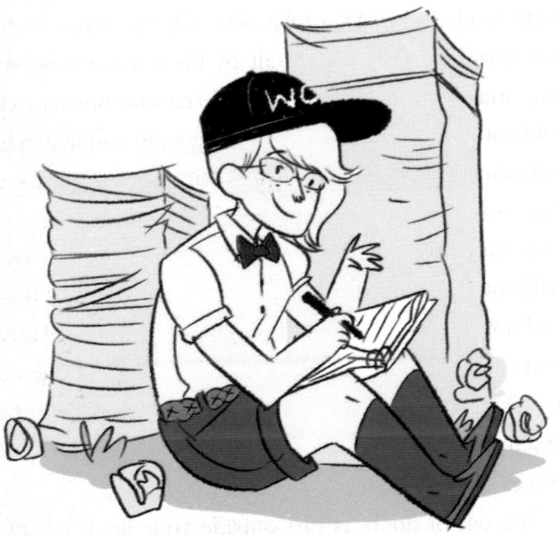
WO

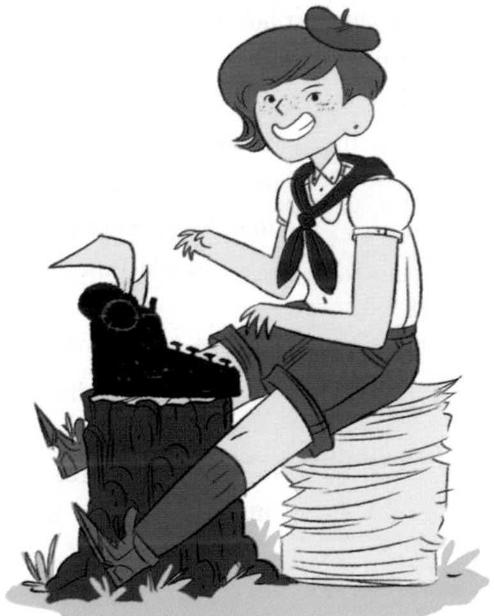

GRACE ELLIS

Grace Ellis is a writer most well-known for co-creating *Lumberjanes* and her work on the site *Autostraddle*. She is from Ohio and when she's not coming up with amazing mix-tapes, she's most likely enjoying camp stories, the zoo and The Great American Musical, of which she's sure to write a hit one someday.

NOELLE STEVENSON

Noelle Stevenson is the *New York Times* bestselling author of *Nimona*, has won two Eisner Awards for the series she co-created; *Lumberjanes*. She's been nominated for Harvey Awards, and was awarded the Slate Cartoonist Studio Prize for Best Web Comic in 2012 for *Nimona*. A graduate of the Maryland Institute College of Art, Noelle is a writer on Disney's *Wander Over Yonder*, she has written for Marvel and DC Comics. She lives in Los Angeles. In her spare time she can be found drawing superheroes and talking about bad TV. **www.gingerhaze.com**

ART BY **BROOKE ALLEN**

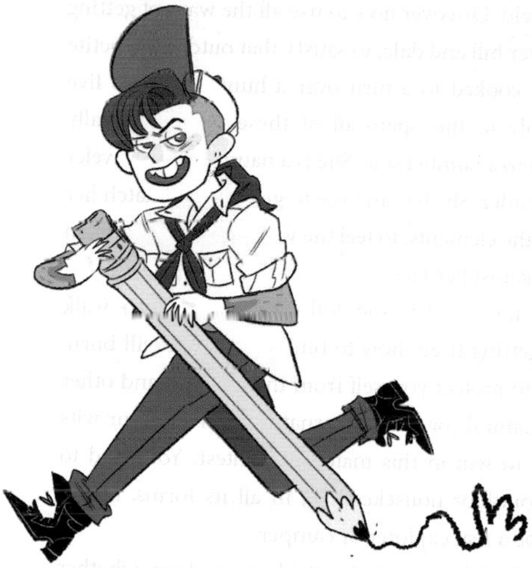

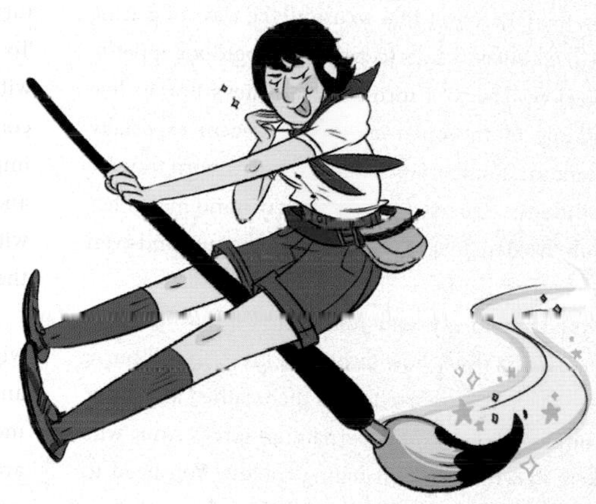

BROOKE ALLEN

Brooke Allen is a co-creator and the artist for *Lumberjanes* and when she is not drawing then she will most likely be found with a saw in her hand making something rad. Currently residing in the "for lovers" state of Virginia, she spends most of her time working on comics with her not-so-helpful assistant Linus...her dog.

CAROLYN NOWAK

Carolyn Nowak is a cartoonist and illustrator who was born in Michigan and currently resides in the best state in the union (Michigan). Beyond Lumberjanes she's most proud of her own self-published comics. She thinks drawing is okay but if she could find someone to pay her to play DDR or watch and analyze T.V. all day she would quit with enthusiasm and never look back. Her only real goals are to live a long time, be happy and die in Michigan.

ART BY **BROOKE ALLEN**

MAARTA LAIHO

Maarta Laiho is a freelance illustrator, who was somehow tricked into becoming a successful comics colorist. She is a graduate from the Savannah College of Art and Design with a BFA in Sequential Art. She, with her chinchilla sidekick, currently resides in the woods of midcoast Maine. In her spare time she draws her webcomic *Madwillow*, hoards houseplants, and complains about the snow. **www.PencilCat.net**

AUBREY AIESE

Aubrey Aiese is an illustrator and hand letterer from Brooklyn, New York currently living in Portland, Oregon. She loves eating ice cream, making comics, and playing with her super cute corgi pups, Ace and Penny. She's been nominated for a Harvey Award for her outstanding lettering on *Lumberjanes* and continues to find new ways to challenge herself in her field. She also puts an absurd amount of ketchup on her french fries. **www.lettersfromaubrey.com**

will co...

The ur...
It help...
appearan...
dress fo...
Further...
Lumber...
to have...
part in...
Thiskv...
Hardo...
have ...
them...

ALRIGHT!

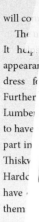

E UNIFORM

...hould be worn at camp
...events when Lumberjanes
...n may also be worn at other
...ions. It should be worn as a
...the uniform dress with
...rect shoes, and stocking or
...out grows her uniform or
...ng ...ter Lumberjane.
...ma she has
... her
... her

WHY DO I ALWAYS DROP THE FLASHLIGHT?

The...
yellow, short sl...
emb...
the w...
choose...
slacks,...
made o...
out-of-do...
green bere...
the colla...
Shoes ma...
heels, rou...
socks shou...
the uniform. Ne... ...es, bracelets, or other jewelry do...
belong with a Lumberjane uniform.

...RGES

HOW TO WEAR THE UNIFORM

To look well in a uniform demans first of...
uniform be kept in good condition—clean ...
pressed. See that the skirt is the right length for your own
height and build, that the belt is adjusted to your waist,
that your shoes and stockings are in keeping with the
uniform, that you watch your posture and carry yourself
with dignity and grace. If the beret is removed indoors,
be sure that your hair is neat and kept in place with an
insonspicuous clip or ribbon. When you wear a
Lumberjane uniform you are identified as a member of
this organization and you should be doubly careful to
conduct yourself in a way that will show everyone that
courtesy and thoughtfullness are part of being a
Lumberjane. People are likely to judge a whole nation by
the selfishness of a few individuals, to criticize a whole
family because of the misconduct of one member, and to
feel unkindly toward and organization because of the

The unifor...
helps to cre...
in a group. ...
active life th...
another bond...
future, and pr...
in order to b...
Lumberjane pr...
Penniquiqul Thi... ...ore Lady
Types, but m... ...es will wish to have one. They
can either b... ...niform, or make it themselves from
materials available at the trading post.

DUCKFACE PRACTICE

LJ

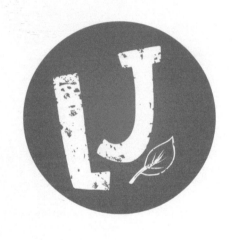